The Editors

FRANCES SMITH FOSTER is Charles Howard Candler Professor Emerita of English and Women's Studies at Emory University. Her books include *Witnessing Slavery: The Development of the Antebellum Slave Narrative*, *Written By Herself: Literary Production by African American Women, 1746–1892*, and *'Til Death or Distance Do Us Part: Love and Marriage in African America.* She is an editor of *The Norton Anthology of African American Literature* and coeditor of the *Oxford Companion to African American Literature*.

RICHARD YARBOROUGH is Professor of English and African American Studies at the University of California, Los Angeles. A prize-winning teacher and scholar, he has published on authors and topics from Frederick Douglass, Harriet Beecher Stowe, and Charles Chesnutt to rock music and black characterization in cinema. He is associate general editor of the *Heath Anthology of American Literature*.

NORTON CRITICAL EDITIONS
AMERICAN REALISM & REFORM

ALCOTT, LITTLE WOMEN
ALGER, RAGGED DICK
ANDERSON, WINESBURG, OHIO
CHESNUTT, THE CONJURE STORIES
CHESNUTT, THE MARROW OF TRADITION
CHOPIN, THE AWAKENING
CRANE, MAGGIE: A GIRL OF THE STREETS
CRANE, THE RED BADGE OF COURAGE
DOUGLASS, NARRATIVE OF THE LIFE OF FREDERICK DOUGLASS
DREISER, SISTER CARRIE
DU BOIS, THE SOULS OF BLACK FOLK
EMERSON, EMERSON'S PROSE AND POETRY
FULLER, WOMAN IN THE NINETEENTH CENTURY
HAWTHORNE, THE BLITHEDALE ROMANCE
HAWTHORNE, THE HOUSE OF THE SEVEN GABLES
HAWTHORNE, NATHANIEL HAWTHORNE'S TALES
HAWTHORNE, THE SCARLET LETTER AND OTHER WRITINGS
HOWELLS, THE RISE OF SILAS LAPHAM
JACOBS, INCIDENTS IN THE LIFE OF A SLAVE GIRL
JAMES, THE AMBASSADORS
JAMES, THE AMERICAN
JAMES, THE PORTRAIT OF A LADY
JAMES, TALES OF HENRY JAMES
JAMES, THE TURN OF THE SCREW
JAMES, THE WINGS OF THE DOVE
LINCOLN, LINCOLN'S SELECTED WRITINGS
MELVILLE, THE CONFIDENCE-MAN
MELVILLE, MELVILLE'S SHORT NOVELS
MELVILLE, MOBY-DICK
MELVILLE, PIERRE
MONTGOMERY, ANNE OF GREEN GABLES
MOODIE, ROUGHING IT IN THE BUSH
NORRIS, MCTEAGUE
NORTHUP, TWELVE YEARS A SLAVE
POE, THE SELECTED WRITINGS OF EDGAR ALLAN POE
RIIS, HOW THE OTHER HALF LIVES
SINCLAIR, THE JUNGLE
STOWE, UNCLE TOM'S CABIN
THOREAU, WALDEN, CIVIL DISOBEDIENCE, AND OTHER WRITINGS
TWAIN, ADVENTURES OF HUCKLEBERRY FINN
TWAIN, THE ADVENTURES OF TOM SAWYER
TWAIN, A CONNECTICUT YANKEE IN KING ARTHUR'S COURT
TWAIN, PUDD'NHEAD WILSON AND THOSE EXTRAORDINARY TWINS
WASHINGTON, UP FROM SLAVERY
WHARTON, THE AGE OF INNOCENCE
WHARTON, ETHAN FROME
WHARTON, THE HOUSE OF MIRTH
WHITMAN, LEAVES OF GRASS AND OTHER WRITINGS

For a complete list of Norton Critical Editions, visit
wwnorton.com/nortoncriticals

A NORTON CRITICAL EDITION

Harriet Jacobs

INCIDENTS IN THE LIFE OF A SLAVE GIRL

AUTHORITATIVE TEXT

CONTEXTS

CRITICISM

SECOND EDITION

Edited by

FRANCES SMITH FOSTER
EMORY UNIVERSITY

and

RICHARD YARBOROUGH
UNIVERSITY OF CALIFORNIA, LOS ANGELES

W • W • NORTON & COMPANY • *New York • London*

W. W. Norton & Company has been independent since its founding in 1923, when William Warder Norton and Mary D. Herter Norton first published lectures delivered at the People's Institute, the adult education division of New York City's Cooper Union. The firm soon expanded its program beyond the Institute, publishing books by celebrated academics from America and abroad. By midcentury, the two major pillars of Norton's publishing program—trade books and college texts—were firmly established. In the 1950s, the Norton family transferred control of the company to its employees, and today—with a staff of four hundred and a comparable number of trade, college, and professional titles published each year—W. W. Norton & Company stands as the largest and oldest publishing house owned wholly by its employees.

Printed in the United States of America

Manufacturing by Maple Press
Book design by Antonina Krass
Production manager: Stephen Sajdak

Library of Congress Cataloging-in-Publication Data

Names: Jacobs, Harriet A. (Harriet Ann), 1813–1897, author. | Foster, Frances Smith, editor. | Yarborough, Richard, editor.
Title: Incidents in the life of a slave girl : authoritative text, contexts, criticism / Harriet Jacobs ; edited by Frances Smith Foster, Emory University, and Richard Yarborough, University of California, Los Angeles.
Description: Second edition. | New York : W.W. Norton & Company, [2019] | Series: A Norton critical edition | Includes bibliographical references.
Identifiers: LCCN 2018019207 | **ISBN 9780393614565 (pbk.)**
Subjects: LCSH: Jacobs, Harriet A. (Harriet Ann), 1813–1897. | Slaves—United States—Biography. | Women slaves—United States—Biography. | Slaves—United States—Social conditions.
Classification: LCC E444 .J17 A3 2019 | DDC 306.3/62092 [B]—dc23
LC record available at https://lccn.loc.gov/2018019207

W. W. Norton & Company, Inc., 500 Fifth Avenue,
New York, N.Y. 10110
www.wwnorton.com
W. W. Norton & Company Ltd., 15 Carlisle Street,
London W1D 3BS

3 4 5 6 7 8 9 0

Contents

Introduction

Were Harriet Jacobs alive today, she would be surprised and pleased that *Incidents in the Life of a Slave Girl* is an international best seller. After she finally surrendered to pleas that public testimony about her experiences in slavery would greatly aid the abolitionist cause, Jacobs worked hard to reach the widest possible audience with her narrative. She had endured condescension, suspicion, and even perfidy from some whom she petitioned or with whom she collaborated. It had taken nearly a decade for her to complete her manuscript, only to have her publisher go out of business before it was printed. Finally appearing in 1861, *Linda: Or, Incidents in the Life of a Slave Girl. Written by Herself* was popular enough for Jacobs to negotiate a British edition, titled *The Deeper Wrong.* Unfortunately, unscrupulous printers produced pirated volumes titled *Incidents in the Life of a Slave Girl* that diverted desperately needed funds from both author and legitimate publisher. Complicating the reception of Jacobs's narrative was the fact that the United States was preoccupied at the time with a crisis that threatened its very existence. The slave states were seceding, and many people blamed slavery for the burgeoning sectional tensions. As a result, interest in the autobiographies of formerly enslaved individuals declined precipitously. Harriet Jacobs's struggle to add her "testimony to that of abler pens to convince the people of the Free States what Slavery really is" seemed labor lost. With the end of the Civil War and the abolition of slavery in 1865, Jacobs, like the rest of the country, turned attention to reconciliation and reconstruction. How could she, then, dream that her "imperfect effort in behalf of her persecuted people" would become quite the international, cross-cultural, multimedia phenomenon, printed in languages and countries worldwide and declared an African American classic?

Harriet Jacobs would be perplexed, if not totally shocked, by the ways and reasons her book is relevant and revelatory today. She had been anxious that readers would consider her disclosures "exaggerated" and that they might indict her for "delicate" or "indelicate" discourse. How astonished she would be that many twenty-first-century readers feel that she had not depicted the violence and despair of enslavement graphically enough and that she did not admit to more extensive sexual experience. She would be horrified to know that secrets she could hardly bear to whisper in a confidante's ear are now openly presented in children's books, in novels, and on stage and screen and that, contrary to her intentions, *Incidents* has drawn attention to Harriet Jacobs herself. However, instead of obloquy, the book generally evokes admiration, imitation, and appropriation. In 1992, Mary E. Lyon's version of *Incidents*, published as *Letters from a Slave Girl*, was chosen as an American Library Association best book. Jacobs's life and writing are prominent in the PBS series *Africans in America* (1998). Lauded as "immensely sophisticated," "searing," and "inspiring," Lydia R. Diamond's *Harriet Jacobs: A Play* (2011) is but one of several theatrical productions. Patina Miller, who plays Charlotte Jenkins in PBS's highly acclaimed television series *Mercy Street* (2016), commented, "What Harriet Jacobs, the main inspiration for my character, went through and suffered in slavery before escaping . . . it was just so powerful."[1] And Colson Whitehead acknowledges *Incidents* as a primary source for his novel *The Underground Railroad*, the 2016 winner of the National Book Award for Fiction.[2] Jacobs's influence is obvious throughout Whitehead's book but is especially conspicuous when Cora, the fugitive protagonist, hides in a small attic cell that, as in *Incidents*, functions as a "Loophole of Retreat" from whence she watches the goings on outside. "It didn't take a lot of energy," Whitehead states, "to find parallels for the language of the slave problem and the inner city problem. All those debates still are going on in different—you know, with coded language."

Whitehead is but one of many who use Jacobs's life and writing to meditate on correspondences between nineteenth-century slavery and twenty-first-century racial subjugation and between their own traumas and those of predecessors who survived them. Harriet Jacobs would be staggered to discover that slavery still exists, that her book continues to inform and motivate antislavery activity against what is now commonly called "human trafficking" or "the prison-industrial complex" but is, in essence, the buying, selling, and exploitation of human beings. Would knowing that her testimony articulates the emotions and experiences of twenty-first-century refugees from the "deep and dark, and foul . . . pit of abominations" alleviate her horror at the persistence of slavery and sexual exploitation? How would Jacobs react to learning that one day in 2005 a

1. John Crook, "Civil War Drama 'Mercy Street' Rises Again on PBS," *Boston Herald*, January 22, 2017.
2. "Colson Whitehead's 'Underground Railroad' Is a Literal Train to Freedom," *Fresh Air* interview with Terry Gross, NPR August 8, 2016.

professor of early Christianity at a predominately Jewish university in the United States would give to a Muslim Sudanese woman a copy of the Norton Critical Edition of *Incidents in the Life of a Slave Girl*, which helped her recover from her own trauma? The professor was Bernadette Brooten and the Sudanese woman was Mende Nazer, a fugitive slave internationally known for her activism and as author of her autobiographical narrative *Slave: My True Story* (2003). Nazer immediately identified with Jacobs's narrative. "I do see the similarity between her story and my story," she says, "And exactly, I feel how Harriet Jacobs must feel about her own story. I read half of the book, and I was crying a lot." Until she read *Incidents in the Life of a Slave Girl,* Nazer had had few resources for coming to terms psychologically with what she had endured, how she felt, and what her future might hold. Jacobs, Nazer said, helped her understand more fully that while the life she recounts in *Slave: My True Story* was hers alone, her experience was not unique.

Truth be told, it is something like a miracle that *Incidents* was resurrected. Not only was its publication in 1861 quickly obscured, but its existence was forgotten in a history that privileges the voices and viewpoints of a gender, race, and class to which "Linda Brent" obviously did not belong. Even when the narrative was rediscovered during the black studies movement of the 1970s, debates over author and authenticity were based more on stereotypical assumptions and the limits of individual credulity than on any concrete research. Knowledgeable nineteenth-century readers had quickly learned that "Linda Brent" was actually Harriet Jacobs. Others generally accepted assurances from the white abolitionist Lydia Maria Child that, as editor, what changes she made to the manuscript were "mainly for purposes of condensation and orderly arrangement" and that she had full confidence in the author, whom she knew personally. Amy Post's and George W. Lowther's assurances that the anonymous author was a woman of "prepossessing" appearance with "remarkable delicacy of feeling and purity of thought" were effective recommendations from prominent figures in the white and the black abolitionist movements respectively. But in the twentieth century, such testimonials had little effect on readers who knew no more about the rectitude of Post and Lowther than they did about the reliability of periodicals such as the *Christian Recorder* and luminaries like William C. Nell and John Greenleaf Whittier, who also affirm *Incidents* and its author.

In the mid-twentieth century, readers found Harriet Jacobs's narrative compelling and controversial, an artful combination of sincerity, sentiment, and sensationalism that should have made her story as famous as those by Olaudah Equiano, Frederick Douglass, or William Wells Brown. However, in the 1970s, when autobiographical writings by formerly enslaved people were being rediscovered, the most accessible were those by and about men. Scholars took to heart these authors' self-identifications as "an American Slave," "a Fugitive Slave," or "The Fugitive Blacksmith" and categorized such works as "slave narratives," defined by the pattern that most followed. Born into slavery, the narrator knows little or nothing about his circumstances—in most cases, not even his birthday or father's name. His relatively carefree childhood abruptly ends, and initiation into the systematic dehumanization of slavery's protocols turns the boy into a "slave." But again something seismic shifts his world. Sometimes it is learning to read. Often it is one too many arbitrary physical assaults. It could be a death, a pending sale, or other shocking event, but something compels the author to reject his identity as chattel, envision himself as a free man, and manifest that identity by making a hazardous and solitary flight from captivity. Even if legally still a "slave," the author demonstrates his manhood by publicly sharing his experiences, becoming an abolitionist warrior, fighting with his writing and rhetoric for justice and freedom. Reading the antebellum fugitive slave narratives was to witness, as Frederick Douglass depicts in his 1845 narrative, "how a man was made a slave and . . . how a slave was made a man."[3]

Incidents does not fit this mode. Harriet Jacobs tells the story of an enslaved woman who never doubted that she was entitled to life, liberty, and the pursuit of happiness—or at least to all the rights and privileges of respectable womanhood. Unlike her own brother and other male fugitive slave narrators, the heroine of *Incidents* refuses to abandon her family and friends by running away. Linda Brent is a young girl—pure, relatively pious, domestically inclined but not submissive—who is sexually harassed by her owner and persecuted by his jealous wife. She is courted by a free African American man who wants to exchange her chains of enslavement for the bonds of a respectable, legal marriage. However, the lecherous Dr. Flint, the white man who claims to own her body and her soul, flatly refuses to sell her or to allow any further contact with her suitor. In despair and revenge, rather than submit to Dr. Flint's advances, the girl allows herself to be seduced by his archrival Mr. Sands, a white lawyer who later became a member of Congress and the father of her two children. Even then Linda is pursued by Flint until in desperation her family hides her in a crude attic crawl space measuring three by seven by nine feet, where she remains for six years and eleven months. Only when she inadvertently exposes herself and family to imminent discovery does she, again with the aid of others,

3. "Narrative of Frederick Douglass, an American Slave," in *Norton Anthology of African American Literature*, 3rd ed., vol. 2 (New York, 2014), p. 366.

escape to the North. There she finds work as a domestic servant to a socially prominent family, reunites with her children, cultivates friendships with abolitionists, and lives discreetly and decorously for as long as she can.

Not only is Jacobs's narrative quite different from those by formerly enslaved males, but in many ways it also resembles the novels of seduction that were so popular during the mid-nineteenth century. Linda's predicament invokes the age-old tale of nefarious, powerful men's attempts to seduce chaste but low-born maidens, a plot in which the innocent girl generally succumbs and loses, if not her life, at least the respect and support of others. In *Incidents*, for example, upon discovering that Linda is pregnant, her grandmother says, "You are a disgrace to your dead mother. . . . Go away. . . . And never come to my house again." Though they are later reconciled, the grandmother pities, but does not forgive, her. Moreover, we encounter a motif central to Jacobs's story: the long stay in an attic, also seen in sentimental novels such as Charlotte Bronte's *Jane Eyre* (1847) and Harriet Beecher Stowe's *Uncle Tom's Cabin* (1852). And like novelists, Jacobs uses dialogue and detailed descriptions as if the decades had not altered or erased them in her memory.

While it seems incredible, *Incidents* is, in broad outline, a true story. Like any good writer, Jacobs selectively shapes or ignores information to achieve her literary ends. She knew that sometimes the best way for truth to be told was through artful alteration of reality and a conscious use of rhetorical and fictive techniques. She is factual, but she selects and articulates facts in ways that suit her desired aesthetic and affective goals. Within the story itself, Linda is a skilled verbal combatant. She hurls insults and writes letters that manipulate Dr. Flint. Linda learns to handle conflicts of opinion with her grandmother and to tell the slanted truth when discretion is paramount. For example, the Reverend Jeremiah Durham, Methodist minister and Underground Railroad conductor, cautions her, saying, "Your straight-forward answers do you credit; but don't answer every body so openly. It might give some heartless people a pretext for treating you with contempt." As Linda learned, and as Harriet Jacobs obviously understood, the kinds of strategic silences and circumlocutions commonly employed in conversations with all but one's most intimate friends were indispensible in life and in literature.

Harriet Jacobs's linguistic agility and literary talents were fairly sophisticated; but moving as she did within circles of other unusually articulate and savvy people, she could not help but hone her communication skills. For example, in 1849, when slave catchers were scouring New York City for her, Jacobs took refuge in Rochester, New York, with Amy and Isaac Post, whose home was an

Underground Railroad station and who hosted such celebrated black abolitionists as Sojourner Truth, Frederick Douglass, and William Nell. In Rochester, Jacobs worked in the Anti-Slavery Office and Reading Room managed by her brother, John, a fugitive who later published his own narrative, "A True Tale of Slavery" (1861), and who, like other male fugitives, frequently spoke at public meetings. The Reading Room was in the same building as the offices of Frederick Douglass's newspaper.

When she finally acceded to the pleas of Amy Post and other activists to share her story publicly, Harriet Jacobs realized that she was jeopardizing her position with her employers as well as her reputation as a respectable African American matron. Even the most decorous white ladies might whisper confidences about sexual violence against people they knew, if not against themselves, but they would resist Jacobs's portrayal of Linda as an innocent victim because prevailing racial stereotypes held that Africans were innately lascivious. Jacobs knew that readers might readily believe her assertion that slavery makes young girls "become prematurely knowing, concerning the evil ways of the world" and that it makes slaveholding husbands betray their wives. Jacobs needed to arouse the sympathies of her Northern, Christian readers while understanding full well that white women, especially, would try to distance their own lived experiences from those of blacks. She knew, also, that her gender was a further handicap because white men, especially prominent ones such as physicians and politicians, were more often believed than women, regardless of race or class.

Harriet Jacobs's sophistication about writing and readers was also influenced by her experience as a live-in servant for the family of Nathaniel Parker Willis, a poet, an editor, and reputedly the highest-paid magazine writer of his day. Willis's sister Sara Payson Willis was the extraordinarily popular author known as Fanny Fern, and the Willis home was a gathering place for literary friends and acquaintances such as Henry Wadsworth Longfellow and Edgar Allan Poe. Perhaps this is why Jacobs decided her project needed a seasoned writer. She was well connected enough to approach Harriet Beecher Stowe, the celebrated author of *Uncle Tom's Cabin,* with a sketch of her personal history and the proposition that Stowe turn Jacobs's testimony into a two-volume narrative. Jacobs stressed the need for confidentiality, but Stowe betrayed her by informing her employer, Cornelia Grinnel Willis, who until then had not known the secrets of Jacobs's past. Even worse, Stowe asked Willis for permission to incorporate Jacobs's story into her own current project, *A Key to Uncle Tom's Cabin.* Rightfully indignant but even more resolved, Jacobs decided to compose her narrative herself. It took Harriet Jacobs ten years to write her story and to have it published, but in 1861 *Linda: Or, Incidents in the Life of a Slave Girl* finally appeared "printed for the author" as a plain, dark green volume with "Linda" on its spine and a title page that proclaimed, "Written by Herself" and that names "L. Maria Child" as editor.

The 1973 edition by Harcourt Brace appears to be the first time in over a century that Harriet Jacobs's book had been reprinted. The introduction by Walter Teller is brief and barely informative, but to his credit he identifies *Incidents* as a slave narrative and the work of "Harriet Brent Jacobs." However, the packaging of the text spoke far louder than Teller's matter-of-fact commentary. The red cover of this paperback edition is emblazoned with a black, slightly blurred, lurid image of a barefoot woman being flogged by three men, while a circle of other men look on intently—a scene that does not appear in the narrative. Replacing the demure title of "Linda," as had the British pirate publishers, with *Incidents in the Life of a Slave Girl* (featuring "Slave Girl" in big, bold letters) encouraged viewing the text as the salacious confessions of "Linda Brent," increasing the chances that readers would judge the book by its cover, purchase it, but consume it as fiction.

It is not hard to understand why or how this happened. In the early 1970s, books about women in U.S. history were rare and generally focused on their lives as wives and mothers, victims, or scandalous rebels. Historians had started viewing the past from the perspectives of average citizens, highlighting experiences of the poor and working class, the immigrants and marginalized, not just those of the rich and the powerful. Some publishers were beginning to promote volumes about or by the disenfranchised and the excluded. Feminist studies, black studies, and other emerging interdisciplinary academic areas were contributing to this democratizing movement; however, books about courageous women of color were rare indeed. In general, the revised histories and the rediscovered literature made it seem, as one Feminist Press anthology proclaims, that "all the blacks were men and all the women were white." But, as that book's title continues, "some of us are brave."[4] Scholar Jean Fagan Yellin was one of those brave women. Knowing what she did about Lydia Maria Child in particular and the abolitionist movement generally, annoyed and troubled by the lack of evidence for dismissing *Incidents* as a white abolitionist novel, Yellin embarked on a remarkable research journey, eventually uncovering a cache of letters, the actual identities of the fictitiously named characters, a photo of Harriet Jacobs, and other information that she published first in a

4. Referencing the title of the pioneering anthology *All the Women Are White, All the Blacks Are Men, But Some of Us Are Brave*, ed. Gloria T. Hull, Patricia Bell Scott, and Barbara Smith (New York: Feminist Press, 1982).

scholarly journal and then in a new edition also titled *Incidents in the Life of a Slave Girl*. In sharp contrast to the 1973 edition, Yellin's was issued by the staid Harvard University Press with a basic brown cover featuring a sepia-toned photograph of a white-haired, grandmotherly Harriet Jacobs. Yellin's work fundamentally altered the scholarly conversation not merely about *Incidents in the Life of a Slave Girl* but about American literary history and culture broadly.

When the first Norton Critical Edition of *Incidents in the Life of a Slave Girl* appeared in 2001, many readers were still fixated on the racier aspects of Jacobs's life, arguing, for example, that a man in Dr. Flint's position may have tried seduction but would have lost patience and resorted to rape. On this issue, following the editors of the first Norton Critical Edition, "We believe as Jacobs must have, that her struggle with Norcom had less to do with sex than her refusal to submit to his will. . . . The success of her efforts offers a compelling case for the effectiveness of literally facing down a great evil" (p. xi). Motivated perhaps by the recent revelations about Sally Hemings and Thomas Jefferson, some readers focused on the long-term relationship between Harriet Jacobs and Samuel Tredwell Sawyer (or, as portrayed in the book, Linda and Mr. Sands). Still others viewed *Incidents* as a fictionalized autobiography that provided a true account of significant experiences in Jacobs's life, even as she was deliberately evasive on particular points, embellishing details and re-creating dialogue that is at least partially improvised. Note that Jacobs is not the only African American author whose credibility has been questioned. From Jarena Lee's *Life and Religious Experience* (1836) to Richard Wright's *Black Boy* (1945) to Barack Obama's *Dreams from My Father* (1995) to the present day, nonblack readers have so regularly required affirmations from prominent, usually white, supporters of black authors that the term "authenticating devices" has seemed invented specifically for the study of African American literature. Eloquent African American testimonies have routinely included copies of birth certificates and other legal documents, images, letters, affidavits, and excerpts from other publications to persuade readers of their authority.

In this Norton Critical Edition, as in the first, we follow the established convention of referring to Harriet Jacobs's text not as *Linda* but simply as *Incidents in the Life of a Slave Girl*. In addition, we continue to offer contextual materials that present Harriet Jacobs as its activist author via a brief chronology of her life and a cluster of other publications and letters that show her intentions and the supportive responses of her contemporaries. In the "Criticism" section of this volume, we provide selected essays that exemplify a wide range of perspectives on *Incidents*. However, now over fifteen years since the publication of the first Norton edition, choosing such material for this second edition has been quite difficult. Thanks in great part to Jean Fagan Yellin's definitive biography, *Harriet Jacobs: A Life* (2004), and her multivolume collection of *The Harriet Jacobs Family Papers* (2008), we have a glorious abundance of relevant information, which has, in turn, spawned a great outpouring of excellent critical analyses. To sample significant and provocative scholarly approaches that have appeared over the past decade or so, we reluctantly cut some articles included in the first edition and supply the appropriate citations in an updated selected bibliography. In choosing new pieces, we viewed quality and diversity as primary criteria, along with originality and relevance. We also sought work that represents ways in which Jacobs has been engaged now that *Incidents* is an African American classic and an established part of the American literary canon.[5]

We begin again with the essay that started it all. Jean Fagan Yellin's "Written by Herself: Harriet Jacobs' Slave Narrative" (1981) proves unequivocally that Harriet Jacobs, a woman enslaved in North Carolina who escaped before the Civil War, was the author of *Incidents* and that the narrative is not fiction. Yellin outlines the nature of her search for the truth of the genesis of the text to dispel further debate on that aspect of its existence. Much of her evidence comes from letters between Jacobs and the white activist Amy Post and from antislavery newspapers and other archival documents. Yellin's essay also includes the story behind Jacobs's brief exchange with Harriet Beecher Stowe, whose attitude toward the formerly enslaved woman so angered Jacobs. "Written by Herself" set in motion the full recovery of Harriet Jacobs and her writings.

Valerie Smith's "Form and Ideology in Three Slave Narratives" (1987) engages *Incidents* along with narratives of Olaudah Equiano and Frederick Douglass, two formerly enslaved men. Smith examines these narratives against a background of such external interventions as authenticating documents, amanuenses, and editors. She also considers how such interventions encouraged some readers to believe that the texts had not been written by the stated authors and did not express the viewpoints of enslaved people themselves. In addition, the hybrid nature of such texts—incorporating elements common to historical, autobiographical, and fictional writing—raises questions of interpretation. Smith argues that Jacobs knew her experiences differed in crucial ways from those of the white heroines in sentimental novels. While Jacobs may have gained by adapting sentimental novel techniques and certain conventions of narratives by formerly enslaved men, Smith states that our understanding

5. For convenience, all page numbers for *Incidents* as cited by other authors are edited to conform to this second edition.

of Jacobs as a black woman who embraced her identity comes through our ability to read the ironies, silences, and spaces in her text.

In "Reading the Fragments in the Fields of History: Harriet Jacobs's *Incidents in the Life of a Slave Girl*" (1995), John Ernest focuses our attention on Jacobs's attempt to appeal to white Northern female readers based on a shared endorsement of Christian motherhood. Complicating this strategy, however, was the extent to which she would somehow have to teach her readers how, in Ernest's words, "to *hear* and understand" her story. This process required that white women move outside of their privilege and sense of security and into an awareness of their own precarious status as well as of their involvement (if only passively) in the maintenance of the ideological system that served to normalize chattel slavery. Jacobs's daunting task, according to Ernest, was to render herself and her experience visible to her white female readers by causing them to interrogate their own experiences, even as doing so might well bring to consciousness their gendered oppression.

Frances Smith Foster's "Resisting *Incidents*" (1996) examines how and why Harriet Jacobs balked at writing her narrative and the extent to which some readers have refused to believe what Jacobs wrote. Using elements of reader-response theory, Foster first discusses examples of reader resistance stemming from habitual attitudes about gender, race, and class. Turning to *Incidents,* she notes that Jacobs's reluctance to write was due at least in part to wanting to protect her privacy, to spare her friends and relatives embarrassment and harassment, and to avoid contributing to negative stereotypes regarding African American morality. In reviewing responses of critics and readers, Foster suggests that Jacobs had good reason to be concerned; for despite her use of rhetorical and literary strategies to focus attention on the antislavery activism that motivated her writing, critics have continued to question Jacobs's authority and the authenticity of her statements. Because much of Foster's discussion focuses on contested readings, her essay helps us identify and perhaps understand moments in which we too might need to examine our interpretations of this text.

In "Reading and Redemption in *Incidents in the Life of a Slave Girl*" (1996), Sandra Gunning demonstrates that African American women have consistently refused white attempts to invalidate them by appropriating their voices and attempting to interpret their experiences for them. Gunning highlights an occasion when activist abolitionist Sojourner Truth brilliantly defied attempts to separate her body and her voice by dramatically disrobing before a gathering of white women and men while verbally confronting her audience with her body as a tangible representation of the crime of American slavery. Gunning suggests that *Incidents* also critiques black powerlessness in the face of white reading practices that separate the black voice from the black body. Gunning points out that in considering the sensitivities of the book's readers in their framing of the text, even Jacobs's white friends Lydia Maria Child and Amy Post silenced Linda Brent. However, the author's preface by Jacobs resists this constraining framework and repositions herself as narrator. By revealing what Child and Post rendered invisible in their statements, Jacobs, like Truth, uses the exploitation of her body to critique the perceived distance that separates white female experiences from those of black enslaved women.

Reminding us that Harriet Jacobs lived as a free woman of color for nineteen years between escaping from North Carolina and publishing her narrative, Mark Rifkin considers *Incidents* in relation to other publications by African American activists, many of whom were, in fact, Jacobs's friends or associates. In "'A Home Made Sacred by Protecting Laws': Black Activist Homemaking and Geographies of Citizenship in *Incidents in the Life of a Slave Girl*" (2007), Rifkin notes common tropes and concerns in terms of how such African American authors articulate and theorize their "complex and uneven" positions as citizens. Jacobs, he finds, explicitly politicized domesticity while revealing and rejecting the "lurking masculinism" in most writings of her peers. In so doing, Rifkin posits, Jacobs relates day-to-day aspects of African American life to more abstract principles and practices of national governance.

In "The Politics of Sex and Representation in Harriet Jacobs's *Incidents in the Life of a Slave Girl*" (2009), P. Gabrielle Foreman urges us to move beyond a reading of the narrative solely for its accurate depiction of Jacobs's life. Instead, Foreman advocates an interpretive approach informed by an awareness of the multiple constructions of what might be considered the *truth* of Jacobs's story, constructions that may indeed stand in contradictory tension. The multivalent nature of Jacobs's text complicates, for instance, her treatment of the sexual exploitation that she contends is endemic to chattel slavery. The narrative dynamic that Foreman dubs "simultextuality" enables an engagement with the complexity of *Incidents* without necessitating an attempt to determine the facticity of Jacobs's rendering of key aspects of her life. The most controversial such instance, and one that Foreman addresses at some length, is the sexual assault to which Jacobs is subjected at the hands of Dr. Flint.

In "'To Tell the Kitchen Version': Architectural Figurations of Race and Gender in Harriet Jacobs's *Incidents in the Life of a Slave Girl*" (2006), Katja Kanzler argues that domestic spheres, especially kitchens, are stages for particularly complex and fluid performances of gender, race, and class. Whereas conventional literary conceits proffer the home as refuge from the vulnerabilities and exposures of public life, Kanzler shows that for enslaved women this is not the case. Rooms in a house, especially kitchens and attics, she writes, are "remarkably marginal spaces." Attics are generally isolated places for secreted storage. In kitchens, such as those in *Incidents*, enslaved people and the wives of slaveholders interact in carefully scripted, complex roles that clearly dramatize the exploitative and abusive nature of slavery. But, as Kanzler demonstrates, in-between spaces such as kitchens and attics can also be stages for resistance and subversion. As in-between spaces, they are rooms that cannot be fully controlled or owned.

Samantha M. Sommers rejects notions of literature as encompassing only the text actually composed by a given author. In "Harriet Jacobs and the Recirculation of Print Culture" (2015), Sommers shows that by inserting previously printed material (sometimes reframed or edited) and by using summaries of her own letters and documents, Jacobs renders as legible her transition from slave subject of print to "an author and arranger of print." Over the course of her analysis, Sommers provocatively argues that Jacobs demonstrates on several occasions the superiority of print over oral texts. Sommers also highlights sections of *Incidents* that have received little examination—for example, Jacobs's comments late in the book regarding the deaths of Aunt Martha and her uncle Phillip.

"Class and Class Awareness in *Incidents in the Life of a Slave Girl*" (2017) represents William L. Andrews's wide-ranging study of what he calls a "striking, though almost never discussed" aspect of many pre–Civil War slave narratives. Focusing on elements in Jacobs's text that reveal her attitudes toward class and caste and on ways that her membership in "The Jacobs-Horniblow clan" inflected her perspectives, Andrews shows how Jacobs's narrative witnesses the power and privileges of enslaved families like hers, which, though restricted and relatively rare, did exist. This essay considers stylistic elements such as dialect and spotlights examples in *Incidents* of social privilege, such as that allowing Aunt Martha to mount the auction block and expose Dr. Flint's duplicity. Andrews's analysis usefully calls attention to the importance of color, class, and caste distinctions within the African American communities even under slavery.

Today, Harriet Jacobs is no longer unknown and her writings are no longer obscure. One finds commemorative historical markers at the site of her house in Cambridge, Massachusetts, and on U.S. Highway 17 in her hometown of Edenton, North Carolina. In cooperation with the National Park Service's Underground Railroad network and other agencies, the Edenton-Chowan County Tourism Development Authority operates the HarrietJacobs.org website and provides tours that highlight not only places mentioned in Jacobs's book but also other significant people and locations in African American communities of her time. In 2013, the town of Edenton held a combined celebration of its tercentennial, the 150th anniversary of the Emancipation Proclamation, and the bicentennial of Jacobs's birth.

Thanks to readers who refused to dismiss *Incidents in the Life of a Slave Girl* as an example of what Nathaniel Hawthorne dubbed fiction by "a damned mob of scribbling [white] women," Jacobs's book has forever altered our sense of American women's writing and of the antebellum fugitive slave narrative. It has helped readers recognize similarities in conditions of enslavement and responses to it across time and space and cultures. As Sissy Helff notes regarding Mende Nazer's *Slave: My True Story* (2003), such writings follow the narrative framework of Harriet Jacobs's narrative and can be read as a "palimpsestic fusion of individual and collective memory." Harriet Jacobs not only articulates experiences and feelings for similarly oppressed individuals but also demonstrates that their futures are not predetermined by their pasts.

Incidents in the Life of a Slave Girl was and continues to be provocative. As a full-length narrative by a formerly enslaved woman, it challenges the acceptance of narratives by formerly enslaved men as representing all enslaved people. Like those by men, Harriet Jacobs's autobiography details trials that she endured and that were suffered (and indeed "far worse") by millions of enslaved women. However, Jacobs also acknowledges hard-won triumphs that she and at least a few other enslaved women achieved. Before Jacobs's *Incidents*, African American writers such as Maria W. Stewart, Jarena Lee, Frances E. W. Harper, and Mary Ann Shadd Cary courageously offered testimony of African American women's lives, desires, opinions, and perspectives, often breaching protocol by entering public conversations on politics, religion, manners, morals, money, and other issues commonly considered the concerns of men only. These women sometimes approach but never quite directly comment on sexual assault, harassment, and exploitation as Harriet Jacobs does. Jacobs's remarkably brave voice is especially significant because of the space out of which it comes and, as many of her modern critics point out, because of her professed ability, beginning at a very early age and continuing throughout her life, to maintain her integrity as a moral human being in the face of seemingly insurmountable odds, to speak truth to power, and to write change into being.

FRANCES SMITH FOSTER
RICHARD YARBOROUGH

Acknowledgments

We acknowledge the work of many people (known and unknown to us) whose efforts enrich this edition of Harriet Jacobs's narrative. The existence of this narrative is something like a miracle that continues to enable understanding of and appreciation for lives and literature worldwide. The richness of literary traditions comes from the continuing work of those who follow after and who add their voices and insights to those of their forerunners. We hope this edition will be worthy of its heritage.

For assisting us in preparing this volume, we thank the many colleagues who offered their suggestions and support; our graduate students of Emory University and University of Wisconsin who did much of the library and other necessary behind-the-scenes work for the first edition as well as Erica Onugha and Brandy Underwood of UCLA, who were invaluable for ensuring this second revised edition came to be. Special thanks to Anthony Parent for telling us about the restored Norcom House. We know that we could not have accomplished our task as thoroughly as we have without the research and personal support of the indefatigable and amazingly generous Jean Fagan Yellin. We recognize the debt we all owe to her.

And to our dearly beloved Nellie Y. McKay, whose spirit stayed with us every moment and influenced every decision we made, we dedicate this volume.

Harriet Jacobs. Image courtesy of Jean Fagan Yellin. Reprinted by permission.

James Norcom (oil portrait attributed to Bass Otis, unknown date). Courtesy of the State Archives of North Carolina. Reprinted with permission of the North Carolina Department of Natural and Cultural Resources.

Who's Who in *Incidents*

Character	Person
Linda Brent	Harriet Jacobs
Mother	Delilah Horniblow
Father	Elijah Knox
William/brother	John S. Jacobs
Ellen/daughter	Louisa Matilda Jacobs
Benjamin/son	Joseph Jacobs
Aunt Martha/Grandmother	Molly Horniblow
Uncle Phillip/ Aunt Martha's son	Mark Ramsey
Uncle Benjamin/ Aunt Martha's son	Joseph
Aunt Nancy/ Aunt Martha's daughter	Betty
Miss Fanny	Hannah Pritchard
Dr. Flint	James Norcom
Mrs. Flint	Mary Matilda Horniblow Norcom
Miss Emily Flint/ Mrs. Dodge	Mary Matilda Norcom/ Mrs. Daniel Messmore
Mr. Sands	Samuel Tredwell Sawyer
Mr. and Mrs. Hobbs/ Sands's cousins	James Iredell Tredwell and Mary Blount Tredwell
Mr. Thorne/ Mrs. Hobbs's brother	Joseph Blount
Mr. Bruce/employer's spouse	Nathaniel Parker Willis
Mrs. Bruce/first employer	Mary Stace Willis
Mrs. Bruce/second employer	Cornelia Grinnell Willis

The Text of
INCIDENTS IN THE LIFE OF A SLAVE GIRL

INCIDENTS

IN THE

LIFE OF A SLAVE GIRL.

WRITTEN BY HERSELF.

"Northerners know nothing at all about Slavery. They think it is perpetual bondage only. They have no conception of the depth of *degradation* involved in that word, SLAVERY; if they had, they would never cease their efforts until so horrible a system was overthrown."

A WOMAN OF NORTH CAROLINA.

"Rise up, ye women that are at ease! Hear my voice, ye careless daughters! Give ear unto my speech."

ISAIAH xxxii. 9.

EDITED BY L. MARIA CHILD.

BOSTON:
PUBLISHED FOR THE AUTHOR.
1861.

Preface by the Author

Reader, be assured this narrative is no fiction. I am aware that some of my adventures may seem incredible; but they are, nevertheless, strictly true. I have not exaggerated the wrongs inflicted by Slavery; on the contrary, my descriptions fall far short of the facts. I have concealed the names of places, and given persons fictitious names. I had no motive for secrecy on my own account, but I deemed it kind and considerate towards others to pursue this course.

I wish I were more competent to the task I have undertaken. But I trust my readers will excuse deficiencies in consideration of circumstances. I was born and reared in Slavery; and I remained in a Slave State twenty-seven years. Since I have been at the North, it has been necessary for me to work diligently for my own support, and the education of my children. This has not left me much leisure to make up for the loss of early opportunities to improve myself; and it has compelled me to write these pages at irregular intervals, whenever I could snatch an hour from household duties.

When I first arrived in Philadelphia, Bishop Paine[1] advised me to publish a sketch of my life, but I told him I was altogether incompetent to such an undertaking. Though I have improved my mind somewhat since that time, I still remain of the same opinion; but I trust my motives will excuse what might otherwise seem presumptuous. I have not written my experiences in order to attract attention to myself; on the contrary, it would have been more pleasant to me to have been silent about my own history. Neither do I care to excite sympathy for my own sufferings. But I do earnestly desire to arouse the women of the North to a realizing sense of the condition of two millions of women at the South, still in bondage, suffering what I suffered, and most of them far worse. I want to add my testimony to that of abler pens to convince the people of the Free States what Slavery really is. Only by experience can any one realize how deep, and dark, and foul is that pit of abominations. May the blessing of God rest on this imperfect effort in behalf of my persecuted people!

LINDA BRENT[2]

1. Daniel A. Payne (1811–1893), a bishop of the African Methodist Episcopal Church and later president of Wilberforce University.
2. The pseudonym adopted by Harriet Jacobs when she initially published *Incidents*.

Introduction by the Editor

The author of the following autobiography is personally known to me, and her conversation and manners inspire me with confidence. During the last seventeen years, she has lived the greater part of the time with a distinguished family in New York, and has so deported herself as to be highly esteemed by them. This fact is sufficient, without further credentials of her character. I believe those who know her will not be disposed to doubt her veracity, though some incidents in her story are more romantic than fiction.

At her request, I have revised her manuscript; but such changes as I have made have been mainly for purposes of condensation and orderly arrangement. I have not added any thing to the incidents, or changed the import of her very pertinent remarks. With trifling exceptions, both the ideas and the language are her own. I pruned excrescences a little, but otherwise I had no reason for changing her lively and dramatic way of telling her own story. The names of both persons and places are known to me; but for good reasons I suppress them.

It will naturally excite surprise that a woman reared in Slavery should be able to write so well. But circumstances will explain this. In the first place, nature endowed her with quick perceptions. Secondly, the mistress, with whom she lived till she was twelve years old, was a kind, considerate friend, who taught her to read and spell. Thirdly, she was placed in favorable circumstances after she came to the North; having frequent intercourse with intelligent persons, who felt a friendly interest in her welfare, and were disposed to give her opportunities for self-improvement.

I am well aware that many will accuse me of indecorum for presenting these pages to the public; for the experiences of this intelligent and much-injured woman belong to a class which some call delicate subjects, and others indelicate. This peculiar phase of Slavery has generally been kept veiled; but the public ought to be made acquainted with its monstrous features, and I willingly take the responsibility of presenting them with the veil withdrawn. I do this for the sake of my sisters in bondage, who are suffering wrongs so foul, that our ears are too delicate to listen to them. I do it with the hope of arousing conscientious and reflecting women at the North to a sense of their duty in the exertion of moral influence on the question of Slavery, on all possible occasions. I do it with the hope that every man who reads this narrative will swear solemnly before God that, so far as he has power to prevent it, no fugitive from Slavery shall ever be sent back to suffer in that loathsome den of corruption and cruelty.

L. Maria Child[1]

1. Lydia Maria Child (1802–1880), novelist, journalist, activist. Child's abolitionist credentials had been established earlier by her editorship of the *National Anti-Slavery Standard* and public support of John Brown.

Contents

Incidents in the Life of a Slave Girl, Seven Years Concealed

I. Childhood

I was born a slave; but I never knew it till six years of happy childhood had passed away. My father was a carpenter, and considered so intelligent and skilful in his trade, that, when buildings out of the common line were to be erected, he was sent for from long distances, to be head workman. On condition of paying his mistress two hundred dollars a year, and supporting himself, he was allowed to work at his trade, and manage his own affairs. His strongest wish was to purchase his children; but, though he several times offered his hard earnings for that purpose, he never succeeded. In complexion my parents were a light shade of brownish yellow, and were termed mulattoes. They lived together in a comfortable home; and, though we were all slaves, I was so fondly shielded that I never dreamed I was a piece of merchandise, trusted to them for safe keeping, and liable to be demanded of them at any moment. I had one brother, William, who was two years younger than myself—a bright, affectionate child. I had also a great treasure in my maternal grandmother, who was a remarkable woman in many respects. She was the daughter of a planter in South Carolina, who, at his death, left her mother and his three children free, with money to go to St. Augustine,[1] where they had relatives. It was during the Revolutionary War; and they were captured on their passage, carried back, and sold to different purchasers. Such was the story my grandmother used to tell me; but I do not remember all the particulars. She was a little girl when she was captured and sold to the keeper of a large hotel. I have often heard her tell how hard she fared during childhood. But as she grew older she evinced so much intelligence, and was so faithful, that her master and mistress could not help seeing it was for their interest to take care of such a valuable piece of property. She became an indispensable personage in the household,

1. St. Augustine (in present-day Florida) was a British port during the Revolutionary War.

officiating in all capacities, from cook and wet nurse to seamstress. She was much praised for her cooking; and her nice crackers became so famous in the neighborhood that many people were desirous of obtaining them. In consequence of numerous requests of this kind, she asked permission of her mistress to bake crackers at night, after all the household work was done; and she obtained leave to do it, provided she would clothe herself and her children from the profits. Upon these terms, after working hard all day for her mistress, she began her midnight bakings, assisted by her two oldest children. The business proved profitable; and each year she laid by a little, which was saved for a fund to purchase her children. Her master died, and the property was divided among his heirs. The widow had her dower[2] in the hotel, which she continued to keep open. My grandmother remained in her service as a slave; but her children were divided among her master's children. As she had five, Benjamin, the youngest one, was sold, in order that each heir might have an equal portion of dollars and cents. There was so little difference in our ages that he seemed more like my brother than my uncle. He was a bright, handsome lad, nearly white; for he inherited the complexion my grandmother had derived from Anglo-Saxon ancestors. Though only ten years old, seven hundred and twenty dollars were paid for him. His sale was a terrible blow to my grandmother; but she was naturally hopeful, and she went to work with renewed energy, trusting in time to be able to purchase some of her children. She had laid up three hundred dollars, which her mistress one day begged as a loan, promising to pay her soon. The reader probably knows that no promise or writing given to a slave is legally binding; for, according to Southern laws, a slave, *being* property, can *hold* no property. When my grandmother lent her hard earnings to her mistress, she trusted solely to her honor. The honor of a slaveholder to a slave!

To this good grandmother I was indebted for many comforts. My brother Willie and I often received portions of the crackers, cakes, and preserves, she made to sell; and after we ceased to be children we were indebted to her for many more important services.

Such were the unusually fortunate circumstances of my early childhood. When I was six years old, my mother died; and then, for the first time, I learned, by the talk around me, that I was a slave. My mother's mistress was the daughter of my grandmother's mistress. She was the foster sister of my mother; they were both nourished at my grandmother's breast. In fact, my mother had been weaned at three months old, that the babe of the mistress might obtain sufficient food. They played together as children; and, when they became women, my mother was a most faithful servant to her

2. The portion of her deceased husband's estate allowed to a widow during her lifetime.

whiter foster sister. On her death-bed her mistress promised that her children should never suffer for any thing; and during her lifetime she kept her word. They all spoke kindly of my dead mother, who had been a slave merely in name, but in nature was noble and womanly. I grieved for her, and my young mind was troubled with the thought who would now take care of me and my little brother. I was told that my home was now to be with her mistress; and I found it a happy one. No toilsome or disagreeable duties were imposed upon me. My mistress was so kind to me that I was always glad to do her bidding, and proud to labor for her as much as my young years would permit. I would sit by her side for hours, sewing diligently, with a heart as free from care as that of any free-born white child. When she thought I was tired, she would send me out to run and jump; and away I bounded, to gather berries or flowers to decorate her room. Those were happy days—too happy to last. The slave child had no thought for the morrow; but there came that blight, which too surely waits on every human being born to be a chattel.

When I was nearly twelve years old, my kind mistress sickened and died. As I saw the cheek grow paler, and the eye more glassy, how earnestly I prayed in my heart that she might live! I loved her; for she had been almost like a mother to me. My prayers were not answered. She died, and they buried her in the little churchyard, where, day after day, my tears fell upon her grave.

I was sent to spend a week with my grandmother. I was now old enough to begin to think of the future; and again and again I asked myself what they would do with me. I felt sure I should never find another mistress so kind as the one who was gone. She had promised my dying mother that her children should never suffer for any thing; and when I remembered that, and recalled her many proofs of attachment to me, I could not help having some hopes that she had left me free. My friends were almost certain it would be so. They thought she would be sure to do it, on account of my mother's love and faithful service. But, alas! we all know that the memory of a faithful slave does not avail much to save her children from the auction block.

After a brief period of suspense, the will of my mistress was read, and we learned that she had bequeathed me to her sister's daughter, a child of five years old. So vanished our hopes. My mistress had taught me the precepts of God's Word: "Thou shalt love thy neighbor as thyself."[3] "Whatsoever ye would that men should do unto you, do ye even so unto them."[4] But I was her slave, and I suppose she did not recognize me as her neighbor. I would give much to blot out

3. Mark 12.31.
4. Matthew 7.12.

from my memory that one great wrong. As a child, I loved my mistress; and, looking back on the happy days I spent with her, I try to think with less bitterness of this act of injustice. While I was with her, she taught me to read and spell; and for this privilege, which so rarely falls to the lot of a slave, I bless her memory.

She possessed but few slaves; and at her death those were all distributed among her relatives. Five of them were my grandmother's children, and had shared the same milk that nourished her mother's children. Notwithstanding my grandmother's long and faithful service to her owners, not one of her children escaped the auction block. These God-breathing machines are no more, in the sight of their masters, than the cotton they plant, or the horses they tend.

II. The New Master and Mistress

Dr. Flint, a physician in the neighborhood, had married the sister of my mistress, and I was now the property of their little daughter. It was not without murmuring that I prepared for my new home; and what added to my unhappiness, was the fact that my brother William was purchased by the same family. My father, by his nature, as well as by the habit of transacting business as a skilful mechanic, had more of the feelings of a freeman than is common among slaves. My brother was a spirited boy; and being brought up under such influences, he early detested the name of master and mistress. One day, when his father and his mistress both happened to call him at the same time, he hesitated between the two; being perplexed to know which had the strongest claim upon his obedience. He finally concluded to go to his mistress. When my father reproved him for it, he said, "You both called me, and I didn't know which I ought to go to first."

"You are *my* child," replied our father, "and when I call you, you should come immediately, if you have to pass through fire and water."

Poor Willie! He was now to learn his first lesson of obedience to a master. Grandmother tried to cheer us with hopeful words, and they found an echo in the credulous hearts of youth.

When we entered our new home we encountered cold looks, cold words, and cold treatment. We were glad when the night came. On my narrow bed I moaned and wept, I felt so desolate and alone.

I had been there nearly a year, when a dear little friend of mine was buried. I heard her mother sob, as the clods fell on the coffin of her only child, and I turned away from the grave, feeling thankful that I still had something left to love. I met my grandmother, who said, "Come with me, Linda;" and from her tone I knew that something sad had happened. She led me apart from the people, and then said, "My child, your father is dead." Dead! How could I believe it? He had died so suddenly I had not even heard that he was sick. I went home with my grandmother. My heart rebelled against God, who had taken from me mother, father, mistress, and friend. The good grandmother tried to comfort me. "Who knows the ways of God?" said she. "Perhaps they have been kindly taken from the evil days to come." Years afterwards I often thought of this. She promised to be a mother to her grandchildren, so far as she might be permitted to do so; and strengthened by her love, I returned to my master's. I thought I should be allowed to go to my father's house the next morning; but I was ordered to go for flowers, that my mistress's house might be decorated for an evening party. I spent the day gathering flowers and weaving them into festoons, while the dead body of my father was lying within a mile of me. What cared my owners for that? he was merely a piece of property. Moreover, they thought he had spoiled his children, by teaching them to feel that they were human beings. This was blasphemous doctrine for a slave to teach; presumptuous in him, and dangerous to the masters.

The next day I followed his remains to a humble grave beside that of my dear mother. There were those who knew my father's worth, and respected his memory.

My home now seemed more dreary than ever. The laugh of the little slave-children sounded harsh and cruel. It was selfish to feel so about the joy of others. My brother moved about with a very grave face. I tried to comfort him, by saying, "Take courage, Willie; brighter days will come by and by."

"You don't know any thing about it, Linda," he replied. "We shall have to stay here all our days; we shall never be free."

I argued that we were growing older and stronger, and that perhaps we might, before long, be allowed to hire our own time, and then we could earn money to buy our freedom. William declared this was much easier to say than to do; moreover, he did not intend to *buy* his freedom. We held daily controversies upon this subject.

Little attention was paid to the slaves' meals in Dr. Flint's house. If they could catch a bit of food while it was going, well and good. I gave myself no trouble on that score, for on my various errands I passed my grandmother's house, where there was always something to spare for me. I was frequently threatened with punishment if I stopped there; and my grandmother, to avoid detaining me, often stood at the gate with something for my breakfast or dinner. I was indebted to *her* for all my comforts, spiritual or temporal. It was *her* labor that supplied my scanty wardrobe. I have a vivid recollection of the linsey-woolsey[1] dress given me every winter by Mrs. Flint. How I hated it! It was one of the badges of slavery.

While my grandmother was thus helping to support me from her hard earnings, the three hundred dollars she had lent her mistress were never repaid. When her mistress died, her son-in-law, Dr. Flint, was appointed executor. When grandmother applied to him for payment, he said the estate was insolvent, and the law prohibited payment. It did not, however, prohibit him from retaining the silver candelabra, which had been purchased with that money. I presume they will be handed down in the family, from generation to generation.

My grandmother's mistress had always promised her that, at her death, she should be free; and it was said that in her will she made good the promise. But when the estate was settled, Dr. Flint told the faithful old servant that, under existing circumstances, it was necessary she should be sold.

On the appointed day, the customary advertisement was posted up, proclaiming that there would be a "public sale of negroes, horses, &c." Dr. Flint called to tell my grandmother that he was unwilling to wound her feelings by putting her up at auction, and that he would prefer to dispose of her at private sale. My grandmother saw through his hypocrisy; she understood very well that he was ashamed of the job. She was a very spirited woman, and if he was base enough to sell her, when her mistress intended she should be free, she was determined the public should know it. She had for a long time supplied many families with crackers and preserves; consequently, "Aunt Marthy," as she was called, was generally known, and every body who knew her respected her intelligence and good character. Her long and faithful service in the family was also well known, and the intention of her mistress to leave her free. When the day of sale came, she took her place among the chattels, and at the first call she sprang upon the auction-block. Many voices called out, "Shame! Shame! Who is going to sell *you*, aunt Marthy? Don't stand there! That is no place for *you*." Without saying a word, she quietly awaited her fate. No one bid for her. At last, a feeble voice said, "Fifty dollars." It came from a maiden lady, seventy years old, the sister of my grandmother's deceased mistress. She had lived forty years under the same roof with my grandmother; she knew how faithfully she had served her owners, and how cruelly she had been defrauded of her rights; and she resolved to protect her. The auctioneer waited for a higher bid; but her wishes were respected; no one bid above her. She could neither read nor write; and when the bill of sale was made out, she signed it with a cross. But what consequence was that,

1. Cheap coarse cloth made of crude linen or cotton fibers mixed with wool.

when she had a big heart overflowing with human kindness? She gave the old servant her freedom.

At that time, my grandmother was just fifty years old. Laborious years had passed since then; and now my brother and I were slaves to the man who had defrauded her of her money, and tried to defraud her of her freedom. One of my mother's sisters, called Aunt Nancy, was also a slave in his family. She was a kind, good aunt to me; and supplied the place of both housekeeper and waiting maid to her mistress. She was, in fact, at the beginning and end of every thing.

Mrs. Flint, like many southern women, was totally deficient in energy. She had not strength to superintend her household affairs; but her nerves were so strong, that she could sit in her easy chair and see a woman whipped, till the blood trickled from every stroke of the lash. She was a member of the church; but partaking of the Lord's supper did not seem to put her in a Christian frame of mind. If dinner was not served at the exact time on that particular Sunday, she would station herself in the kitchen, and wait till it was dished, and then spit in all the kettles and pans that had been used for cooking. She did this to prevent the cook and her children from eking out their meagre fare with the remains of the gravy and other scrapings. The slaves could get nothing to eat except what she chose to give them. Provisions were weighed out by the pound and ounce, three times a day. I can assure you she gave them no chance to eat wheat bread from her flour barrel. She knew how many biscuits a quart of flour would make, and exactly what size they ought to be.

Dr. Flint was an epicure.[2] The cook never sent a dinner to his table without fear and trembling; for if there happened to be a dish not to his liking, he would either order her to be whipped, or compel her to eat every mouthful of it in his presence. The poor, hungry creature might not have objected to eating it; but she did object to having her master cram it down her throat till she choked.

They had a pet dog, that was a nuisance in the house. The cook was ordered to make some Indian mush[3] for him. He refused to eat, and when his head was held over it, the froth flowed from his mouth into the basin. He died a few minutes after. When Dr. Flint came in, he said the mush had not been well cooked, and that was the reason the animal would not eat it. He sent for the cook, and compelled her to eat it. He thought that the woman's stomach was stronger than the dog's; but her sufferings afterwards proved that he was mistaken. This poor woman endured many cruelties from her master and mistress; sometimes she was locked up, away from her nursing baby, for a whole day and night.

2. A person who enjoys fine food; a gourmet.
3. A corn porridge.

When I had been in the family a few weeks, one of the plantation slaves was brought to town, by order of his master. It was near night when he arrived, and Dr. Flint ordered him to be taken to the work house, and tied up to the joist, so that his feet would just escape the ground. In that situation he was to wait till the doctor had taken his tea. I shall never forget that night. Never before, in my life, had I heard hundreds of blows fall, in succession, on a human being. His piteous groans, and his "O, pray don't, massa," rang in my ear for months afterwards. There were many conjectures as to the cause of this terrible punishment. Some said master accused him of stealing corn; others said the slave had quarrelled with his wife, in presence of the overseer, and had accused his master of being the father of her child. They were both black, and the child was very fair.

I went into the work house next morning, and saw the cowhide still wet with blood, and the boards all covered with gore. The poor man lived, and continued to quarrel with his wife. A few months afterwards Dr. Flint handed them both over to a slave-trader. The guilty man put their value into his pocket, and had the satisfaction of knowing that they were out of sight and hearing. When the mother was delivered into the trader's hands, she said, "You *promised* to treat me well." To which he replied, "You have let your tongue run too far; damn you!" She had forgotten that it was a crime for a slave to tell who was the father of her child.

From others than the master persecution also comes in such cases. I once saw a young slave girl dying soon after the birth of a child nearly white. In her agony she cried out, "O Lord, come and take me!" Her mistress stood by, and mocked at her like an incarnate fiend. "You suffer, do you?" she exclaimed. "I am glad of it. You deserve it all, and more too."

The girl's mother said, "The baby is dead, thank God; and I hope my poor child will soon be in heaven, too."

"Heaven!" retorted the mistress. "There is no such place for the like of her and her bastard."

The poor mother turned away, sobbing. Her dying daughter called her, feebly, and as she bent over her, I heard her say, "Don't grieve so, mother; God knows all about it; and HE will have mercy upon me."

Her sufferings, afterwards, became so intense, that her mistress felt unable to stay; but when she left the room, the scornful smile was still on her lips. Seven children called her mother. The poor black woman had but the one child, whose eyes she saw closing in death, while she thanked God for taking her away from the greater bitterness of life.

III. The Slaves' New Year's Day

Dr. Flint owned a fine residence in town, several farms, and about fifty slaves, besides hiring a number by the year.

Hiring-day at the south takes place on the 1st of January. On the 2d, the slaves are expected to go to their new masters. On a farm, they work until the corn and cotton are laid. They then have two holidays. Some masters give them a good dinner under the trees. This over, they work until Christmas eve. If no heavy charges are meantime brought against them, they are given four or five holidays, whichever the master or overseer may think proper. Then comes New Year's eve; and they gather together their little alls, or more properly speaking, their little nothings, and wait anxiously for the dawning of day. At the appointed hour the grounds are thronged with men, women, and children, waiting, like criminals, to hear their doom pronounced. The slave is sure to know who is the most humane, or cruel master, within forty miles of him.

It is easy to find out, on that day, who clothes and feeds his slaves well; for he is surrounded by a crowd, begging, "Please, massa, hire me this year. I will work *very* hard, massa."

If a slave is unwilling to go with his new master, he is whipped, or locked up in jail, until he consents to go, and promises not to run away during the year. Should he chance to change his mind, thinking it justifiable to violate an extorted promise, woe unto him if he is caught! The whip is used till the blood flows at his feet; and his stiffened limbs are put in chains, to be dragged in the field for days and days!

If he lives until the next year, perhaps the same man will hire him again, without even giving him an opportunity of going to the hiring-ground. After those for hire are disposed of, those for sale are called up.

O, you happy free women, contrast *your* New Year's day with that of the poor bond-woman! With you it is a pleasant season, and the light of the day is blessed. Friendly wishes meet you every where, and gifts are showered upon you. Even hearts that have been estranged from you soften at this season, and lips that have been silent echo back, "I wish you a happy New Year." Children bring their little offerings, and raise their rosy lips for a caress. They are your own, and no hand but that of death can take them from you.

But to the slave mother New Year's day comes laden with peculiar sorrows. She sits on her cold cabin floor, watching the children who may all be torn from her the next morning; and often does she wish that she and they might die before the day dawns. She may be an ignorant creature, degraded by the system that has brutalized her from childhood; but she has a mother's instincts, and is capable of feeling a mother's agonies.

On one of these sale days, I saw a mother lead seven children to the auction-block. She knew that *some* of them would be taken from her; but they took *all*. The children were sold to a slave-trader, and their mother was bought by a man in her own town. Before night her children were all far away. She begged the trader to tell her where he intended to take them; this he refused to do. How *could* he, when he knew he would sell them, one by one, wherever he could command the highest price? I met that mother in the street, and her wild, haggard face lives to-day in my mind. She wrung her hands in anguish, and exclaimed, "Gone! All gone! Why *don't* God kill me?" I had no words wherewith to comfort her. Instances of this kind are of daily, yea, of hourly occurrence.

Slaveholders have a method, peculiar to their institution, of getting rid of *old* slaves, whose lives have been worn out in their service. I knew an old woman, who for seventy years faithfully served her master. She had become almost helpless, from hard labor and disease. Her owners moved to Alabama, and the old black woman was left to be sold to any body who would give twenty dollars for her.

IV. The Slave Who Dared to Feel like a Man

Two years had passed since I entered Dr. Flint's family, and those years had brought much of the knowledge that comes from experience, though they had afforded little opportunity for any other kinds of knowledge.

My grandmother had, as much as possible, been a mother to her orphan grandchildren. By perseverance and unwearied industry, she was now mistress of a snug little home, surrounded with the necessaries of life. She would have been happy could her children have shared them with her. There remained but three children and two grandchildren, all slaves. Most earnestly did she strive to make us feel that it was the will of God: that He had seen fit to place us under such circumstances; and though it seemed hard, we ought to pray for contentment.

It was a beautiful faith, coming from a mother who could not call her children her own. But I, and Benjamin, her youngest boy, condemned it. We reasoned that it was much more the will of God that we should be situated as she was. We longed for a home like hers. There we always found sweet balsam[1] for our troubles. She was so loving, so sympathizing! She always met us with a smile, and listened

1. A healing plant resin, balm.

with patience to all our sorrows. She spoke so hopefully, that unconsciously the clouds gave place to sunshine. There was a grand big oven there, too, that baked bread and nice things for the town, and we knew there was always a choice bit in store for us.

But, alas! even the charms of the old oven failed to reconcile us to our hard lot. Benjamin was now a tall, handsome lad, strongly and gracefully made, and with a spirit too bold and daring for a slave. My brother William, now twelve years old, had the same aversion to the word master that he had when he was an urchin of seven years. I was his confidant. He came to me with all his troubles. I remember one instance in particular. It was on a lovely spring morning, and when I marked the sunlight dancing here and there, its beauty seemed to mock my sadness. For my master, whose restless, craving, vicious nature roved about day and night, seeking whom to devour, had just left me, with stinging, scorching words; words that scathed ear and brain like fire. O, how I despised him! I thought how glad I should be, if some day when he walked the earth, it would open and swallow him up, and disencumber the world of a plague.

When he told me that I was made for his use, made to obey his command in *every* thing; that I was nothing but a slave, whose will must and should surrender to his, never before had my puny arm felt half so strong.

So deeply was I absorbed in painful reflections afterwards, that I neither saw nor heard the entrance of any one, till the voice of William sounded close beside me. "Linda," said he, "what makes you look so sad? I love you. O, Linda, isn't this a bad world? Every body seems so cross and unhappy. I wish I had died when poor father did."

I told him that every body was *not* cross, or unhappy; that those who had pleasant homes, and kind friends, and who were not afraid to love them, were happy. But we, who were slave-children, without father or mother, could not expect to be happy. We must be good; perhaps that would bring us contentment.

"Yes," he said, "I try to be good; but what's the use? They are all the time troubling me." Then he proceeded to relate his afternoon's difficulty with young master Nicholas. It seemed that the brother of master Nicholas had pleased himself with making up stories about William. Master Nicholas said he should be flogged, and he would do it. Whereupon he went to work; but William fought bravely, and the young master, finding he was getting the better of him, undertook to tie his hands behind him. He failed in that likewise. By dint of kicking and fisting, William came out of the skirmish none the worse for a few scratches.

He continued to discourse on his young master's *meanness*; how he whipped the *little* boys, but was a perfect coward when a tussle ensued between him and white boys of his own size. On such occasions he always took to his legs. William had other charges to make against him. One was his rubbing up pennies with quicksilver,[2] and passing them off for quarters of a dollar on an old man who kept a fruit stall. William was often sent to buy fruit, and he earnestly inquired of me what he ought to do under such circumstances. I told him it was certainly wrong to deceive the old man, and that it was his duty to tell him of the impositions practised by his young master. I assured him the old man would not be slow to comprehend the whole, and there the matter would end. William thought it might with the old man, but not with *him*. He said he did not mind the smart of the whip, but he did not like the *idea* of being whipped.

While I advised him to be good and forgiving I was not unconscious of the beam in my own eye.[3] It was the very knowledge of my own shortcomings that urged me to retain, if possible, some sparks of my brother's God-given nature. I had not lived fourteen years in slavery for nothing. I had felt, seen, and heard enough, to read the characters, and question the motives, of those around me. The war of my life had begun; and though one of God's most powerless creatures, I resolved never to be conquered. Alas, for me!

If there was one pure, sunny spot for me, I believed it to be in Benjamin's heart, and in another's, whom I loved with all the ardor of a girl's first love. My owner knew of it, and sought in every way to render me miserable. He did not resort to corporal punishment, but to all the petty, tyrannical ways that human ingenuity could devise.

I remember the first time I was punished. It was in the month of February. My grandmother had taken my old shoes, and replaced them with a new pair. I needed them; for several inches of snow had fallen, and it still continued to fall. When I walked through Mrs. Flint's room, their creaking grated harshly on her refined nerves. She called me to her, and asked what I had about me that made such a horrid noise. I told her it was my new shoes. "Take them off," said she; "and if you put them on again, I'll throw them into the fire."

I took them off, and my stockings also. She then sent me a long distance, on an errand. As I went through the snow, my bare feet tingled. That night I was very hoarse; and I went to bed thinking the next day would find me sick, perhaps dead. What was my grief on waking to find myself quite well!

I had imagined if I died, or was laid up for some time, that my mistress would feel a twinge of remorse that she had so hated "the little imp," as she styled me. It was my ignorance of that mistress that gave rise to such extravagant imaginings.

2. Mercury.
3. Matthew 7.3–5, Luke 6.41–42.

Dr. Flint occasionally had high prices offered for me; but he always said, "She don't belong to me. She is my daughter's property, and I have no right to sell her." Good, honest man! My young mistress was still a child, and I could look for no protection from her. I loved her, and she returned my affection. I once heard her father allude to her attachment to me; and his wife promptly replied that it proceeded from fear. This put unpleasant doubts into my mind. Did the child feign what she did not feel? or was her mother jealous of the mite of love she bestowed on me? I concluded it must be the latter. I said to myself, "Surely, little children are true."

One afternoon I sat at my sewing, feeling unusual depression of spirits. My mistress had been accusing me of an offence, of which I assured her I was perfectly innocent; but I saw, by the contemptuous curl of her lip, that she believed I was telling a lie.

I wondered for what wise purpose God was leading me through such thorny paths, and whether still darker days were in store for me. As I sat musing thus, the door opened softly, and William came in. "Well, brother," said I, "what is the matter this time?"

"O Linda, Ben and his master have had a dreadful time!" said he.

My first thought was that Benjamin was killed. "Don't be frightened, Linda," said William; "I will tell you all about it."

It appeared that Benjamin's master had sent for him, and he did not immediately obey the summons. When he did, his master was angry, and began to whip him. He resisted. Master and slave fought, and finally the master was thrown. Benjamin had cause to tremble; for he had thrown to the ground his master—one of the richest men in town. I anxiously awaited the result.

That night I stole to my grandmother's house, and Benjamin also stole thither from his master's. My grandmother had gone to spend a day or two with an old friend living in the country.

"I have come," said Benjamin, "to tell you good by. I am going away."

I inquired where.

"To the north," he replied.

I looked at him to see whether he was in earnest. I saw it all in his firm, set mouth. I implored him not to go, but he paid no heed to my words. He said he was no longer a boy, and every day made his yoke more galling. He had raised his hand against his master, and was to be publicly whipped for the offence. I reminded him of the poverty and hardships he must encounter among strangers. I told him he might be caught and brought back; and that was terrible to think of.

He grew vexed, and asked if poverty and hardships with freedom, were not preferable to our treatment in slavery. "Linda," he continued, "we are dogs here; foot-balls, cattle, every thing that's mean. No, I will not stay. Let them bring me back. We don't die but once."

He was right; but it was hard to give him up. "Go," said I, "and break your mother's heart."

I repented of my words ere they were out.

"Linda," said he, speaking as I had not heard him speak that evening, "how *could* you say that? Poor mother! be kind to her, Linda; and you, too, cousin Fanny."

Cousin Fanny was a friend who had lived some years with us.

Farewells were exchanged, and the bright, kind boy, endeared to us by so many acts of love, vanished from our sight.

It is not necessary to state how he made his escape. Suffice it to say, he was on his way to New York when a violent storm overtook the vessel. The captain said he must put into the nearest port. This alarmed Benjamin, who was aware that he would be advertised in every port near his own town. His embarrassment was noticed by the captain. To port they went. There the advertisement met the captain's eye. Benjamin so exactly answered its description, that the captain laid hold on him, and bound him in chains. The storm passed, and they proceeded to New York. Before reaching that port Benjamin managed to get off his chains and throw them overboard. He escaped from the vessel, but was pursued, captured, and carried back to his master.

When my grandmother returned home and found her youngest child had fled, great was her sorrow; but, with characteristic piety, she said, "God's will be done." Each morning, she inquired if any news had been heard from her boy. Yes, news *was* heard. The master was rejoicing over a letter, announcing the capture of his human chattel.

That day seems but as yesterday, so well do I remember it. I saw him led through the streets in chains, to jail. His face was ghastly pale, yet full of determination. He had begged one of the sailors to go to his mother's house and ask her not to meet him. He said the sight of her distress would take from him all self-control. She yearned to see him, and she went; but she screened herself in the crowd, that it might be as her child had said.

We were not allowed to visit him; but we had known the jailer for years, and he was a kind-hearted man. At midnight he opened the jail door for my grandmother and myself to enter, in disguise. When we entered the cell not a sound broke the stillness. "Benjamin, Benjamin!" whispered my grandmother. No answer. "Benjamin!" she again faltered. There was a jingle of chains. The moon had just risen, and cast an uncertain light through the bars of the window. We knelt down and took Benjamin's cold hands in ours. We did not speak.

Sobs were heard, and Benjamin's lips were unsealed; for his mother was weeping on his neck. How vividly does memory bring back that sad night! Mother and son talked together. He asked her pardon for the suffering he had caused her. She said she had nothing to forgive; she could not blame his desire for freedom. He told her that when he was captured, he broke away, and was about casting himself into the river, when thoughts of *her* came over him, and he desisted. She asked if he did not also think of God. I fancied I saw his face grow fierce in the moonlight. He answered, "No, I did not think of him. When a man is hunted like a wild beast he forgets there is a God, a heaven. He forgets every thing in his struggle to get beyond the reach of the bloodhounds."

"Don't talk so, Benjamin," said she. "Put your trust in God. Be humble, my child, and your master will forgive you."

"Forgive me for *what*, mother? For not letting him treat me like a dog? No! I will never humble myself to him. I have worked for him for nothing all my life, and I am repaid with stripes and imprisonment. Here I will stay till I die, or till he sells me."

The poor mother shuddered at his words. I think he felt it; for when he next spoke, his voice was calmer. "Don't fret about me, mother. I ain't worth it," said he. "I wish I had some of your goodness. You bear every thing patiently, just as though you thought it was all right. I wish I could."

She told him she had not always been so; once, she was like him; but when sore troubles came upon her, and she had no arm to lean upon, she learned to call on God, and he lightened her burdens. She besought him to do likewise.

We overstaid our time, and were obliged to hurry from the jail.

Benjamin had been imprisoned three weeks, when my grandmother went to intercede for him with his master. He was immovable. He said Benjamin should serve as an example to the rest of his slaves; he should be kept in jail till he was subdued, or be sold if he got but one dollar for him. However, he afterwards relented in some degree. The chains were taken off, and we were allowed to visit him.

As his food was of the coarsest kind, we carried him as often as possible a warm supper, accompanied with some little luxury for the jailer.

Three months elapsed, and there was no prospect of release or of a purchaser. One day he was heard to sing and laugh. This piece of indecorum was told to his master, and the overseer was ordered to re-chain him. He was now confined in an apartment with other prisoners, who were covered with filthy rags. Benjamin was chained near them, and was soon covered with vermin. He worked at his chains till he succeeded in getting out of them. He passed them through the bars of the window, with a request that they should be taken to his master, and he should be informed that he was covered with vermin.

This audacity was punished with heavier chains, and prohibition of our visits.

My grandmother continued to send him fresh changes of clothes. The old ones were burned up. The last night we saw him in jail his mother still begged him to send for his master, and beg his pardon. Neither persuasion nor argument could turn him from his purpose. He calmly answered, "I am waiting his time."

Those chains were mournful to hear.

Another three months passed, and Benjamin left his prison walls. We that loved him waited to bid him a long and last farewell. A slave trader had bought him. You remember, I told you what price he brought when ten years of age. Now he was more than twenty years old, and sold for three hundred dollars. The master had been blind to his own interest. Long confinement had made his face too pale, his form too thin; moreover, the trader had heard something of his character, and it did not strike him as suitable for a slave. He said he would give any price if the handsome lad was a girl. We thanked God that he was not.

Could you have seen that mother clinging to her child, when they fastened the irons upon his wrists; could you have heard her heart-rending groans, and seen her bloodshot eyes wander wildly from face to face, vainly pleading for mercy; could you have witnessed that scene as I saw it, you would exclaim, *Slavery is damnable!*

Benjamin, her youngest, her pet, was forever gone! She could not realize it. She had had an interview with the trader for the purpose of ascertaining if Benjamin could be purchased. She was told it was impossible, as he had given bonds not to sell him till he was out of the state. He promised that he would not sell him till he reached New Orleans.

With a strong arm and unvaried trust, my grandmother began her work of love. Benjamin must be free. If she succeeded, she knew they would still be separated; but the sacrifice was not too great. Day and night she labored. The trader's price would treble that he gave; but she was not discouraged.

She employed a lawyer to write to a gentleman, whom she knew, in New Orleans. She begged him to interest himself for Benjamin, and he willingly favored her request. When he saw Benjamin, and stated his business, he thanked him; but said he preferred to wait a while before making the trader an offer. He knew he had tried to obtain a high price for him, and had invariably failed. This encouraged him to make another effort for freedom. So one morning, long before day, Benjamin was missing. He was riding over the blue billows, bound for Baltimore.

For once his white face did him a kindly service. They had no suspicion that it belonged to a slave; otherwise, the law would have been followed out to the letter, and the *thing* rendered back to slavery. The brightest skies are often overshadowed by the darkest clouds. Benjamin was taken sick, and compelled to remain in Baltimore three weeks. His strength was slow in returning; and his desire to continue his journey seemed to retard his recovery. How could he get strength without air and exercise? He resolved to venture on a short walk. A by-street was selected, where he thought himself secure of not being met by any one that knew him; but a voice called out, "Halloo, Ben, my boy! what are you doing *here*?"

His first impulse was to run; but his legs trembled so that he could not stir. He turned to confront his antagonist, and behold, there stood his old master's next door neighbor! He thought it was all over with him now; but it proved otherwise. That man was a miracle. He possessed a goodly number of slaves, and yet was not quite deaf to that mystic clock, whose ticking is rarely heard in the slaveholder's breast.

"Ben, you are sick," said he. "Why, you look like a ghost. I guess I gave you something of a start. Never mind, Ben, I am not going to touch you. You had a pretty tough time of it, and you may go on your way rejoicing for all me. But I would advise you to get out of this place plaguy quick,[4] for there are several gentlemen here from our town." He described the nearest and safest route to New York, and added, "I shall be glad to tell your mother I have seen you. Good by, Ben."

Benjamin turned away, filled with gratitude, and surprised that the town he hated contained such a gem—a gem worthy of a purer setting.

This gentleman was a Northerner by birth, and had married a southern lady. On his return, he told my grandmother that he had seen her son, and of the service he had rendered him.

Benjamin reached New York safely, and concluded to stop there until he had gained strength enough to proceed further. It happened that my grandmother's only remaining son had sailed for the same city on business for his mistress. Through God's providence, the brothers met. You may be sure it was a happy meeting. "O Phil," exclaimed Benjamin, "I am here at last." Then he told him how near he came to dying, almost in sight of free land, and how he prayed that he might live to get one breath of free air. He said life was worth something now, and it would be hard to die. In the old jail he had not valued it; once, he was tempted to destroy it; but something, he did not know what, had prevented him; perhaps it was fear. He had heard those who profess to be religious declare there was no heaven

4. Very quickly.

for self-murderers; and as his life had been pretty hot here, he did not desire a continuation of the same in another world. "If I die now," he exclaimed, "thank God, I shall die a freeman!"

He begged my uncle Phillip not to return south; but stay and work with him, till they earned enough to buy those at home. His brother told him it would kill their mother if he deserted her in her trouble. She had pledged her house, and with difficulty had raised money to buy him. Would he be bought?

"No, never!" he replied. "Do you suppose, Phil, when I have got so far out of their clutches, I will give them one red cent? No! And do you suppose I would turn mother out of her home in her old age? That I would let her pay all those hard-earned dollars for me, and never to see me? For you know she will stay south as long as her other children are slaves. What a good mother! Tell her to buy *you*, Phil. You have been a comfort to her, and I have been a trouble. And Linda, poor Linda; what'll become of her? Phil, you don't know what a life they lead her. She has told me something about it, and I wish old Flint was dead, or a better man. When I was in jail, he asked her if she didn't want *him* to ask my master to forgive me, and take me home again. She told him, No; that I didn't want to go back. He got mad, and said we were all alike. I never despised my own master half as much as I do that man. There is many a worse slaveholder than my master; but for all that I would not be his slave."

While Benjamin was sick, he had parted with nearly all his clothes to pay necessary expenses. But he did not part with a little pin I fastened in his bosom when we parted. It was the most valuable thing I owned, and I thought none more worthy to wear it. He had it still.

His brother furnished him with clothes, and gave him what money he had.

They parted with moistened eyes; and as Benjamin turned away, he said, "Phil, I part with all my kindred." And so it proved. We never heard from him again.

Uncle Phillip came home; and the first words he uttered when he entered the house were, "Mother, Ben is free! I have seen him in New York." She stood looking at him with a bewildered air. "Mother, don't you believe it?" he said, laying his hand softly upon her shoulder. She raised her hands, and exclaimed, "God be praised! Let us thank him." She dropped on her knees, and poured forth her heart in prayer. Then Phillip must sit down and repeat to her every word Benjamin had said. He told her all; only he forbore to mention how sick and pale her darling looked. Why should he distress her when she could do him no good?

The brave old woman still toiled on, hoping to rescue some of her other children. After a while she succeeded in buying Phillip. She paid eight hundred dollars, and came home with the precious document that secured his freedom. The happy mother and son sat together by the old hearthstone that night, telling how proud they were of each other, and how they would prove to the world that they could take care of themselves, as they had long taken care of others. We all concluded by saying, "He that is *willing* to be a slave, let him be a slave."

V. The Trials of Girlhood

During the first years of my service in Dr. Flint's family, I was accustomed to share some indulgences with the children of my mistress. Though this seemed to me no more than right, I was grateful for it, and tried to merit the kindness by the faithful discharge of my duties. But I now entered on my fifteenth year—a sad epoch in the life of a slave girl. My master began to whisper foul words in my ear. Young as I was, I could not remain ignorant of their import. I tried to treat them with indifference or contempt. The master's age, my extreme youth, and the fear that his conduct would be reported to my grandmother, made him bear this treatment for many months. He was a crafty man, and resorted to many means to accomplish his purposes. Sometimes he had stormy, terrific ways, that made his victims tremble; sometimes he assumed a gentleness that he thought must surely subdue. Of the two, I preferred his stormy moods, although they left me trembling. He tried his utmost to corrupt the pure principles my grandmother had instilled. He peopled my young mind with unclean images, such as only a vile monster could think of. I turned from him with disgust and hatred. But he was my master. I was compelled to live under the same roof with him—where I saw a man forty years my senior daily violating the most sacred commandments of nature. He told me I was his property; that I must be subject to his will in all things. My soul revolted against the mean tyranny. But where could I turn for protection? No matter whether the slave girl be as black as ebony or as fair as her mistress. In either case, there is no shadow of law to protect her from insult, from violence, or even from death; all these are inflicted by fiends who bear the shape of men. The mistress, who ought to protect the helpless victim, has no other feelings towards her but those of jealousy and rage. The degradation, the wrongs, the vices, that grow out of slavery, are more than I can describe. They are greater than you would willingly believe. Surely, if you credited one half the truths that are told you concerning the helpless millions suffering in this cruel bondage, you at the north would not help to tighten the yoke. You surely would refuse to do for the master, on your own soil, the mean and cruel work which trained bloodhounds and the lowest class of whites do for him at the south.

Every where the years bring to all enough of sin and sorrow; but in slavery the very dawn of life is darkened by these shadows. Even the little child, who is accustomed to wait on her mistress and her children, will learn, before she is twelve years old, why it is that her mistress hates such and such a one among the slaves. Perhaps the child's own mother is among those hated ones. She listens to violent outbreaks of jealous passion, and cannot help understanding what is the cause. She will become prematurely knowing in evil things. Soon she will learn to tremble when she hears her master's footfall. She will be compelled to realize that she is no longer a child: If God has bestowed beauty upon her, it will prove her greatest curse. That which commands admiration in the white woman only hastens the degradation of the female slave. I know that some are too much brutalized by slavery to feel the humiliation of their position; but many slaves feel it most acutely, and shrink from the memory of it. I cannot tell how much I suffered in the presence of these wrongs, nor how I am still pained by the retrospect. My master met me at every turn, reminding me that I belonged to him, and swearing by heaven and earth that he would compel me to submit to him. If I went out for a breath of fresh air, after a day of unwearied toil, his footsteps dogged me. If I knelt by my mother's grave, his dark shadow fell on me even there. The light heart which nature had given me became heavy with sad forebodings. The other slaves in my master's house noticed the change. Many of them pitied me; but none dared to ask the cause. They had no need to inquire. They knew too well the guilty practices under that roof; and they were aware that to speak of them was an offence that never went unpunished.

I longed for some one to confide in. I would have given the world to have laid my head on my grandmother's faithful bosom, and told her all my troubles. But Dr. Flint swore he would kill me, if I was not as silent as the grave. Then, although my grandmother was all in all to me, I feared her as well as loved her. I had been accustomed to look up to her with a respect bordering upon awe. I was very young, and felt shamefaced about telling her such impure things, especially as I knew her to be very strict on such subjects. Moreover, she was a woman of a high spirit. She was usually very quiet in her demeanor; but if her indignation was once roused, it was not very easily quelled. I had been told that she once chased a white gentleman with a loaded pistol, because he insulted one of her daughters. I dreaded the consequences of a violent outbreak; and both pride and fear kept me silent. But though I did not confide in my grandmother, and even evaded her vigilant watchfulness and inquiry, her presence in the neighborhood was some protection to me. Though she had been a slave, Dr. Flint was afraid of her. He dreaded her scorching rebukes. Moreover, she was known and patronized by many people; and he did not wish to have his villainy made public. It was lucky for me that I did not live on a distant plantation, but in a town not so large that the inhabitants were ignorant of each other's affairs. Bad as are the laws and customs in a slaveholding community, the doctor, as a professional man, deemed it prudent to keep up some outward show of decency.

O, what days and nights of fear and sorrow that man caused me! Reader, it is not to awaken sympathy for myself that I am telling you truthfully what I suffered in slavery. I do it to kindle a flame of compassion in your hearts for my sisters who are still in bondage, suffering as I once suffered.

I once saw two beautiful children playing together. One was a fair white child; the other was her slave, and also her sister. When I saw them embracing each other, and heard their joyous laughter, I turned sadly away from the lovely sight. I foresaw the inevitable blight that would fall on the little slave's heart. I knew how soon her laughter would be changed to sighs. The fair child grew up to be a still fairer woman. From childhood to womanhood her pathway was blooming with flowers, and overarched by a sunny sky. Scarcely one day of her life had been clouded when the sun rose on her happy bridal morning.

How had those years dealt with her slave sister, the little playmate of her childhood? She, also, was very beautiful; but the flowers and sunshine of love were not for her. She drank the cup of sin, and shame, and misery, whereof her persecuted race are compelled to drink.

In view of these things, why are ye silent, ye free men and women of the north? Why do your tongues falter in maintenance of the right? Would that I had more ability! But my heart is so full, and my pen is so weak! There are noble men and women who plead for us, striving to help those who cannot help themselves. God bless them! God give them strength and courage to go on! God bless those, every where, who are laboring to advance the cause of humanity!

VI. The Jealous Mistress

I would ten thousand times rather that my children should be the half-starved paupers of Ireland[1] than to be the most pampered among the slaves of America. I would rather drudge out my life on a cotton plantation, till the grave opened to give me rest, than to live with an unprincipled master and a jealous mistress. The felon's home in a penitentiary is preferable. He may repent, and turn from

1. Abolitionists frequently compared the situation of American slaves to the Irish sufferings during the potato famine of 1845–49.

the error of his ways, and so find peace; but it is not so with a favorite slave. She is not allowed to have any pride of character. It is deemed a crime in her to wish to be virtuous.

Mrs. Flint possessed the key to her husband's character before I was born. She might have used this knowledge to counsel and to screen the young and the innocent among her slaves; but for them she had no sympathy. They were the objects of her constant suspicion and malevolence. She watched her husband with unceasing vigilance; but he was well practised in means to evade it. What he could not find opportunity to say in words he manifested in signs. He invented more than were ever thought of in a deaf and dumb asylum. I let them pass, as if I did not understand what he meant; and many were the curses and threats bestowed on me for my stupidity. One day he caught me teaching myself to write. He frowned, as if he was not well pleased; but I suppose he came to the conclusion that such an accomplishment might help to advance his favorite scheme. Before long, notes were often slipped into my hand. I would return them, saying, "I can't read them, sir." "Can't you?" he replied; "then I must read them to you." He always finished the reading by asking, "Do you understand?" Sometimes he would complain of the heat of the tea room, and order his supper to be placed on a small table in the piazza.[2] He would seat himself there with a well-satisfied smile, and tell me to stand by and brush away the flies. He would eat very slowly, pausing between the mouthfuls. These intervals were employed in describing the happiness I was so foolishly throwing away, and in threatening me with the penalty that finally awaited my stubborn disobedience. He boasted much of the forbearance he had exercised towards me, and reminded me that there was a limit to his patience. When I succeeded in avoiding opportunities for him to talk to me at home, I was ordered to come to his office, to do some errand. When there, I was obliged to stand and listen to such language as he saw fit to address to me. Sometimes I so openly expressed my contempt for him that he would become violently enraged, and I wondered why he did not strike me. Circumstanced as he was, he probably thought it was better policy to be forbearing. But the state of things grew worse and worse daily. In desperation I told him that I must and would apply to my grandmother for protection. He threatened me with death, and worse than death, if I made any complaint to her. Strange to say, I did not despair. I was naturally of a buoyant disposition, and always I had a hope of somehow getting out of his clutches. Like many a poor, simple slave before me, I trusted that some threads of joy would yet be woven into my dark destiny.

2. An open patio or courtyard.

I had entered my sixteenth year, and every day it became more apparent that my presence was intolerable to Mrs. Flint. Angry words frequently passed between her and her husband. He had never punished me himself, and he would not allow any body else to punish me. In that respect, she was never satisfied; but, in her angry moods, no terms were too vile for her to bestow upon me. Yet I, whom she detested so bitterly, had far more pity for her than he had, whose duty it was to make her life happy. I never wronged her, or wished to wrong her; and one word of kindness from her would have brought me to her feet.

After repeated quarrels between the doctor and his wife, he announced his intention to take his youngest daughter, then four years old, to sleep in his apartment. It was necessary that a servant should sleep in the same room, to be on hand if the child stirred. I was selected for that office, and informed for what purpose that arrangement had been made. By managing to keep within sight of people, as much as possible, during the day time, I had hitherto succeeded in eluding my master, though a razor was often held to my throat to force me to change this line of policy. At night I slept by the side of my great aunt, where I felt safe. He was too prudent to come into her room. She was an old woman, and had been in the family many years. Moreover, as a married man, and a professional man, he deemed it necessary to save appearances in some degree. But he resolved to remove the obstacle in the way of his scheme; and he thought he had planned it so that he should evade suspicion. He was well aware how much I prized my refuge by the side of my old aunt, and he determined to dispossess me of it. The first night the doctor had the little child in his room alone. The next morning, I was ordered to take my station as nurse the following night. A kind Providence interposed in my favor. During the day Mrs. Flint heard of this new arrangement, and a storm followed. I rejoiced to hear it rage.

After a while my mistress sent for me to come to her room. Her first question was, "Did you know you were to sleep in the doctor's room?"

"Yes, ma'am."

"Who told you?"

"My master."

"Will you answer truly all the questions I ask?"

"Yes, ma'am."

"Tell me, then, as you hope to be forgiven, are you innocent of what I have accused you?"

"I am."

She handed me a Bible, and said, "Lay your hand on your heart, kiss this holy book, and swear before God that you tell me the truth."

I took the oath she required, and I did it with a clear conscience.

"You have taken God's holy word to testify your innocence," said she. "If you have deceived me, beware! Now take this stool, sit down, look me directly in the face, and tell me all that has passed between your master and you."

I did as she ordered. As I went on with my account her color changed frequently, she wept, and sometimes groaned. She spoke in tones so sad, that I was touched by her grief. The tears came to my eyes; but I was soon convinced that her emotions arose from anger and wounded pride. She felt that her marriage vows were desecrated, her dignity insulted; but she had no compassion for the poor victim of her husband's perfidy. She pitied herself as a martyr; but she was incapable of feeling for the condition of shame and misery in which her unfortunate, helpless slave was placed.

Yet perhaps she had some touch of feeling for me; for when the conference was ended, she spoke kindly, and promised to protect me. I should have been much comforted by this assurance if I could have had confidence in it; but my experiences in slavery had filled me with distrust. She was not a very refined woman, and had not much control over her passions. I was an object of her jealousy, and, consequently, of her hatred; and I knew I could not expect kindness or confidence from her under the circumstances in which I was placed. I could not blame her. Slaveholders' wives feel as other women would under similar circumstances. The fire of her temper kindled from small sparks, and now the flame became so intense that the doctor was obliged to give up his intended arrangement.

I knew I had ignited the torch, and I expected to suffer for it afterwards; but I felt too thankful to my mistress for the timely aid she rendered me to care much about that. She now took me to sleep in a room adjoining her own. There I was an object of her especial care, though not of her especial comfort, for she spent many a sleepless night to watch over me. Sometimes I woke up, and found her bending over me. At other times she whispered in my ear, as though it was her husband who was speaking to me, and listened to hear what I would answer. If she startled me, on such occasions, she would glide stealthily away; and the next morning she would tell me I had been talking in my sleep, and ask who I was talking to. At last, I began to be fearful for my life. It had been often threatened; and you can imagine, better than I can describe, what an unpleasant sensation it must produce to wake up in the dead of night and find a jealous woman bending over you. Terrible as this experience was, I had fears that it would give place to one more terrible.

My mistress grew weary of her vigils; they did not prove satisfactory. She changed her tactics. She now tried the trick of accusing my master of crime, in my presence, and gave my name as the author of the accusation. To my utter astonishment, he replied, "I don't believe it; but if she did acknowledge it, you tortured her into exposing me." Tortured into exposing him! Truly, Satan had no difficulty in distinguishing the color of his soul! I understood his object in making this false representation. It was to show me that I gained nothing by seeking the protection of my mistress; that the power was still all in his own hands. I pitied Mrs. Flint. She was a second wife, many years the junior of her husband; and the hoary-headed miscreant was enough to try the patience of a wiser and better woman. She was completely foiled, and knew not how to proceed. She would gladly have had me flogged for my supposed false oath; but, as I have already stated, the doctor never allowed any one to whip me. The old sinner was politic. The application of the lash might have led to remarks that would have exposed him in the eyes of his children and grandchildren. How often did I rejoice that I lived in a town where all the inhabitants knew each other! If I had been on a remote plantation, or lost among the multitude of a crowded city, I should not be a living woman at this day.

The secrets of slavery are concealed like those of the Inquisition.[3] My master was, to my knowledge, the father of eleven slaves. But did the mothers dare to tell who was the father of their children? Did the other slaves dare to allude to it, except in whispers among themselves? No, indeed! They knew too well the terrible consequences.

My grandmother could not avoid seeing things which excited her suspicions. She was uneasy about me, and tried various ways to buy me; but the never-changing answer was always repeated: "Linda does not belong to *me*. She is my daughter's property, and I have no legal right to sell her." The conscientious man! He was too scrupulous to *sell* me; but he had no scruples whatever about committing a much greater wrong against the helpless young girl placed under his guardianship, as his daughter's property. Sometimes my persecutor would ask me whether I would like to be sold. I told him I would rather be sold to any body than to lead such a life as I did. On such occasions he would assume the air of a very injured individual, and reproach me for my ingratitude. "Did I not take you into the house, and make you the companion of my own children?" he would say. "Have I ever treated you like a negro? I have never allowed you to be punished, not even to please your mistress. And this is the recompense I get, you ungrateful girl!" I answered that he had reasons of his own for screening me from punishment, and that the course he pursued made my mistress hate me and persecute me. If I wept, he would say, "Poor child! Don't cry! don't cry! I will make peace for you with

3. A period in Western Europe from the Middle Ages through the eighteenth century that was marked by a series of trials convened by the Catholic Church and aimed at identifying and punishing heretics, often through torture and execution.

your mistress. Only let me arrange matters in my own way. Poor, foolish girl! you don't know what is for your own good. I would cherish you. I would make a lady of you. Now go, and think of all I have promised you."

I did think of it.

Reader, I draw no imaginary pictures of southern homes. I am telling you the plain truth. Yet when victims make their escape from this wild beast of Slavery, northerners consent to act the part of bloodhounds, and hunt the poor fugitive back into his den, "full of dead men's bones, and all uncleanness."[4] Nay, more, they are not only willing, but proud, to give their daughters in marriage to slaveholders. The poor girls have romantic notions of a sunny clime, and of the flowering vines that all the year round shade a happy home. To what disappointments are they destined! The young wife soon learns that the husband in whose hands she has placed her happiness pays no regard to his marriage vows. Children of every shade of complexion play with her own fair babies, and too well she knows that they are born unto him of his own household. Jealousy and hatred enter the flowery home, and it is ravaged of its loveliness.

Southern women often marry a man knowing that he is the father of many little slaves. They do not trouble themselves about it. They regard such children as property, as marketable as the pigs on the plantation; and it is seldom that they do not make them aware of this by passing them into the slave-trader's hands as soon as possible, and thus getting them out of their sight. I am glad to say there are some honorable exceptions.

I have myself known two southern wives who exhorted their husbands to free those slaves towards whom they stood in a "parental relation;" and their request was granted. These husbands blushed before the superior nobleness of their wives' natures. Though they had only counselled them to do that which it was their duty to do, it commanded their respect, and rendered their conduct more exemplary. Concealment was at an end, and confidence took the place of distrust.

Though this bad institution deadens the moral sense, even in white women, to a fearful extent, it is not altogether extinct. I have heard southern ladies say of Mr. Such a one, "He not only thinks it no disgrace to be the father of those little niggers,[5] but he is not ashamed to call himself their master. I declare, such things ought not to be tolerated in any decent society!"

4. Matthew 23.27. "Bloodhounds": a breed of hunting dogs that were frequently used to track slaves.
5. "Nigger" was a highly derogatory word used to refer to blacks. The term was also adopted by many enslaved persons and employed, some commentators argue, without the racist connotations. This epithet remains controversial today.

VII. The Lover

Why does the slave ever love? Why allow the tendrils of the heart to twine around objects which may at any moment be wrenched away by the hand of violence? When separations come by the hand of death, the pious soul can bow in resignation, and say, "Not my will, but thine be done, O Lord!" But when the ruthless hand of man strikes the blow, regardless of the misery he causes, it is hard to be submissive. I did not reason thus when I was a young girl. Youth will be youth. I loved, and I indulged the hope that the dark clouds around me would turn out a bright lining. I forgot that in the land of my birth the shadows are too dense for light to penetrate. A land

> "Where laughter is not mirth; nor thought the mind;
> Nor words a language; nor e'en men mankind.
> Where cries reply to curses, shrieks to blows,
> And each is tortured in his separate hell."[1]

There was in the neighborhood a young colored carpenter; a free born man. We had been well acquainted in childhood, and frequently met together afterwards. We became mutually attached, and he proposed to marry me. I loved him with all the ardor of a young girl's first love. But when I reflected that I was a slave, and that the laws gave no sanction to the marriage of such, my heart sank within me. My lover wanted to buy me; but I knew that Dr. Flint was too wilful and arbitrary a man to consent to that arrangement. From him, I was sure of experiencing all sorts of opposition, and I had nothing to hope from my mistress. She would have been delighted to have got rid of me, but not in that way. It would have relieved her mind of a burden if she could have seen me sold to some distant state, but if I was married near home I should be just as much in her husband's power as I had previously been,—for the husband of a slave has no power to protect her. Moreover, my mistress, like many others, seemed to think that slaves had no right to any family ties of their own; that they were created merely to wait upon the family of the mistress. I once heard her abuse a young slave girl, who told her that a colored man wanted to make her his wife. "I will have you peeled and pickled, my lady," said she, "if I ever hear you mention that subject again. Do you suppose that I will have you tending *my* children with the children of that nigger?" The girl to whom she said this had a mulatto child, of course not acknowledged by its father. The poor black man who loved her would have been proud to acknowledge his helpless offspring.

1. Lord Byron, "The Lament of Tasso" (1817).

Many and anxious were the thoughts I revolved in my mind. I was at a loss what to do. Above all things, I was desirous to spare my lover the insults that had cut so deeply into my own soul. I talked with my grandmother about it, and partly told her my fears. I did not dare to tell her the worst. She had long suspected all was not right, and if I confirmed her suspicions I knew a storm would rise that would prove the overthrow of all my hopes.

This love-dream had been my support through many trials; and I could not bear to run the risk of having it suddenly dissipated. There was a lady in the neighborhood, a particular friend of Dr. Flint's, who often visited the house. I had a great respect for her, and she had always manifested a friendly interest in me. Grandmother thought she would have great influence with the doctor. I went to this lady, and told her my story. I told her I was aware that my lover's being a free-born man would prove a great objection; but he wanted to buy me; and if Dr. Flint would consent to that arrangement, I felt sure he would be willing to pay any reasonable price. She knew that Mrs. Flint disliked me; therefore, I ventured to suggest that perhaps my mistress would approve of my being sold, as that would rid her of me. The lady listened with kindly sympathy, and promised to do her utmost to promote my wishes. She had an interview with the doctor, and I believe she pleaded my cause earnestly; but it was all to no purpose.

How I dreaded my master now! Every minute I expected to be summoned to his presence; but the day passed, and I heard nothing from him. The next morning, a message was brought to me: "Master wants you in his study." I found the door ajar, and I stood a moment gazing at the hateful man who claimed a right to rule me, body and soul. I entered, and tried to appear calm. I did not want him to know how my heart was bleeding. He looked fixedly at me, with an expression which seemed to say, "I have half a mind to kill you on the spot." At last he broke the silence, and that was a relief to both of us.

"So you want to be married, do you?" said he, "and to a free nigger."

"Yes, sir."

"Well, I'll soon convince you whether I am your master, or the nigger fellow you honor so highly. If you *must* have a husband, you may take up with one of my slaves."

What a situation I should be in, as the wife of one of *his* slaves, even if my heart had been interested!

I replied, "Don't you suppose, sir, that a slave can have some preference about marrying? Do you suppose that all men are alike to her?"

"Do you love this nigger?" said he, abruptly.

"Yes, sir."

"How dare you tell me so!" he exclaimed, in great wrath. After a slight pause, he added, "I supposed you thought more of yourself; that you felt above the insults of such puppies."

I replied, "If he is a puppy I am a puppy, for we are both of the negro race. It is right and honorable for us to love each other. The man you call a puppy never insulted me, sir; and he would not love me if he did not believe me to be a virtuous woman."

He sprang upon me like a tiger, and gave me a stunning blow. It was the first time he had ever struck me; and fear did not enable me to control my anger. When I had recovered a little from the effects, I exclaimed, "You have struck me for answering you honestly. How I despise you!"

There was silence for some minutes. Perhaps he was deciding what should be my punishment; or, perhaps, he wanted to give me time to reflect on what I had said, and to whom I had said it. Finally, he asked, "Do you know what you have said?"

"Yes, sir; but your treatment drove me to it."

"Do you know that I have a right to do as I like with you,—that I can kill you, if I please?"

"You have tried to kill me, and I wish you had; but you have no right to do as you like with me."

"Silence!" he exclaimed, in a thundering voice. "By heavens, girl, you forget yourself too far! Are you mad? If you are, I will soon bring you to your senses. Do you think any other master would bear what I have borne from you this morning? Many masters would have killed you on the spot. How would you like to be sent to jail for your insolence?"

"I know I have been disrespectful, sir," I replied; "but you drove me to it; I couldn't help it. As for the jail, there would be more peace for me there than there is here."

"You deserve to go there," said he, "and to be under such treatment, that you would forget the meaning of the word *peace*. It would do you good. It would take some of your high notions out of you. But I am not ready to send you there yet, notwithstanding your ingratitude for all my kindness and forbearance. You have been the plague of my life. I have wanted to make you happy, and I have been repaid with the basest ingratitude; but though you have proved yourself incapable of appreciating my kindness, I will be lenient towards you, Linda. I will give you one more chance to redeem your character. If you behave yourself and do as I require, I will forgive you and treat you as I always have done; but if you disobey me, I will punish you as I would the meanest slave on my plantation. Never let me hear that fellow's name mentioned again. If I ever know of your speaking to him, I will cowhide you both; and if I catch him lurking about my premises, I will shoot him as soon as I would a dog. Do you hear what I say? I'll teach you a lesson about marriage and free niggers! Now go, and let this be the last time I have occasion to speak to you on this subject."

Reader, did you ever hate? I hope not. I never did but once; and I trust I never shall again. Somebody has called it "the atmosphere of hell;"[2] and I believe it is so.

For a fortnight the doctor did not speak to me. He thought to mortify me; to make me feel that I had disgraced myself by receiving the honorable addresses of a respectable colored man, in preference to the base proposals of a white man. But though his lips disdained to address me, his eyes were very loquacious. No animal ever watched its prey more narrowly than he watched me. He knew that I could write, though he had failed to make me read his letters; and he was now troubled lest I should exchange letters with another man. After a while he became weary of silence; and I was sorry for it. One morning, as he passed through the hall, to leave the house, he contrived to thrust a note into my hand. I thought I had better read it, and spare myself the vexation of having him read it to me. It expressed regret for the blow he had given me, and reminded me that I myself was wholly to blame for it. He hoped I had become convinced of the injury I was doing myself by incurring his displeasure. He wrote that he had made up his mind to go to Louisiana; that he should take several slaves with him, and intended I should be one of the number. My mistress would remain where she was; therefore I should have nothing to fear from that quarter. If I merited kindness from him, he assured me that it would be lavishly bestowed. He begged me to think over the matter, and answer the following day.

The next morning I was called to carry a pair of scissors to his room. I laid them on the table, with the letter beside them. He thought it was my answer, and did not call me back. I went as usual to attend my young mistress to and from school. He met me in the street, and ordered me to stop at his office on my way back. When I entered, he showed me his letter, and asked me why I had not answered it. I replied, "I am your daughter's property, and it is in your power to send me, or take me, wherever you please." He said he was very glad to find me so willing to go, and that we should start early in the autumn. He had a large practice in the town, and I rather thought he had made up the story merely to frighten me. However that might be, I was determined that I would never go to Louisiana with him.

Summer passed away, and early in the autumn Dr. Flint's eldest son was sent to Louisiana to examine the country, with a view to

2. Martin Tupper, "Of Hatred and Anger," *Proverbial Philosophy* (1837).

emigrating. That news did not disturb me. I knew very well that I should not be sent with *him*. That I had not been taken to the plantation before this time, was owing to the fact that his son was there. He was jealous of his son; and jealousy of the overseer had kept him from punishing me by sending me into the fields to work. Is it strange that I was not proud of these protectors? As for the overseer, he was a man for whom I had less respect than I had for a bloodhound.

Young Mr. Flint did not bring back a favorable report of Louisiana, and I heard no more of that scheme. Soon after this, my lover met me at the corner of the street, and I stopped to speak to him. Looking up, I saw my master watching us from his window. I hurried home, trembling with fear. I was sent for, immediately, to go to his room. He met me with a blow. "When is mistress to be married?" said he, in a sneering tone. A shower of oaths and imprecations followed. How thankful I was that my lover was a free man! that my tyrant had no power to flog him for speaking to me in the street!

Again and again I revolved in my mind how all this would end. There was no hope that the doctor would consent to sell me on any terms. He had an iron will, and was determined to keep me, and to conquer me. My lover was an intelligent and religious man. Even if he could have obtained permission to marry me while I was a slave, the marriage would give him no power to protect me from my master. It would have made him miserable to witness the insults I should have been subjected to. And then, if we had children, I knew they must "follow the condition of the mother."[3] What a terrible blight that would be on the heart of a free, intelligent father! For *his* sake, I felt that I ought not to link his fate with my own unhappy destiny. He was going to Savannah to see about a little property left him by an uncle; and hard as it was to bring my feelings to it, I earnestly entreated him not to come back. I advised him to go to the Free States, where his tongue would not be tied, and where his intelligence would be of more avail to him. He left me, still hoping the day would come when I could be bought. With me the lamp of hope had gone out. The dream of my girlhood was over. I felt lonely and desolate.

Still I was not stripped of all. I still had my good grandmother, and my affectionate brother. When he put his arms round my neck, and looked into my eyes, as if to read there the troubles I dared not tell, I felt that I still had something to love. But even that pleasant emotion was chilled by the reflection that he might be torn from me at any moment, by some sudden freak of my master. If he had known how we loved each other, I think he would have exulted in separating

3. Whether a child was free or enslaved was determined by the legal status of his or her mother.

us. We often planned together how we could get to the north. But, as William remarked, such things are easier said than done. My movements were very closely watched, and we had no means of getting any money to defray our expenses. As for grandmother, she was strongly opposed to her children's undertaking any such project. She had not forgotten poor Benjamin's sufferings, and she was afraid that if another child tried to escape, he would have a similar or a worse fate. To me, nothing seemed more dreadful than my present life. I said to myself, "William *must* be free. He shall go to the north, and I will follow him." Many a slave sister has formed the same plans.

VIII. What Slaves Are Taught to Think of the North

Slaveholders pride themselves upon being honorable men; but if you were to hear the enormous lies they tell their slaves, you would have small respect for their veracity. I have spoken plain English. Pardon me. I cannot use a milder term. When they visit the north, and return home, they tell their slaves of the runaways they have seen, and describe them to be in the most deplorable condition. A slaveholder once told me that he had seen a runaway friend of mine in New York, and that she besought him to take her back to her master, for she was literally dying of starvation; that many days she had only one cold potato to eat, and at other times could get nothing at all. He said he refused to take her, because he knew her master would not thank him for bringing such a miserable wretch to his house. He ended by saying to me, "This is the punishment she brought on herself for running away from a kind master."

This whole story was false. I afterwards staid with that friend in New York, and found her in comfortable circumstances. She had never thought of such a thing as wishing to go back to slavery. Many of the slaves believe such stories, and think it is not worth while to exchange slavery for such a hard kind of freedom. It is difficult to persuade such that freedom could make them useful men, and enable them to protect their wives and children. If those heathen in our Christian land had as much teaching as some Hindoos, they would think otherwise. They would know that liberty is more valuable than life. They would begin to understand their own capabilities, and exert themselves to become men and women.

But while the Free States sustain a law which hurls fugitives back into slavery, how can the slaves resolve to become men? There are some who strive to protect wives and daughters from the insults of their masters; but those who have such sentiments have had advantages above the general mass of slaves. They have been partially civilized and Christianized by favorable circumstances. Some are bold enough to *utter* such sentiments to their masters. O, that there were more of them!

Some poor creatures have been so brutalized by the lash that they will sneak out of the way to give their masters free access to their wives and daughters. Do you think this proves the black man to belong to an inferior order of beings? What would *you* be, if you had been born and brought up a slave, with generations of slaves for ancestors? I admit that the black man *is* inferior. But what is it that makes him so? It is the ignorance in which white men compel him to live; it is the torturing whip that lashes manhood out of him; it is the fierce bloodhounds of the South, and the scarcely less cruel human bloodhounds of the north, who enforce the Fugitive Slave Law. *They* do the work.

Southern gentlemen indulge in the most contemptuous expressions about the Yankees, while they, on their part, consent to do the vilest work for them, such as the ferocious bloodhounds and the despised negro-hunters are employed to do at home. When southerners go to the north, they are proud to do them honor; but the northern man is not welcome south of Mason and Dixon's line, unless he suppresses every thought and feeling at variance with their "peculiar institution." Nor is it enough to be silent. The masters are not pleased, unless they obtain a greater degree of subservience than that; and they are generally accomodated. Do they respect the northerner for this? I trow[1] not. Even the slaves despise "a northern man with southern principles;" and that is the class they generally see. When northerners go to the south to reside, they prove very apt scholars. They soon imbibe the sentiments and disposition of their neighbors, and generally go beyond their teachers. Of the two, they are proverbially the hardest masters.

They seem to satisfy their consciences with the doctrine that God created the Africans to be slaves. What a libel upon the heavenly Father, who "made of one blood all nations of men!"[2] And then who *are* Africans? Who can measure the amount of Anglo-Saxon blood coursing in the veins of American slaves?

I have spoken of the pains slaveholders take to give their slaves a bad opinion of the north; but, notwithstanding this, intelligent slaves are aware that they have many friends in the Free States. Even the most ignorant have some confused notions about it. They knew that I could read; and I was often asked if I had seen any thing in the

1. I believe.
2. Acts 17.26.

newspapers about white folks over in the big north, who were trying to get their freedom for them. Some believe that the abolitionists have already made them free, and that it is established by law, but that their masters prevent the law from going into effect. One woman begged me to get a newspaper and read it over. She said her husband told her that the black people had sent word to the queen of 'Merica that they were all slaves; that she didn't believe it, and went to Washington city to see the president about it. They quarrelled; she drew her sword upon him, and swore that he should help her to make them all free.

That poor, ignorant woman thought that America was governed by a Queen, to whom the President was subordinate. I wish the President was subordinate to Queen Justice.

IX. Sketches of Neighboring Slaveholders

There was a planter in the country, not far from us, whom I will call Mr. Litch. He was an ill-bred, uneducated man, but very wealthy. He had six hundred slaves, many of whom he did not know by sight. His extensive plantation was managed by well-paid overseers. There was a jail and a whipping post on his grounds; and whatever cruelties were perpetrated there, they passed without comment. He was so effectually screened by his great wealth that he was called to no account for his crimes, not even for murder.

Various were the punishments resorted to. A favorite one was to tie a rope round a man's body, and suspend him from the ground. A fire was kindled over him, from which was suspended a piece of fat pork. As this cooked, the scalding drops of fat continually fell on the bare flesh. On his own plantation, he required very strict obedience to the eighth commandment.[1] But depredations on the neighbors were allowable, provided the culprit managed to evade detection or suspicion. If a neighbor brought a charge of theft against any of his slaves, he was browbeaten by the master, who assured him that his slaves had enough of every thing at home, and had no inducement to steal. No sooner was the neighbor's back turned, than the accused was sought out, and whipped for his lack of discretion. If a slave stole from him even a pound of meat or a peck of corn, if detection followed, he was put in chains and imprisoned, and so kept till his form was attenuated by hunger and suffering.

A freshet[2] once bore his wine cellar and meat house miles away from the plantation. Some slaves followed, and secured bits of meat

1. Exodus 20.15: "Thou shalt not steal."
2. Freshwater stream.

and bottles of wine. Two were detected; a ham and some liquor being found in their huts. They were summoned by their master. No words were used, but a club felled them to the ground. A rough box was their coffin, and their interment was a dog's burial. Nothing was said.

Murder was so common on his plantation that he feared to be alone after nightfall. He might have believed in ghosts.

His brother, if not equal in wealth, was at least equal in cruelty. His bloodhounds were well trained. Their pen was spacious, and a terror to the slaves. They were let loose on a runaway, and if they tracked him, they literally tore the flesh from his bones. When this slaveholder died, his shrieks and groans were so frightful that they appalled his own friends. His last words were, "I am going to hell; bury my money with me."

After death his eyes remained open. To press the lids down, silver dollars were laid on them. These were buried with him. From this circumstance, a rumor went abroad that his coffin was filled with money. Three times his grave was opened, and his coffin taken out. The last time, his body was found on the ground, and a flock of buzzards were pecking at it. He was again interred, and a sentinel set over his grave. The perpetrators were never discovered.

Cruelty is contagious in uncivilized communities. Mr. Conant, a neighbor of Mr. Litch, returned from town one evening in a partial state of intoxication. His body servant gave him some offence. He was divested of his clothes, except his shirt, whipped, and tied to a large tree in front of the house. It was a stormy night in winter. The wind blew bitterly cold, and the boughs of the old tree crackled under falling sleet. A member of the family, fearing he would freeze to death, begged that he might be taken down; but the master would not relent. He remained there three hours; and, when he was cut down, he was more dead than alive. Another slave, who stole a pig from this master, to appease his hunger, was terribly flogged. In desperation, he tried to run away. But at the end of two miles, he was so faint with loss of blood, he thought he was dying. He had a wife, and he longed to see her once more. Too sick to walk, he crept back that long distance on his hands and knees. When he reached his master's, it was night. He had not strength to rise and open the gate. He moaned, and tried to call for help. I had a friend living in the same family. At last his cry reached her. She went out and found the prostrate man at the gate. She ran back to the house for assistance, and two men returned with her. They carried him in, and laid him on the floor. The back of his shirt was one clot of blood. By means of lard, my friend loosened it from the raw flesh. She bandaged him, gave him cool drink, and left him to rest. The master said he deserved a hundred more lashes. When his own labor was stolen from him, he had stolen food to appease his hunger. This was his crime.

Another neighbor was a Mrs. Wade. At no hour of the day was there cessation of the lash on her premises. Her labors began with the dawn, and did not cease till long after nightfall. The barn was her particular place of torture. There she lashed the slaves with the might of a man. An old slave of hers once said to me, "It is hell in missis's house. 'Pears I can never get out. Day and night I prays to die."

The mistress died before the old woman, and, when dying, entreated her husband not to permit any one of her slaves to look on her after death. A slave who had nursed her children, and had still a child in her care, watched her chance, and stole with it in her arms to the room where lay her dead mistress. She gazed a while on her, then raised her hand and dealt two blows on her face, saying, as she did so, "The devil is got you *now!*" She forgot that the child was looking on. She had just begun to talk; and she said to her father, "I did see ma, and mammy did strike ma, so," striking her own face with her little hand. The master was startled. He could not imagine how the nurse could obtain access to the room where the corpse lay; for he kept the door locked. He questioned her. She confessed that what the child had said was true, and told how she had procured the key. She was sold to Georgia.

In my childhood I knew a valuable slave, named Charity, and loved her, as all children did. Her young mistress married, and took her to Louisiana. Her little boy, James, was sold to a good sort of master. He became involved in debt, and James was sold again to a wealthy slaveholder, noted for his cruelty. With this man he grew up to manhood, receiving the treatment of a dog. After a severe whipping, to save himself from further infliction of the lash, with which he was threatened, he took to the woods. He was in a most miserable condition—cut by the cowskin, half naked, half starved, and without the means of procuring a crust of bread.

Some weeks after his escape, he was captured, tied, and carried back to his master's plantation. This man considered punishment in his jail, on bread and water, after receiving hundreds of lashes, too mild for the poor slave's offence. Therefore he decided, after the overseer should have whipped him to his satisfaction, to have him placed between the screws of the cotton gin, to stay as long as he had been in the woods. This wretched creature was cut with the whip from his head to his feet, then washed with strong brine, to prevent the flesh from mortifying, and make it heal sooner than it otherwise would. He was then put into the cotton gin, which was screwed down, only allowing him room to turn on his side when he could not lie on his back. Every morning a slave was sent with a piece of bread and bowl of water, which were placed within reach of the poor fellow. The slave was charged, under penalty of severe punishment, not to speak to him.

Four days passed, and the slave continued to carry the bread and water. On the second morning, he found the bread gone, but the water untouched. When he had been in the press four days and five nights, the slave informed his master that the water had not been used for four mornings, and that a horrible stench came from the gin house. The overseer was sent to examine into it. When the press was unscrewed, the dead body was found partly eaten by rats and vermin. Perhaps the rats that devoured his bread had gnawed him before life was extinct. Poor Charity! Grandmother and I often asked each other how her affectionate heart would bear the news, if she should ever hear of the murder of her son. We had known her husband, and knew that James was like him in manliness and intelligence. These were the qualities that made it so hard for him to be a plantation slave. They put him into a rough box, and buried him with less feeling than would have been manifested for an old house dog. Nobody asked any questions. He was a slave; and the feeling was that the master had a right to do what he pleased with his own property. And what did *he* care for the value of a slave? He had hundreds of them. When they had finished their daily toil, they must hurry to eat their little morsels, and be ready to extinguish their pine knots before nine o'clock, when the overseer went his patrol rounds. He entered every cabin, to see that men and their wives had gone to bed together, lest the men, from over-fatigue, should fall asleep in the chimney corner, and remain there till the morning horn called them to their daily task. Women are considered of no value, unless they continually increase their owner's stock. They are put on a par with animals. This same master shot a woman through the head, who had run away and been brought back to him. No one called him to account for it. If a slave resisted being whipped, the bloodhounds were unpacked, and set upon him, to tear his flesh from his bones. The master who did these things was highly educated, and styled a perfect gentleman. He also boasted the name and standing of a Christian, though Satan never had a truer follower.

I could tell of more slaveholders as cruel as those I have described. They are not exceptions to the general rule. I do not say there are no humane slaveholders. Such characters do exist, notwithstanding the hardening influences around them. But they are "like angels' visits—few and far between."[3]

I knew a young lady who was one of these rare specimens. She was an orphan, and inherited as slaves a woman and her six children.

3. John Norris, *The Parting* (1678): "Like angels' visits, short and bright"; Robert Blair, *The Grave* (1743): "Like those of angels, short and far between."

Their father was a free man. They had a comfortable home of their own, parents and children living together. The mother and eldest daughter served their mistress during the day, and at night returned to their dwelling, which was on the premises. The young lady was very pious, and there was some reality in her religion. She taught her slaves to lead pure lives, and wished them to enjoy the fruit of their own industry. *Her* religion was not a garb put on for Sunday, and laid aside till Sunday returned again. The eldest daughter of the slave mother was promised in marriage to a free man; and the day before the wedding this good mistress emancipated her, in order that her marriage might have the sanction of *law*.

Report said that this young lady cherished an unrequited affection for a man who had resolved to marry for wealth. In the course of time a rich uncle of hers died. He left six thousand dollars to his two sons by a colored woman, and the remainder of his property to this orphan niece. The metal soon attracted the magnet. The lady and her weighty purse became his. She offered to manumit her slaves—telling them that her marriage might make unexpected changes in their destiny, and she wished to insure their happiness. They refused to take their freedom, saying that she had always been their best friend, and they could not be so happy any where as with her. I was not surprised. I had often seen them in their comfortable home, and thought that the whole town did not contain a happier family. They had never felt slavery; and, when it was too late, they were convinced of its reality.

When the new master claimed this family as his property, the father became furious, and went to his mistress for protection. "I can do nothing for you now, Harry," said she. "I no longer have the power I had a week ago. I have succeeded in obtaining the freedom of your wife; but I cannot obtain it for your children." The unhappy father swore that nobody should take his children from him. He concealed them in the woods for some days; but they were discovered and taken. The father was put in jail, and the two oldest boys sold to Georgia. One little girl, too young to be of service to her master, was left with the wretched mother. The other three were carried to their master's plantation. The eldest soon became a mother; and, when the slaveholder's wife looked at the babe, she wept bitterly. She knew that her own husband had violated the purity she had so carefully inculcated. She had a second child by her master, and then he sold her and his offspring to his brother. She bore two children to the brother, and was sold again. The next sister went crazy. The life she was compelled to lead drove her mad. The third one became the mother of five daughters. Before the birth of the fourth the pious mistress died. To the last, she rendered every kindness to the slaves that her unfortunate circumstances permitted. She passed away peacefully, glad to close her eyes on a life which had been made so wretched by the man she loved.

This man squandered the fortune he had received, and sought to retrieve his affairs by a second marriage; but, having retired after a night of drunken debauch, he was found dead in the morning. He was called a good master; for he fed and clothed his slaves better than most masters, and the lash was not heard on his plantation so frequently as on many others. Had it not been for slavery, he would have been a better man, and his wife a happier woman.

No pen can give an adequate description of the all-pervading corruption produced by slavery. The slave girl is reared in an atmosphere of licentiousness and fear. The lash and the foul talk of her master and his sons are her teachers. When she is fourteen or fifteen, her owner, or his sons, or the overseer, or perhaps all of them, begin to bribe her with presents. If these fail to accomplish their purpose, she is whipped or starved into submission to their will. She may have had religious principles inculcated by some pious mother or grandmother, or some good mistress; she may have a lover, whose good opinion and peace of mind are dear to her heart; or the profligate men who have power over her may be exceedingly odious to her. But resistance is hopeless.

> "The poor worm
> Shall prove her contest vain. Life's little day
> Shall pass, and she is gone!"[4]

The slaveholder's sons are, of course, vitiated, even while boys, by the unclean influences every where around them. Nor do the master's daughters always escape. Severe retributions sometimes come upon him for the wrongs he does to the daughters of the slaves. The white daughters early hear their parents quarrelling about some female slave. Their curiosity is excited, and they soon learn the cause. They are attended by the young slave girls whom their father has corrupted; and they hear such talk as should never meet youthful ears, or any other ears. They know that the women slaves are subject to their father's authority in all things; and in some cases they exercise the same authority over the men slaves. I have myself seen the master of such a household whose head was bowed down in shame; for it was known in the neighborhood that his daughter had selected one of the meanest slaves on his plantation to be the father of his first grandchild. She did not make her advances to her equals, nor even to her father's more intelligent servants. She selected the most brutalized, over whom her authority could be exercised with less fear of exposure. Her father, half frantic with rage, sought

4. William Mason, *Elfrida, A Dramatic Poem* (1752).

to revenge himself on the offending black man; but his daughter, foreseeing the storm that would arise, had given him free papers, and sent him out of the state.

In such cases the infant is smothered, or sent where it is never seen by any who know its history. But if the white parent is the *father*, instead of the mother, the offspring are unblushingly reared for the market. If they are girls, I have indicated plainly enough what will be their inevitable destiny.

You may believe what I say; for I write only that whereof I know. I was twenty-one years in that cage of obscene birds. I can testify, from my own experience and observation, that slavery is a curse to the whites as well as to the blacks. It makes the white fathers cruel and sensual; the sons violent and licentious; it contaminates the daughters, and makes the wives wretched. And as for the colored race, it needs an abler pen than mine to describe the extremity of their sufferings, the depth of their degradation.

Yet few slaveholders seem to be aware of the widespread moral ruin occasioned by this wicked system. Their talk is of blighted cotton crops—not of the blight on their children's souls.

If you want to be fully convinced of the abominations of slavery, go on a southern plantation, and call yourself a negro trader. Then there will be no concealment; and you will see and hear things that will seem to you impossible among human beings with immortal souls.

X. A Perilous Passage in the Slave Girl's Life

After my lover went away, Dr. Flint contrived a new plan. He seemed to have an idea that my fear of my mistress was his greatest obstacle. In the blandest tones, he told me that he was going to build a small house for me, in a secluded place, four miles away from the town. I shuddered; but I was constrained to listen, while he talked of his intention to give me a home of my own, and to make a lady of me. Hitherto, I had escaped my dreaded fate, by being in the midst of people. My grandmother had already had high words with my master about me. She had told him pretty plainly what she thought of his character, and there was considerable gossip in the neighborhood about our affairs, to which the open-mouthed jealousy of Mrs. Flint contributed not a little. When my master said he was going to build a house for me, and that he could do it with little trouble and expense, I was in hopes something would happen to frustrate his scheme; but I soon heard that the house was actually begun. I vowed before my Maker that I would never enter it. I had rather toil on the plantation from dawn till dark; I had rather live and die in jail, than drag on, from day to day, through such a living death. I was determined that the master, whom I so hated and loathed, who had blighted the prospects of my youth, and made my life a desert, should not, after my long struggle with him, succeed at last in trampling his victim under his feet. I would do any thing, every thing, for the sake of defeating him. What *could* I do? I thought and thought, till I became desperate, and made a plunge into the abyss.

And now, reader, I come to a period in my unhappy life, which I would gladly forget if I could. The remembrance fills me with sorrow and shame. It pains me to tell you of it; but I have promised to tell you the truth, and I will do it honestly, let it cost me what it may. I will not try to screen myself behind the plea of compulsion from a master; for it was not so. Neither can I plead ignorance or thoughtlessness. For years, my master had done his utmost to pollute my mind with foul images, and to destroy the pure principles inculcated by my grandmother, and the good mistress of my childhood. The influences of slavery had had the same effect on me that they had on other young girls; they had made me prematurely knowing, concerning the evil ways of the world. I knew what I did, and I did it with deliberate calculation.

But, O, ye happy women, whose purity has been sheltered from childhood, who have been free to choose the objects of your affection, whose homes are protected by law, do not judge the poor desolate slave girl too severely! If slavery had been abolished, I, also, could have married the man of my choice; I could have had a home shielded by the laws; and I should have been spared the painful task of confessing what I am now about to relate; but all my prospects had been blighted by slavery. I wanted to keep myself pure; and, under the most adverse circumstances, I tried hard to preserve my self-respect; but I was struggling alone in the powerful grasp of the demon Slavery; and the monster proved too strong for me. I felt as if I was forsaken by God and man; as if all my efforts must be frustrated; and I became reckless in my despair.

I have told you that Dr. Flint's persecutions and his wife's jealousy had given rise to some gossip in the neighborhood. Among others, it chanced that a white unmarried gentleman had obtained some knowledge of the circumstances in which I was placed. He knew my grandmother, and often spoke to me in the street. He became interested for me, and asked questions about my master, which I answered in part. He expressed a great deal of sympathy, and a wish to aid me. He constantly sought opportunities to see me, and wrote to me frequently. I was a poor slave girl, only fifteen years old.

So much attention from a superior person was, of course, flattering; for human nature is the same in all. I also felt grateful for his sympathy, and encouraged by his kind words. It seemed to me a great thing to have such a friend. By degrees, a more tender feeling crept into my heart. He was an educated and eloquent gentleman; too eloquent, alas, for the poor slave girl who trusted in him. Of course I saw whither all this was tending. I knew the impassable gulf between us; but to be an object of interest to a man who is not married, and who is not her master, is agreeable to the pride and feelings of a slave, if her miserable situation has left her any pride or sentiment. It seems less degrading to give one's self, than to submit to compulsion. There is something akin to freedom in having a lover who has no control over you, except that which he gains by kindness and attachment. A master may treat you as rudely as he pleases, and you dare not speak; moreover, the wrong does not seem so great with an unmarried man, as with one who has a wife to be made unhappy. There may be sophistry in all this; but the condition of a slave confuses all principles of morality, and, in fact, renders the practice of them impossible.

When I found that my master had actually begun to build the lonely cottage, other feelings mixed with those I have described. Revenge, and calculations of interest, were added to flattered vanity and sincere gratitude for kindness. I knew nothing would enrage Dr. Flint so much as to know that I favored another; and it was something to triumph over my tyrant even in that small way. I thought he would revenge himself by selling me, and I was sure my friend, Mr. Sands, would buy me. He was a man of more generosity and feeling than my master, and I thought my freedom could be easily obtained from him. The crisis of my fate now came so near that I was desperate. I shuddered to think of being the mother of children that should be owned by my old tyrant. I knew that as soon as a new fancy took him, his victims were sold far off to get rid of them; especially if they had children. I had seen several women sold, with his babies at the breast. He never allowed his offspring by slaves to remain long in sight of himself and his wife. Of a man who was not my master I could ask to have my children well supported; and in this case, I felt confident I should obtain the boon.[1] I also felt quite sure that they would be made free. With all these thoughts revolving in my mind, and seeing no other way of escaping the doom I so much dreaded, I made a headlong plunge. Pity me, and pardon me, O virtuous reader! You never knew what it is to be a slave; to be entirely unprotected by law or custom; to have the laws reduce you to the condition of a chattel, entirely subject to the will of another. You never exhausted your ingenuity in avoiding the snares, and eluding the power of a hated tyrant; you never shuddered at the sound of his footsteps, and trembled within hearing of his voice. I know I

1. Request or favor.

did wrong. No one can feel it more sensibly than I do. The painful and humiliating memory will haunt me to my dying day. Still, in looking back, calmly, on the events of my life, I feel that the slave woman ought not to be judged by the same standard as others.

The months passed on. I had many unhappy hours. I secretly mourned over the sorrow I was bringing on my grandmother, who had so tried to shield me from harm. I knew that I was the greatest comfort of her old age, and that it was a source of pride to her that I had not degraded myself, like most of the slaves. I wanted to confess to her that I was no longer worthy of her love; but I could not utter the dreaded words.

As for Dr. Flint, I had a feeling of satisfaction and triumph in the thought of telling *him*. From time to time he told me of his intended arrangements, and I was silent. At last, he came and told me the cottage was completed, and ordered me to go to it. I told him I would never enter it. He said, "I have heard enough of such talk as that. You shall go, if you are carried by force; and you shall remain there."

I replied, "I will never go there. In a few months I shall be a mother."

He stood and looked at me in dumb amazement, and left the house without a word. I thought I should be happy in my triumph over him. But now that the truth was out, and my relatives would hear of it, I felt wretched. Humble as were their circumstances, they had pride in my good character. Now, how could I look them in the face? My self-respect was gone! I had resolved that I would be virtuous, though I was a slave. I had said, "Let the storm beat! I will brave it till I die." And now, how humiliated I felt!

I went to my grandmother. My lips moved to make confession, but the words stuck in my throat. I sat down in the shade of a tree at her door and began to sew. I think she saw something unusual was the matter with me. The mother of slaves is very watchful. She knows there is no security for her children. After they have entered their teens she lives in daily expectation of trouble. This leads to many questions. If the girl is of a sensitive nature, timidity keeps her from answering truthfully, and this well-meant course has a tendency to drive her from maternal counsels. Presently, in came my mistress, like a mad woman, and accused me concerning her husband. My grandmother, whose suspicions had been previously awakened, believed what she said. She exclaimed, "O Linda! has it come to this? I had rather see you dead than to see you as you now are. You are a disgrace to your dead mother." She tore from my fingers my mother's wedding ring and her silver thimble. "Go away!" she exclaimed, "and never come to my house, again." Her reproaches fell so hot and heavy, that they left me no chance to answer. Bitter tears, such as the eyes never shed but once, were my only answer. I rose from my seat, but fell back again, sobbing. She did not speak to me; but the tears were running down her furrowed cheeks, and they scorched me like fire. She had always been so kind to me! *So* kind! How I longed to throw myself at her feet, and tell her all the truth! But she had ordered me to go, and never to come there again. After a few minutes, I mustered strength, and started to obey her. With what feelings did I now close that little gate, which I used to open with such an eager hand in my childhood! It closed upon me with a sound I never heard before.

Where could I go? I was afraid to return to my master's. I walked on recklessly, not caring where I went, or what would become of me. When I had gone four or five miles, fatigue compelled me to stop. I sat down on the stump of an old tree. The stars were shining through the boughs above me. How they mocked me, with their bright, calm light! The hours passed by, and as I sat there alone a chilliness and deadly sickness came over me. I sank on the ground. My mind was full of horrid thoughts. I prayed to die; but the prayer was not answered. At last, with great effort I roused myself, and walked some distance further, to the house of a woman who had been a friend of my mother. When I told her why I was there, she spoke soothingly to me; but I could not be comforted. I thought I could bear my shame if I could only be reconciled to my grandmother. I longed to open my heart to her. I thought if she could know the real state of the case, and all I had been bearing for years, she would perhaps judge me less harshly. My friend advised me to send for her. I did so; but days of agonizing suspense passed before she came. Had she utterly forsaken me? No. She came at last. I knelt before her, and told her the things that had poisoned my life; how long I had been persecuted; that I saw no way of escape; and in an hour of extremity I had become desperate. She listened in silence. I told her I would bear any thing and do any thing, if in time I had hopes of obtaining her forgiveness. I begged of her to pity me, for my dead mother's sake. And she did pity me. She did not say, "I forgive you;" but she looked at me lovingly, with her eyes full of tears. She laid her old hand gently on my head, and murmured, "Poor child! Poor child!"

XI. The New Tie to Life

I returned to my good grandmother's house. She had an interview with Mr. Sands. When she asked him why he could not have left her one ewe lamb,[1]—whether there were not plenty of slaves who did not care about character,—he made no answer; but he spoke

1. 2 Samuel 12.3.

kind and encouraging words. He promised to care for my child, and to buy me, be the conditions what they might.

I had not seen Dr. Flint for five days. I had never seen him since I made the avowal to him. He talked of the disgrace I had brought on myself; how I had sinned against my master, and mortified my old grandmother. He intimated that if I had accepted his proposals, he, as a physician, could have saved me from exposure. He even condescended to pity me. Could he have offered wormwood[2] more bitter? He, whose persecutions had been the cause of my sin!

"Linda," said he, "though you have been criminal towards me, I feel for you, and I can pardon you if you obey my wishes. Tell me whether the fellow you wanted to marry is the father of your child. If you deceive me, you shall feel the fires of hell."

I did not feel as proud as I had done. My strongest weapon with him was gone. I was lowered in my own estimation, and had resolved to bear his abuse in silence. But when he spoke contemptuously of the lover who had always treated me honorably; when I remembered that but for *him* I might have been a virtuous, free, and happy wife, I lost my patience. "I have sinned against God and myself," I replied; "but not against you."

He clinched his teeth, and muttered, "Curse you!" He came towards me, with ill-suppressed rage, and exclaimed, "You obstinate girl! I could grind your bones to powder! You have thrown yourself away on some worthless rascal. You are weak-minded, and have been easily persuaded by those who don't care a straw for you. The future will settle accounts between us. You are blinded now; but hereafter you will be convinced that your master was your best friend. My lenity towards you is a proof of it. I might have punished you in many ways. I might have had you whipped till you fell dead under the lash. But I wanted you to live; I would have bettered your condition. Others cannot do it. You are my slave. Your mistress, disgusted by your conduct, forbids you to return to the house; therefore I leave you here for the present; but I shall see you often. I will call tomorrow."

He came with frowning brows, that showed a dissatisfied state of mind. After asking about my health, he inquired whether my board was paid, and who visited me. He then went on to say that he had neglected his duty; that as a physician there were certain things that he ought to have explained to me. Then followed talk such as would have made the most shameless blush. He ordered me to stand up before him. I obeyed. "I command you," said he, "to tell me whether the father of your child is white or black." I hesitated. "Answer me this instant!" he exclaimed. I did answer. He sprang upon me like a

2. Bitter plant used as a tonic.

wolf, and grabbed my arm as if he would have broken it. "Do you love him?" said he, in a hissing tone.

"I am thankful that I do not despise him," I replied.

He raised his hand to strike me; but it fell again. I don't know what arrested the blow. He sat down, with lips tightly compressed. At last he spoke. "I came here," said he, "to make you a friendly proposition; but your ingratitude chafes me beyond endurance. You turn aside all my good intentions towards you. I don't know what it is that keeps me from killing you." Again he rose, as if he had a mind to strike me.

But he resumed. "On one condition I will forgive your insolence and crime. You must henceforth have no communication of any kind with the father of your child. You must not ask any thing from him, or receive any thing from him. I will take care of you and your child. You had better promise this at once, and not wait till you are deserted by him. This is the last act of mercy I shall show towards you."

I said something about being unwilling to have my child supported by a man who had cursed it and me also. He rejoined, that a woman who had sunk to my level had no right to expect any thing else. He asked, for the last time, would I accept his kindness? I answered that I would not.

"Very well," said he; "then take the consequences of your wayward course. Never look to me for help. You are my slave, and shall always be my slave. I will never sell you, that you may depend upon."

Hope died away in my heart as he closed the door after him. I had calculated that in his rage he would sell me to a slave-trader; and I knew the father of my child was on the watch to buy me.

About this time my uncle Phillip was expected to return from a voyage. The day before his departure I had officiated as bridesmaid to a young friend. My heart was then ill at ease, but my smiling countenance did not betray it. Only a year had passed; but what fearful changes it had wrought! My heart had grown gray in misery. Lives that flash in sunshine, and lives that are born in tears, receive their hue from circumstances. None of us know what a year may bring forth.

I felt no joy when they told me my uncle had come. He wanted to see me, though he knew what had happened. I shrank from him at first; but at last consented that he should come to my room. He received me as he always had done. O, how my heart smote me when I felt his tears on my burning cheeks! The words of my grandmother came to my mind,—"Perhaps your mother and father are taken from the evil days to come." My disappointed heart could now praise God that it was so. But why, thought I, did my relatives ever cherish hopes for me? What was there to save me from the usual fate of slave girls? Many more beautiful and more intelligent than I had experienced a similar fate, or a far worse one. How could they hope that I should escape?

My uncle's stay was short, and I was not sorry for it. I was too ill in mind and body to enjoy my friends as I had done. For some weeks I was unable to leave my bed. I could not have any doctor but my master, and I would not have him sent for. At last, alarmed by my increasing illness, they sent for him. I was very weak and nervous; and as soon as he entered the room, I began to scream. They told him my state was very critical. He had no wish to hasten me out of the world, and he withdrew.

When my babe was born, they said it was premature. It weighed only four pounds; but God let it live. I heard the doctor say I could not survive till morning. I had often prayed for death; but now I did not want to die, unless my child could die too. Many weeks passed before I was able to leave my bed. I was a mere wreck of my former self. For a year there was scarcely a day when I was free from chills and fever. My babe also was sickly. His little limbs were often racked with pain. Dr. Flint continued his visits, to look after my health; and he did not fail to remind me that my child was an addition to his stock of slaves.

I felt too feeble to dispute with him, and listened to his remarks in silence. His visits were less frequent; but his busy spirit could not remain quiet. He employed my brother in his office, and he was made the medium of frequent notes and messages to me. William was a bright lad, and of much use to the doctor. He had learned to put up medicines, to leech, cup, and bleed.[3] He had taught himself to read and spell. I was proud of my brother; and the old doctor suspected as much. One day, when I had not seen him for several weeks, I heard his steps approaching the door. I dreaded the encounter, and hid myself. He inquired for me, of course; but I was nowhere to be found. He went to his office, and despatched William with a note. The color mounted to my brother's face when he gave it to me; and he said, "Don't you hate me, Linda, for bringing you these things?" I told him I could not blame him; he was a slave, and obliged to obey his master's will. The note ordered me to come to his office. I went. He demanded to know where I was when he called. I told him I was at home. He flew into a passion, and said he knew better. Then he launched out upon his usual themes,—my crimes against him, and my ingratitude for his forbearance. The laws were laid down to me anew, and I was dismissed. I felt humiliated that my brother should stand by, and listen to such language as would be addressed only to a slave. Poor boy! He was powerless to defend

3. Bloodletting (or bleeding) was thought to cure many illnesses. "Leech": to apply leeches, as a bloodletting agent, for medicinal purposes. "Cup": to apply heated cups to the skin as a counterirritant. "Bleed": to drain blood from a patient.

me; but I saw the tears, which he vainly strove to keep back. This manifestation of feeling irritated the doctor. William could do nothing to please him. One morning he did not arrive at the office so early as usual; and that circumstance afforded his master an opportunity to vent his spleen.[4] He was put in jail. The next day my brother sent a trader to the doctor, with a request to be sold. His master was greatly incensed at what he called his insolence. He said he had put him there to reflect upon his bad conduct, and he certainly was not giving any evidence of repentance. For two days he harassed himself to find somebody to do his office work; but every thing went wrong without William. He was released, and ordered to take his old stand, with many threats, if he was not careful about his future behavior.

As the months passed on, my boy improved in health. When he was a year old, they called him beautiful. The little vine was taking deep root in my existence, though its clinging fondness excited a mixture of love and pain. When I was most sorely oppressed I found a solace in his smiles. I loved to watch his infant slumbers; but always there was a dark cloud over my enjoyment. I could never forget that he was a slave. Sometimes I wished that he might die in infancy. God tried me. My darling became very ill. The bright eyes grew dull, and the little feet and hands were so icy cold that I thought death had already touched them. I had prayed for his death, but never so earnestly as I now prayed for his life; and my prayer was heard. Alas, what mockery it is for a slave mother to try to pray back her dying child to life! Death is better than slavery. It was a sad thought that I had no name to give my child. His father caressed him and treated him kindly, whenever he had a chance to see him. He was not unwilling that he should bear his name; but he had no legal claim to it; and if I had bestowed it upon him, my master would have regarded it as a new crime, a new piece of insolence, and would, perhaps, revenge it on the boy. O, the serpent of Slavery has many and poisonous fangs!

XII. Fear of Insurrection

Not far from this time Nat Turner's[1] insurrection broke out; and the news threw our town into great commotion. Strange that they should be alarmed, when their slaves were so "contented and happy"! But so it was.

4. Once considered the seat of the emotions in the body, later associated with rage.
1. The slave leader of an 1831 insurrection in Southampton County, Virginia, during which several whites were killed. In the aftermath, Turner and his allies were tried and executed; in a flood of punitive violence all across the South, dozens, maybe hundreds, of black people were killed.

It was always the custom to have a muster[2] every year. On that occasion every white man shouldered his musket. The citizens and the so-called country gentlemen wore military uniforms. The poor whites took their places in the ranks in every-day dress, some without shoes, some without hats. This grand occasion had already passed; and when the slaves were told there was to be another muster, they were surprised and rejoiced. Poor creatures! They thought it was going to be a holiday. I was informed of the true state of affairs, and imparted it to the few I could trust. Most gladly would I have proclaimed it to every slave; but I dared not. All could not be relied on. Mighty is the power of the torturing lash.

By sunrise, people were pouring in from every quarter within twenty miles of the town. I knew the houses were to be searched; and I expected it would be done by country bullies and the poor whites. I knew nothing annoyed them so much as to see colored people living in comfort and respectability; so I made arrangements for them with especial care. I arranged every thing in my grandmother's house as neatly as possible. I put white quilts on the beds, and decorated some of the rooms with flowers. When all was arranged, I sat down at the window to watch. Far as my eye could reach, it rested on a motley crowd of soldiers. Drums and fifes were discoursing martial music. The men were divided into companies of sixteen, each headed by a captain. Orders were given, and the wild scouts rushed in every direction, wherever a colored face was to be found.

It was a grand opportunity for the low whites, who had no negroes of their own to scourge. They exulted in such a chance to exercise a little brief authority, and show their subserviency to the slaveholders; not reflecting that the power which trampled on the colored people also kept themselves in poverty, ignorance, and moral degradation. Those who never witnessed such scenes can hardly believe what I know was inflicted at this time on innocent men, women, and children, against whom there was not the slightest ground for suspicion. Colored people and slaves who lived in remote parts of the town suffered in an especial manner. In some cases the searchers scattered powder and shot among their clothes, and then sent other parties to find them, and bring them forward as proof that they were plotting insurrection. Every where men, women, and children were whipped till the blood stood in puddles at their feet. Some received five hundred lashes; others were tied hands and feet, and tortured with a bucking paddle, which blisters the skin terribly. The dwellings of the colored people, unless they happened to be protected by some influential white person, who was nigh at hand, were robbed of clothing and everything else the marauders thought worth

2. A gathering for display, inspection, drill, or service.

carrying away. All day long these unfeeling wretches went round, like a troop of demons, terrifying and tormenting the helpless. At night, they formed themselves into patrol bands, and went wherever they chose among the colored people, acting out their brutal will. Many women hid themselves in woods and swamps, to keep out of their way. If any of the husbands or fathers told of these outrages, they were tied up to the public whipping post, and cruelly scourged for telling lies about white men. The consternation was universal. No two people that had the slightest tinge of color in their faces dared to be seen talking together.

I entertained no positive fears about our household, because we were in the midst of white families who would protect us. We were ready to receive the soldiers whenever they came. It was not long before we heard the tramp of feet and the sound of voices. The door was rudely pushed open; and in they tumbled, like a pack of hungry wolves. They snatched at every thing within their reach. Every box, trunk, closet, and corner underwent a thorough examination. A box in one of the drawers containing some silver change was eagerly pounced upon. When I stepped forward to take it from them, one of the soldiers turned and said angrily, "What d'ye foller us fur? D'ye s'pose white folks is come to steal?"

I replied, "You have come to search; but you have searched that box, and I will take it, if you please."

At that moment I saw a white gentleman who was friendly to us; and I called to him, and asked him to have the goodness to come in and stay till the search was over. He readily complied. His entrance into the house brought in the captain of the company, whose business it was to guard the outside of the house, and see that none of the inmates left it. This officer was Mr. Litch, the wealthy slaveholder whom I mentioned, in the account of neighboring planters, as being notorious for his cruelty. He felt above soiling his hands with the search. He merely gave orders; and, if a bit of writing was discovered, it was carried to him by his ignorant followers, who were unable to read.

My grandmother had a large trunk of bedding and table cloths. When that was opened, there was a great shout of surprise; and one exclaimed, "Where'd the damned niggers git all dis sheet an' table clarf?"

My grandmother, emboldened by the presence of our white protector, said, "You may be sure we didn't pilfer 'em from *your* houses."

"Look here, mammy," said a grim-looking fellow without any coat, "you seem to feel mighty gran' 'cause you got all them 'ere fixens. White folks oughter have 'em all."

His remarks were interrupted by a chorus of voices shouting, "We's got 'em! We's got 'em! Dis 'ere yaller gal's got letters!"

There was a general rush for the supposed letter, which, upon examination, proved to be some verses written to me by a friend. In packing away my things, I had overlooked them. When their captain informed them of their contents, they seemed much disappointed. He inquired of me who wrote them. I told him it was one of my friends. "Can you read them?" he asked. When I told him I could, he swore, and raved, and tore the paper into bits. "Bring me all your letters!" said he, in a commanding tone. I told him I had none. "Don't be afraid," he continued, in an insinuating way. "Bring them all to me. Nobody shall do you any harm." Seeing I did not move to obey him, his pleasant tone changed to oaths and threats. "Who writes to you? half free niggers?" inquired he. I replied, "O, no; most of my letters are from white people. Some request me to burn them after they are read, and some I destroy without reading."

An exclamation of surprise from some of the company put a stop to our conversation. Some silver spoons which ornamented an old-fashioned buffet had just been discovered. My grandmother was in the habit of preserving fruit for many ladies in the town, and of preparing suppers for parties; consequently she had many jars of preserves. The closet that contained these was next invaded, and the contents tasted. One of them, who was helping himself freely, tapped his neighbor on the shoulder, and said, "Wal done! Don't wonder de niggers want to kill all de white folks, when dey live on 'sarves" [meaning preserves]. I stretched out my hand to take the jar, saying, "You were not sent here to search for sweetmeats."[3]

"And what *were* we sent for?" said the captain, bristling up to me. I evaded the question.

The search of the house was completed, and nothing found to condemn us. They next proceeded to the garden, and knocked about every bush and vine, with no better success. The captain called his men together, and, after a short consultation, the order to march was given. As they passed out of the gate, the captain turned back, and pronounced a malediction on the house. He said it ought to be burned to the ground, and each of its inmates receive thirty-nine lashes. We came out of this affair very fortunately; not losing any thing except some wearing apparel.

Towards evening the turbulence increased. The soldiers, stimulated by drink, committed still greater cruelties. Shrieks and shouts continually rent the air. Not daring to go to the door, I peeped under the window curtain. I saw a mob dragging along a number of colored people, each white man, with his musket upraised, threatening instant death if they did not stop their shrieks. Among the prisoners was a respectable old colored minister. They had found a

3. Confections rich in sugar, such as the preserves.

few parcels of shot in his house, which his wife had for years used to balance her scales. For this they were going to shoot him on Court House Green. What a spectacle was that for a civilized country! A rabble, staggering under intoxication, assuming to be the administrators of justice!

The better class of the community exerted their influence to save the innocent, persecuted people; and in several instances they succeeded, by keeping them shut up in jail till the excitement abated. At last the white citizens found that their own property was not safe from the lawless rabble they had summoned to protect them. They rallied the drunken swarm, drove them back into the country, and set a guard over the town.

The next day, the town patrols were commissioned to search colored people that lived out of the city; and the most shocking outrages were committed with perfect impunity. Every day for a fortnight, if I looked out, I saw horsemen with some poor panting negro tied to their saddles, and compelled by the lash to keep up with their speed, till they arrived at the jail yard. Those who had been whipped too unmercifully to walk were washed with brine, tossed into a cart, and carried to jail. One black man, who had not fortitude to endure scourging, promised to give information about the conspiracy. But it turned out that he knew nothing at all. He had not even heard the name of Nat Turner. The poor fellow had, however, made up a story, which augmented his own sufferings and those of the colored people.

The day patrol continued for some weeks, and at sundown a night guard was substituted. Nothing at all was proved against the colored people, bond or free. The wrath of the slaveholders was somewhat appeased by the capture of Nat Turner. The imprisoned were released. The slaves were sent to their masters, and the free were permitted to return to their ravaged homes. Visiting was strictly forbidden on the plantations. The slaves begged the privilege of again meeting at their little church in the woods, with their burying ground around it. It was built by the colored people, and they had no higher happiness than to meet there and sing hymns together, and pour out their hearts in spontaneous prayer. Their request was denied, and the church was demolished. They were permitted to attend the white churches, a certain portion of the galleries being appropriated to their use. There, when every body else had partaken of the communion, and the benediction had been pronounced, the minister said, "Come down, now, my colored friends." They obeyed the summons, and partook of the bread and wine, in commemoration of the meek and lowly Jesus, who said, "God is your Father, and all ye are brethren."[4]

4. Matthew 23.8.

XIII. The Church and Slavery

After the alarm caused by Nat Turner's insurrection had subsided, the slaveholders came to the conclusion that it would be well to give the slaves enough of religious instruction to keep them from murdering their masters. The Episcopal clergyman offered to hold a separate service on Sundays for their benefit. His colored members were very few, and also very respectable—a fact which I presume had some weight with him. The difficulty was to decide on a suitable place for them to worship. The Methodist and Baptist churches admitted them in the afternoon; but their carpets and cushions were not so costly as those at the Episcopal church. It was at last decided that they should meet at the house of a free colored man, who was a member.

I was invited to attend, because I could read. Sunday evening came, and, trusting to the cover of night, I ventured out. I rarely ventured out by daylight, for I always went with fear, expecting at every turn to encounter Dr. Flint, who was sure to turn me back, or order me to his office to inquire where I got my bonnet, or some other article of dress. When the Rev. Mr. Pike came, there were some twenty persons present. The reverend gentleman knelt in prayer, then seated himself, and requested all present, who could read, to open their books, while he gave out the portions he wished them to repeat or respond to.

His text was, "Servants, be obedient to them that are your masters according to the flesh, with fear and trembling, in singleness of your heart, as unto Christ."[1]

Pious Mr. Pike brushed up his hair till it stood upright, and, in deep, solemn tones, began: "Hearken, ye servants! Give strict heed unto my words. You are rebellious sinners. Your hearts are filled with all manner of evil. 'Tis the devil who tempts you. God is angry with you, and will surely punish you, if you don't forsake your wicked ways. You that live in town are eye-servants behind your master's back. Instead of serving your masters faithfully, which is pleasing in the sight of your heavenly Master, you are idle, and shirk your work. God sees you. You tell lies. God hears you. Instead of being engaged in worshipping him, you are hidden away somewhere, feasting on your master's substance; tossing coffee-grounds with some wicked fortuneteller, or cutting cards with another old hag. Your masters may not find you out, but God sees you, and will punish you. O, the depravity of your hearts! When your master's work is done, are you quietly together, thinking of the goodness of God to such

1. Ephesians 6.5.

sinful creatures? No; you are quarrelling, and tying up little bags of roots to bury under the door-steps to poison each other with. God sees you. You men steal away to every grog[2] shop to sell your master's corn, that you may buy rum to drink. God sees you. You sneak into the back streets, or among the bushes, to pitch coppers. Although your masters may not find you out, God sees you; and he will punish you. You must forsake your sinful ways, and be faithful servants. Obey your old master and your young master—your old mistress and your young mistress. If you disobey your earthly master, you offend your heavenly Master. You must obey God's commandments. When you go from here, don't stop at the corners of the streets to talk, but go directly home, and let your master and mistress see that you have come."

The benediction was pronounced. We went home, highly amused at brother Pike's gospel teaching, and we determined to hear him again. I went the next Sabbath evening, and heard pretty much a repetition of the last discourse. At the close of the meeting, Mr. Pike informed us that he found it very inconvenient to meet at the friend's house, and he should be glad to see us, every Sunday evening, at his own kitchen.

I went home with the feeling that I had heard the Reverend Mr. Pike for the last time. Some of his members repaired to his house, and found that the kitchen sported two tallow candles; the first time, I am sure, since its present occupant owned it, for the servants never had any thing but pine knots. It was so long before the reverend gentleman descended from his comfortable parlor that the slaves left, and went to enjoy a Methodist shout. They never seem so happy as when shouting and singing at religious meetings. Many of them are sincere, and nearer to the gate of heaven than sanctimonious Mr. Pike, and other long-faced Christians, who see wounded Samaritans,[3] and pass by on the other side.

The slaves generally compose their own songs and hymns; and they do not trouble their heads much about the measure. They often sing the following verses:

"Old Satan is one busy ole man;
He rolls dem blocks all in my way;
But Jesus is my bosom friend;
He rolls dem blocks away.

"If I had died when I was young,
Den how my stam'ring tongue would have sung;

2. Home-brewed alcoholic beverage.
3. Possibly a misstating of the biblical story in which a traveler from Samaria stops to help a wounded man whom he sees on the road.

But I am ole, and now I stand
A narrow chance for to tread dat heavenly land."

I well remember one occasion when I attended a Methodist class meeting.[4] I went with a burdened spirit, and happened to sit next a poor, bereaved mother, whose heart was still heavier than mine. The class leader was the town constable—a man who bought and sold slaves, who whipped his brethren and sisters of the church at the public whipping post, in jail or out of jail. He was ready to perform that Christian office any where for fifty cents. This white-faced, black-hearted brother came near us, and said to the stricken woman, "Sister, can't you tell us how the Lord deals with your soul? Do you love him as you did formerly?"

She rose to her feet, and said, in piteous tones, "My Lord and Master, help me! My load is more than I can bear. God has hid himself from me, and I am left in darkness and misery." Then, striking her breast, she continued, "I can't tell you what is in here! They've got all my children. Last week they took the last one. God only knows where they've sold her. They let me have her sixteen years, and then—O! O! Pray for her brothers and sisters! I've got nothing to live for now. God make my time short!"

She sat down, quivering in every limb. I saw that constable class leader become crimson in the face with suppressed laughter, while he held up his handkerchief, that those who were weeping for the poor woman's calamity might not see his merriment. Then, with assumed gravity, he said to the bereaved mother, "Sister, pray to the Lord that every dispensation of his divine will may be sanctified to the good of your poor needy soul!"

The congregation struck up a hymn, and sung as though they were as free as the birds that warbled round us,—

"Ole Satan thought he had a mighty aim;
He missed my soul, and caught my sins.
Cry Amen, cry Amen, cry Amen to God!

"He took my sins upon his back;
Went muttering and grumbling down to hell.
Cry Amen, cry Amen, cry Amen to God!

"Ole Satan's church is here below.
Up to God's free church I hope to go.
Cry Amen, cry Amen, cry Amen to God!"

4. In some denominations, members were assigned to small groups called "classes," with whom they studied, socialized, and practiced various religious activities.

Precious are such moments to the poor slaves. If you were to hear them at such times, you might think they were happy. But can that hour of singing and shouting sustain them through the dreary week, toiling without wages, under constant dread of the lash?

The Episcopal clergyman, who, ever since my earliest recollection, had been a sort of god among the slaveholders, concluded, as his family was large, that he must go where money was more abundant. A very different clergyman took his place. The change was very agreeable to the colored people, who said, "God has sent us a good man this time." They loved him, and their children followed him for a smile or a kind word. Even the slaveholders felt his influence. He brought to the rectory five slaves. His wife taught them to read and write, and to be useful to her and themselves. As soon as he was settled, he turned his attention to the needy slaves around him. He urged upon his parishioners the duty of having a meeting expressly for them every Sunday, with a sermon adapted to their comprehension. After much argument and importunity, it was finally agreed that they might occupy the gallery of the church on Sunday evenings. Many colored people, hitherto unaccustomed to attend church, now gladly went to hear the gospel preached. The sermons were simple, and they understood them. Moreover, it was the first time they had ever been addressed as human beings. It was not long before his white parishioners began to be dissatisfied. He was accused of preaching better sermons to the negroes than he did to them. He honestly confessed that he bestowed more pains upon those sermons than upon any others; for the slaves were reared in such ignorance that it was a difficult task to adapt himself to their comprehension. Dissensions arose in the parish. Some wanted he should preach to them in the evening, and to the slaves in the afternoon. In the midst of these disputings his wife died, after a very short illness. Her slaves gathered round her dying bed in great sorrow. She said, "I have tried to do you good and promote your happiness; and if I have failed, it has not been for want of interest in your welfare. Do not weep for me; but prepare for the new duties that lie before you. I leave you all free. May we meet in a better world." Her liberated slaves were sent away, with funds to establish them comfortably. The colored people will long bless the memory of that truly Christian woman. Soon after her death her husband preached his farewell sermon, and many tears were shed at his departure.

Several years after, he passed through our town and preached to his former congregation. In his afternoon sermon he addressed the colored people. "My friends," said he, "it affords me great happiness to have an opportunity of speaking to you again. For two years I have been striving to do something for the colored people of my own parish; but nothing is yet accomplished. I have not even preached a sermon to them. Try to live according to the word of God, my friends. Your skin is darker than mine; but God judges men by their hearts, not by the color of their skins." This was strange doctrine from a southern pulpit. It was very offensive to slaveholders. They said he and his wife had made fools of their slaves, and that he preached like a fool to the negroes.

I knew an old black man, whose piety and childlike trust in God were beautiful to witness. At fifty-three years old he joined the Baptist church. He had a most earnest desire to learn to read. He thought he should know how to serve God better if he could only read the Bible. He came to me, and begged me to teach him. He said he could not pay me, for he had no money; but he would bring me nice fruit when the season for it came. I asked him if he didn't know it was contrary to law; and that slaves were whipped and imprisoned for teaching each other to read. This brought the tears into his eyes. "Don't be troubled, uncle Fred,"[5] said I. "I have no thoughts of refusing to teach you. I only told you of the law, that you might know the danger, and be on your guard." He thought he could plan to come three times a week without its being suspected. I selected a quiet nook, where no intruder was likely to penetrate, and there I taught him his A, B, C. Considering his age, his progress was astonishing. As soon as he could spell in two syllables he wanted to spell out words in the Bible. The happy smile that illuminated his face put joy into my heart. After spelling out a few words, he paused, and said, "Honey, it 'pears when I can read dis good book I shall be nearer to God. White man is got all de sense. He can larn easy. It ain't easy for ole black man like me. I only wants to read dis book, dat I may know how to live; den I hab no fear 'bout dying."

I tried to encourage him by speaking of the rapid progress he had made. "Hab patience, child," he replied. "I larns slow."

I had no need of patience. His gratitude, and the happiness I imparted, were more than a recompense for all my trouble.

At the end of six months he had read through the New Testament, and could find any text in it. One day, when he had recited unusually well, I said, "Uncle Fred, how do you manage to get your lessons so well?"

"Lord bress you, chile," he replied. "You nebber gibs me a lesson dat I don't pray to God to help me to understan' what I spells and what I reads. And he *does* help me, chile. Bress his holy name!"

There are thousands, who, like good uncle Fred, are thirsting for the water of life; but the law forbids it, and the churches withhold it. They send the Bible to heathen abroad, and neglect the heathen at home. I am glad that missionaries go out to the dark corners of

5. "Uncle," like "aunt," can be used as a title of respect, as here.

the earth; but I ask them not to overlook the dark corners at home. Talk to American slaveholders as you talk to savages in Africa. Tell *them* it is wrong to traffic in men. Tell them it is sinful to sell their own children, and atrocious to violate their own daughters. Tell them that all men are brethren, and that man has no right to shut out the light of knowledge from his brother. Tell them they are answerable to God for sealing up the Fountain of Life from souls that are thirsting for it.

There are men who would gladly undertake such missionary work as this; but, alas! their number is small. They are hated by the south, and would be driven from its soil, or dragged to prison to die, as others have been before them. The field is ripe for the harvest, and awaits the reapers. Perhaps the great grandchildren of uncle Fred may have freely imparted to them the divine treasures, which he sought by stealth, at the risk of the prison and the scourge.

Are doctors of divinity blind, or are they hypocrites? I suppose some are the one, and some the other; but I think if they felt the interest in the poor and the lowly, that they ought to feel, they would not be so *easily* blinded. A clergyman who goes to the south, for the first time, has usually some feeling, however vague, that slavery is wrong. The slaveholder suspects this, and plays his game accordingly. He makes himself as agreeable as possible; talks on theology, and other kindred topics. The reverend gentleman is asked to invoke a blessing on a table loaded with luxuries. After dinner he walks round the premises, and sees the beautiful groves and flowering vines, and the comfortable huts of favored household slaves. The southerner invites him to talk with these slaves. He asks them if they want to be free, and they say, "O, no, massa." This is sufficient to satisfy him. He comes home to publish a "South-Side View of Slavery,"[6] and to complain of the exaggerations of abolitionists. He assures people that he has been to the south, and seen slavery for himself; that it is a beautiful "patriarchal institution;"[7] that the slaves don't want their freedom; that they have hallelujah meetings, and other religious privileges.

What does *he* know of the half-starved wretches toiling from dawn till dark on the plantations? of mothers shrieking for their children, torn from their arms by slave traders? of young girls dragged down into moral filth? of pools of blood around the whipping post? of hounds trained to tear human flesh? of men screwed into cotton gins to die? The slaveholder showed him none of these things, and the slaves dared not tell of them if he had asked them.

6. Published by the Reverend Nehemiah Adams of Boston in 1854, after his tour of the South.
7. A euphemism for chattel slavery in the United States.

There is a great difference between Christianity and religion at the south. If a man goes to the communion table, and pays money into the treasury of the church, no matter if it be the price of blood, he is called religious. If a pastor has offspring by a woman not his wife, the church dismiss him, if she is a white woman; but if she is colored, it does not hinder his continuing to be their good shepherd.

When I was told that Dr. Flint had joined the Episcopal church, I was much surprised. I supposed that religion had a purifying effect on the character of men; but the worst persecutions I endured from him were after he was a communicant. The conversation of the doctor, the day after he had been confirmed, certainly gave *me* no indication that he had "renounced the devil and all his works."[8] In answer to some of his usual talk, I reminded him that he had just joined the church. "Yes, Linda," said he. "It was proper for me to do so. I am getting in years, and my position in society requires it, and it puts an end to all the damned slang.[9] You would do well to join the church, too, Linda."

"There are sinners enough in it already," rejoined I. "If I could be allowed to live like a Christian, I should be glad."

"You can do what I require; and if you are faithful to me, you will be as virtuous as my wife," he replied.

I answered that the Bible didn't say so.

His voice became hoarse with rage. "How dare you preach to me about your infernal Bible!" he exclaimed. "What right have you, who are my negro, to talk to me about what you would like, and what you wouldn't like? I am your master, and you shall obey me."

No wonder the slaves sing,—

> "Ole Satan's church is here below;
> Up to God's free church I hope to go."

XIV. Another Link to Life

I had not returned to my master's house since the birth of my child. The old man raved to have me thus removed from his immediate power; but his wife vowed, by all that was good and great, she would kill me if I came back; and he did not doubt her word. Sometimes he would stay away for a season. Then he would come and renew the old threadbare discourse about his forbearance and my ingratitude. He labored, most unnecessarily, to convince me that I had lowered myself. The venomous old reprobate had no need of descanting on that theme. I felt humiliated enough. My unconscious

8. A pledge taken upon conversion.
9. Vulgar language.

babe was the ever-present witness of my shame. I listened with silent contempt when he talked about my having forfeited *his* good opinion; but I shed bitter tears that I was no longer worthy of being respected by the good and pure. Alas! slavery still held me in its poisonous grasp. There was no chance for me to be respectable. There was no prospect of being able to lead a better life.

Sometimes, when my master found that I still refused to accept what he called his kind offers, he would threaten to sell my child. "Perhaps that will humble you," said he.

Humble *me!* Was I not already in the dust? But his threat lacerated my heart. I knew the law gave him power to fulfil it; for slaveholders have been cunning enough to enact that "the child shall follow the condition of the *mother*," not of the *father*; thus taking care that licentiousness shall not interfere with avarice. This reflection made me clasp my innocent babe all the more firmly to my heart. Horrid visions passed through my mind when I thought of his liability to fall into the slave trader's hands. I wept over him, and said, "O my child! perhaps they will leave you in some cold cabin to die, and then throw you into a hole, as if you were a dog."

When Dr. Flint learned that I was again to be a mother, he was exasperated beyond measure. He rushed from the house, and returned with a pair of shears. I had a fine head of hair; and he often railed about my pride of arranging it nicely. He cut every hair close to my head, storming and swearing all the time. I replied to some of his abuse, and he struck me. Some months before, he had pitched me down stairs in a fit of passion; and the injury I received was so serious that I was unable to turn myself in bed for many days. He then said, "Linda, I swear by God I will never raise my hand against you again;" but I knew that he would forget his promise.

After he discovered my situation, he was like a restless spirit from the pit. He came every day; and I was subjected to such insults as no pen can describe. I would not describe them if I could; they were too low, too revolting. I tried to keep them from my grandmother's knowledge as much as I could. I knew she had enough to sadden her life, without having my troubles to bear. When she saw the doctor treat me with violence, and heard him utter oaths terrible enough to palsy a man's tongue, she could not always hold her peace. It was natural and motherlike that she should try to defend me; but it only made matters worse.

When they told me my new-born babe was a girl, my heart was heavier than it had ever been before. Slavery is terrible for men; but it is far more terrible for women. Superadded to the burden common to all, *they* have wrongs, and sufferings, and mortifications peculiarly their own.

Dr. Flint had sworn that he would make me suffer, to my last day, for this new crime against *him*, as he called it; and as long as he had me in his power he kept his word. On the fourth day after the birth of my babe, he entered my room suddenly, and commanded me to rise and bring my baby to him. The nurse who took care of me had gone out of the room to prepare some nourishment, and I was alone. There was no alternative. I rose, took up my babe, and crossed the room to where he sat. "Now stand there," said he, "till I tell you to go back!" My child bore a strong resemblance to her father, and to the deceased Mrs. Sands, her grandmother. He noticed this; and while I stood before him, trembling with weakness, he heaped upon me and my little one every vile epithet he could think of. Even the grandmother in her grave did not escape his curses. In the midst of his vituperations I fainted at his feet. This recalled him to his senses. He took the baby from my arms, laid it on the bed, dashed cold water in my face, took me up, and shook me violently, to restore my consciousness before any one entered the room. Just then my grandmother came in, and he hurried out of the house. I suffered in consequence of this treatment; but I begged my friends to let me die, rather than send for the doctor. There was nothing I dreaded so much as his presence. My life was spared; and I was glad for the sake of my little ones. Had it not been for these ties to life, I should have been glad to be released by death, though I had lived only nineteen years.

Always it gave me a pang that my children had no lawful claim to a name. Their father offered his; but, if I had wished to accept the offer, I dared not while my master lived. Moreover, I knew it would not be accepted at their baptism. A Christian name they were at least entitled to; and we resolved to call my boy for our dear good Benjamin, who had gone far away from us.

My grandmother belonged to the church; and she was very desirous of having the children christened. I knew Dr. Flint would forbid it, and I did not venture to attempt it. But chance favored me. He was called to visit a patient out of town, and was obliged to be absent during Sunday. "Now is the time," said my grandmother; "we will take the children to church, and have them christened."

When I entered the church, recollections of my mother came over me, and I felt subdued in spirit. There she had presented me for baptism, without any reason to feel ashamed. She had been married, and had such legal rights as slavery allows to a slave. The vows had at least been sacred to *her*, and she had never violated them. I was glad she was not alive, to know under what different circumstances her grandchildren were presented for baptism. Why had my lot been so different from my mother's? *Her* master had died when she was a child; and she remained with her mistress till she married. She was never in the power of any master; and thus she escaped one class of the evils that generally fall upon slaves.

When my baby was about to be christened, the former mistress of my father stepped up to me, and proposed to give it her Christian name. To this I added the surname of my father, who had himself no legal right to it; for my grandfather on the paternal side was a white gentleman. What tangled skeins are the genealogies of slavery! I loved my father; but it mortified me to be obliged to bestow his name on my children.

When we left the church, my father's old mistress invited me to go home with her. She clasped a gold chain round my baby's neck. I thanked her for this kindness; but I did not like the emblem. I wanted no chain to be fastened on my daughter, not even if its links were of gold. How earnestly I prayed that she might never feel the weight of slavery's chain, whose iron entereth into the soul!

XV. Continued Persecutions

My children grew finely; and Dr. Flint would often say to me, with an exulting smile, "These brats will bring me a handsome sum of money one of these days."

I thought to myself that, God being my helper, they should never pass into his hands. It seemed to me I would rather see them killed than have them given up to his power. The money for the freedom of myself and my children could be obtained; but I derived no advantage from that circumstance. Dr. Flint loved money, but he loved power more. After much discussion, my friends resolved on making another trial. There was a slaveholder about to leave for Texas, and he was commissioned to buy me. He was to begin with nine hundred dollars, and go up to twelve. My master refused his offers. "Sir," said he, "she don't belong to me. She is my daughter's property, and I have no right to sell her. I mistrust that you come from her paramour. If so, you may tell him that he cannot buy her for any money; neither can he buy her children."

The doctor came to see me the next day, and my heart beat quicker as he entered. I never had seen the old man tread with so majestic a step. He seated himself and looked at me with withering scorn. My children had learned to be afraid of him. The little one would shut her eyes and hide her face on my shoulder whenever she saw him; and Benny, who was now nearly five years old, often inquired, "What makes that bad man come here so many times? Does he want to hurt us?" I would clasp the dear boy in my arms, trusting that he would be free before he was old enough to solve the problem. And now, as the doctor sat there so grim and silent, the child left his play and came and nestled up by me. At last my tormentor spoke. "So you are left in disgust, are you?" said he. "It is no more than I expected. You remember I told you years ago that you would be treated so. So he is tired of you? Ha! ha! ha! The virtuous madam don't like to hear about it, does she? Ha! ha! ha!" There was a sting in his calling me virtuous madam. I no longer had the power of answering him as I had formerly done. He continued: "So it seems you are trying to get up another intrigue. Your new paramour came to me, and offered to buy you; but you may be assured you will not succeed. You are mine; and you shall be mine for life. There lives no human being that can take you out of slavery. I would have done it; but you rejected my kind offer."

I told him I did not wish to get up any intrigue; that I had never seen the man who offered to buy me.

"Do you tell me I lie?" exclaimed he, dragging me from my chair. "Will you say again that you never saw that man?"

I answered, "I do say so."

He clinched my arm with a volley of oaths. Ben began to scream, and I told him to go to his grandmother.

"Don't you stir a step, you little wretch!" said he. The child drew nearer to me, and put his arms round me, as if he wanted to protect me. This was too much for my enraged master. He caught him up and hurled him across the room. I thought he was dead, and rushed towards him to take him up.

"Not yet!" exclaimed the doctor. "Let him lie there till he comes to."

"Let me go! Let me go!" I screamed, "or I will raise the whole house." I struggled and got away; but he clinched me again. Somebody opened the door, and he released me. I picked up my insensible child, and when I turned my tormentor was gone. Anxiously I bent over the little form, so pale and still; and when the brown eyes at last opened, I don't know whether I was very happy.

All the doctor's former persecutions were renewed. He came morning, noon, and night. No jealous lover ever watched a rival more closely than he watched me and the unknown slaveholder, with whom he accused me of wishing to get up an intrigue. When my grandmother was out of the way he searched every room to find him.

In one of his visits, he happened to find a young girl, whom he had sold to a trader a few days previous. His statement was, that he sold her because she had been too familiar with the overseer. She had had a bitter life with him, and was glad to be sold. She had no mother, and no near ties. She had been torn from all her family years before. A few friends had entered into bonds for her safety, if the trader would allow her to spend with them the time that intervened between her sale and the gathering up of his human stock. Such a favor was rarely granted. It saved the trader the expense of board and jail fees, and though the amount was small, it was a weighty consideration in a slave-trader's mind.

Dr. Flint always had an aversion to meeting slaves after he had sold them. He ordered Rose out of the house; but he was no longer her master, and she took no notice of him. For once the crushed Rose was the conqueror. His gray eyes flashed angrily upon her; but that was the extent of his power. "How came this girl here?" he exclaimed. "What right had you to allow it, when you knew I had sold her?"

I answered, "This is my grandmother's house, and Rose came to see her. I have no right to turn any body out of doors, that comes here for honest purposes."

He gave me the blow that would have fallen upon Rose if she had still been his slave. My grandmother's attention had been attracted by loud voices, and she entered in time to see a second blow dealt. She was not a woman to let such an outrage, in her own house, go unrebuked. The doctor undertook to explain that I had been insolent. Her indignant feelings rose higher and higher, and finally boiled over in words. "Get out of my house!" she exclaimed. "Go home, and take care of your wife and children, and you will have enough to do, without watching my family."

He threw the birth of my children in her face, and accused her of sanctioning the life I was leading. She told him I was living with her by compulsion of his wife; that he needn't accuse her, for he was the one to blame; he was the one who had caused all the trouble. She grew more and more excited as she went on. "I tell you what, Dr. Flint," said she, "you ain't got many more years to live, and you'd better be saying your prayers. It will take 'em all, and more too, to wash the dirt off your soul."

"Do you know whom you are talking to?" he exclaimed.

She replied, "Yes, I know very well who I am talking to."

He left the house in a great rage. I looked at my grandmother. Our eyes met. Their angry expression had passed away, but she looked sorrowful and weary—weary of incessant strife. I wondered that it did not lessen her love for me; but if it did she never showed it. She was always kind, always ready to sympathize with my troubles. There might have been peace and contentment in that humble home if it had not been for the demon Slavery.

The winter passed undisturbed by the doctor. The beautiful spring came; and when Nature resumes her loveliness, the human soul is apt to revive also. My drooping hopes came to life again with the flowers. I was dreaming of freedom again; more for my children's sake than my own. I planned and I planned. Obstacles hit against plans. There seemed no way of overcoming them; and yet I hoped.

Back came the wily doctor. I was not at home when he called. A friend had invited me to a small party, and to gratify her I went. To my great consternation, a messenger came in haste to say that Dr. Flint was at my grandmother's, and insisted on seeing me. They did not tell him where I was, or he would have come and raised a disturbance in my friend's house. They sent me a dark wrapper; I threw it on and hurried home. My speed did not save me; the doctor had gone away in anger. I dreaded the morning, but I could not delay it; it came, warm and bright. At an early hour the doctor came and asked me where I had been last night. I told him. He did not believe me, and sent to my friend's house to ascertain the facts. He came in the afternoon to assure me he was satisfied that I had spoken the truth. He seemed to be in a facetious mood, and I expected some jeers were coming. "I suppose you need some recreation," said he, "but I am surprised at your being there, among those negroes. It was not the place for *you*. Are you *allowed* to visit such people?"

I understood this covert fling at the white gentleman who was my friend; but I merely replied, "I went to visit my friends, and any company they keep is good enough for me."

He went on to say, "I have seen very little of you of late, but my interest in you is unchanged. When I said I would have no more mercy on you I was rash. I recall my words. Linda, you desire freedom for yourself and your children, and you can obtain it only through me. If you agree to what I am about to propose, you and they shall be free. There must be no communication of any kind between you and their father. I will procure a cottage, where you and the children can live together. Your labor shall be light, such as sewing for my family. Think what is offered you, Linda—a home and freedom! Let the past be forgotten. If I have been harsh with you at times, your wilfulness drove me to it. You know I exact obedience from my own children, and I consider you as yet a child."

He paused for an answer, but I remained silent.

"Why don't you speak?" said he. "What more do you wait for?"

"Nothing, sir."

"Then you accept my offer?"

"No, sir."

His anger was ready to break loose; but he succeeded in curbing it, and replied. "You have answered without thought. But I must let you know there are two sides to my proposition; if you reject the bright side, you will be obliged to take the dark one. You must either accept my offer, or you and your children shall be sent to your young master's plantation, there to remain till your young mistress is married; and your children shall fare like the rest of the negro children. I give you a week to consider of it."

He was shrewd; but I knew he was not to be trusted. I told him I was ready to give my answer now.

"I will not receive it now," he replied. "You act too much from impulse. Remember that you and your children can be free a week from to-day if you choose."

On what a monstrous chance hung the destiny of my children! I knew that my master's offer was a snare, and that if I entered it escape would be impossible. As for his promise, I knew him so well that I was sure if he gave me free papers, they would be so managed as to have no legal value. The alternative was inevitable. I resolved to go to the plantation. But then I thought how completely I should be in his power, and the prospect was appalling. Even if I should kneel before him, and implore him to spare me, for the sake of my children, I knew he would spurn me with his foot, and my weakness would be his triumph.

Before the week expired, I heard that young Mr. Flint was about to be married to a lady of his own stamp. I foresaw the position I should occupy in his establishment. I had once been sent to the plantation for punishment, and fear of the son had induced the father to recall me very soon. My mind was made up; I was resolved that I would foil my master and save my children, or I would perish in the attempt. I kept my plans to myself; I knew that friends would try to dissuade me from them, and I would not wound their feelings by rejecting their advice.

On the decisive day the doctor came, and said he hoped I had made a wise choice.

"I am ready to go to the plantation, sir," I replied.

"Have you thought how important your decision is to your children?" said he.

I told him I had.

"Very well. Go to the plantation, and my curse go with you," he replied. "Your boy shall be put to work, and he shall soon be sold; and your girl shall be raised for the purpose of selling well. Go your own ways!" He left the room with curses, not to be repeated.

As I stood rooted to the spot, my grandmother came and said, "Linda, child, what did you tell him?"

I answered that I was going to the plantation.

"*Must* you go?" said she. "Can't something be done to stop it?"

I told her it was useless to try; but she begged me not to give up. She said she would go to the doctor, and remind him how long and how faithfully she had served in the family, and how she had taken her own baby from her breast to nourish his wife. She would tell him I had been out of the family so long they would not miss me; that she would pay them for my time, and the money would procure a woman who had more strength for the situation than I had. I begged her not to go; but she persisted in saying, "He will listen to *me*, Linda." She went, and was treated as I expected. He coolly listened to what she said, but denied her request. He told her that what he did was for my good, that my feelings were entirely above my situation, and that on the plantation I would receive treatment that was suitable to my behavior.

My grandmother was much cast down. I had my secret hopes; but I must fight my battle alone. I had a woman's pride, and a mother's love for my children; and I resolved that out of the darkness of this hour a brighter dawn should rise for them. My master had power and law on his side; I had a determined will. There is might in each.

XVI. Scenes at the Plantation

Early the next morning I left my grandmother's with my youngest child. My boy was ill, and I left him behind. I had many sad thoughts as the old wagon jolted on. Hitherto, I had suffered alone; now, my little one was to be treated as a slave. As we drew near the great house, I thought of the time when I was formerly sent there out of revenge. I wondered for what purpose I was now sent. I could not tell. I resolved to obey orders so far as duty required; but within myself, I determined to make my stay as short as possible. Mr. Flint was waiting to receive us, and told me to follow him up stairs to receive orders for the day. My little Ellen was left below in the kitchen. It was a change for her, who had always been so carefully tended. My young master said she might amuse herself in the yard. This was kind of him, since the child was hateful to his sight. My task was to fit up the house for the reception of the bride. In the midst of sheets, tablecloths, towels, drapery, and carpeting, my head was as busy planning, as were my fingers with the needle. At noon I was allowed to go to Ellen. She had sobbed herself to sleep. I heard Mr. Flint say to a neighbor, "I've got her down here, and I'll soon take the town notions out of her head. My father is partly to blame for her nonsense. He ought to have broke her in long ago." The remark was made within my hearing, and it would have been quite as manly to have made it to my face. He *had* said things to my face which might, or might not, have surprised his neighbor if he had known of them. He was "a chip of the old block."

I resolved to give him no cause to accuse me of being too much of a lady, so far as work was concerned. I worked day and night, with wretchedness before me. When I lay down beside my child, I felt how much easier it would be to see her die than to see her master beat her about, as I daily saw him beat other little ones. The spirit of the mothers was so crushed by the lash, that they stood by, without courage to remonstrate. How much more must I suffer, before I should be "broke in" to that degree?

I wished to appear as contented as possible. Sometimes I had an opportunity to send a few lines home; and this brought up recollections that made it difficult, for a time, to seem calm and indifferent to my lot. Notwithstanding my efforts, I saw that Mr. Flint regarded me with a suspicious eye. Ellen broke down under the trials of her new life. Separated from me, with no one to look after her, she wandered about, and in a few days cried herself sick. One day, she sat under the window where I was at work, crying that weary cry which makes a mother's heart bleed. I was obliged to steel myself to bear it. After a while it ceased. I looked out, and she was gone. As it was near noon, I ventured to go down in search of her. The great house was raised two feet above the ground. I looked under it, and saw her about midway, fast asleep. I crept under and drew her out. As I held her in my arms, I thought how well it would be for her if she never waked up; and I uttered my thought aloud. I was startled to hear some one say, "Did you speak to me?" I looked up, and saw Mr. Flint standing beside me. He said nothing further, but turned, frowning, away. That night he sent Ellen a biscuit and a cup of sweetened milk. This generosity surprised me. I learned afterwards, that in the afternoon he had killed a large snake, which crept from under the house; and I supposed that incident had prompted his unusual kindness.

The next morning the old cart was loaded with shingles for town. I put Ellen into it, and sent her to her grandmother. Mr. Flint said I ought to have asked his permission. I told him the child was sick, and required attention which I had no time to give. He let it pass; for he was aware that I had accomplished much work in a little time.

I had been three weeks on the plantation, when I planned a visit home. It must be at night, after every body was in bed. I was six miles from town and the road was very dreary. I was to go with a young man, who, I knew often stole to town to see his mother. One night, when all was quiet, we started. Fear gave speed to our steps, and we were not long in performing the journey. I arrived at my grandmother's. Her bed room was on the first floor, and the window was open, the weather being warm. I spoke to her and she awoke. She let me in and closed the window, lest some late passer-by should see me. A light was brought, and the whole household gathered round me, some smiling and some crying. I went to look at my children, and thanked God for their happy sleep. The tears fell as I leaned over them. As I moved to leave, Benny stirred. I turned back, and whispered, "Mother is here." After digging at his eyes with his little fist, they opened, and he sat up in bed, looking at me curiously.

Having satisfied himself that it was I, he exclaimed, "O mother! you ain't dead, are you? They didn't cut off your head at the plantation, did they?"

My time was up too soon, and my guide was waiting for me. I laid Benny back in his bed, and dried his tears by a promise to come again soon. Rapidly we retraced our steps back to the plantation. About half way we were met by a company of four patrols.[1] Luckily we heard their horse's hoofs before they came in sight, and we had time to hide behind a large tree. They passed, hallooing and shouting in a manner that indicated a recent carousal. How thankful we were that they had not their dogs with them! We hastened our footsteps, and when we arrived on the plantation we heard the sound of the hand-mill. The slaves were grinding their corn. We were safely in the house before the horn summoned them to their labor. I divided my little parcel of food with my guide, knowing that he had lost the chance of grinding his corn, and must toil all day in the field.

Mr. Flint often took an inspection of the house, to see that no one was idle. The entire management of the work was trusted to me, because he knew nothing about it; and rather than hire a superintendent he contented himself with my arrangements. He had often urged upon his father the necessity of having me at the plantation to take charge of his affairs, and make clothes for the slaves; but the old man knew him too well to consent to that arrangement.

When I had been working a month at the plantation, the great aunt of Mr. Flint came to make him a visit. This was the good old lady who paid fifty dollars for my grandmother, for the purpose of making her free, when she stood on the auction block. My grandmother loved this old lady, whom we all called Miss Fanny. She often came to take tea with us. On such occasions the table was spread with a snow-white cloth, and the china cups and silver spoons were taken from the old-fashioned buffet. There were hot muffins, tea rusks,[2] and delicious sweetmeats. My grandmother kept two cows, and the fresh cream was Miss Fanny's delight. She invariably declared that it was the best in town. The old ladies had cosey times together. They would work and chat, and sometimes, while talking over old times, their spectacles would get dim with tears, and would have to be taken off and wiped. When Miss Fanny bade us good by, her bag was filled with grandmother's best cakes, and she was urged to come again soon.

There had been a time when Dr. Flint's wife came to take tea with us, and when her children were also sent to have a feast of "Aunt Marthy's" nice cooking. But after I became an object of her jealousy

1. Groups of whites employed to monitor roads for enslaved people traveling without permission.
2. Delicate, twice-baked biscuits.

and spite, she was angry with grandmother for giving a shelter to me and my children. She would not even speak to her in the street. This wounded my grandmother's feelings, for she could not retain ill will against the woman whom she had nourished with her milk when a babe. The doctor's wife would gladly have prevented our intercourse[3] with Miss Fanny if she could have done it, but fortunately she was not dependent on the bounty of the Flints. She had enough to be independent; and that is more than can ever be gained from charity, however lavish it may be.

Miss Fanny was endeared to me by many recollections, and I was rejoiced to see her at the plantation. The warmth of her large, loyal heart made the house seem pleasanter while she was in it. She staid a week, and I had many talks with her. She said her principal object in coming was to see how I was treated, and whether any thing could be done for me. She inquired whether she could help me in any way. I told her I believed not. She condoled with me in her own peculiar way; saying she wished that I and all my grandmother's family were at rest in our graves, for not until then should she feel any peace about us. The good old soul did not dream that I was planning to bestow peace upon her, with regard to myself and my children; not by death, but by securing our freedom.

Again and again I had traversed those dreary twelve miles, to and from the town; and all the way, I was meditating upon some means of escape for myself and my children. My friends had made every effort that ingenuity could devise to effect our purchase, but all their plans had proved abortive. Dr. Flint was suspicious, and determined not to loosen his grasp upon us. I could have made my escape alone; but it was more for my helpless children than for myself that I longed for freedom. Though the boon would have been precious to me, above all price, I would not have taken it at the expense of leaving them in slavery. Every trial I endured, every sacrifice I made for their sakes, drew them closer to my heart, and gave me fresh courage to beat back the dark waves that rolled and rolled over me in a seemingly endless night of storms.

The six weeks were nearly completed, when Mr. Flint's bride was expected to take possession of her new home. The arrangements were all completed, and Mr. Flint said I had done well. He expected to leave home on Saturday, and return with his bride the following Wednesday. After receiving various orders from him, I ventured to ask permission to spend Sunday in town. It was granted; for which favor I was thankful. It was the first I had ever asked of him, and I intended it should be the last. It needed more than one night to accomplish the project I had in view; but the whole of Sunday would

3. Contact or conversation.

give me an opportunity. I spent the Sabbath with my grandmother. A calmer, more beautiful day never came down out of heaven. To me it was a day of conflicting emotions. Perhaps it was the last day I should ever spend under that dear, old sheltering roof! Perhaps these were the last talks I should ever have with the faithful old friend of my whole life! Perhaps it was the last time I and my children should be together! Well, better so, I thought, than that they should be slaves. I knew the doom that awaited my fair baby in slavery, and I determined to save her from it, or perish in the attempt. I went to make this vow at the graves of my poor parents, in the burying-ground of the slaves. "There the wicked cease from troubling, and there the weary be at rest. There the prisoners rest together; they hear not the voice of the oppressor; the servant is free from his master."[4] I knelt by the graves of my parents, and thanked God, as I had often done before, that they had not lived to witness my trials, or to mourn over my sins. I had received my mother's blessing when she died; and in many an hour of tribulation I had seemed to hear her voice, sometimes chiding me, sometimes whispering loving words into my wounded heart. I have shed many and bitter tears, to think that when I am gone from my children they cannot remember me with such entire satisfaction as I remembered my mother.

The graveyard was in the woods, and twilight was coming on. Nothing broke the death-like stillness except the occasional twitter of a bird. My spirit was overawed by the solemnity of the scene. For more than ten years I had frequented this spot, but never had it seemed to me so sacred as now. A black stump, at the head of my mother's grave, was all that remained of a tree my father had planted. His grave was marked by a small wooden board, bearing his name, the letters of which were nearly obliterated. I knelt down and kissed them, and poured forth a prayer to God for guidance and support in the perilous step I was about to take. As I passed the wreck of the old meeting house, where, before Nat Turner's time, the slaves had been allowed to meet for worship, I seemed to hear my father's voice come from it, bidding me not to tarry till I reached freedom or the grave. I rushed on with renovated hopes. My trust in God had been strengthened by that prayer among the graves.

My plan was to conceal myself at the house of a friend, and remain there a few weeks till the search was over. My hope was that the doctor would get discouraged, and, for fear of losing my value, and also of subsequently finding my children among the missing, he would consent to sell us; and I knew somebody would buy us. I had done all in my power to make my children comfortable during the time I expected to be separated from them. I was packing my things,

4. Job 3.17–18.

when grandmother came into the room, and asked what I was doing. "I am putting my things in order," I replied. I tried to look and speak cheerfully; but her watchful eye detected something beneath the surface. She drew me towards her, and asked me to sit down. She looked earnestly at me, and said, "Linda, do you want to kill your old grandmother? Do you mean to leave your little, helpless children? I am old now, and cannot do for your babies as I once did for you."

I replied, that if I went away, perhaps their father would be able to secure their freedom.

"Ah, my child," said she, "don't trust too much to him. Stand by your own children, and suffer with them till death. Nobody respects a mother who forsakes her children; and if you leave them, you will never have a happy moment. If you go, you will make me miserable the short time I have to live. You would be taken and brought back, and your sufferings would be dreadful. Remember poor Benjamin. Do give it up, Linda. Try to bear a little longer. Things may turn out better than we expect."

My courage failed me, in view of the sorrow I should bring on that faithful, loving old heart. I promised that I would try longer, and that I would take nothing out of her house without her knowledge.

Whenever the children climbed on my knee, or laid their heads on my lap, she would say, "Poor little souls! what would you do without a mother? She don't love you as I do." And she would hug them to her own bosom, as if to reproach me for my want of affection; but she knew all the while that I loved them better than my life. I slept with her that night, and it was the last time. The memory of it haunted me for many a year.

On Monday I returned to the plantation, and busied myself with preparations for the important day. Wednesday came. It was a beautiful day, and the faces of the slaves were as bright as the sunshine. The poor creatures were merry. They were expecting little presents from the bride, and hoping for better times under her administration. I had no such hopes for them. I knew that the young wives of slaveholders often thought their authority and importance would be best established and maintained by cruelty; and what I had heard of young Mrs. Flint gave me no reason to expect that her rule over them would be less severe than that of the master and overseer. Truly, the colored race are the most cheerful and forgiving people on the face of the earth. That their masters sleep in safety is owing to their superabundance of heart; and yet they look upon their sufferings with less pity than they would bestow on those of a horse or a dog.

I stood at the door with others to receive the bridegroom and bride. She was a handsome, delicate-looking girl, and her face flushed with emotion at sight of her new home. I thought it likely that visions of a happy future were rising before her. It made me sad;

for I knew how soon clouds would come over her sunshine. She examined every part of the house, and told me she was delighted with the arrangements I had made. I was afraid old Mrs. Flint had tried to prejudice her against me, and I did my best to please her.

All passed off smoothly for me until dinner time arrived. I did not mind the embarrassment of waiting on a dinner party, for the first time in my life, half so much as I did the meeting with Dr. Flint and his wife, who would be among the guests. It was a mystery to me why Mrs. Flint had not made her appearance at the plantation during all the time I was putting the house in order. I had not met her, face to face, for five years, and I had no wish to see her now. She was a praying woman, and, doubtless, considered my present position a special answer to her prayers. Nothing could please her better than to see me humbled and trampled upon. I was just where she would have me—in the power of a hard, unprincipled master. She did not speak to me when she took her seat at table; but her satisfied, triumphant smile, when I handed her plate, was more eloquent than words. The old doctor was not so quiet in his demonstrations. He ordered me here and there, and spoke with peculiar emphasis when he said "your *mistress*." I was drilled like a disgraced soldier. When all was over, and the last key turned, I sought my pillow, thankful that God had appointed a season of rest for the weary.

The next day my new mistress began her housekeeping. I was not exactly appointed maid of all work; but I was to do whatever I was told. Monday evening came. It was always a busy time. On that night the slaves received their weekly allowance of food. Three pounds of meat, a peck of corn, and perhaps a dozen herring were allowed to each man. Women received a pound and half of meat, a peck of corn, and the same number of herring. Children over twelve years old had half the allowance of the women. The meat was cut and weighed by the foreman of the field hands, and piled on planks before the meat house. Then the second foreman went behind the building, and when the first foreman called out, "Who takes this piece of meat?" he answered by calling somebody's name. This method was resorted to as a means of preventing partiality in distributing the meat. The young mistress came out to see how things were done on her plantation, and she soon gave a specimen of her character. Among those in waiting for their allowance was a very old slave, who had faithfully served the Flint family through three generations. When he hobbled up to get his bit of meat, the mistress said he was too old to have any allowance; that when niggers were too old to work, they ought to be fed on grass. Poor old man! He suffered much before he found rest in the grave.

My mistress and I got along very well together. At the end of a week, old Mrs. Flint made us another visit, and was closeted a long time with her daughter-in-law. I had my suspicions what was the subject of the conference. The old doctor's wife had been informed that I could leave the plantation on one condition, and she was very desirous to keep me there. If she had trusted me, as I deserved to be trusted by her, she would have had no fears of my accepting that condition. When she entered her carriage to return home, she said to young Mrs. Flint, "Don't neglect to send for them as quick as possible." My heart was on the watch all the time, and I at once concluded that she spoke of my children. The doctor came the next day, and as I entered the room to spread the tea table, I heard him say, "Don't wait any longer. Send for them to-morrow." I saw through the plan. They thought my children's being there would fetter me to the spot, and that it was a good place to break us all in to abject submission to our lot as slaves. After the doctor left, a gentleman called, who had always manifested friendly feelings towards my grandmother and her family. Mr. Flint carried him over the plantation to show him the results of labor performed by men and women who were unpaid, miserably clothed, and half famished. The cotton crop was all they thought of. It was duly admired, and the gentleman returned with specimens to show his friends. I was ordered to carry water to wash his hands. As I did so, he said, "Linda, how do you like your new home?" I told him I liked it as well as I expected. He replied, "They don't think you are contented, and to-morrow they are going to bring your children to be with you. I am sorry for you, Linda. I hope they will treat you kindly." I hurried from the room, unable to thank him. My suspicions were correct. My children were to be brought to the plantation to be "broke in."

To this day I feel grateful to the gentleman who gave me this timely information. It nerved me to immediate action.

XVII. The Flight

Mr. Flint was hard pushed for house servants, and rather than lose me he had restrained his malice. I did my work faithfully, though not, of course, with a willing mind. They were evidently afraid I should leave them. Mr. Flint wished that I should sleep in the great house instead of the servants' quarters. His wife agreed to the proposition, but said I mustn't bring my bed into the house, because it would scatter feathers on her carpet. I knew when I went there that they would never think of such a thing as furnishing a bed of any kind for me and my little one. I therefore carried my own bed, and now I was forbidden to use it. I did as I was ordered. But now that I was certain my children were to be put in their power, in order to give them a stronger hold on me, I resolved to leave them that night.

I remembered the grief this step would bring upon my dear old grandmother; and nothing less than the freedom of my children would have induced me to disregard her advice. I went about my evening work with trembling steps. Mr. Flint twice called from his chamber door to inquire why the house was not locked up. I replied that I had not done my work. "You have had time enough to do it," said he. "Take care how you answer me!"

I shut all the windows, locked all the doors, and went up to the third story, to wait till midnight. How long those hours seemed, and how fervently I prayed that God would not forsake me in this hour of utmost need! I was about to risk every thing on the throw of a die;[1] and if I failed, O what would become of me and my poor children? They would be made to suffer for my fault.

At half past twelve I stole softly down stairs. I stopped on the second floor, thinking I heard a noise. I felt my way down into the parlor, and looked out of the window. The night was so intensely dark that I could see nothing. I raised the window very softly and jumped out. Large drops of rain were falling, and the darkness bewildered me. I dropped on my knees, and breathed a short prayer to God for guidance and protection. I groped my way to the road, and rushed towards the town with almost lightning speed. I arrived at my grandmother's house, but dared not see her. She would say, "Linda, you are killing me;" and I knew that would unnerve me. I tapped softly at the window of a room, occupied by a woman, who had lived in the house several years. I knew she was a faithful friend, and could be trusted with my secret. I tapped several times before she heard me. At last she raised the window, and I whispered, "Sally, I have run away. Let me in, quick." She opened the door softly, and said in low tones, "For God's sake, don't. Your grandmother is trying to buy you and de chillern. Mr. Sands was here last week. He tole her he was going away on business, but he wanted her to go ahead about buying you and de chillern, and he would help her all he could. Don't run away, Linda. Your grandmother is all bowed down wid trouble now."

I replied, "Sally, they are going to carry my children to the plantation to-morrow; and they will never sell them to any body so long as they have me in their power. Now, would you advise me to go back?"

"No, chile, no," answered she. "When dey finds you is gone, dey won't want de plague[2] ob de chillern; but where is you going to hide? Dey knows ebery inch ob dis house."

I told her I had a hiding-place, and that was all it was best for her to know. I asked her to go into my room as soon as it was light, and

1. Singular of "dice": small cubes used in games, often gambling.
2. Bother, inconvenience.

take all my clothes out of my trunk, and pack them in hers; for I knew Mr. Flint and the constable would be there early to search my room. I feared the sight of my children would be too much for my full heart; but I could not go out into the uncertain future without one last look. I bent over the bed where lay my little Benny and baby Ellen. Poor little ones! fatherless and motherless! Memories of their father came over me. He wanted to be kind to them; but they were not all to him, as they were to my womanly heart. I knelt and prayed for the innocent little sleepers. I kissed them lightly, and turned away.

As I was about to open the street door, Sally laid her hand on my shoulder, and said, "Linda, is you gwine all alone? Let me call your uncle."

"No, Sally," I replied, "I want no one to be brought into trouble on my account."

I went forth into the darkness and rain. I ran on till I came to the house of the friend who was to conceal me.

Early the next morning Mr. Flint was at my grandmother's inquiring for me. She told him she had not seen me, and supposed I was at the plantation. He watched her face narrowly, and said, "Don't you know any thing about her running off?" She assured him that she did not. He went on to say, "Last night she ran off without the least provocation. We had treated her very kindly. My wife liked her. She will soon be found and brought back. Are her children with you?" When told that they were, he said, "I am very glad to hear that. If they are here, she cannot be far off. If I find out that any of my niggers have had any thing to do with this damned business, I'll give 'em five hundred lashes." As he started to go to his father's, he turned round and added, persuasively, "Let her be brought back, and she shall have her children to live with her."

The tidings made the old doctor rave and storm at a furious rate. It was a busy day for them. My grandmother's house was searched from top to bottom. As my trunk was empty, they concluded I had taken my clothes with me. Before ten o'clock every vessel northward bound was thoroughly examined, and the law against harboring fugitives was read to all on board. At night a watch was set over the town. Knowing how distressed my grandmother would be, I wanted to send her a message; but it could not be done. Every one who went in or out of her house was closely watched. The doctor said he would take my children, unless she became responsible for them; which of course she willingly did. The next day was spent in searching. Before night, the following advertisement was posted at every corner, and in every public place for miles round:—

"$300 REWARD! Ran away from the subscriber, an intelligent, bright, mulatto girl, named Linda, 21 years of age. Five feet four inches high. Dark eyes, and black hair inclined to curl; but it can be made straight. Has a decayed spot on a front tooth. She can read and write, and in all probability will try to get to the Free States. All persons are forbidden, under penalty of the law, to harbor or employ said slave. $150 will be given to whoever takes her in the state, and $300 if taken out of the state and delivered to me, or lodged in jail.

Dr. Flint."

XVIII. Months of Peril

The search for me was kept up with more perseverance than I had anticipated. I began to think that escape was impossible. I was in great anxiety lest I should implicate the friend who harbored me. I knew the consequences would be frightful; and much as I dreaded being caught, even that seemed better than causing an innocent person to suffer for kindness to me. A week had passed in terrible suspense, when my pursuers came into such close vicinity that I concluded they had tracked me to my hiding-place. I flew out of the house, and concealed myself in a thicket of bushes. There I remained in an agony of fear for two hours. Suddenly, a reptile of some kind seized my leg. In my fright, I struck a blow which loosened its hold, but I could not tell whether I had killed it; it was so dark, I could not see what it was; I only knew it was something cold and slimy. The pain I felt soon indicated that the bite was poisonous. I was compelled to leave my place of concealment, and I groped my way back into the house. The pain had become intense, and my friend was startled by my look of anguish. I asked her to prepare a poultice of warm ashes and vinegar, and I applied it to my leg, which was already much swollen. The application gave me some relief, but the swelling did not abate. The dread of being disabled was greater than the physical pain I endured. My friend asked an old woman, who doctored among the slaves, what was good for the bite of a snake or a lizard. She told her to steep a dozen coppers in vinegar, over night, and apply the cankered vinegar to the inflamed part.[1]

I had succeeded in cautiously conveying some messages to my relatives. They were harshly threatened, and despairing of my having a chance to escape, they advised me to return to my master, ask his forgiveness, and let him make an example of me. But such counsel had no influence with me. When I started upon this hazardous undertaking, I had resolved that, come what would, there should be

1. The poison of a snake is a powerful acid, and is counteracted by powerful alkalies, such as potash, ammonia, &c. The Indians are accustomed to apply wet ashes, or plunge the limb into strong lie. White men, employed to lay out railroads in snaky places, often carry ammonia with them as an antidote.—Editor [Child's note].

no turning back. "Give me liberty, or give me death," was my motto. When my friend contrived to make known to my relatives the painful situation I had been in for twenty-four hours, they said no more about my going back to my master. Something must be done, and that speedily; but where to turn for help, they knew not. God in his mercy raised up "a friend in need."

Among the ladies who were acquainted with my grandmother, was one who had known her from childhood, and always been very friendly to her. She had also known my mother and her children, and felt interested for them. At this crisis of affairs she called to see my grandmother, as she not unfrequently did. She observed the sad and troubled expression of her face, and asked if she knew where Linda was, and whether she was safe. My grandmother shook her head, without answering. "Come, Aunt Martha," said the kind lady, "tell me all about it. Perhaps I can do something to help you." The husband of this lady held many slaves, and bought and sold slaves. She also held a number in her own name; but she treated them kindly, and would never allow any of them to be sold. She was unlike the majority of slaveholders' wives. My grandmother looked earnestly at her. Something in the expression of her face said "Trust me!" and she did trust her. She listened attentively to the details of my story, and sat thinking for a while. At last she said, "Aunt Martha, I pity you both. If you think there is any chance of Linda's getting to the Free States, I will conceal her for a time. But first you must solemnly promise that my name shall never be mentioned. If such a thing should become known, it would ruin me and my family. No one in my house must know of it, except the cook. She is so faithful that I would trust my own life with her; and I know she likes Linda. It is a great risk; but I trust no harm will come of it. Get word to Linda to be ready as soon as it is dark, before the patrols are out. I will send the housemaids on errands, and Betty shall go to meet Linda." The place where we were to meet was designated and agreed upon. My grandmother was unable to thank the lady for this noble deed; overcome by her emotions, she sank on her knees and sobbed like a child.

I received a message to leave my friend's house at such an hour, and go to a certain place where a friend would be waiting for me. As a matter of prudence no names were mentioned. I had no means of conjecturing who I was to meet, or where I was going. I did not like to move thus blindfolded, but I had no choice. It would not do for me to remain where I was. I disguised myself, summoned up courage to meet the worst, and went to the appointed place. My friend Betty was there; she was the last person I expected to see. We hurried along in silence. The pain in my leg was so intense that it seemed as if I should drop; but fear gave me strength. We reached the house and entered unobserved. Her first words were: "Honey, now you is safe. Dem devils ain't coming to search *dis* house. When I get you into missis' safe place, I will bring some nice hot supper. I specs you need it after all dis skeering." Betty's vocation led her to think eating the most important thing in life. She did not realize that my heart was too full for me to care much about supper.

The mistress came to meet us, and led me up stairs to a small room over her own sleeping apartment. "You will be safe here, Linda," said she; "I keep this room to store away things that are out of use. The girls are not accustomed to be sent to it, and they will not suspect any thing unless they hear some noise. I always keep it locked, and Betty shall take care of the key. But you must be very careful, for my sake as well as your own; and you must never tell my secret; for it would ruin me and my family. I will keep the girls busy in the morning, that Betty may have a chance to bring your breakfast; but it will not do for her to come to you again till night. I will come to see you sometimes. Keep up your courage. I hope this state of things will not last long." Betty came with the "nice hot supper," and the mistress hastened down stairs to keep things straight till she returned. How my heart overflowed with gratitude! Words choked in my throat; but I could have kissed the feet of my benefactress. For that deed of Christian womanhood, may God forever bless her!

I went to sleep that night with the feeling that I was for the present the most fortunate slave in town. Morning came and filled my little cell with light. I thanked the heavenly Father for this safe retreat. Opposite my window was a pile of feather beds. On the top of these I could lie perfectly concealed, and command a view of the street through which Dr. Flint passed to his office. Anxious as I was, I felt a gleam of satisfaction when I saw him. Thus far I had outwitted him, and I triumphed over it. Who can blame slaves for being cunning? They are constantly compelled to resort to it. It is the only weapon of the weak and oppressed against the strength of their tyrants.

I was daily hoping to hear that my master had sold my children; for I knew who was on the watch to buy them. But Dr. Flint cared even more for revenge than he did for money. My brother William, and the good aunt who had served in his family twenty years, and my little Benny, and Ellen, who was a little over two years old, were thrust into jail, as a means of compelling my relatives to give some information about me. He swore my grandmother should never see one of them again till I was brought back. They kept these facts from me for several days. When I heard that my little ones were in a loathsome jail, my first impulse was to go to them. I was encountering dangers for the sake of freeing them, and must I be the cause of their death? The thought was agonizing. My benefactress tried to soothe me by telling me that my aunt would take good care of the children while they remained in jail. But it added to my pain to think that the good old aunt, who had always been so kind to her sister's orphan children, should be shut up in prison for no other crime than loving them. I suppose my friends feared a reckless movement on my part, knowing, as they did, that my life was bound up in my children. I received a note from my brother William. It was scarcely legible, and ran thus: "Wherever you are, dear sister, I beg of you not to come here. We are all much better off than you are. If you come, you will ruin us all. They would force you to tell where you had been, or they would kill you. Take the advice of your friends; if not for the sake of me and your children, at least for the sake of those you would ruin."

Poor William! He also must suffer for being my brother. I took his advice and kept quiet. My aunt was taken out of jail at the end of a month, because Mrs. Flint could not spare her any longer. She was tired of being her own housekeeper. It was quite too fatiguing to order her dinner and eat it too. My children remained in jail, where brother William did all he could for their comfort. Betty went to see them sometimes, and brought me tidings. She was not permitted to enter the jail; but William would hold them up to the grated window while she chatted with them. When she repeated their prattle, and told me how they wanted to see their ma, my tears would flow. Old Betty would exclaim, "Lors, chile! what's you crying 'bout? Dem young uns vil kill you dead. Don't be so chick'n hearted! If you does, you vil nebber git thro' dis world."

Good old soul! She had gone through the world childless. She had never had little ones to clasp their arms around her neck; she had never seen their soft eyes looking into hers; no sweet little voices had called her mother; she had never pressed her own infants to her heart, with the feeling that even in fetters there was something to live for. How could she realize my feelings? Betty's husband loved children dearly, and wondered why God had denied them to him. He expressed great sorrow when he came to Betty with the tidings that Ellen had been taken out of jail and carried to Dr. Flint's. She had the measles a short time before they carried her to jail, and the disease had left her eyes affected. The doctor had taken her home to attend to them. My children had always been afraid of the doctor and his wife. They had never been inside of their house. Poor little Ellen cried all day to be carried back to prison. The instincts of childhood are true. She knew she was loved in the jail. Her screams and sobs annoyed Mrs. Flint. Before night she called one of the slaves, and said, "Here, Bill, carry this brat back to the jail. I can't stand her noise. If she would be quiet I should like to keep the little minx. She would make a handy waiting-maid for my daughter by and by. But if she staid here, with her white face, I suppose I should either kill her or spoil her. I hope the doctor will sell them as far as wind and water can carry them. As for their mother, her ladyship will find out yet what she gets by running away. She hasn't so much feeling for her children as a cow has for its calf. If she had, she would have come back long ago, to get them out of jail, and save all this expense and trouble. The good-for-nothing hussy! When she is caught, she shall stay in jail, in irons, for one six months, and then be sold to a sugar plantation. I shall see her broke in yet. What do you stand there for, Bill? Why don't you go off with the brat? Mind, now, that you don't let any of the niggers speak to her in the street!"

When these remarks were reported to me, I smiled at Mrs. Flint's saying that she should either kill my child or spoil her. I thought to myself there was very little danger of the latter. I have always considered it as one of God's special providences that Ellen screamed till she was carried back to jail.

That same night Dr. Flint was called to a patient, and did not return till near morning. Passing my grandmother's, he saw a light in the house, and thought to himself, "Perhaps this has something to do with Linda." He knocked, and the door was opened. "What calls you up so early?" said he. "I saw your light, and I thought I would just stop and tell you that I have found out where Linda is. I know where to put my hands on her, and I shall have her before twelve o'clock." When he had turned away, my grandmother and my uncle looked anxiously at each other. They did not know whether or not it was merely one of the doctor's tricks to frighten them. In their uncertainty, they thought it was best to have a message conveyed to my friend Betty. Unwilling to alarm her mistress, Betty resolved to dispose of me herself. She came to me, and told me to rise and dress quickly. We hurried down stairs, and across the yard, into the kitchen. She locked the door, and lifted up a plank in the floor. A buffalo skin and a bit of carpet were spread for me to lie on, and a quilt thrown over me. "Stay dar," said she, "till I sees if dey know 'bout you. Dey say dey vil put thar hans on you afore twelve o'clock. If dey *did* know whar you are, dey won't know *now*. Dey'll be disapinted dis time. Dat's all I got to say. If dey comes rummagin 'mong *my* tings, dey'll get one bressed sarssin from dis 'ere nigger." In my shallow bed I had but just room enough to bring my hands to my face to keep the dust out of my eyes; for Betty walked over me twenty times in an hour, passing from the dresser to the fireplace. When she was alone, I could hear her pronouncing anathemas over Dr. Flint and all his tribe, every now and then saying, with a chuckling laugh, "Dis nigger's too cute for 'em dis time." When the housemaids were about, she had sly ways of drawing them out, that I might hear what they would say. She would repeat stories she had heard about my being in this, or that, or the other place. To which they would answer, that I was not fool enough to be staying round there; that I was in Philadelphia or New York before this time. When all were abed and asleep, Betty raised the plank, and said, "Come out, chile; come out. Dey don't know nottin 'bout you. 'Twas only white folks' lies, to skeer de niggers."

Some days after this adventure I had a much worse fright. As I sat very still in my retreat above stairs, cheerful visions floated through my mind. I thought Dr. Flint would soon get discouraged, and would be willing to sell my children, when he lost all hopes of making them the means of my discovery. I knew who was ready to buy them. Suddenly I heard a voice that chilled my blood. The sound was too familiar to me, it had been too dreadful, for me not to recognize at once my old master. He was in the house, and I at once concluded he had come to seize me. I looked round in terror. There was no way of escape. The voice receded. I supposed the constable was with him, and they were searching the house. In my alarm I did not forget the trouble I was bringing on my generous benefactress. It seemed as if I were born to bring sorrow on all who befriended me, and that was the bitterest drop in the bitter cup of my life. After a while I heard approaching footsteps; the key was turned in my door. I braced myself against the wall to keep from falling. I ventured to look up, and there stood my kind benefactress alone. I was too much overcome to speak, and sunk down upon the floor.

"I thought you would hear your master's voice," she said; "and knowing you would be terrified, I came to tell you there is nothing to fear. You may even indulge in a laugh at the old gentleman's expense. He is so sure you are in New York, that he came to borrow five hundred dollars to go in pursuit of you. My sister had some money to loan on interest. He has obtained it, and proposes to start for New York to-night. So, for the present, you see you are safe. The doctor will merely lighten his pocket hunting after the bird he has left behind."

XIX. The Children Sold

The doctor came back from New York, of course without accomplishing his purpose. He had expended considerable money, and was rather disheartened. My brother and the children had now been in jail two months, and that also was some expense. My friends thought it was a favorable time to work on his discouraged feelings. Mr. Sands sent a speculator to offer him nine hundred dollars for my brother William, and eight hundred for the two children. These were high prices, as slaves were then selling; but the offer was rejected. If it had been merely a question of money, the doctor would have sold any boy of Benny's age for two hundred dollars; but he could not bear to give up the power of revenge. But he was hard pressed for money, and he revolved the matter in his mind. He knew that if he could keep Ellen till she was fifteen, he could sell her for a high price; but I presume he reflected that she might die, or might be stolen away. At all events, he came to the conclusion that he had better accept the slave-trader's offer. Meeting him in the street, he inquired when he would leave town. "To-day, at ten o'clock," he replied. "Ah, do you go so soon?" said the doctor; "I have been reflecting upon your proposition, and I have concluded to let you have the three negroes if you will say nineteen hundred dollars." After some parley, the trader agreed to his terms. He wanted the bill of sale drawn up and signed immediately, as he had a great deal to attend to during the short time he remained in town. The doctor went to the jail and told William he would take him back into his service if he would promise to behave himself; but he replied that he would rather be sold. "And you *shall* be sold, you ungrateful rascal!" exclaimed the doctor. In less than an hour the money was paid, the papers were signed, sealed, and delivered, and my brother and children were in the hands of the trader.

It was a hurried transaction; and after it was over, the doctor's characteristic caution returned. He went back to the speculator, and said, "Sir, I have come to lay you under obligations of a thousand dollars not to sell any of those negroes in this state." "You come too late," replied the trader; "our bargain is closed." He had, in fact, already sold them to Mr. Sands, but he did not mention it. The doctor required him to put irons on "that rascal, Bill," and to pass through the back streets when he took his gang out of town. The trader was privately instructed to concede to his wishes. My good old aunt went to the jail to bid the children good by, supposing them to be the speculator's property, and that she should never see them again. As she held Benny in her lap, he said, "Aunt Nancy, I want to show you something." He led her to the door and showed her a long row of marks, saying, "Uncle Will taught me to count. I have made a mark for every day I have been here, and it is sixty days. It is a long time; and the speculator is going to take me and Ellen away. He's a bad man. It's wrong for him to take grandmother's children. I want to go to my mother."

My grandmother was told that the children would be restored to her, but she was requested to act as if they were really to be sent away. Accordingly, she made up a bundle of clothes and went to the jail. When she arrived, she found William handcuffed among the gang, and the children in the trader's cart. The scene seemed too much like reality. She was afraid there might have been some deception or mistake. She fainted, and was carried home.

When the wagon stopped at the hotel, several gentlemen came out and proposed to purchase William, but the trader refused their offers, without stating that he was already sold. And now came the trying hour for that drove of human beings, driven away like cattle, to be sold they knew not where. Husbands were torn from wives, parents from children, never to look upon each other again this side the grave. There was wringing of hands and cries of despair.

Dr. Flint had the supreme satisfaction of seeing the wagon leave town, and Mrs. Flint had the gratification of supposing that my children were going "as far as wind and water would carry them." According to agreement, my uncle followed the wagon some miles, until they came to an old farm house. There the trader took the irons from William, and as he did so, he said, "You are a damned clever fellow. I should like to own you myself. Them gentlemen that wanted to buy you said you was a bright, honest chap, and I must git you a good home. I guess your old master will swear to-morrow, and call himself an old fool for selling the children. I reckon he'll never git their mammy back agin. I expect she's made tracks for the north. Good by, old boy. Remember, I have done you a good turn. You must thank me by coaxing all the pretty gals to go with me next fall. That's going to be my last trip. This trading in niggers is a bad business for a fellow that's got any heart. Move on, you fellows!" And the gang went on, God alone knows where.

Much as I despise and detest the class of slave-traders, whom I regard as the vilest wretches on earth, I must do this man the justice to say that he seemed to have some feeling. He took a fancy to William in the jail, and wanted to buy him. When he heard the story of my children, he was willing to aid them in getting out of Dr. Flint's power, even without charging the customary fee.

My uncle procured a wagon and carried William and the children back to town. Great was the joy in my grandmother's house! The curtains were closed, and the candles lighted. The happy grandmother cuddled the little ones to her bosom. They hugged her, and kissed her, and clapped their hands, and shouted. She knelt down and poured forth one of her heartfelt prayers of thanksgiving to God. The father was present for a while; and though such a "parental relation" as existed between him and my children takes slight hold of the hearts or consciences of slaveholders, it must be that he experienced some moments of pure joy in witnessing the happiness he had imparted.

I had no share in the rejoicings of that evening. The events of the day had not come to my knowledge. And now I will tell you something that happened to me; though you will, perhaps, think it illustrates the superstition of slaves. I sat in my usual place on the floor near the window, where I could hear much that was said in the street without being seen. The family had retired for the night, and all was still. I sat there thinking of my children, when I heard a low strain of music. A band of serenaders were under the window, playing "Home, sweet home." I listened till the sounds did not seem like music, but like the moaning of children. It seemed as if my heart would burst. I rose from my sitting posture, and knelt. A streak of moonlight was on the floor before me, and in the midst of it appeared the forms of my two children. They vanished; but I had seen them distinctly. Some will call it a dream, others a vision. I know not how to account for it, but it made a strong impression on my mind, and I felt certain something had happened to my little ones.

I had not seen Betty since morning. Now I heard her softly turning the key. As soon as she entered, I clung to her, and begged her to let me know whether my children were dead, or whether they were sold; for I had seen their spirits in my room, and I was sure something had happened to them. "Lor, chile," said she, putting her arms round me, "you's got de highsterics. I'll sleep wid you to-night, 'cause you'll make a noise, and ruin missis. Something has stirred you up mightily. When you is done cryin, I'll talk wid you. De chillern is well, and mighty happy. I seed 'em myself. Does dat satisfy you? Dar, chile, be still! Somebody vill hear you." I tried to obey her. She lay down, and was soon sound asleep; but no sleep would come to my eyelids.

At dawn, Betty was up and off to the kitchen. The hours passed on, and the vision of the night kept constantly recurring to my thoughts. After a while I heard the voices of two women in the entry. In one of them I recognized the housemaid. The other said to her, "Did you know Linda Brent's children was sold to the speculator yesterday. They say ole massa Flint was mighty glad to see 'em drove out of town; but they say they've come back agin. I 'spect it's all their daddy's doings. They say he's bought William too. Lor! how it will take hold of ole massa Flint! I'm going roun' to aunt Marthy's to see 'bout it."

I bit my lips till the blood came to keep from crying out. Were my children with their grandmother, or had the speculator carried them off? The suspense was dreadful. Would Betty *never* come, and tell me the truth about it? At last she came, and I eagerly repeated what I had overheard. Her face was one broad, bright smile. "Lor, you foolish ting!" said she. "I'se gwine to tell you all 'bout it. De gals is eating thar breakfast, and missus tole me to let her tell you; but, poor creeter! t'aint right to keep you waitin', and I'se gwine to tell you. Brudder, chillern, all is bought by de daddy! I'se laugh more dan nuff, tinking 'bout ole massa Flint. Lor, how he *vill* swar! He's got ketched dis time, any how; but I must be getting out o' dis, or dem gals vill come and ketch *me*."

Betty went off laughing; and I said to myself, "Can it be true that my children are free? I have not suffered for them in vain. Thank God!"

Great surprise was expressed when it was known that my children had returned to their grandmother's. The news spread through the town, and many a kind word was bestowed on the little ones.

Dr. Flint went to my grandmother's to ascertain who was the owner of my children, and she informed him. "I expected as much," said he. "I am glad to hear it. I have had news from Linda lately, and I shall soon have her. You need never expect to see *her* free. She shall be my slave as long as I live, and when I am dead she shall be the slave of my children. If I ever find out that you or Phillip had any thing to do with her running off I'll kill him. And if I meet William in the street, and he presumes to look at me, I'll flog him within an inch of his life. Keep those brats out of my sight!"

As he turned to leave, my grandmother said something to remind him of his own doings. He looked back upon her, as if he would have been glad to strike her to the ground.

I had my season of joy and thanksgiving. It was the first time since my childhood that I had experienced any real happiness. I heard of the old doctor's threats, but they no longer had the same power to trouble me. The darkest cloud that hung over my life had rolled away. Whatever slavery might do to me, it could not shackle my children. If I fell a sacrifice, my little ones were saved. It was well for me that my simple heart believed all that had been promised for their welfare. It is always better to trust than to doubt.

XX. New Perils

The doctor, more exasperated than ever, again tried to revenge himself on my relatives. He arrested uncle Phillip on the charge of having aided my flight. He was carried before a court, and swore truly that he knew nothing of my intention to escape, and that he had not seen me since I left my master's plantation. The doctor then demanded that he should give bail for five hundred dollars that he would have nothing to do with me. Several gentlemen offered to be security for him; but Mr. Sands told him he had better go back to jail, and he would see that he came out without giving bail.

The news of his arrest was carried to my grandmother, who conveyed it to Betty. In the kindness of her heart, she again stowed me away under the floor; and as she walked back and forth, in the performance of her culinary duties, she talked apparently to herself, but with the intention that I should hear what was going on. I hoped that my uncle's imprisonment would last but few days; still I was anxious. I thought it likely Dr. Flint would do his utmost to taunt and insult him, and I was afraid my uncle might lose control of himself, and retort in some way that would be construed into a punishable offence; and I was well aware that in court his word would not be taken against any white man's. The search for me was renewed. Something had excited suspicions that I was in the vicinity. They searched the house I was in. I heard their steps and their voices. At night, when all were asleep, Betty came to release me from my place of confinement. The fright I had undergone, the constrained posture, and the dampness of the ground, made me ill for several days. My uncle was soon after taken out of prison; but the movements of all my relatives, and of all our friends, were very closely watched.

We all saw that I could not remain where I was much longer. I had already staid longer than was intended, and I knew my presence must be a source of perpetual anxiety to my kind benefactress. During this time, my friends had laid many plans for my escape, but the extreme vigilance of my persecutors made it impossible to carry them into effect.

One morning I was much startled by hearing somebody trying to get into my room. Several keys were tried, but none fitted. I instantly conjectured it was one of the housemaids; and I concluded she must either have heard some noise in the room, or have noticed the entrance of Betty. When my friend came, at her usual time, I told her what had happened. "I knows who it was," said she. "'Pend upon it, 'twas dat Jenny. Dat nigger allers got de debble in her." I suggested that she might have seen or heard something that excited her curiosity.

"Tut! tut! chile!" exclaimed Betty, "she ain't seen notin', nor hearn notin'. She only 'spects something. Dat's all. She wants to fine out who hab cut and make my gownd. But she won't nebber know. Dat's sartin. I'll git missis to fix her."

I reflected a moment, and said, "Betty, I must leave here to-night."

"Do as you tink best, poor chile," she replied. "I'se mighty 'fraid dat 'ere nigger vill pop on you some time."

She reported the incident to her mistress, and received orders to keep Jenny busy in the kitchen till she could see my uncle Phillip. He told her he would send a friend for me that very evening. She told him she hoped I was going to the north, for it was very dangerous for me to remain any where in the vicinity. Alas, it was not an easy thing, for one in my situation, to go to the north. In order to leave the coast quite clear for me, she went into the country to spend the day with her brother, and took Jenny with her. She was afraid to come and bid me good by, but she left a kind message with Betty. I heard her carriage roll from the door, and I never again saw her who had so generously befriended the poor, trembling fugitive! Though she was a slaveholder, to this day my heart blesses her!

I had not the slightest idea where I was going. Betty brought me a suit of sailor's clothes,—jacket, trowsers, and tarpaulin hat. She gave me a small bundle, saying I might need it where I was going. In cheery tones, she exclaimed, "I'se *so* glad you is gwine to free parts! Don't forget ole Betty. P'raps I'll come 'long by and by."

I tried to tell her how grateful I felt for all her kindness, but she interrupted me. "I don't want no tanks, honey. I'se glad I could help you, and I hope de good Lord vill open de path for you. I'se gwine wid you to de lower gate. Put your hands in your pockets, and walk ricketty, like de sailors."

I performed to her satisfaction. At the gate I found Peter, a young colored man, waiting for me. I had known him for years. He had been an apprentice to my father, and had always borne a good character. I was not afraid to trust to him. Betty bade me a hurried good by, and we walked off. "Take courage, Linda," said my friend Peter. "I've got a dagger, and no man shall take you from me, unless he passes over my dead body."

It was a long time since I had taken a walk out of doors, and the fresh air revived me. It was also pleasant to hear a human voice speaking to me above a whisper. I passed several people whom I knew, but they did not recognize me in my disguise. I prayed internally that, for Peter's sake, as well as my own, nothing might occur to bring out his dagger. We walked on till we came to the wharf. My aunt Nancy's husband was a seafaring man, and it had been deemed necessary to let him into our secret. He took me into his boat, rowed out to a vessel not far distant, and hoisted me on board. We three were the only occupants of the vessel. I now ventured to ask what they proposed to do with me. They said I was to remain on board till near dawn, and then they would hide me in Snaky Swamp, till my uncle Phillip had prepared a place of concealment for me. If the vessel had been bound north, it would have been of no avail to me, for it would certainly have been searched. About four o'clock, we were again seated in the boat, and rowed three miles to the swamp. My fear of snakes had been increased by the venomous bite I had received, and I dreaded to enter this hiding-place. But I was in no situation to choose, and I gratefully accepted the best that my poor, persecuted friends could do for me.

Peter landed first, and with a large knife cut a path through bamboos and briers of all descriptions. He came back, took me in his arms, and carried me to a seat made among the bamboos. Before we reached it, we were covered with hundreds of mosquitos. In an hour's time they had so poisoned my flesh that I was a pitiful sight to behold. As the light increased, I saw snake after snake crawling round us. I had been accustomed to the sight of snakes all my life, but these were larger than any I had ever seen. To this day I shudder when I remember that morning. As evening approached, the number of snakes increased so much that we were continually obliged to thrash them with sticks to keep them from crawling over us. The bamboos were so high and so thick that it was impossible to see beyond a very short distance. Just before it became dark we procured a seat nearer to the entrance of the swamp, being fearful of losing our way back to the boat. It was not long before we heard the paddle of oars, and the low whistle, which had been agreed upon as a signal. We made haste to enter the boat, and were rowed back to the vessel. I passed a wretched night; for the heat of the swamp, the mosquitos, and the constant terror of snakes, had brought on a burning fever. I had just dropped asleep, when they came and told me it was time to go back to that horrid swamp. I could scarcely summon courage to rise. But even those large, venomous snakes were less dreadful to my imagination than the white men in that community called civilized. This time Peter took a quantity of tobacco to burn, to keep off the mosquitos. It produced the desired effect on them, but gave me nausea and severe headache. At dark we returned to the vessel. I had been so sick during the day, that Peter declared I should go home that night, if the devil himself was on patrol. They told me a place of concealment had been provided for me at my grandmother's. I could not imagine how it was possible to hide me in her house, every nook and corner of which was known to the Flint family. They told me to wait and see. We were rowed ashore, and went boldly through the streets, to my grandmother's. I wore my sailor's clothes, and had blackened my face with charcoal. I passed several people whom I knew. The father of my children came so near that I brushed against his arm; but he had no idea who it was.

"You must make the most of this walk," said my friend Peter, "for you may not have another very soon."

I thought his voice sounded sad. It was kind of him to conceal from me what a dismal hole was to be my home for a long, long time.

XXI. The Loophole of Retreat

A small shed had been added to my grandmother's house years ago. Some boards were laid across the joists at the top, and between these boards and the roof was a very small garret, never occupied by any thing but rats and mice. It was a pent roof, covered with nothing but shingles, according to the southern custom for such buildings. The garret was only nine feet long and seven wide. The highest part was three feet high, and sloped down abruptly to the loose board floor. There was no admission for either light or air. My uncle Philip, who was a carpenter, had very skilfully made a concealed trap-door, which communicated with the storeroom. He had been doing this while I was waiting in the swamp. The storeroom opened upon a piazza. To this hole I was conveyed as soon as I entered the house. The air was stifling; the darkness total. A bed had been spread on the floor. I could sleep quite comfortably on one side; but the slope was so sudden that I could not turn on the other without hitting the roof. The rats and mice ran over my bed; but I was weary, and I slept such sleep as the wretched may, when a tempest has passed over them. Morning came. I knew it only by the noises I heard; for in my small den day and night were all the same. I suffered for air even more than for light. But I was not comfortless. I heard the voices of my children. There was joy and there was sadness in the sound. It made my tears flow. How I longed to speak to them! I was eager to look on their faces; but there was no hole, no crack, through which I could peep. This continued darkness was oppressive. It seemed horrible to sit or lie in a cramped position day after day, without one gleam of light. Yet I would have chosen this, rather than my lot as a slave, though white people considered it an easy one; and it was so compared with the fate of others. I was never cruelly over-worked; I was never lacerated with the whip from head to foot; I was never so beaten and bruised that I could not turn from one side to the other; I never had my heel-strings[1] cut to prevent my running away; I was never chained to a log and forced to drag it about, while I toiled in the fields from morning till night; I was never branded with hot iron, or torn by bloodhounds. On the contrary, I had always been kindly treated, and tenderly cared for, until I came into the hands of Dr. Flint. I had never wished for freedom till then. But though my life in slavery was comparatively devoid of hardships, God pity the woman who is compelled to lead such a life!

My food was passed up to me through the trap-door my uncle had contrived; and my grandmother, my uncle Phillip, and aunt Nancy would seize such opportunities as they could, to mount up there and chat with me at the opening. But of course this was not safe in the daytime. It must all be done in darkness. It was impossible for me to move in an erect position, but I crawled about my den for exercise. One day I hit my head against something, and found it was a gimlet.[2] My uncle had left it sticking there when he made the trap-door. I was as rejoiced as Robinson Crusoe[3] could have been at finding such a treasure. It put a lucky thought into my head. I said to myself, "Now I will have some light. Now I will see my children." I did not dare to begin my work during the daytime, for fear of attracting

1. Achilles tendons.
2. A small, metal tool used to bore holes.
3. The protagonist of Daniel Defoe's 1719 novel of the same name, who finds himself shipwrecked on an island.

attention. But I groped round; and having found the side next the street, where I could frequently see my children, I stuck the gimlet in and waited for evening. I bored three rows of holes, one above another; then I bored out the interstices between. I thus succeeded in making one hole about an inch long and an inch broad. I sat by it till late into the night, to enjoy the little whiff of air that floated in. In the morning I watched for my children. The first person I saw in the street was Dr. Flint. I had a shuddering, superstitious feeling that it was a bad omen. Several familiar faces passed by. At last I heard the merry laugh of children, and presently two sweet little faces were looking up at me, as though they knew I was there, and were conscious of the joy they imparted. How I longed to *tell* them I was there!

My condition was now a little improved. But for weeks I was tormented by hundreds of little red insects, fine as a needle's point, that pierced through my skin, and produced an intolerable burning. The good grandmother gave me herb teas and cooling medicines, and finally I got rid of them. The heat of my den was intense, for nothing but thin shingles protected me from the scorching summer's sun. But I had my consolations. Through my peeping-hole I could watch the children, and when they were near enough, I could hear their talk. Aunt Nancy brought me all the news she could hear at Dr. Flint's. From her I learned that the doctor had written to New York to a colored woman, who had been born and raised in our neighborhood, and had breathed his contaminating atmosphere. He offered her a reward if she could find out any thing about me. I know not what was the nature of her reply; but he soon after started for New York in haste, saying to his family that he had business of importance to transact. I peeped at him as he passed on his way to the steamboat. It was a satisfaction to have miles of land and water between us, even for a little while; and it was a still greater satisfaction to know that he believed me to be in the Free States. My little den seemed less dreary than it had done. He returned, as he did from his former journey to New York, without obtaining any satisfactory information. When he passed our house next morning, Benny was standing at the gate. He had heard them say that he had gone to find me, and he called out, "Dr. Flint, did you bring my mother home? I want to see her." The doctor stamped his foot at him in a rage, and exclaimed, "Get out of the way, you little damned rascal! If you don't, I'll cut off your head."

Benny ran terrified into the house, saying, "You can't put me in jail again. I don't belong to you now." It was well that the wind carried the words away from the doctor's ear. I told my grandmother of it, when we had our next conference at the trap-door; and begged of her not to allow the children to be impertinent to the irascible old man.

Autumn came, with a pleasant abatement of heat. My eyes had become accustomed to the dim light, and by holding my book or work in a certain position near the aperture I contrived to read and sew. That was a great relief to the tedious monotony of my life. But when winter came, the cold penetrated through the thin shingle roof, and I was dreadfully chilled. The winters there are not so long, or so severe, as in northern latitudes; but the houses are not built to shelter from cold, and my little den was peculiarly comfortless. The kind grandmother brought me bed-clothes and warm drinks. Often I was obliged to lie in bed all day to keep comfortable; but with all my precautions, my shoulders and feet were frostbitten. O, those long, gloomy days, with no object for my eye to rest upon, and no thoughts to occupy my mind, except the dreary past and the uncertain future! I was thankful when there came a day sufficiently mild for me to wrap myself up and sit at the loophole to watch the passers by. Southerners have the habit of stopping and talking in the streets, and I heard many conversations not intended to meet my ears. I heard slave-hunters planning how to catch some poor fugitive. Several times I heard allusions to Dr. Flint, myself, and the history of my children, who, perhaps, were playing near the gate. One would say, "I wouldn't move my little finger to catch her, as old Flint's property." Another would say, "I'll catch *any* nigger for the reward. A man ought to have what belongs to him, if he *is* a damned brute." The opinion was often expressed that I was in the Free States. Very rarely did any one suggest that I might be in the vicinity. Had the least suspicion rested on my grandmother's house, it would have been burned to the ground. But it was the last place they thought of. Yet there was no place, where slavery existed, that could have afforded me so good a place of concealment.

Dr. Flint and his family repeatedly tried to coax and bribe my children to tell something they had heard said about me. One day the doctor took them into a shop, and offered them some bright little silver pieces and gay handkerchiefs if they would tell where their mother was. Ellen shrank away from him, and would not speak; but Benny spoke up, and said, "Dr. Flint, I don't know where my mother is. I guess she's in New York; and when you go there again, I wish you'd ask her to come home, for I want to see her; but if you put her in jail, or tell her you'll cut her head off, I'll tell her to go right back."

XXII. Christmas Festivities

Christmas was approaching. Grandmother brought me materials, and I busied myself making some new garments and little playthings for my children. Were it not that hiring day is near at hand, and many families are fearfully looking forward to the probability of separation in a few days, Christmas might be a happy season for the poor slaves. Even slave mothers try to gladden the hearts of their little ones on that occasion. Benny and Ellen had their Christmas stockings filled. Their imprisoned mother could not have the privilege of witnessing their surprise and joy. But I had the pleasure of peeping at them as they went into the street with their new suits on. I heard Benny ask a little playmate whether Santa Claus brought him any thing. "Yes," replied the boy; "but Santa Claus ain't a real man. It's the children's mothers that put things into the stockings." "No, that can't be," replied Benny, "for Santa Claus brought Ellen and me these new clothes, and my mother has been gone this long time."

How I longed to tell him that his mother made those garments, and that many a tear fell on them while she worked!

Every child rises early on Christmas morning to see the Johnkannaus.[1] Without them, Christmas would be shorn of its greatest attraction. They consist of companies of slaves from the plantations, generally of the lower class. Two athletic men, in calico wrappers, have a net thrown over them, covered with all manner of bright-colored stripes. Cows' tails are fastened to their backs, and their heads are decorated with horns. A box, covered with sheepskin, is called the gumbo box. A dozen beat on this, while others strike triangles and jawbones, to which bands of dancers keep time. For a month previous they are composing songs, which are sung on this occasion. These companies, of a hundred each, turn out early in the morning, and are allowed to go round till twelve o'clock, begging for contributions. Not a door is left unvisited where there is the least chance of obtaining a penny or a glass of rum. They do not drink while they are out, but carry the rum home in jugs, to have a carousal. These Christmas donations frequently amount to twenty or thirty dollars. It is seldom that any white man or child refuses to give them a trifle. If he does, they regale his ears with the following song:—

"Poor massa, so dey say;
Down in de heel, so dey say;
Got no money, so dey say;
Not one shillin, so dey say;
God A'mighty bress you, so dey say."

Christmas is a day of feasting, both with white and colored people. Slaves, who are lucky enough to have a few shillings, are sure to spend them for good eating; and many a turkey and pig is captured, without saying, "By your leave, sir." Those who cannot obtain these,

1. Also "junkanoos." Celebrations featuring costumes and masks originating in African culture.

cook a 'possum, or a raccoon, from which savory dishes can be made. My grandmother raised poultry and pigs for sale; and it was her established custom to have both a turkey and a pig roasted for Christmas dinner.

On this occasion, I was warned to keep extremely quiet, because two guests had been invited. One was the town constable, and the other was a free colored man, who tried to pass himself off for white, and who was always ready to do any mean work for the sake of currying favor with white people. My grandmother had a motive for inviting them. She managed to take them all over the house. All the rooms on the lower floor were thrown open for them to pass in and out; and after dinner, they were invited up stairs to look at a fine mocking bird my uncle had just brought home. There, too, the rooms were all thrown open, that they might look in. When I heard them talking on the piazza, my heart almost stood still. I knew this colored man had spent many nights hunting for me. Every body knew he had the blood of a slave father in his veins; but for the sake of passing himself off for white, he was ready to kiss the slaveholders' feet. How I despised him! As for the constable, he wore no false colors. The duties of his office were despicable, but he was superior to his companion, inasmuch as he did not pretend to be what he was not. Any white man, who could raise money enough to buy a slave, would have considered himself degraded by being a constable; but the office enabled its possessor to exercise authority. If he found any slave out after nine o'clock, he could whip him as much as he liked; and that was a privilege to be coveted. When the guests were ready to depart, my grandmother gave each of them some of her nice pudding, as a present for their wives. Through my peep-hole I saw them go out of the gate, and I was glad when it closed after them. So passed the first Christmas in my den.

XXIII. Still in Prison

When spring returned, and I took in the little patch of green the aperture commanded, I asked myself how many more summers and winters I must be condemned to spend thus. I longed to draw in a plentiful draught of fresh air, to stretch my cramped limbs, to have room to stand erect, to feel the earth under my feet again. My relatives were constantly on the lookout for a chance of escape; but none offered that seemed practicable, and even tolerably safe. The hot summer came again, and made the turpentine drop from the thin roof over my head.

During the long nights I was restless for want of air, and I had no room to toss and turn. There was but one compensation; the atmosphere was so stifled that even mosquitos would not condescend to buzz in it. With all my detestation of Dr. Flint, I could hardly wish him a worse punishment, either in this world or that which is to come, than to suffer what I suffered in one single summer. Yet the laws allowed *him* to be out in the free air, while I, guiltless of crime, was pent up here, as the only means of avoiding the cruelties the laws allowed him to inflict upon me! I don't know what kept life within me. Again and again, I thought I should die before long; but I saw the leaves of another autumn whirl through the air, and felt the touch of another winter. In summer the most terrible thunder storms were acceptable, for the rain came through the roof, and I rolled up my bed that it might cool the hot boards under it. Later in the season, storms sometimes wet my clothes through and through, and that was not comfortable when the air grew chilly. Moderate storms I could keep out by filling the chinks with oakum.[1]

But uncomfortable as my situation was, I had glimpses of things out of doors, which made me thankful for my wretched hiding-place. One day I saw a slave pass our gate, muttering, "It's his own, and he can kill it if he will." My grandmother told me that woman's history. Her mistress had that day seen her baby for the first time, and in the lineaments of its fair face she saw a likeness to her husband. She turned the bondwoman and her child out of doors, and forbade her ever to return. The slave went to her master, and told him what had happened. He promised to talk with her mistress, and make it all right. The next day she and her baby were sold to a Georgia trader.

Another time I saw a woman rush wildly by, pursued by two men. She was a slave, the wet nurse of her mistress's children. For some trifling offence her mistress ordered her to be stripped and whipped. To escape the degradation and the torture, she rushed to the river, jumped in, and ended her wrongs in death.

Senator Brown,[2] of Mississippi, could not be ignorant of many such facts as these, for they are of frequent occurrence in every Southern State. Yet he stood up in the Congress of the United States, and declared that slavery was "a great moral, social, and political blessing; a blessing to the master, and a blessing to the slave!"

I suffered much more during the second winter than I did during the first. My limbs were benumbed by inaction, and the cold filled them with cramp. I had a very painful sensation of coldness in my head; even my face and tongue stiffened, and I lost the power of speech. Of course it was impossible, under the circumstances, to summon any physician. My brother William came and did all he

1. Loose fiber picked from rope and used to caulk ships or fill holes.
2. Albert G. Brown (1830–1880), a Mississippi senator.

could for me. Uncle Phillip also watched tenderly over me; and poor grandmother crept up and down to inquire whether there were any signs of returning life. I was restored to consciousness by the dashing of cold water in my face, and found myself leaning against my brother's arm, while he bent over me with streaming eyes. He afterwards told me he thought I was dying, for I had been in an unconscious state sixteen hours. I next became delirious, and was in great danger of betraying myself and my friends. To prevent this, they stupefied me with drugs. I remained in bed six weeks, weary in body and sick at heart. How to get medical advice was the question. William finally went to a Thompsonian doctor,[3] and described himself as having all my pains and aches. He returned with herbs, roots, and ointment. He was especially charged to rub on the ointment by a fire; but how could a fire be made in my little den? Charcoal in a furnace was tried, but there was no outlet for the gas, and it nearly cost me my life. Afterwards coals, already kindled, were brought up in an iron pan, and placed on bricks. I was so weak, and it was so long since I had enjoyed the warmth of a fire, that those few coals actually made me weep. I think the medicines did me some good; but my recovery was very slow. Dark thoughts passed through my mind as I lay there day after day. I tried to be thankful for my little cell, dismal as it was, and even to love it, as part of the price I had paid for the redemption of my children. Sometimes I thought God was a compassionate Father, who would forgive my sins for the sake of my sufferings. At other times, it seemed to me there was no justice or mercy in the divine government. I asked why the curse of slavery was permitted to exist, and why I had been so persecuted and wronged from youth upward. These things took the shape of mystery, which is to this day not so clear to my soul as I trust it will be hereafter.

In the midst of my illness, grandmother broke down under the weight of anxiety and toil. The idea of losing her, who had always been my best friend and a mother to my children, was the sorest trial I had yet had. O, how earnestly I prayed that she might recover! How hard it seemed, that I could not tend upon her, who had so long and so tenderly watched over me!

One day the screams of a child nerved me with strength to crawl to my peeping-hole, and I saw my son covered with blood. A fierce dog, usually kept chained, had seized and bitten him. A doctor was sent for, and I heard the groans and screams of my child while the wounds were being sewed up. O, what torture to a mother's heart, to listen to this and be unable to go to him!

3. Samuel Thomson (1763–1843) treated illnesses by hyperthermia, or raising the patient's body temperature.

But childhood is like a day in spring, alternately shower and sunshine. Before night Benny was bright and lively, threatening the destruction of the dog; and great was his delight when the doctor told him the next day that the dog had bitten another boy and been shot. Benny recovered from his wounds; but it was long before he could walk.

When my grandmother's illness became known, many ladies, who were her customers, called to bring her some little comforts, and to inquire whether she had every thing she wanted. Aunt Nancy one night asked permission to watch with her sick mother, and Mrs. Flint replied, "I don't see any need of your going. I can't spare you." But when she found other ladies in the neighborhood were so attentive, not wishing to be outdone in Christian charity, she also sallied forth, in magnificent condescension, and stood by the bedside of her who had loved her in her infancy, and who had been repaid by such grievous wrongs. She seemed surprised to find her so ill, and scolded uncle Phillip for not sending for Dr. Flint. She herself sent for him immediately, and he came. Secure as I was in my retreat, I should have been terrified if I had known he was so near me. He pronounced my grandmother in a very critical situation, and said if her attending physician wished it, he would visit her. Nobody wished to have him coming to the house at all hours, and we were not disposed to give him a chance to make out a long bill.

As Mrs. Flint went out, Sally told her the reason Benny was lame was, that a dog had bitten him. "I'm glad of it," replied she. "I wish he had killed him. It would be good news to send to his mother. *Her* day will come. The dogs will grab *her* yet." With these Christian words she and her husband departed, and, to my great satisfaction, returned no more.

I heard from uncle Phillip, with feelings of unspeakable joy and gratitude, that the crisis was passed and grandmother would live. I could now say from my heart, "God is merciful. He has spared me the anguish of feeling that I caused her death."

XXIV. The Candidate for Congress

The summer had nearly ended, when Dr. Flint made a third visit to New York, in search of me. Two candidates were running for Congress, and he returned in season to vote. The father of my children was the Whig candidate. The doctor had hitherto been a stanch Whig; but now he exerted all his energies for the defeat of Mr. Sands. He invited large parties of men to dine in the shade of his trees, and supplied them with plenty of rum and brandy. If any poor fellow drowned his wits in the bowl, and, in the openness of his convivial heart, proclaimed that he did not mean to vote the Democratic ticket, he was shoved into the street without ceremony.

The doctor expended his liquor in vain. Mr. Sands was elected; an event which occasioned me some anxious thoughts. He had not emancipated my children, and if he should die they would be at the mercy of his heirs. Two little voices, that frequently met my ear, seemed to plead with me not to let their father depart without striving to make their freedom secure. Years had passed since I had spoken to him. I had not even seen him since the night I passed him, unrecognized, in my disguise of a sailor. I supposed he would call before he left, to say something to my grandmother concerning the children, and I resolved what course to take.

The day before his departure for Washington I made arrangements, towards evening, to get from my hiding-place into the storeroom below. I found myself so stiff and clumsy that it was with great difficulty I could hitch from one resting place to another. When I reached the storeroom my ankles gave way under me, and I sank exhausted on the floor. It seemed as if I could never use my limbs again. But the purpose I had in view roused all the strength I had. I crawled on my hands and knees to the window, and, screened behind a barrel, I waited for his coming. The clock struck nine, and I knew the steamboat would leave between ten and eleven. My hopes were failing. But presently I heard his voice, saying to some one, "Wait for me a moment. I wish to see aunt Martha." When he came out, as he passed the window, I said, "Stop one moment, and let me speak for my children." He started, hesitated, and then passed on, and went out of the gate. I closed the shutter I had partially opened, and sank down behind the barrel. I had suffered much; but seldom had I experienced a keener pang than I then felt. Had my children, then, become of so little consequence to him? And had he so little feeling for their wretched mother that he would not listen a moment while she pleaded for them? Painful memories were so busy within me, that I forgot I had not hooked the shutter, till I heard some one opening it. I looked up. He had come back. "Who called me?" said he, in a low tone. "I did," I replied. "Oh, Linda," said he, "I knew your voice; but I was afraid to answer, lest my friend should hear me. Why do you come here? Is it possible you risk yourself in this house? They are mad to allow it. I shall expect to hear that you are all ruined." I did not wish to implicate him, by letting him know my place of concealment; so I merely said, "I thought you would come to bid grandmother good by, and so I came here to speak a few words to you about emancipating my children. Many changes may take place during the six months you are gone to Washington, and it does not seem right for you to expose them to the risk of such changes.

I want nothing for myself; all I ask is, that you will free my children, or authorize some friend to do it, before you go."

He promised he would do it, and also expressed a readiness to make any arrangements whereby I could be purchased.

I heard footsteps approaching, and closed the shutter hastily. I wanted to crawl back to my den, without letting the family know what I had done; for I knew they would deem it very imprudent. But he stepped back into the house, to tell my grandmother that he had spoken with me at the storeroom window, and to beg of her not to allow me to remain in the house over night. He said it was the height of madness for me to be there; that we should certainly all be ruined. Luckily, he was in too much of a hurry to wait for a reply, or the dear old woman would surely have told him all.

I tried to go back to my den, but found it more difficult to go up than I had to come down. Now that my mission was fulfilled, the little strength that had supported me through it was gone, and I sank helpless on the floor. My grandmother, alarmed at the risk I had run, came into the storeroom in the dark, and locked the door behind her. "Linda," she whispered, "where are you?"

"I am here by the window," I replied. "I *couldn't* have him go away without emancipating the children. Who knows what may happen?"

"Come, come, child," said she, "it won't do for you to stay here another minute. You've done wrong; but I can't blame you, poor thing!"

I told her I could not return without assistance, and she must call my uncle. Uncle Phillip came, and pity prevented him from scolding me. He carried me back to my dungeon, laid me tenderly on the bed, gave me some medicine, and asked me if there was any thing more he could do. Then he went away, and I was left with my own thoughts—starless as the midnight darkness around me.

My friends feared I should become a cripple for life; and I was so weary of my long imprisonment that, had it not been for the hope of serving my children, I should have been thankful to die; but, for their sakes, I was willing to bear on.

XXV. Competition in Cunning

Dr. Flint had not given me up. Every now and then he would say to my grandmother that I would yet come back, and voluntarily surrender myself; and that when I did, I could be purchased by my relatives, or any one who wished to buy me. I knew his cunning nature too well not to perceive that this was a trap laid for me; and so all my friends understood it. I resolved to match my cunning against his cunning. In order to make him believe that I was in New York, I resolved to write him a letter dated from that place. I sent for my friend Peter, and asked him if he knew any trustworthy seafaring person, who would carry such a letter to New York, and put it in the post office there. He said he knew one that he would trust with his own life to the ends of the world. I reminded him that it was a hazardous thing for him to undertake. He said he knew it, but he was willing to do any thing to help me. I expressed a wish for a New York paper, to ascertain the names of some of the streets. He run his hand into his pocket, and said, "Here is half a one, that was round a cap I bought of a pedler yesterday." I told him the letter would be ready the next evening. He bade me good by, adding, "Keep up your spirits, Linda; brighter days will come by and by."

My uncle Phillip kept watch over the gate until our brief interview was over. Early the next morning, I seated myself near the little aperture to examine the newspaper. It was a piece of the New York Herald;[1] and, for once, the paper that systematically abuses the colored people, was made to render them a service. Having obtained what information I wanted concerning streets and numbers, I wrote two letters, one to my grandmother, the other to Dr. Flint. I reminded him how he, a gray-headed man, had treated a helpless child, who had been placed in his power, and what years of misery he had brought upon her. To my grandmother, I expressed a wish to have my children sent to me at the north, where I could teach them to respect themselves, and set them a virtuous example; which a slave mother was not allowed to do at the south. I asked her to direct her answer to a certain street in Boston, as I did not live in New York, though I went there sometimes. I dated these letters ahead, to allow for the time it would take to carry them, and sent a memorandum of the date to the messenger. When my friend came for the letters, I said, "God bless and reward you, Peter, for this disinterested kindness. Pray be careful. If you are detected, both you and I will have to suffer dreadfully. I have not a relative who would dare to do it for me." He replied, "You may trust to me, Linda. I don't forget that your father was my best friend, and I will be a friend to his children so long as God lets me live."

It was necessary to tell my grandmother what I had done, in order that she might be ready for the letter, and prepared to hear what Dr. Flint might say about my being at the north. She was sadly troubled. She felt sure mischief would come of it. I also told my plan to aunt Nancy, in order that she might report to us what was said at Dr. Flint's house. I whispered it to her through a crack, and she

1. The *Herald* was considered a proslavery newspaper.

whispered back, "I hope it will succeed. I shan't mind being a slave all *my* life, if I can only see you and the children free."

I had directed that my letters should be put into the New York post office on the 20th of the month. On the evening of the 24th my aunt came to say that Dr. Flint and his wife had been talking in a low voice about a letter he had received, and that when he went to his office he promised to bring it when he came to tea. So I concluded I should hear my letter read the next morning. I told my grandmother Dr. Flint would be sure to come, and asked her to have him sit near a certain door, and leave it open, that I might hear what he said. The next morning I took my station within sound of that door, and remained motionless as a statue. It was not long before I heard the gate slam, and the well-known footsteps enter the house. He seated himself in the chair that was placed for him, and said, "Well, Martha, I've brought you a letter from Linda. She has sent me a letter, also. I know exactly where to find her; but I don't choose to go to Boston for her. I had rather she would come back of her own accord, in a respectable manner. Her uncle Phillip is the best person to go for her. With *him*, she would feel perfectly free to act. I am willing to pay his expenses going and returning. She shall be sold to her friends. Her children are free; at least I suppose they are; and when you obtain her freedom, you'll make a happy family. I suppose, Martha, you have no objection to my reading to you the letter Linda has written to you."

He broke the seal, and I heard him read it. The old villain! He had suppressed the letter I wrote to grandmother, and prepared a substitute of his own, the purport of which was as follows:—

"Dear Grandmother: I have long wanted to write to you; but the disgraceful manner in which I left you and my children made me ashamed to do it. If you knew how much I have suffered since I ran away, you would pity and forgive me. I have purchased freedom at a dear rate. If any arrangement could be made for me to return to the south without being a slave, I would gladly come. If not, I beg of you to send my children to the north. I cannot live any longer without them. Let me know in time, and I will meet them in New York or Philadelphia, whichever place best suits my uncle's convenience. Write as soon as possible to your unhappy daughter,

Linda."

"It is very much as I expected it would be," said the old hypocrite, rising to go. "You see the foolish girl has repented of her rashness, and wants to return. We must help her to do it, Martha. Talk with Phillip about it. If he will go for her, she will trust to him, and come back. I should like an answer tomorrow. Good morning, Martha."

As he stepped out on the piazza, he stumbled over my little girl. "Ah, Ellen, is that you?" he said, in his most gracious manner. "I didn't see you. How do you do?"

"Pretty well, sir," she replied. "I heard you tell grandmother that my mother is coming home. I want to see her."

"Yes, Ellen, I am going to bring her home very soon," rejoined he; "and you shall see her as much as you like, you little curly-headed nigger."

This was as good as a comedy to me, who had heard it all; but grandmother was frightened and distressed, because the doctor wanted my uncle to go for me.

The next evening Dr. Flint called to talk the matter over. My uncle told him that from what he had heard of Massachusetts, he judged he should be mobbed if he went there after a runaway slave. "All stuff and nonsense, Phillip!" replied the doctor. "Do you suppose I want you to kick up a row in Boston? The business can all be done quietly. Linda writes that she wants to come back. You are her relative, and she would trust *you*. The case would be different if I went. She might object to coming with *me*; and the damned abolitionists, if they knew I was her master, would not believe me, if I told them she had begged to go back. They would get up a row; and I should not like to see Linda dragged through the streets like a common negro. She has been very ungrateful to me for all my kindness; but I forgive her, and want to act the part of a friend towards her. I have no wish to hold her as my slave. Her friends can buy her as soon as she arrives here."

Finding that his arguments failed to convince my uncle, the doctor "let the cat out of the bag,"[2] by saying that he had written to the mayor of Boston, to ascertain whether there was a person of my description at the street and number from which my letter was dated. He had omitted this date in the letter he had made up to read to my grandmother. If I had dated from New York, the old man would probably have made another journey to that city. But even in that dark region, where knowledge is so carefully excluded from the slave, I had heard enough about Massachusetts to come to the conclusion that slaveholders did not consider it a comfortable place to go to in search of a runaway. That was before the Fugitive Slave Law was passed; before Massachusetts had consented to become a "nigger hunter" for the south.[3]

2. Revealed his secret.
3. Part of a package of legislation known as the Compromise of 1850, the Fugitive Slave Act made aiding blacks fleeing slavery a federal offense. Abolitionists expressed particular outrage at the support of the Compromise provided by Senator Daniel Webster of Massachusetts, a state that was home to considerable antislavery activity.

My grandmother, who had become skittish by seeing her family always in danger, came to me with a very distressed countenance, and said, "What will you do if the mayor of Boston sends him word that you haven't been there? Then he will suspect the letter was a trick; and maybe he'll find out something about it, and we shall all get into trouble. O Linda, I wish you had never sent the letters."

"Don't worry yourself, grandmother," said I. "The mayor of Boston won't trouble himself to hunt niggers for Dr. Flint. The letters will do good in the end. I shall get out of this dark hole some time or other."

"I hope you will, child," replied the good, patient old friend. "You have been here a long time; almost five years; but whenever you do go, it will break your old grandmother's heart. I should be expecting every day to hear that you were brought back in irons and put in jail. God help you, poor child! Let us be thankful that some time or other we shall go 'where the wicked cease from troubling, and the weary are at rest.'"[4] My heart responded, Amen.

The fact that Dr. Flint had written to the mayor of Boston convinced me that he believed my letter to be genuine, and of course that he had no suspicion of my being any where in the vicinity. It was a great object to keep up this delusion, for it made me and my friends feel less anxious, and it would be very convenient whenever there was a chance to escape. I resolved, therefore, to continue to write letters from the north from time to time.

Two or three weeks passed, and as no news came from the mayor of Boston, grandmother began to listen to my entreaty to be allowed to leave my cell, sometimes, and exercise my limbs to prevent my becoming a cripple. I was allowed to slip down into the small storeroom, early in the morning, and remain there a little while. The room was all filled up with barrels, except a small open space under my trap-door. This faced the door, the upper part of which was of glass, and purposely left uncurtained, that the curious might look in. The air of this place was close; but it was so much better than the atmosphere of my cell, that I dreaded to return. I came down as soon as it was light, and remained till eight o'clock, when people began to be about, and there was danger that some one might come on the piazza. I had tried various applications to bring warmth and feeling into my limbs, but without avail. They were so numb and stiff that it was a painful effort to move; and had my enemies come upon me during the first mornings I tried to exercise them a little in the small unoccupied space of the storeroom, it would have been impossible for me to have escaped.

4. Job 3.17.

XXVI. Important Era in My Brother's Life

I missed the company and kind attentions of my brother William, who had gone to Washington with his master, Mr. Sands. We received several letters from him, written without any allusion to me, but expressed in such a manner that I knew he did not forget me. I disguised my hand, and wrote to him in the same manner. It was a long session; and when it closed, William wrote to inform us that Mr. Sands was going to the north, to be gone some time, and that he was to accompany him. I knew that his master had promised to give him his freedom, but no time had been specified. Would William trust to a slave's chances? I remembered how we used to talk together, in our young days, about obtaining our freedom, and I thought it very doubtful whether he would come back to us.

Grandmother received a letter from Mr. Sands, saying that William had proved a most faithful servant, and he would also say a valued friend; that no mother had ever trained a better boy. He said he had travelled through the Northern States and Canada; and though the abolitionists had tried to decoy him away, they had never succeeded. He ended by saying they should be at home shortly.

We expected letters from William, describing the novelties of his journey, but none came. In time, it was reported that Mr. Sands would return late in the autumn, accompanied by a bride. Still no letters from William. I felt almost sure I should never see him again on southern soil; but had he no word of comfort to send to his friends at home? to the poor captive in her dungeon? My thoughts wandered through the dark past, and over the uncertain future. Alone in my cell, where no eye but God's could see me, I wept bitter tears. How earnestly I prayed to him to restore me to my children, and enable me to be a useful woman and a good mother!

At last the day arrived for the return of the travellers. Grandmother had made loving preparations to welcome her absent boy back to the old hearthstone. When the dinner table was laid, William's plate occupied its old place. The stage coach went by empty. My grandmother waited dinner. She thought perhaps he was necessarily detained by his master. In my prison I listened anxiously, expecting every moment to hear my dear brother's voice and step. In the course of the afternoon a lad was sent by Mr. Sands to tell grandmother that William did not return with him; that the abolitionists had decoyed him away. But he begged her not to feel troubled about it, for he felt confident she would see William in a few days. As soon as he had time to reflect he would come back, for he could never expect to be so well off at the north as he had been with him.

If you had seen the tears, and heard the sobs, you would have thought the messenger had brought tidings of death instead of freedom. Poor old grandmother felt that she should never see her darling boy again. And I was selfish. I thought more of what I had lost, than of what my brother had gained. A new anxiety began to trouble me. Mr. Sands had expended a good deal of money, and would naturally feel irritated by the loss he had incurred. I greatly feared this might injure the prospects of my children, who were now becoming valuable property. I longed to have their emancipation made certain. The more so, because their master and father was now married. I was too familiar with slavery not to know that promises made to slaves, though with kind intentions, and sincere at the time, depend upon many contingencies for their fulfilment.

Much as I wished William to be free, the step he had taken made me sad and anxious. The following Sabbath was calm and clear; so beautiful that it seemed like a Sabbath in the eternal world. My grandmother brought the children out on the piazza, that I might hear their voices. She thought it would comfort me in my despondency; and it did. They chatted merrily, as only children can. Benny said, "Grandmother, do you think uncle Will has gone for good? Won't he ever come back again? May be he'll find mother. If he does, *won't* she be glad to see him! Why don't you and uncle Phillip, and all of us, go and live where mother is? I should like it; wouldn't you, Ellen?"

"Yes, I should like it," replied Ellen; "but how could we find her? Do you know the place, grandmother? I don't remember how mother looked—do you, Benny?"

Benny was just beginning to describe me when they were interrupted by an old slave woman, a near neighbor, named Aggie. This poor creature had witnessed the sale of her children, and seen them carried off to parts unknown, without any hopes of ever hearing from them again. She saw that my grandmother had been weeping, and she said, in a sympathizing tone, "What's the matter, aunt Marthy?"

"O Aggie," she replied, "it seems as if I shouldn't have any of my children or grandchildren left to hand me a drink when I'm dying, and lay my old body in the ground. My boy didn't come back with Mr. Sands. He staid at the north."

Poor old Aggie clapped her hands for joy. "Is *dat* what you's crying fur?" she exclaimed. "Git down on your knees and bress de Lord! I don't know whar my poor chillern is, and I nebber 'spect to know. You don't know whar poor Linda's gone to; but you *do* know whar her brudder is. He's in free parts; and dat's de right place. Don't murmur at de Lord's doings, but git down on your knees and tank him for his goodness."

My selfishness was rebuked by what poor Aggie said. She rejoiced over the escape of one who was merely her fellow-bondman, while his own sister was only thinking what his good fortune might cost her children. I knelt and prayed God to forgive me; and I thanked him from my heart, that one of my family was saved from the grasp of slavery.

It was not long before we received a letter from William. He wrote that Mr. Sands had always treated him kindly, and that he had tried to do his duty to him faithfully. But ever since he was a boy, he had longed to be free; and he had already gone through enough to convince him he had better not lose the chance that offered. He concluded by saying, "Don't worry about me, dear grandmother. I shall think of you always; and it will spur me on to work hard and try to do right. When I have earned money enough to give you a home, perhaps you will come to the north, and we can all live happy together."

Mr. Sands told my uncle Phillip the particulars about William's leaving him. He said, "I trusted him as if he were my own brother, and treated him as kindly. The abolitionists talked to him in several places; but I had no idea they could tempt him. However, I don't blame William. He's young and inconsiderate, and those Northern rascals decoyed him. I must confess the scamp was very bold about it. I met him coming down the steps of the Astor House with his trunk on his shoulder, and I asked him where he was going. He said he was going to change his old trunk. I told him it was rather shabby, and asked if he didn't need some money. He said, No, thanked me, and went off. He did not return so soon as I expected; but I waited patiently. At last I went to see if our trunks were packed, ready for our journey. I found them locked, and a sealed note on the table informed me where I could find the keys. The fellow even tried to be religious. He wrote that he hoped God would always bless me, and reward me for my kindness; that he was not unwilling to serve me; but he wanted to be a free man; and that if I thought he did wrong, he hoped I would forgive him. I intended to give him his freedom in five years. He might have trusted me. He has shown himself ungrateful; but I shall not go for him, or send for him. I feel confident that he will soon return to me."

I afterwards heard an account of the affair from William himself. He had not been urged away by abolitionists. He needed no information they could give him about slavery to stimulate his desire for freedom. He looked at his hands, and remembered that they were once in irons. What security had he that they would not be so again? Mr. Sands was kind to him; but he might indefinitely postpone the promise he had made to give him his freedom. He might come under pecuniary embarrassments, and his property be seized by creditors; or he might die, without making any arrangements in his favor. He had too often known such accidents to happen to slaves who had kind masters, and he wisely resolved to make sure of the present opportunity to own himself. He was scrupulous about taking any money from his master on false pretences; so he sold his best clothes to pay for his passage to Boston. The slaveholders pronounced him a base, ungrateful wretch, for thus requiting his master's indulgence. What would *they* have done under similar circumstances?

When Dr. Flint's family heard that William had deserted Mr. Sands, they chuckled greatly over the news. Mrs. Flint made her usual manifestations of Christian feeling, by saying, "I'm glad of it. I hope he'll never get him again. I like to see people paid back in their own coin. I reckon Linda's children will have to pay for it. I should be glad to see them in the speculator's hands again, for I'm tired of seeing those little niggers march about the streets."

XXVII. New Destination for the Children

Mrs. Flint proclaimed her intention of informing Mrs. Sands who was the father of my children. She likewise proposed to tell her what an artful devil I was; that I had made a great deal of trouble in her family; that when Mr. Sands was at the north, she didn't doubt I had followed him in disguise, and persuaded William to run away. She had some reason to entertain such an idea; for I had written from the north, from time to time, and I dated my letters from various places. Many of them fell into Dr. Flint's hands, as I expected they would; and he must have come to the conclusion that I travelled about a good deal. He kept a close watch over my children, thinking they would eventually lead to my detection.

A new and unexpected trial was in store for me. One day, when Mr. Sands and his wife were walking in the street, they met Benny. The lady took a fancy to him, and exclaimed, "What a pretty little negro! Whom does he belong to?"

Benny did not hear the answer; but he came home very indignant with the stranger lady, because she had called him a negro. A few days afterwards, Mr. Sands called on my grandmother, and told her he wanted her to take the children to his house. He said he had informed his wife of his relation to them, and told her they were motherless; and she wanted to see them.

When he had gone, my grandmother came and asked what I would do. The question seemed a mockery. What *could* I do? They were Mr. Sands's slaves, and their mother was a slave, whom he had represented to be dead. Perhaps he thought I was. I was too much pained and puzzled to come to any decision; and the children were carried without my knowledge.

Mrs. Sands had a sister from Illinois staying with her. This lady, who had no children of her own, was so much pleased with Ellen, that she offered to adopt her, and bring her up as she would a daughter. Mrs. Sands wanted to take Benjamin. When grandmother reported this to me, I was tried almost beyond endurance. Was this all I was to gain by what I had suffered for the sake of having my children free? True, the prospect *seemed* fair; but I knew too well how lightly slaveholders held such "parental relations." If pecuniary troubles should come, or if the new wife required more money than could conveniently be spared, my children might be thought of as a convenient means of raising funds. I had no trust in thee, O Slavery! Never should I know peace till my children were emancipated with all due formalities of law.

I was too proud to ask Mr. Sands to do any thing for my own benefit; but I could bring myself to become a supplicant for my children. I resolved to remind him of the promise he had made me, and to throw myself upon his honor for the performance of it. I persuaded my grandmother to go to him, and tell him I was not dead, and that I earnestly entreated him to keep the promise he had made me; that I had heard of the recent proposals concerning my children, and did not feel easy to accept them; that he had promised to emancipate them, and it was time for him to redeem his pledge. I knew there was some risk in thus betraying that I was in the vicinity; but what will not a mother do for her children? He received the message with surprise, and said, "The children are free. I have never intended to claim them as slaves. Linda may decide their fate. In my opinion, they had better be sent to the north. I don't think they are quite safe here. Dr. Flint boasts that they are still in his power. He says they were his daughter's property, and as she was not of age when they were sold, the contract is not legally binding."

So, then, after all I had endured for their sakes, my poor children were between two fires; between my old master and their new master! And I was powerless. There was no protecting arm of the law for me to invoke. Mr. Sands proposed that Ellen should go, for the present, to some of his relatives, who had removed to Brooklyn, Long Island. It was promised that she should be well taken care of, and sent to school. I consented to it, as the best arrangement I could make for her. My grandmother, of course, negotiated it all; and Mrs. Sands knew of no other person in the transaction. She proposed that they should take Ellen with them to Washington, and keep her till they had a good chance of sending her, with friends, to Brooklyn. She had an infant daughter. I had had a glimpse of it, as the nurse passed with it in her arms. It was not a pleasant thought to me, that the bondwoman's child should tend her free-born sister; but there was no alternative. Ellen was made ready for the journey.

O, how it tried my heart to send her away, so young, alone, among strangers! Without a mother's love to shelter her from the storms of life; almost without memory of a mother! I doubted whether she and Benny would have for me the natural affection that children feel for a parent. I thought to myself that I might perhaps never see my daughter again, and I had a great desire that she should look upon me, before she went, that she might take my image with her in her memory. It seemed to me cruel to have her brought to my dungeon. It was sorrow enough for her young heart to know that her mother was a victim of slavery, without seeing the wretched hiding-place to which it had driven her. I begged permission to pass the last night in one of the open chambers, with my little girl. They thought I was crazy to think of trusting such a young child with my perilous secret. I told them I had watched her character, and I felt sure she would not betray me; that I was determined to have an interview, and if they would not facilitate it, I would take my own way to obtain it. They remonstrated against the rashness of such a proceeding; but finding they could not change my purpose, they yielded. I slipped through the trap-door into the storeroom, and my uncle kept watch at the gate, while I passed into the piazza and went up stairs, to the room I used to occupy. It was more than five years since I had seen it; and how the memories crowded on me! There I had taken shelter when my mistress drove me from her house; there came my old tyrant, to mock, insult, and curse me; there my children were first laid in my arms; there I had watched over them, each day with a deeper and sadder love; there I had knelt to God, in anguish of heart, to forgive the wrong I had done. How vividly it all came back! And after this long, gloomy interval, I stood there such a wreck!

In the midst of these meditations, I heard footsteps on the stairs. The door opened, and my uncle Phillip came in, leading Ellen by the hand. I put my arms round her, and said, "Ellen, my dear child, I am your mother." She drew back a little, and looked at me; then, with sweet confidence, she laid her cheek against mine, and I folded her to the heart that had been so long desolated. She was the first to speak. Raising her head, she said, inquiringly, "You really *are* my mother?" I told her I really was; that during all the long time she had not seen me, I had loved her most tenderly; and that now she was going away, I wanted to see her and talk with her, that she might remember me. With a sob in her voice, she said, "I'm glad you've come to see me; but why didn't you ever come before? Benny and I have wanted so much to see you! He remembers you, and sometimes he tells me about you. Why didn't you come home when Dr. Flint went to bring you?"

I answered, "I couldn't come before, dear. But now that I am with you, tell me whether you like to go away." "I don't know," said she, crying. "Grandmother says I ought not to cry; that I am going to a good place, where I can learn to read and write, and that by and by I can write her a letter. But I shan't have Benny, or grandmother, or uncle Phillip, or any body to love me. Can't you go with me? O, *do* go, dear mother!"

I told her I couldn't go now; but sometime I would come to her, and then she and Benny and I would live together, and have happy times. She wanted to run and bring Benny to see me now. I told her he was going to the north, before long, with uncle Phillip, and then I would come to see him before he went away. I asked if she would like to have me stay all night and sleep with her. "O, yes," she replied. Then, turning to her uncle, she said, pleadingly, "*May* I stay? Please, uncle! She is my own mother." He laid his hand on her head, and said, solemnly, "Ellen, this is the secret you have promised grandmother never to tell. If you ever speak of it to any body, they will never let you see your grandmother again, and your mother can never come to Brooklyn." "Uncle," she replied, "I will never tell." He told her she might stay with me; and when he had gone, I took her in my arms and told her I was a slave, and that was the reason she must never say she had seen me. I exhorted her to be a good child, to try to please the people where she was going, and that God would raise her up friends. I told her to say her prayers, and remember always to pray for her poor mother, and that God would permit us to meet again. She wept, and I did not check her tears. Perhaps she would never again have a chance to pour her tears into a mother's bosom. All night she nestled in my arms, and I had no inclination to slumber. The moments were too precious to lose any of them. Once, when I thought she was asleep, I kissed her forehead softly, and she said, "I am not asleep, dear mother."

Before dawn they came to take me back to my den. I drew aside the window curtain, to take a last look of my child. The moonlight shone on her face, and I bent over her, as I had done years before, that wretched night when I ran away. I hugged her close to my throbbing heart; and tears, too sad for such young eyes to shed, flowed down her cheeks, as she gave her last kiss, and whispered in my ear, "Mother, I will never tell." And she never did.

When I got back to my den, I threw myself on the bed and wept there alone in the darkness. It seemed as if my heart would burst. When the time for Ellen's departure drew nigh, I could hear neighbors and friends saying to her, "Good by, Ellen. I hope your poor mother will find you out. *Won't* you be glad to see her!" She replied, "Yes, ma'am;" and they little dreamed of the weighty secret that weighed down her young heart. She was an affectionate child, but naturally very reserved, except with those she loved, and I felt secure that my secret would be safe with her. I heard the gate close after her, with such feelings as only a slave mother can experience. During the day my meditations were very sad. Sometimes I feared I had been very selfish not to give up all claim to her, and let her go to Illinois, to be adopted by Mrs. Sands's sister. It was my experience of slavery that decided me against it. I feared that circumstances might arise that would cause her to be sent back. I felt confident that I should go to New York myself; and then I should be able to watch over her, and in some degree protect her.

Dr. Flint's family knew nothing of the proposed arrangement till after Ellen was gone, and the news displeased them greatly. Mrs. Flint called on Mrs. Sands's sister to inquire into the matter. She expressed her opinion very freely as to the respect Mr. Sands showed for his wife, and for his own character, in acknowledging those "young niggers." And as for sending Ellen away, she pronounced it to be just as much stealing as it would be for him to come and take a piece of furniture out of her parlor. She said her daughter was not of age to sign the bill of sale, and the children were her property; and when she became of age, or was married, she could take them, wherever she could lay hands on them.

Miss Emily Flint, the little girl to whom I had been bequeathed, was now in her sixteenth year. Her mother considered it all right and honorable for her, or her future husband, to steal my children; but she did not understand how any body could hold up their heads in respectable society, after they had purchased their own children, as Mr. Sands had done. Dr. Flint said very little. Perhaps he thought that Benny would be less likely to be sent away if he kept quiet. One of my letters, that fell into his hands, was dated from Canada; and he seldom spoke of me now. This state of things enabled me to slip down into the storeroom more frequently, where I could stand upright, and move my limbs more freely.

Days, weeks, and months passed, and there came no news of Ellen. I sent a letter to Brooklyn, written in my grandmother's name, to inquire whether she had arrived there. Answer was returned that she had not. I wrote to her in Washington; but no notice was taken of it. There was one person there, who ought to have had some sympathy with the anxiety of the child's friends at home; but the links of such relations as he had formed with me, are easily broken and cast away as rubbish. Yet how protectingly and persuasively he once talked to the poor, helpless slave girl! And how entirely I trusted him! But now suspicions darkened my mind. Was my child dead, or had they deceived me, and sold her?

If the secret memoirs of many members of Congress should be published, curious details would be unfolded. I once saw a letter from a member of Congress to a slave, who was the mother of six of his children. He wrote to request that she would send her children away from the great house before his return, as he expected to be accompanied by friends. The woman could not read, and was obliged to employ another to read the letter. The existence of the colored children did not trouble this gentleman, it was only the fear that friends might recognize in their features a resemblance to him.

At the end of six months, a letter came to my grandmother, from Brooklyn. It was written by a young lady in the family, and announced that Ellen had just arrived. It contained the following message from her: "I do try to do just as you told me to, and I pray for you every night and morning." I understood that these words were meant for me; and they were a balsam to my heart. The writer closed her letter by saying, "Ellen is a nice little girl, and we shall like to have her with us. My cousin, Mr. Sands, has given her to me, to be my little waiting maid. I shall send her to school, and I hope some day she will write to you herself." This letter perplexed and troubled me. Had my child's father merely placed her there till she was old enough to support herself? Or had he given her to his cousin, as a piece of property? If the last idea was correct, his cousin might return to the south at any time, and hold Ellen as a slave. I tried to put away from me the painful thought that such a foul wrong could have been done to us. I said to myself, "Surely there must be *some* justice in man;" then I remembered, with a sigh, how slavery perverted all the natural feelings of the human heart. It gave me a pang to look on my light-hearted boy. He believed himself free; and to have him brought under the yoke of slavery, would be more than I could bear. How I longed to have him safely out of the reach of its power!

XXVIII. Aunt Nancy

I have mentioned my great-aunt, who was a slave in Dr. Flint's family, and who had been my refuge during the shameful persecutions I suffered from him. This aunt had been married at twenty years of age; that is, as far as slaves *can* marry. She had the consent of her master and mistress, and a clergyman performed the ceremony. But it was a mere form, without any legal value. Her master or mistress could annul it any day they pleased. She had always slept on the floor in the entry, near Mrs. Flint's chamber door, that she might be within call. When she was married, she was told she might have the use of a small room in an out-house. Her mother and her husband furnished it. He was a seafaring man, and was allowed to sleep there when he was at home. But on the wedding evening, the bride was ordered to her old post on the entry floor.

Mrs. Flint, at that time, had no children; but she was expecting to be a mother, and if she should want a drink of water in the night, what could she do without her slave to bring it? So my aunt was compelled to lie at her door, until one midnight she was forced to leave, to give premature birth to a child. In a fortnight, she was required to resume her place on the entry floor, because Mrs. Flint's babe needed her attentions. She kept her station there through summer and winter, until she had given premature birth to six children; and all the while she was employed as night-nurse to Mrs. Flint's children. Finally, toiling all day, and being deprived of rest at night, completely broke down her constitution, and Dr. Flint declared it was impossible she could ever become the mother of a living child. The fear of losing so valuable a servant by death, now induced them to allow her to sleep in her little room in the out-house, except when there was sickness in the family. She afterwards had two feeble babes, one of whom died in a few days, and the other in four weeks. I well remember her patient sorrow as she held the last dead baby in her arms. "I wish it could have lived," she said; "it is not the will of God that any of my children should live. But I will try to be fit to meet their little spirits in heaven."

Aunt Nancy was housekeeper and waiting-maid in Dr. Flint's family. Indeed, she was the *factotum* of the household. Nothing went on well without her. She was my mother's twin sister, and, as far as was in her power, she supplied a mother's place to us orphans. I slept with her all the time I lived in my old master's house, and the bond between us was very strong. When my friends tried to discourage me from running away, she always encouraged me. When they thought I had better return and ask my master's pardon, because there was no possibility of escape, she sent me word never to yield. She said if I persevered I might, perhaps, gain the freedom of my children; and even if I perished in doing it, that was better than to leave them to groan under the same persecutions that had blighted my own life. After I was shut up in my dark cell, she stole away, whenever she could, to bring me the news and say something cheering. How often did I kneel down to listen to her words of consolation, whispered through a crack! "I am old, and have not long to live," she used to say; "and I could die happy if I could only see you and the children free. You must pray to God, Linda, as I do for you, that he will lead you out of this darkness." I would beg her not to worry herself on my account; that there was an end of all suffering sooner or later, and that whether I lived in chains or in freedom, I should always remember her as the good friend who had been the comfort of my life. A word from her always strengthened me; and not me only. The whole family relied upon her judgment, and were guided by her advice.

I had been in my cell six years when my grandmother was summoned to the bedside of this, her last remaining daughter. She was very ill, and they said she would die. Grandmother had not entered Dr. Flint's house for several years. They had treated her cruelly, but she thought nothing of that now. She was grateful for permission to watch by the death-bed of her child. They had always been devoted to each other; and now they sat looking into each other's eyes, longing to speak of the secret that had weighed so much on the hearts of both. My aunt had been stricken with paralysis. She lived but two days, and the last day she was speechless. Before she lost the power of utterance, she told her mother not to grieve if she could not speak to her; that she would try to hold up her hand, to let her know that all was well with her. Even the hard-hearted doctor was a little softened when he saw the dying woman try to smile on the aged mother, who was kneeling by her side. His eyes moistened for a moment, as he said she had always been a faithful servant, and they should never be able to supply her place. Mrs. Flint took to her bed, quite overcome by the shock. While my grandmother sat alone with the dead, the doctor came in, leading his youngest son, who had always been a great pet with aunt Nancy, and was much attached to her. "Martha," said he, "aunt Nancy loved this child, and when he comes where you are, I hope you will be kind to him, for her sake." She replied, "Your wife was my foster-child, Dr. Flint, the foster-sister of my poor Nancy, and you little know me if you think I can feel any thing but good will for her children."

"I wish the past could be forgotten, and that we might never think of it," said he; "and that Linda would come to supply her aunt's place. She would be worth more to us than all the money that could be paid for her. I wish it for your sake also, Martha. Now that Nancy is taken away from you, she would be a great comfort to your old age."

He knew he was touching a tender chord. Almost choking with grief, my grandmother replied, "It was not I that drove Linda away. My grandchildren are gone; and of my nine children only one is left. God help me!"

To me, the death of this kind relative was an inexpressible sorrow. I knew that she had been slowly murdered; and I felt that my troubles had helped to finish the work. After I heard of her illness, I listened constantly to hear what news was brought from the great house; and the thought that I could not go to her made me utterly miserable. At last, as uncle Phillip came into the house, I heard some one inquire, "How is she?" and he answered, "She is dead." My little cell seemed whirling round, and I knew nothing more till I opened my eyes and found uncle Phillip bending over me. I had no need to ask any questions. He whispered, "Linda, she died happy." I could not weep. My fixed gaze troubled him. "Don't look *so*," he said. "Don't add to my poor mother's trouble. Remember how much she has to bear, and that we ought to do all we can to comfort her." Ah, yes, that blessed old grandmother, who for seventy-three years had borne the pelting storms of a slave-mother's life. She did indeed need consolation!

Mrs. Flint had rendered her poor foster-sister childless, apparently without any compunction; and with cruel selfishness had ruined her health by years of incessant, unrequited toil, and broken rest. But now she became very sentimental. I suppose she thought it would be a beautiful illustration of the attachment existing between slave-holder and slave, if the body of her old worn-out servant was buried at her feet. She sent for the clergyman and asked if he had any objection to burying aunt Nancy in the doctor's family burial-place. No colored person had ever been allowed interment in the white people's burying-ground, and the minister knew that all the deceased of our family reposed together in the old graveyard of the slaves. He therefore replied, "I have no objection to complying with your wish; but perhaps aunt Nancy's *mother* may have some choice as to where her remains shall be deposited."

It had never occurred to Mrs. Flint that slaves could have any feelings. When my grandmother was consulted, she at once said she wanted Nancy to lie with all the rest of her family, and where her own old body would be buried. Mrs. Flint graciously complied with her wish, though she said it was painful to her to have Nancy buried away from *her*. She might have added with touching pathos, "I was so long *used* to sleep with her lying near me, on the entry floor."

My uncle Phillip asked permission to bury his sister at his own expense; and slaveholders are always ready to grant *such* favors to slaves and their relatives. The arrangements were very plain, but perfectly respectable. She was buried on the Sabbath, and Mrs. Flint's minister read the funeral service. There was a large concourse of colored people, bond and free, and a few white persons who had always been friendly to our family. Dr. Flint's carriage was in the procession; and when the body was deposited in its humble resting place, the mistress dropped a tear, and returned to her carriage, probably thinking she had performed her duty nobly.

It was talked of by the slaves as a mighty grand funeral. Northern travellers, passing through the place, might have described this tribute of respect to the humble dead as a beautiful feature in the "patriarchal institution;" a touching proof of the attachment between slaveholders and their servants; and tender-hearted Mrs. Flint would have confirmed this impression, with handkerchief at her eyes. *We* could have told them a different story. We could have given them a chapter of wrongs and sufferings, that would have touched their hearts, if they *had* any hearts to feel for the colored people. We could have told them how the poor old slave-mother had toiled, year after year, to earn eight hundred dollars to buy her son Phillip's right to his own earnings; and how that same Phillip paid the expenses of the funeral, which they regarded as doing so much credit to the master. We could also have told them of a poor, blighted young creature, shut up in a living grave for years, to avoid the tortures that would be inflicted on her, if she ventured to come out and look on the face of her departed friend.

All this, and much more, I thought of, as I sat at my loophole, waiting for the family to return from the grave; sometimes weeping, sometimes falling asleep, dreaming strange dreams of the dead and the living.

It was sad to witness the grief of my bereaved grandmother. She had always been strong to bear, and now, as ever, religious faith supported her. But her dark life had become still darker, and age and trouble were leaving deep traces on her withered face. She had four places to knock for me to come to the trap-door, and each place had a different meaning. She now came oftener than she had done, and talked to me of her dead daughter, while tears trickled slowly down her furrowed cheeks. I said all I could to comfort her; but it was a sad reflection, that instead of being able to help her, I was a constant source of anxiety and trouble. The poor old back was fitted to its burden. It bent under it, but did not break.

XXIX. Preparations for Escape

I hardly expect that the reader will credit me, when I affirm that I lived in that little dismal hole, almost deprived of light and air, and with no space to move my limbs, for nearly seven years. But it is a fact; and to me a sad one, even now; for my body still suffers from the effects of that long imprisonment, to say nothing of my soul. Members of my family, now living in New York and Boston, can testify to the truth of what I say.

Countless were the nights that I sat late at the little loophole scarcely large enough to give me a glimpse of one twinkling star. There, I heard the patrols and slave-hunters conferring together about the capture of runaways, well knowing how rejoiced they would be to catch me.

Season after season, year after year, I peeped at my children's faces, and heard their sweet voices, with a heart yearning all the while to say, "Your mother is here." Sometimes it appeared to me as if ages had rolled away since I entered upon that gloomy, monotonous existence. At times, I was stupefied and listless; at other times I became very impatient to know when these dark years would end, and I should again be allowed to feel the sunshine, and breathe the pure air.

After Ellen left us, this feeling increased. Mr. Sands had agreed that Benny might go to the north whenever his uncle Phillip could go with him; and I was anxious to be there also, to watch over my children, and protect them so far as I was able. Moreover, I was likely to be drowned out of my den, if I remained much longer; for the slight roof was getting badly out of repair, and uncle Phillip was afraid to remove the shingles, lest some one should get a glimpse of me. When storms occurred in the night, they spread mats and bits of carpet, which in the morning appeared to have been laid out to dry; but to cover the roof in the daytime might have attracted attention. Consequently, my clothes and bedding were often drenched; a process by which the pains and aches in my cramped and stiffened limbs were greatly increased. I revolved various plans of escape in my mind, which I sometimes imparted to my grandmother, when she came to whisper with me at the trap-door. The kind-hearted old woman had an intense sympathy for runaways. She had known too much of the cruelties inflicted on those who were captured. Her memory always flew back at once to the sufferings of her bright and handsome son, Benjamin, the youngest and dearest of her flock. So, whenever I alluded to the subject, she would groan out, "O, don't think of it, child. You'll break my heart." I had no good old aunt Nancy now to encourage me; but my brother William and my children were continually beckoning me to the north.

And now I must go back a few months in my story. I have stated that the first of January was the time for selling slaves, or leasing them out to new masters. If time were counted by heart-throbs, the poor slaves might reckon years of suffering during that festival so joyous to the free. On the New Year's day preceding my aunt's death, one of my friends, named Fanny, was to be sold at auction, to pay her master's debts. My thoughts were with her during all the day, and at night I anxiously inquired what had been her fate. I was told that she had been sold to one master, and her four little girls to another master, far distant; that she had escaped from her purchaser, and was not to be found. Her mother was the old Aggie I have spoken of. She lived in a small tenement belonging to my grandmother, and built on the same lot with her own house. Her dwelling was searched and watched, and that brought the patrols so near me that I was obliged to keep very close in my den. The hunters were somehow eluded; and not long afterwards Benny accidentally caught sight of Fanny in her mother's hut. He told his grandmother, who charged him never to speak of it, explaining to him the frightful consequences; and he never betrayed the trust. Aggie little dreamed that my grandmother knew where her daughter was concealed, and that the stooping form of her old neighbor was bending under a similar burden of anxiety and fear; but these dangerous secrets deepened the sympathy between the two old persecuted mothers.

My friend Fanny and I remained many weeks hidden within call of each other; but she was unconscious of the fact. I longed to have her share my den, which seemed a more secure retreat than her own; but I had brought so much trouble on my grandmother, that it seemed wrong to ask her to incur greater risks. My restlessness increased. I had lived too long in bodily pain and anguish of spirit. Always I was in dread that by some accident, or some contrivance, slavery would succeed in snatching my children from me. This thought drove me nearly frantic, and I determined to steer for the North Star at all hazards. At this crisis, Providence opened an unexpected way for me to escape. My friend Peter came one evening, and asked to speak with me. "Your day has come, Linda," said he. "I have found a chance for you to go to the Free States. You have a fortnight to decide." The news seemed too good to be true; but Peter explained his arrangements, and told me all that was necessary was for me to say I would go. I was going to answer him with a joyful yes, when the thought of Benny came to my mind. I told him the temptation was exceedingly strong, but I was terribly afraid of Dr. Flint's alleged power over my child, and that I could not go and leave him behind. Peter remonstrated earnestly. He said such a good chance might never occur again; that Benny was free, and could be sent to me; and that for the sake of my children's welfare I ought not to hesitate a moment. I told him I would consult with uncle Phillip. My uncle rejoiced in the plan, and bade me go by all means. He promised, if his life was spared, that he would either bring or send my son to me as soon as I reached a place of safety. I resolved to go, but thought nothing had better be said to my grandmother till very near the time of departure. But my uncle thought she would feel it more keenly if I left her so suddenly. "I will reason with her," said he, "and convince her how necessary it is, not only for your sake, but for hers also. You cannot be blind to the fact that she is sinking under her burdens." I was not blind to it. I knew that my concealment was an ever-present source of anxiety, and that the older she grew the more nervously fearful she was of discovery. My uncle talked with her, and finally succeeded in persuading her that it was absolutely necessary for me to seize the chance so unexpectedly offered.

The anticipation of being a free woman proved almost too much for my weak frame. The excitement stimulated me, and at the same time bewildered me. I made busy preparations for my journey, and for my son to follow me. I resolved to have an interview with him before I went, that I might give him cautions and advice, and tell him how anxiously I should be waiting for him at the north.

Grandmother stole up to me as often as possible to whisper words of counsel. She insisted upon my writing to Dr. Flint, as soon as I arrived in the Free States, and asking him to sell me to her. She said she would sacrifice her house, and all she had in the world, for the sake of having me safe with my children in any part of the world. If she could only live to know *that* she could die in peace. I promised the dear old faithful friend that I would write to her as soon as I arrived, and put the letter in a safe way to reach her; but in my own mind I resolved that not another cent of her hard earnings should be spent to pay rapacious slaveholders for what they called their property. And even if I had not been unwilling to buy what I had already a right to possess, common humanity would have prevented me from accepting the generous offer, at the expense of turning my aged relative out of house and home, when she was trembling on the brink of the grave.

I was to escape in a vessel; but I forbear to mention any further particulars. I was in readiness, but the vessel was unexpectedly detained several days. Meantime, news came to town of a most horrible murder committed on a fugitive slave, named James. Charity, the mother of this unfortunate young man, had been an old acquaintance of ours. I have told the shocking particulars of his death, in my description of some of the neighboring slaveholders. My grandmother, always nervously sensitive about runaways, was terribly frightened. She felt sure that a similar fate awaited me, if I did not desist from my enterprise. She sobbed, and groaned, and entreated me not to go. Her excessive fear was somewhat contagious, and my heart was not proof against her extreme agony. I was grievously disappointed, but I promised to relinquish my project.

When my friend Peter was apprised of this, he was both disappointed and vexed. He said, that judging from our past experience, it would be a long time before I had such another chance to throw away. I told him it need not be thrown away; that I had a friend concealed near by, who would be glad enough to take the place that had been provided for me. I told him about poor Fanny, and the kind-hearted, noble fellow, who never turned his back upon any body in distress, white or black, expressed his readiness to help her. Aggie was much surprised when she found that we knew her secret. She was rejoiced to hear of such a chance for Fanny, and arrangements were made for her to go on board the vessel the next night. They both supposed that I had long been at the north, therefore my name was not mentioned in the transaction. Fanny was carried on board at the appointed time, and stowed away in a very small cabin. This accommodation had been purchased at a price that would pay for a voyage to England. But when one proposes to go to fine old England, they stop to calculate whether they can afford the cost of the pleasure; while in making a bargain to escape from slavery, the trembling victim is ready to say, "Take all I have, only don't betray me!"

The next morning I peeped through my loophole, and saw that it was dark and cloudy. At night I received news that the wind was ahead, and the vessel had not sailed. I was exceedingly anxious about Fanny, and Peter too, who was running a tremendous risk at my instigation. Next day the wind and weather remained the same. Poor Fanny had been half dead with fright when they carried her on board, and I could readily imagine how she must be suffering now. Grandmother came often to my den, to say how thankful she was I did not go. On the third morning she rapped for me to come down to the storeroom. The poor old sufferer was breaking down under her weight of trouble. She was easily flurried now. I found her in a nervous, excited state, but I was not aware that she had forgotten to lock the door behind her, as usual. She was exceedingly worried about the detention of the vessel. She was afraid all would be discovered, and then Fanny, and Peter, and I, would all be tortured to death, and Phillip would be utterly ruined, and her house would be torn down. Poor Peter! If he should die such a horrible death as the poor slave James had lately done, and all for his kindness in trying to help me, how dreadful it would be for us all! Alas, the thought was familiar to me, and had sent many a sharp pang through my heart. I tried to suppress my own anxiety, and speak soothingly to her. She brought in some allusion to aunt Nancy, the dear daughter she had recently buried, and then she lost all control of herself. As she stood there, trembling and sobbing, a voice from the piazza called out, "Whar is you, aunt Marthy?" Grandmother was startled, and in her agitation opened the door, without thinking of me. In stepped Jenny, the mischievous housemaid, who had tried to enter my room, when I was concealed in the house of my white benefactress. "I's bin huntin ebery whar for you, aunt Marthy," said she. "My missis wants you to send her some crackers." I had slunk down behind a barrel, which entirely screened me, but I imagined that Jenny was looking directly at the spot, and my heart beat violently. My grandmother immediately thought what she had done, and went out quickly with Jenny to count the crackers, locking the door after her. She returned to me, in a few minutes, the perfect picture of despair. "Poor child!" she exclaimed, "my carelessness has ruined you. The boat ain't gone yet. Get ready immediately, and go with Fanny. I ain't got another word to say against it now; for there's no telling what may happen this day."

Uncle Phillip was sent for, and he agreed with his mother in thinking that Jenny would inform Dr. Flint in less than twenty-four hours. He advised getting me on board the boat, if possible; if not, I had better keep very still in my den, where they could not find me without tearing the house down. He said it would not do for him to move in the matter, because suspicion would be immediately excited; but he promised to communicate with Peter. I felt reluctant to apply to him again, having implicated him too much already; but there seemed to be no alternative. Vexed as Peter had been by my indecision, he was true to his generous nature, and said at once that he would do his best to help me, trusting I should show myself a stronger woman this time.

He immediately proceeded to the wharf, and found that the wind had shifted, and the vessel was slowly beating down stream. On some pretext of urgent necessity, he offered two boatmen a dollar apiece to catch up with her. He was of lighter complexion than the boatmen he hired, and when the captain saw them coming so rapidly, he thought officers were pursuing his vessel in search of the runaway slave he had on board. They hoisted sails, but the boat gained upon them, and the indefatigable Peter sprang on board.

The captain at once recognized him. Peter asked him to go below, to speak about a bad bill he had given him. When he told his errand, the captain replied, "Why, the woman's here already; and I've put her where you or the devil would have a tough job to find her."

"But it is another woman I want to bring," said Peter. "*She* is in great distress, too, and you shall be paid any thing within reason, if you'll stop and take her."

"What's her name?" inquired the captain.

"Linda," he replied.

"That's the name of the woman already here," rejoined the captain. "By George! I believe you mean to betray me."

"O!" exclaimed Peter, "God knows I wouldn't harm a hair of your head. I am too grateful to you. But there really *is* another woman in great danger. Do have the humanity to stop and take her!"

After a while they came to an understanding. Fanny, not dreaming I was any where about in that region, had assumed my name, though she called herself Johnson. "Linda is a common name," said Peter, "and the woman I want to bring is Linda Brent."

The captain agreed to wait at a certain place till evening, being handsomely paid for his detention.

Of course, the day was an anxious one for us all. But we concluded that if Jenny had seen me, she would be too wise to let her mistress know of it; and that she probably would not get a chance to see Dr. Flint's family till evening, for I knew very well what were the rules in that household. I afterwards believed that she did not see me; for nothing ever came of it, and she was one of those base characters that would have jumped to betray a suffering fellow being for the sake of thirty pieces of silver.[1]

I made all my arrangements to go on board as soon as it was dusk. The intervening time I resolved to spend with my son. I had not spoken to him for seven years, though I had been under the same roof, and seen him every day, when I was well enough to sit at the loophole. I did not dare to venture beyond the storeroom; so they brought him there, and locked us up together, in a place concealed from the piazza door. It was an agitating interview for both of us. After we had talked and wept together for a little while, he said, "Mother, I'm glad you're going away. I wish I could go with you. I knew you was here; and I have been *so* afraid they would come and catch you!"

I was greatly surprised, and asked him how he had found it out.

He replied, "I was standing under the eaves, one day, before Ellen went away, and I heard somebody cough up over the wood shed. I don't know what made me think it was you, but I did think so. I missed Ellen, the night before she went away; and grandmother brought her back into the room in the night; and I thought maybe she'd been to see *you*, before she went, for I heard grandmother whisper to her, 'Now go to sleep; and remember never to tell.' "

I asked him if he ever mentioned his suspicions to his sister. He said he never did; but after he heard the cough, if he saw her playing with other children on that side of the house, he always tried to coax her round to the other side, for fear they would hear me cough, too. He said he had kept a close lookout for Dr. Flint, and if he saw him speak to a constable, or a patrol, he always told grandmother. I now recollected that I had seen him manifest uneasiness, when people were on that side of the house, and I had at the time been puzzled to conjecture a motive for his actions. Such prudence may seem extraordinary in a boy of twelve years, but slaves, being surrounded by mysteries, deceptions, and dangers, early learn to be suspicious and watchful, and prematurely cautious and cunning. He had never asked a question of grandmother, or uncle Phillip, and I had often heard him chime in with other children, when they spoke of my being at the north.

I told him I was now really going to the Free States, and if he was a good, honest boy, and a loving child to his dear old grandmother, the Lord would bless him, and bring him to me, and we and Ellen would live together. He began to tell me that grandmother had not eaten any thing all day. While he was speaking, the door was unlocked, and she came in with a small bag of money, which she wanted me to take. I begged her to keep a part of it, at least, to pay for Benny's being sent to the north; but she insisted, while her tears

1. Zechariah 11.12–13; Matthew 26.15, 27.3, 27.9.

were falling fast, that I should take the whole. "You may be sick among strangers," she said, "and they would send you to the poor-house to die." Ah, that good grandmother!

For the last time I went up to my nook. Its desolate appearance no longer chilled me, for the light of hope had risen in my soul. Yet, even with the blessed prospect of freedom before me, I felt very sad at leaving forever that old homestead, where I had been sheltered so long by the dear old grandmother; where I had dreamed my first young dream of love; and where, after that had faded away, my children came to twine themselves so closely round my desolate heart. As the hour approached for me to leave, I again descended to the storeroom. My grandmother and Benny were there. She took me by the hand, and said, "Linda, let us pray." We knelt down together, with my child pressed to my heart, and my other arm round the faithful, loving old friend I was about to leave forever. On no other occasion has it ever been my lot to listen to so fervent a supplication for mercy and protection. It thrilled through my heart, and inspired me with trust in God.

Peter was waiting for me in the street. I was soon by his side, faint in body, but strong of purpose. I did not look back upon the old place, though I felt that I should never see it again.

XXX. Northward Bound

I never could tell how we reached the wharf. My brain was all of a whirl, and my limbs tottered under me. At an appointed place we met my uncle Phillip, who had started before us on a different route, that he might reach the wharf first, and give us timely warning if there was any danger. A row-boat was in readiness. As I was about to step in, I felt something pull me gently, and turning round I saw Benny, looking pale and anxious. He whispered in my ear, "I've been peeping into the doctor's window, and he's at home. Good by, mother. Don't cry; I'll come." He hastened away. I clasped the hand of my good uncle, to whom I owed so much, and of Peter, the brave, generous friend who had volunteered to run such terrible risks to secure my safety. To this day I remember how his bright face beamed with joy, when he told me he had discovered a safe method for me to escape. Yet that intelligent, enterprising, noble-hearted man was a chattel! liable, by the laws of a country that calls itself civilized, to be sold with horses and pigs! We parted in silence. Our hearts were all too full for words!

Swiftly the boat glided over the water. After a while, one of the sailors said, "Don't be down-hearted, madam. We will take you safely to your husband, in ——." At first I could not imagine what he meant;

but I had presence of mind to think that it probably referred to something the captain had told him; so I thanked him, and said I hoped we should have pleasant weather.

When I entered the vessel the captain came forward to meet me. He was an elderly man, with a pleasant countenance. He showed me to a little box of a cabin, where sat my friend Fanny. She started as if she had seen a spectre. She gazed on me in utter astonishment, and exclaimed, "Linda, can this be *you*? or is it your ghost?" When we were locked in each other's arms, my overwrought feelings could no longer be restrained. My sobs reached the ears of the captain, who came and very kindly reminded us, that for his safety, as well as our own, it would be prudent for us not to attract any attention. He said that when there was a sail in sight he wished us to keep below; but at other times, he had no objection to our being on deck. He assured us that he would keep a good lookout, and if we acted prudently, he thought we should be in no danger. He had represented us as women going to meet our husbands in ——. We thanked him, and promised to observe carefully all the directions he gave us.

Fanny and I now talked by ourselves, low and quietly, in our little cabin. She told me of the sufferings she had gone through in making her escape, and of her terrors while she was concealed in her mother's house. Above all, she dwelt on the agony of separation from all her children on that dreadful auction day. She could scarcely credit me, when I told her of the place where I had passed nearly seven years. "We have the same sorrows," said I. "No," replied she, "you are going to see your children soon, and there is no hope that I shall ever even hear from mine."

The vessel was soon under way, but we made slow progress. The wind was against us. I should not have cared for this, if we had been out of sight of the town; but until there were miles of water between us and our enemies, we were filled with constant apprehensions that the constables would come on board. Neither could I feel quite at ease with the captain and his men. I was an entire stranger to that class of people, and I had heard that sailors were rough, and sometimes cruel. We were so completely in their power, that if they were bad men, our situation would be dreadful. Now that the captain was paid for our passage, might he not be tempted to make more money by giving us up to those who claimed us as property? I was naturally of a confiding disposition, but slavery had made me suspicious of every body. Fanny did not share my distrust of the captain or his men. She said she was afraid at first, but she had been on board three days while the vessel lay in the dock, and nobody had betrayed her, or treated her otherwise than kindly.

The captain soon came to advise us to go on deck for fresh air. His friendly and respectful manner, combined with Fanny's testimony, reassured me, and we went with him. He placed us in a comfortable seat, and occasionally entered into conversation. He told us he was a Southerner by birth, and had spent the greater part of his life in the Slave States, and that he had recently lost a brother who traded in slaves. "But," said he, "it is a pitiable and degrading business, and I always felt ashamed to acknowledge my brother in connection with it." As we passed Snaky Swamp, he pointed to it, and said, "There is a slave territory that defies all the laws." I thought of the terrible days I had spent there, and though it was not called Dismal Swamp,[1] it made me feel very dismal as I looked at it.

I shall never forget that night. The balmy air of spring was so refreshing! And how shall I describe my sensations when we were fairly sailing on Chesapeake Bay? O, the beautiful sunshine! the exhilarating breeze! and I could enjoy them without fear or restraint. I had never realized what grand things air and sunlight are till I had been deprived of them.

Ten days after we left land we were approaching Philadelphia. The captain said we should arrive there in the night, but he thought we had better wait till morning, and go on shore in broad daylight, as the best way to avoid suspicion.

I replied, "You know best. But will you stay on board and protect us?"

He saw that I was suspicious, and he said he was sorry, now that he had brought us to the end of our voyage, to find I had so little confidence in him. Ah, if he had ever been a slave he would have known how difficult it was to trust a white man. He assured us that we might sleep through the night without fear; that he would take care we were not left unprotected. Be it said to the honor of this captain, Southerner as he was, that if Fanny and I had been white ladies, and our passage lawfully engaged, he could not have treated us more respectfully. My intelligent friend, Peter, had rightly estimated the character of the man to whose honor he had intrusted us.

The next morning I was on deck as soon as the day dawned. I called Fanny to see the sun rise, for the first time in our lives, on free soil; for such I *then* believed it to be. We watched the reddening sky, and saw the great orb come up slowly out of the water, as it seemed. Soon the waves began to sparkle, and every thing caught the beautiful glow. Before us lay the city of strangers. We looked at each other, and the eyes of both were moistened with tears. We had escaped from slavery, and we supposed ourselves to be safe from the hunters. But we were alone in the world, and we had left dear ties behind us; ties cruelly sundered by the demon Slavery.

1. Ranging across Virginia and North Carolina, it sometimes served as a hiding place for those fleeing slavery.

XXXI. Incidents in Philadelphia

I had heard that the poor slave had many friends at the north. I trusted we should find some of them. Meantime, we would take it for granted that all were friends, till they proved to the contrary. I sought out the kind captain, thanked him for his attentions, and told him I should never cease to be grateful for the service he had rendered us. I gave him a message to the friends I had left at home, and he promised to deliver it. We were placed in a row-boat, and in about fifteen minutes were landed on a wood wharf in Philadelphia. As I stood looking round, the friendly captain touched me on the shoulder, and said, "There is a respectable-looking colored man behind you. I will speak to him about the New York trains, and tell him you wish to go directly on." I thanked him, and asked him to direct me to some shops where I could buy gloves and veils. He did so, and said he would talk with the colored man till I returned. I made what haste I could. Constant exercise on board the vessel, and frequent rubbing with salt water, had nearly restored the use of my limbs. The noise of the great city confused me, but I found the shops, and bought some double veils and gloves for Fanny and myself. The shopman told me they were so many levies.[1] I had never heard the word before, but I did not tell him so. I thought if he knew I was a stranger he might ask me where I came from. I gave him a gold piece, and when he returned the change, I counted it, and found out how much a levy was. I made my way back to the wharf, where the captain introduced me to the colored man, as the Rev. Jeremiah Durham, minister of Bethel church. He took me by the hand, as if I had been an old friend. He told us we were too late for the morning cars to New York, and must wait until the evening, or the next morning. He invited me to go home with him, assuring me that his wife would give me a cordial welcome; and for my friend he would provide a home with one of his neighbors. I thanked him for so much kindness to strangers, and told him if I must be detained, I should like to hunt up some people who formerly went from our part of the country. Mr. Durham insisted that I should dine with him, and then he would assist me in finding my friends. The sailors came to bid us good by. I shook their hardy hands, with tears in my eyes. They had all been kind to us, and they had rendered us a greater service than they could possibly conceive of.

I had never seen so large a city, or been in contact with so many people in the streets. It seemed as if those who passed looked at us

1. Short for "eleven-penny bit," a levy was a coin used in Pennsylvania, Maryland, and Virginia worth between 11 and 12½ cents.

with an expression of curiosity. My face was so blistered and peeled, by sitting on deck, in wind and sunshine, that I thought they could not easily decide to what nation I belonged.

Mrs. Durham met me with a kindly welcome, without asking any questions. I was tired, and her friendly manner was a sweet refreshment. God bless her! I was sure that she had comforted other weary hearts, before I received her sympathy. She was surrounded by her husband and children, in a home made sacred by protecting laws. I thought of my own children, and sighed.

After dinner Mr. Durham went with me in quest of the friends I had spoken of. They went from my native town, and I anticipated much pleasure in looking on familiar faces. They were not at home, and we retraced our steps through streets delightfully clean. On the way, Mr. Durham observed that I had spoken to him of a daughter I expected to meet; that he was surprised, for I looked so young he had taken me for a single woman. He was approaching a subject on which I was extremely sensitive. He would ask about my husband next, I thought, and if I answered him truly, what would he think of me? I told him I had two children, one in New York the other at the south. He asked some further questions, and I frankly told him some of the most important events of my life. It was painful for me to do it; but I would not deceive him. If he was desirous of being my friend, I thought he ought to know how far I was worthy of it. "Excuse me, if I have tried your feelings," said he. "I did not question you from idle curiosity. I wanted to understand your situation, in order to know whether I could be of any service to you, or your little girl. Your straight-forward answers do you credit; but don't answer every body so openly. It might give some heartless people a pretext for treating you with contempt."

That word *contempt* burned me like coals of fire. I replied, "God alone knows how I have suffered; and He, I trust, will forgive me. If I am permitted to have my children, I intend to be a good mother, and to live in such a manner that people cannot treat me with contempt."

"I respect your sentiments," said he. "Place your trust in God, and be governed by good principles, and you will not fail to find friends."

When we reached home, I went to my room, glad to shut out the world for a while. The words he had spoken made an indelible impression upon me. They brought up great shadows from the mournful past. In the midst of my meditations I was startled by a knock at the door. Mrs. Durham entered, her face all beaming with kindness, to say that there was an anti-slavery friend down stairs, who would like to see me. I overcame my dread of encountering strangers, and went with her. Many questions were asked concerning my experiences, and my escape from slavery; but I observed how careful they all were not to say any thing that might wound my feelings. How gratifying this was, can be fully understood only by those who have been accustomed to be treated as if they were not included within the pale of human beings. The anti-slavery friend had come to inquire into my plans, and to offer assistance, if needed. Fanny was comfortably established, for the present, with a friend of Mr. Durham. The Anti-Slavery Society agreed to pay her expenses to New York. The same was offered to me, but I declined to accept it; telling them that my grandmother had given me sufficient to pay my expenses to the end of my journey. We were urged to remain in Philadelphia a few days, until some suitable escort could be found for us. I gladly accepted the proposition, for I had a dread of meeting slaveholders, and some dread also of railroads. I had never entered a railroad car in my life, and it seemed to me quite an important event.

That night I sought my pillow with feelings I had never carried to it before. I verily believed myself to be a free woman. I was wakeful for a long time, and I had no sooner fallen asleep, than I was roused by fire-bells. I jumped up, and hurried on my clothes. Where I came from, every body hastened to dress themselves on such occasions. The white people thought a great fire might be used as a good opportunity for insurrection, and that it was best to be in readiness; and the colored people were ordered out to labor in extinguishing the flames. There was but one engine in our town, and colored women and children were often required to drag it to the river's edge and fill it. Mrs. Durham's daughter slept in the same room with me, and seeing that she slept through all the din, I thought it was my duty to wake her. "What's the matter?" said she, rubbing her eyes.

"They're screaming fire in the streets, and the bells are ringing," I replied.

"What of that?" said she, drowsily. "We are used to it. We never get up, without the fire is very near. What good would it do?"

I was quite surprised that it was not necessary for us to go and help fill the engine. I was an ignorant child, just beginning to learn how things went on in great cities.

At daylight, I heard women crying fresh fish, berries, radishes, and various other things. All this was new to me. I dressed myself at an early hour, and sat at the window to watch that unknown tide of life. Philadelphia seemed to me a wonderfully great place. At the breakfast table, my idea of going out to drag the engine was laughed over, and I joined in the mirth.

I went to see Fanny, and found her so well contented among her new friends that she was in no haste to leave. I was also very happy with my kind hostess. She had had advantages for education, and was vastly my superior. Every day, almost every hour, I was adding to my little stock of knowledge. She took me out to see the city as much as she deemed prudent. One day she took me to an artist's room, and showed me the portraits of some of her children. I had never seen any paintings of colored people before, and they seemed to me beautiful.

At the end of five days, one of Mrs. Durham's friends offered to accompany us to New York the following morning. As I held the hand of my good hostess in a parting clasp, I longed to know whether her husband had repeated to her what I had told him. I supposed he had, but she never made any allusion to it. I presume it was the delicate silence of womanly sympathy.

When Mr. Durham handed us our tickets, he said, "I am afraid you will have a disagreeable ride; but I could not procure tickets for the first class cars."

Supposing I had not given him money enough, I offered more. "O, no," said he, "they could not be had for any money. They don't allow colored people to go in the first-class cars."

This was the first chill to my enthusiasm about the Free States. Colored people were allowed to ride in a filthy box, behind white people, at the south, but there they were not required to pay for the privilege. It made me sad to find how the north aped the customs of slavery.

We were stowed away in a large, rough car, with windows on each side, too high for us to look out without standing up. It was crowded with people, apparently of all nations. There were plenty of beds and cradles, containing screaming and kicking babies. Every other man had a cigar or pipe in his mouth, and jugs of whiskey were handed round freely. The fumes of the whiskey and the dense tobacco smoke were sickening to my senses, and my mind was equally nauseated by the coarse jokes and ribald songs around me. It was a very disagreeable ride. Since that time there has been some improvement in these matters.

XXXII. The Meeting of Mother and Daughter

When we arrived in New York, I was half crazed by the crowd of coachmen calling out, "Carriage, ma'am?" We bargained with one to take us to Sullivan Street for twelve shillings. A burly Irishman stepped up and said, "I'll tak' ye for sax shillings." The reduction of half the price was an object to us, and we asked if he could take us right away. "Troth an I will, ladies," he replied. I noticed that the hackmen smiled at each other, and I inquired whether his conveyance was decent. "Yes, it's dacent it is, marm. Devil a bit would I be after takin' ladies in a cab that was not dacent." We gave him our checks. He went for the baggage, and soon reappeared, saying, "This way, if you plase, ladies." We followed, and found our trunks on a truck,[1] and we were invited to take our seats on them. We told him that was not what we bargained for, and he must take the trunks off. He swore they should not be touched till we had paid him six shillings. In our situation it was not prudent to attract attention, and I was about to pay him what he required, when a man near by shook his head for me not to do it. After a great ado we got rid of the Irishman, and had our trunks fastened on a hack. We had been recommended to a boarding-house in Sullivan Street, and thither we drove. There Fanny and I separated. The Anti-Slavery Society[2] provided a home for her, and I afterwards heard of her in prosperous circumstances. I sent for an old friend from my part of the country, who had for some time been doing business in New York. He came immediately. I told him I wanted to go to my daughter, and asked him to aid me in procuring an interview.

I cautioned him not to let it be known to the family that I had just arrived from the south, because they supposed I had been at the north seven years. He told me there was a colored woman in Brooklyn who came from the same town I did, and I had better go to her house, and have my daughter meet me there. I accepted the proposition thankfully, and he agreed to escort me to Brooklyn. We crossed Fulton ferry, went up Myrtle Avenue, and stopped at the house he designated. I was just about to enter, when two girls passed. My friend called my attention to them. I turned, and recognized in the eldest, Sarah, the daughter of a woman who used to live with my grandmother, but who had left the south years ago. Surprised and rejoiced at this unexpected meeting, I threw my arms round her, and inquired concerning her mother.

"You take no notice of the other girl," said my friend. I turned, and there stood my Ellen! I pressed her to my heart, then held her away from me to take a look at her. She had changed a good deal in the two years since I parted from her. Signs of neglect could be discerned by eyes less observing than a mother's. My friend invited us all to go into the house; but Ellen said she had been sent of an errand, which she would do as quickly as possible, and go home and ask Mrs. Hobbs to let her come and see me. It was agreed that I should send for her the next day. Her companion, Sarah, hastened to tell her mother of my arrival. When I entered the house, I found the mistress of it absent, and I waited for her return. Before I saw her, I heard her saying, "Where is Linda Brent? I used to know her father and mother." Soon Sarah came with her mother. So there was quite

1. An open cart meant for hauling heavy cargo.
2. The American Anti-Slavery Society, founded in 1833.

a company of us, all from my grandmother's neighborhood. These friends gathered round me and questioned me eagerly. They laughed, they cried, and they shouted. They thanked God that I had got away from my persecutors and was safe on Long Island. It was a day of great excitement. How different from the silent days I had passed in my dreary den!

The next morning was Sunday. My first waking thoughts were occupied with the note I was to send to Mrs. Hobbs, the lady with whom Ellen lived. That I had recently come into that vicinity was evident; otherwise I should have sooner inquired for my daughter. It would not do to let them know I had just arrived from the south, for that would involve the suspicion of my having been harbored there, and might bring trouble, if not ruin, on several people.

I like a straightforward course, and am always reluctant to resort to subterfuges. So far as my ways have been crooked, I charge them all upon slavery. It was that system of violence and wrong which now left me no alternative but to enact a falsehood. I began my note by stating that I had recently arrived from Canada, and was very desirous to have my daughter come to see me. She came and brought a message from Mrs. Hobbs, inviting me to her house, and assuring me that I need not have any fears. The conversation I had with my child did not leave my mind at ease. When I asked if she was well treated, she answered yes; but there was no heartiness in the tone, and it seemed to me that she said it from an unwillingness to have me troubled on her account. Before she left me, she asked very earnestly, "Mother, when will you take me to live with you?" It made me sad to think that I could not give her a home till I went to work and earned the means; and that might take me a long time. When she was placed with Mrs. Hobbs, the agreement was that she should be sent to school. She had been there two years, and was now nine years old, and she scarcely knew her letters. There was no excuse for this, for there were good public schools in Brooklyn, to which she could have been sent without expense.

She staid with me till dark, and I went home with her. I was received in a friendly manner by the family, and all agreed in saying that Ellen was a useful, good girl. Mrs. Hobbs looked me coolly in the face, and said, "I suppose you know that my cousin, Mr. Sands, has *given* her to my eldest daughter. She will make a nice waiting-maid for her when she grows up." I did not answer a word. How *could* she, who knew by experience the strength of a mother's love, and who was perfectly aware of the relation Mr. Sands bore to my children,—how *could* she look me in the face, while she thrust such a dagger into my heart?

I was no longer surprised that they had kept her in such a state of ignorance. Mr. Hobbs had formerly been wealthy, but he had failed, and afterwards obtained a subordinate situation in the Custom House. Perhaps they expected to return to the south some day; and Ellen's knowledge was quite sufficient for a slave's condition. I was impatient to go to work and earn money, that I might change the uncertain position of my children. Mr. Sands had not kept his promise to emancipate them. I had also been deceived about Ellen. What security had I with regard to Benjamin? I felt that I had none.

I returned to my friend's house in an uneasy state of mind. In order to protect my children, it was necessary that I should own myself. I called myself free, and sometimes felt so; but I knew I was insecure. I sat down that night and wrote a civil letter to Dr. Flint, asking him to state the lowest terms on which he would sell me; and as I belonged by law to his daughter, I wrote to her also, making a similar request.

Since my arrival at the north I had not been unmindful of my dear brother William. I had made diligent inquiries for him, and having heard of him in Boston, I went thither. When I arrived there, I found he had gone to New Bedford. I wrote to that place, and was informed he had gone on a whaling voyage, and would not return for some months. I went back to New York to get employment near Ellen. I received an answer from Dr. Flint, which gave me no encouragement. He advised me to return and submit myself to my rightful owners, and then any request I might make would be granted. I lent this letter to a friend, who lost it; otherwise I would present a copy to my readers.

XXXIII. A Home Found

My greatest anxiety now was to obtain employment. My health was greatly improved, though my limbs continued to trouble me with swelling whenever I walked much. The greatest difficulty in my way was, that those who employed strangers required a recommendation; and in my peculiar position, I could, of course, obtain no certificates from the families I had so faithfully served.

One day an acquaintance told me of a lady who wanted a nurse for her babe, and I immediately applied for the situation. The lady told me she preferred to have one who had been a mother, and accustomed to the care of infants. I told her I had nursed two babes of my own. She asked me many questions, but, to my great relief, did not require a recommendation from my former employers. She told me she was an English woman, and that was a pleasant circumstance to me, because I had heard they had less prejudice against color than Americans entertained. It was agreed that we should try each other for a week. The trial proved satisfactory to both parties, and I was engaged for a month.

The heavenly Father had been most merciful to me in leading me to this place. Mrs. Bruce was a kind and gentle lady, and proved a true and sympathizing friend. Before the stipulated month expired, the necessity of passing up and down stairs frequently, caused my limbs to swell so painfully, that I became unable to perform my duties. Many ladies would have thoughtlessly discharged me; but Mrs. Bruce made arrangements to save me steps, and employed a physician to attend upon me. I had not yet told her that I was a fugitive slave. She noticed that I was often sad, and kindly inquired the cause. I spoke of being separated from my children, and from relatives who were dear to me; but I did not mention the constant feeling of insecurity which oppressed my spirits. I longed for some one to confide in; but I had been so deceived by white people, that I had lost all confidence in them. If they spoke kind words to me, I thought it was for some selfish purpose. I had entered this family with the distrustful feelings I had brought with me out of slavery; but ere six months had passed, I found that the gentle deportment of Mrs. Bruce and the smiles of her lovely babe were thawing my chilled heart. My narrow mind also began to expand under the influences of her intelligent conversation, and the opportunities for reading, which were gladly allowed me whenever I had leisure from my duties. I gradually became more energetic and more cheerful.

The old feeling of insecurity, especially with regard to my children, often threw its dark shadow across my sunshine. Mrs. Bruce offered me a home for Ellen; but pleasant as it would have been, I did not dare to accept it, for fear of offending the Hobbs family. Their knowledge of my precarious situation placed me in their power; and I felt that it was important for me to keep on the right side of them, till, by dint of labor and economy, I could make a home for my children. I was far from feeling satisfied with Ellen's situation. She was not well cared for. She sometimes came to New York to visit me; but she generally brought a request from Mrs. Hobbs that I would buy her a pair of shoes, or some article of clothing. This was accompanied by a promise of payment when Mr. Hobbs's salary at the Custom House became due; but some how or other the pay-day never came. Thus many dollars of my earnings were expended to keep my child comfortably clothed. That, however, was a slight trouble, compared with the fear that their pecuniary embarrassments might induce them to sell my precious young daughter. I knew they were in constant communication with Southerners, and had frequent opportunities to do it. I have stated that when Dr. Flint put Ellen in jail, at two years old, she had an inflammation of the eyes, occasioned by measles. This disease still troubled her; and kind Mrs. Bruce proposed that she should come to New York for a while, to be under the care of Dr. Elliott, a well known oculist. It did not occur to me that there was any thing improper in a mother's making such a request; but Mrs. Hobbs was very angry, and refused to let her go. Situated as I was, it was not politic to insist upon it. I made no complaint, but I longed to be entirely free to act a mother's part towards my children. The next time I went over to Brooklyn, Mrs. Hobbs, as if to apologize for her anger, told me she had employed her own physician to attend to Ellen's eyes, and that she had refused my request because she did not consider it safe to trust her in New York. I accepted the explanation in silence; but she had told me that my child *belonged* to her daughter, and I suspected that her real motive was a fear of my conveying her property away from her. Perhaps I did her injustice; but my knowledge of Southerners made it difficult for me to feel otherwise.

Sweet and bitter were mixed in the cup of my life, and I was thankful that it had ceased to be entirely bitter. I loved Mrs. Bruce's babe. When it laughed and crowed in my face, and twined its little tender arms confidingly about my neck, it made me think of the time when Benny and Ellen were babies, and my wounded heart was soothed. One bright morning, as I stood at the window, tossing baby in my arms, my attention was attracted by a young man in sailor's dress, who was closely observing every house as he passed. I looked at him earnestly. Could it be my brother William? It *must* be he—and yet, how changed! I placed the baby safely, flew down stairs, opened the front door, beckoned to the sailor, and in less than a minute I was clasped in my brother's arms. How much we had to tell each other! How we laughed, and how we cried, over each other's adventures! I took him to Brooklyn, and again saw him with Ellen, the dear child whom he had loved and tended so carefully, while I was shut up in my miserable den. He staid in New York a week. His old feelings of affection for me and Ellen were as lively as ever. There are no bonds so strong as those which are formed by suffering together.

XXXIV. The Old Enemy Again

My young mistress, Miss Emily Flint, did not return any answer to my letter requesting her to consent to my being sold. But after a while, I received a reply, which purported to be written by her younger brother. In order rightly to enjoy the contents of this letter, the reader must bear in mind that the Flint family supposed I had been at the north many years. They had no idea that I knew of the doctor's three excursions to New York in search of me; that I had heard his voice, when he came to borrow five hundred dollars for that purpose; and that I had seen him pass on his way to the steamboat. Neither were they aware that all the particulars of aunt Nancy's death and burial were conveyed to me at the time they occurred. I have kept the letter, of which I herewith subjoin a copy:—

"Your letter to sister was received a few days ago. I gather from it that you are desirous of returning to your native place, among your friends and relatives. We were all gratified with the contents of your letter; and let me assure you that if any members of the family have had any feeling of resentment towards you, they feel it no longer. We all sympathize with you in your unfortunate condition, and are ready to do all in our power to make you contented and happy. It is difficult for you to return home as a free person. If you were purchased by your grandmother, it is doubtful whether you would be permitted to remain, although it would be lawful for you to do so. If a servant should be allowed to purchase herself, after absenting herself so long from her owners, and return free, it would have an injurious effect. From your letter, I think your situation must be hard and uncomfortable. Come home. You have it in your power to be reinstated in our affections. We would receive you with open arms and tears of joy. You need not apprehend any unkind treatment, as we have not put ourselves to any trouble or expense to get you. Had we done so, perhaps we should feel otherwise. You know my sister was always attached to you, and that you were never treated as a slave. You were never put to hard work, nor exposed to field labor. On the contrary, you were taken into the house, and treated as one of us, and almost as free; and we, at least, felt that you were above disgracing yourself by running away. Believing you may be induced to come home voluntarily has induced me to write for my sister. The family will be rejoiced to see you; and your poor old grandmother expressed a great desire to have you come, when she heard your letter read. In her old age she needs the consolation of having her children round her. Doubtless you have heard of the death of your aunt. She was a faithful servant, and a faithful member of the Episcopal church. In her Christian life she taught us how to live—and, O, too high the price of knowledge, she taught us how to die! Could you have seen us round her death bed, with her mother, all mingling our tears in one common stream, you would have thought the same heartfelt tie existed between a master and his servant, as between a mother and her child. But this subject is too painful to dwell upon. I must bring my letter to a close. If you are contented to stay away from your old grandmother, your child, and the friends who love you, stay where you are. We shall never trouble ourselves to apprehend you. But should you prefer to come home, we will do all that we can to make you happy. If you do not wish to remain in the family, I know that father, by our persuasion, will be induced to let you be purchased by any person you may choose in our community. You will please answer this as soon as possible, and let us know your decision. Sister sends much love to you. In the mean time believe me your sincere friend and well wisher."

This letter was signed by Emily's brother, who was as yet a mere lad. I knew, by the style, that it was not written by a person of his age, and though the writing was disguised, I had been made too unhappy by it, in former years, not to recognize at once the hand of Dr. Flint. O, the hypocrisy of slaveholders! Did the old fox suppose I was goose enough to go into such a trap? Verily, he relied too much on "the stupidity of the African race." I did not return the family of Flints any thanks for their cordial invitation—a remissness for which I was, no doubt, charged with base ingratitude.

Not long afterwards I received a letter from one of my friends at the south, informing me that Dr. Flint was about to visit the north. The letter had been delayed, and I supposed he might be already on the way. Mrs. Bruce did not know I was a fugitive. I told her that important business called me to Boston, where my brother then was, and asked permission to bring a friend to supply my place as nurse, for a fortnight. I started on my journey immediately; and as soon as I arrived, I wrote to my grandmother that if Benny came, he must be sent to Boston. I knew she was only waiting for a good chance to send him north, and, fortunately, she had the legal power to do so, without asking leave of any body. She was a free woman; and when my children were purchased, Mr. Sands preferred to have the bill of sale drawn up in her name. It was conjectured that he advanced the money, but it was not known. At the south, a gentleman may have a shoal of colored children without any disgrace; but if he is known to purchase them, with the view of setting them free, the example is thought to be dangerous to their "peculiar institution," and he becomes unpopular.

There was a good opportunity to send Benny in a vessel coming directly to New York. He was put on board with a letter to a friend, who was requested to see him off to Boston. Early one morning, there was a loud rap at my door, and in rushed Benjamin, all out of breath. "O mother!" he exclaimed, "here I am! I run all the way; and I come all alone. How d'you do?"

O reader, can you imagine my joy? No, you cannot, unless you have been a slave mother. Benjamin rattled away as fast as his tongue could go. "Mother, why don't you bring Ellen here? I went over to Brooklyn to see her, and she felt very bad when I bid her good by. She said, 'O Ben, I wish I was going too.' I thought she'd know ever so much; but she don't know so much as I do; for I can read, and she can't. And, mother, I lost all my clothes coming. What can I do to get some more? I 'spose free boys can get along here at the north as well as white boys."

I did not like to tell the sanguine, happy little fellow how much he was mistaken. I took him to a tailor, and procured a change of clothes. The rest of the day was spent in mutual asking and answering of questions, with the wish constantly repeated that the good old grandmother was with us, and frequent injunctions from Benny to write to her immediately, and be sure to tell her every thing about his voyage, and his journey to Boston.

Dr. Flint made his visit to New York, and made every exertion to call upon me, and invite me to return with him; but not being able to ascertain where I was, his hospitable intentions were frustrated, and the affectionate family, who were waiting for me with "open arms," were doomed to disappointment.

As soon as I knew he was safely at home, I placed Benjamin in the care of my brother William, and returned to Mrs. Bruce. There I remained through the winter and spring, endeavoring to perform my duties faithfully, and finding a good degree of happiness in the attractions of baby Mary, the considerate kindness of her excellent mother, and occasional interviews with my darling daughter.

But when summer came, the old feeling of insecurity haunted me. It was necessary for me to take little Mary out daily, for exercise and fresh air, and the city was swarming with Southerners, some of whom might recognize me. Hot weather brings out snakes and slaveholders, and I like one class of the venomous creatures as little as I do the other. What a comfort it is, to be free to *say* so!

XXXV. Prejudice against Color

It was a relief to my mind to see preparations for leaving the city. We went to Albany in the steamboat Knickerbocker. When the gong sounded for tea, Mrs. Bruce said, "Linda, it is late, and you and baby had better come to the table with me." I replied, "I know it is time baby had her supper, but I had rather not go with you, if you please. I am afraid of being insulted." "O no, not if you are with *me*," she said. I saw several white nurses go with their ladies, and I ventured to do the same. We were at the extreme end of the table. I was no sooner seated, than a gruff voice said, "Get up! You know you are not allowed to sit here." I looked up, and, to my astonishment and indignation, saw that the speaker was a colored man. If his office required him to enforce the by-laws of the boat, he might, at least, have done it politely. I replied, "I shall not get up, unless the captain comes and takes me up." No cup of tea was offered me, but

Mrs. Bruce handed me hers and called for another. I looked to see whether the other nurses were treated in a similar manner. They were all properly waited on.

Next morning, when we stopped at Troy for breakfast, every body was making a rush for the table. Mrs. Bruce said, "Take my arm, Linda, and we'll go in together." The landlord heard her, and said, "Madam, will you allow your nurse and baby to take breakfast with my family?" I knew this was to be attributed to my complexion; but he spoke courteously, and therefore I did not mind it.

At Saratoga we found the United States Hotel crowded, and Mr. Bruce took one of the cottages belonging to the hotel. I had thought, with gladness, of going to the quiet of the country, where I should meet few people, but here I found myself in the midst of a swarm of Southerners. I looked round me with fear and trembling, dreading to see some one who would recognize me. I was rejoiced to find that we were to stay but a short time.

We soon returned to New York, to make arrangements for spending the remainder of the summer at Rockaway. While the laundress was putting the clothes in order, I took an opportunity to go over to Brooklyn to see Ellen. I met her going to a grocery store, and the first words she said, were, "O, mother, don't go to Mrs. Hobbs's. Her brother, Mr. Thorne, has come from the south, and may be he'll tell where you are." I accepted the warning. I told her I was going away with Mrs. Bruce the next day, and would try to see her when I came back.

Being in servitude to the Anglo-Saxon race, I was not put into a "Jim Crow car,"[1] on our way to Rockaway, neither was I invited to ride through the streets on the top of trunks in a truck; but every where I found the same manifestations of that cruel prejudice, which so discourages the feelings, and represses the energies of the colored people. We reached Rockaway before dark, and put up at the Pavilion—a large hotel, beautifully situated by the sea-side—a great resort of the fashionable world. Thirty or forty nurses were there, of a great variety of nations. Some of the ladies had colored waiting-maids and coachmen, but I was the only nurse tinged with the blood of Africa. When the tea bell rang, I took little Mary and followed the other nurses. Supper was served in a long hall. A young man, who had the ordering of things, took the circuit of the table two or three times, and finally pointed me to a seat at the lower end of it. As there was but one chair, I sat down and took the child in my lap. Whereupon the young man came to me and said, in the blandest manner possible, "Will you please to seat the little girl in the chair, and stand behind it and feed her? After they have done, you will be shown to the kitchen, where you will have a good supper."

1. A train car to which black passengers were restricted.

This was the climax! I found it hard to preserve my self-control, when I looked round, and saw women who were nurses, as I was, and only one shade lighter in complexion, eyeing me with a defiant look, as if my presence were a contamination. However, I said nothing. I quietly took the child in my arms, went to our room, and refused to go to the table again. Mr. Bruce ordered meals to be sent to the room for little Mary and I. This answered for a few days; but the waiters of the establishment were white, and they soon began to complain, saying they were not hired to wait on negroes. The landlord requested Mr. Bruce to send me down to my meals, because his servants rebelled against bringing them up, and the colored servants of other boarders were dissatisfied because all were not treated alike.

My answer was that the colored servants ought to be dissatisfied with *themselves,* for not having too much self-respect to submit to such treatment; that there was no difference in the price of board for colored and white servants, and there was no justification for difference of treatment. I staid a month after this, and finding I was resolved to stand up for my rights, they concluded to treat me well. Let every colored man and woman do this, and eventually we shall cease to be trampled under foot by our oppressors.

XXXVI. The Hair-Breadth Escape

After we returned to New York, I took the earliest opportunity to go and see Ellen. I asked to have her called down stairs; for I supposed Mrs. Hobbs's southern brother might still be there, and I was desirous to avoid seeing him, if possible. But Mrs. Hobbs came to the kitchen, and insisted on my going up stairs. "My brother wants to see you," said she, "and he is sorry you seem to shun him. He knows you are living in New York. He told me to say to you that he owes thanks to good old aunt Martha for too many little acts of kindness for him to be base enough to betray her grandchild."

This Mr. Thorne had become poor and reckless long before he left the south, and such persons had much rather go to one of the faithful old slaves to borrow a dollar, or get a good dinner, than to go to one whom they consider an equal. It was such acts of kindness as these for which he professed to feel grateful to my grandmother. I wished he had kept at a distance, but as he was here, and knew where I was, I concluded there was nothing to be gained by trying to avoid him; on the contrary, it might be the means of exciting his ill will. I followed his sister up stairs. He met me in a very friendly manner, congratulated me on my escape from slavery, and hoped I had a good place, where I felt happy.

I continued to visit Ellen as often as I could. She, good thoughtful child, never forgot my hazardous situation, but always kept a vigilant lookout for my safety. She never made any complaint about her own inconveniences and troubles; but a mother's observing eye easily perceived that she was not happy. On the occasion of one of my visits I found her unusually serious. When I asked her what was the matter, she said nothing was the matter. But I insisted upon knowing what made her look so very grave. Finally, I ascertained that she felt troubled about the dissipation that was continually going on in the house. She was sent to the store very often for rum and brandy, and she felt ashamed to ask for it so often; and Mr. Hobbs and Mr. Thorne drank a great deal, and their hands trembled so that they had to call her to pour out the liquor for them. "But for all that," said she, "Mr. Hobbs is good to me, and I can't help liking him. I feel sorry for him." I tried to comfort her, by telling her that I had laid up a hundred dollars, and that before long I hoped to be able to give her and Benjamin a home, and send them to school. She was always desirous not to add to my troubles more than she could help, and I did not discover till years afterwards that Mr. Thorne's intemperance was not the only annoyance she suffered from him. Though he professed too much gratitude to my grandmother to injure any of her descendants, he had poured vile language into the ears of her innocent great-grandchild.

I usually went to Brooklyn to spend Sunday afternoon. One Sunday, I found Ellen anxiously waiting for me near the house. "O, mother," said she, "I've been waiting for you this long time. I'm afraid Mr. Thorne has written to tell Dr. Flint where you are. Make haste and come in. Mrs. Hobbs will tell you all about it!"

The story was soon told. While the children were playing in the grape-vine arbor, the day before, Mr. Thorne came out with a letter in his hand, which he tore up and scattered about. Ellen was sweeping the yard at the time, and having her mind full of suspicions of him, she picked up the pieces and carried them to the children, saying, "I wonder who Mr. Thorne has been writing to."

"I'm sure I don't know, and don't care," replied the oldest of the children; "and I don't see how it concerns you."

"But it does concern me," replied Ellen; "for I'm afraid he's been writing to the south about my mother."

They laughed at her, and called her a silly thing, but good-naturedly put the fragments of writing together, in order to read them to her. They were no sooner arranged, than the little girl exclaimed, "I declare, Ellen, I believe you are right."

The contents of Mr. Thorne's letter, as nearly as I can remember, were as follows: "I have seen your slave, Linda, and conversed with her. She can be taken very easily, if you manage prudently. There are enough of us here to swear to her identity as your property. I am a patriot, a lover of my country, and I do this as an act of justice to the laws." He concluded by informing the doctor of the street and number where I lived. The children carried the pieces to Mrs. Hobbs, who immediately went to her brother's room for an explanation. He was not to be found. The servants said they saw him go out with a letter in his hand, and they supposed he had gone to the post office. The natural inference was, that he had sent to Dr. Flint a copy of those fragments. When he returned, his sister accused him of it, and he did not deny the charge. He went immediately to his room, and the next morning he was missing. He had gone over to New York, before any of the family were astir.

It was evident that I had no time to lose; and I hastened back to the city with a heavy heart. Again I was to be torn from a comfortable home, and all my plans for the welfare of my children were to be frustrated by that demon Slavery! I now regretted that I never told Mrs. Bruce my story. I had not concealed it merely on account of being a fugitive; that would have made her anxious, but it would have excited sympathy in her kind heart. I valued her good opinion, and I was afraid of losing it, if I told her all the particulars of my sad story. But now I felt that it was necessary for her to know how I was situated. I had once left her abruptly, without explaining the reason, and it would not be proper to do it again. I went home resolved to tell her in the morning. But the sadness of my face attracted her attention, and, in answer to her kind inquiries, I poured out my full heart to her, before bed time. She listened with true womanly sympathy, and told me she would do all she could to protect me. How my heart blessed her!

Early the next morning, Judge Vanderpool and Lawyer Hopper were consulted. They said I had better leave the city at once, as the risk would be great if the case came to trial. Mrs. Bruce took me in a carriage to the house of one of her friends, where she assured me I should be safe until my brother could arrive, which would be in a few days. In the interval my thoughts were much occupied with Ellen. She was mine by birth, and she was also mine by Southern law, since my grandmother held the bill of sale that made her so. I did not feel that she was safe unless I had her with me. Mrs. Hobbs, who felt badly about her brother's treachery, yielded to my entreaties, on condition that she should return in ten days. I avoided making any promise. She came to me clad in very thin garments, all outgrown, and with a school satchel on her arm, containing a few articles. It was late in October, and I knew the child must suffer; and not daring to go out in the streets to purchase any thing, I took off my own flannel skirt and converted it into one for her. Kind Mrs. Bruce came to bid me good by, and when she saw that I had taken off my clothing for my child, the tears came to her eyes. She said, "Wait for me, Linda," and went out. She soon returned with a nice warm shawl and hood for Ellen. Truly, of such souls as hers are the kingdom of heaven.

My brother reached New York on Wednesday. Lawyer Hopper advised us to go to Boston by the Stonington route, as there was less Southern travel in that direction. Mrs. Bruce directed her servants to tell all inquirers that I formerly lived there, but had gone from the city.

We reached the steamboat Rhode Island in safety. That boat employed colored hands, but I knew that colored passengers were not admitted to the cabin. I was very desirous for the seclusion of the cabin, not only on account of exposure to the night air, but also to avoid observation. Lawyer Hopper was waiting on board for us. He spoke to the stewardess, and asked, as a particular favor, that she would treat us well. He said to me, "Go and speak to the captain yourself by and by. Take your little girl with you, and I am sure that he will not let her sleep on deck." With these kind words and a shake of the hand he departed.

The boat was soon on her way, bearing me rapidly from the friendly home where I had hoped to find security and rest. My brother had left me to purchase the tickets, thinking that I might have better success than he would. When the stewardess came to me, I paid what she asked, and she gave me three tickets with clipped corners. In the most unsophisticated manner I said, "You have made a mistake; I asked you for cabin tickets. I cannot possibly consent to sleep on deck with my little daughter." She assured me there was no mistake. She said on some of the routes colored people were allowed to sleep in the cabin, but not on this route, which was much travelled by the wealthy. I asked her to show me to the captain's office, and she said she would after tea. When the time came, I took Ellen by the hand and went to the captain, politely requesting him to change our tickets, as we should be very uncomfortable on deck. He said it was contrary to their custom, but he would see that we had berths below; he would also try to obtain comfortable seats for us in the cars; of that he was not certain, but he would speak to the conductor about it, when the boat arrived. I thanked him, and returned to the ladies' cabin. He came afterwards and told me that the conductor of the cars was on board, that he had spoken to him, and he had promised to take care of us. I was very much surprised at receiving so much kindness. I don't know whether the pleasing face of my little girl had won his heart, or whether the stewardess inferred from Lawyer Hopper's manner that I was a fugitive, and had pleaded with him in my behalf.

When the boat arrived at Stonington, the conductor kept his promise, and showed us to seats in the first car, nearest the engine.

He asked us to take seats next the door, but as he passed through, we ventured to move on toward the other end of the car. No incivility was offered us, and we reached Boston in safety.

The day after my arrival was one of the happiest of my life. I felt as if I was beyond the reach of the bloodhounds; and, for the first time during many years, I had both my children together with me. They greatly enjoyed their reunion, and laughed and chatted merrily. I watched them with a swelling heart. Their every motion delighted me.

I could not feel safe in New York, and I accepted the offer of a friend, that we should share expenses and keep house together. I represented to Mrs. Hobbs that Ellen must have some schooling, and must remain with me for that purpose. She felt ashamed of being unable to read or spell at her age, so instead of sending her to school with Benny, I instructed her myself till she was fitted to enter an intermediate school. The winter passed pleasantly, while I was busy with my needle, and my children with their books.

XXXVII. A Visit to England

In the spring, sad news came to me. Mrs. Bruce was dead. Never again, in this world, should I see her gentle face, or hear her sympathizing voice. I had lost an excellent friend, and little Mary had lost a tender mother. Mr. Bruce wished the child to visit some of her mother's relatives in England, and he was desirous that I should take charge of her. The little motherless one was accustomed to me, and attached to me, and I thought she would be happier in my care than in that of a stranger. I could also earn more in this way than I could by my needle. So I put Benny to a trade, and left Ellen to remain in the house with my friend and go to school.

We sailed from New York, and arrived in Liverpool after a pleasant voyage of twelve days. We proceeded directly to London, and took lodgings at the Adelaide Hotel. The supper seemed to me less luxurious than those I had seen in American hotels; but my situation was indescribably more pleasant. For the first time in my life I was in a place where I was treated according to my deportment, without reference to my complexion. I felt as if a great millstone had been lifted from my breast. Ensconced in a pleasant room, with my dear little charge, I laid my head on my pillow, for the first time, with the delightful consciousness of pure, unadulterated freedom.

As I had constant care of the child, I had little opportunity to see the wonders of that great city; but I watched the tide of life that flowed through the streets, and found it a strange contrast to the stagnation in our Southern towns. Mr. Bruce took his little daughter to spend some days with friends in Oxford Crescent, and of course it was necessary for me to accompany her. I had heard much of the systematic method of English education, and I was very desirous that my dear Mary should steer straight in the midst of so much propriety. I closely observed her little playmates and their nurses, being ready to take any lessons in the science of good management. The children were more rosy than American children, but I did not see that they differed materially in other respects. They were like all children—sometimes docile and sometimes wayward.

We next went to Steventon, in Berkshire. It was a small town, said to be the poorest in the county. I saw men working in the fields for six shillings, and seven shillings, a week, and women for sixpence, and sevenpence, a day, out of which they boarded themselves. Of course they lived in the most primitive manner; it could not be otherwise, where a woman's wages for an entire day were not sufficient to buy a pound of meat. They paid very low rents, and their clothes were made of the cheapest fabrics, though much better than could have been procured in the United States for the same money. I had heard much about the oppression of the poor in Europe. The people I saw around me were, many of them, among the poorest poor. But when I visited them in their little thatched cottages, I felt that the condition of even the meanest and most ignorant among them was vastly superior to the condition of the most favored slaves in America. They labored hard; but they were not ordered out to toil while the stars were in the sky, and driven and slashed by an overseer, through heat and cold, till the stars shone out again. Their homes were very humble; but they were protected by law. No insolent patrols could come, in the dead of night, and flog them at their pleasure. The father, when he closed his cottage door, felt safe with his family around him. No master or overseer could come and take from him his wife, or his daughter. They must separate to earn their living; but the parents knew where their children were going, and could communicate with them by letters. The relations of husband and wife, parent and child, were too sacred for the richest noble in the land to violate with impunity. Much was being done to enlighten these poor people. Schools were established among them, and benevolent societies were active in efforts to ameliorate their condition. There was no law forbidding them to learn to read and write; and if they helped each other in spelling out the Bible, they were in no danger of thirty-nine lashes, as was the case with myself and poor, pious, old uncle Fred. I repeat that the most ignorant and the most destitute of these peasants was a thousand fold better off than the most pampered American slave.

I do not deny that the poor are oppressed in Europe. I am not disposed to paint their condition so rose-colored as the Hon. Miss

Murray[1] paints the condition of the slaves in the United States. A small portion of *my* experience would enable her to read her own pages with anointed eyes. If she were to lay aside her title, and, instead of visiting among the fashionable, become domesticated, as a poor governess, on some plantation in Louisiana or Alabama, she would see and hear things that would make her tell quite a different story.

My visit to England is a memorable event in my life, from the fact of my having there received strong religious impressions. The contemptuous manner in which the communion had been administered to colored people, in my native place; the church membership of Dr. Flint, and others like him; and the buying and selling of slaves, by professed ministers of the gospel, had given me a prejudice against the Episcopal church. The whole service seemed to me a mockery and a sham. But my home in Steventon was in the family of a clergyman, who was a true disciple of Jesus. The beauty of his daily life inspired me with faith in the genuineness of Christian professions. Grace entered my heart, and I knelt at the communion table, I trust, in true humility of soul.

I remained abroad ten months, which was much longer than I had anticipated. During all that time, I never saw the slightest symptom of prejudice against color. Indeed, I entirely forgot it, till the time came for us to return to America.

XXXVIII. Renewed Invitation to Go South

We had a tedious winter passage, and from the distance spectres seemed to rise up on the shores of the United States. It is a sad feeling to be afraid of one's native country. We arrived in New York safely, and I hastened to Boston to look after my children. I found Ellen well, and improving at her school; but Benny was not there to welcome me. He had been left at a good place to learn a trade, and for several months every thing worked well. He was liked by the master, and was a favorite with his fellow-apprentices; but one day they accidentally discovered a fact they had never before suspected—that he was colored! This at once transformed him into a different being. Some of the apprentices were Americans, others American-born Irish; and it was offensive to their dignity to have a "nigger" among them, after they had been told that he *was* a "nigger." They began by treating him with silent scorn, and finding that he returned the same, they resorted to insults and abuse. He was too spirited a boy

1. Amelia Matilda Murray (1795–1884), British author, portrayed slavery positively in her writings about her travels in the United States.

to stand that, and he went off. Being desirous to do something to support himself, and having no one to advise him, he shipped for a whaling voyage. When I received these tidings I shed many tears, and bitterly reproached myself for having left him so long. But I had done it for the best, and now all I could do was to pray to the heavenly Father to guide and protect him.

Not long after my return, I received the following letter from Miss Emily Flint, now Mrs. Dodge:—

"In this you will recognized the hand of your friend and mistress. Having heard that you had gone with a family to Europe, I have waited to hear of your return to write to you. I should have answered the letter you wrote to me long since, but as I could not then act independently of my father, I knew there could be nothing done satisfactory to you. There were persons here who were willing to buy you and run the risk of getting you. To this I would not consent. I have always been attached to you, and would not like to see you the slave of another, or have unkind treatment. I am married now, and can protect you. My husband expects to move to Virginia this spring, where we think of settling. I am very anxious that you should come and live with me. If you are not willing to come, you may purchase yourself; but I should prefer having you live with me. If you come, you may, if you like, spend a month with your grandmother and friends, then come to me in Norfolk, Virginia. Think this over, and write as soon as possible, and let me know the conclusion. Hoping that your children are well, I remain your friend and mistress."

Of course I did not write to return thanks for this cordial invitation. I felt insulted to be thought stupid enough to be caught by such professions.

> "'Come up into my parlor,' said the spider to the fly;
> ''Tis the prettiest little parlor that ever you did spy.'"[1]

It was plain that Dr. Flint's family were apprised of my movements, since they knew of my voyage to Europe. I expected to have further trouble from them; but having eluded them thus far, I hoped to be as successful in future. The money I had earned, I was desirous to devote to the education of my children, and to secure a home for them. It seemed not only hard, but unjust, to pay for myself. I could not possibly regard myself as a piece of property. Moreover, I had worked many years without wages, and during that time had been

1. Reference to Mary Howitt's poem "The Spider and the Fly" (1844), which ends with the following advice: "And now, dear little children, who may this story read, / To idle, silly flattering words I pray you ne'er give heed; / Unto an evil counselor close heart and ear and eye, / And take a lesson from this tale of the spider and the fly."

obliged to depend on my grandmother for many comforts in food and clothing. My children certainly belonged to me; but though Dr. Flint had incurred no expense for their support, he had received a large sum of money for them. I knew the law would decide that I was his property, and would probably still give his daughter a claim to my children; but I regarded such laws as the regulations of robbers, who had no rights that I was bound to respect.[2]

The Fugitive Slave Law had not then passed. The judges of Massachusetts had not then stooped under chains to enter her courts of justice, so called. I knew my old master was rather skittish of Massachusetts. I relied on her love of freedom, and felt safe on her soil. I am now aware that I honored the old Commonwealth beyond her deserts.

XXXIX. The Confession

For two years my daughter and I supported ourselves comfortably in Boston. At the end of that time, my brother William offered to send Ellen to a boarding school. It required a great effort for me to consent to part with her, for I had few near ties, and it was her presence that made my two little rooms seem home-like. But my judgment prevailed over my selfish feelings. I made preparations for her departure. During the two years we had lived together I had often resolved to tell her something about her father; but I had never been able to muster sufficient courage. I had a shrinking dread of diminishing my child's love. I knew she must have curiosity on the subject, but she had never asked a question. She was always very careful not to say any thing to remind me of my troubles. Now that she was going from me, I thought if I should die before she returned, she might hear my story from some one who did not understand the palliating circumstances; and that if she were entirely ignorant on the subject, her sensitive nature might receive a rude shock.

When we retired for the night, she said, "Mother, it is very hard to leave you alone. I am almost sorry I am going, though I do want to improve myself. But you will write to me often; won't you, mother?"

I did not throw my arms round her. I did not answer her. But in a calm, solemn way, for it cost me great effort, I said, "Listen to me, Ellen; I have something to tell you!" I recounted my early sufferings in slavery, and told her how nearly they had crushed me. I began to tell her how they had driven me into a great sin, when she clasped

2. A sarcastic play on the wording of the notorious 1857 U.S. Supreme Court *Dred Scott v. Sanford* decision that pronounced blacks to be "so far inferior, that they had no rights which the white man was bound to respect."

me in her arms, and exclaimed, "O, don't, mother! Please don't tell me any more."

I said, "But, my child, I want you to know about your father."

"I know all about it, mother," she replied; "I am nothing to my father, and he is nothing to me. All my love is for you. I was with him five months in Washington, and he never cared for me. He never spoke to me as he did to his little Fanny. I knew all the time he was my father, for Fanny's nurse told me so; but she said I must never tell any body, and I never did. I used to wish he would take me in his arms and kiss me, as he did Fanny; or that he would sometimes smile at me, as he did at her. I thought if he was my own father, he ought to love me. I was a little girl then, and didn't know any better. But now I never think any thing about my father. All my love is for you." She hugged me closer as she spoke, and I thanked God that the knowledge I had so much dreaded to impart had not diminished the affection of my child. I had not the slightest idea she knew that portion of my history. If I had, I should have spoken to her long before; for my pent-up feelings had often longed to pour themselves out to some one I could trust. But I loved the dear girl better for the delicacy she had manifested towards her unfortunate mother.

The next morning, she and her uncle started on their journey to the village in New York, where she was to be placed at school. It seemed as if all the sunshine had gone away. My little room was dreadfully lonely. I was thankful when a message came from a lady, accustomed to employ me, requesting me to come and sew in her family for several weeks. On my return, I found a letter from brother William. He thought of opening an anti-slavery reading room in Rochester, and combining with it the sale of some books and stationery; and he wanted me to unite with him. We tried it, but it was not successful. We found warm anti-slavery friends there, but the feeling was not general enough to support such an establishment. I passed nearly a year in the family of Isaac and Amy Post,[1] practical believers in the Christian doctrine of human brotherhood. They measured a man's worth by his character, not by his complexion. The memory of those beloved and honored friends will remain with me to my latest hour.

XL. The Fugitive Slave Law

My brother, being disappointed in his project, concluded to go to California; and it was agreed that Benjamin should go with him. Ellen liked her school, and was a great favorite there. They did not

1. Amy Post (1802–1889) was a Quaker abolitionist and women's rights activist.

know her history, and she did not tell it, because she had no desire to make capital out of their sympathy. But when it was accidentally discovered that her mother was a fugitive slave, every method was used to increase her advantages and diminish her expenses.

I was alone again. It was necessary for me to be earning money, and I preferred that it should be among those who knew me. On my return from Rochester, I called at the house of Mr. Bruce, to see Mary, the darling little babe that had thawed my heart, when it was freezing into a cheerless distrust of all my fellow-beings. She was growing a tall girl now, but I loved her always. Mr. Bruce had married again, and it was proposed that I should become nurse to a new infant. I had but one hesitation, and that was my feeling of insecurity in New York, now greatly increased by the passage of the Fugitive Slave Law. However, I resolved to try the experiment. I was again fortunate in my employer. The new Mrs. Bruce was an American, brought up under aristocratic influences, and still living in the midst of them; but if she had any prejudice against color, I was never made aware of it; and as for the system of slavery, she had a most hearty dislike of it. No sophistry of Southerners could blind her to its enormity. She was a person of excellent principles and a noble heart. To me, from that hour to the present, she has been a true and sympathizing friend. Blessings be with her and hers!

About the time that I reëntered the Bruce family an event occurred of disastrous import to the colored people. The slave Hamlin,[1] the first fugitive that came under the new law, was given up by the bloodhounds of the north to the bloodhounds of the south. It was the beginning of a reign of terror to the colored population. The great city rushed on in its whirl of excitement, taking no note of the "short and simple annals of the poor."[2] But while fashionables were listening to the thrilling voice of Jenny Lind[3] in Metropolitan Hall, the thrilling voices of poor hunted colored people went up, in an agony of supplication, to the Lord, from Zion's church. Many families, who had lived in the city for twenty years, fled from it now. Many a poor washerwoman, who, by hard labor, had made herself a comfortable home, was obliged to sacrifice her furniture, bid a hurried farewell to friends, and seek her fortune among strangers in Canada. Many a wife discovered a secret she had never known before—that her husband was a fugitive, and must leave her to insure his own safety. Worse still, many a husband discovered that his wife had fled from slavery years ago, and as "the child follows the condition of its mother," the children of his love were liable to be seized and carried

1. A misspelling of the name of James Hamelt, who was purportedly the first person recaptured in New York under the provisions of the Fugitive Slave Act.
2. Thomas Gray, "Elegy Written in a Country Churchyard" (1751).
3. Popular singer known as the "Swedish Nightingale."

into slavery. Every where, in those humble homes, there was consternation and anguish. But what cared the legislators of the "dominant race" for the blood they were crushing out of trampled hearts?

When my brother William spent his last evening with me, before he went to California, we talked nearly all the time of the distress brought on our oppressed people by the passage of this iniquitous law; and never had I seen him manifest such bitterness of spirit, such stern hostility to our oppressors. He was himself free from the operation of the law; for he did not run from any Slaveholding State, being brought into the Free States by his master. But I was subject to it; and so were hundreds of intelligent and industrious people all around us. I seldom ventured into the streets; and when it was necessary to do an errand for Mrs. Bruce, or any of the family, I went as much as possible through back streets and by-ways. What a disgrace to a city calling itself free, that inhabitants, guiltless of offence, and seeking to perform their duties conscientiously, should be condemned to live in such incessant fear, and have nowhere to turn for protection! This state of things, of course, gave rise to many impromptu vigilance committees. Every colored person, and every friend of their persecuted race, kept their eyes wide open. Every evening I examined the newspapers carefully, to see what Southerners had put up at the hotels. I did this for my own sake, thinking my young mistress and her husband might be among the list; I wished also to give information to others, if necessary; for if many were "running to and fro," I resolved that "knowledge should be increased."[4]

This brings up one of my Southern reminiscences, which I will here briefly relate. I was somewhat acquainted with a slave named Luke, who belonged to a wealthy man in our vicinity. His master died, leaving a son and daughter heirs to his large fortune. In the division of the slaves, Luke was included in the son's portion. This young man became a prey to the vices growing out of the "patriarchal institution," and when he went to the north, to complete his education, he carried his vices with him. He was brought home, deprived of the use of his limbs, by excessive dissipation. Luke was appointed to wait upon his bed-ridden master, whose despotic habits were greatly increased by exasperation at his own helplessness. He kept a cowhide beside him, and, for the most trivial occurrence, he would order his attendant to bare his back, and kneel beside the couch, while he whipped him till his strength was exhausted. Some days he was not allowed to wear any thing but his shirt, in order to be in readiness to be flogged. A day seldom passed without his

4. Daniel 12.4.

receiving more or less blows. If the slightest resistance was offered, the town constable was sent for to execute the punishment, and Luke learned from experience how much more the constable's strong arm was to be dreaded than the comparatively feeble one of his master. The arm of his tyrant grew weaker, and was finally palsied; and then the constable's services were in constant requisition. The fact that he was entirely dependent on Luke's care, and was obliged to be tended like an infant, instead of inspiring any gratitude or compassion towards his poor slave, seemed only to increase his irritability and cruelty. As he lay there on his bed, a mere degraded wreck of manhood, he took into his head the strangest freaks of despotism; and if Luke hesitated to submit to his orders, the constable was immediately sent for. Some of these freaks were of a nature too filthy to be repeated. When I fled from the house of bondage, I left poor Luke still chained to the bedside of this cruel and disgusting wretch.

One day, when I had been requested to do an errand for Mrs. Bruce, I was hurrying through back streets, as usual, when I saw a young man approaching, whose face was familiar to me. As he came nearer, I recognized Luke. I always rejoiced to see or hear of any one who had escaped from the black pit; but, remembering this poor fellow's extreme hardships, I was peculiarly glad to see him on Northern soil, though I no longer called it *free* soil. I well remembered what a desolate feeling it was to be alone among strangers, and I went up to him and greeted him cordially. At first, he did not know me; but when I mentioned my name, he remembered all about me. I told him of the Fugitive Slave Law, and asked him if he did not know that New York was a city of kidnappers.

He replied, "De risk ain't so bad for me, as 'tis fur you. 'Cause I runned away from de speculator, and you runned away from de massa. Dem speculators vont spen dar money to come here fur a runaway, if dey ain't sartin sure to put dar hans right on him. An I tell you I's tuk good car 'bout dat. I had too hard times down dar, to let 'em ketch dis nigger."

He then told me of the advice he had received, and the plans he had laid. I asked if he had money enough to take him to Canada. "'Pend upon it, I hab," he replied. "I tuk car fur dat. I'd bin workin all my days fur dem cussed whites, an got no pay but kicks and cuffs. So I tought dis nigger had a right to money nuff to bring him to de Free States. Massa Henry he lib till ebery body vish him dead; an ven he did die, I knowed de debbil would hab him, an vouldn't vant him to bring his money 'long too. So I tuk some of his bills, and put 'em in de pocket of his ole trousers. An ven he was buried, dis nigger ask fur dem ole trousers, an dey gub 'em to me." With a low, chuckling laugh, he added, "You see I didn't *steal* it; dey *gub* it to me. I tell you, I had mighty hard time to keep de speculator from findin it; but he didn't git it."

This is a fair specimen of how the moral sense is educated by slavery. When a man has his wages stolen from him, year after year, and the laws sanction and enforce the theft, how can he be expected to have more regard to honesty than has the man who robs him? I have become somewhat enlightened, but I confess that I agree with poor, ignorant, much-abused Luke, in thinking he had a *right* to that money, as a portion of his unpaid wages. He went to Canada forthwith, and I have not since heard from him.

All that winter I lived in a state of anxiety. When I took the children out to breathe the air, I closely observed the countenances of all I met. I dreaded the approach of summer, when snakes and slaveholders make their appearance. I was, in fact, a slave in New York, as subject to slave laws as I had been in a Slave State. Strange incongruity in a State called free!

Spring returned, and I received warning from the south that Dr. Flint knew of my return to my old place, and was making preparations to have me caught. I learned afterwards that my dress, and that of Mrs. Bruce's children, had been described to him by some of the Northern tools, which slaveholders employ for their base purposes, and then indulge in sneers at their cupidity and mean servility.

I immediately informed Mrs. Bruce of my danger, and she took prompt measures for my safety. My place as nurse could not be supplied immediately, and this generous, sympathizing lady proposed that I should carry her baby away. It was a comfort to me to have the child with me; for the heart is reluctant to be torn away from every object it loves. But how few mothers would have consented to have one of their own babes become a fugitive, for the sake of a poor, hunted nurse, on whom the legislators of the country had let loose the bloodhounds! When I spoke of the sacrifice she was making, in depriving herself of her dear baby, she replied, "It is better for you to have baby with you, Linda; for if they get on your track, they will be obliged to bring the child to me; and then, if there is a possibility of saving you, you shall be saved."

This lady had a very wealthy relative, a benevolent gentleman in many respects, but aristocratic and proslavery. He remonstrated with her for harboring a fugitive slave; told her she was violating the laws of her country; and asked her if she was aware of the penalty. She replied, "I am very well aware of it. It is imprisonment and one thousand dollars fine. Shame on my country that it *is* so! I am ready to incur the penalty. I will go to the state's prison, rather than have any poor victim torn from *my* house, to be carried back to slavery."

The noble heart! The brave heart! The tears are in my eyes while I write of her. May the God of the helpless reward her for her sympathy with my persecuted people!

I was sent into New England, where I was sheltered by the wife of a senator, whom I shall always hold in grateful remembrance. This honorable gentleman would not have voted for the Fugitive Slave Law, as did the senator in "Uncle Tom's Cabin;"[5] on the contrary, he was strongly opposed to it; but he was enough under its influence to be afraid of having me remain in his house many hours. So I was sent into the country, where I remained a month with the baby. When it was supposed that Dr. Flint's emissaries had lost track of me, and given up the pursuit for the present, I returned to New York.

XLI. Free at Last

Mrs. Bruce, and every member of her family, were exceedingly kind to me. I was thankful for the blessings of my lot, yet I could not always wear a cheerful countenance. I was doing harm to no one; on the contrary, I was doing all the good I could in my small way; yet I could never go out to breathe God's free air without trepidation at my heart. This seemed hard; and I could not think it was a right state of things in any civilized country.

From time to time I received news from my good old grandmother. She could not write; but she employed others to write for her. The following is an extract from one of her last letters:—

"Dear Daughter: I cannot hope to see you again on earth; but I pray to God to unite us above, where pain will no more rack this feeble body of mine; where sorrow and parting from my children will be no more. God has promised these things if we are faithful unto the end. My age and feeble health deprive me of going to church now; but God is with me here at home. Thank your brother for his kindness. Give much love to him, and tell him to remember the Creator in the days of his youth, and strive to meet me in the Father's kingdom. Love to Ellen and Benjamin. Don't neglect him. Tell him for me, to be a good boy. Strive, my child, to train them for God's children. May he protect and provide for you, is the prayer of your loving old mother."

These letters both cheered and saddened me. I was always glad to have tidings from the kind, faithful old friend of my unhappy youth; but her messages of love made my heart yearn to see her

5. In Harriet Beecher Stowe's *Uncle Tom's Cabin* (1852), a white legislator named Senator Bird comes to question the morality of slavery, despite his commitment to the rule of law, after he meets a young mother and her child fleeing captivity.

before she died, and I mourned over the fact that it was impossible. Some months after I returned from my flight to New England, I received a letter from her, in which she wrote, "Dr. Flint is dead. He has left a distressed family. Poor old man! I hope he made his peace with God."

I remembered how he had defrauded my grandmother of the hard earnings she had loaned; how he had tried to cheat her out of the freedom her mistress had promised her, and how he had persecuted her children; and I thought to myself that she was a better Christian than I was, if she could entirely forgive him. I cannot say, with truth, that the news of my old master's death softened my feelings towards him. There are wrongs which even the grave does not bury. The man was odious to me while he lived, and his memory is odious now.

His departure from this world did not diminish my danger. He had threatened my grandmother that his heirs should hold me in slavery after he was gone; that I never should be free so long as a child of his survived. As for Mrs. Flint, I had seen her in deeper afflictions than I supposed the loss of her husband would be, for she had buried several children; yet I never saw any signs of softening in her heart. The doctor had died in embarrassed circumstances, and had little to will to his heirs, except such property as he was unable to grasp. I was well aware what I had to expect from the family of Flints; and my fears were confirmed by a letter from the south, warning me to be on my guard, because Mrs. Flint openly declared that her daughter could not afford to lose so valuable a slave as I was.

I kept close watch of the newspapers for arrivals; but one Saturday night, being much occupied, I forgot to examine the Evening Express as usual. I went down into the parlor for it, early in the morning, and found the boy about to kindle a fire with it. I took it from him and examined the list of arrivals. Reader, if you have never been a slave, you cannot imagine the acute sensation of suffering at my heart, when I read the names of Mr. and Mrs. Dodge, at a hotel in Courtland Street. It was a third-rate hotel, and that circumstance convinced me of the truth of what I had heard, that they were short of funds and had need of my value, as *they* valued me; and that was by dollars and cents. I hastened with the paper to Mrs. Bruce. Her heart and hand were always open to every one in distress, and she always warmly sympathized with mine. It was impossible to tell how near the enemy was. He might have passed and repassed the house while we were sleeping. He might at that moment be waiting to pounce upon me if I ventured out of doors. I had never seen the husband of my young mistress, and therefore I could not distinguish him from any other stranger. A carriage was hastily ordered; and, closely veiled, I followed Mrs. Bruce, taking the baby again with me into exile. After various turnings and crossings, and returnings, the carriage stopped at the house of one of Mrs. Bruce's friends, where I was kindly received. Mrs. Bruce returned immediately, to instruct the domestics what to say if any one came to inquire for me.

It was lucky for me that the evening paper was not burned up before I had a chance to examine the list of arrivals. It was not long after Mrs. Bruce's return to her house, before several people came to inquire for me. One inquired for me, another asked for my daughter Ellen, and another said he had a letter from my grandmother, which he was requested to deliver in person.

They were told, "She *has* lived here, but she has left."

"How long ago?"

"I don't know, sir."

"Do you know where she went?"

"I do not, sir." And the door was closed.

This Mr. Dodge, who claimed me as his property, was originally a Yankee pedler in the south; then he became a merchant, and finally a slaveholder. He managed to get introduced into what was called the first society, and married Miss Emily Flint. A quarrel arose between him and her brother, and the brother cowhided him. This led to a family feud, and he proposed to remove to Virginia. Dr. Flint left him no property, and his own means had become circumscribed, while a wife and children depended upon him for support. Under these circumstances, it was very natural that he should make an effort to put me into his pocket.

I had a colored friend, a man from my native place, in whom I had the most implicit confidence. I sent for him, and told him that Mr. and Mrs. Dodge had arrived in New York. I proposed that he should call upon them to make inquiries about his friends at the south, with whom Dr. Flint's family were well acquainted. He thought there was no impropriety in his doing so, and he consented. He went to the hotel, and knocked at the door of Mr. Dodge's room, which was opened by the gentleman himself, who gruffly inquired, "What brought you here? How came you to know I was in the city?"

"Your arrival was published in the evening papers, sir; and I called to ask Mrs. Dodge about my friends at home. I didn't suppose it would give any offence."

"Where's that negro girl, that belongs to my wife?"

"What girl, sir?"

"You know well enough. I mean Linda, that ran away from Dr. Flint's plantation, some years ago. I dare say you've seen her, and know where she is."

"Yes, sir, I've seen her, and know where she is. She is out of your reach, sir."

"Tell me where she is, or bring her to me, and I will give her a chance to buy her freedom."

"I don't think it would be of any use, sir. I have heard her say she would go to the ends of the earth, rather than pay any man or woman for her freedom, because she thinks she has a right to it. Besides, she couldn't do it, if she would, for she has spent her earnings to educate her children."

This made Mr. Dodge very angry, and some high words passed between them. My friend was afraid to come where I was; but in the course of the day I received a note from him. I supposed they had not come from the south, in the winter, for a pleasure excursion; and now the nature of their business was very plain.

Mrs. Bruce came to me and entreated me to leave the city the next morning. She said her house was watched, and it was possible that some clew to me might be obtained. I refused to take her advice. She pleaded with an earnest tenderness, that ought to have moved me; but I was in a bitter, disheartened mood. I was weary of flying from pillar to post. I had been chased during half my life, and it seemed as if the chase was never to end. There I sat, in that great city, guiltless of crime, yet not daring to worship God in any of the churches. I heard the bells ringing for afternoon service, and, with contemptuous sarcasm, I said, "Will the preachers take for their text, 'Proclaim liberty to the captive, and the opening of prison doors to them that are bound'?[1] or will they preach from the text, 'Do unto others as ye would they should do unto you'?"[2] Oppressed Poles and Hungarians could find a safe refuge in that city; John Mitchell[3] was free to proclaim in the City Hall his desire for "a plantation well stocked with slaves;" but there I sat, an oppressed American, not daring to show my face. God forgive the black and bitter thoughts I indulged on that Sabbath day! The Scripture says, "Oppression makes even a wise man mad;"[4] and I was not wise.

I had been told that Mr. Dodge said his wife had never signed away her right to my children, and if he could not get me, he would take them. This it was, more than any thing else, that roused such a tempest in my soul. Benjamin was with his uncle William in California, but my innocent young daughter had come to spend a vacation with me. I thought of what I had suffered in slavery at her age, and my heart was like a tiger's when a hunter tries to seize her young.

Dear Mrs. Bruce! I seem to see the expression of her face, as she turned away discouraged by my obstinate mood. Finding her expostulations unavailing, she sent Ellen to entreat me. When ten o'clock in the evening arrived and Ellen had not returned, this watchful and unwearied friend became anxious. She came to us in a carriage,

1. Isaiah 61.1.
2. Matthew 7.12.
3. John Mitchel (1815–1875), an Irish revolutionary who expressed support for American slavery.
4. Ecclesiastes 7.7.

bringing a well-filled trunk for my journey—trusting that by this time I would listen to reason. I yielded to her, as I ought to have done before.

The next day, baby and I set out in a heavy snow storm, bound for New England again. I received letters from the City of Iniquity, addressed to me under an assumed name. In a few days one came from Mrs. Bruce, informing me that my new master was still searching for me, and that she intended to put an end to this persecution by buying my freedom. I felt grateful for the kindness that prompted this offer, but the idea was not so pleasant to me as might have been expected. The more my mind had become enlightened, the more difficult it was for me to consider myself an article of property; and to pay money to those who had so grievously oppressed me seemed like taking from my sufferings the glory of triumph. I wrote to Mrs. Bruce, thanking her, but saying that being sold from one owner to another seemed too much like slavery; that such a great obligation could not be easily cancelled; and that I preferred to go to my brother in California.

Without my knowledge, Mrs. Bruce employed a gentleman in New York to enter into negotiations with Mr. Dodge. He proposed to pay three hundred dollars down, if Mr. Dodge would sell me, and enter into obligations to relinquish all claim to me or my children forever after. He who called himself my master said he scorned so small an offer for such a valuable servant. The gentleman replied, "You can do as you choose, sir. If you reject this offer you will never get any thing; for the woman has friends who will convey her and her children out of the country."

Mr. Dodge concluded that "half a loaf was better than no bread,"[5] and he agreed to the proffered terms. By the next mail I received this brief letter from Mrs. Bruce: "I am rejoiced to tell you that the money for your freedom has been paid to Mr. Dodge. Come home to-morrow. I long to see you and my sweet babe."

My brain reeled as I read these lines. A gentleman near me said, "It's true; I have seen the bill of sale." "The bill of sale!" Those words struck me like a blow. So I was *sold* at last! A human being *sold* in the free city of New York! The bill of sale is on record, and future generations will learn from it that women were articles of traffic in New York, late in the nineteenth century of the Christian religion. It may hereafter prove a useful document to antiquaries,[6] who are seeking to measure the progress of civilization in the United States. I well know the value of that bit of paper; but much as I love freedom, I do not like to look upon it. I am deeply grateful to the

5. That is, something is better than nothing at all.
6. Historians.

generous friend who procured it, but I despise the miscreant who demanded payment for what never rightfully belonged to him or his.

I had objected to having my freedom bought, yet I must confess that when it was done I felt as if a heavy load had been lifted from my weary shoulders. When I rode home in the cars I was no longer afraid to unveil my face and look at people as they passed. I should have been glad to have met Daniel Dodge himself; to have had him seen me and known me, that he might have mourned over the untoward circumstances which compelled him to sell me for three hundred dollars.

When I reached home, the arms of my benefactress were thrown round me, and our tears mingled. As soon as she could speak, she said, "O Linda, I'm *so* glad it's all over! You wrote to me as if you thought you were going to be transferred from one owner to another. But I did not buy you for your services. I should have done just the same, if you had been going to sail for California to-morrow. I should, at least, have the satisfaction of knowing that you left me a free woman."

My heart was exceedingly full. I remembered how my poor father had tried to buy me, when I was a small child, and how he had been disappointed. I hoped his spirit was rejoicing over me now. I remembered how my good old grandmother had laid up her earnings to purchase me in later years, and how often her plans had been frustrated. How that faithful, loving old heart would leap for joy, if she could look on me and my children now that we were free! My relatives had been foiled in all their efforts, but God had raised me up a friend among strangers, who had bestowed on me the precious, long-desired boon. Friend! It is a common word, often lightly used. Like other good and beautiful things, it may be tarnished by careless handling; but when I speak of Mrs. Bruce as my friend, the word is sacred.

My grandmother lived to rejoice in my freedom; but not long after, a letter came with a black seal. She had gone "where the wicked cease from troubling, and the weary are at rest."[7]

Time passed on, and a paper came to me from the south, containing an obituary notice of my uncle Phillip. It was the only case I ever knew of such an honor conferred upon a colored person. It was written by one of his friends, and contained these words: "Now that death has laid him low, they call him a good man and a useful citizen; but what are eulogies to the black man, when the world has faded from his vision? It does not require man's praise to obtain rest in God's kingdom." So they called a colored man a *citizen!* Strange words to be uttered in that region!

7. Job 3.17.

Reader, my story ends with freedom; not in the usual way, with marriage. I and my children are now free! We are as free from the power of slaveholders as are the white people of the north; and though that, according to my ideas, is not saying a great deal, it is a vast improvement in *my* condition. The dream of my life is not yet realized. I do not sit with my children in a home of my own. I still long for a hearthstone of my own, however humble. I wish it for my children's sake far more than for my own. But God so orders circumstances as to keep me with my friend Mrs. Bruce. Love, duty, gratitude, also bind me to her side. It is a privilege to serve her who pities my oppressed people, and who has bestowed the inestimable boon of freedom on me and my children.

It has been painful to me, in many ways, to recall the dreary years I passed in bondage. I would gladly forget them if I could. Yet the retrospection is not altogether without solace; for with those gloomy recollections come tender memories of my good old grandmother, like light, fleecy clouds floating over a dark and troubled sea.

Appendix

The following statement is from Amy Post, a member of the Society of Friends[1] in the State of New York, well known and highly respected by friends of the poor and the oppressed. As has been already stated, in the preceding pages, the author of this volume spent some time under her hospitable roof. L. M. C.[2]

"The author of this book is my highly-esteemed friend. If its readers knew her as I know her, they could not fail to be deeply interested in her story. She was a beloved inmate of our family nearly the whole of the year 1849. She was introduced to us by her affectionate and conscientious brother, who had previously related to us some of the almost incredible events in his sister's life. I immediately became much interested in Linda; for her appearance was prepossessing, and her deportment indicated remarkable delicacy of feeling and purity of thought.

"As we became acquainted, she related to me, from time to time some of the incidents in her bitter experiences as a slave-woman. Though impelled by a natural craving for human sympathy, she passed through a baptism of suffering, even in recounting her trials to me, in private confidential conversations. The burden of these memories lay heavily upon her spirit—naturally virtuous and refined.

1. Also referred to as Quakers, a religious group known for its opposition to slavery. See note 1, p. 156
2. Lydia Maria Child.

I repeatedly urged her to consent to the publication of her narrative; for I felt that it would arouse people to a more earnest work for the disinthralment of millions still remaining in that soul-crushing condition, which was so unendurable to her. But her sensitive spirit shrank from publicity. She said, 'You know a woman can whisper her cruel wrongs in the ear of a dear friend much easier than she can record them for the world to read.' Even in talking with me, she wept so much, and seemed to suffer such mental agony, that I felt her story was too sacred to be drawn from her by inquisitive questions, and I left her free to tell as much, or as little, as she chose. Still, I urged upon her the duty of publishing her experience, for the sake of the good it might do; and, at last, she undertook the task.

"Having been a slave so large a portion of her life, she is unlearned; she is obliged to earn her living by her own labor, and she has worked untiringly to procure education for her children; several times she has been obliged to leave her employments, in order to fly from the man-hunters and woman-hunters of our land; but she pressed through all these obstacles and overcame them. After the labors of the day were over, she traced secretly and wearily, by the midnight lamp, a truthful record of her eventful life.

"This Empire State[3] is a shabby place of refuge for the oppressed; but here, through anxiety, turmoil, and despair, the freedom of Linda and her children was finally secured, by the exertions of a generous friend. She was grateful for the boon; but the idea of having been *bought* was always galling to a spirit that could never acknowledge itself to be a chattel. She wrote to us thus, soon after the event: 'I thank you for your kind expressions in regard to my freedom; but the freedom I had before the money was paid was dearer to me. God gave me *that* freedom; but man put God's image in the scales with the paltry sum of three hundred dollars. I served for my liberty as faithfully as Jacob served for Rachel.[4] At the end, he had large possessions; but I was robbed of my victory; I was obliged to resign my crown, to rid myself of a tyrant.'

"Her story, as written by herself, cannot fail to interest the reader. It is a sad illustration of the condition of this country, which boasts of its civilization, while it sanctions laws and customs which make the experiences of the present more strange than any fictions of the past.

AMY POST.

3. New York.
4. Genesis 29.18–20. Jacob serves Laban for seven years in order to gain permission to marry his daughter, Rachel. Jacobs spent seven years in hiding.

"ROCHESTER, N. Y., Oct. 30th, 1859."

The following testimonial is from a man who is now a highly respectable colored citizen of Boston. L. M. C.

"This narrative contains some incidents so extraordinary, that, doubtless, many persons, under whose eyes it may chance to fall, will be ready to believe that it is colored highly, to serve as special purpose. But, however it may be regarded by the incredulous, I know that it is full of living truths. I have been well acquainted with the author from my boyhood. The circumstances recounted in her history are perfectly familiar to me. I knew of her treatment from her master; of the imprisonment of her children; of their sale and redemption; of her seven years' concealment; and of her subsequent escape to the North. I am now a resident of Boston, and am a living witness to the truth of this interesting narrative.

GEORGE W. LOWTHER"[5]

5. A free black man (1822–1898) who was raised in Jacobs's hometown of Edenton, North Carolina. In 1878, he was elected by Massachusetts to the House of Representatives.

CONTEXTS

Public Statements

HARRIET JACOBS

Letter from a Fugitive Slave†

Slaves Sold under Peculiar Circumstances.

[We publish the subjoined communication exactly as written by the author, with the exception of corrections in punctuation and spelling, and the omission of one or two passages—Ed.]

To the Editor of the N.Y. Tribune.

SIR: Having carefully read your paper for some months I became very much interested in some of the articles and comments written on Mrs. Tyler's Reply to the Ladies of England.[1] Being a slave myself, I could not have felt otherwise. Would that I could write an article worthy of notice in your columns. As I never enjoyed the advantages of an education, therefore I could not study the arts of reading and writing, yet poor as it may be, I had rather give it from my own hand, than have it said that I employed others to do it for me. The truth can never be told so well through the second and third person as from yourself. But I am straying from the question. In that Reply to the Ladies of England, Mrs. Tyler said that slaves were never sold only under very peculiar circumstances. As Mrs. Tyler and her friend Bhains were so far used up, that he could not explain what those peculiar circumstances were, let one whose peculiar suffering justifies her in explaining it for Mrs. Tyler.

I was born a slave, reared in the Southern hot-bed until I was the mother of two children, sold at the early age of two and four years old. I have been hunted through all of the Northern States, but no, I will not tell you of my own suffering—no, it would harrow up my soul, and defeat the object that I wish to pursue. Enough—the dregs of that bitter cup have been my bounty for many years.

† *New York Tribune*, June 21, 1853.

1. Julia G. Tyler, wife of the former U.S. president John Tyler, had written a rebuttal to an abolitionist appeal for British women's support.

And as this is the first time that I ever took my pen in hand to make such an attempt, you will not say that it is fiction, for had I the inclination, I have neither the brain or talent to write it. But to this very peculiar circumstance under which slaves are sold.

My mother was held as property by a maiden lady; when she married, my younger sister was in her fourteenth year, whom they took into the family. She was as gentle as she was beautiful. Innocent and guileless child, the light of our desolate hearth! But oh, my heart bleeds to tell you of the misery and degradation she was forced to suffer in slavery. The monster who owned her had no humanity in his soul. The most sincere affection that his heart was capable of, could not make him faithful to his beautiful and wealthy bride the short time of three months, but every stratagem was used to seduce my sister. Mortified and tormented beyond endurance, this child came and threw herself on her mother's bosom, the only place where she could seek refuge from her persecutor; and yet she could not protect her child that she bore into the world. On that bosom with *bitter tears* she told her troubles, and entreated her mother to save her. And oh, Christian mothers! you that have daughters of your own, can you think of your sable sisters without offering a prayer to that God who created all in their behalf! My poor mother, naturally high-spirited, smarting under what she considered as the wrongs and outrages which her child had to bear, sought her master, entreating him to spare her child. Nothing could exceed his rage at this what he called impertinence. My mother was dragged to jail, there remained twenty-five days, with negro traders to come in as they liked to examine her, as she was offered for sale. My sister was told that she must yield, or never expect to see her mother again. There were three younger children; on no other condition could she be restored to them without the sacrifice of one. That child gave herself up to her master's bidding, to save one that was dearer to her than life itself. And can you, Christian, find it in your heart to despise her? Ah, no! not even Mrs. Tyler; for though we believe that the vanity of a name would lead her to bestow her hand where her heart could never go with it, yet, with all her faults and follies, she is nothing more than a *woman*. For if her domestic hearth is surrounded with slaves, ere long before this she has opened her eyes to the evils of slavery, and that the mistress as well as the slave must submit to the indignities and vices imposed on them by their lords of body and soul. But to one of those peculiar circumstances.

At fifteen, my sister held to her bosom an innocent offspring of her guilt and misery. In this way she dragged a miserable existence of two years, between the fires of her mistress's jealousy and her master's brutal passion. At seventeen, she gave birth to another helpless infant, heir to all the evils of slavery. Thus life and its sufferings were meted out to her until her twenty-first year. Sorrow and suffering had made its ravages upon her—she was less the object to be desired by the fiend who had crushed her to the earth; and as her children grew, they bore too strong a resemblance to him who desired to give them no other inheritance save Chains and Handcuffs, and in the dead hour of the night, when this young, deserted mother lay with her little ones clinging around her, little dreaming of the dark and inhuman plot that would be carried into execution before another dawn, and when the sun rose on God's beautiful earth, that broken-hearted mother was far on her way to the capitol of Virginia. That day should have refused her light to so disgraceful and inhuman an act in your boasted country of Liberty. Yet, reader, it is true, those two helpless children were the *sons* of one of your sainted Members in Congress; that agonized mother, his victim and slave. And where she now is God only knows, who has kept a record on high of all that she has suffered on earth.

And, you would exclaim, Could not the master have been more merciful to his children? God is merciful to all of his children, but it is seldom that a slaveholder has any mercy for his slave child. And you will believe it when I tell you that mother and her children were sold to make room for another sister, who was now the age of that mother when she entered the family. And this selling appeased the mistress's wrath, and satisfied her desire for *revenge*, and made the path more smooth for her young rival at first. For there is a strong rivalry between a handsome mulatto girl and a jealous and *faded* mistress, and her liege lord sadly neglects those little attentions for a while that once made her happy. For the master will either neglect his wife or double his attentions, to save him from being suspected by his wife. Would you not think that Southern women had cause to despise that Slavery which forces them to bear so much deception practiced by their *husbands*? Yet all this is true, for a slaveholder seldom takes a white mistress, for she is an expensive commodity, not submissive as he would like to have her, but more apt to be tyrannical; and when his passion seeks another object, he must leave her in quiet possession of all the gewgaws that she has sold herself for. But not so with his poor *slave victim*, that he has robbed of everything that could make life desirable; she must be torn from the little that is left to bind her to life, and sold by her *seducer* and *master*, caring not where, so that it puts him in possession of enough to purchase another victim. And such are the peculiar circumstances of American Slavery—of all the evils in God's sight the most to be abhorred.

Perhaps while I am writing this, you too, dear Emily, may be on your way to the Mississippi River, for those peculiar circumstances occur every day in the midst of my poor oppressed fellow-creatures in bondage. And oh ye Christians, while your arms are extended to receive the oppressed of all nations, while you exert every power of your soul to assist them to raise funds, put weapons in their hands, tell them to return to their own country to slay every foe until they break the accursed yoke from off their necks, not buying and selling; this they never do under any circumstances. But while Americans do all this, they forget the millions of slaves they have at home, bought and sold under very peculiar circumstances.

And because one friend of the slave has dared to tell of their wrongs you would annihilate her. But in Uncle Tom's Cabin[2] she has not told the half. Would that I had one spark from her storehouse of genius and talent, I would tell you of my own sufferings—I would tell you of wrongs that Hungary has never inflicted, nor England ever dreamed of in this free country where all nations fly for liberty, equal rights and protection under your stripes and stars. It should be stripes and scars, for they go along with Mrs. Tyler's peculiar circumstances, of which I have told you only one.

A FUGITIVE SLAVE.

HARRIET JACOBS

Cruelty to Slaves†

To the Editor of The N. Y. Tribune.

SIR: Having seen an article, a few days ago, that was going the rounds in some of the daily papers, denying the truth of an advertisement wherein Slaves were outlawed in North Carolina. I wish to reply to it through your columns. I was born in that good old State, and less than 20 years since I left it, and it is not that length of time since I witnessed there a sight which I can never forget. It was a slave that been a runaway from his master twelvemonths. After that time a white man is justified in shooting a slave as he is considered an outlaw. This slave man was brought to the wharf, placed in a small boat, by two white men, early in the morning, with his *head* severed from his body, and remained there in an August sun until noon, before an inquest was held. Then he was buried, and not a word of murder or of arrest was heard. He was a negro and runaway slave, and it was all right. It mattered not who murdered him—if he was a white man he was sure of the reward, and the name of being a brave fellow, truly. The writer of that article has said, the people of North Carolina have hearts and souls like our own. Surely, many of them have. The poor slave, however, who had his head severed from his body was owned by a merchant in New York.

A FUGITIVE.

2. Title of the 1852 antislavery novel by Harriet Beecher Stowe (1811–1896).
† *New York Tribune,* July 25, 1853.

WILLIAM C. NELL

Linda, the Slave Girl†

Boston, January 21, 1861.

Dear Mr. Garrison:

Crowded though I know the *Liberator* columns to be just now, I am constrained to solicit space for a word in announcement of a book just issued from the press, entitled "LINDA: *Incidents in the Life of a Slave Girl, seven years concealed in Slavery.*" It is a handsome volume of 306 pages, and is on sale at the Anti-Slavery Office, price $1.00. I feel confident that its circulation at this crisis in our country's history will render a signal and most acceptable service.

The lamented Mrs. Follen,[1] in her admirable tract addressed to Mothers in the Free States, and with which that indefatigable colporteur,[2] Miss Putnam,[3] is doing so much good in her visits to families, seems to have anticipated just such a contribution to anti-slavery literature as this book, "Linda." It presents features more attractive than many of its predecessors purporting to be histories of slave life in America, because, in contrast with their mingling of fiction with fact, this record of complicated experience in the life of a young woman, a doomed victim to America's peculiar institution—her seven years' concealment in slavery—continued persecutions—hopes, often deferred, but which at length culminated in her freedom—surely need not the charms that any pen of fiction, however gifted and graceful, could lend. They shine by the lustre of their own truthfulness—a rhetoric which always commends itself to the wise head and honest heart. In furtherance of the object of its author, LYDIA MARIA CHILD has furnished a graceful introduction, and AMY POST a well-written letter; and wherever the names of these two devoted friends of humanity are known, no higher credentials can be required or given. My own acquaintance, too, with the author and her relatives, of whom special mention is made in the book, warrants an expression of the hope that it will find its way into every family, where all, especially mothers and daughters, may learn yet more of the barbarism of American slavery and the character of its victims.

Yours, for breaking every yoke,
WM. C. NELL.[4]

† *Liberator,* January 21, 1861.
1. Eliza Lee Cabot Follen (1787–1860), antislavery author of *To Mothers in the Free States* (1855).
2. An itinerant bookseller.
3. The abolitionist Caroline F. Putnam (1826–1917).
4. William Cooper Nell (1816–1874) was a black Boston author, activist, and Jacobs family friend.

ANONYMOUS

From the *Anti-Slavery Bugle*†

INCIDENTS IN THE LIFE OF A SLAVE GIRL; the narrative of Linda Brent—

We have read this unpretending work with much pleasure. It is a veritable history of the trials and sufferings to which a slave girl was subjected, but who finally triumphed over all discouragements, and obtained freedom for herself and her two children. The manuscript was revised by Mrs. Child, who is acquainted with the author, and who assures the reader that she "has not added anything to the incidents, or changed the import of her very pertinent remarks," the revision being merely for condensation and orderly arrangement. The style is simple and attractive—you feel less as though you were reading a book, than talking with the woman herself. Her revelations of the *domestic* character of the domestic institution unfolds a fearful sum of infamy, that demands the active opposition of every wife and mother in our land.

The work, which forms a handsome volume of over 300 pages, is published for the benefit of the author, and those who desire to benefit themselves as well as the writer, can procure a copy for $1, at the Anti-Slavery office, 221 Washingon St. Boston.

ANONYMOUS

From Our Boston Correspondence‡

Confessions from Boston by an Ordinary Man

BOSTON, February 11, 1861.

* * *

To go to a more serious subject, have you read "Linda." These "Incidents in the Life of a Slave Girl" are nearly as absorbing, from the simple interest of the narrative, as Uncle Tom was from the genius which reproduced the life of the lowly. It is by no means an extreme picture of the delicate institution. The writer never suffers personal chastisement, and meets with white friends who comfort and assist. Her chief persecutor, a physician in good repute and practice, seems to have been subjected to all restraints that Southern public opinion

† *Anti-Slavery Bugle*, February 9, 1861.
‡ *National Anti-Slavery Standard*, February 16, 1861.

can put upon a professional man directly dependent upon it for support. That it did exert a restraint that one in this exceptional position would never have felt, is very evident. The book has a vivid dramatic power as a narrative, and should have a wide circulation. The writer's truth and character are indorsed by persons of the highest social station, who have long known her. A few sentences, in which the moral is rather oppressively displayed, might have been omitted with advantage. These, it is to be wished, Mrs. Child had felt herself authorized to expunge. They are the strongest witnesses who leave the summing up to the judge, and the verdict to the jury. These slight excrescences are the only exceptions to the power and directness of this most interesting testimony.

* * *

ANONYMOUS

Literature†

The Deeper Wrong; or, Incidents in the Life of a Slave Girl. Written by Herself.
Edited by LYDIA MARIA CHILD. London: TWEEDIE. 1862.

In South Carolina, during the Revolutionary War, a planter died, leaving, with other goods and chattels, a slave woman and her three children. The children were his as well as hers; and at his death he bequeathed the mother and her offspring their freedom, with a sum of money to carry them to St. Augustine,[1] where they had relatives. They were captured, however, on their passage, and sold to different purchasers. One of the children, a girl, was bought by the landlord of a large hotel, in which she grew up to great usefulness, as cook, seamstress, wet nurse, &c. The favour was granted to her by her owner of exercising her skill in making "crackers" at night, when her day's work was done, and selling them for her own profit, on condition that she clothed herself and children at her own charge. This she did, and saved money besides; and when her master died, she was the owner of a small hoard. The widow continued to carry on

† *Newcastle* [England] *Daily Chronicle and Northern Counties Advertiser,* March 13, 1862; reprinted in *The Harriet Jacobs Family Papers*, ed. Jean Fagan Yellin, vol. 1 (Chapel Hill: U of North Carolina P, 2008), 375–78. All notes are Yellin's. Page numbers in brackets refer to this Norton Critical Edition.

1. St. Augustine, Florida, founded in 1565 as a Spanish territory, mission, and later Spain's military headquarters in North America, was held as a British possession from 1763 to 1783. See note 1, p. 9.

the hotel, retaining the invaluable cook and needlewoman in the house as a slave; but four of her children were shared up among the children of her master and mistress; and there was a fifth, named Benjamin, the youngest, almost white, who was sold for 720 dollars, to facilitate the equal division of the estate. One of his sisters found a kind mistress in the lady, her foster-sister,[2] to whose lot she fell; and when this sister died, the same kindness was experienced by the child she left behind her, a girl of six years old. The little slave was taught, not only needlework, but to read; and, unconsciously, the gentle mistress was educating a woman who was destined to write her autobiography, and exhibit one more picture of slavery from the life. Such, in brief, is the pedigree of Linda Brent, the author of "The Deeper Wrong."

Linda, at the age of 12, had the misfortune to lose her mistress, who left her by will to a niece of five years old, the daughter of a physician. Whilst she lived in this family, her father, a mulatto carpenter, died. He had for some years worked on his own account, paying his master 200 dollars a-year for the privilege, and keeping himself, and laying by money, with which he would fain have bought the freedom of his family, but could not obtain permission.

At the death of her widowed landlady, her cook, of whom she had borrowed three hundred dollars, lost the loan; and she herself was sold by her grandchild's master, whose real name is veiled under that of "Dr. Flint." He gained little more, however, than discredit by the transaction. The widow's sister, who knew all the circumstances of the case, appeared before the auction-block, and started the sale by a bid of "fifty dollars." Nobody would bid against her; her motive was known and appreciated; and "Aunt Marthy" was knocked down to her new owner, who gave her her freedom.

Linda's mistress, the wife of Dr. Flint, was a contrast to her first. She was easy and listless, but with nerves that could bear the whipping of a woman in her presence till the blood followed the lash. Her master was a libertine; and his slave paints the degradation and wrongs of her order, the natural consequences of the "peculiar institution," and also the domestic jealousy and discord which it engenders. "I draw no imaginary pictures," says the author, "of Southern homes. I am telling the plain truth. Yet, when victims make their escape from this wild beast of Slavery, Northerners consent to act the part of bloodhounds, and hunt the poor fugitive back into his den, 'full of dead men's bones and all uncleanness.' Nay, more! they are not only willing, but proud, to give their daughters in marriage

2. "A female child nursed at the same breast as, or reared together with, another of different parentage." (*The Oxford English Dictionary*, 2nd ed., 2. vols. [New York: Oxford University Press, 1989].)

to slaveholders. The poor girls have romantic notions of a sunny clime, and of the flowering vines that all the year round shade a happy home. To what disappointments are they destined! The young wife soon learns that the husband in whose hands she has placed her happiness pays no regard to his marriage vows. Children of every shade of complexion play with her own fair babies; and too well she knows that they are born unto him of his own household. Jealousy and hatred enter the flowery home and it is ravaged of its loveliness. Southern women often marry a man, knowing that he is the father of many little slaves. They do not trouble themselves about it. They regard such children as property, as marketable as the pigs on the plantation; and it is seldom that they do not make them aware of this by passing them into the slavetrader's hands as soon as possible, and thus getting them out of their sight. I am glad to say there are some honourable exceptions." "You may believe," says Linda to her readers (after entering into details of Southern life), "you may believe what I say; for I write only that which I know. I was twenty-one years in that cage of obscene birds. I can testify, from my own experience and observation, that slavery is a curse to the whites as well as to the blacks. It makes the white fathers cruel and sensual, the sons violent and licentious; it contaminates the daughters, and makes the wives wretched. And as for the coloured race it needs an abler pen than mine to describe the extremity of their sufferings, the depth of their degradation."

Linda's life, from the time of her escape out of the hands of Dr. Flint, down to her emancipation, frankly told as it is, has all the interest of romance and the instruction of history. The credibility of the author is attested by unexceptionable vouchers;[3] and every one who reads "The Deeper Wrong" will all the more rejoice that the Slave Power in America, fighting for its foul existence, is threatened with destruction.

HARRIET JACOBS

Life among the Contrabands[†]

DEAR MR. GARRISON:

I thank you for the request of a line on the condition of the contrabands,[1] and what I have seen while among them. When we parted at that pleasant gathering of the Progressive Friends at Longwood, you

3. Testimonials by Amy Kirby Post and George W. Lowther are included in the appendix to *Incidents*, 203–5 [167–69].
† *Liberator*, September 5, 1862.
1. A term applied to slaves liberated from Confederates during the Civil War.

to return to the Old Bay State,[2] to battle for freedom and justice to the slave, I to go to the District of Columbia, where the shackles had just fallen,[3] I hoped that the glorious echo from the blow had aroused the spirit of freedom, if a spark slumbered in its bosom. Having purchased my ticket through to Washington at the Philadelphia station, I reached the capital without molestation. Next morning, I went to Duff Green's Row, Government head-quarters for the contrabands here. I found men, women and children all huddled together, without any distinction or regard to age or sex. Some of them were in the most pitiable condition. Many were sick with measles, diptheria, scarlet and typhoid fever. Some had a few filthy rags to lie on; others had nothing but the bare floor for a couch. There seemed to be no established rules among them; they were coming in at all hours, often through the night, in large numbers, and the Superintendent had enough to occupy his time in taking the names of those who came in, and of those who were sent out. His office was thronged through the day by persons who came to hire these poor creatures, who they say will not work and take care of themselves. Single women hire at four dollars a month; a woman with one child, two and a half or three dollars a month. Men's wages are ten dollars per month. Many of them, accustomed as they have been to field labor, and to living almost entirely out of doors, suffer much from the confinement in this crowded building. The little children pine like prison birds for their native element. It is almost impossible to keep the building in a healthy condition. Each day brings its fresh additions of the hungry, naked and sick. In the early part of June, there were, some days, as many as ten deaths reported at this place in twenty-four hours. At this time, there was no matron in the house, and nothing at hand to administer to the comfort of the sick and dying. I felt that their sufferings must be unknown to the people. I did not meet kindly, sympathizing people, trying to soothe the last agonies of death. Those tearful eyes often looked up to me with the language, "Is this freedom?"

A new Superintendent was engaged, Mr. Nichol, who seemed to understand what these people most needed. He laid down rules, went to work in earnest pulling down partitions to enlarge the rooms, that he might establish two hospitals, one for the men and another for the women. This accomplished, cots and matresses were needed. There is a small society in Washington—the Freedman's Association—who are doing all they can; but remember, Washington is not New England. I often met Rev. W. H. Channing,[4] whose hands and heart are earnestly in the cause of the enslaved of his country. This gentleman was always

2. Massachusetts.
3. Slavery had been declared illegal in the District of Columbia on April 16, 1862.
4. William Henry Channing (1810–1884), Unitarian clergyman and abolitionist.

ready to act in their behalf. Through these friends, an order was obtained from Gen. Wadsworth for cots for the contraband hospitals.

At this time, I met in Duff Green Row, Miss Hannah Stevenson, of Boston, and Miss Kendall. The names of these ladies need no comment. They were the first white females whom I had seen among these poor creatures, except those who had come in to hire them. These noble ladies had come to work, and their names will be lisped in prayer by many a dying slave. Hoping to help a little in the good work they had begun, I wrote to a lady in New York, a true and tried friend of the slave, who from the first moment had responded to every call of humanity. This letter was to ask for such articles as would make comfortable the sick and dying in the hospital. On the Saturday following, the cots were put up. A few hours after, an immense box was received from New York. Before the sun went down, those ladies who have labored so hard for the comfort of these people had the satisfaction of seeing every man, woman and child with clean garments, lying in a clean bed. What a contrast! They seemed different beings. Every countenance beamed with gratitude and satisfied rest. To me, it was a picture of holy peace within. The next day was the first Christian Sabbath they had ever known. One mother passed away as the setting sun threw its last rays across her dying bed, and as I looked upon her, I could not but say—"One day of freedom, and gone to her God." Before the dawn, others were laid beside her. It was a comfort to know that some effort had been made to soothe their dying pillows. Still, there were other places in which I felt, if possible, more interest, where the poor creatures seemed so far removed from the immediate sympathy of those who would help them. These were the contrabands in Alexandria. This place is strongly secesh;[5] the inhabitants are kept quiet only at the point of Northern bayonets. In this place, the contrabands are distributed more over the city. In visiting those places, I had the assistance of two kind friends, women. True at heart, they felt the wrongs and degradation of their race. These ladies were always ready to aid me, as far as lay in their power. To Mrs. Brown, of 3d street, Washington, and Mrs. Dagans, of Alexandria, the contrabands owe much gratitude for the kindly aid they gave me in serving them. In this place, the men live in an old foundry, which does not afford protection from the weather. The sick lay on boards on the ground floor; some, through the kindness of the soldiers, have an old blanket. I did not hear a complaint among them. They said it was much better than it had been. All expressed a willingness to work, and were anxious to know what was to be done with them after the work was done. All of them said they had not received pay for

5. A term applied to those who seceded from the Union and joined the Confederacy.

their work, and some wanted to know if I thought it would be paid to their masters. One old man said, "I don't kere if dey don't pay, so dey give me freedom. I bin working for ole mass all de time; he nebber gib me five cent. I like de Unions fuss rate. If de Yankee Unions didn't come long, I'd be working tu de ole place now." All said they had plenty to eat, but no clothing, and no money to buy any.

Another place, the old school-house in Alexandria, is the Government head-quarters for the women. This I thought the most wretched of all the places. Any one who can find an apology for slavery should visit this place, and learn its curse. Here you see them from infancy up to a hundred years old. What but the love of freedom could bring these old people hither? One old man, who told me he was a hundred, said he had come to be free with his children. The journey proved too much for him. Each visit, I found him sitting in the same spot, under a shady tree, suffering from rheumatism. Unpacking a barrel, I found a large coat, which I thought would be so nice for the old man, that I carried it to him. I found him sitting in the same spot, with his head on his bosom. I stooped down to speak to him. Raising his head, I found him dying. I called his wife. The old woman, who seems in her second childhood, looked on as quietly as though we were placing him for a night's rest. In this house are scores of women and children, with nothing to do, and nothing to do with. Their husbands are at work for the Government. Here they have food and shelter, but they cannot get work. The slaves who come into Washington from Maryland are sent here to protect them from the Fugitive Slave Law. These people are indebted to Mr. Rufus Leighton, formerly of Boston, for many comforts. But for their Northern friends, God pity them in their wretched and destitute condition! The Superintendent, Mr. Clarke, a Pennsylvanian, seems to feel much interest in them, and is certainly very kind. They told me they had confidence in him as a friend. That is much for a slave to say.

From this place, I went to Birch's slave-pen, in Alexandria. This place forms a singular contrast with what it was two years ago. The habitable part of the building is filled with contrabands; the old jail is filled with secesh prisoners—all within speaking distance of each other. Many a compliment is passed between them on the change in their positions. There is another house on Cameron street, which is filled with very destitute people. To these places I distributed large supplies of clothing, given me by the ladies of New York, New Bedford, and Boston. They have made many a desolate heart glad. They have clothed the naked, fed the hungry. To them, God's promise is sufficient.

Let me tell you of another place, to which I always planned my last visit for the day. There was something about this house to make you forget that you came to it with a heavy heart. The little children you meet at this door bring up pleasant memories when you leave it; from the older ones you carry pleasant recollections. These were what the people call the more favored slaves, and would boast of having lived in the first families in Virginia.[6] They certainly had reaped some advantage from the contact. It seemed by a miracle that they had all fallen together. They were intelligent, and some of the young women and children beautiful. One young girl, whose beauty I cannot describe, although its magnetism often drew me to her side, I loved to talk with, and look upon her sweet face, covered with blushes; besides, I wanted to learn her true position, but her gentle shyness I had to respect. One day, while trying to draw her out, a fine-looking woman, with all the pride of a mother, stepped forward, and said—"Madam, this young woman is my son's wife." It was a relief. I thanked God that this young creature had an arm to lean upon for protection. Here I looked upon slavery, and felt the curse of their heritage was what is considered the best blood of Virginia. On one of my visits here, I met a mother who had just arrived from Virginia, bringing with her four daughters. Of course, they belonged to one of the first families. This man's strong attachment to this woman and her children caused her, with her children, to be locked up one month. She made her escape one day while her master had gone to learn the news from the Union army. She fled to the Northern army for freedom and protection. These people had earned for themselves many little comforts. Their houses had an inviting aspect. The clean floors, the clean white spreads on their cots, and the general tidiness throughout the building, convinced me they had done as well as any other race could have done, under the same circumstances.

Let me tell you of another place—Arlington Heights. Every lady has heard of Gen. Lee's beautiful residence, which has been so faithfully guarded by our Northern army. It looks as though the master had given his orders every morning. Not a tree around that house has fallen. About the forts and camps they have been compelled to use the axe. At the quarters, there are many contrabands. The men are employed, and most of the women. Here they have plenty of exercise in the open air, and seem very happy. Many of the regiments are stationed here. It is a delightful place for both the soldier and the contraband. Looking around this place, and remembering what I had heard of the character of the man who owned it before it passed into the hands of its present owner, I was much inclined to say, Although the wicked prosper for a season, the way of the transgressor is hard.[7]

When in Washington for the day, my morning visit would be up at Duff Green's Row. My first business would be to look into a small

6. Refers to white, elite families in Virginia who trace their ancestors back to the colonial period.
7. Proverbs 13.15.

room on the ground floor. This room was covered with lime. Here I would learn how many deaths had occurred in the last twenty-four hours. Men, women and children lie here together, without a shadow of those rites which we give to our poorest dead. There they lie, in the filthy rags they wore from the plantation. Nobody seems to give it a thought. It is an every-day occurrence, and the scenes have become familiar. One morning, as I looked in, I saw lying there five children. By the side of them lay a young man. He escaped, was taken back to Virginia, whipped nearly to death, escaped again the next night, dragged his body to Washington, and died, literally cut to pieces. Around his feet I saw a rope; I could not see that put into the grave with him. Other cases similar to this came to my knowledge, but this I saw.

Amid all this sadness, we sometimes would hear a shout of joy. Some mother had come in, and found her long-lost child; some husband his wife. Brothers and sisters meet. Some, without knowing it, had lived years within twenty miles of each other.

A word about the schools. It is pleasant to see that eager group of old and young, striving to learn their A, B, C, and Scripture sentences. Their great desire is to learn to read. While in the schoolroom, I could not but feel how much these young women and children needed female teachers who could do something more than teach them their A, B, C. They need to be taught the right habits of living and the true principles of life.

My last visit intended for Alexandria was on Saturday. I spent the day with them, and received showers of thanks for myself and the good ladies who had sent me; for I had been careful to impress upon them that these kind friends sent me, and that all that was given by me was from them. Just as I was on the point of leaving, I found a young woman, with an infant, who had just been brought in. She lay in a dying condition, with nothing but a piece of an old soldier coat under her head. Must I leave her in this condition? I could not beg in Alexandria. It was time for the last boat to leave for Washington, and I promised to return in the morning. The Superintendent said he would meet me at the landing. Early next morning, Mrs. Brown and myself went on a begging expedition, and some old quilts were given us. Mr. Clarke met us, and offered the use of his large Government wagon, with the horses and driver, for the day, and said he would accompany us, if agreeable. I was delighted, and felt I should spend a happy Sabbath in exploring Dixie, while the large bundles that I carried with me would help make others happy. After attending to the sick mother and child, we started for Fairfax Seminary. They send many of the convalescent soldiers to this place. The houses are large, and the location is healthy. Many of the contrabands are here. Their condition is much better than that of those kept in the city. They soon gathered around Mr. Clarke, and begged him to come back and be their boss. He said, "Boys, I want you all to go to Hayti." They said, "You gwine wid us, Mr. Clarke?" "No, I must stay here, and take care of the rest of the boys." "Den, if you aint gwine, de Lord knows I aint a gwine." Some of them will tell Uncle Abe[8] the same thing. Mr. Clarke said they would do anything for him—seldom gave him any trouble. They spoke kindly of Mr. Thomas, who is constantly employed in supplying their wants, as far as he can. To the very old people at this place, I gave some clothing, returned to Alexandria, and bade all good bye. Begging me to come back they promised to do all they could to help themselves. One old woman said—"Honey tink, when all get still, I kin go an fine de old place? Tink de Union 'stroy it? You can't get nothin on dis place. Down on de ole place, you can raise ebery ting. I ain't seen bacca since I bin here. Neber git a libin here, where de peoples eben buy pasly." This poor old woman thought it was nice to live where tobacco grew, but it was dreadful to be compelled to buy a bunch of parsley. Here they have preaching once every Sabbath. They must have a season to sing and pray, and we need true faith in Christ to go among them and do our duty. How beautiful it is to find it among themselves! Do not say the slaves take no interest in each other. Like other people, some of them are designedly selfish, some are ignorantly selfish. With the light and instruction you give them, you will see this selfishness disappear. Trust them, make them free, and give them the responsibility of caring for themselves, and they will soon learn to help each other. Some of them have been so degraded by slavery that they do not know the usages of civilized life: they know little else than the handle of the hoe, the plough, the cotton pad, and the overseer's lash. Have patience with them. You have helped to make them what they are; teach them civilization. You owe it to them, and you will find them as apt to learn as any other people that come to you stupid from oppression. The negroes' strong attachment no one doubts; the only difficulty is, they have cherished it too strongly. Let me tell you of an instance among the contrabands. One day, while in the hospital, a woman came in to ask that she might take a little orphan child. The mother had just died, leaving two children, the eldest three years old. This woman had five children in the house with her. In a few days, the number would be six. I said to this mother, "What can you do with this child, shut up here with your own? They are as many as you can attend to." She looked up with tears in her eyes, and said—"The child's mother was a stranger; none of her friends cum wid her from de ole place. I took one boy down on de plantation; he is a big boy now, working mong de Unions. De Lord help me to bring up dat boy, and he will help me to take care dis child.

8. President Abraham Lincoln.

My husband work for de Unions when dey pay him. I can make home for all. Dis child shall hab part ob de crust." How few white mothers, living in luxury, with six children, could find room in her heart for a seventh, and that child a stranger!

In this house there are scores of children, too young to help themselves, from eight years old down to the little one-day freeman, born at railroad speed, while the young mother was flying from Virginia to save her babe from breathing its tainted air.

I left the contrabands, feeling that the people were becoming more interested in their behalf, and much had been done to make their condition more comfortable. On my way home, I stopped a few days in Philadelphia. I called on a lady who had sent a large supply to the hospital, and told her of the many little orphans who needed a home. This lady advised me to call and see the Lady Managers of an institution for orphan children supported by those ladies. I did so, and they agreed to take the little orphans. They employed a gentleman to investigate the matter, and it was found impossible to bring them through Baltimore. This gentleman went to the captains of the propellers in Philadelphia, and asked if those orphan children could have a passage on their boats. Oh no, it could not be; it would make an unpleasant feeling among the people! Some of those orphans have died since I left, but the number is constantly increasing. Many mothers, on leaving the plantations, pick up the little orphans, and bring them with their own children; but they cannot provide for them; they come very destitute themselves.

To the ladies who have so nobly interested themselves in behalf of my much oppressed race, I feel the deepest debt of gratitude. Let me beg the reader's attention to these orphans. They are the innocent and helpless of God's poor. If you cannot take one, you can do much by contributing your mite to the institution that will open its doors to receive them.

LINDA.

ANONYMOUS

School at Alexandria†

Mrs. Jacobs (Linda) has sent us an admirable photograph of the school in Alexandria which she aided in establishing, and which is so ably conducted by Mr. Banfield, and his assistants, the Misses Lawton. It is delightful to see this group of neatly dressed children, of all ages, and with faces of every variety of the African and mixed type, all intelligent, eager, and happy. Mrs. Jacobs's honest, beaming countenance

† *Freedmen's Record,* September 1865.

irradiates the whole picture; and the good teacher stands in the background looking over his scholars with great complacency. It is a whole volume of answers to the sceptical and superficial questions often put as to the desire and capacity of the negro race for improvement.

The picture may be seen at our office by any friends wishing to know how a freedman's school looks.

ANONYMOUS

A Milestone of Progress†

We have before referred to Mrs. Harriet Jacobs, whose autobiography is well known under the title of "Linda." For the last three years she has been working among the freedmen of Alexandria, having established a school there whose teachers have been supplied by this society. The people at Alexandria are now so far advanced towards education and self-support, that she feels justified in leaving them, that she may carry the blessings of her influence to those more in need. She has lately paid a visit to her early home in Edenton, N.C., where her years of slavery were passed. All was changed; only a few old people remembered "the chile who had been gone so long." But she looked up to her old prison-house, and thanked God for the deliverance vouchsafed her that she might lead her people, and felt that she would willingly bear seven years more of such misery, for such recompense. The son of her old master came to see her. He has lost all his property, and professes to have been all through the war a good Union man, and a great friend of the negro. He asks the influence of his former slave to procure him an office under the Freedmen's Bureau. We have seen a set of German pictures, called "The World Turned Upside Down." We think this incident would add another scene to the series.

THE REVEREND FRANCIS J. GRIMKÉ

Eulogy for Harriet Jacobs‡

It has been some years since I first made the acquaintance of Mrs. Jacobs. She was then living in Cambridge Mass. I took to her a letter of introduction from an intimate friend, who a few years

† *Freedmen's Record*, December 1865.

‡ From the Francis J. Grimké Papers, Moorland-Spingarn Research Center, Howard University. Transcribed by the editors of the first Norton Critical Edition. Francis J. Grimké (1850–1937) was minister of the prominent and socially active Fifteenth Street Presbyterian Church in Washington, DC, and husband of Jacobs's close friend Charlotte Forten Grimké.

afterwards passed into the silent land, into which she has now also entered. I remember as distinctly, as though it were yesterday, our first meeting. The cordiality with which she received me and made me welcome to her pleasant and hospitable home, I shall never forget. I soon felt, in her presence, as much at home as though I had known her all my life. And from that day to the present, as I came to know her more intimately, to get a clearer and fuller insight into the inner workings of her soul, the more strongly was I drawn towards her, and the more highly did I come to esteem her. Since her residence in this city I have seen much of her. I called frequently at her home; and it was always a pleasure to meet her, to get a glimpse of her kind, benevolent face; to feel the pressure of the warm grasp of her friendly hand; and to hear her speak of the stirring times before the war when the great struggle for freedom was going on, and of the events immediately after the war. She was thoroughly alive to all that was transforming, and had a most vivid recollection of the events and of the actors, the prominent men and women, who figured on the stage of action at that time. She herself at the close of the war took an active interest in, and played a most important part in caring for the freedmen, in looking out for their physical needs, and in providing schools for the training of their children. My purpose however, is not to attempt a sketch of her life; that will be done at another time, and by other hands. All I desire to do, in the few moments that I shall occupy, is to state simply in a word, the impression she has left upon me, as I have come in contact with her during the years that I have known her.

She impressed me as a woman of marked individuality. There was never any danger of overlooking her, or of mistaking her for anybody else. Some people are mere nonentities, or, are merely negative quantities. They leave no very clear or marked impression upon those with whom they are associated. It was not so however, in her case. She was always a positive quantity, easily recognizable, and always sure to be felt wherever her lot was cast. She rose above the dead level of mediocrity, like the mountain peaks that shoot above the mountain range.

She was a woman of strong character. She possessed all the elements that go to make up such a character. She had great will power. She knew how to say, No, when it was necessary, and how to adhere to it. She was no reed shaken by the wind, vacillating, easily moved from a position. She did her own thinking; had opinions of her own, and held to them with great tenacity. Only when her judgment was convinced could she be moved.

With great strength of character, there was also combined in her a heart as tender as that of a little child. How wonderfully sympathetic she was; how readily did she enter into the sorrows, the heartaches of others; how natural it seemed for her to take up in the arms of her great love, all who needed to be soothed and comforted. The very Sprit of the Lord was upon her, that Spirit to which the prophet referred when he said: "The spirit of the Lord God is upon me, because he hath sent me to bind up the broken hearted; to comfort all that mourn; to give unto them beauty for ashes, the oil of joy for mourning, the garment of praise for the spirit of heaviness."[1] How divinely beautiful was her sympathy, her tenderness.

She was also the very soul of generosity; she possessed in a remarkable degree, what we sometimes call the milk of human kindness. Especially did her sympathies go out towards the poor, the suffering, the destitute. She never hesitated to share what she had with others, to deny herself for the sake of helping a suffering fellow creature. There are hundreds, who if they had the opportunity to day, would rise up and call her blessed, to whom she has been a real sister of charity, a veritable Dorcas. As I think of her, I am reminded of that impressive scene which took place in the upper room at Joppa, so touchingly recounted in the Acts of the Apostles. How, as that noble woman lay in the icy embrace of death, those whom she had ministered to with her own hands came around and with tears in their eyes spoke of her kind, loving deeds.[2] It is one of the most beautiful pictures presented in the whole word of God: and that which gives it its beauty, is the spirit of unselfish love which animated that noble woman while she lived,—beautiful because it is illumined with that divinest thing in the universe, unselfish love. And it is that love which made that life beautiful, and radiant, and divine, that is one of the crowning glories of this life which has just come to a close, and which has filled it with light and beauty. The estimate which the Master himself placed upon this quality may be seen in the summing up which he makes in the twenty fifth of Matthew, "Come ye blessed of my father, inherit the kingdom prepared for you from the foundation of the world: for I was an hungered and ye gave me meat: I was thirsty and ye gave me drink: I was naked and ye clothed me."[3] And when they protested that they had no recollection of ever having thus ministering to him, his reply was, "In as much as ye have done it unto one of the least of these my brethren, ye have done it unto me." Surely this is what he will say to this departed friend. She ministered to such poor and suffering ones, as God gave her the ability.

I remember some years ago,—it was on Thanksgiving day,—how she gathered into her home a goodly company of old people, who were in destitute circumstances, and made a feast for them. Thus

1. Isaiah 61.1–3.
2. Acts 9.36–39.
3. Matthew 25.34–36.

carrying out the Savior's [. . .] And I remember also how happy it made her to see the old people enjoy themselves. It was a real pleasure to her. How her face lighted up as she looked upon their bright, happy countenances. She seemed even happier than the old people themselves, though their hearts were overflowing with joy. And that is but a sample of what she was constantly doing. The alabaster box of precious ointment which Mary broke and poured out upon the head of Jesus, as an expression of her love, she was constantly breaking and pouring out, in his name, upon the poor, the suffering, the destitute.[4] And like the odor of that precious ointment, the influence of her beautiful and unselfish life shall long continue to be felt amongst us.

As a friend, she was true to the heart's core. She could always be depended upon. She was absolutely loyal. There was not the slightest trace of insincerity about her. There was not a false note in all her make up. She grappled her friends to her soul with hooks of steel.

Religiously, she was a woman of real, genuine piety, of deep heartfelt spirituality. Hers was no mere empty profession: she lived the life of a Christian; hers was the faith that works by love, and that purifies the heart. She believed in God; she believed in Jesus Christ; she rested upon him as her only and all-sufficient Saviour. She desired to please him; to live to his glory; to be wholly conformed to his image; she was constantly reaching forth, ever pressing towards the mark, for the prize of the high calling of God, in Christ Jesus.

This is the life she lived; and with faith unshaken—the faith that looks death in the face and says, where is thy sting? grave, where is thy victory?[5] she fell asleep on last Sabbath morning, in the beautiful realization of the fact that it was well with her soul.

"Asleep in Jesus, blessed sleep
From which none ever wakes to weep,
A calm and undisturbed repose
Unbroken by the last of foes."[6]

We say farewell to her, but it is only for a little time. We sorrow not like those without hope. Ours is the hope, not only of an inheritance that is incorruptible, undefiled and that fadeth not away; but also of a glorious reunion beyond, the smiling and the weeping.

"We shall reach the summer-land,
Some sweet day, by and by;
We shall press the golden strand,
Some sweet day, by and by;

4. Matthew 26.7.
5. I Corinthians 15.55.
6. Margaret Mackay, "Asleep in Jesus! Blessed Sleep" (1832).

Oh, the loved ones watching there,
By the tree of life so fair;
Till we come their joy to share,
Some sweet day, by and by.

At the crystal river's brink,
Some sweet day, by and by;
We shall find each broken link,
Some sweet day, by and by;
Then the star which faded here,
Left our hearts and homes so drear,
We shall see more bright and clear,
Some sweet day, by and by."[7]

7. Fanny Crosby, "We Shall Reach the Summerland." As a hymn, set to music by W. Howard Doane.

Correspondence

HARRIET JACOBS

To Amy Post[†]

Cornwall, [New York] June 25th, [1853]

My Dearest Amy,

I stop in the midst of all kind of care and perplexities to scratch you a line and commit to you a breach of trust which I have never breathed to anyone therefore I cannot ask the favor of anyone else without appearing very ludicrous in their opinion. I love you and can bear your severest criticism because you know what my advantages have been and what they have not been. When I was in New York last week I picked up a paper with a piece alluding to the buying and selling of slaves mixed up with some of Mrs. Tylers views. I felt so indignant. With the impulse of the moment I determined to reply to it.[1] Were to leave next day. I had no time for thought but as soon as every body was safe in bed I began to look back that I might tell the truth. And every word was true accept my Mother and sisters. It was one whom I dearly loved. It was my first attempt and when morning found me I had not time to correct it or copy it. I must send it or leave it to some future time. The spelling I believe was every word correct. Punctuation I did not attempt for I never studied grammar therefore I know nothing about it. But I have taken the hint and will commence that one study with all my soul. This letter I wrote in reply I sent it to the Tribune. I left the same morning. The second day it was in the paper. It came here while Mr W[2] was at dinner. I glanced at it. After dinner he took the paper with him. It is headed Slaves Sold under Peculiar Circumstances. It was Tuesday 21st. I thought

† From the manuscripts found in the Isaac and Amy Post Family Papers (see note 1, p. 156), University of Rochester, New York, and reprinted in the microfilms of *Black Abolitionist Papers, 1830–1865* (Sanford, NC: Microfilming Corporation of America, 1981). Transcribed by the editors of the first edition of this Norton Critical Edition. For clarity and convenience, we have silently edited certain mechanical or grammatical inconsistencies.

1. Jacobs refers here to her letter published in the *New York Tribune* on June 21, 1853, and reprinted in this text as "Letter from a Fugitive Slave" (pp. 173–76).

2. Nathaniel P. Willis, her employer.

perhaps it might be copied in the North Star.[3] If so will you get two and cut the articles out and enclose them to me? I have another but I can not offer it before I can read over the first to see more of its imperfections. Please answer this dear Amy as soon as possible. I want to write you a long letter but I am working very hard preparing the new house. Mrs W cant give me any assistance. She is so feeble. Give a great deal of love to all my much loved friends. Kiss dear Willie for Dah[?] and a heart full of warmest and happiest congratulations to Dear Sarah and [I] beg you to give them for me.[4] I must stop. God bless is my prayer.

Harriet

HARRIET JACOBS

To Amy Post[†]

Oct. 9th [1853]

My Dear Friend,

I was more than glad to receive your welcome letter for I must acknowledge that your long silence had troubled me much. I should have written before this but we have had a little member added to the family and I have had little time for anything besides the extras. It makes my heart sad to tell you that I have not heard from my brother and Joseph.[1] And, dear Amy, I have lost that dear old grandmother that I so dearly loved. Oh, her life has been one of sorrow and trial but he in whom she trusted has never forsaken her. Her death was beautiful. May my last end be like hers. Louisa is with me.[2] I don't know how long she will remain. I shall try and keep her all winter as I want to try and make arrangements to have some of my time.

Mrs. Stowe never answered any of my letters after I refused to have my history in her key.[3] Perhaps, it's for the best. At least I will try and

3. A newspaper edited by Frederick Douglass.
4. Willett ("Willie") Post was Amy's son. Sarah Kirby was Amy's sister, who was also active in the abolition movement.

† From the manuscripts found in the Isaac and Amy Post Family Papers, University of Rochester, New York, and reprinted in the microfilms of *Black Abolitionist Papers, 1830–1865* (Sanford, NC: Microfilming Corporation of America, 1981). Transcribed by the editors of the first edition of this Norton Critical Edition. For clarity and convenience, we have silently edited certain mechanical or grammatical inconsistencies.

1. Her brother, John S. Jacobs, and her son, Joseph.
2. Louisa was Jacobs's daughter.
3. Originally Jacobs had wanted Harriet Beecher Stowe to help write her narrative. Stowe, however, sought to incorporate Jacobs's story into her own *A Key to "Uncle Tom's Cabin."* Jacobs refused.

think so. Have you seen any more of my scribbling? They were marked "fugitive."[4] William Nell[5] told Louisa about the piece and sent her a copy. I was careful to keep it from her and no one here never suspected me. I would not have Mrs. W.[6] to know it before I had undertaken my history for I must write just what I have lived and witnessed myself. Don't expect much of me, Dear Amy. You shall have truth but not talent. God did not give me that gift, but he gave me a soul that burned for freedom and a heart nerved with determination to suffer even unto death in pursuit of that liberty which without makes life an intolerable burden. But, dear A, I fear that I am burdening you. The request in your letter—I told you it was true in all its statements except its being my mother and sister. But we grew up together. The answer to the slave's being outlawed in North Carolina [is] I was home when the poor outlawed was brought in town with his head severed from his body. The piece on Colonisation was just what my poor little indignant heart felt towards the society. And now, my dear friend, don't flatter me. I am aware of my many mistakes and willing to be told of them. Only let me come before the world as I have been, an uneducated oppressed slave. But I must stop. Love to all. God bless you. Excuse the hasty scrawl.

Yours,
Harriet

1 o'clock

HARRIET JACOBS

To Amy Post†

Cornwall [N.Y.] March [1854]

My Dear Friend

I recieved your kind and welcome ↑letter↓ and should have replied to it much earlier but various hindrances have prevented me and when I would have written I was in Bed with a severe attack of

4. Jacobs refers here to the letters published in the *New York Tribune*. They are reprinted in this volume (pp. 173–76).
5. William C. Nell (1816–1874), African American writer and abolitionist who had assisted Jacobs in her attempts to find a publisher.
6. Cornelia Willis, Jacobs's employer.

† From *The Harriet Jacobs Family Papers*, ed. Jean Fagan Yellin, vol. 1 (Chapel Hill: U of North Carolina P, 2008), 212–15. The letter is held in the Isaac and Amy Post Family Papers, University of Rochester, New York. All notes are Yellin's. Interlineations are indicated by arrows (↑↓), although raised letters after dates and raised initials in abbreviations have been silently brought to the line.

Rheumatism so that I could not raise my hands to my head I am still suffering with it in my Shoulders and we have had much sickness in the family this winter I know my plea for want of time will find its way to your heart

my dear friend let me thank you for your kind and generous offer of the hospitality of your pleasant home which would afford me much pleasure to accept but as yet I . . . [*obliterated*] ~~not~~ ↑cannot↓ decide my friends Mr & Mrs Brockett is very anxious that I should go to their home and write they live very quietly and retired they were here and spent a day and night with me and saw from my daily duties that it was hard for me to find much time to write as yet I have not written a single page by daylight Mrs W[1] dont know from my lips that I am writing for a Book and has never seen a line of what I have written I told her in the Autumn that I would give her Louisa services through the winter if she would allow me my winter evenings to myself but with the care of the little baby and the big Babies[2] and at the houshold calls I have but a little time to think or write but I have tried in my poor way to do my best and that is not much

And you my dear friend must not expect much where there has been so little given Yes dear Amy there has been more than a bountiful share of suffering given enough to crush the finer feelings of stouter hearts than this poor timid one of mine but I will try and not send you a portriature of feelings just now the poor Book is in its Chrysalis state[3] and though I can never make it a butterfly I am satisfied to have it creep meekly among some of the humbler bugs I sometimes wish that I could fall into a Rip Van Winkle sleep[4] and awake with the blest belief of that little Witch Topsy[5] that I never was born but you will say it is too late in the day I have outgrown the belief oh yes and outlived it too but you know that my bump of hope[6] is large how is my dear old friend Mr Post I have no doubt but

1. Cornelia Grinnell Willis.
2. The little baby and big babies are the four Willis children alive in 1854: Imogen, Grinnell, Lilian, and Edith, the youngest. (William M. Emery, *The Howland Heirs* [New Bedford, Mass.: E. Anthony and Sons, 1895], 254.)
3. The chrysalis state is "the state into which the larva of most insects passes before becoming an imago or perfect insect. In this state the insect is inactive and takes no food, and is wrapped in a hard sheath or case."(*Oxford English Dictionary.*)
4. Rip Van Winkle is the title character who sleeps for twenty years in a Washington Irving story. (Washington Irving, *Rip Van Winkle and Other Sketches* [Chicago: W. B. Conkey, 1800].)
5. Topsy is the young African American girl in *Uncle Tom's Cabin*, who proclaims that she "never was born" but instead "just growed." (Harriet Beecher Stowe, *Uncle Tom's Cabin*, ed. Jean Fagan Yellin [New York: Oxford University Press, 1998], 249–50.)
6. The "bump of hope" is a reference to phrenology, the nineteenth-century pseudoscience, whose practitioners believed they could understand people's personalities through an examination of the shape of their skulls. A large bump of hope would indicate that a person is an optimist who expects much out of life and has strong self-esteem. (O. S. and L. N. Fowler, *Phrenology: A Practical Guide to Your Head* [New York: Chelsea House Publishers, 1969], vi–vii, 128.)

that he is at his Post perhaps heading a mighty Phalanx to put the Nebraska bill[7] through well he shall have my vote 1856 when Arnold[8] and Belshazzar[9] rools down the avalanche[1] remember me with much kindness to all the family tell Willie[2] I want to see him very much when you write tell me if I know the friend[3] that you spoke of in your letter as soon as my plans are more matured I will write you again it will be very difficult for to get some one in my place yet it will be left for me to do I know of but one person[4] she is a Ladys nurse and her wages would be high but I think that can get her she is a nice person I must stop this rambling letter let no one see it Lou sends much love to you I am sorry you dont know her better you would love her [*along right margin*] *god bless you write as soon as you can yours

H Jacobs*

7. The initial version of the Nebraska Bill, introduced in January 1854 by Senator Stephen A. Douglas, asserted that when the state or states that formed from the Nebraska Territory were admitted into the United States, their constitutions would determine whether they allowed slavery. The plan met with fierce resistance from southern congressmen, and a new version of the bill explicitly repealed the Missouri Compromise's ban on slavery north of 36°30′ and split Nebraska into two territories, with Nebraska in the north and Kansas in the south. Supporters of the Missouri Compromise and the Compromise of 1850 perceived the Kansas-Nebraska Bill, as it was renamed, as a betrayal and joined the abolitionists to oppose it, but the bill was passed in May 1854. (James M. McPherson, *Battle Cry of Freedom* [New York: Oxford University Press, 1988], 121–25.)
8. Benedict Arnold (1741–1801) is famed as a Revolutionary War traitor. An effigy of Stephen Douglas was found suspended from the top of the flagpole on Boston Common, with the inscription, "Stephen A. Douglas, author of the Nebraska Bill—the Benedict Arnold of 1854." (*DAB*, s.v. "Arnold, Benedict"; "Hung in Effigy," *Liberator*, Mar. 31, 1854.)
9. Belshazzar was the dissipated leader in the book of Daniel who, ignoring the needs of his people, ruled blindly, precipitately fell, and whose empire was destroyed. Here he may signify President Franklin Pierce, who supported the Nebraska Bill. (Daniel 11:11, 27.)
1. The "avalanche" is a reference to a poem published in the *Liberator* entitled, "The Presidential Chair for Sale," which ended, "Just then, an avalanche of indignation fell / From an insulted nation on their heads / And buried them in everlasting shame. / It was an avalanche of freemen's votes, / Which rolled from granite hills and mountains green." (George W. Bungay, "The Presidential Chair for Sale," *Liberator*, Feb. 17, 1854.)
2. Willet Post.
3. Amy Post's friend has not been identified.
4. The woman has not been identified.

HARRIET JACOBS

To Amy Post[†]

June 21st [1857]

My Dear Friend

A heart full of thanks for your kind and welcome—letter which would have been answered immediately—but for want of time to think a moment. I would dearly love to talk with you as it would be more satisfactory—but as I cannot I will try to explain myself on paper as well as I can—

I have My dear friend— . . . [*obliterated*] Striven faithfully to give a true and just account of my own life in slavry— God knows I have tried to do it in a Christian spirit— there are somethings that I might have made plainer I know— woman can whisper—her cruel wrongs into the ear of a very dear friend—much easier than she can record them for the world to read— I have left nothing out but what I thought—the world might believe that a Slave woman ↑was↓ too willing to pour out—that she might ↑gain↓ their sympathies I ask nothing— I have placed myself before you to be judged as a woman . . . [*obliterated*] ↑whether↓ I deserve your pity or contempt. I have another object in view— it is to come to you just as I am a poor slave Mother— not to tell you what I have heard but what I have seen— and what I have suffered— and if their is any sympathy to give—let it be given to the thousands—of of Slave Mothers that are still in bondage—suffering far more than I have— let it plead for their helpless Children that they ↑ . . . [*obliterated*]↓ may enjoy the same liberties that my Children now enjoy— Say anything of me that you have had from a truthful source that you think best— ask me any question you like—in regard to the father of my Children I think I have stated all perhaps I did not tell you—that he was a member of Congress—at that time all ~~that~~ of this I have writen— I think it would be best for you to begin with our acquaintance and the length of time that I was in your family you advice ~~about~~ about giving the history of my life in Slavry mention that I lived at service ↑all the↓ while that I was striving to get the Book out but do not say with whom I lived as I would not use the Willis name neither would I like to have people think that I was living an Idle life—and had got this book out merely to make money— my kind friend I do not restrict you in anything for

† From *The Harriet Jacobs Family Papers*, ed. Jean Fagan Yellin, vol. 1 (Chapel Hill: U of North Carolina P, 2008), 236–38. Copyright © 2008 by Jean Fagan Yellin. Used by permission of the University of North Carolina Press. The letter is held in the Isaac and Amy Post Family Papers, University of Rochester, New York. All notes are Yellin's. Interlineations are indicated by arrows (↑↓), although raised letters after dates and raised initials in abbreviations have been silently brought to the line.

you know far better than I do what to say I am only too happy to think that I am going to have it from ↑you—↓

I hope you will be able to read my unconnected scrool— I have been interupted and called away so often—that I hardly know what I have written but I must send it for fear the opportunity will not come to morrow—to do better— Proffessor Botta and Lady[1] with Ole Bull eldest ↑son↓[2] is here—on a visit from the City— beside three other persons that we have had in to spend the day— and Baby[3] is just 4 weeks old this morning— houskeping and looking after the Children—occupy every moment of my time we have in all five Children—three Girls—and two boys. Imogen is at home for the Summer Louise came up and spent a week—with me she desired much love to you— she is not well but looking miserably thin—

I have been thinking that I would so like to go away and sell my Book— I could then secure a copywright—to sell it both here and in England—and by identifying myself with—it I might do something for the Antislavry Cause— to do this I would have to ~~have of~~ ↑get letters of↓ introduction. from some of the leading Abolitionist of this Country to those of the Old— when you write tell me what you think of it I must stop for I am in the only spot where I can have a light—and the mosquitoes have taken possession of me— much love to all my friends—and Willie— and believe me ever yours

Harriet

1. Vincenzo Botta (1818–94), an Italian-born professor of literature at the University of the City of New York, married Anne Charlotte Lynch, a writer and a teacher, in 1855. Anne, author of *A Handbook of Universal Literature* (1860), held a celebrated weekly salon; a contributor to the *Home Journal*, she developed a close friendship with Cornelia Grinnell and Nathaniel Parker Willis. ("Botta, Vincenzo," *Dictionary of American Biography*, 20 vols., eds. Allen Johnson and Dumas Malone [New York: Charles Scribner's Sons, 1928–36]; "Botta, Vincenzo," *Notable American Women, 1607–1950: A Biographical Dictionary*, 3 vols., eds. Edward T. James, Janet Wilson James, and Paul S. Boyer [Cambridge, Mass.: Belknap Press of Harvard University Press, 1971]; Henry R. Beers, *Nathaniel Parker Willis* [1885; New York: AMS Press, 1969], 293.)
2. Ole Bull (1810–80), a Norwegian concert violinist, toured extensively in the United States. In 1852 he attempted to build a community for Norwegian immigrants, Oleana, in Pennsylvania, but the venture quickly failed. Alexander (ca. 1839–?), Bull's eldest son with his first wife, Alexandrine Félicité Villeminot, joined his father in the United States in late 1856. Anne Botta became very close to Alexander before he and his father returned to Norway on July 29, 1857. ("Bull, Ole," *American National Biography*, 24 vols., eds. John A. Garraty and Mark C. Carnes [New York: Oxford University Press, 1999]; Mortimer Smith, *The Life of Ole Bull* [Princeton, N.J.: Princeton University Press, 1943].)
3. In addition to the newborn baby Bailey, Cornelia and Nathaniel Parker Willis had three other children together: Grinnell, born in 1848, Lilian, born in 1850, and Edith, born in 1853. The family also included Imogen, born in 1842, the daughter of Willis and his first wife, Mary Stace. (*Howland Heirs*, 254; *Nathaniel Parker Willis*, 264.)

LYDIA MARIA CHILD

To Harriet Jacobs†

Wayland, Aug. 13th 1860

Dear Mrs. Jacobs,

I have been busy with your M.S. ever since I saw you; and have only done one third of it. I have very little occasion to alter the language, which is wonderfully good, for one whose opportunities for education have been so limited. The events are interesting, and well told; the remarks are also good, and to the purpose. But I am copying a great deal of it, for the purpose of transposing sentences and pages, so as to bring the story into continuous *order*, and the remarks into *appropriate* places. I think you will see that this renders the story much more clear and entertaining.

I should not take so much pains, if I did not consider the book unusually interesting, and likely to do much service to the Anti-Slavery cause. So you need not feel under great personal obligations. You know I would go through fire and water to help give a blow to Slavery. I suppose you will want to see the M.S. after I have exercised my bump of mental order[1] upon it; and I will send it wherever you direct, a fortnight hence.

My object in writing at this time is to ask you to write what you can recollect of the outrages committed on the colored people, in Nat Turner's time.[2] You say the reader would not believe what you saw "inflicted on men, women, and children, without the slightest ground of suspicion against them." What *were* those inflictions? Were any tortured to make them confess? and how? Where [*sic*] any killed? Please write down some of the most striking particulars, and let me have them to insert.

I think the last Chapter, about John Brown,[3] had better be omitted. It does not naturally come into your story, and the M.S. is already too long. Nothing can be so appropriate to end with, as the death of your grandmother.

† The following letters are from the Isaac and Amy Post Family Papers, University of Rochester, New York, and reprinted in the microfilms of *Black Abolitionist Papers, 1830–1865* (Sanford, NC: Micofilming Corporation of America, 1981). Transcribed by the editors of this Norton Critical Edition. For clarity and convenience, we have silently edited certain mechanical or grammatical inconsistencies.

1. A reference to the site on the skull identified with this capacity by phrenologists.
2. Nat Turner (1800–1831) was the leader of a major slave uprising in Southampton County, Virginia, in August 1831.
3. John Brown (1800–1859), a radical white abolitionist who sought to end slavery by armed rebellion.

Mr. Child desires to be respectfully remembered to you.

Very cordially your friend,
L. Maria Child.

Wayland, Sep 27th, 1860

Dear Mrs. Jacobs,

I have signed and sealed the contract with Thayer & Eldridge, in my name, and told them to take out the copyright in my name. Under the circumstances *your* name could not be used, you know. I inquired of other booksellers, and could find none that were willing to undertake it, except Thayer & Eldridge. I have never heard a word to the disparagement of either of them, and I do not think you could do better than to let them have it. They *ought* to have the monopoly of it for some time, if they *stereotype* it, because that process involves considerable expense, and if you changed publishers, their plates would be worth nothing to them. When I spoke of limiting them to an edition of 2000, I did not suppose they intended to stereotype it. They have agreed to pay you ten per cent on the retail price of all sold, and to let you have as many as you want, at the lowest wholesale price. On your part, I have agreed that they may publish it for five years on those terms, and that you will not print any abridgement, or altered copy, meanwhile.

I have no reason whatever to think that Thayer & Eldridge are likely to fail. I merely made the suggestion because they were *beginners*. However, several of the *oldest* bookselling firms have failed within the last three years; mine among the rest. We must run for luck in these matters.

I have promised to correct the proof-sheets, and I don't think it would be of any use to the book to have you here at this time. They say they shall get it out by the 1'st of Nov.

. . .

I want you to sign the following paper, and send it back to me. It will make Thayer and Eldridge safe about the contract in *my* name, and in case of my death, will prove that the book is *your* property, not *mine*.

Cordially your friend,

L. Maria Child.

HARRIET JACOBS

To Amy Post†

New York
June 18th [1861]

My Dear Friends,

I have just received a letter from my brother[1] and one enclosed to his friend Mr. Post. As it was not under cover, I read it myself. I then read mine which was only a few scolding lines—because I had not sent my book to different people in England. In the first place it costs too much to send them while in debt, and in the next I did not care to give it a circulation then before I tried to turn it to some account. So I have taken it very patiently—but I don't give up as I used to. The trouble is I begin to find out we poor women have always been too meek. When I hear a man call a woman an Angel when she is out of sight—I begin to think about poor Leah of the Bible,[2] not Leah of the Spirits.[3] I told our spirit friend it was better to be born lucky than rich—but to my letter. I read mine and a part of yours to Oliver Johnson.[4] He wanted me to take some notes from it. With your permission, may I give them for the *Liberator* and the *Standard*?[5] What my brother says about me is true, in his letter. I am going to Statten Island tomorrow for the first time. I shall register my brother's letter. There is fifteen pounds enclosed in it. I meant to write you a long letter but they are waiting for me. I am so tired. I long to see you. Kindest remembrance to my friends.
With much love,

Harriet

† From the manuscripts found in the Isaac and Amy Post Family Papers, University of Rochester, New York, and reprinted in the microfilms of *Black Abolitionist Papers, 1830–1865:* (Sanford, NC: Microfilming Corporation of America, 1981). Transcribed by the editors of the first edition of this Norton Critical Edition. For clarity and convenience, we have silently edited certain mechanical or grammatical inconsistencies.

1. Harriet's brother, John Jacobs, was living in England at the time.
2. Wife of Jacob in the Old Testament of the Bible.
3. Leah Fox (1813–1890), a well-known spiritualist.
4. Oliver Johnson (1809–1889), an editor of the *Liberator*, an antislavery newspaper.
5. The *National Anti-Slavery Standard* had once been edited by L. Maria Child.

JOHN GREENLEAF WHITTIER

To Lydia Maria Child†

April 1, 1861

A thousand thanks for giving us that wonderful book 'Linda.' We have read it with the deepest interest. It ought to be circulated broadcast over the land. I laid it down with a deeper abhorrence than ever of the Fugitive Slave Law. Has thee seen Dr. Adams's new book?[1] It is the foulest blasphemy ever put in type—but weak as it is wicked. Get it; it is a curiosity of devilish theology worth studying.— What is to be the end of this disunion turmoil?[2] I cannot but hope that, in spite of the efforts of politicians and compromises, the Great Nuisance[3] is to fall off from us; and we are to be a free people.

† From *The Harriet Jacobs Family Papers*, ed. Jean Fagan Yellin, vol. 1 (Chapel Hill: U of North Carolina P, 2008), 341–42. Copyright © 2008 by Jean Fagan Yellin. Used by permission of the University of North Carolina Press. All notes are Yellin's. Yellin's original source note credits "Samuel Pickard, ed., *The Life and Letters of John Greenleaf Whittier*, 2 vols. (Boston: Houghton Mifflin, 1907), 1:436–37," and a further note explains: "The Lydia Maria Child Papers also presents this document and cites Pickard's edition of Whittier's *Life and Letters* as its source. The *Life and Letters* version contains a sentence not found in the Child Papers version. The original has not been located. (Lydia Maria Child Papers, Library of Congress.)"

1. *The Sable Cloud* (1861), by Nehemiah Adams (1806–78)—pastor, from 1834 until his death, of the Essex Street, or Union Congregational Church in Boston—was a response to the sharp criticism he had received for publishing *A South-Side View of Slavery* (1854). While not technically a defense of slavery, *A South-Side View*, which Harriet Jacobs sharply condemns in *Incidents*, attempted to highlight positive aspects of the institution and criticized what Adams believed to be the excesses of northern abolitionists. His last writings on slavery, a volume of sermons titled *At Eventide* (1877), was composed at the request of clergymen in Charleston, S.C., to promote better feelings between the North and the South. (Nehemiah Adams, *The Sable Cloud: A Southern Tale with Northern Comments* [Boston: Ticknor and Fields, 1861]; Nehemiah Adams, *A South-Side View of Slavery* [Boston: T. R. Marvin and B. B. Mussey, 1854]; "Adams, Nehemiah," *Dictionary of American Biography*, edited by Johnson and Malone; *Incidents*, 74, 294 [66]; John B. Pickard, ed., *The Letters of John Greenleaf Whittier*, 3 vols. [Cambridge, Mass.: Belknap Press of Harvard University Press, 1975], 2:17.)
2. Whittier's letter comes less than two weeks before the Confederate attack on Fort Sumter, beginning the Civil War, on Apr. 12, 1861. (*Civil War Day by Day*, 56; James D. Richardson, ed., *A Compilation of the Messages and Papers of the Presidents, 1789–1897*, 10 vols. [Washington, D.C.: published by the authority of Congress, 1899], 6:20–31.)
3. In an 1829 debate on slavery in the District of Columbia, Representative Charles Miner of Pennsylvania referred to blacks as "great nuisance to the community" and "a degraded class [that] will gradually disappear." Here, rhetorically, Whittier applies the phrase to the institution of chattel slavery. (Rogan Kersh, *Dreams of a More Perfect Union* [Ithaca, N.Y.: Cornell University Press, 2001], 118.)

LYDIA MARIA CHILD

To John Greenleaf Whittier†

Medford, April 4'th 1861

Dear Friend Whittier,

I thank you for your friendly letter, and your gentle sister also for her kindly greeting.

I am glad you liked "Linda". I have taken a good deal of pains to publish it, and circulate it, because it seemed to me well calculated to take hold of many minds, that will not attend to *arguments* against slavery. The author is a quick-witted, intelligent woman, with great refinement and propriety of manner. Her daughter, now a young woman grown, is a stylish-looking, attractive young person, white as an Italian lady, and very much *like* an Italian of refined education. If she were the daughter of any of the Beacon St. gentry,[1] she would produce a sensation in the fashionable world. The Mrs. *Bruce*, with whom the mother is described as living in New York, is in fact Mrs. *Willis*; for in fact my protegée has for many years been the factotum in the family of N.P. Willis, the distinguished poet. He has mentioned her incidentally in "Letters from Idlewild," in the Home Journal, as "our intelligent housekeeper," our "household oracle," &c. He would not have *dared* to mention that she had ever been a fugitive slave. The Home Journal is not *violently* pro-slavery, but it is very *insidiously* and *systematically* so. The N.Y. Herald, the Day Book, and the Home Journal, are announced by the Jeff. Davis organs[2] to be the *only* Northern papers that the South can securely *trust*. Mr. Willis entertains many Southerners at Idlewild, and is a favorite with them; for that reason, the author of "Linda" did not ask *him* to help her about her M.S. though he has always been very friendly to her, and would have far more influence than I have. *Mrs.* Willis is decidedly *Anti* Slavery in her feelings. The advent of *any* truth into society is always a Messiah, which divides families, and brings "not peace, but a sword."[3] These things ought not to be mentioned in the *papers*. I use fictitious names in the book; first, lest the Southern family, who secreted Linda some months, should be brought into difficulty; secondly, lest some of her surviving relatives at the South should be

† From *Lydia Maria Child: Selected Letters, 1817–1880*, ed. Milton Meltzer and P. S. Holland (Amherst: U of Massachusetts P, 1982), 378–79. Notes are by the editors of this Norton Critical Edition. The original letter can be found in the Manuscript Division, Library of Congress (microfiche 48/1300).

1. Boston's Beacon Street was a fashionable, white neighborhood.
2. Pro-Confederacy periodicals.
3. Matthew 10.34.

persecuted; and thirdly, out of delicacy to Mrs. Willis, who would not like to have her name bandied about in the newspapers, perhaps to the injury of her husband's *interests*, and certainly to the injury of his *feelings*.

The publishers of "Linda," failed, before a copy had been sold. The author succeeded in buying the plates, paying half the money down. The Boston booksellers are dreadfully afraid of soiling their hands with an Anti-Slavery book; so we have a good deal of trouble in getting the book into the market. Do you think any bookseller, or other *responsible* person in Newburyport, would be answerable for a few? They sell here, at retail, $1 a volume. Whoever would take one or two dozen of them might have them at 68 cts per vol. If you think it worth while to send any to Newburyport or Amesbury, please inform me to whom to send.

With regard to the present crisis of affairs,[4] I think the *wisest* can hardly foresee what turn events will take; but *whatever* way they may develope, I have faith that the present agitation will shorten the existence of slavery; and we ought to be willing to suffer *any*thing to bring about *that* result. The ancient proverb declares that "whom the gods would destroy, they first make mad"; and surely the South are mad enough to secure destruction. My *own* soul utters but *one* prayer; and that is, that we may be effectually separated from *all* the Slave-States. My reasons are, first, that we can in no *other* way present to the world a fair experiment of a free Republic; second, that if the Border-States[5] remain with us, we shall be just as much bound to deliver up fugitives as we now are; third those Border-States will form a line of armed sentinels between us and the New Confederacy of "Slave-own-ia", (as Punch[6] wittily calls it) preventing the escape of slaves from the far south, just as they now do; lastly, we shall continue to be demoralized, politically and socially, by a *few* slave-states, as much as we should by *all* of them; they will always be demanding concessions of principle, and our politicians will always be finding reasons for compromise. There is no *health* for us, unless we can get *rid* of the accursed thing. My prayer is, "Deliver us, O Lord, from this body of Death![″][7]

This does not arise from any sectional or partisan feeling; but simply because my reason, my heart, and my conscience, *all* pronounce this Union to be *wicked*. The original compact is *wrong*; and the attempt to obey the laws of *man*, when they are in open

4. Though the Civil War had not yet officially begun, several states had already seceded from the Union and established themselves as the Confederate States of America.
5. Delaware, Kentucky, Maryland, and Missouri were slave states that had not yet decided whether to stay with the Union or join the Confederacy.
6. A British periodical famous for satiric humor.
7. Romans 7.24.

conflict with the laws of *God*, must *inevitably* demoralize a nation, and ultimately undermine all true prosperity, even in a material point of view.

* * *

HARRIET JACOBS

To J. Sella Martin†

The following letter from Mrs. Jacobs—the "Linda" of the "Deeper Wrong"—to the Rev. Sella Martin,[1] is just received. We think she will not blame us for its publication when she knows how useful it will be.

"Alexandria, April 13th.

"My Esteemed Friend,

"Accept my sincere thanks for the very kind manner in which you spoke of me before the anti-slavery friends in England. The memory of the past in my early life, the cruel wrongs that a slave must suffer, has served to bind me more closely to those around me; whatever I have done or may do, is a christian duty I owe to my race—I owe it to God's suffering poor. When these grateful creatures gather around me, some looking so sad and desolate, while others with their faces beaming happiness, and their condition so much improved by the blessings of freedom, I can but feel within my heart the last chain is to be broken, the accursed blot wiped out. This lightens my labours, and if any sacrifices have been made, they are forgotten. I have often wished you were here,—the field is large, but the labourers are few. We have passed through a trying season;—may I never again behold the misery I have witnessed this winter. When I wrote to our little Society in Boston, the small pox raged fearfully—death met you at every turn. From the 20th of October to the 4th of March, 800 refugees were buried in this town by the Government, beside many private burials, that were not put in the list, but were refugees. The authorities really do not know the number of ex-slaves in this place. We have no superintendent appointed by the Government to look after them: this we need sadly in a place like this, where the citizens are so strongly secessionist—kept down only at the point of northern bayonets. You may imagine there is little sympathy among them for these poor creatures. I found them packed together in the most

† *Black Abolitionist Papers*, 13 April 1863.

1. John Sella Martin (1832–1876), formerly enslaved abolitionist leader and pastor of Boston's Joy Street Baptist, to which Jacobs belonged.

miserable quarters, dying without the commonest necessities of life; for most of the comforts they have had, we are indebted to the Society of Orthodox Friends in New York. They have indeed proved themselves friends to this poor neglected race.

"When I hear the many eloquent appeals made from the pulpit and the forum in behalf of the soldiers, stating our duty to them ought to be paramount to all others, I feel it is right: thank God! I am proud to know the coloured man is helping to fill up these ranks, and he, too, will be acknowledged a man.

"I am gratified to know we are remembered with sympathy by our friends across the water. England has been the coloured man's boast of freedom; we will still believe our English friends true to their declared principles.

"How I should like to talk with you! I have been ill here, and it has left my eyes so weak, I can use them but very little.

"I must say one word about our schools. We have 125 scholars; we have no paid teachers as yet, the children have been taught by convalescent soldiers, who kindly volunteer their services until called to join their regiment. We need female teachers: the little ones are apt; it is surprising to see what progress some of them make. I have a large sewing class of children and adults. I had a long battle about the marriage rites for the poor people, at length I carried my point. The first wedding took place in the school-house; the building was so densely crowded, the rafters above gave way; the excitement was intense for a few moments, the poor creatures thought the rebels were upon them."

CRITICISM

JEAN FAGAN YELLIN

Written by Herself: Harriet Jacobs' Slave Narrative†

I

> Your proposal to me has been thought over and over again, but not without some most painful remembrance. Dear Amy, if it was the life of a heroine with no degradation associated with it! Far better to have been one of the starving poor of Ireland whose bones had to bleach on the highways than to have been a slave with the curse of slavery stamped upon yourself and children. . . . I have tried for the last two years to conquer . . . [my stubborn pride] and I feel that God has helped me, or I never would consent to give my past life to anyone, for I would not do it without giving the whole truth. If it could help save another from my fate, it would be selfish and unChristian in me to keep it back.[1]

With these words, more than a century ago the newly emancipated fugitive slave Harriet Jacobs expressed conflicting responses to a friend's suggestion that she make her life story public. Although she finally succeeded in writing and publishing her sensational tale, its authenticity—long questioned—has recently been denied. Jacobs' *Incidents in the Life of a Slave Girl: Written By Herself* has just been transformed from a questionable slave narrative into a well-documented pseudonymous autobiography, however, by the discovery of a cache of her letters.[2]

† From *American Literature* 53.3 (November 1981): 479–486. Reprinted courtesy of Jean Fagan Yellin.

1. This passage comes from one of thirty letters from Harriet Jacobs to Amy Post in the Post Family Papers recently acquired by the University of Rochester Library. Labeled a.d. #84, it was probably written at the end of 1852 or the beginning of 1853. All of the letters cited from Jacobs to Post are in this collection. Most note only day and month; my attempts to supply missing dates may be in error. Editing Jacobs' letters, I have regularized paragraphing, capitalization, punctuation, and spelling, but not otherwise tampered with text.

   I hasten to record my considerable debt to Dorothy Sterling who includes some of Jacobs' letters in [*We Are Your Sisters* (New York: Norton, 1997)] and with whom I am writing a book on Jacobs; to Karl Kabelac of the University of Rochester Library; and to Patricia G. Holland, co-editor of *The Collected Correspondence of Lydia Maria Child, 1817–1880* (Millwood, N.Y.: K.T.O. Microform, 1979).

2. [Harriet Jacobs], *Incidents in the Life of a Slave Girl. Written by Herself.* Ed. L. Maria Child (Boston: For the Author, 1861). An English edition appeared the following year: [Harriet Jacobs], *The Deeper Wrong: Or, Incidents in the Life of a Slave Girl. Written by Herself.* Ed. L. Maria Child. (London: W. Tweedie, 1862).

   Examining *Incidents* in a discussion of "fictional accounts . . . in which the major character may have been a real fugitive, but the narrative of his life is probably false," John Blassingame recently judged that "the work is not credible." See *The Slave Community* (New York: Oxford Univ. Press, 1972), pp. 233–34.

This correspondence establishes Jacobs' authorship and clarifies the role of her editor. In doing so, it provides us with a new perspective on an unlikely grouping of nineteenth-century writers—Nathaniel P. Willis, Harriet Beecher Stowe, William C. Nell, and L. Maria Child—and enriches our literary history by presenting us with a unique chronicle of the efforts of an underclass black woman to write and publish her autobiography in antebellum America.

II

The appearance of Jacobs' letters has made it possible to trace her life. She was born near Edenton, North Carolina, about 1815. In *Incidents*, she writes that her parents died while she was a child, and that at the death of her beloved mistress (who had taught her to read and spell) she was sent to a licentious master. He subjected her to unrelenting sexual harassment. In her teens she bore two children to another white man. When her jealous master threatened her with concubinage, Jacobs ran away. Aided by sympathetic black and white neighbors, she was sheltered by her family and for years remained hidden in the home of her grandmother, a freed slave. During this time the father of her children, who had bought them from her master, allowed them to live with her grandmother. Although later he took their little girl to a free state, he failed to keep his promise to emancipate the children.

About 1842, Harriet Jacobs finally escaped North, contacted her daughter, was joined by her son, and found work in New York City. Because the baby she was hired to tend was the daughter of litterateur N.P. Willis, it has been possible to use Willis' materials to piece out—and to corroborate—Jacobs' story.[3] In 1849 she moved to Rochester, New York, where the Women's Rights Convention had recently met and where Frederick Douglass' *North Star* was being published each week. With her brother, a fugitive active in the abolitionist movement, she ran an antislavery reading room and met other reformers. Jacobs made the Rochester Quaker Amy Post, a feminist and abolitionist, her confidante; her letters to Post date from this period. In September 1850 Jacobs returned to New York and resumed work in the Willis household. When she was again hounded by her owner, she and her children were purchased and manumitted by Willis.

It was following this—between 1853 and 1858—that Jacobs acquiesced to Post's urgings; after a brush with Harriet Beecher Stowe, she wrote out the story of her life by herself. With the help of black abolitionist writer William C. Nell and white abolitionist woman of letters

3. Willis referred to Jacobs directly—though not by name—in a *House and Home* column reprinted in *Outdoors at Idlewild* (New York: Scribner's, 1855), pp. 275–76.

L. Maria Child (whose correspondence, too, corroborates Jacobs'), her narrative was finally published early in 1861.[4] As the national crisis deepened, Jacobs attempted to swell sentiment for Emancipation by publicizing and circulating her book. During the Civil War she went to Washington, D.C., to nurse black troops; she later returned South to help the freedmen. Jacobs remained actively engaged for the next thirty years. She died at Washington, D.C., in 1897.

III

The primary literary importance of Harriet Jacobs' letters to Amy Post is that they establish her authorship of *Incidents* and define the role of her editor, L. Maria Child. They also yield a fascinating account of the experiences of this underclass black female autobiographer with several antebellum writers.

Jacobs' letters express her conviction that, unlike both his first and his second wife, Nathaniel P. Willis was "pro-slavery," and writings like his picturesque 1859 account of slave life entitled "Negro Happiness in Virginia" must have confirmed her judgment.[5] Because of this—although she repeatedly sought help to win the time and privacy to write, and even requested introductions to public figures in hope that they would effect the publication of her book—Jacobs consistently refused to ask for Willis' aid. She did not even want him to know that she was writing. For years, while living under his roof, she worked on her book secretly and at night.

Her brief involvement with Harriet Beecher Stowe was decisive in the genesis of *Incidents*. When Jacobs first agreed to a public account of her life, she did not plan to write it herself, but to enlist Stowe's aid in helping her produce a dictated narrative. To this end, Jacobs asked Post to approach Uncle Tom's creator with the suggestion that Jacobs be invited to Stowe's home so they could become acquainted. Then, reading in the papers of the author's plan to travel abroad, Jacobs persuaded Mrs. Willis to write suggesting that Stowe permit Jacobs' daughter Louisa to accompany her to England as a "representative southern slave."

Harriet Beecher Stowe evidently responded by writing to Mrs. Willis that she would not take Jacobs' daughter with her, by forwarding to Mrs. Willis Post's sketch of Jacobs' sensational life for verification, and by proposing that if it was true, she herself use Jacobs' story

4. Nell reviewed *Incidents* in *The Liberator*, 25 Jan. 1861. Other reviews include *The National Anti-Slavery Standard*, 23 Feb. 1861, and *The Weekly Anglo-African*, 13 April 1861. Relevant passages from Child's correspondence are cited below.

5. For Jacobs on Willis, see Jacobs to Post, Cornwall, Orange County (late 1852–early 1853?) n.d. #84. Child commented on Jacobs' relationship with Willis in a letter to John G. Whittier dated 4 April 1861, now in the Child Papers, Manuscript Division, the Library of Congress. Willis' article was anthologized in *The Convalescent* (New York: Scribner's, 1859), pp. 410–16.

in *The Key to Uncle Tom's Cabin*, which she was rushing to complete. Reporting all of this to Post, Jacobs suggests that she felt denigrated as a mother, betrayed as a woman, and threatened as a writer by Stowe's action.

> [Mrs. Stowe] said it would be much care to her to take Louisa. As she went by invitation, it would not be right, and she was afraid that if . . . [Louisa's] situation as a slave should be known, it would subject her to much petting and patronizing, which would be more pleasing to a young girl than useful; and the English were very apt to do it, and . . . [Mrs. Stowe] was very much opposed to it with this class of people. . . .
>
> I had never opened my life to Mrs. Willis concerning my children. . . . It embarrassed me at first, but I told her the truth; but we both thought it wrong in Mrs. Stowe to have sent your letter. She might have written to inquire if she liked.
>
> Mrs. Willis wrote her a very kind letter begging that she would not use any of the facts in her *Key*, saying that I wished it to be a history of my life entirely by itself, which would do more good, and it needed no romance; but if she wanted some facts for her book, that I would be most happy to give her some. She never answered the letter. She [Mrs. Willis] wrote again, and I wrote twice, with no better success. . . .
>
> I think she did not like my objection. I can't help it.[6]

Jacobs later expressed her racial outrage: "Think, dear Amy, that a visit to Stafford House would spoil me, as Mrs. Stowe thinks petting is more than my race can bear? Well, what a pity we poor blacks can't have the firmness and stability of character that you white people have!"[7]

Jacobs' distrust of Willis and disillusionment with Stowe contrast with her confidence in William C. Nell and L. Maria Child. After the Stowe episode, Jacobs decided to write her story herself. She spent years on the manuscript and, when it was finished, more years trying to get it published in England and America. Finally, in a letter spelling out the cost of her lack of an endorsement from Willis or Stowe, she reported to Post that Nell and Child were helping arrange for the publication of her autobiography.

> Difficulties seemed to thicken, and I became discouraged. . . . My manuscript was read at Phillips and Sampson. They agreed

6. My discussion of Jacobs and Stowe is based on five letters from Jacobs to Post: Cornwall, Orange County (late 1852–early 1853?) n.d. #84; 14 Feb. (1853?); 4 April (1853?); New Bedford, Mass. (Spring, 1853?) n.d. #80; 31 July (1854?) n.d. #88. The lengthy quotation is from Jacobs to Post, 4 April (1853?). I have been unable to locate any letters to Stowe from Post, Cornelia Willis, or Jacobs, or from Stowe to Cornelia Willis.
7. Jacobs to Post, New Bedford, Mass. (Spring, 1853?) n.d. #80.

> to take it if I could get Mrs. Stowe or Mr. Willis to write a preface for it. The former I had the second clinch [?] from, and the latter I would not ask, and before anything was done, this establishment failed. So I gave up the effort until this autumn [when] I sent it to Thayer and Eldridge of Boston. They were willing to publish it if I could obtain a preface from Mrs. Child. . . .
>
> I had never seen Mrs. Child. Past experience made me tremble at the thought of approaching another satellite of so great magnitude . . . [but] through W. C. Nell's ready kindness, I met Mrs. Child at the antislavery office. Mrs. C. is like yourself, a whole-souled woman. We soon found the way to each other's heart. I will send you some of her letters. . . . [8]

Accompanying this correspondence are two letters from L. Maria Child to Harriet Jacobs. These, I believe, resolve the questions historians have repeatedly raised concerning the editing of Jacobs' manuscript. Child begins the first by describing her editorial procedures in much the same way she later discussed them in her Introduction to *Incidents*.

> I have been busy with your M.S. ever since I saw you; and have only done one-third of it. I have very little occasion to alter the language, which is wonderfully good, for one whose opportunities for education have been so limited. The events are interesting, and well told; the remarks are also good, and to the purpose. But I am copying a great deal of it, for the purpose of transposing sentences and pages, so as to bring the story into continuous *order*, and the remarks into *appropriate* places. I think you will see that this renders the story much more clear and entertaining.

Child's second letter is a detailed explanation of the publisher's contract.[9]

Jacobs' letters are also of value in providing a unique running account of the efforts of this newly emancipated Afro-American woman to produce her autobiography. After deciding to write the

8. Jacobs to Post, 8 Oct. (1860?). I have not been able to document a second attempt to gain Stowe's backing. Jacobs discusses her efforts to publish her book abroad in letters to Post dated 21 June (1857?) n.d. #90; New Bedford, 9 August (1857?); 1 March (1858?); and Cambridge, 3 May (1858?) n.d. #87.
9. Child to Jacobs, Wayland, 13 August 1860; and Wayland, 27 Sept. 1860. Any remaining doubts concerning Child's role must, I think, rest on an undated plea for secrecy from Jacobs to Post: "Please let no one see these letters. I am pledged to Mrs. Child that I will tell no one what she has done, as she is beset by so many people, and it would affect the book. It must be the slave's own story—which it truly is." To my mind, this reflects an effort to shield Child from interruption while she edits the manuscript, not an attempt to hide editorial improprieties. Also see Child to Lucy [Searle], 4 Feb. 1861 in the Lydia Maria Child Papers, Anti-Slavery Collection of Cornell University Libraries.

manuscript herself, she followed the long-standing practice of sending apprentice pieces to the newspapers. In style and in subject, her first public letter reflects her private correspondence and prefigures her book by using the language of polite letters to discuss the sexual exploitation of women in slavery. Jacobs begins with an announcement of her newly found determination to tell her tale by herself. Then—as in the letters and the book—she expresses the pain she feels as she recalls and writes about her life.

> Poor as it may be, I had rather give . . . [my story] from my own hand, than have it said that I employed others to do it for me. . . .
> I was born a slave, raised in the Southern hot-bed until I was the mother of two children, sold at the early age of two and four years old. I have been hunted through all of the Northern States—but no, I will not tell you of my own suffering—no, it would harrow up my soul. . . . [1]

Encouraged by the publication of this letter, Jacobs secretly composed others. Her correspondence during this period reveals that she was at once determined to write, apprehensive about her ability to do so, and fearful of being discovered: "No one here ever suspected me [of writing to the *Tribune*]. I would not have Mrs. W. to know it before I had undertaken my history, for I must write just what I have lived and witnessed myself. Don't expect much of me, dear Amy. You shall have truth, but not talent."[2]

The letters record other pressures. During the years Jacobs composed her extraordinary memoirs, Mr. and Mrs. Willis moved into an eighteen-room estate and added two more children to their family; Jacobs' work load increased accordingly. Writing to Post, she voiced the frustrations of a would-be writer who earned her living as a nursemaid: "Poor Hatty's name is so much in demand that I cannot accomplish much; if I could steal away and have two quiet months to myself, I would work night and day though it should all fall to the ground." She went on, however, to say that she preferred the endless interruptions to revealing her project to her employers: "To get this time I should have to explain myself, and no one here except Louisa knows that I have ever written anything to be put in print. I have not the courage to meet the criticism and ridicule of educated people."[3]

Her distress about the content of her book was even worse than her embarrassment about its formal flaws. As her manuscript neared

1. "Letter From a Fugitive Slave," New York *Tribune*, 21 June 1853. Jacobs' second letter appeared on 25 July 1853.
2. Jacobs to Post, 9 Oct. (1853?) n.d. #85. Also see Jacobs to Post, Cornwall, 25 June (1853?).
3. Jacobs to Post, Cornwall, 11 Jan. (1854?).

completion, Jacobs asked Post to identify herself with the book in a letter expressing her concern about its sensational aspects and her need for the acceptance of another woman: "I have thought that I wanted some female friend to write a preface or some introductory remarks . . . yet believe me, dear friend, there are many painful things in . . . [my book] that make me shrink from asking the sacrifice from one so good and pure as yourself."[4]

IV

While *Incidents* embodies the general characteristics of the slave narrative, it has long been judged a peculiar example of this American genre. It is not, like most, the story of a life but, as its title announces, of incidents in a life. Like other narrators, Jacobs asserted her authorship in her subtitle, wrote in the first person, and addressed the subject of the oppression of chattel slavery and the struggle for freedom from the perspective of one who had been enslaved. But in her title she identified herself by gender, and in her text addressed a specific aspect of this subject. *Incidents* is an account by a woman of her struggle against her oppression in slavery as a sexual object and as a mother. Thus it presents a double critique of our nineteenth-century ideas and institutions. It inevitably challenges not only the institution of chattel slavery and its supporting ideology of white racism; it also challenges traditional patriarchal institutions and ideas.

Publication of this book marked, I think, a unique moment in our literary history. *Incidents* defied the taboos prohibiting women from discussing their sexuality—much less their sexual exploitation—in print. Within its pages, a well-known woman writer presented to the public the writing of a pseudonymous "impure woman" on a "forbidden subject." Here a black American woman, defying barriers of caste and class, defying rules of sexual propriety, was joined by a white American woman to make her history known in an attempt to effect social change. It is ironic that this narrative, which was painfully written in an effort to give "the whole truth," has been branded false. Now that the discovery of Harriet Jacobs' letters has established that her book was indeed *Written By Herself*, we can reexamine its place within women's writings, Afro-American literature, and the body of our national letters.

4. Jacobs to Post, 18 May and 8 June (1857?). Post's signed statement in the Appendix to *Incidents* was written in response to this request.

VALERIE SMITH

From Form and Ideology in Three Slave Narratives†

The way in which the narratives of freed and fugitive slaves were produced has been largely responsible for their uncertain status as subjects of critical inquiry. In form they most closely resemble autobiographies. But if we expect autobiographies to present us with rhetorical figures and thematic explorations that reveal the author's sense of what his or her life means, then these stories disappoint. In each stage of their history, the presence of an intermediary renders the majority of the narratives not artistic constructions of personal experience but illustrations of someone else's view of slavery.

In the earliest examples of the genre, as William L. Andrews has shown, the relationship between narrator and text was triangulated through the ordering intelligence of a white amanuensis or editor. Relying on a model of slavery as a fundamentally benevolent institution, the early narratives portray the slave as either an outlaw or a wayfarer in need of the protection that only white paternal authority could provide.[1] Most of the middle-period accounts, published from the 1830s through the 1860s, claim to be written by the narrators themselves, yet these cases too serve an outside interest: the stories are shaped according to the requirements of the abolitionists who published them and provided them with readers. And as Marion Wilson Starling and Dorothy Sterling have acknowledged, even the narratives transcribed in the twentieth century by the Federal Writers' Project of the Works Progress Administration (WPA) bear more than their share of the interviewers' influence.[2] As Sterling remarks:

> Few of the interviewers were linguists. They transcribed the ex-slaves' speech as they heard it, as they thought they heard it, or as they thought it should have been said—and sometimes, the whiter the interviewer's skin, the heavier the dialect and the more erratic the spelling. A number of the interviews also went

† From *Self-Discovery and Authority in Afro-American Narrative* (Cambridge: Harvard UP, 1987) 9–12, 28–43. Copyright © 1987 by the President and Fellows of Harvard College. Reprinted by permission of the publisher, Harvard University Press. Page numbers in brackets refer to this Norton Critical Edition.

1. William L. Andrews, "The First Fifty Years of the Slave Narrative, 1760–1810," in *The Art of Slave Narrative: Original Essays in Criticism and Theory*, ed. John Sekora and Darwin T. Turner (Macomb, Ill.: Western Illinois University Press, 1982), p. 7.
2. Marion Wilson Starling, *The Slave Narrative: Its Place in American History* (Boston: G. K. Hall, 1981), pp. xvii–xviii; Dorothy Sterling, ed., *We Are Your Sisters: Black Women in the Nineteenth Century* (New York: W. W. Norton, 1984), pp. 3–4.

> through an editorial process in which dialect was cleaned up or exaggerated, depending on the editors' judgment. To attempt to make the language of the interviews consistent or to "translate" them into standard English would add still another change.[3]

It is not surprising that a scholarly tradition that values the achievements of the classically educated, middle-class white male has dismissed the transcriptions of former slaves' oral accounts. Nor is it surprising that even those narratives that purport to be written by slaves themselves have come into disrepute: when three popular narratives were exposed as inauthentic between 1836 and 1838, serious doubts arose about authorship in the genre as a whole.[4] But the intrusive abolitionist influence has interfered with the critical reception of even those narratives that are demonstrably genuine. The former slaves may have seized upon the writing of their life stories as an opportunity to celebrate their escape and to reveal the coherence and meaning of their lives. These personal motives notwithstanding, the narratives were also (if not primarily) literary productions that documented the antislavery crusade. Their status as both popular art and propaganda imposed upon them a repetitiveness of structure, tone, and content that obscured individual achievements and artistic merit.[5]

As Henry Louis Gates, Jr., has shown, apologists and detractors alike have failed to attend to the formal dimensions of black texts:

> For all sorts of complex historical reasons, the very act of writing has been a "political" act for the black author. Even our most solipsistic texts, at least since the Enlightenment in Europe, have been treated as political evidence of one sort or another both implicitly and explicitly. And because our life in the West has been one struggle after another, our literature has been defined from without, and rather often from within, as primarily just one more polemic in those struggles.[6]

The formulaic and hybrid quality of the narratives has rendered their status as critical subjects even more elusive than that of other examples of Afro-American literary expression. Combining elements of history, autobiography, and fiction, they raise unique questions of

3. Sterling, *We Are Your Sisters*, p. 4. For a compelling discussion of ways in which the WPA narratives might be used, see Paul D. Escott, "The Art and Science of Reading WPA Slave Narratives," in *The Slave's Narrative*, ed. Charles T. Davis and Henry Louis Gates, Jr. (New York: Oxford University Press, 1985), pp. 40–48.
4. Starling, *The Slave Narrative*, pp. 226–232.
5. See James Olney's provocative discussion of this tension in "'I Was Born': The Slave Narratives, Their Status as Autobiography and as Literature," *Callaloo*, 20 (Winter 1984), 46–73.
6. Henry Louis Gates, Jr., "Criticism in the Jungle," in *Black Literature and Literary Theory* (New York: Methuen, 1984), p. 5.

interpretation. To study them as, for example, sustained images of an author's experience ignores the fact that they conform rather programmatically to a conventional pattern. Or to talk about the unity of an individual narrative is to ignore the fact that the texts as we read them contain numerous authenticating documents that create a panoply of other voices. Only by beginning from a clear sense of the narratives' generic properties does one capture the subtlety and achievement of the most compelling accounts.[7]

[Some] narratives, [however, like Harriet Jacobs's *Incidents in the Life of a Slave Girl* (1861),] elude the domination of received generic structures and conventions. * * * [Such] narratives * * * test the limits of the formula [and] tell us most about what those conventions signify. Furthermore, the narrators who transform the conventions into an image of what they believe their lives mean most closely resemble autobiographers; they leave the impress of their personal experience on the structure in which they tell their story. Perhaps most important, these narratives are of interest because in their variations on the formula they provide a figure for the author's liberation from slavery, the central act of the accounts themselves. In these places of difference, the narrators of these stories of freedom reveal their resistance even to the domination of their white allies.

* * *

* * * Harriet Jacobs's freedom to reconstruct her life was limited by a genre that suppressed subjective experience in favor of abolitionist polemics. But if slave narrators in general were restricted by

7. The narratives first emerge as a subject in critical literature in the 1970s. The nature of the commentary bespeaks their troublesomeness as a literary category more precisely than does their omission from earlier studies. Two seminal books, Stephen Butterfield's *Black Autobiography in America* (Amherst: University of Massachusetts Press, 1974) and Sidonie Ann Smith's *Where I'm Bound: Patterns of Slavery and Freedom in Black American Autobiography* (Westport, Conn.: Greenwood Press, 1974) explore the connections between the narratives and modern black autobiography. Neither acknowledges the characteristics of the narratives that distinguish them from either history or autobiography; both present an image of the narratives as a monolithic body of work.

More recent studies seek to establish the relationship of the accounts to the conditions out of which they arose. Frances Smith Foster's *Witnessing Slavery* (Westport, Conn.: Greenwood Press, 1979) and Starling's *Slave Narrative: Its Place in American History* contribute immeasurably to our understanding of the narratives in their political, cultural, and literary contexts. Both provide detailed summaries of the themes and plots of the narratives, but neither discusses the common rhetorical structures that bind the texts as a genre.

H. Bruce Franklin in *The Victim as Criminal and Artist: Literature from the American Prison* (New York: Oxford University Press, 1978) and Houston A. Baker, Jr., in *The Journey Back: Issues in Black Literature and Criticism* (Chicago: University of Chicago Press, 1980), in contrast, demonstrate ways in which the texts respond to the ideological context in which they were produced. By analyzing the resonance and textual strategies of the Douglass and Jacobs narratives in the one case and of the Equiano and Douglass narratives in the other, they offer the most persuasive evidence of their literariness. To borrow Franklin's formulation (p. 7), by using methods that ordinarily illuminate our readings of classic texts, they make a strong argument for the narratives' subtlety and complexity.

the antislavery agenda, she was doubly bound by the form in which she wrote, for it contained a plot more compatible with received notions of masculinity than with those of womanhood. As Niemtzow has suggested, Jacobs incorporated the rhetoric of the sentimental novel into her account, at least in part because it provided her with a way of talking about her vulnerability to the constant threat of rape. This form imposed upon her restrictions of its own.[8] Yet she seized authority over her literary restraints in much the same way that she seized power in life. From within her ellipses and ironies—equivalents of the garret in which she concealed herself for seven years—she expresses the complexity of her experience as a black woman.

In *Incidents in the Life of a Slave Girl*, the account of her life as a slave and her escape to freedom, Harriet Jacobs refers to the crawl space in which she concealed herself for seven years as a "loophole of retreat."[9] The phrase calls attention both to the closeness of her hiding place—three feet high, nine feet long, and seven feet wide—and the passivity that even voluntary confinement imposes. For if the combined weight of racism and sexism have already placed inexorable restrictions upon her as a black female slave in the antebellum South, her options seem even narrower after she conceals herself in the garret, where just to speak to her loved ones jeopardizes her own and her family's welfare.

And yet Jacobs's phrase "the loophole of retreat" possesses an ambiguity of meaning that extends to the literal loophole as well. For if a loophole signifies for Jacobs a place of withdrawal, it signifies in common parlance an avenue of escape. Likewise, and perhaps more important, the garret, a place of confinement, also renders the narrator spiritually independent of her master, and makes possible her ultimate escape to freedom. It is thus hardly surprising that Jacobs finds her imprisonment, however uncomfortable, an improvement over her "lot as a slave" (p. 117) [98]. As her statement implies, she dates her emancipation from the time she entered her loophole, even though she did not cross into the free states until seven years later. Given the constraints that framed her life, even the act of choosing her own mode of confinement constitutes an exercise of will, an indirect assault against her master's domination.[1]

8. Niemtzow, "The Problematic of Self," pp. 105–108.
9. Linda Brent [Harriet Jacobs], *Incidents in the Life of a Slave Girl* (New York: Harcourt Brace Jovanovich, 1973), p. 117 [97]. Subsequent references will be given in the text.
1. As I completed revisions of this discussion, I read Houston A. Baker, Jr.'s, *Blues, Ideology, and Afro-American Literature: A Vernacular Theory* (Chicago: University of Chicago Press, 1984). He too considers the significance of this image to Jacobs's account, but he focuses on Jacobs's ability to transform the economics of her oppression, whereas I concentrate on her use of received literary conventions.

The plot of Jacobs's narrative, her journey from slavery to freedom, is punctuated by a series of similar structures of confinement, both literal and figurative. Not only does she spend much of her time in tiny rooms (her grandmother's garret, closets in the homes of two friends), but she seems as well to have been penned in by the importunities of Dr. Flint, her master: "My master met me at every turn, reminding me that I belonged to him, and swearing by heaven and earth that he would compel me to submit to him. If I went out for a breath of fresh air after a day of unwearied toil, his footsteps dogged me. If I knelt by my mother's grave, his dark shadow fell on me even there" (p. 27) [28]. Repeatedly she escapes overwhelming persecutions only by choosing her own space of confinement: the stigma of unwed motherhood over sexual submission to her master; concealment in one friend's home, another friend's closet, and her grandmother's garret over her own and her children's enslavement on a plantation; Jim Crowism and the threat of the Fugitive Slave Law in the North over institutionalized slavery at home. Yet each moment of apparent enclosure actually empowers Jacobs to redirect her own and her children's destiny. To borrow Elaine Showalter's formulation, she inscribes a subversive plot of empowerment beneath the more orthodox, public plot of weakness and vulnerability.[2]

It is not surprising that both literal and figurative enclosures proliferate in Jacobs's narrative. As a nineteenth-century black woman, former slave, and writer, she labored under myriad social and literary restrictions that shaped the art she produced.[3] Feminist scholarship has shown that, in general, women's writing in the nineteenth and twentieth centuries has been strongly marked by imagery of confinement, a pattern of imagery that reflects the limited cultural options available to the authors because of their gender and chosen profession. Sandra Gilbert and Susan Gubar, for instance, describe the prodigious restraints historically imposed upon women that led to the recurrence of structures of concealment and evasion in their literature.[4] Not only were they denied access to the professions, civic responsibilities, and higher education, but also their secular and religious instruction encouraged them from childhood to adopt the "feminine," passive virtues of "submissiveness, modesty, selflessness."[5] Taken to its extreme, such an idealization of female weakness and

2. Elaine Showalter, "Review Essay," *Signs*, I (1975), 435.
3. Only recently have scholars accepted the authenticity of Jacobs's account, thanks largely to Jean Fagan Yellin's meticulous and illuminating documentation of Jacobs's life and writing. See her essay "Texts and Contexts of Harriet Jacobs's *Incidents in the Life of a Slave Girl; Written by Herself*," in Davis and Gates, *The Slave's Narrative*, pp. 262–282. See also Yellin's edition of this text (Cambridge, Mass.: Harvard University Press, 1987).
4. Sandra M. Gilbert and Susan Gubar, *The Madwoman in the Attic* (New Haven: Yale University Press, 1979), pp. 3–104 passim.
5. Ibid., p. 23.

self-effacement contributed to what Ann Douglas has called a "domestication of death," characterized by the prevalence in literature of a hagiography of dying women and children, and the predilection in life for dietary, sartorial, and medical practices that led to actual or illusory weakness and illness.[6]

Literary women confronted additional restraints, given the widespread cultural identification of creativity with maleness. As Gubar argues elsewhere, our "culture is steeped in . . . myths of male primacy in theological, artistic, and scientific creativity," myths that present women as art objects, perhaps, but never as creators.[7] These ideological restraints, made concrete by inhospitable editors, publishers, and reviewers and disapproving relatives and friends have, as Gilbert and Gubar demonstrate, traditionally invaded women's literary undertakings with all manner of tensions. The most obvious sign of nineteenth-century women writers' anxiety about their vocation (but one that might also be attributed to the demands of the literary marketplace) is the frequency with which they published either anonymously or under a male pseudonym. Their sense of engaging in an improper enterprise is evidenced as well by their tendency both to disparage their own accomplishments in autobiographical remarks and to inscribe deprecations of women's creativity within their fictions. Moreover, they found themselves in a curious relation to the implements of their own craft. The literary conventions they received from genres dominated by male authors perpetuated reductive, destructive images of women that cried out to be revised. Yet the nature of women writer's socialization precluded their confronting problematic stereotypes directly. Instead, as Patricia Meyer Spacks, Carolyn Heilbrun, and Catherine Stimpson, as well as Showalter and Gilbert and Gubar have shown, the most significant women writers secreted revisions of received plots and assumptions either within or behind the more accessible content of their work.[8]

Jacobs's *Incidents* reveals just such a tension between the manifest and the concealed plot. Jacobs explicitly describes her escape as a progression from one small space to another. As if to underscore her helplessness and vulnerability, she indicates that although she ran alone to her first friend's home, she left each of her hiding

6. Ann Douglas, *The Feminization of American Culture* (New York: Avon Books, 1977), pp. 240–273 passim.
7. Susan Gubar, "'The Blank Page' and the Issues of Female Creativity," in *Writing and Sexual Difference*, ed. Elizabeth Abel (Chicago: University of Chicago Press, 1982), p. 74.
8. See Showalter, "Review Essay," and Gilbert and Gubar, *The Madwoman in the Attic*. See also Patricia Meyer Spacks, *The Female Imagination* (New York: Knopf, 1975), p. 317, and Carolyn Heilbrun and Catharine Stimpson, "Theories of Feminist Criticism: A Dialogue," in *Feminist Literary Criticism*, ed. Josephine Donovan (Lexington, Ky.: University Press of Kentucky, 1975), p. 62.

places only with the aid of someone else. In fact, when she goes to her second and third hiding places, she is entirely at the mercy of her companion, for she is kept ignorant of her destination. Yet each closet, while at one level a prison, may be seen as well as a station on her journey to freedom. Moreover, from the garret of her seven-year imprisonment she uses to her advantage all the power of the voyeur—the person who sees but remains herself unseen. When she learns that Sands, her white lover and the father of her children, is about to leave town, she descends from her hiding place and, partly because she catches him unawares, is able to secure his promise to help free her children. In addition, she prevents her own capture not merely by remaining concealed but, more important, by embroiling her master, Dr. Flint, in an elaborate plot that deflects his attention. Fearing that he suspects her whereabouts, she writes him letters that she then has postmarked in Boston and New York to send him off in hot pursuit in the wrong direction. Despite her grandmother's trepidation, Jacobs clearly delights in exerting some influence over the man who has tried to control her.

Indeed, if the architectural close places are at once prisons and exits, then her relationship to Sands is both as well. She suggests that when she decides to take him as her lover, she is caught between Scylla and Charybdis. Forbidden to marry the free black man she loves, she knows that by becoming Sands's mistress she will compromise her virtue and reputation. But, she remarks, since her alternative is to yield to the master she loathes, she has no choice but to have sexual relations with Sands. As she writes: "It seems less degrading to give one's self, than to submit to compulsion. There is something akin to freedom in having a lover who has no control over you, except that which he gains by kindness and attachment" (p. 55) [50].

One might argue that Jacobs's dilemma encapsulates the slave woman's sexual victimization and vulnerability. I do not mean to impugn that reading, but I would suggest that her relationship with Sands provides her with a measure of power. Out of his consideration for her, he purchases her children and her brother from Flint. William, her brother, eventually escapes from slavery on his own, but Sands frees the children in accordance with their mother's wishes. In a system that allowed the buying and selling of people as if they were animals, Jacobs's influence was clearly minimal. Yet even at the moments when she seems most vulnerable, she exercises some degree of control.

* * *

* * * [Still,] Jacobs's tale is not the classic story of the triumph of the individual will; rather it is more a story of a triumphant

self-in-relation.[9] With the notable exception of the narrative of William and Ellen Craft, most of the narratives by men represent the life in slavery and the escape as essentially solitary journeys. This is not to suggest that male slaves were more isolated than their female counterparts, but it does suggest that they were attempting to prove their equality, their manhood, in terms acceptable to their white, middle-class readers.

Under different, equally restrictive injunctions, Jacobs readily acknowledges the support and assistance she received, as the description of her escape makes clear. Not only does she diminish her own role in her escape, but she is also quick to recognize the care and generosity of her family in the South and her friends in the North. The opening chapter of her account focuses not on the solitary "I" of so many narratives but on Jacobs's relatives. And she associates her desire for freedom with her desire to provide opportunities for her children.

By mythologizing rugged individuality, physical strength, and geographical mobility, the narratives enshrine cultural definitions of masculinity.[1] The plot of the standard narrative may thus be seen as not only the journey from slavery to freedom but also the journey from slavehood to manhood. Indeed, that rhetoric explicitly informs some of the best known and most influential narratives. In the key scene in William Wells Brown's account, for example, a Quaker friend and supporter renames the protagonist, saying, "Since thee has got out of slavery, thee has become a man, and men always have two names."[2] Douglass also explicitly contrasts slavehood with manhood, for he argues that learning to read made him a man but being beaten made him a slave. Only by overpowering his overseer was he able to become a man—thus free—again.

Simply by underscoring her reliance on other people, Jacobs reveals another way in which the story of slavery and escape might be written. But in at least one place in the narrative she makes obvious her problematic relation to the rhetoric she uses. The fourth chapter, "The Slave Who Dared to Feel Like a Man," bears a title reminiscent of one of the most familiar lines from Douglass's 1845 *Narrative*. Here Jacobs links three anecdotes that illustrate the fact that independence of mind is incompatible with the demands of life

9. I draw here on the vocabulary of recent feminist psychoanalytic theory, which revises traditional accounts of female psychosexual development. See Jean Baker Miller, *Toward a New Psychology of Women* (Boston: Beacon Press, 1976); Nancy Chodorow, *The Reproduction of Mothering: Psychoanalysis and the Sociology of Gender* (Berkeley: University of California Press, 1978); and Carol Gilligan, *In a Different Voice* (Cambridge, Mass.: Harvard University Press, 1982).
1. I acknowledge here my gratitude to Mary Helen Washington for pointing out to me this characteristic of the narratives.
2. William Wells Brown, *Narrative of William W. Brown* (Boston: The Anti-Slavery Office, 1847; rpt. New York: Arno Press, 1968), p. 105.

as a slave. She begins with a scene in which her grandmother urges her family to content themselves with their lot as slaves; her son and grandchildren, however, cannot help resenting her admonitions. The chapter then centers on the story of her Uncle Ben, a slave who retaliates when his master tries to beat him and eventually escapes to the North.

The chapter title thus refers explicitly to Ben, the slave who, by defending himself, dares to feel like a man. And yet it might also refer to the other two stories included in the chapter. In the first, Jacobs's brother, William, refuses to capitulate to his master's authority. In the second, Jacobs describes her own earliest resolution to resist her master's advances. Although the situation does not yet require her to fight back, she does say that her young arm never felt half so strong. Like her uncle and brother, she determines to remain unconquered.

The chapter focuses on Ben's story, then, but it indicates also that his niece and nephew can resist authority. Its title might therefore refer to either of them as well. As Jacobs suggests by indirection, as long as the rhetoric of the genre identifies freedom and independence of thought with manhood, it lacks a category for describing the achievements of the tenacious black woman.

As L. Maria Child's introduction, Jacobs's own preface, and the numerous asides in the narrative make clear, Jacobs was writing for an audience of northern white women, a readership that by midcentury had grown increasingly leisured, middle class, and accustomed to the conventions of the novel of domestic sentiment. Under the auspices of Child, herself an editor and writer of sentimental fiction, Jacobs constructed the story of her life in terms that her reader would find familiar. Certainly Jacobs's *Incidents* contains conventional apostrophes that call attention to the interests she shares with her readers. But as an additional strategy for enlisting their sympathy, she couches her story in the rhetoric and structures of popular fiction.

The details of the narrator's life that made her experience as a slave more comfortable than most are precisely those that render her story particularly amenable to the conventions and assumptions of the sentimental novel. Like Douglass's, slave narratives often begin with an absence, the narrator announcing from the first that he has no idea where or when he was born or who his parents were. But Jacobs was fortunate enough to have been born into a stable family at once nuclear and extended. Although both of her parents died young, she nurtured vivid, pleasant memories of them. Moreover, she remained close to her grandmother, an emancipated, self-supporting, property-owning black woman, and to her uncles and aunts, until she escaped to the North.

Jacobs's class affiliation, and the fact that she was subjected to relatively minor forms of abuse as a slave, enabled her to locate a point of identification both with her readers and with the protagonists of sentimental fiction. Like them, she aspired to chastity and piety as consummate feminine virtues and hoped that marriage and family would be her earthly reward. Her master, for some reason reluctant to force her to submit sexually, harassed her, pleaded with her, and tried to bribe her into capitulating in the manner of an importunate suitor like Richardson's seducer. He tells her, for example, that he would be within his rights to kill her or have her imprisoned for resisting his advances, but he wishes to make her happy and thus will be lenient toward her. She likens his behavior to that of a jealous lover on one occasion when he becomes violent with her son. And he repeatedly offers to make a lady of her if she will grant him her favors, volunteering to set her up in a cottage of her own where she can raise her children.

By pointing up the similarities between her own story and those plots with which her readers would have been familiar, Jacobs could thus expect her readers to identify with her suffering. Moreover, this technique would enable them to appreciate the ways in which slavery converts into liabilities the very qualities of virtue and beauty that women were taught to cultivate. This tactic has serious limitations, however. As is always the case when one attempts to universalize a specific political point, Jacobs here trivializes the complexity of her situation when she likens it to a familiar paradigm. Like Richardson's Pamela, Jacobs is her pursuer's servant. But Pamela is free to escape, if she chooses, to the refuge of her parents' home, while as Dr. Flint's property, Jacobs has severely limited options. Moreover, Mr. B., in the terms the novel constructs, can redeem his importunities by marrying Pamela and elevating her and their progeny to his position. No such possibility exists for Jacobs and her master. Indeed, the system of slavery, conflating as it does the categories of property and sexual relationships, ensures that her posterity will become his material possessions.

For other reasons as well, the genre seems inappropriate for Jacobs's purposes. As the prefatory documents imply, Jacobs's readers were accustomed to a certain degree of propriety and circumlocution in fiction. In keeping with cultural injunctions against women's assertiveness and directness in speech, the literature they wrote and read tended to be "exercises in euphemism" that excluded certain subjects from the purview of fiction.[3] But Jacobs's purpose was to celebrate her freedom to express what she had undergone, and to engender additional abolitionist support. Child and Jacobs

3. Niemtzow, "The Problematic of Self," pp. 105–106.

both recognized that Jacobs's story might well violate the rules of decorum in the genre. Their opening statements express the tension between the content of the narrative and the form in which it appears.

Child's introduction performs the function conventional to the slave narrative of establishing the narrator's veracity and the reliability of the account. What is unusual about her introduction, however, is the basis of her authenticating statement: she establishes her faith in Jacobs's story on the correctness and delicacy of the author's manner.

> The author of the following autobiography is personally known to me, and her conversation and manners inspire me with confidence. During the last seventeen years, she has lived the greater part of the time with a distinguished family in New York, and has so deported herself as to be highly esteemed by them. This fact is sufficient, without further credentials of her character. I believe those who know her will not be disposed to doubt her veracity, though some incidents in her story are more romantic than fiction. (p. xi) [6]

This paragraph attempts to equate contradictory notions; Child implies not only that Jacobs is both truthful and a model of decorous behavior but also that her propriety ensures her veracity. Child's assumption is troublesome, since ordinarily decorousness connotes the opposite of candor: one equates propriety not with openness but with concealment in the interest of taste.

Indeed, later in her introduction Child seems to recognize that an explicit political imperative may well be completely incompatible with bourgeois notions of propriety. While in the first paragraph she suggests that Jacobs's manner guarantees her veracity, by the last she has begun to ask if questions of delicacy have any place at all in discussions of human injustice. In the last paragraph, for example, she writes, "I am well aware that many will accuse me of indecorum for presenting these pages to the public." Here, rather than equating truthfulness with propriety, she acknowledges somewhat apologetically that candor about her chosen subject may well violate common rules of decorum. From this point she proceeds tactfully but firmly to dismantle the usefulness of delicacy as a category where subjects of urgency are concerned. She remarks, for instance, that "the experiences of this intelligent and much-injured woman belong to a class which some call delicate subjects, and others indelicate." By pointing to the fact that one might identify Jacobs's story as either delicate or its opposite, she acknowledges the superfluity of this particular label.

In the third and fourth sentences of this paragraph Child offers her most substantive critique of delicacy, for she suggests that it allows the reader an excuse for insensitivity and self-involvement. The third sentence reads as follows: "This peculiar phase of slavery has generally been kept veiled; but the public ought to be made acquainted with its monstrous features, and I willingly take the responsibility of presenting them with the veil withdrawn." Here she invokes and reverses the traditional symbol of feminine modesty. A veil (read: euphemism) is ordinarily understood to protect the wearer (read: reader) from the ravages of a threatening world. Child suggests, however, that a veil (or euphemism) may also work the other way, concealing the hideous countenance of truth from those who choose ignorance above discomfort.

In the fourth sentence she pursues further the implication that considerations of decorum may well excuse the reader's self-involvement. She writes, "I do this for the sake of my sisters in bondage, who are suffering wrongs so foul, that our ears are too delicate to listen to them." The structure of this sentence is especially revealing, for it provides a figure for the narcissism of which she implicitly accuses the reader. A sentence that begins, as Child's does, "I do this for the sake of my sisters in bondage, who are suffering wrongs so foul that . . ." would ordinarily conclude with some reference to the "sisters" or the wrongs they endure. We would thus expect the sentence to read something like: "I do this for the sake of my sisters in bondage, who are suffering wrongs so foul that they must soon take up arms against their master," or "that they no longer believe in a moral order." Instead, Child's sentence rather awkwardly imposes the reader in the precise grammatical location where the slave woman ought to be. This usurpation of linguistic space parallels the potential for narcissism of which Child suggests her reader is guilty.

Child, the editor, the voice of form and convention in the narrative—the one who revised, condensed, and ordered the manuscript and "pruned [its] excrescences" (p. xi) [6]—thus prepares the reader for its straightforwardness. Jacobs, whose life provides the narrative subject, in apparent contradiction to Child calls attention in her preface to her book's silences. Rather conventionally she admits to concealing the names of places and people to protect those who aided in her escape. And, one might again be tempted to say conventionally, she apologizes for the inadequacy of her literary skills. But in fact, when Jacobs asserts that her narrative is no fiction, that her adventures may seem incredible but are nevertheless true, and that only experience can reveal the abomination of slavery, she underscores the inability of her form adequately to capture her experience.

Although Child and Jacobs are aware of the limitations of genre, the account often rings false. Characters speak like figures out of a romance. Moreover, the form allows Jacobs to talk about her sexual experiences only when they are the result of her victimization. She becomes curiously silent about the fact that her relationship with Sands continued even after Flint no longer seemed a threat.

Its ideological assumptions are the most serious problem the form presents. Jacobs invokes a plot initiated by Richardson's *Pamela*, and recapitulated in nineteenth-century American sentimental novels, in which a persistent male of elevated social rank seeks to seduce a woman of a lower class. Through her resistance and piety, she educates her would-be seducer into an awareness of his own depravity and his capacity for true, honorable love. In the manner of Pamela's Mr. B, the reformed villain rewards the heroine's virtue by marrying her.

As is true with popular literature generally, this paradigm affirms the dominant ideology, in this instance (as in Douglass's case) the power of patriarchy.[4] As Tania Modleski and Janice Radway have shown, the seduction plot typically represents pursuit or harassment as love, allowing the protagonist and reader alike to interpret the male's abusiveness as a sign of his inability to express his profound love for the heroine.[5] The problem is one that Ann Douglas attributes to sentimentalism as a mode of discourse, in that it never challenges fundamental assumptions and structures: "Sentimentalism is a complex phenomenon. It asserts that the values a society's activity denies are precisely the ones it cherishes; it attempts to deal with the phenomenon of cultural bifurcation by the manipulation of nostalgia. Sentimentalism provides a way to protest a power to which one has already in part capitulated."[6] Like Douglass, Jacobs does not intend to capitulate, especially since patriarchy is for her synonymous with slavocracy. But to invoke that plot is to invoke the clusters of associations and assumptions that surround it.

As Jacobs exercises authority over the limits of the male narrative, however, she triumphs as well over the limits of the sentimental novel, a genre more suited to the experience of her white, middle-class reader than to her own. From at least three narrative spaces, analogs to the garret in which she concealed herself, she displays her power over the forms at her disposal.

4. See Douglas, *The Feminization of American Culture*, p. 72.
5. See Tania Modleski, *Loving with a Vengeance: Mass-Produced Fantasies for Women* (New York: Archon Books, 1982), p. 17, and Janice Radway, *Reading the Romance: Women, Patriarchy, and Popular Literature* (Chapel Hill: University of North Carolina Press, 1984), p. 75.
6. See Douglas, *The Feminization of American Culture*, p. 12.

In a much-quoted line from the penultimate paragraph of her account she writes: "Reader, my story ends with freedom, not in the usual way, with marriage" (p. 207) [167]. In this sentence she calls attention to the space between the traditional happy ending of the novel of domestic sentiment and the ending of her story. She acknowledges that however much her story may resemble superficially the story of the sentimental heroine, as a black woman she plays for different stakes; marriage is not the ultimate reward she seeks.

Another gap occurs at the point where she announces her second pregnancy. She describes her initial involvement with Sands as a conundrum. The brutality of neighboring masters, the indifference of the legal system, and her own master's harassment have forced her to take a white man as her lover. Both in the way she leads up to this revelation and in the apostrophes to the reader, she presents it as a situation in which she had no choice. Her explanation for taking Sands as her lover is accompanied by expressions of the appropriate regret and chagrin and then followed by two general chapters about slave religion and the local response to the Nat Turner rebellion. When we return to Jacobs's story, she remarks that Flint's harassment has persisted, and she announces her second pregnancy by saying simply, "When Dr. Flint learned that I was again to be a mother, he was exasperated beyond measure" (p. 79) [68]. Her continued relationship with Sands and her own response to her second pregnancy are submerged in the subtext of the two previous chapters and in the space between paragraphs. By consigning to the narrative silences those aspects of her own sexuality for which the genre does not allow, Jacobs points to an inadequacy in the form.

The third such gap occurs a bit later, just before she leaves the plantation. Her master's great aunt, Miss Fanny, a kind-hearted elderly woman who is a great favorite with Jacobs's grandmother, comes to visit. Jacobs is clearly fond of this woman, but as she tells the story, she admits that she resents Miss Fanny's attempts to sentimentalize her situation. As Jacobs tells it, Miss Fanny remarks at one point that she "wished that I and all my grandmother's family were at rest in our graves, for not until then should she feel any peace about us" (p. 91) [78]. Jacobs then reflects privately that "the good old soul did not dream that I was planning to bestow peace upon her, with regard to myself and my children; not by death, but by securing our freedom." Here, Jacobs resists becoming the object of someone else's sentimentality and calls attention to the inappropriateness of this response. Although she certainly draws on the conventions of sentimentalism when they suit her purposes, she is also capable of replacing the self-indulgent mythicization of death with the more practical solution of freedom.

The complex experience of the black woman has eluded analyses and theories that focus on any one of the variables of race, class, and gender alone. As Barbara Smith has remarked, the effect of the multiple oppression of race, class, and gender is not merely arithmetic.[7] That is, one cannot say only that in addition to racism, black women have had to confront the problem of sexism. Rather, issues of class and race alter one's experience of gender, just as gender alters the experience of class and race. Whatever the limitations of her narrative, Jacobs anticipates recent developments in class, race, and gender analysis. Her account indicates that this story of a black woman does not emerge from the superimposition of a slave narrative on a sentimental novel. Rather, in the ironies and silences and spaces of her book, she makes not quite adequate forms more truly her own.

JOHN ERNEST

From Reading the Fragments in the Fields of History: Harriet Jacobs's *Incidents in the Life of a Slave Girl*[†]

In 1837, at the Anti-Slavery Convention of American Women,[1] Mrs. A. L. Cox put forth a resolution proclaiming that "there is no class of women to whom the anti-slavery cause makes so direct and powerful an appeal as to *mothers*." Responding to this appeal, the

7. See Barbara Smith, "Notes for Yet Another Paper on Black Feminism, or Will the Real Enemy Please Stand Up," *Conditions: Five*, 3 (October 1978), 123–132. For further discussion of this issue see Paula Giddings, *When and Where I Enter: The Impact of Black Women on Race and Sex in America* (New York: William Morrow, 1984); Angela Davis, *Women, Race, and Class* (New York: Vintage Books, 1983); and Elizabeth V. Spelman, "Theories of Race and Gender: The Erasure of Black Women," *Quest*, 5 (1979), 36–62.

† From *Resistance and Reformation in Nineteenth-Century African-American Literature: Brown, Wilson, Jacobs, Delany, Douglass, and Harper* (Jackson: U P of Mississippi, 1995), 81–108. Copyright © 1995 by the University Press of Mississippi. Reprinted with permission of the University Press of Mississippi. Page numbers in brackets refer to this Norton Critical Edition.

1. Dorothy Sterling has called the convention not only "the first public political meeting of U.S. women" but also "the first interracial gathering of any consequence" (*Turning* 3). *Incidents*' editor, Lydia Maria Child, attended the convention, as did many other prominent women. The convention passed resolutions denouncing prejudices against color, promoting the renewal and practice of Christian principles, and arguing against the practice of many churches. The convention delegates also "organized a campaign to collect a million signatures on petitions to Congress asking for the abolition of slavery in the District of Columbia and the Florida Territory," and "prepared six pamphlets and 'open letters' for publication" (Sterling, *Turning* 4). Significantly, agreements about the public efficacy of Christian virtue and sympathetic motherhood were more easily reached than agreements about attendant redefinitions of women's social role. On the 1837 convention in the context of women's reform activism generally, see Ginzberg, ch. 1; on the 1837 convention and the justification and political influence of petitions, see Ginzberg, ch. 3 and Lerner, ch. 8.

resolution calls for women to "lift up their hearts to God on behalf of the captive, as often as they pour them out over their own children in a joy with which 'no stranger may intermeddle.'" The same resolution warns women to "guard with jealous care the minds of their children from the ruining influences of the spirit of pro-slavery and prejudice, let those influences come in what name, or through what connexions they may" (Sterling, *Turning* 17). The dual directive here—for hearts to be lifted upward to God's purifying realm, and for jealous care to be directed outward against humankind's *corrupting* realm—directs us in turn to what Jean Fagan Yellin calls the "double tale" in Harriet Jacobs's 1861 narrative *Incidents in the Life of a Slave Girl*. As Yellin notes, Jacobs dramatizes "the triumph of her efforts to prevent her master from raping her," but she also presents the story of "her failure to adhere to sexual standards in which she believed" (Introduction xiv). In other words, although Jacobs might hope that the story of her "triumph" would lift up her readers' hearts, she knew also that her "failure" would cause her readers to guard those same hearts with jealous care, and to turn God's realm against Jacobs in judgment.

It is this other double story, her white readers' inevitably dual response of approbation and judgment, that complicates Jacobs's attempt to "be honest and tell the whole truth,"[2] and that qualifies any common bond she might claim as a mother. Certainly, resistance to the institution of slavery required mothers to protest the habitual violation of an ideologically sanctified relationship—in effect, a matter of insisting upon the enslaved woman's right to the privileges and duties of motherhood. But Jacobs knew well that many antislavery white women, in their search for injustice, did not even think to look beyond the visible violation of the sacred relationship of mother and child. In other words, they saw only those horrors that threatened the ideological security of the domestic sphere, and from that sphere they judged such horrors. To maintain the sphere, the horrors (including both the act of violating and the act of being violated) must remain outside. As Robert B. Stepto argues, "The risks that written storytelling undertakes are . . . at least twofold: one is that the reader will become a hearer but not manage an authenticating response; the other is that the reader will *remain a reader* and not only belittle or reject storytelling's particular 'keen disturbance,' but also issue confrontational responses which sustain altogether different definitions of literature, of literacy, and of appropriate reader response" ("Distrust" 308). Thus distanced, Jacobs could not hope to "tell the whole truth" unless she could teach her readers to *hear* and understand the whole truth.

2. The phrase is from a letter from Jacobs to Amy Post; in *Incidents*, 232.

If Jacobs was to present something more than an object lesson in the horrors of slavery, she would have to inspire her readers to trace to their own homes the "ruining influences of the spirit of pro-slavery and prejudice," and to question not only their willingness but even their ability to fulfill the duties of motherhood in a culture that sanctions slavery. In other words, motherhood, as viewed from Jacobs's perspective, does not provide an unproblematic bond between narrator and reader, for Linda Brent, the pseudonymous author and subject of this story, cannot help but represent the most threatening and pervasive vice. No reader, no matter how sympathetic, can change Brent's cultural identity; the progression available to Linda Brent is that from a slave girl to a concubine to a slave mother to a fugitive slave to a "free black." Each new phase is a resounding echo of her previous condition: a restricted identity, the terms of which Brent can try to adapt to her needs but can never hope to control. Nor can Brent offer the dubious protection or comfort of a closing moral, for such closure was not available to her or to the larger community whose story she represents. Instead, the lesson of *Incidents* is that white mothers and daughters *cannot* identify with Brent, but that they must learn to do so if they are to achieve their own moral ideals, if they are to fulfill the terms of their own self-definition.[3]

Incidents directs itself towards this paradox, and operates in the space it at once opens and closes, thereby creating a need for the perspective that only Jacobs, and others like her, can offer. The choice for white women and mothers concerned about the immorality of slavery—the choice between taking the high moral ground of, say, an Esther and being the victim of a prophecy—cannot be accomplished by way of a sympathetic engagement in Brent's story, a self-assuring response to what Joanne M. Braxton terms "outraged motherhood."[4] Rather, this choice requires white women to learn from Brent not only a new language but also a new mode of understanding, one characterized not by a separation of subject and object but rather by a reciprocal relationship between two differently knowing subjects. Ultimately, Jacobs issues to her readers an epistemic challenge to change the nature of their knowledge by changing the way they look at and learn from African Americans.

* * *

In 1859 one of the many attacks on the increasing public prominence of women was an article published in the *Southern Literary*

3. On Jacobs's/Brent's relation to her readers, see Yellin, *Women & Sisters*, 92; Carby, *Reconstructing*, 51; Andrews, *To Tell a Free Story*, 253–54; and Sidonie Smith.
4. Braxton presents "the archetype of the outraged mother" as "a counterpart to the articulate hero," noting of this archetype that "She is a mother because motherhood was virtually unavoidable under slavery; she is outraged because of the intimacy of her oppression" (19).

Messenger on the "Intellectual Culture of Woman," an article designed ultimately to argue that it is the mother's role, within the context of domestic education, to defend the institution of slavery. Asserting that "it is no slight duty . . . to which woman is called, in the discharge of her offices to society," the author strategically amplifies the implicit responsibilities inherent in the ideology of femininity, arguing that "the social problems which are the subject and the origin of laws, the manners and customs of the people which originate and produce these laws, are the product, directly or indirectly, of the women" (329). As this appropriation demonstrates, the ideology of motherhood—like religion itself, like law, like republican philosophy—proved infinitely flexible. Whether or not a woman accepted the role of a true woman, the task of applying this generalized role to the concerns of the day was unavoidably political. To be a mother in opposition to law and custom was to announce an ideological reconstitution of motherhood.

At the 1837 Anti-Slavery Convention of American Women, for example, agreements about the public efficacy of Christian virtue and sympathetic motherhood were more easily reached than agreements about attendant redefinitions of woman's social role. On the second day of the convention, Angelina Grimké offered the following resolution relating to such redefinitions of woman's sphere:

> RESOLVED, That as certain rights and duties are common to all moral beings, the time has come for women to move in that sphere which Providence has assigned her, and no longer remain satisfied in the circumscribed limits with which corrupt custom and a perverted application of Scripture have encircled her; therefore that it is the duty of woman, and the province of woman, to plead the cause of the oppressed in our land, and to do all that she can by her voice, and her pen, and her purse, and the influence of her example, to overthrow the horrible system of American slavery. (Sterling, *Turning* 13)

According to the convention notes, this resolution, and the suggested amendments that followed, "called forth an animated and interesting debate respecting the rights and duties of women. The resolution was finally adopted, without amendment, though *not anonymously*" (13). On the next day, the minutes record that "L.M. Child in consideration of the wishes of some members, who were opposed to the adoption of the resolution on the province of women, moved that the same be reconsidered. The motion was seconded by A. W. Weston, but after discussion was lost" (17). Twelve women asked that their opposition to the resolution be recorded, with their names, in the minutes.

Grimké had directed a similar argument—and had demonstrated a careful awareness of the tensions it creates—toward a much less receptive audience in her "Appeal to the Christian Women of the South," which appeared in *The Anti-Slavery Examiner* in 1836. Noting that southern women are likely to wonder what they, who lack political and legislative power, can do, Grimké argues that they can do "four things": read, pray, speak, and act on the subject (16–17).[5] The first three things Grimké explains in three paragraphs; the fourth occupies much of the rest of the essay—not merely because there was so much to be done, but because Grimké had to justify and situate ideologically the concept of action by women against the state. What follows is a history of heroic women, grounded ultimately in the example of the male apostles, beginning with biblical women and proceeding to Protestant women in the time of Catholic Inquisitions; and then to English women who worked for "the great and glorious cause of Emancipation"; and finally to "The Ladies' Anti-Slavery Society of Boston" (18–24).

In effect, Grimké presents a brief history of activist women in order to *dehistoricize* the concept of activism, placing the concept, with good abolitionist logic, within an eschatological framework. Referring to the courage of the apostles Peter and John to preach the gospel regardless of the threat of persecution, Grimké argues that "*Consequences*, my friends, belong no more to *you*, than they did to these apostles. Duty is ours and events are God's" (19). Duty thus becomes a matter of stepping outside of human history and entering into providential history. Specifically, it becomes the moral human agency by which biblical prophecies will be fulfilled on earth. Beginning with the prophecy of Psalm 68:31 ("Ethiopia shall stretch forth her hands unto God") Grimké proceeds to the prophecy of judgment near the end of the book of Daniel (12:4): "Many shall run to and fro, and *knowledge* shall be increased."[6] Grimké then concludes this section of her essay significantly by alluding to another prophecy, from the book of Isaiah—that book that warns against luxury and fashion, a country under peril of judgment, and that prophecizes that "a virgin shall conceive, and bear a son, and shall call his name Immanuel" (7:14). The verse Grimké quotes is one of communal hope, of Isaiah's prophecy of a messianic kingdom (11:9): "They shall *not* hurt nor destroy in all my holy mountain" (27). Having placed slavery in this Old Testament prophetic framework, Grimké argues that "*Slavery, then, must be overthrown before* the

5. Drawing attention to the sequence of this list, Grimké notes that "I have not placed reading before praying because I regard it more important, but because, in order to pray aright, we must understand what we are praying for; it is only then we can 'pray with the understanding and the spirit also'" (17).

6. Perhaps it is worth noting that Grimké doesn't quote further from this chapter of Daniel; verse 10 reads: "Many shall be purified, and made white, and tried; but the wicked shall do wickedly: and none of the wicked shall understand; but the wise shall understand."

prophecies can be accomplished" (27). Womanhood, in other words, can justify an activist stance not by abandoning the "cardinal virtues" of true womanhood but rather by tracing these virtues to their theological roots. By this formulation, womanhood is not ushered into history, nor is it separated from its relation to the state, nor is the relationship between womanhood and the state provided a new ideological configuration. Rather, the existing ideological configuration for defining the relationship between womanhood and state is intensified, urging women to serve not the historical state but the philosophical state, the nation viewed as a potential fulfillment of providential history, a nation blessed by God (and therefore open to particularly harsh judgment if it should fail in its mission).

The need for this transition from the domestic to the biblical sphere is central to *Incidents in the Life of a Slave Girl*, but Brent (and Jacobs) cannot claim the cultural authority of motherhood; she can only struggle to call into question her readers' own claims to authority. Jacobs's self-representation undermines the ideological foundation by which womanhood can be comfortably reconfigured, offering no entrance into biblical womanhood except by way of an unprotected entrance into social and political history. As Hazel V. Carby reminds us, at the end of her narrative Brent remains "excluded from the domain of the home, the sphere within which womanhood and motherhood were defined. Without a 'woman's sphere,' both were rendered meaningless" (*Reconstructing* 49).[7] However, the unspoken assertion behind Jacobs's self-presentation is that her white motherly readers themselves cannot claim the power of reified womanhood because the ideological vessel of that power is falsely constructed. Accordingly, as Brent promises not "to try to screen [herself] behind the plea of compulsion of a master" (54 [49]), so Brent's female readers must learn to step out from behind their own ideological screens. To do so means to confront the actual conditions and events of their world, in all their disturbing and disruptive ideological contradictions, and, more to the point, to acknowledge responsibility for these contradictions. The screens themselves, woven of coarse ideological threads, provide a unified public diorama to cover the many private stories that would reveal the nation's failure to live up to its professed ideals. And as Jacobs knew well, yet another screen—in some ways, the most deceptive of all, and most capable of undermining the individual sense of moral responsibility—was the abolitionist belief in the possibility of understanding the "monstrous features" of slavery once the "veil" of propriety is

7. Similarly, J. Sherman refers to Brent's double bind of slavery and true womanhood, noting that "Both systems denied her a selfhood; neither had words to authorize her choices" (168). As I argue, to create choices, Jacobs (through Brent) had to reconfigure authorized modes of discourse and knowledge.

"withdrawn," as [Lydia Maria] Child puts it in her introduction to the narrative (*Incidents* 4 [6]). For the "monstrous" is always the Other; and as the Other, Jacobs would have no real voice, no way to penetrate the screen between narrator and reader. White readers would need to learn to see the monstrous at home before Jacobs could extend her own cultural identity beyond that of a representative and victimized site of monstrous exchanges.

By all cultural standards, ideological motherhood in *this* narrative of national life has been violated and corrupted, and Jacobs argues that it is only by acknowledging and studying the terms of that violation and corruption that motherhood can be restored to integrity. After all, *Incidents*' central character, Linda Brent, has no living mother, and can look for her maternal guidance only from her grandmother. Indeed, Brent notes early in the narrative that "if I knelt by my mother's grave, [Flint's] dark shadow fell on me even there" (28 [28]). Instead of providing the moral entrance into history, motherhood in this narrative marks the violent intrusion of history into a woman's life. For Brent, the state does not await the performance of motherhood; rather, the state has become sexually implicated in the condition of womanhood and the conception of motherhood. When telling of her attempt to avoid Flint's demands by submitting herself to relations with a future statesman,[8] Brent notes significantly that without slavery she would have nothing to confess. Asserting that her own deliberate moral transgression was the only avenue for self-determination, Brent reminds the reader again that "the condition of a slave confuses all principles of morality, and, in fact, renders the practice of them impossible" [50]. Her grandmother's own rejection of Brent after this transgression emphasizes the strictness with which American Christianity defines that which it creates, forcing Brent outside the moral sanctuary of the domestic sphere.

Banished from that culturally determined domestic sphere, Brent leaves her grandmother's house, and as the gate closes behind her—"with a sound I never heard before" [52]—she enters into a new stage in her relation to her grandmother, history, and selfhood. Jacobs's readers seemingly are left within the gate, with little more to offer than sympathetic echoes of the grandmother's lamentation after the two are reconciled: "Poor child! Poor child!" [52]. Brent herself is left with the experience that will produce the children who will motivate her eventual escape from the South. But the internal logic of *Incidents* comes to a point here, as Brent completes her identity as a highly determined product of the American Christian slave

8. Mr. Sands (identified by Yellin as Samuel Tredwell Sawyer) runs for and is elected to Congress as the Whig candidate (*Incidents* 189 [105]).

culture, literally embodying its moral and social contradictions in the children she soon carries. Jacobs's task is to draw her readers themselves beyond the gate, to show that they reside there already, and thereby to make Brent their representative and her quest theirs as well.[9]

SILENT UNDERSTANDING AND LOCKED EYES

To perform this task, Jacobs must re-educate her readers, teaching them to see the invisible by giving voice to the unspeakable, forcing them beyond the gate of moral security and into a realm where all is uncertain, and where nothing can be addressed directly. What is needed is not merely the familiar argument that slaves and whites alike are taught in the "school of slavery" to accept and participate in the moral corruption of the system. Although Jacobs indeed works to reveal the baseness of these lessons learned in school, she argues further that the mode of thought one acquires in this school is inadequate to change the course of these lessons. Whereas Harriet Beecher Stowe argued that her readers should "*feel right*" (515), Jacobs (perhaps fortified by her own disillusioning experience with Stowe, and certainly by her attenuated enslavement as a "free black" in domestic service)[1] begins with the assumption that it will matter little if readers "feel right" if they do not also challenge fundamentally the nature and terms of their self-definition. Drawing her readers into an awareness of their own identities as U.S. citizens, Jacobs challenges the reader's ability even to know whether he or she does "feel right." If one is produced by this culture, then "feeling right" is a matter of aligning one's behavior (both physical and intellectual) with one's conception of moral law. As Stowe argues through her characterization of Marie St. Clare in *Uncle Tom's Cabin*, if one's conception of moral law is distorted, then so too is one's "conscience," and feeling right will mean simply that this dual distortion is perfectly aligned.

Jacobs could not simply appeal to a true application of Christian precepts, for the "all-pervading corruption produced by slavery" (51 [47]) made such appeals, in and of themselves, worthless. The dominant culture's ability even to understand those precepts was itself in question. Moreover, the many "Christian" slaveholders and proslavery ministers throughout both the northern and southern states demonstrated daily that such appeals could easily be redirected

9. On Jacobs's use of the "perspective of the homeless," see Sidonie Smith, 94–102; and Becker.

1. On Jacobs's experiences with and comments about Stowe, and on her situation after reaching the North, see the letters collected in the Appendix of Yellin's edition of *Incidents*; see also Yellin's Introduction; *Women & Sisters*, ch. 4; and "Texts and Contexts." See also Carby, *Reconstructing*, 47–61.

back at the enslaved. Well versed in the multifarious ways in which slavery is capable of "[perverting] all the natural feelings of the human heart" (142 [120]) Jacobs has little hope of appealing to that heart for justice. She knows that the justice of the heart can only echo, even at its best, the conceptions of justice defined by culture and habit. The ideological system that both requires and sustains the figurative heart would be the interpretive filter through which any appeal must pass. As Carby argues, not only white southern women but also the northern women "who formed Jacobs's audience were implicated in the preservation of this [ideological] oppression" (*Reconstructing* 55). Unable to trust in relationships engendered by the fundamental commonalities of women's condition and experiences, Jacobs needed to reshape the ways in which women relate their individual experience to the concept of gendered commonality.

The problem was that many, blinded by custom, could not see what they were doing to blacks; in fact, many were incapable of imagining that the dominant culture's ethical standards could even apply to blacks. Early in *Incidents*, Brent notes that her otherwise solicitous and kind original mistress had taught her "the precepts of God's Word: 'Thou shalt love thy neighbor as thyself,'" and "'Whatsoever ye would that men should do unto you, do ye even so unto them'" (8 [11]). The mistress commits her "one great wrong" (bequeathing Brent to her sister's daughter) not because she fails to believe in the "precepts of God's Word," but rather because she does not recognize Brent as her neighbor in the moral sphere (8 [11]). Brent's later mistress, worried about Dr. Flint's interest in the girl, forces her to act as a moral agent by swearing on the Bible and "before God" to tell the truth; but this episode is fundamentally similar to the earlier one, for Brent's account simply leads Mrs. Flint to "[pity] herself as a martyr." Brent adds pointedly that Mrs. Flint "was incapable of feeling for the condition of shame and misery in which her unfortunate, helpless slave was placed" (33 [32]).

Certainly, Jacobs writes in the hope that the exposure of immorality will inspire in her readers a renewal of moral character, leading to reformative actions. At its most basic level, *Incidents* follows the signifyin(g) strategy of motivated repetition and exposure that Linda Brent had learned from her grandmother. When Dr. Flint informs "Aunt Marthy" that, out of respect for her feelings, he will sell her at a private rather than a public auction, Brent's grandmother realizes that "he was ashamed of the job," not only because he was selling her, but also because "every body who knew her respected her intelligence and good character" (11 [14]). She had, in other words, become visible to the community, and the ethical transgressions inherent in slave auctions had accordingly become visible as well. Grandmother uses this visibility to advantage, standing on the auction block, leading observers (who otherwise were willing participants in this socioeconomic ritual) to remark, "Shame! Shame! Who is going to sell *you*, aunt Marthy? Don't stand there! That is no place for *you*" (11 [14]). Finally, she is purchased by one who recognizes that "she had been defrauded of her rights," a "maiden lady" who can sign the bill of sale only with a cross (11–12 [14]). This pivotal morality play, in which the dominant culture refuses to apply to one the corrupt standards it willingly applies to others, is central to *Incidents* as to other slave narratives. Indeed, Jacobs presents American Christianity and American slavery as symbiotic ideological systems, mutually dependent for ideological integrity. She presents American Christianity not as the system that enables her to *see* her wrongs, but rather as the system that forces her to *commit* her wrongs—a closed system that requires transgression, thereby making visible the terms of moral self-definition. Like the Inquisition to which she compares it, American Christian slavery requires a conspicuous institutional emphasis of moral standards, a public ritual that all but requires sins that must be punished, and that veils the sins of the institutional body itself, the "secrets of slavery" (35 [33]). Although there are many, Brent reminds her readers, who "are thirsting for the water of life," "the law forbids it, and the churches withhold it" (73 [65]). These many are assigned instead to "inferior" roles in which moral self-awareness cannot lead to repentance. Comparing the life of a "favorite slave" to that of a "[felon] in a penitentiary," Brent notes that the felon "may repent, and turn from the error of his ways, and so find peace," while for the slave "it is deemed a crime in her to wish to be virtuous" (31 [30]).

Jacobs signals her awareness also that this effort to reform by exposing wrongs relies on a rather tenuous hope. Christian "precepts" can be applied to African Americans for the purposes of intellectual and spiritual colonization, but the flexible logic by which those precepts are applied belongs to the dominant culture, the members of which determine—at times consciously, at times not—which aspects of black bodies and black lives shall be visible. Dehumanized enough to be viewed as a slave, Brent was still human and woman enough to be the object of Flint's lust; still invisible, however, remained the human heart and divine soul that would make it impossible for Flint to fulfill his desires without sacrificing his community standing. Jacobs had long been in the North when she wrote *Incidents*, and Northerners, she notes through Linda Brent, are all too ready to "satisfy their consciences with the doctrine that God created the Africans to be slaves" (44 [41]). And those who could see more than a slave often had trouble seeing more than a servant. Jacobs knew that exposure simply uncovered one layer of black invisibility, one more dimension of the fullness of human experience that whites had not learned (or did not care) to recognize in blacks.

At issue is not only *what* knowledge the reader gains from this text, but also *how* the reader conceptualizes the acquisition of that knowledge. In *What Can She Know*?, Lorraine Code joins many looking to construct a feminist epistemology in arguing that "the subject-object relation that the autonomy-of-reason credo underwrites is at once its most salient and its most politically significant epistemological consequence" (139). In traditional approaches to knowledge acquisition, Code argues, "the subject is removed from, detached from, positions himself at a distance from the object; and knows the object as other than himself" (139). This subject/object relation characterized the nineteenth-century relationship between white reader and black author. In this highly politicized relationship, the black author served as the ostensibly self-voicing object of knowledge. However, the tenor and quality of that voice was itself an object of knowledge, obliged to obey the demand that Thoreau complains of in *Walden*: "that you shall speak so that they can understand you" (216).[2] The conventions of cultural communication carry with them the cultural assumptions and prejudices that can undermine true communication between white and black. As Karen Sanchez-Eppler argues compellingly, the "moments of identification" that characterized the feminist/abolitionist alliance led easily and invisibly to "acts of appropriation" (31). Jacobs's task was to redefine the terms of this identification by reappropriating the authority to define the experience of oppression.

She approaches this task by redefining knowledge—replacing, in effect, the gaze as the central perspectival figure for acquiring knowledge, drawing instead on the visual mode sometimes referred to as "locking eyes." As Lorraine Code notes, "direct eye contact between people" is "a symmetrical act of mutual recognition in which neither need be passive and neither in control. Such contact is integral to the way people position themselves in relation to one another and signify the meaning of their encounters. Through it, they engage with one another, convey feelings, and establish and maintain, or renegotiate, their relationships" (144). The most familiar experience of "locking eyes" might be the intimate contact that two people can discover through love—a discovery both revealed and developed when each discovers her or his ability to look into the eyes of the other, to meet intent look with intent look. Out of this symmetrical act of mutual recognition, the two create something more than the sum of one-plus-one. And if the relationship thus formed

2. See Andrews on the differences between Thoreau's concept of autobiography and that of black autobiographers (*To Tell a Free Story* 2).

fails to develop or is not sustained, the unavoidable sign of the failure is the couple's inability to look each other in the eye.[3] * * *

Throughout *Incidents*, working behind the screens of their official relationship, Jacobs looks to establish intimate and reciprocal contact with her women readers, which requires that she first break through their subject/object mode of knowing. If this project seems most clearly delimited by Jacobs's cultural position, Jacobs actually works on the assumption that those closer to the cultural center—the white northern women she and Child appeal to in *Incidents*' Preface and Introduction—are yet more delimited. In this, Jacobs acts upon a recognition that is associated today with feminist standpoint theory. "The starting point of standpoint theory," as Sandra Harding explains,

> is that in societies stratified by race, ethnicity, class, gender, sexuality, or some other such politics shaping the very structure of society, the *activities* of those at the top both organize and set limits on what persons who perform such activities can understand about themselves and the world around them. . . . In contrast, the activities of those at the bottom of such social hierarchies can provide starting points for thought—for *everyone's* research and scholarship—from which humans' relations with each other and the natural world can become visible. . . . These experiences and lives have been devalued or ignored as a source of objectivity-maximizing questions—the answers to which are not necessarily to be found in those experiences or lives but elsewhere in the beliefs and activities of people at the center who make policies and engage in social practices that shape marginal lives. (54)

Certainly, this is a just description of the cultural field by which Jacobs's experiences are contained and defined—and Jacobs can only work in that field. But as she cannot hope to have any readers actively value her "standpoint," she must work towards a fundamental breakthrough in the ways in which knowledge about this field is grounded and constructed.

To initiate such a breakthrough, Jacobs must rely upon the power of the stories *suggested* by the stories one tells. By saying indirectly that which she cannot communicate directly, Jacobs deflects the

3. My example here is not as strange as it might seem. In her discussion of scientific ways of knowing, its "epistemological positions" (50), Code quotes from scientist Anna Brito's "accounts of her work with lymphocytes," in which Brito claims that "'the nearest an ordinary person gets to the essence of the scientific process is when they fall in love. . . . You, the scientist, don't know you're falling in love, but suddenly you become attracted to that cell, or to that problem. Then you are going to have to go through an active process in relationship to it, and this leads to discovery'" (qtd. in Code, 152).

reader's attempt to acquire knowledge from her text; she disrupts the subject/object dynamic of the gaze, and locks eyes, if only momentarily, in a quiet glance of mutual understanding. Through this indirect mode, Jacobs accomplishes what might be called *deferred* discourse, a suspended communication that first addresses unspeakable bonds, formed of common experiences, between (black) narrator and (white) reader, so that later the task of truly reciprocal discourse might be possible. These unspeakable bonds, formed of the gendered experiences for which women have no recognized public language, provide Jacobs with a possible mode of communication beyond the words contained and defined by the dominant, patriarchal culture, as if to exchange knowing looks with those female readers gazing at her pages.

* * *

In the silent reciprocity of locked eyes, Jacobs could speak through the stories she tells and, yet more powerfully, through those untold and untellable stories she implicitly draws from her readers. In the most intimate chapter of *Incidents*, under the decidedly objectified title "A Perilous Passage in the Slave Girl's Life," Brent argues that the reader cannot understand the "deliberate calculation" by which she chose to take Mr. Sands as her lover (54 [49]). Certainly, her readers will want to stand at a distance from such calculated transgressions of the ideology of moral relations between the sexes. And yet, as Brent explains *why* they cannot understand her motives, her language echoes not only feminist/abolitionist rhetoric but also the rhetoric and plot of many a sentimental romance:[4] "Pity me, and pardon me, O virtuous reader! You never knew what it is to be a slave; to be entirely unprotected by law or custom; to have the laws reduce you to the condition of a chattel, entirely subject to the will of another. You never exhausted your ingenuity in avoiding the snares, and eluding the power of a hated tyrant; you never shuddered at the sound of his footsteps, and trembled within hearing of his voice" (55 [50]). This passage can change depending on whether one approaches it after having read other slave narratives or after having read sentimental or seduction fiction—literature also replete with ominous footsteps and threatening voices.[5] Jacobs's appeal for understanding, that is, sends a covert message to the many women who have either read about or experienced the stratagems of a "hated tyrant," and who have felt the consequences of being "unprotected by

4. Many critics have noted Jacobs's use of sentimental conventions, though the implications of this feature of her narrative have not been fully explored. See especially Nudelman; Vermillion; Foster, *Written by Herself*, ch. 6; Tate, 26–32; and Andrews, "The Changing Moral Discourse."
5. For backgrounds on sentimental fiction, see Baym, *Woman's Fiction*; and Reynolds.

law or custom," "subject to the will of another." Her readers' unspoken, responding narratives are likely to begin in sympathy when Brent confesses "I know I did wrong," and to extend in empathy when she claims, "No one can feel it more sensibly than I do" (55 [51]). Critics looking at this passage have noted the assertion that ends the paragraph—"I feel that the slave woman ought not to be judged by the same standards as others" (56 [51])—and have rightly argued that Jacobs suggests that such standards are inadequate to account for the reality of the black subject's life.[6] In this regard, of course, Jacobs simply echoes Douglass's own assertion, voiced by Madison Washington in "The Heroic Slave," that "'Your moral code may differ from mine, as your customs and usages are different'" (50); and Douglass is yet more direct when he speaks in his own voice in *My Bondage and My Freedom*: "The morality of *free* society can have no application to *slave* society. Slaveholders have made it almost impossible for the slave to commit any crime, known either to the laws of God or to the laws of man" (248). Jacobs, who might emphasize the word "almost" here, takes the point still further, indicating not only the inapplicability of the morality of free to slave society but also that of patriarchical society to women's actual lives. The moral codes of this culture—by which men idealize white women while dominating, restricting, and generally holding to a double standard the actual women around them—are inadequate to account for the reality of *any* woman's life. Seeing their own experiences behind the veil of this confession, Jacobs's white female readers could see also the failure of their own culture to provide them with a sense of moral closure, let alone justice.

Moral closure, in the form of mutual understanding and a truly reciprocal relationship, comes when Brent confesses a second time, not to the presumably Christian reader but rather to her daughter Ellen. This time, in the brief chapter entitled "The Confession," Brent addresses herself to someone who neither needs nor wants to hear the confession, someone who understands the world that necessitated and shaped Brent's decision. The reader gazes on as an informed spectator, waiting, perhaps, to see Ellen's reaction. But Brent and the reader alike discover that the confession is unnecessary—at least as an *informative* act. Ellen knows of her mother's past, and she knows who her father is. But Brent's confession still has value as a *moral* act, the act of confessing one's sins for the sake of those who listen. Ellen's experience has provided her with a different knowledge of the world than that known by Brent's white readers, and therefore with a different standard for judgment. "I thanked God,"

6. See, for example, Yellin, "Text and Contexts," 274; and *Women & Sisters*, 93; see also Carby, *Reconstructing*, 58.

Brent tells us, "that the knowledge I had so much dreaded to impart had not diminished the affection of my child" (189 [156]). Ellen, after all, knows the world well enough to say of her former belief that a father should love his child, "'I was a little girl then, and didn't know any better'" (189 [156]). In this case, Brent's confession makes possible the reciprocity of trust: "I had not the slightest idea she knew that portion of my history. If I had, I should have spoken to her long before; for my pent-up feelings had often longed to pour themselves out to some one I could trust. But I loved the dear girl better for the delicacy she had manifested towards her unfortunate mother" (189 [156]). Reading this chapter, we see Ellen's reading of her world, an understanding born of experience that strengthens her relationship with her mother. Far from endangering the relationship, Brent's confession signals an unspoken understanding between mother and daughter that both had suspected but not fully realized. Through this exchange, the two give voice, and a shared consciousness, to the history of a relationship that might otherwise have seemed always imminent, always unfulfilled.

Jacobs's point is that different standards of judgment, capable of accounting for the actual lives concealed behind the moral and behavioral screens of reified womanhood, will not come from the dominant culture; they can come only from "the knowledge that comes from experience" in slavery (17 [18]). Certainly, Jacobs's readers still do not know any better than to hold to a belief in the natural love of a parent for a child, a love to be expressed according to established cultural codes of behavior. Transgression of the codes constitutes transgression of parental duty and love. Even Brent's own grandmother warns her that her plans to escape constitute a double blow to motherhood, damaging Brent's role and reputation as a mother, and hurting her grandmother in the bargain. "'Nobody,'" her grandmother informs her, "'respects a mother who forsakes her children'" (91 [80]). Aware of this, and in spite of the rewards of her confession to her daughter, Brent still hesitates when the time comes to tell the reader. She knows that the white reader's judgment, even when directed at the system of slavery, necessarily encompasses herself as well. But as Brent, writing "only that whereof I know," describes the "all-pervading corruption produced by slavery," her readers may find themselves encompassed by their own standards of judgment, wondering who has forsaken whose children. For the sins enabled by slavery are both individual and systemic, extending beyond individual families to pervert the roles and relationships that give meaning to the *concept* of family: "It makes the white fathers cruel and sensual; the sons violent and licentious; it contaminates the daughters, and makes the wives wretched" (52 [48]). Clearly, history has invaded not only Brent's life but those of her readers as well.

Brent's point is that she is valuable to those contained by the ideological American home precisely because she stands outside that home and therefore knows it differently than those inside.

READING THE FRAGMENTED TEXT

It is here, in this moral realm born of her struggles, that Jacobs works to transform herself from the object of knowledge to a subject of mutual understanding. In this narrative that is celebrated for its frank depiction of the experiences of enslaved women, Brent works to train her readers to read their world and themselves indirectly. For as experience shapes knowledge, so knowledge, in turn, shapes experience; that is, her white readers' "knowledge" of themselves and their world tells them what to see in Brent's story, and how to understand it. White readers must learn to read their way out of the self-fulfilling prophecies of racialized knowledge and into the world of Brent's experience. This, of course, requires a heightened state of self-consciousness, which Brent encourages by emphasizing the necessity of considering one's response to Brent's confessions. For example, when she meets with Mr. Durham in Philadelphia, Brent "frankly" tells him of her life, noting that "it was painful for me to do it; but I would not deceive him" (160 [135]). Mr. Durham's response is significant, the last word of which burns Brent "like coals of fire": "'Your straightforward answers do you credit; but don't answer every body so openly. It might give some heartless people a pretext for treating you with contempt'" (160–61 [135]). As Jacobs makes painfully clear, this advice still stood as she wrote this narrative.

Equally clear was the extent to which apparently straightforward discourse could prove threatening. When Brent looks to recover her daughter, who is staying with Mrs. Hobbs, she makes a point of noting that she had to contrive a story to present in her note. It was important, she emphasizes, that no one know that she had recently arrived from the South, "for that would involve the suspicion," she explains to the reader, "of my having been harbored there, and might bring trouble, if not ruin, on several people" (165 [139]). And having thus presented this reading of the cultural text, Brent explains the necessity of deception in her response to this text: "I like a straightforward course, and am always reluctant to resort to subterfuges. So far as my ways have been crooked, I charge them all upon slavery. It was that system of violence and wrong which now left me no alternative but to enact a falsehood" (165 [139]). Straightforwardness may be best, but experience has taught her when to practice it and when to avoid it. In a system based on deception, straightforwardness can be dangerous, opening one not only to contempt but also to violence. All that is stated directly in such a system is held to the logic of the dominant ideology, in which anything Brent might say is held to be either inconsequential or threatening to the standing order. Brent's security, and the security of her extended community, depends upon careful reading, and equally careful narration.

Appealing to the deferred narratives of women's actual lives, the encoded stories that they can whisper to one another but not reveal to the world,[7] Jacobs draws her female readers into an unspoken realm contained and silenced by the ideological boundaries of cultural womanhood, a realm with its own mode of discourse (for communication both behind and across gender lines) and of knowledge. Wounded and sexually violated by Mr. Flint's words, Brent is "made . . . prematurely knowing, concerning the evil ways of the world" (54 [49]); in writing *Incidents* she uses the conventions of sentimental discourse to suggest the evil beneath the smooth patriarchal veneer. But she learns also that the subterranean realm of the actual "ways of the world" has its own silent codes, its own system of relations—the sensual vortex not only of the "secrets of slavery" but also of the secrets of women's experience. The second Mrs. Flint, Brent notes, "possessed the key to her husband's character before I was born," and "she might have used this knowledge to counsel and to screen the young and the innocent among her slaves" (31 [30]). Instead, Mrs. Flint carries her struggle to the visible cultural apparatus for assigning guilt and maintaining order: she punishes the female slaves and watches her husband "with unceasing vigilance" (31 [30]). Mr. Flint himself, when under his wife's eye, simply takes his violations to the subterranean realm of communication: "What he could not find opportunity to say in words he manifested in signs. He invented more than were ever thought of in a deaf and dumb asylum" (31 [30]). Jacobs knew the power of this mode of discourse not only as a slave but also as a "free" black in the North where she lived daily with unspoken signs of prejudice. If *Incidents* was to be transformative, this is the realm it would need to transform, and this the discourse it would need to appropriate.

Incidents offers its readers ample opportunity to practice Brent's mode of interpretation—that is, to reread apparently straightforward discourse, to question and interpret the cultural text guided by the hermeneutical map of Brent's narrative. Consider, for example, this one of many examples, towards the end of the narrative, when Brent receives a letter from her former enslavers. Brent copies the letter, and then comments on it, though telling her readers nothing they could not have determined from the letter itself:

7. I am referring, of course, to Jacobs's letter to Amy Post, in which she says that "Woman can whisper—her cruel wrongs into the ear of a very dear friend—much easier than she can record them for the world to read" (*Incidents* 242 [168]).

> The letter was signed by Emily's brother, who was as yet a mere lad. I knew, by the style, that it was not written by a person of his age, and though the writing was disguised, I had been made too unhappy by it, in former years, not to recognize at once the hand of Dr. Flint. O, the hypocrisy of slaveholders! Did the old fox suppose that I was goose enough to go into such a trap? Verily, he relied too much on "the stupidity of the African race." I did not return the family of Flints any thanks for their cordial invitation—a remissness for which I was, no doubt, charged with base ingratitude. (172 [144])

Note that before she reprints the letter, Brent hints that it is a veiled text, a letter "which purported to be written by her younger brother," but she does not tell the reader that "though the writing was disguised" she "recognized at once the hand of Dr. Flint" (171–72 [144]). The reader guesses the identity of the writer, and sees through the feigned affection and cordiality of the letter, simply noting these characteristics associated with the mythology of the paternalistic southern system. Brent simply affirms this reading after she presents the letter, and adds at the end her own ironic rendition of formal courtesy, concerning their "cordial invitation," as an inside joke for the reader to enjoy.

But however threatening Flint's duplicitous letter may be, yet more threatening are those whose straightforwardness serves as simply the most direct example of a well-trained, restrictive perspective, as when Mrs. Hobbs, a northern woman and mother, looks Brent "coolly in the face" to inform her that Ellen has been "*given*" to Hobbs's eldest daughter (166 [139]). In so doing, Mrs. Hobbs exemplifies the limited hopes one could place in the justice that might come of *enraged* motherhood. If Jacobs had hoped to appeal to mothers through this narrative, this experience certainly reminded her how tenuous the power of that appeal might be. As Brent puts it, questioning the very bond of motherhood that she seems to count on for understanding elsewhere in the narrative, "How *could* she, who knew by experience the strength of a mother's love, and who was perfectly aware of the relation Mr. Sands bore to my children,—how *could* she look me in the face, while she thrust such a dagger into my heart?" (166 [139]). A partial answer, of course, is that Mrs. Hobbs's experience is insufficient for understanding the very injustice of which she is aware. One could say that she is fundamentally incapable of looking Brent in the face, for she can *look into* only the face her experience has prepared her to see. She lacks the knowledge that comes from the experience of slavery, and she *cannot attain* this knowledge. As Brent puts it when she is reunited with her son Benjamin, "O reader, can you imagine my joy? No, you cannot, unless you have been a slave mother" (173 [144]).

Brent's experience has trained her differently; she is able to recognize Mrs. Hobbs's gaze for what it is, even though she is astounded to encounter it. More significantly, Brent's experience enables her to read the broader cultural text from an informed rather than a merely theoretical perspective. Consider Brent's discussion of the relative condition of American slaves and the European laboring classes, a comparison that dominated debates about slavery, and that was therefore a standard feature of many slave narratives. Brent ends by emphasizing that she will address only the relative condition of the two groups, and not the actual experience of European laborers. She does so to contrast her account of the laborers from uninformed accounts of slavery in America: "I do not deny that the poor are oppressed in Europe. I am not disposed to paint their condition so rose-colored as the Hon. Miss Murray paints the condition of the slaves in the United States. A small portion of *my* experience would enable her to read her own pages with anointed eyes" (184–85 [152–53]). Without such experience, one lacks the eyes to read not only Brent's experience but also one's own pages, one's *own* experience. And can we imagine? No, we cannot. At best, we can recognize that we are incapable of reading our world without the "small portion" of Brent's experience that we gain by reading this narrative. We need Brent's help if we are to read "with anointed eyes" not only the system of slavery but also the broader system that has informed our identities.[8]

Brent underscores this need for a "small portion" of her experience not only by reminding her readers that the act of interpretation is a moral act but also by emphasizing the fragmentation of the cultural text. One might take as the symbol of this text the letter that Mr. Thorne writes to Dr. Flint, informing him of Brent's whereabouts. Thorne tears up the letter, and Ellen retrieves the fragments, telling Mrs. Hobbs's children that Thorne is out to expose her mother. The children do not believe that she can be right until they "put the fragments of writing together, in order to read them to her" (179 [148]). Similarly, Brent argues throughout *Incidents* that we are faced with a fragmented cultural text, and that we cannot read it until we reassemble the fragments. Moreover, we cannot put the fragments together without Brent's help. Earlier in the narrative, when William accompanies Mr. Sands to Washington and then runs away, Brent presents us with varying accounts of William's

8. On Jacobs's attempt to "structure an alternate vantage of understanding, an alternative epistemology, that mirrors Linda's reconstituted Subjectivity," particularly as it relates to the relation between (black) author and (white) reader, see Nelson, ch. 7. As Nelson argues, "The text repeatedly appeals to the sympathy of its readers, but at the same time it warns them to be careful about the motives and critical of the results of that sympathetic identification" (144, 142).

escape. She presents the reader first with William's letter to his family; next with Mr. Sands's account to Brent's Uncle Philip; and, finally, with William's unwritten account to Brent herself when later they meet. The first is a conditioned account, for one could not afford to assume that the letter would be read only by one's intended audience. The second is a version of the dominant culture's interpretation of the event. The third is a frank account—to one who knew how to read the situation, one who had experienced enslavement—that deconstructs the authorized explanation. The true account of this event is not the last but the combined implications of all three. Brent presents the reader with a series of conditioned readings, each of which works to encompass, undermine, or otherwise account for the others. The fragmented text, in other words, is not simply a puzzle waiting to be pieced together; rather, it is a series of overlapping pieces that together form no single picture but indicate pictures that must be envisioned.

If Linda Brent cannot claim the knowledge of cultural privilege and education, she can claim the knowledge that forms the contours of her readers' lives, the knowledge gained from moral and ideological transgression, the transgression by which the dominant culture defines the enclosing boundaries of social order. Ostensibly, *Incidents*, like other works produced and endorsed by the abolitionist movement, argued that stories of experience will arm empowered white readers with the knowledge they need to struggle for the right. Brent herself acknowledges this possibility of empowering knowledge, noting that "never before had my puny arm felt half so strong" as when she understood Flint's implicit demand that she was "made for his use, made to obey his command in *every* thing" (18 [19]). But Brent shows also the limited value of this forearming knowledge when she becomes the victim of knowledge. Resolving "never to be conquered," able to "read the characters, and question the motives, of those around me" (19 [20]), she resists Dr. Flint by taking up with Mr. Sands (whose motives she also reads and understands). Thus she accepts the same situation she had tried to resist, with only the comfort of knowing that she had deliberately chosen, from a strictly limited field, her sexual partner. As the object of knowledge, Brent embodies the significations of both official cultural discourse and the more intimate subterranean codes, both order and its underlying chaos. Public discourse defines her; private whispers surround her. She is the Other that embodies the unspeakable experiences of the Self. In short, she is the fully determined product of the will to know—so determined, in fact, that she stands at the other side of the gate of knowledge, where the imminence of sexual and social violation is brought not only to consummation but also to public display. And it is from this public platform that she gazes back at the reader, locking eyes to begin the mutual task of re-forming knowledge, discourse, and community.

* * *

Works Cited

Andrews, William L. "The Changing Moral Discourse of Nineteenth-Century African American Women's Autobiography: Harriet Jacobs and Elizabeth Keckley." In *De/Colonizing the Subject: The Politics of Gender in Women's Autobiography*. Minneapolis: University of Minnesota Press, 1992. 225–41.

———. *To Tell a Free Story: The First Century of Afro-American Autobiography, 1760–1865*. Urbana: University of Illinois Press, 1986.

Baym, Nina. *Woman's Fiction: A Guide to Novels by and about Women in America, 1820–70*. Urbana: University of Illinois Press, 1993.

Becker, Elizabeth C. "Harriet Jacobs's Search for Home." *CLA Journal* 35 (June 1992): 411–21.

Braxton, Joanne M. *Black Women Writing Autobiography: A Tradition within a Tradition*. Philadelphia: Temple University Press, 1989.

Carby, Hazel V. *Reconstructing Womanhood: The Emergence of the Afro-American Novelist*. New York: Oxford University Press, 1987.

Code, Lorraine. *What Can She Know? Feminist Theory and the Construction of Knowledge*. Ithaca: Cornell University Press, 1991.

Foster, Frances Smith. *Written by Herself: Literary Production by African American Women, 1746–1892*. Bloomington: Indiana University Press, 1993.

Ginzberg, Lori D. *Women and the Work of Benevolence: Morality, Politics, and Class in the 19th–Century United States*. New Haven, Conn.: Yale University Press, 1990.

Grimké, A[ngelina] E. "Appeal to the Christian Women of the South." *The Anti-Slavery Examiner: Nos. 7–14, 1838–1845*. Westport, Conn.: Negro Universities Press, 1970. 1–36.

"Intellectual Culture of Woman." *Southern Literary Messenger: A Magazine Devoted to Literature, Science and Art* 28 (May 1859): 321–32.

Jacobs, Harriet A. *Incidents in the Life of a Slave Girl, Written by Herself*. Ed. Jean Fagan Yellin. Cambridge: Harvard University Press, 1987.

Lerner, Gerda. *The Majority Finds Its Past: Placing Women in History*. Oxford: Oxford University Press, 1979.

Nelson, Dana D. *The Word in Black and White: Reading "Race" in American Literature, 1638–1867*. New York: Oxford University Press, 1992.

Nudelman, Franny. "Harriet Jacobs and the Sentimental Politics of Female Suffering." *ELH* 59 (1992): 939–64.
Reynolds, David S. *Beneath the American Renaissance: The Subversive Imagination in the Age of Emerson and Melville*. Cambridge: Harvard University Press, 1989.
Sherman, Joan R. *Invisible Poets: Afro-Americans of the Nineteenth Century*. 2d ed. Urbana: University of Illinois Press, 1989.
Smith, Sidonie. "Resisting the Gaze of Embodiment: Women's Autobiography in the Nineteenth Century." In *American Women's Autobiography: Fea(s)ts of Memory*. Ed. Margo Culley. Madison: University of Wisconsin Press, 1992. 75–110.
Sterling, Dorothy. *Turning the World Upside Down: The Anti-Slavery Convention of American Women*. New York: Feminist Press, 1987.
Tate, Claudia. *Domestic Allegories of Political Desire: The Black Heroine's Text at the Turn of the Century*. New York: Oxford University Press, 1992.
Vermillion, Mary. "Reembodying the Self: Representations of Rape in *Incidents in the Life of a Slave Girl* and *I Know Why the Caged Bird Sings*." *Biography* 15 (Summer 1992): 243–60.
Yellin, Jean Fagan. Introduction. In *Incidents in the Life of a Slave Girl*. By Harriet A. Jacobs. Ed. Jean Fagan Yellin. Cambridge: Harvard University Press, 1987. xiii–xxxiv.
———. "Texts and Contexts of Harriet Jacobs' *Incidents in the Life of a Slave Girl: Written by Herself*." In *The Slave's Narrative*. Ed. Charles T. Davis and Henry Louis Gates, Jr. Oxford: Oxford University Press, 1985. 262–82.
———. *Women & Sisters: The Antislavery Feminists in American Culture*. New Haven, Conn.: Yale University Press, 1989.

FRANCES SMITH FOSTER

Resisting *Incidents*†

Particular communicative contexts seem inevitably to trigger resistance. When a writer or narrator is different in race, gender, or class from the implied or actual reader, questions about authority and authenticity multiply. As Susan Lanser points out in *The Narrative Act*, a writer's or a narrator's social identity is never totally

† From *Harriet Jacobs and* Incidents in the Life of a Slave Girl: *New Critical Essays*, ed. Deborah M. Garfield and Rafia Zafar (New York: Cambridge UP, 1996) 57–75. Page numbers in brackets refer to this Norton Critical Edition, with the exception of references to extratext material included in the Yellin edition.

irrelevant, but readers automatically assume that the "unmarked" narrator is a literate white male.[1] When the title page, the book jacket, or any other source marks one as not white, not a man, or not to the manor born, different sets of cultural assumptions "determined by the ideological system and the norms of social dominance in a given society" (Lanser, 166) come into play. When the topic or the general development of the text coincides thematically with the readers' assumptions about the writer's or narrator's social identity, status becomes particularly significant to the discursive context. "Social identity and textual behavior," Lanser concludes, "combine to provide the reader with a basis for determining the narrator's mimetic authority" (Lanser, 169).

Lanser uses gender as her primary focus, but her thesis applies as well to other writers whose race or class places them outside the courts of power and privilege. Any attempt by an individual who is not white, male, and at least middle class to be acknowledged as part of the literary or intellectual community is inevitably challenged, even by readers who share their racial, social, or gender status. When a readership is invited into communicative contexts with writers of a race, gender, or class that it assumes to be equal or inferior to its own, questions about authority and authenticity take on an intensity and texture that obscure other aspects of the discourse. Readers tend to assume that cultural landscapes not dominated by written texts are inferior and individuals native to such cultures can hardly be expected to represent the best thoughts of the best minds or to create things of beauty that are joys to behold. When, as they often do, such writers do not replicate that with which readers are already familiar, claims and challenges to authorial prerogatives and to the authenticity of their depictions may become contentious. More readers try to compete with the writers, to rearrange the writers' words, details, and intentions to make them more compatible with the readers' own experiences and expectations. Oppositional intensity varies by time, place, and circumstance, but African Americans inevitably encounter a significant number of obstinate readers. From the publication of *Poems on Various Subjects, Religious and Moral*, the earliest extant volume by an African American, to the present time, the mimetic details, social relevance, and political implications of their texts have been particularly challenged.

Although resistance may be absolutely the right way to read a particular text or a particular author, the fact that literary productions of African American writers, particularly of those who were or had been slaves, are habitually greeted with resistance is provoking and

1. Susan Lanser, *The Narrative Act: Point of View in Prose Fiction* (Princeton: Princeton University Press, 1981). Subsequent references are found in the text.

problematic. Consider the case of Phillis Wheatley, the author of the earliest extant volume of poetry by an African American. In order to convince readers to accept Wheatley as the author of *Poems on Various Subjects, Religious and Moral*, before the book was published (1773), it was deemed necessary to include various authenticating documents, including her picture, a biographical sketch from her master that explains how she came to acquire literacy, and an affidavit from eighteen of "the most respectable characters in Boston,"[2] who had examined her and determined that Wheatley was indeed capable of writing the poems.

Once her authorship was established, Wheatley became a celebrity, but the significance of her contributions, even her identification as a poet, were not unequivocally granted. Phillis Wheatley wrote *Poems on Various Subjects, Religious and Moral* (emphasis mine), but eighteenth-century readers, especially, were inclined to read her words as those of a former pagan who could testify to acquired piety but could contribute nothing original about theology or morality. Thomas Jefferson spoke for many when he stated, "Religion, indeed, has produced a Phyllis Whately [*sic*]; but it could not produce a poet." In order to bar Wheatley from poetic society, Jefferson had to ignore the consensus of Western aesthetics that *utile and dulce* were essential literary components and that *utile*, especially in the New England colonies, had always meant that the writings serve a religious and moral purpose. To demonstrate that religion may have inspired Wheatley to write but that her writing about religion precluded her acceptability as a poet, Jefferson defined not religion or morality but romantic love as the "peculiar oestrum of the poet." Romantic love, Jefferson then pontificated, could kindle the senses of blacks but not their imaginations.[3]

Whether Phillis Wheatley was surprised by her readers' reactions is a matter of conjecture, but that misreadings and misinterpretations of her work and worth continue to this day should shock more people than it does. Today, Phillis Wheatley is lauded as the first African American and the second woman in colonial America to publish a volume of poetry. Her works are included in virtually every anthology that purports to be "inclusive." Her debts to Greek and Roman mythology, to evangelical Methodist rhetoric, and to neoclassicism are frequently cited as evidence that, when given the opportunity, she—and by implication other blacks—could and did learn as well as or better than whites. But until recently, most

2. Phillis Wheatley, *Poems on Various Subjects, Religious and Moral*, in *The Poems of Phillis Wheatley*, ed. Julian D. Mason, Jr. (Chapel Hill: University of North Carolina Press, 1989), 48. Subsequent references to Wheatley's poems and letters are from this source and noted in the text.
3. Thomas Jefferson, *The Writings of Thomas Jefferson*, ed. Albert Ellery Bergh (Washington, D.C., 1907), Vol. 2, 196; quoted in Mason, *The Poems of Phillis Wheatley*, 30, n. 10.

readers considered her to be of "the mockingbird school," able to imitate but not to interpret or debate. Until recently, few scholars would entertain the notion that Phillis Wheatley made original contributions to eighteenth-century theology, to the rhetoric of the U.S. Revolution, and to the discourse on race and gender.

The standard interpretation of "On Being Brought from Africa to America," the most anthologized of Phillis Wheatley's poems, demonstrates this. The poem is an eight-line monologue addressed to Christians by an African convert. It has three distinct parts with three increasingly authoritative tones. The poem begins as a hymn of gratitude for the divine mercy that brought the speaker from a "benighted land" to one where she learned to seek and to know spiritual redemption. In line five the narrator switches from grateful testimony and reproves those who believe that the "sable" skins of Africans signify diabolical natures. The last two lines are didactic and ominous: "Remember, *Christians, Negroes*, black as *Cain*, / May be refin'd, and join th' angelic train" (emphasis hers). In this poem, a newly enlightened member does not simply recite catechism but argues theology and warns the entire congregation against presumptions of exclusivity by declaring that the gift of salvation makes all converts joint heirs in Christ. Despite, or perhaps because of, the simple diction and the authority manifest in the tonal changes, readers have historically misinterpreted the text. They have emphasized the first lines and read the poem as Wheatley's disavowal of her African heritage and as evidence of her "pious sentimentalizing about Truth, Salvation, Mercy, and Goodness"[4] while ignoring the changes in tone and focus that begin with line five and saying nothing of the audacity of the last two lines, which claim divine authority to testify for racial equality. Although summaries or interpretations that take into account only part of the text subvert literary convention and violate basic tenets of exposition, it seems easier for readers to ignore half of a poem than to acknowledge that an African slave girl barely out of her teens would be audacious enough not only to write poetry, but also to use it to instruct and to chastise her readers.

For African American women writers, the resistance to the authority of blacks or of slaves was compounded by gender prejudices. Even if the authorship were acknowledged and their accounts were verified, their writings were still perceived through a veil of sexism that obscured their individuality and revealed only the shadowy contours their readers expected to see. As African American women proved their imaginativeness with romantic prose and poetry and

4. Richard Barksdale and Keneth Kinnamon, *Black American Writers* (New York: Macmillan, 1972), 39–40.

their political acumen with logical and incisive analyses, nineteenth-century audiences struggled desperately against the belief that black women could be intelligent and eloquent. The nineteenth-century author and orator Frances Ellen Watkins Harper provides another example of the lengths to which some audiences would go to deny what they saw and heard. By all accounts she was very lady-like in appearance and few contemporary reporters failed to note her "slender and graceful" form and her "soft musical voice" when recounting her public presentations. Harper's writings have often been summarized as sentimental, moral, and chaste. Some of them were. But Frances Harper was also a militant evangelist for equality. She worked with the Underground Railroad, staged sit-ins on public transportation, and supported John Brown's Harper's Ferry attack. During Reconstruction, Frances Harper went around the South lecturing on political and social change. Hers was not a pitiful plea for acceptance. "We are all bound up together in one great bundle of humanity, and society cannot trample on the weakest and feeblest of its members without receiving the curse in its own soul," she argued. Her writings and her speeches explained why the fate of the country rested in its solution to the economic problems of poor whites and blacks, the suffrage demands of women of all races, and a variety of other major issues. For a black woman to speak publicly and aggressively on political, economic, and social issues was so alien to traditional expectation that many simply could not believe their ears or eyes. In a letter to a friend, Harper writes, "I don't know but that you would laugh if you were to hear some of the remarks which my lectures call forth: 'She is a man,' again, 'She is not colored, she is painted.'"[5]

Other African Americans learned from the experiences of writers such as Wheatley and Harper. African Americans who wrote for publication in the eighteenth and nineteenth centuries knew as well as, if not better than, other writers that successful communication required appropriate attention to content and context. They knew that some readers would be unable or unwilling to concede that they legitimately could or would act, think, and write in ways contrary to the ideas with which those readers approach that text. African Americans quickly understood that in order to employ the power of the pen, they had not only to seize it but to wield it with courage, skill, and cunning. Unable to trust their readers to respond to their texts as peers, they developed literary strategies to compensate.

It is beyond the scope of this paper to entertain all the manifestations of resistance or to speculate about their motivations. This

5. Frances E. W. Harper, "Almost Constantly Either Traveling or Speaking," in *A Brighter Coming Day: A Frances Ellen Watkins Harper Reader*, ed. Frances Smith Foster (New York: Feminist Press, 1990), 126–7.

discussion will focus upon examples of reader and writer resistance as demonstrated in Harriet Jacobs's *Linda; Or, Incidents in the Life of a Slave Girl*. The case of this author and this text has its own unique aspects, but it is a good representation of the more general situation. Resistance to Jacobs's *Incidents*, like that to Wheatley's *Poems on Various Subjects*, to Harper's lectures, and to other African American writers, stems in large measure not from the text or its author's manifest ability but from the readers' response to both. Resistance to *Incidents* is rooted in a usually unspoken, perhaps unconscious, recognition that the book exposes as fabrications many of the truths which we hold to be self-evident and that the writer expects us to reconsider both the grounds for our perceptions of reality and the limitations of our abilities to accept competing versions.

Resistance characterized both Jacobs's life and the genesis and the renaissance of her autobiography. Both her biographers and her autobiography demonstrate that she was born into a family that refused to accept others' definitions of who they were and how they ought to live. Jacobs's self-esteem was strong enough that she could reject her master's edict that she consider herself his property and submit to his will in both thought and deed. When her resources dwindled and the confrontations seemed unending, she chose confinement in a nine-by-seven-foot attic for more than six years rather than live as her master commanded her. Eventually she did flee to the North. Harriet Jacobs was regularly asked to contribute her story to the antislavery effort, but she withstood those pleas for almost twelve years before she agreed to testify. It was only after the Compromise of 1850 created the Fugitive Slave Law, which made it possible for slave owners to claim individuals as their private property even in states where slavery was illegal, that Jacobs agreed to publicize some of her most personal experiences.

Hers was a particularly difficult decision because Harriet Jacobs valued her privacy and believed that "no one had a right to question" her.[6] She was proud of her triumphs and her achievements, but she did not consider hers to be "the life of a Heroine with no degradation associated with it" (Jacobs, 232 [200]). Although she could justify her actions in her own mind, Jacobs was reluctant to explain them to strangers and unwilling to accept their pity or censure. When she finally decided to reveal some of her personal history, however, Jacobs resolved to "give a true and just account . . . in a Christian spirit" (Jacobs, 242 [200]), but not to pander to her audience. As a former slave, she knew that stereotypes about people of

6. Letter from Harriet Jacobs to Amy Post in 1852. Quoted in *Incidents in the Life of a Slave Girl: Written by Herself*, ed. Jean Fagan Yellin (Cambridge, MA: Harvard University Press, 1987), p. 232. Unless otherwise noted, all quotations from Jacobs's letters and from her book are from this source and noted in the text.

her race and class encouraged her audience to expect a certain kind of testimony, yet Jacobs refused to divulge the kinds of things that she thought "the world might believe that a Slave Woman was too willing to pour out" (Jacobs, 242 [200]). She decided to use her position as one of a very few antislavery writers who could relate from personal experience incidents in the life of a slave girl to introduce a different perspective on slavery and slave women. Like other antislavery writers, she did not deny the prevalence of rape and seduction. In fact, her text appears to be unprecedented in its use of sexual liaisons and misadventures as a prime example of the perils of slave womanhood. But hers was a story of a slave woman who refused to be victimized. Harriet Jacobs used her own experiences to create a book that would correct and enlist support against prevailing social myths and political ideologies.

Another reason for her original resistance to writing her narrative was that Harriet Jacobs knew that writing a well-crafted autobiography required more time and talent than she had. During an era in which the majority of Americans could barely write their names, Jacobs enjoyed reading, corresponding, and conversing with a coterie of intellectuals, artists, and social activists, and she had enough literary sophistication to know that literacy was but one requirement for authorship. She was well acquainted with many of the attitudes and assumptions of the Anglo-American literary establishment, for not only did she read widely, but she lived in the household of Nathaniel Willis; the editor and writer whose home was a rendezvous for New York literati. She knew also the conventions of abolitionist and African American literature. Jacobs had worked for a year in her brother's Rochester antislavery reading room. Since it was located over the offices of Frederick Douglass, she may have heard the history of the resistance that Douglass had encountered; especially from his most ardent abolitionist friends, when he decided to tell his story his way. Because Jacobs was a live-in domestic worker, stealing the time and marshalling the energy to develop her own writing skills to the level that she judged adequate for her intentions were more complicated for her than for many others. As a fugitive slave, she also knew that friends or employers, who were willing to adhere to the "Don't ask, don't tell" philosophy in her case, might not be supportive if she went public about her status. And if Jacobs had not known about professional jealousy and competition, she soon learned that she had to fight to protect her story and to establish her right to determine what should be told and how to tell it. In the process of getting her story told, she had to defy such opportunists as Harriet Beecher Stowe, who wanted to appropriate her narrative in order to enhance Stowe's own authority.

Harriet Jacobs had ample reason to know the perils that African American writers, especially women, faced, and it would have been very strange indeed had she not carefully considered the rhetorical and narrative strategies that they had used as she outlined her own story. When she stated in the preface that "I want to add my testimony to that of abler pens to convince the people of the Free States what Slavery really is" (Jacobs, 1–20 [5]), the words "convince" and "really" were undoubtedly chosen with care. She knew she could not trust her readers to understand or to accept what she would relate. She also knew that there was no literary model to fit her task and her temperament. Nonetheless, Harriet Jacobs chose to record her history as she had lived it, to confront her readers with an alternative truth, and to demand that they not only acknowledge it but act upon it. To that end, Harriet Jacobs created a new literary form, one that challenged her audiences' social and aesthetic assumptions even as it delighted and reaffirmed them.

Jacobs's narrative records the struggle of a young girl to resist the sexual advances of a man who was thirty-five years older, better educated, and socially superior. Obviously its story of a young virgin's attempts to defend her chastity against the wiles and assaults of an older, more experienced, and socially privileged male makes it clear kin to Fielding's *Pamela* and other such seduction stories. However, Linda never confuses a threatened loss of chastity with a loss of self-worth or reason for living. Harriet Jacobs colors the plot even further by painting the man—Flint—as driven by more than lust or moral turpitude and the girl—Linda—as resisting from motives only partially shaded by fear of social censure or pregnancy. Perhaps she had learned from fireside stories of Brer Rabbit or from observations within the slave quarters, perhaps it was just common sense, but Linda understood that physical superiority or social status is not necessarily the deciding factor in any contest.

With *Incidents in the Life of a Slave Girl* Harriet Jacobs reconstructs the standard seduction pattern of urbane seducer versus naive maiden. Jacobs expands the peasant or proletariat categories to include the slaves in the United States. Moreover, she makes it clear that the impoverished are not the only oppressed and that slaves are not the only victims. Mrs. Flint is driven to distraction by her husband's infidelity, and the narrator informs us that the seventh is not the only commandment violated in such situations, that young white boys follow the grown men's examples, and so do some white women. Jacobs asserts that slave girls are not the only ones to be prematurely robbed of their innocence. The daughters of slaveholders, she warns, overhear the quarrels between their parents, learn about sexual oppression from slave girls, and sometimes "exercise the same authority over the men slaves" (Jacobs, 52 [47]). While she writes to encourage Northern women to resist slavery, Harriet Jacobs does not allow them to distance themselves too thoroughly. She reminds her readers that they sometimes marry and ofttimes are kin to slaveholders. She explains how the Fugitive Slave Law represents an attack upon the freedom of Northerners. And in noting that Linda technically belonged to Dr. Flint's daughter, who was not able either as a child or as an adult to claim or to direct her inheritance, Jacobs suggests a larger definition of "slave girl." Linda is the heroine who struggles against evil, but Harriet Jacobs identifies other women and men, white and black, Northern and Southern, who are similarly victimized or are potential victims.

Once Harriet Jacobs had completed the narrative of her life in bondage and her struggle for freedom, she spent several years trying to find a publisher. Although publishers, especially those of antislavery leanings, were generally eager to print slave narratives, Jacobs's account was so original and so striking that they required more than the usual endorsements by others. Two prominent friends, one a white woman and the other a black man, had written ten letters of recommendation to be published along with Jacobs's text. But as Jacobs reported in a letter to a friend, the publishers wanted "a Satellite of so great magnitude" as Harriet Beecher Stowe, Nathaniel Willis, or Lydia Maria Child before they would issue her account (Yellin, xxii). With the help of William C. Nell, another African American writer and activist, Jacobs contacted Lydia Maria Child, who agreed to serve as her editor. With Child's support, the firm of Thayer and Eldridge contracted to print two thousand copies. In 1861, nearly a decade after she had decided to write the book, Harriet Jacobs's narrative was finally published. It appeared as the anonymous testimony of "A Slave Girl: Written by Herself." Child was identified as its editor. The publication immediately stirred controversies that have waxed and waned but continue to this day. Despite the testimonies of Jacobs's contemporaries and the meticulous evidence of present-day scholars, a good many readers continue to resist identifying the book as an autobiography by a former slave woman named Harriet Jacobs.

Some antebellum reader caution is understandable. Slave narratives were written to help destroy an institution, swaddled in myth and mystery, and deeply rooted in U.S. culture. Slave narrators, like other purposeful writers, were particularly careful to select incidents and language for maximum persuasive value. Readers of such texts had the privilege and probably the obligation to consider carefully the arguments and the motivations of those whom they read. Especially when faced with direct statements of intention, readers, then as now, should not be expected to squelch their inclinations to contest the validity or the relevance of surprising revelations. Not surprisingly, even the most sympathetic readers wanted then, as they do now, to have certain expectations met and some assumptions confirmed. Moreover, in the mid-1850s, resistance to women writers was decreasing but still pervasive, and Harriet Jacobs presented more than the usual challenge to literary tradition. She was one of those strange, modern, and frightening women who dared to take pen to paper about politics and moral values, to urge resistance to laws and social mores. And, finally, questions of authority and authenticity were not then, as they are not now, intrinsically inappropriate or unimportant to the study of any literature and especially not to the study of autobiographical writings. Such scholars as Albert E. Stone have demonstrated that autobiography is a "mode of storytelling" and that any given autobiography is "simultaneously historical record and literary artifact, psychological case history and spiritual confession, didactic essay and ideological testament."[7]

The modifications in genre that Jacobs made probably did not bother antebellum readers as much as they seem to bother twentieth-century ones, but they certainly must have noticed them. Since she was obviously not an educated white male, the resistance that other writers routinely inspire was certainly augmented by her daring to tamper with traditional literary forms. Jacobs obviously borrowed from the novel of seduction, the criminal confessional, the American jeremiad, the slave narrative, and other popular forms. The melodramatic and feminist elements in *Incidents in the Life of a Slave Girl* were fairly common in antislavery novels. Harriet Beecher Stowe's *Uncle Tom's Cabin* was the most famous, but neither the first nor the last to enlist melodrama in the antislavery cause. Harriet Jacobs began her book at about the same time that William Wells Brown was writing *Clotel* and Harriet E. Wilson was writing *Our Nig*, but by the time *Incidents* was published in 1861, these two writers and others had already introduced the heroic African American woman protagonist. Brown had already demonstrated that an African American female slave might be morally superior to the white man who claimed both social superiority and physical ownership. But Harriet Jacobs claimed more social prestige than did Harriet E. Wilson and Linda is less compromising or compromised than Clotel. Jacobs wrote not to secure money to save her sickly son but to convince readers to heal their ailing society. Dr. Flint's offer of a cottage in the woods and an almost-marriage is comparable to what Brown's heroine accepts, but Linda is not in the least tempted, and the relationship between Linda and Congressman Sands may be

7. Albert E. Stone, "Introduction: American Autobiographies as Individual Stories and Cultural Narratives," in *The American Autobiography: A Collection of Critical Essays*, ed. Albert E. Stone (Englewood Cliffs, NJ: Prentice Hall, 1981), 1–2.

read as a deliberately empowered version of the Clotel and Horatio affair. The struggle between Linda and the father of her children, like that between her and Dr. Flint, is a true contest. Sands, like Flint, had "power and law on his side," but Linda says, "I had a determined will. There is might in each" (Jacobs, 85 [75]).

The changes that Harriet Jacobs wrought in the slave narrative genre were even more remarkable. When she agreed to write her personal narrative, Jacobs set out to wrestle with the "serpent of Slavery" and to expose and detoxify its "many and poisonous fangs" (Jacobs, 62 [56]). To accomplish this, she incorporated the basic elements of the slave narrative genre, but modified them to fit the experiences of those who did not resist by fleeing the site of conflict. The antebellum slave narrative featured a protagonist best described as a heroic male fugitive. The usual pattern of the narrative was to demonstrate examples of the cruelty and degradation inherent in the institution of slavery, then to chronicle an individual's discovery that the concept and the condition of slavery were neither inevitable or irrevocable. Following that revelation, the typical slave narrator secretly plotted his escape and, at the opportune time, struck out alone but resolved to follow the North Star to freedom. Slave narratives generally ended when, upon arrival in the free territory, the former slave assumed a new name, obtained a job, married, and began a new happy-ever-after life.

In contrast, Jacobs's female fugitive refuses to abandon her loved ones and spends the first several years of her escape hiding in places provided by family and friends. When her grandmother accidentally jeopardizes the security of her retreat, Linda has to flee to the North. Even then she does not run alone. Instead, she leaves the South on a ship in the company of another fugitive woman, her friend Fanny. Jacobs does not report a name change, and Linda does not marry. And although she does set about the task of creating a new life for herself and for her children, that task is complicated by failing health and persistent pursuit from those who claim her as their property. Jacobs's narrative makes it clear that racial discrimination and the Fugitive Slave Law ensured that the North was not the Promised Land. The passages in which Jacobs chronicles the abuses of slaves are common to antebellum slave narratives, but her personal testimony of will power and peer protection proving stronger than physical might and legal right are unique. She weaves incidents that she experienced or witnessed into a narrative that was common to the "two millions of women at the South, still in bondage, suffering what [she] suffered, and most of them far worse" (Jacobs, 1 [5]).

In appropriating the elements of various genres into one more suitable for her intents, Harriet Jacobs was following a convention that African American writers had been using for at least a century before her, and it was this tradition of improvisation and invention that also provided her with the techniques that she could adapt to meet her particular circumstances. Some of these African American rhetorical devices have been described quite aptly by others as "sass,"[8] "signifying,"[9] or "discourse of distrust."[1] I say more about the discourse of distrust later; the focus of this discussion is upon specific ways in which *Incidents* resists and is resisted. Like flies or mosquitoes, many of these incidents of resistance would be obvious but insignificant were they not so numerous, did they not unexpectedly appear in inappropriate places, and did their persistent buzzing not distract our attention from more productive occupations.

One example that gains importance when considered in relation to myriad other small instances is the way in which twentieth-century readers have insisted upon renaming Jacobs's book. In 1861 the work was published and reviewed as *Linda: Or, Incidents in the Life of a Slave Girl* and it was as "Linda" that Harriet Jacobs came to be known by the reading public. She signed autographs, letters, and other publications with that name. Today, however, readers know the text only by its subtitle, *Incidents in the Life of a Slave Girl*, and it is by its subtitle that the book is now reprinted, discussed, and claimed as "a classic slave narrative," "one of the major autobiographies in the Afro-American tradition," or simply as a "classic" of African American literature.[2] Although not unprecedented nor without merit, this renaming is a little odd. Referring to the book as *Incidents in the Life of a Slave Girl* subordinates the individual protagonist to the general type, as its author intended. Rather than use her experiences as representative of others, however, too many scholars and critics have used the experiences of others to invalidate those that Jacobs recounted. Their interest revolves almost

8. Joanne M. Braxton defines "sass" as "a mode of verbal discourse and as a weapon of self defense." Sass and "the outraged mother" are key to her discussion of *Incidents*. Joanne M. Braxton, *Black Women Writing Autobiography: A Tradition within a Tradition* (Philadelphia: Temple University Press, 1989), 10.
9. The most famous discussion of "signifying" is from that of Henry Louis Gates, Jr., in *The Signifying Monkey: A Theory of Afro-American Literary Criticism* (New York: Oxford University Press, 1988). Gates is building upon the work of several people, but two are particularly helpful: Claudia Mitchell-Kernan, "Signifying as a Form of Verbal Art" in *Mother Wit from the Laughing Barrel: Readings in the Interpretation of Afro-American Folklore*, ed. Alan Dundes (Englewood Cliffs, NJ: Prentice Hall, 1973), 310–28, and Geneva Smitherman, *Talkin and Testifyin: The Language of Black America* (Boston: Houghton Mifflin, 1977).
1. Robert B. Stepto, "Distrust of the Reader in Afro-American Narratives," in *Reconstructing American Literary History*, ed. Sacvan Bercovitch (Cambridge, MA: Harvard University Press, 1986), 305. Subsequent references are from this source and found in the text.
2. Here I am quoting from Henry Louis Gates, Jr., *The Classic Slave Narratives* (New York: New American Library, 1987), xvi. I, too, find it easier to go along with the tide than to swim against it. In this discussion, I too will refer to the text as "*Incidents in the Life of a Slave Girl*."

exclusively around Harriet Jacobs as both author and subject and around how her victories and her values contrast with prevailing theories and opinions of slave life. Since the author/narrator is of such interest, it is particularly noteworthy that the work is not known by the narrator's name and that Jacobs's authorship is continually questioned. To cite racial prejudice would be an inadequate explanation for this because slave narratives do tend to be known by the names of their authors. Nor is gender bias a satisfactory conclusion, for the formal and functional similarities of Jacobs's narrative to those of nineteenth-century sentimental fiction is consistently mentioned. Still, unlike *Pamela, Clotel, Ramona*, and others, *"Linda"* is not the name by which Jacobs's tale is known. Harriet Stowe's book is linked in content and context to Harriet Jacobs's and has undergone a similar transformation. Despite the fact that Eliza's escape, Eva's death, and Topsy's devilment all eclipse Uncle Tom's crucifixion, we do not normally refer to Stowe's work by its more appropriate subtitle, *Life Among the Lowly*. We accept *Uncle Tom's Cabin*.

Complicating Jacobs's situation is the fact that even while the narrative no longer carries the title "Linda" and while the authenticity of Jacobs's recitations is questioned, it is with Linda or Harriet that readers are most concerned. Given the extraordinary character of most slave narrators and the uniqueness of many of the incidents they relate, one is not overly surprised when their narratives are treated as documentaries and their self-depictions are taken as fact. But even in the case of one so unique as Frederick Douglass, readers tend to accept their personal narratives as representative of at least one particular kind or group of slaves. In the *Narrative of the Life of Frederick Douglass, an American Slave*, the climactic scene is one in which the slave boy physically resists punishment by his white boss. Douglass introduces the fight between him and Covey as if it were representative by saying, "You have seen how a man was made a slave; you shall see how a slave was made a man."[3] Readers have accepted this unusual rite of passage as archetypal even though almost no other narrator admits to such an experience. Douglass's narrative is considered a "master narrative," a model against which all others should be measured, while in fact, though not unheard of, scenes of physical combat between blacks and whites are rare in the genre.[4] With Harriet Jacobs, however, the concerns and consensus are different. Since it is a common belief that slave women were routinely raped and that slaves generally did not know their

3. *Narrative of the Life of Frederick Douglass, an American Slave* (1845; rpt., New York: Doubleday, 1963), 68.
4. Another example is that of Elizabeth Keckley in *Behind the Scenes* (1867; rpt., New York: Oxford University Press, 1988), whose graphic accounts of a series of incidents in which she physically resisted beatings despite the inherent sensationalism of the gender differences has excited virtually no comment.

ancestry or other details of their personal histories, Jacobs's family pride and self-confidence are considered aberrations. Moreover, Harriet Jacobs has more than once been accused of having omitted or distorted details of her own life in order to enhance her personal reputation or to achieve artistic effect. Historian Elizabeth Fox-Genovese, for example, has declared that Jacobs's "pivotal authentication of self probably rested upon a great factual lie, for it stretches the limits of all credibility that Linda Brent actually eluded her master's sexual advances."[5]

Another and more worrisome form of resistance has been the skepticism and concern about authorship that has become more pronounced in the twentieth century. That the book was first published anonymously and its editor was herself a prominent figure would provide some excuse were it not in such contrast to the reception of other anonymously published books, including Richard Hildreth's *Archy Moore; or The White Slave*, Mattie Griffiths's *Autobiography of a Female Slave*, and James Weldon Johnson's *Autobiography of an Ex-Colored Man*. That she consulted with and sometimes accepted the advice of her editor should pose no more serious concerns about authorship for Jacobs's text than it does for D. H. Lawrence's *Sons and Lovers*, certain poems signed by T. S. Eliot, or virtually any book authored by Thomas Wolfe.[6] Neither the decision to publish the book anonymously, the reputation of Lydia Maria Child, nor the generic modifications and innovations such as changing names and creating dialogue in an autobiography account sufficiently for the resistance that *Incidents* continues to encounter.

Arguments presented in recent studies of women's and of African American narrative strategies help clarify the reasons for such reader resistance while offering insight into specific techniques by which writers have combated it. Jeanne Kammer's discussion of the diaphoric imagination and the aesthetic of silence suggests two.[7] Like many of the women poets that Kammer discusses, Jacobs adopts an oratorical model and "depends on the capacity of the voice, not only to invest the words with a persuasive *timbre*, but to sustain the performance over a long enough time to move the listener to the desired conclusions" (Kammer, 159). Harriet Jacobs was writing prose of fact rather than poetry; therefore, she could substitute

5. *Within the Plantation Household* (Chapel Hill: University of North Carolina Press, 1988), 392.

6. Scholars have long acknowledged that these writers, like many others, relied heavily upon the advice and sometimes the revisions of their friends and editors. This has not been a major impediment to their reputations as writers or to the acceptance of their work as serious contributions.

7. Jeanne Kammer, "The Art of Silence and the Forms of Women's Poetry," in *Shakespeare's Sisters: Feminist Essays on Women Poets*, ed. Sandra M. Gilbert and Susan Gubar (Bloomington: Indiana University Press, 1979), 153–164. Subsequent references are from this edition and found in the text.

incidents for images, but she too produces "new meaning by the juxtaposition alone of two (or more) images, each term concrete, their joining unexplained" (Kammer, 157). She too elevates the speaker into a focus of interest in the text. She presents that speaker as "the only available guide through its ambiguities, and the source of its human appeal" (Kammer, 159).

Jacobs's text also provides an opportunity for "the broader look at the historical and literary contexts" that Robyn R. Warhol intends her discussion of the "engaging narrator" to stimulate.[8] Warhol's examination is limited to a pattern of narrative intervention used by three novelists of Jacobs's time, but its similarities to this nonfiction text are several and significant. Like Stowe, Gaskell, and Eliot, Jacobs wrote "to inspire belief in the situations their [texts] describe" and "to move actual readers to sympathize with real-life slaves, workers, or ordinary middle-class people" (Warhol, 811). Each writer uses her narrator as a "surrogate" working "to engage 'you' through the substance and, failing that, the stance of their narrative interventions and addresses to 'you'" (Warhol, 813). Such an "engaging narrator" intrudes into the text, and although neither she nor her reader is a participant in the narrative itself, the narrator engages the reader in dialogue and sometimes implies "imperfections in the narratee's ability to comprehend, or sympathize with, the contents of the text, even while expressing confidence that the narratee will rise to the challenge" (Warhol, 814).

Both Kammer and Warhol focus their discussions on texts by white women, but they agree that diaphor, oratory, and narrative engagement are employed, with some variation, by other writers. Race and class are two very salient variables for Harriet Jacobs. That she was African American and a former slave was vital to her message and to her mission. Yet, in emphasizing both of these factors, she was stirring up attitudes that she preferred to ignore. Like other African Americans and former slaves, Harriet Jacobs did not subscribe to the racial and literary stereotypes that formed the collective consciousness of her white readers. There may be exceptions that prove the rule but, as Raymond Hedin explains, "Black writers have never relished the need to take into account the racial assumptions of white readers, but their minority status and their unavoidable awareness of those assumptions have made it all but inevitable that they do so. The notion of black inferiority has become the 'countertext' of black writing."[9] "One constant among the variables,"

8. Robyn R. Warhol, "Towards a Theory of the Engaging Narrator: Earnest Interventions in Gaskell, Stowe, and Eliot," *PMLA* 101:5 (October 1988): 811–17. Subsequent references are in the text.

9. Raymond Hedin, "The Structuring of Emotion in Black American Fiction," *Novel* 10 (Fall 1982): 36. Subsequent references to Hedin's argument are from this source and noted in the text.

Hedin notes, is "a distinctive continuing tradition of narrative strategy deriving from black writers' continuing awareness that a significant part of their audience, whatever its proportions—or at the very least a significant part of the larger culture they find themselves in—clings to reservations about the full humanity of blacks" (Hedin, 36). The result is "an implicitly argumentative tradition" that manifests in the fact that African American writers "felt [an often vehement] need to confront and alter the white reader's possible racial biases" (Hedin, 37).

Hedin's "implicitly argumentative tradition" is quite similar to what Robert B. Stepto calls a "discourse of distrust," for both approaches are derived from the same speech acts regularly used by blacks in conversation with whites. In a discourse of distrust, Stepto tells us, "distrust is not so much a subject as a basis for specific narrative plottings and rhetorical strategies . . . the texts are fully 'about' the communicative prospects of Afro-Americans writing for American readers, black and white, given the race rituals which color reading and/or listening" (Stepto, 305). Such writers often try to initiate "creative communication" by getting readers "told" or "told off" in such a way that they do not stop reading but do begin to "hear" the writer. In Jacobs's text the telling off begins with the title and the prefatory material. That aspect of "authority," with its implicit claims to accuracy and reliability, is then supplemented by the characterizations and the reconstructed relations among the characters.

The spines of the original editions of Harriet Jacobs's book are imprinted only with the word "Linda." The title pages carry only the subtitle, *Incidents in the Life of a Slave Girl: Written by Herself.*[1] Together the title and subtitle offer a balance of the exemplar and the example. Without the proper name, the subtitle emphasizes the generic and general over the personal and individual. The subtitle in concert with the title also challenges more explicitly the usual hierarchy of race, class, and gender. "Written by Herself" invests authority in the author/narrator's participant/observer status while simultaneously subordinating that of the readers. *Incidents in the Life* also implies that the narrator is not simply reporting her life history, but she is selecting from a multitude of possibilities those events that she chooses to share. *A Slave Girl* establishes this narrative as one common to or representative of a class. "Girl" is a term rarely applied to slaves in literature; thus, it disrupts the expected

1. Here I am assuming that if the presentation of the book was not orchestrated by Jacobs, it certainly met her approval. Although it is possible that the cover and the title page were her publisher's or her editor's design, Jean Fagan Yellin's documentation of the relationship between Jacobs and Child suggests that Jacobs was actively concerned with every aspect of the production of her text. Moreover, since the original publisher went bankrupt and Jacobs purchased the plates, she had the opportunity to change the design had it been contrary to her intentions.

discourse by resisting more common epithets such as "pickaninny" or "young slave." There may even be a subtle suggestion about the intelligence of African Americans, since there were even fewer girls than there were women being published at that time. But with "Linda," the subtitle more readily establishes this as a female slave's narrative whose authority is not easily disputed since it is *her* life of which she writes. The unnamed author writes as a mediator, a first-person narrator now more experienced but still sympathetic, who looks back upon her girlhood and selects those experiences that she deems most appropriate for her audience and her literary intentions. Reading the words "Written by Herself" that follow the subtitle and the words "Published for the author" that come at the bottom of that page, a reader confronts not only the exercise of literary prerogative, of claiming authorial responsibility for the text's selection and arrangement, but also an assumption of self-worth, of meaning and interest in her personal experiences that exceed the specific or personal.

The title page carries two epigrams that are compelling when read in light of what Karlyn Kohrs Campbell has termed " 'feminine' rhetoric."[2] Such writing, Campbell asserts, is

> usually grounded in personal experience. In most instances, personal experience is tested against the pronouncements of male authorities (who can be used for making accusations and indictments that would be impermissible from a woman) . . . [It] may appeal to biblical authority . . . The tone tends to be personal and somewhat tentative, rather than objective or authoritative . . . tends to plead, to appeal to the sentiments of the audience, to "court" the audience by being "seductive." . . . [to invite] female audiences to act, to draw their own conclusions and make their own decisions, in contrast to a traditionally "Masculine" style that approaches the audience as inferiors to be told what is right or to be led.

What Campbell terms "feminine rhetoric" is comparable to the "discourse of distrust" and certain other rhetorical strategies developed by African Americans. It too strives to thwart the resisting reader's urge to compete with the author for authority and to enlist the reader instead as a collaborator. But for Jacobs, as for other African Americans, not all the strategies of "feminine rhetoric" would work for her purposes. Though she was a woman writing primarily to other women, she was also a black woman writing to white women. Racism exacerbates distrust. Racial stereotypes would make certain conventions,

2. Karlyn Kohrs Campbell, "Style and Content in the Rhetoric of Early Afro-American Feminists," *Quarterly Journal of Speech* 72 (1986): 434–45. Subsequent references are from this source and found in the text.

such as the seductive speaker, the tentative tone, and the laissez-faire lecturer, work against her. But the use of quoted authority to state the more accusatory or unflattering conclusions had great potential. And, those "feminine" literary conventions that Jacobs does adopt are adapted to project images more in line with her purposes as a writer and her status as a black woman.

Consider, for example, the ways in which Jacobs employs verification, the process of using quotations from others to state the more accusatory or unflattering conclusions. As Campbell notes, women writers frequently used references from scripture to validate their claims and they often cited the words of others, especially the pronouncements of men, to state directly the accusations or indictments that the women writers were implying. Jacobs includes two quotations on her title page. The first declares that "Northerners know nothing at all about SLAVERY . . . They have no conception of the depth of *degradation* involved . . . if they had, they would never cease their efforts until so horrible a system was overthrown."[3] This quotation is unmistakably patronizing if not actually accusatory or indicting. However, Harriet Jacobs does not attribute these words to a man, but cites, instead, an anonymous "woman of North Carolina." Sophisticated readers of abolitionist literature would recognize these words as those quoted by Angelina E. Grimké in her *Appeal to the Christian Women of the South* in 1836. Such a scholarly reference would enhance the author's claim to learnedness. But in 1861, it is doubtful that many readers would have recognized the source of this quote. Jacobs's decision not to identify the speaker with any more accuracy than that of gender and geography allows a more powerful use of verification even as it demonstrates elements of "sass" and "signifying." Given the assumed inferiority of blacks to whites, this modification would be acceptable to most of her readers. They would assume that a black woman's appeal to authority by citing a white woman was comparable to a white woman's seeking verification from a white man and, given the racism of that time, they would undoubtedly assume that the anonymous woman was in fact white. But, the woman's race is not stated, and although there are at least two Southern white women in *Incidents* who surreptitiously work against slavery, none is as outspokenly antislavery as the black women in Jacobs's narrative or the Northern white women who wrote the authenticating statements that frame Jacobs's narrative. The only women from North Carolina in Harriet Jacobs's text who exhibit the

3. I am grateful to Elizabeth Spelman for recognizing this quotation as having been published by Angelina Grimké. While it may correct my earlier theory that Jacobs was quoting herself, the fact that I originally read it that way supports the overall concept. Attributing the quote to an anonymous woman of North Carolina in a text where the most assertive and "real" women are black allows and encourages readers to make such assumptions.

spirit and audacity of the woman quoted on her title page are black. Since Harriet Jacobs was a "woman of North Carolina" and her book is designed to effect the kind of awareness and action referred to in the quotation, it is quite likely that readers, especially those who were African American, might assume that Jacobs is quoting another slave woman or herself. Such a reading would be subtly empowering.

Jacobs's second quotation is Biblical. It too functions as verification, to increase her authority. The words are those of Isaiah 32:6: "Rise up, ye women that are at ease! Hear my voice, ye careless daughters! Give ear unto my speech." The relationship between this command and the theme of *Incidents* is fairly obvious. But the quotation does more than refer to a precedent for women becoming politically active. This quotation comes from the section of Isaiah that warns directly against alliances with Egypt, a word synonymous in the antebellum United States with "slavery." And in this chapter, Isaiah's prophecy is actually a warning. The women "that are at ease," the "careless daughters" who fail to rise up and support the rights of the poor and the oppressed, will find themselves enslaved. Again, Jacobs has revised the "feminine" rhetorical convention, for this citation is more demanding and declarative than it is seductive or suggestive.

The author's preface follows the title page. As is expected in the discourse of distrust, Jacobs's first words "tell off" the reader in ways that she or he must "hear." "Reader, be assured this narrative is no fiction." This statement is neither apology nor request. It is a polite command, soothingly stated but nonetheless an imperative. The next sentence neither explains nor defends: "I am aware that some of my adventures may seem incredible; but they are, nevertheless, strictly true." Instead of elaborating upon her claim to authenticity in the preface, Jacobs requires an even higher level of trust, for she advises her readers that she has not told all that she knows. "I have not exaggerated the wrongs inflicted by Slavery," she writes, "on the contrary, my descriptions fall far short of the facts." With these words, the author claims superior knowledge and plainly privileges her own interpretation over any contrary ideas that the reader may have as to the text's authenticity.

At the conclusion of her narrative, Jacobs's struggle has gained her a conditional freedom. "We are as free from the power of slave holders," she argues, "as are the white people of the north." But she continues, "that, according to my ideas, is not saying a great deal. . . . The dream of my life is not yet realized" (Jacobs, 201 [167]). Ironically, her authorial efforts, as creative and effective as they are, have not achieved an unmitigated success either.

The situation with *Incidents in the Life of a Slave Girl* is an extreme example of that faced by "other" writers. Especially with African

American women, reader resistance seems neverending. However, I am convinced that Harriet Jacobs, like many others, anticipated a hostile and incredulous reception to her narrative. And using techniques from her multiple cultures, she created a transcultural[4] text that begged, borrowed, stole, and devised the techniques that would allow her maximum freedom to tell her story in her own way and to her own ends. Jacobs may well have underestimated the persistence of resistance, but she did in fact create a brilliantly innovative autobiography. That the incidents of resistance were not quelled may say more about the perspicaciousness of her readers than about imperfections in the text itself.

SANDRA GUNNING

Reading and Redemption in *Incidents in the Life of a Slave Girl*†

The post–Civil War version of Olive Gilbert's *Narrative of Sojourner Truth* included a curious letter by Indiana abolitionist William Hayward describing an 1858 confrontation between Truth and proslavery forces: During a rural antislavery meeting, a Dr. T. W. Strain declared "that a doubt existed in the minds of many persons present respecting the sex of the speaker"; according to Strain, Truth should "submit her breast to the inspection of some of the ladies present, that the doubt may be removed by their testimony."[1] When Truth inquired about the basis for his opinion, Strain

4. Here I am adapting definitions that Masao Miyoshi posits in his discussion of transnational and multinational corporations. The distinction, he argues, is "problematic" and frequently the terms may be used interchangeably. The differences are "in the degrees of alienation from the countries of origin." Multinational corporations belong to one nation and operate in several. Transnational corporations, on the other hand, are not tied to their nations of origin but are more self-contained and self-serving. Although there may be obvious incompatibilities between the discussion of multicultural and multinational businesses and discourse, Miyoshi's discussion stimulated my own thinking in this matter. See his "A Borderless World? From Colonialism to Transnationalism and the Decline of the Nation-State," *Critical Inquiry* 19 (Summer 1993): 726–51.

† From *Harriet Jacobs and* Incidents in the Life of a Slave Girl: *New Critical Essays,* ed. Deborah M. Garfield and Rafia Zafar (New York: Cambridge UP, 1996) 131–54. Page numbers in brackets refer to this Norton Critical Edition, with the exception of references to extratext material included in the Yellin edition. [My thanks to Keith L. T. Alexander, Barbara Christian, M. Giulia Fabi, and Stephanie Smith for their sensitive commentary on early drafts of this essay (Gunning's acknowledgment).]

1. [Olive Gilbert, ed.], "Book of Life" in *Narrative of Sojourner Truth; A bondswoman of Olden times, With a History of Her Labors and Correspondence Drawn from Her "Book of Life"* (1878; rpt., New York: Oxford University Press, 1991), 138. Cited in text henceforth as *Narrative,* followed by page number.

continued: '"Your voice is not the voice of a woman, it is the voice of a man, and we believe you to be a man'" (*Narrative*, 138).

Facing an unruly crowd, the indefatigable Truth replied

> that her breasts had suckled many a white babe, to the exclusion of her own offspring; that some of those white babies had grown to man's estate; that although they had sucked her colored breasts they were . . . far more manly than they (her persecutors) appeared to be; and she quietly asked them, as she disrobed her bosom, if they too, wished to suck!

Truth thus uncovers herself before the crowd, "not to her shame . . . but to their shame" (*Narrative*, 139). With Truth's sex verified, Hayward gloats that Strain loses a forty-dollar bet on her masculinity.

Though undoubtedly included by the *Narrative*'s white editors as a testimonial to Truth's courage, Hayward's anecdote speaks ironically to the ways in which the ostensibly opposing elements of abolition and slavery could rely on the same mechanism for self-enhancement: On the one hand Strain set out to discredit anti-slavery activists by the obliteration of Truth's voice through a deliberate misreading of her body, a misreading firmly set within a context of de-sexualization provided by slavery, where male bodies became interchangeable with female, where gender was acknowledged only for the convenience of sexual and reproductive exploitation.[2] But on the other hand Hayward ignores the assault on Truth's modesty and makes the issue instead Truth's willingness to combat slavery by any means available—even with her body. At the same time, however, Hayward is quick to recognize that a physical examination of an unclothed black body by female audience members is an attack on white female modesty: "a large number of ladies present . . . appeared to be ashamed and indignant at such a proposition" (*Narrative*, 138). When he proudly reports on the proslavery advocate's loss of face through the public revelation of Truth's breasts, he inadvertently confirms that Truth's own credibility as an abolitionist speaker must rest finally not with her testimony as an ex-slave, but on the white reading of her body. Whether the incident ends in favor of the proslavery supporters or the abolitionists, successful political agitation seems destined to occur through the medium of Truth's body, the body of the slave interlocutor.

Although abolitionist objectification appears to win out over proslavery fetishization, there is a crucial dimension to this incident produced by Truth's decision to disrobe publicly. Challenging the objectifying gaze of the hostile Indiana audience (and with the publication of Hayward's letter, future generations of white readers

2. See Hortense J. Spillers's "Mama's Baby, Papa's Maybe: An American Grammar Book," *Diacritics* 17 (Summer 1987): 65–81, for an excellent discussion of the popular construction of black women.

also), Truth reunites the ex-slave's body with its voice through an articulation of bodily secrets that confirm white links with black physicality. Truth appropriates the linguistic moment by reinterpreting her breasts not as markers of biological identity, but as signifiers of the long American history of exploitative sexual and maternal contact between black and white bodies. As the crowd insists on their moral obligation to know the truth of her body, Truth's invitation to suckle the crowd recontextualizes that white desire for knowledge as pruriently sexual, as exploitative of her maternity. Thus under Truth's bodily language of critique the distinction between the North and South as ideological opposites in their attention to the slave begins to blur as the black abolitionist resembles the denuded slave woman on a Northern auction block, and the false ideal of slavery as the patriarchal institution merges with and consequently begins to falsify white middle-class idealization of domesticity and maternity.[3]

If we move from this narrated incident in the life of Sojourner Truth to the self-authored narrative of Harriet Jacobs in *Incidents in the Life of a Slave Girl* (1861), we find Jacobs confronting, through the voice of her alter ego Linda Brent, the very similar challenge of a white audience intent on replacing her interpreting voice with her already overinterpreted black body. However, as I argue in this essay, if for Truth the ability to assert herself as a social critic rests on the capacity to interpret the black female body's history as a narrative about masked relations, a similar strategy is employed by Jacobs to highlight and to challenge her audience's unwillingness to accept the authority of a slave speaker. Like Truth, Harriet Jacobs uses the story of her body's exploitation in slavery as a critical moment to call into question the supposed distances between black and white bodies, and especially the Northerners' (especially Northern white women's) conception of themselves as ideologically distinguished from their Southern neighbors on the subject of slavery. Working to make visible the seemingly invisible, disembodied white reader through the medium of the physically exploited Linda Brent, Jacobs achieves a critique of Northern models of white female domestic activism that in the end establishes hers as the true voice of reform, to which all whites must attend if they are concerned about moral salvation.[4]

Ironically, Jacobs's credibility as a social commentator is compromised not by doubts about her sex, but by the fact of her identity and

3. Truth had been a slave in New York state before the abolition of slavery in that region. She escaped in 1827.

4. In her book *The Word in Black and White: Reading "Race" in American Literature, 1638–1867* (New York: Oxford University Press, 1992), Dana D. Nelson also addresses Jacobs's critique of traditional notions of racial difference, and the complacency of readers. Although she and I arrive at what I feel are complementary conclusions, Nelson focuses more on the notion of how "sympathy" mediates Jacobs's critique of the reader: "The text repeatedly appeals to the sympathy of its readers, but at the same time it warns them to be careful about the motives and critical of the results of that sympathetic identification" (142).

experience as a female ex-slave. According to the narrative, as a young woman in Edenton, North Carolina, Jacobs (represented through Linda Brent in the story) chooses to escape a lascivious master by encouraging the affections of a sympathetic white admirer.[5] Eventually, in an effort to secure the freedom of their resulting two children, as well as in a final bid to put a stop to her master's continued sexual advances, Jacobs confines herself to an attic hiding place. Only after spending almost seven years in hiding does Jacobs finally escape to the North.

But as Jacobs and some of her supporters well knew, Northern white readers of the narrative would ignore her analysis of slavery's criminality and instead fix upon her "immoral" black body and her apparently willful complicity in sexual relations with a white man. Indeed, the problem was that instead of defining Jacobs as she defined herself, that is, as a mother who has led her children out of slavery and who now seeks to create a subjective role as an abolitionist writer and social critic, her white audience would construct her as the contaminated product of slavery's moral decadence—an object of white scrutiny, of white contempt for her violation of moral codes of female conduct, but certainly not an authoritative commentator on slavery, much less Northern morality.

Like Truth, Harriet Jacobs aims, as she enters the political arena, to become the interpreter of her own body's experience of slavery. But in Jacobs's case, the female ex-slave is determined to provide readings of her sexual conduct that compete with the already established white middle-class patterns of judging correct female behavior. As virtually all modern readers of *Incidents* have noted, Jacobs's commentaries are strategically embedded within Linda Brent's language of domesticity, a language imported into the text to highlight the black female slave as mother, all in an effort to make her acceptable to a Northern audience. Indeed "it is not surprising," Jean Fagan Yellin suggests, "that Jacobs presents Linda Brent in terms of motherhood, the most valued 'feminine' role" of the antebellum period, given the need to enlist white sympathy for a story which many might find outrageous.[6] As an escaped slave Jacobs confronts

5. Recalling her "deliberate calculation" to choose a sexual partner in order to maintain control over her life, Jacobs remarks through Linda Brent's narration that "it seemed less degrading to give one's self, than to submit to compulsion"; in Harriet Jacobs, *Incidents in the Life of a Slave Girl, Written by Herself* (1861; rpt., Cambridge: Harvard University Press, 1987), 54, 55 [46, 47]. Cited in this essay henceforth as *I* followed by page number.

6. Jean Fagan Yellin, "Introduction," *Incidents in the Life of a Slave Girl, Written by Herself* (Cambridge: Harvard University Press, 1987), xxvi. See also Bruce Mills, "Lydia Maria Child and the Endings of Harriet Jacobs's *Incidents in the Life of a Slave Girl*," *American Literature* 64:2 (June 1992): 255–72. Standard discussions of the cultural binary constructions of black and white womanhood include Barbara Christian, *Black Women Novelists: The Development of a Tradition, 1892–1976* (Westport, CT: Greenwood, 1980), specifically 7–14; Paula Giddings, *When and Where I Enter: The Impact of Black Women on Race and Sex in America* (Bantam, 1985), 47–55; Hazel Carby, *Reconstructing Womanhood: The Emergence of the Afro-American Woman Novelist* (New York: Oxford University Press, 1987), chapter 2.

an American cultural setting that defines black femininity as everything white womanhood was not: publicly exposed, sexualized, unable or unwilling to create a domestic space of its own.

Jacobs's presentation of the black woman as mother is not simply an attempt to embrace a white cultural icon of respectibility. Within the narrative Jacobs appears to fall into line behind such women as Harriet Beecher Stowe and Lydia Maria Child in using the language of domesticity to build a platform from which to agitate for social justice. Yet the text's political aims are continually at odds with the format of the domestic novel, which precludes discussions of sexual exploitation and miscegenation as subjects unmentionable in a white familial setting, despite their importance to any discussion of slavery. Instead of submission to silence, however, *Incidents in the Life of a Slave Girl* uses the continual conflict between form and content to problematize the position of white readers with respect to their role as private spectators to the public story of Linda Brent and her exploitation as a slave, and, as a result, their political identity as Northern, supposedly antislavery advocates.[7] In the end, *Incidents in the Life of a Slave Girl* gives special meaning to a black woman's physical flight from slavery to freedom and a home by contextualizing such experiences within a continuum of moral corruption where racism, wrongful persecution, and sexual exploitation flourish. This pattern of suffering begins in North Carolina but, as the narrative works to emphasize, it extends even to Northern cities, despite the strong presence of abolitionists. In the narrative, the same terrible hardships that Jacobs and her children must endure regardless of whether they live in the North or the South suggest that the regions might be similar in their moral and indeed their political treatment of black slaves.

And yet *Incidents* does not merely set out to condemn Northern white readers; rather, it is a critique of the traditional practices of

7. According to Karen Sanchez-Eppler, "the acceptability [of stories from slavery] . . . depends upon their adherence to a feminine and domestic demeanor that softens the cruelty they describe and makes their political goals more palatable to a less politicized readership." See "Bodily Bonds: The Intersecting Rhetorics of Feminism and Abolition," *Representations* 24 (Fall 1988): 35. For other discussions of Harriet Jacobs, Linda Brent, and their relationship to the narrative's audience, see Carby, *Reconstructing Womanhood*, 45–61; Valerie Smith, "'Loopholes of Retreat': Architecture and Ideology in Harriet Jacobs's *Incidents in the Life of a Slave Girl*," in *Reading Black, Reading Feminist: A Critical Anthology*, ed. Henry Louis Gates, Jr. (New York: Meridian, 1990): 212–26; P. Gabrielle Foreman, "The Spoken and the Silenced in *Incidents in the Life of a Slave Girl* and *Our Nig*," *Callaloo* 13 (Spring 1990): 313–24; Beth Maclay Doriani, "Black Womanhood in Nineteenth-Century America: Subversion and Self-Construction in Two Women's Autobiographies," *American Quarterly* 43 (June 1991): 199–222; Fanny Nudelman, "Harriet Jacobs and the Sentimental Politics of Female Suffering," *ELH* (59) 1992: 939–64; Harryette Mullen, "Runaway Tongue: Resistant Orality in *Uncle Tom's Cabin, Our Nig, Incidents in the Life of a Slave Girl*, and *Beloved*" in *The Culture of Sentiment: Race, Gender, and Sentimentality in Nineteenth-Century America*, ed. Shirley Samuels (New York: Oxford University Press, 1992): 244–64, 332–5.

reading blackness as a severed relationship between voice and body, as the epitome of powerless victimization. And if Jacobs's text calls into question the patterns of representation for blackness, then it does so for representations of whiteness as well: On what foundation is white privacy based within the context of race? What is the basis of white political self-constructions with regard to liberty and slavery? Why is agency racialized as white with regard to abolitionists? These are some of the questions Jacobs addresses in her narrative, and they are designed to lead readers beyond inane stereotyping of black victimization or black culpability, beyond deluding self-constructions, toward a sense of Northern white moral and political self-scrutiny.

I

Jacobs's project of re-reading posed a challenge to mid-nineteenth-century literary and social ideologies that fetishized the black female body. White women agitating for suffrage employed the image of the chained, denuded, helpless black female slave as a metaphor to describe their own perceived position as patriarchal wards without the social and political power to control their economic and physical lives.[8] Although these representations also epitomized Southern slavery, visions of chained black women did not necessarily encourage white women to empathize with the material condition of female slaves. For example, even though Harriet Beecher Stowe set out in *Uncle Tom's Cabin* (1851) and the 1853 *Key* to the novel to demonstrate black exploitation during slavery, her own dealings with real black women (and Jacobs in particular) suggests that Stowe was not always inclined toward sensitivity, or antiracist feelings.[9]

For most Northerners, black enslavement (as opposed to the figurative "slavery" of marriage) was made vivid through the numerous descriptions of public slave auctions, the violation of black families, beatings, and allusions to rape and incest within the pages of popular male-authored slave narratives and antislavery fiction by white abolitionists.[1] Such scenes of moral chaos no doubt provided a

8. See Yellin's *Woman and Sisters: The Antislavery Feminists in American Culture* (New Haven: Yale University Press, 1989). Also, Ronald G. Walters, "The Erotic South: Civilization and Sexuality in American Abolitionism," *American Quarterly* 25 (May 1973): 177–201. For a useful look at the rhetoric of white feminist abolitionists and its relationship to the bodies of male and female slaves see Sanchez-Eppler, "Bodily Bonds," and William Andrews, *To Tell a Free Story: The First Century of Afro-American Autobiography, 1760–1865* (Urbana: University of Illinois Press, 1988), 241–7.
9. See Stowe's rebuff of Jacobs over the publication of the latter's story in the *Key to Uncle Tom's Cabin* in Yellin, "Introduction," xviii–xix. Jacobs's letters to Amy Post also reveal her anger and distrust for Stowe. They are reprinted in *Incidents*, 233–37.
1. See Frances Foster's "'In Respect to Females . . .': Differences in the Portrayals of Women by Male and Female Narrators," *Black American Literature Forum* 15:2 (Summer 1981): 66–70.

comforting contrast for Northern whites between their life and the life of the degraded South, a contrast abolitionists capitalized on by presenting slavery as a national threat to traditional concepts of family and personal liberty; indeed slavery marked "the outer limits of disorder and debauchery," and if left unchecked it might spread moral pollution even to the North.[2] Certainly although whites in the North were not necessarily hostile to slaves, blackness and black women in particular signified victimization (hence, as Jean Fagan Yellin and Karen Sánchez-Eppler have shown, the need to act on behalf of the slave, especially the slave-mother), but also the threat of racial pollution (hence the need to keep the de facto miscegenation practices of the South out of the North).[3]

When Lydia Maria Child (who served as the narrative's editor) and Jacobs's white friend Amy Post composed the literary addresses that frame *Incidents*, their presentations of the ex-slave as Linda Brent were clearly shaped by dual Northern attitudes to black women as pariahs and victims.[4] Lydia Maria Child recognized the problem of audience reception, no doubt from her own experience as an abolitionist writer shunned for the publication of her controversial *An Appeal in Favor of That Class of Americans Called Africans* (1833).[5] In the "Editor's Introduction" to *Incidents* Child instructs white readers to look beyond the ex-slave's narration of offending horrors and interpret *Incidents* so as to focus on the injustice of slavery. Indeed, in her role as editor Child reorganized certain aspects of the narrative as part of a strategy against audience alienation, putting "savage cruelties into one chapter . . . in order that those who shrink from 'supping upon horrors' might omit them, without interrupting the thread of the story."[6]

Nevertheless, as her own introduction suggests, Child recognizes that even with the "savage cruelties" pruned, the story of Linda Brent might itself be offensive:

2. Walters, "Erotic South," 189. According to Carolyn L. Karcher, one of the many challenges faced by white abolitionist writers was the problem of even discussing the occurrences of rape, torture, incest, or murder under slavery, since any representation of these issues would have been insulting to the sensibilities of American white women of the North. See her "Rape, Murder and Revenge in 'Slavery's Pleasant Homes': Lydia Maria Child's Antislavery Fiction and the Limits of Genre," *Women's Studies International Forum* 9:4 (1986): 323.
3. See Yellin, *Women and Sisters*, and Sánchez-Eppler, "Bodily Bonds."
4. Whereas Child and Post see Harriet Jacobs and Linda Brent as the same person, I would argue that to some extent Jacobs is fictionalizing her life experiences through the character of Brent, or, according to P. Gabrielle Foreman, at least shielding herself through the narrator. See Foreman's "The Spoken and the Silenced."
5. See Carolyn L. Karcher's discussion in "Censorship, American Style: the Case of Lydia Maria Child," *Studies in the American Renaissance, 1986*; ed. Joel Myerson (Charlottesville: University Press of Virginia, 1986), 283–303.
6. Quoted in Yellin, "Introduction," xxii. Karcher also discusses this practice in the context of antislavery fiction in "Rape, Murder and Revenge," 330. Bruce Mill's "Lydia Maria Child and the Endings to Harriet Jacobs's *Incidents*" is the most recent discussion of Child's role as editor.

> I am well aware that many will accuse me of indecorum for presenting these pages to the public; for the experiences of this intelligent and much-injured woman belong to a class which some call delicate subjects, and others indelicate. . . . [B]ut the public ought to be made acquainted with . . . [slavery's] monstrous features, and I willingly take the responsibility of presenting them with the veil withdrawn. (*I*, 3–4 [6])

In her effort to protect Jacobs and justify the publication of *Incidents*, Child bypasses Jacobs's authorship—and therefore the notion of Jacobs as a self-conscious critic of an American political and social system—altogether, thereby constructing Linda Brent as an anonymous woman defined not by her role as speaker, but by her (presumed) bodily "experiences" in slavery.[7] These are the real issues of the narrative, according to Child. By focusing on the problem of audience reception (the problem of indecorousness), Child draws attention not to the slave narrator's authority to determine the meaning of her slavery, but to the privatized privilege of the white reader to interpret and pass judgment on Brent's life and—if we follow the gist of Child's metaphor of the unveiling—on Brent's body as well.[8] The white reader's authority (especially that of the white female reader) is constructed through the metaphoric presentation of the unveiled slave woman: Her location within the public realm signifies female contamination, racialized in this context as black, while their location within the realm of shielding domesticity signifies spirituality and moral purity.[9]

At the same time, if Child unveils the "monstrous features" of slavery made visible upon the body of a slave woman, this woman is both an object of charity and a pariah, as her life story vacillates between the "delicate" and the "indelicate"—categories that move the white audience either to protect the victimized Brent or to protect their own sensibilities from her offending presence. The problem here is Child's appeal to the conscience of the white reader and her or his interpretation of the narrative; the success of the narrative rests not on Brent's telling, but on how the white reader chooses to read the meaning of the narrative, in effect the meaning of Brent's body as it is exposed in the text.

7. For other readings of Child's introduction, see Valerie Smith, "Loopholes of Retreat," 218–23, and Foreman, "The Spoken and the Silenced," 316–17.
8. Child is acting the part of the conscientious editor, given the traditional expectations of white readers. According to William Andrews, "nineteenth century whites read slave narratives more to get a firsthand look at the institution of slavery than to become acquainted with an individual slave." Indeed, a "reliable slave narrative would be one that seemed purely mimetic, in which the self is on the periphery instead of at the center of attention, . . . transcribing rather than interpreting a set of objective facts" (*To Tell a Free Story*, 5–6).
9. Though he fails to underscore the importance of race in the determination of privacy, Richard H. Brodhead nevertheless offers an important discussion on the subject of (un)veiled presentations in "Veiled Ladies: Towards a History of Antebellum Entertainment," *American Literary History* 1 (Summer 1989): 273–94.

Child's strategy of mediation becomes clear when she phrases her final appeal to the audience as a celebration of the power of Northern whites to effect correct moral judgments:

> I do this for the sake of my sisters in bondage, who are suffering wrongs so foul, that our ears are too delicate to listen to them. I do it with the hope of arousing conscientious and reflecting women at the North to a sense of their duty in the exertion of moral influence on the question of Slavery, on all possible occasions. (*I*, 4 [6])

Child's final proposal for the proper response to her "unveiling" of Brent identifies the "indelicate" (the offensiveness of Jacobs's story) with the slave testimony ("our ears are too delicate to listen to them"), since the pronoun "them" refers both to the black speakers and to the atrocities committed under slavery. At the same time, since Child has described the readers' proposed encounter with stories of slavery through the visual metaphor of gazing at unveiled images, the suggestion then is that within *Incidents* the mere sight of Brent's enslaved body, unadorned with commentary, will be less offensive than hearing about it from Brent herself. What is indelicate, then, is the black eye-witness interpretation of slavery, the notion of the authoritative voice of the slave narrator.[1]

Only when Brent is silenced can she become the object of charity. Her situation can be perceived as "delicate" (and therefore worthy of sensitivity) only when thoughtful white women readers are allowed to contemplate safely the transparent text of Brent's life for themselves, and in so doing assign what whites would consider to be proper meaning to the ex-slave's experience. In other words, the public body of the slave woman, the site of the grossly physical, becomes the site of intervention and mystification for the disembodied white female reader to "exert" protective moral influence.

If in her "Introduction" Child attempts to win audience support by validating the white right to assign correct meaning to the "monstrous features" of slavery through the construction of a silenced Brent as literally a physical specimen for sympathetic white consideration, Amy Post tries a seemingly different tactic in her appendix. In a statement of support for the slave narrator that attempts to remain faithful to Jacobs's directives from an 1857 letter, Post seems at first to destabilize the terms of Child's introduction by completely

1. In a letter to the *National Anti-Slavery Standard*, one reader of *Incidents* objected to the existence of slave commentary: "A few sentences in which the moral is rather oppressively displayed, might have been omitted with advantage. These, it is to be wished, Mrs. Child had felt herself authorized to expunge. They are the strongest witnesses who leave the summing up to the judge, and the verdict to the jury" (quoted in Yellin, "Introduction," xxiv–xxv).

submerging the notion of Brent's physicality.[2] Referring directly to Jacobs through the pseudonym of Linda Brent, Post stresses the slave narrator's perfect assimilation into the private world of Northern middle-class white true womanhood.

As "a beloved inmate" of Post's house, Brent's physical characteristics are referred to in passing as "prepossessing," but in large part the testimonial constructs Brent as a spiritual creature with "remarkable delicacy of feeling and purity of thought" whose body responds to the more acceptable somatic sensations of grief and modesty, rather than to sexual exploitation (*I*, 203 [167]). But whereas the evidence of slavery is concealed in the suppression of bodily knowledge, such suppression seems to have rendered Brent inarticulate and even mute—this after the "incidents" themselves have just been delivered in the ex-slave's own words: "she passed through a baptism of suffering . . . in private confidential conversations"; "even in talking with me, she wept so much, and seemed to suffer such mental agony, that I felt her story was too sacred to be drawn from her by inquisitive questions" (*I*, 203–4 [167–68]).[3] Even though she is ethereal, Brent is being read for what is unsaid about her body. Indeed, her tears and shrinking modesty, even as they signify her rightful place in a white domestic setting, might also betray incriminating secrets. After all, though she is accepted into Post's female community, Brent's claim to true womanhood is always mediated by her race.

Brent's body seems to have been recouped by Post's narrative strategy, yet the slave narrator's interpreting voice is still depicted as nonexistent, since the political foresight to write and publish the narrative is unmistakably stressed as Post's rather than Brent's. In the end, though Brent performs the manual labor of tracing "secretly and wearily . . . a truthful record of her eventful life" (204 [168]), Post takes the credit by constantly harping on "the [moral] duty of publishing" *Incidents*. As such, though Brent occupies the favored place of adopted white daughter, though she displays the necessary spiritual grace of white women, she still lacks the moral strength that defines the ideal of white domestic feminism. Thus Post's

2. In her letter to Post, Jacobs writes: "I think it would be best for you to begin with our acquaintance and the length of time I was in your family your advice about giving the history of my life in Slavery mention that I lived at service all the while that I was striving to get the Book out . . . —my kind friend I do not restrict you in anything for you know far better than I do what to say" (reprinted in *I*, 242 [201]).

3. In an earlier letter to Post in 1852, which mentions Post's "proposal" that Jacobs make her story public, the latter says: "dear Amy if it was the life of a Heroine with no degradation associated with it far better to have been one of the starving poor of Ireland whose bones had to bleach on the highways than to have been a slave with the curse of slavery stamped upon yourself and Children" (reprinted in *I*, 232). Is Jacobs just ashamed of her experience under slavery, as Post's appendix seems to imply, or is she instead trustful of the Northern reading public?

appendix suggests that Brent may be the daughter, but it is the white mother who leads her toward political action.[4]

Despite the disturbing implications of their testimonials, Child and Post offer their respective construction of the slave narrator from a genuine commitment to assisting Jacobs with the publication of her text. Jacobs was no doubt grateful to both women for their encouragement and assistance in helping her with *Incidents*, and she describes them affectionately as "whole souled."[5] However, her own discussion of the writing of the narrative and her implied instructions to the audience about what, who, or how to "read" with regard to her autobiography contradict the interpretive practices employed by Child and Post, and also clearly foreground her awareness of the problems of writing for a Northern audience not likely to grant her respect as a competent social commentator.

Through the persona of Linda Brent in the "Author's Preface," Jacobs's terse description of her past and present condition suggests a woman who has survived physically and intellectually the hardships of drudgery and denial imposed by life in both the North and the South:

> I was born and reared in Slavery. . . . Since I have been at the North, it has been necessary for me to work diligently for my own support, and the education of my children. This has not left me much leisure to make up for the loss of early opportunities to improve myself; and it has compelled me to write these pages at irregular intervals, whenever I could snatch an hour from household duties. (*I*, 1 [5])

In describing her confinement to domestic service Jacobs does not focus on physical tortures, but instead makes clear her dedication to political action ("I want to add my testimony to that of abler pens to convince the people of the Free States what Slavery really is"), and her desire to claim for herself the role of the moral and intellectual authority who will lead the audience to a proper understanding of the complex issue contained within the narrative: "I do earnestly desire to arouse the women of the North to a realizing sense of the condition of two millions of women at the South, still in bondage" (*I*, 1–2 [5]).

4. Although Post did urge Jacobs to write the narrative, Jacobs had never doubted the need for her own political activism: "My conscience approved it but my stubborn pride would not yield I have tried for the past two years to conquer it and I feel that God has helped me or I never would consent to give my past life to any one for I would not do it without giving the whole truth if it could help save another from my fate it would be selfish and unchristian in me to keep it back" (reprinted in *I*, 232). One of the chief causes she lists for not writing is her situation on the household staff of proslavery Nathaniel P. Willis.

5. Harriet Jacobs's 1860 letter to Amy Post, reprinted in *I*, 247.

In an 1857 letter to Amy Post, Jacobs describes the persona she has created for herself in *Incidents* as "a poor Slave Mother [who comes] not to tell you what I have heard but what I have seen—and what I have suffered" (*I*, 243). The oxymoronic appellation Slave/Mother ironically gestures toward the two entities split in Child's introduction and racialized as opposites: the sexually degraded, commercialized body that Child would unveil, and the intuitive, disembodied nurturing image of female moral force.[6] In the public body of the narrator Linda Brent, both mother and slave will be united as witness and participant. And it is precisely Jacobs's experience as a participant (the same experience which might repulse the audience) that her preface argues is the premiere qualification for assigning her the role of judge: "Only by experience can any one realize how deep, and dark, and foul is that pit of abominations" (*I*, 2 [5]). Clearly, what Child sees as the point of danger for white women becomes a source of authority for Jacobs.

II

In her effort to problematize the authority of a white audience that deems itself empowered by the privatized moral force of domestic feminism, the narrator Linda Brent situates both the Southern and Northern portions of *Incidents* within the interior spaces of the home. Her tactic here is to highlight that setting as the special context of black female exploitation. Representational patterns begin shifting from the very opening of the text, when Brent's first owner turns out to be a godly woman having more in common with the mothers among the audience than with slaveholders like Simon Legree. In her introduction Lydia Maria Child identifies her as Brent's first benefactor who, along with many white Northerners, provides the slave with "opportunities for self-improvement" by teaching her to read and educating her in "the precepts of God's Word" after the death of Brent's parents (*I*, 3, 8 [6, 11]).

But Brent herself is quick to discuss the full extent of her "opportunities" when as a surrogate daughter within the white family unit she is bequeathed to the white woman's niece, the infant daughter of the infamous Dr. Flint. Unlike Brent's former mistress, who is

6. While acknowledging for a moment the critical explanation that Brent/Jacobs embraces maternity within her narrative as a strategy to engage Northern sympathies, we need to recognize that maternity itself is a highly problematic category in *Incidents*. Although she has been acting in the capacity of a mother since the birth of her children during slavery, Brent is not officially allowed to accept the status of mother until the final pages of the narrative when, as a free woman, she can own herself and so own her children. The category of the slave-mother embodied by the character Linda Brent functions not just as a category for her presentation to American readers, but also as a metaphor for instability to describe Brent's lifelong struggle against social processes that govern her identity.

ultimately disappointing in her actions because she appears to be falsely the ideal white mother, Flint and his wife take on demonic proportions from the start: the doctor tries to sell Brent's grandmother after her mistress's death, even though both blacks and whites know that the mistress had intended to free Aunt Martha. A fitting consort to Dr. Flint, Mrs. Flint has no "strength to superintend her household affairs," but she is strong enough to "sit in her easy chair and see a woman whipped, till the blood trickled from every stroke of the lash" (*I*, 12 [15]).

Brent's description of life in the Flint household lifts Child's metaphoric veil of decency to reveal not just brutalized slave bodies, but the nature of the victimization process developed and sustained as part of the means of constructing white privacy. Her first discussion of Dr. Flint's sexual misconduct in the slave quarters makes clear this connection. After only a short time in the Flint household, she witnesses the torture of a male slave:

> There were many conjectures as to the cause of this terrible punishment. Some said master accused him of stealing corn; others said the slave had quarreled with his wife, in presence of the overseer, and had accused his master of being the father of her child. They were both black, and the child was very fair. (*I*, 13 [16])

Eventually Flint sells both husband and wife:

> The guilty man put their value into his pocket, and had the satisfaction of knowing that they were out of sight and hearing. When the mother was delivered into the trader's hands, she said, "you *promised* to treat me well." To which he replied, "You have let your tongue run too far; damn you!" (*I*, 13 [16])

Flint conceals his indiscretion by prohibiting the woman from speaking of the crime, so that even the slave community must whisper and conjecture about what has really occurred. Under this system of reversals the pregnant slave bears the guilt of sexual misconduct. Indeed the protection of Flint's private life as father and husband is predicated on the exposure and punishment of black female bodies; they become criminalized, while white paternity is replaced by irresponsible, immoral black maternity. However, Brent's narration works to undermine the careful protection Flint has constructed for himself by moving the narrative beyond the public exhibition of the slaves (the man who is beaten, the woman who is sold), an exhibition that, in its reliance on stereotypical images of victimization, suppresses rather than facilitates truth. Her vocalization finally allows the lost story of the slave couple to surface, despite

Flint's prohibition. Brent's motive for speaking out in the case of the slave couple becomes the context for the telling of her own experiences: clearly, as in the case of the slave woman who is sold away, for Brent *not* to reveal the details of her relationship with Flint would be to allow her (potential) bodily corruption to stand as a means of shielding his moral degradation.

Though regional and political differences seem to separate the degenerate Flints from the apparently purer communities of Northern white readers, Brent's emphasis throughout her narrative on Flint's obsession with the silencing of black (especially black female) speech about sexual exploitation suggests frightening parallels in the Northern white readers' own resistance to *hearing* about the horrifying details of slavery as they read the narrative within a familial setting. Indeed, if they resist Brent's authority as narrator, the morally righteous audience addressed by Child's introduction, who are appealed to as saviors but whose ears will be contaminated by slave accounts of oppression under slavery, ironically risk appearing in collusion with Flint, the evil slavemaster so often vilified in abolitionist literature.

This implication has important consequences with respect to how white readers supportive of familial harmony can claim to be innocent spectators to the perversion of their ideals in the Southern patriarchal "family" of slavery. Brent's narrative continually seeks to implicate them in a racial conspiracy against black female modesty that undermines the notion of white sectional difference. She begins by appropriating the concept of delicacy and assigning it to black femininity. Then she depicts this delicacy under assault by the white master "father" who seeks to suppress the detailed discussion of sexual—and therefore incestuous—exploitation of a surrogate daughter: "My master began to *whisper* foul words in *my ear*. . . . He tried his utmost to corrupt the pure principles my grandmother had instilled" (emphasis added; *I*, 27 [27]):

> I saw a man forty years my senior daily violating the most sacred commandments of nature. He told me I was his property; that I must be subject to his will in all things. . . . But where could I turn for protection? No matter whether the slave girl be as black as ebony or as fair as her mistress. In either case, there is no shadow of law to protect her from insult, from violence, or even from death. . . . The degradation, the wrongs, the vices, that grow of slavery, are more than I can describe. They are greater than you would willingly believe. (*I*, 27–8 [27])

The penultimate sentence of this passage re-echoes Flint's own silencing of his victim: "Dr. Flint swore he would kill me, if I was not as silent as the grave" (*I*, 28 [28]).[7] And since decency, or more precisely "delicacy," is the same watchword mediating between the audience/slave master and the slave narrator (neither wants their home contaminated by Brent's story), then in the North as well as the South discretion rather than justice remains the better part of valor. Thus, white readers, who shy away from full disclosures from the mouth of the slave narrator, could well be accused of an identical acceptance of a hypocritical standard of public morality.

With regard to Brent's reticence concerning the details of Flint's attempted seduction, her silence cannot be attributed solely to her desire to avoid reliving a distressing situation.[8] Precisely because Flint's prohibition occurs within the context of white middle-class privacy, which is dependent on the annihilation of the slave family and the poisoning of black female morality, Brent seems compelled to speak. Her silence is therefore dramatized as an imposed one—in the past by Flint, in the present moment of *Incidents in the Life of a Slave Girl* by the antislavery audience itself: "The degradation, the wrongs, the vices that grow out of slavery, are more than I can describe. They are greater than you would willingly believe."

In many ways Brent's compelled silence forces her to be the guardian of the white reader's morality, since she keeps to herself all the unpleasant, unseemly details that insult a pure sensibility. Consequently, the exploited slave girl is transformed into the physical receptacle of slavery's contamination, standing as the victim abolitionists want to rescue, the pariah they feel compelled to keep at arm's length.[9] But it is precisely in dramatizing how the protection of both Northern and Southern white morality is constructed through the particular usage of the slave body in tandem with the silencing of the slave's voice that Brent resurrects herself as social critic. This point is made clearer when we read the rest of her comments to a disbelieving audience:

> Surely, if you credited one half the truths that are told you concerning the helpless millions suffering in this cruel bondage, you at the north would not help to tighten the yoke. You surely would refuse to do for the master, on your own soil, the mean

7. For an illuminating recent discussion of Southern etiquette around miscegenation and the rape of slave women by white men, see Catherine Clinton, "'Southern Dishonor': Flesh, Blood, Race, and Bondage," in *In Joy and in Sorrow: Women, Family, and Marriage in the Victorian South, 1830–1900*, ed. Carol Bleser (New York: Oxford University Press, 1991): 52–68, 281–84.
8. Certainly the descriptions of Flint's initial attempts to corrupt Brent are marked with what other readers have called "omissions and circumlocution" designed to give some modicum of protection to the narrator—who seems unwilling to relive the details of the event—or to encourage the potential voyeurism of the white reader regarding Brent's experience of a distressing situation. See Yellin, "Introduction," xxi, and especially Foreman, "The Spoken and the Silenced," 317.
9. I am grateful to M. Giulia Fabi for helping me develop this idea.

> and cruel work which trained bloodhounds and the lowest class of whites do for him at the south. (*I*, 28 [27])

Thus Brent, artless, reticent, bowed down by shame, uses the apparently limiting construction of herself as mute victim to reveal her binary opposite, the depraved tyrant whose "monstrous features" depict not just Flint, but also the moral citizens of the North who tolerate the Fugitive Slave Law. So when Brent describes Flint as a fiend, Northerners, because of their own hypocrisy and their refusal to listen to "truths," are likewise constructed as the monstrous bloodhounds and uncivilized slave-catchers in antislavery territory.

This refiguration of the well-meaning readers is particularly devastating with respect to its implication for white women. Their participation, as readers, in the silencing of Brent sanctions her sexual exploitation by Flint; the identification of their need for silence with his recontextualizes these women's popular representation as saviors. They have, in fact, joined the ranks of Brent's male tormentors, a shift that threatens to defeminize them. So, clearly, Brent's appeal is not solely for the protection of the slave victim: What is at risk also is the very notion of femininity and true womanhood white Americans have hitherto idealized.

Since Brent wants to arrest the attention of her audience without alienating it, she provides a vivid but distanced dramatization of white female collusion in a half-sarcastic, half-regretful description of Mrs. Flint as the failed maternal figure who might protect her from the doctor's torments. When her husband's sexual designs on Brent become too obvious, Mrs. Flint's anger is aroused. Up to this point Brent has represented Flint's sexual harassment as incestuous, a violation of the codes of familial decency. He demands to have his four-year-old daughter sleep in his chamber, as an excuse for Brent to remain in the room; here one wonders if Flint expects the child to be present while he tries to rape her nurse. The narrative thus creates the need for a response from Mrs. Flint, the family's moral guardian, not just to save Linda, but indeed to save the white family as well.

Brent has already painted Mrs. Flint as the stereotypically lethargic but cruel slave mistress; here she urges the need to understand the secrets of slavery and to act against the institution as a necessary self-protective measure. Mrs. Flint's (and the white female reader's) salvation as the moral center of the family will depend on her ability to uncover the master's secrets, despite his subterfuge. If she depends on her own abilities of discernment, she will fail: Mrs. Flint "watched her husband with unceasing vigilance; but he was well practiced in means to evade it" (*I*, 31 [30]). Her only hope of comprehending the problem and shifting her position from accommodating ignorance to effecting change is to allow herself to heed the words of the slave narrator.

Significantly, in the same chapter in which Brent teaches herself to write (and thus begins her journey to the present white audience as author/commentator), Mrs. Flint finally allows a painful interview with Brent that lays bare the details of her husband's debauchery. Brent's words also suggest their commonality as virtuous females who have been violated by exposure to a slaveholder's conduct:

> As I went on with my account her color changed frequently, she wept, and sometimes groaned. She spoke in tones so sad, that I was touched by her grief. The tears came to my eyes. . . . She felt that her marriage vows were desecrated, her dignity insulted. (*I*, 33 [32])

But because Mrs. Flint is a model of white female ineptitude, she is unable to grasp the connection between herself and Brent: "She pitied herself as a martyr; but she was incapable of feeling for the condition of shame and misery in which her unfortunate, helpless slave was placed" (*I*, 33 [32]).

Rather than trust the testimony of a slave who has raised the first blow against the master's evasions by disobeying the order of silence, an angry Mrs. Flint becomes obsessed with observing Brent's body, a move that links her unmistakably with the readers addressed in Child's introduction. Mimicking her husband's construction of the slave woman as the object of (sexual) desire, Mrs. Flint situates Brent "in a room adjoining her own," keeping a constant watch on the slave victim, rather than on her husband. Enacting an "especial care" of Brent, Mrs. Flint scrutinizes Brent's body in hopes of a more comforting version of events that will somehow contradict what she has already heard. And when her attention parallels Flint's own lascivious obsession with Brent ("Sometimes I woke up, and found her bending over me"), Mrs. Flint is transformed into the corrupting seducer intent on tricking Brent into becoming the site of sexual contamination (*I*, 34 [32]).[1]

But in a clever repositioning of herself as the reader of Mrs. Flint's body, Brent carefully describes the slave mistress's self-seduction by the details of her own falsely constructed narrative of sexual misconduct. Working under the delusion that Brent is the corrupter of Dr. Flint, the slave mistress attempts to elicit unconscious responses from her (at night "she whispered in my ear, as though it was her husband who was speaking to me, and listened to hear what I would answer"), responses that will confirm her "truth" that Brent is the

1. Though Hortense Spillers gives a different but related reading of Mrs. Flint's role as seducer, I am indebted to her discussion for the formulation of my own.

real threat to the sanctity of her marriage and home (*I*, 34 [32]). But when Brent is represented as the seducer, Dr. Flint is shielded once more by an "audience's" refusal to listen to slave testimony. With the unwitting Mrs. Flint working hard to support her husband's deceptive practices, Brent becomes the only resister holding out for a true account of the events.

Brent's narrative suggests that, as an ideal method of misreading, Mrs. Flint's self-consoling validation of white interpretive powers through an invalidation of the black voice reinforces white visions of racial superiority, but it has little to do with the freeing of slaves or with national moral reform. The story of Mrs. Flint's failure stands as a textual lesson for Brent's readers about how Northern domestic morality can quickly become ineffective (indeed self-annihilating) when whites fail to recognize the folly of designating the victim's, rather than the slaveholder's, testimony as the source of offense. At moments such as these the text forces a confrontation between the dual myths of a manifestly present white authority and a manifestly absent black authority to interpret the meaning of slave speech. The interview between Mrs. Flint and Brent provides the Northern audience with two choices: either they participate in the exploitation of the slave body and remain deaf to the only credible interpreter available (Brent herself), in which case they are identified with the duped and demonic slave mistress, or they admit to the necessity of allowing Brent not just to speak to but to guide them, as part of the initial step toward abolition.

If we are indeed meant to read this failed interview between Mrs. Flint and Brent as a representation of the reader's rejection of the black female slave narrator, what is at stake finally is not Mrs. Flint's (and the Northern audience's) misplaced obsession with the artificial dichotomy of white spiritual morality versus black bodily immorality, but rather the hope that there might exist a national moral landscape where respect and protection for white ideals will translate into respect and protection for the black victim. I am not suggesting here that *Incidents in the Life of a Slave Girl* is voicing a simplistic call to interracial unity. Rather, I am suggesting that the text questions the character of a white nation that establishes its moral ideals on a victimizing construction of blackness.

Earlier, in describing her plight as an unprotected slave girl, Brent has evoked the traditional contrasts between the sexually exploited female slave and her supposedly more fortunate white counterpart: The black slave accepts "the cup of sin, and shame, and misery," whereas the white child becomes "a still fairer woman" whose life is "blooming with flowers, and overarched by a sunny sky" up until the moment of her marriage (*I*, 29 [29]). But although the ideal of the white true womanhood depends on the perceived existence of its opposite, the sexualized black female, how ideal an image is sanctified, privatized white ladyhood, and thus domesticity, if it has to be safeguarded through the silencing of slave discourse on rape and sexual terror, and a tolerance of slavery?

The notion that white ladyhood will have no real value in any community supporting slavery is made clear by Brent when she analyzes the implication of Flint's attempt to bribe her with promises of fair treatment: "'Have I ever treated you like a negro? . . . I would cherish you. I would make a lady of you.'" (*I*, 33 [33–34]). Brent suggests that Flint's offer of a falsified female respectability is not that of the pampered quadroon mistress but that of white femininity itself. At this point Brent drops the personification of corrupted white womanhood as exclusively Southern by referring directly to Northerners supportive of slavery through acceptance of the Fugitive Slave Law. They willingly jeopardize the sensibilities of their own women when they "proud[ly] . . . give their daughters in marriage to slaveholders" (*I*, 36 [34]). Lulled into ignorance by "romantic notions" about Southern life, these woman (again note the connection with Mrs. Flint) enter brothellike settings: "The young wife soon learns that the husband in whose hands she has placed her happiness pays no regard to his marriage vows. Children of every shade and complexion play with her own fair babies. . . . Jealousy and hatred enter the flowery home, and it is *ravaged* of its loveliness" (*I*, 36 [34]); emphasis added). Brent's choice of words unmistakably implies that through white moral neglect, the rape of the slave woman will translate into the rape of the Northern/Southern home.

III

In recounting her life with the Flints, Brent demonstrates the futility of white analyses that address neither the sexual politics of slavery nor the right of slaves to speak. Such avoidance cannot lead whites to effective agency in the abolition of slavery and, in the face of the audience's failure to act its part (as exemplified by Mrs. Flint), *Incidents in the Life of a Slave Girl* suggests that without white sympathy Brent is not only compelled to enact her own strategy for emancipation; she must succeed on the very terms of what whites perceive to be black female moral failure. In contrast to those who interpret black bodies as merely metaphors for slavery, Linda Brent works to achieve her own liberation by dictating a radical resignification of black physicality against the fundamentally linked expectations of both Dr. Flint and Northern white readers. Though the moral vacuum created by Mrs. Flint's retreat forces Brent to take a white lover to save herself from Flint, this moment of the female slave's apparent physical self-abasement is transformed by the narrative into an articulation of staunch resistance: "I knew nothing would enrage Dr. Flint so much as to know that I favored another; and it was something to triumph over my tyrant even in that small way" (*I*, 55 [50]).

To authorize her appropriation of the white power to liberate, Brent enacts a second moment of confrontation when she addresses offended readers who, like Mrs. Flint, come across distasteful information (her decision to submit to Sands's overtures). Will the readers blame Linda for sexual promiscuity, or will they accept her pronouncement that "the slave woman ought not to be judged by the same standards as others" (*I*, 56 [51]) in the struggle for her freedom? At this point the narrative exhibits an oft-noted schizophrenic quality, retreating back and forth between a very matter-of-fact, dispassionate detailing of a material strategy of manipulation and admissions of guilt and emotional appeals for the audience's forgiveness:

> I thought he [Dr. Flint] would revenge himself by selling me, and I was sure my friend, Mr. Sands, would buy me. . . . Pity me, and pardon me, O virtuous reader! . . . I know I did wrong. No one can feel it more sensibly than I do. (*I*, 55 [50–51])[2]

But does such a duality signify regret for mistaken action and a desire to be seen as a truthful, virtuous witness, or does it dramatize the conflict between, on the one hand, Brent's desire to record in her own words the transformation from victim to actor on the very terms of the slave woman's oppression (that is, her sexuality), and, on the other, her white audience's determination to reject that transformation and its implied transference of agency from the abolitionist to the slave? *Incidents* is patterned after novels of domesticity but, as Carolyn Karcher has shown, Brent's literary tradition is the domestic novel specifically politicized as antislavery fiction.[3] Thus, although Brent's problematic apologies would seem to refer to the indelicacy of her sexual choices, they stress that such acts of self-liberation are unacceptable only within the context of antislavery fiction that would value the passivity rather than the resistance of the exploited female slave.

Up to this moment, Brent's role as victim is crucial to effect the construction of the white savior. Up to this moment, the fairly

2. Contemporary scholars have long been fascinated by Brent's discussion of her affair with Mr. Sands, because it seems to be a curious mixture of shame, regret, defiance, and "deliberate calculation" (*I*, 24) [49]. For illuminating discussions of Brent's description of her affair with Sands in the context of a domestic narrative that shuns any discussion of sexuality, see Yellin, "Introduction," xxix–xxxi; Foreman, "The Spoken and the Silenced," 322–3; Valerie Smith, "Loopholes of Retreat," 222; Andrews, *To Tell a Free Story*, 254–6. See also Laura E. Tanner, "Self-Conscious Representation in The Slave Narrative," *Black American Literature Forum* 21:4 (Winter 1987): 415–24.
3. See her "Rape, Murder and Revenge," esp. 330.

traditional presentation of Brent as the silent, shamefaced slave girl whose ordeal remains inoffensive as long as it is discreetly unvoiced has exemplified, at least superficially, Child's promised history of bodily horrors presented in the slave's silence. But Brent's body becomes offensive in the text precisely when the narrative begins to articulate a different system of bodily representation, one that jeopardizes the political role of the reader. Thus what is now offensive in Brent's account is her claim to agency: the move toward self-ownership that transforms her body from an emblem for white self-construction to the enabling tool for black action. Again, the implied sense of the Northern reader's affront to, condemnation of, and even anger at Brent is also shared by Dr. Flint, revealing that even as Brent appears to pay homage to pure Northern sensibilities, she questions those sensibilities by aligning them with a designated foe of domestic morality. Such an alignment also implies that anger at her action must come from the same basic source: a resentment for her defiance of white power over the slave.

After the narrative's indictment of the reader's authority to comprehend Brent's situation or to act on her behalf, the slave suggests an alternative audience and agent of salvation: female slaves themselves. If Mrs. Flint is a failed reader, Aunt Martha is cautiously styled as her opposite—cautiously, because even though she receives Brent's story of sexual manipulation with "an understanding and compassion readers are meant to share," she does not grant Brent her forgiveness.[4] Nevertheless Aunt Martha's acceptance of Brent's narrative (which has a cathartic effect for Brent) signals the potential for a transformed relationship between speaker and reader and provides the next step in Brent's achievement of physical freedom from the Flint household.

Once she acknowledges the conditions from which Brent has emerged, Aunt Martha—along with other women in her community—offers her shelter as Brent enacts a scheme to free her two children by Sands. In her effort to disappear from sight and thereby convince Flint he has nothing to gain by refusing to sell her children, Brent retreats to an attic crawl space of Aunt Martha's house. What is important here is the fact that Brent removes her body from the relations between herself and Flint, so that the master's power is now diminished precisely because the material basis for his role has vanished. In a narrative dramatizing the struggle to tell a supposedly sympathetic audience about the need to abolish slavery, Brent demonstrates the power of her voice as Flint is forced to follow the directives of her discourse via letters sent from various Northern locations by

4. Mills, "Lydia Marie Child . . . ," 259.

the "escaped" slave Linda. When her manipulations eventually lead a frustrated Flint to sell the children to Mr. Sands, Brent emerges as the true liberator in the narrative.

It is important that as a mother herself, Brent achieves her children's freedom by both enacting and critiquing the central metaphor of maternity which describes the abolitionist platform for social reform. From her hiding place Brent watches over her children, appears mysteriously to urge their father to take them north, and visits them at night as if she were an apparition. As the "disembodied" matron who must literally watch her children from above, Brent ridicules Northern white metaphoric self-construction (abolitionists supposedly watch over the slaves) as "maternal" saviors. In describing herself as the ethereal mother within the relative privacy of her grandmother's home, Brent continually indicates the white impediments to safeguarding that privacy, as Aunt Martha's domestic peace is regularly violated by Dr. Flint and other enforcers of white law. Brent's self-construction here registers a warning against an idealization of the spirit of maternity that severs it from the material conditions of the body. Lest we romanticize her role as maternal figure in the "Loophole of Retreat," Brent continually reminds us that she is actually cut off from her children and that she also suffers a confinement of the body that is tortuous: enduring sickness, painful insect bites, extremes of heat and cold, and frostbite, she has to accept that her limbs might never recover from their imprisonment (*I*, 114 [97]).

Her articulation of bodily torture in the performance of maternal duty becomes a plea for a new construction of maternal power that includes black women; idealized maternity, like idealized womanhood, cannot function for black women if it celebrates moral action but denigrates attempts at physical survival. Brent acts like a mother while she is hiding, but she achieves liberating motherhood for her children only when she is reunited with them. Otherwise Brent is destined to imitate in part the life of her deceased Aunt Nancy, whose physical connection to motherhood has been stolen by slavery until she is "stricken with paralysis" (*I*, 144 [122]), and finally dies without the ability to speak.

The text stresses the need to attend to the slave woman's body, as well as her soul, when Brent's position is juxtaposed with that of the dead Nancy: she calls herself "a poor, blighted young creature, shut up in a living grave for years" (*I*, 147 [124]). Although some readers have recently argued that Brent's confinement can be read partially as a metaphor of birth in that Aunt Martha has provided "a protective womb for Linda's birth to freedom," or that Brent "manages to convert that tomb into a womb" by reaffirming ties with her family, by remaining in the attic she risks a still-birth into inertia, rather than physical freedom or active motherhood.[5] Eventually, when Brent goes north, her escape from slavery is framed within the specific context of the need to address the alienated black body. Indeed, the freedom signified by the North can be tangible only if it signals a reclamation, a reversal of that alienation.

Brent goes north in 1842, after her daughter has been sent to New York to live with relatives of Mr. Sands, where she is later joined by her son. Yet what will become of her ultimate search in the North for "a home and freedom," a material situation first promised by Dr. Flint when he tried to bribe Brent into sexual submission (*I*, 83 [73])? Her search for the genuine article beyond the South is constantly frustrated by Northern conditions that duplicate almost exactly those survived by Brent and her family in North Carolina. Even before the passing of the Fugitive Slave Law in 1850, these conditions of "free" life included fear of physical capture, constant confinement, subterfuge, racism, and—for Brent's daughter Ellen—direct enslavement and even the threat of sexual harassment from white relatives. When Brent obtains a post as nursemaid in the Bruce household (the same post she occupied with the Flints), she must accept the position of surrogate mother. Such characterizations of Brent's experiences as essentially repetitions of slave life, despite the shift in region, demonstrate the narrative's active critique of the "freedom" offered to blacks by the North.

An important variation within the text's repetitive moments is Ellen's shift into Brent's former role, and Brent's into that of her grandmother. While Brent's own position improves (she has a kind employer), Ellen's condition worsens. Evoking a tangle of blood, capital, and control that characterized Brent's position in the Flint household, Mr. Sands's relative Mrs. Hobbs echoes Flint in her insistence on a tie of ownership between her family and their cousin Ellen: "I suppose you know that . . . Mr. Sands, has *given* her to my eldest daughter. She will make a nice waiting maid for her when she grows up" (*I*, 166 [139]). In addition, to hide their own alcoholism, Mr. Hobbs and his Southern brother-in-law Mr. Thorne employ Ellen to fetch their liquor, so much so that "she felt ashamed to ask for it so often" (*I*, 179 [148]). Though she suppresses this information so as not to burden her mother, Ellen is distressed by such concealment. This situation recalls Brent's own discomfort about, and concealment of, similar experiences during her girlhood: "I did not

5. Ibid.; see also Stephanie A. Smith, "Conceived in Liberty: Maternal Iconography and American Literature, 1830–1900" (Ph.D. dissertation, University of California, Berkeley, 1990), 179.

discover till years afterwards that Mr. Thorne's intemperance was not the only annoyance she suffered from him. . . . He had poured vile language into the ears" of the young girl (*I*, 179 [148]).

Brent's metaphoric description of the exchange between Thorne and Ellen exactly mirrors those she used earlier in describing Dr. Flint's attempts to seduce her. Such reoccurrences challenge the notion of regional and political differences (Brent will soon call New York under the Fugitive Slave Law "the City of Iniquity"), since the use of the silenced black "slave" Ellen as a shield for white sins provides a parallel between the domestic life of slavery in the South and the domestic life of "freedom" in the North.

This pattern of duplicated suffering occurs in the vacuum created by white inaction, a vacuum that again demands that Brent emerge as the liberator. When it is discovered that Mr. Thorne has betrayed her location to Dr. Flint, Brent goes into hiding, but this time she takes Ellen with her. This rescue of another "slave girl" is achieved through "a mother's observing eye" (*I*, 178 [148]), since Brent has read distress on Ellen's face: Replaying both the failed role of Mrs. Flint and the problematic role of Aunt Martha, Brent again defines the ideal of liberating maternity as one that must be informed by a willingness to come to terms with the physical nature of black female exploitation. Because of her own experience in slavery, she alone can claim the power of bodily interpretation. Also, Brent's recognition of Ellen's pain is mirrored by the daughter's own attempt to quiet her mother's silent fears about revealing the circumstance of her birth: "I know all about it mother. . . . All my love is for you" (*I*, 189 [156]). Thus the acknowledged suffering of mother and daughter enables isolating silences to be replaced with mutual understanding and comfort. In a sense Ellen and her mother do not need to speak of their experiences: the nature of their slavery—and Brent's ability to understand the terms of black female exploitation and to use them as the basis for a successful rescue of herself and her family—has already been voiced by the narrative's account of their reunion.

Long before Brent obtains her legal freedom, then, she articulates a particular kind of salvation that reunites the voice with the body of the slave, celebrates black actions against slavery, and finally appropriates the domestic discourse of maternity in order to reform it for the use of black women. But if Brent is now the successful mother, the successful speaker, and the successful abolitionist (at least in the sense of obtaining a relative freedom for herself and her children), what role then does the Northerner play? Although *Incidents* suggests that Northern whites might actually represent a negative social force against the abolition of the slave's condition, the text does not finally accept rigid binaries as the only ground for black–white interaction. Throughout Brent has been helped in small ways by Southern slave mistresses, slave traders, and others who empathize with the slave's plight. But for Brent effective white empathy must be accompanied with an activism that acknowledges a connection rather than a dislocation between black and white bodies.

After the death of his English wife, Mr. Bruce remarries, and Brent's new American mistress serves as the narrative's closing model for the ideal white abolitionist. When Brent is forced into hiding to escape the Flint family, the new Mrs. Bruce, like her Southern counterpart, is called upon to offer protection. However, unlike Mrs. Flint, who recoiled from any connection to Brent, Mrs. Bruce embraces a strategy of redemption that causes her to risk her own domestic peace for the sake of resisting the North's moral ineptitude.

Mrs. Bruce allows her own child to accompany Brent into hiding as a scheme to force the slave-catchers to alert the white mother should the slave be caught. For Brent this is not a paternalistic act, but one of self-sacrifice: "How few mothers would have consented to have one of their own babes become a fugitive, for the sake of a poor, hunted nurse, on whom the legislators of the country had let loose the bloodhounds" (*I*, 194 [160]). Mrs. Bruce's temporary abandonment of her child for the sake of a slave's freedom redefines the possibility of domestic feminism's role in abolition, because it forces Mrs. Bruce, even in a limited way, to experience the same sense of maternal loss that Brent experienced when she left her children in pursuit of their freedom. By breaking the Fugitive Slave Law, Mrs. Bruce invites imprisonment and financial penalties, and in doing so she demonstrates a willingness to endure a kind of physical suffering that does not duplicate slavery, but comes close to it: "I will go to the state's prison, rather than have any poor victim torn from *my* house, to be carried back to slavery" (*I*, 194 [160]).[6] Yet, although Brent's representation of Mrs. Bruce's active sympathy suggests that whites can help through a more sincere and deliberate sharing of risks, the fact that the slave's freedom can be secured only by a bill of sale between her benefactress and the Flint family still indicts the North: "the bill of sale is on record, and future generations will learn from it that women were articles of traffic in

6. Interestingly, Jacobs originally ended her narrative with a chapter on John Brown, the white militant abolitionist executed for his attack on Harper's Ferry. In a letter to Jacobs, Child said she thought it "had better be omitted," adding that "Nothing could be so appropriate to end with, as the death of your grandmother" (reprinted in *I*, 244). [Reprinted on p. 202 of this Norton Critical Edition (*Editor*).] Arguing for the appeasement of the audience through an appeal to their sympathies, Child wanted to steer Jacobs away from discussions about direct political action by encouraging her to end with "tender memories of my good old grandmother, like light fleecy clouds floating over a dark and troubled sea" (*I*, 201 [167]). For a discussion of Child's reaction to John Brown see Mills, "Lydia Marie Child . . . ," 255–72.

New York, late in the nineteenth century of the Christian religion" (*I*, 200 [165]).[7]

In concluding her critique, Brent refuses to validate the freedom offered to her in the North, but instead problematizes this freedom almost to the last sentence: "We are as free from the power of slaveholders as are the white people of the north; and though that . . . is not saying a great deal, it is a vast improvement in *my* condition" (*I*, 201 [167]). Brent's ambivalence arises from the fact that "the dream of my life is not yet realized. I do not sit with my children in a home of my own" (*I*, 201 [167]). These bitter reflections (Is the North really free of slavery? Do homelessness and the struggle to overcome poverty in the North represent a major improvement?) challenge naive notions of freedom and as such affirm the black critiques Jacobs has been working to uncover through the narrative of Linda Brent. Revering the memory of Aunt Martha, and fully aware of the new struggles that await her on the "dark and troubled sea" signified by Northern black life, Brent ends the narrative by validating herself as a survivor and an active critic of both the North's and the South's peculiar forms of social injustice.

MARK RIFKIN

From "A Home Made Sacred by Protecting Laws": Black Activist Homemaking and Geographies of Citizenship in *Incidents in the Life of a Slave Girl*[†]

* * *

Activist Genealogies and the Problematic of Citizenship

In situating *Incidents* in the social terrain of the antebellum u.s., critics have tended to contextualize it in relation to two primary

7. Echoing William Andrews, Dana D. Nelson argues that Mrs. Bruce is still a slaveholder and that for Brent, "serving, whether under compulsion or privilege, remains servitude: the structure of this sympathetic identification is one of hierarchy, not equality." However, although Brent articulates an unmistakable resentment by the narrative's end, her anger is directed not at Mrs. Bruce herself, as some critics have suggested, but at the contradictory legal and social "circumstances" allowed to develop in the North, so that Mrs. Bruce's genuine act against the slaveholders is itself compromised by its resemblance to slavery. For Nelson's comments, see *The Word in Black and White*, 141. See also Andrews, *To Tell a Free Story*, 260–2.

† From *differences: A Journal of Feminist Cultural Studies* 18.2 (2007): 76–77, 80–94, 100–03. Page numbers in brackets refer to this Norton Critical Edition.

formations—sentimentalism and slave law.[1] While these areas are certainly relevant in reading the text, what is striking is the relative absence of attempts to think about the narrative in light of the work of free people of color, Jacobs's contemporaries and associates for the nineteen years between her escape from the South and the publication of her narrative. As Carla Peterson has argued in *"Doers of the Word": African American Women Speakers and Writers in the North (1830–1880)*, a focus on slavery and slave narrative, while clearly crucial to a consideration of African American life and self-representation in the antebellum u.s., can obfuscate the cultural presence, political work, and textual production of free people of color. She proposes a new kind of investigation whose

> point of departure lies in the premise that resistant "civil rights movements" are not a modern phenomenon but can be traced at least as far back as the early nineteenth century, and that investigations of African American culture in the "free" North provide an important counterweight to the more numerous histories of Southern slavery, where power relations between blacks and whites took on a highly specific and codified configuration. (4)[2]

The corollary to Peterson's intervention, though, is to begin to read slave narratives within the context of the forms of activism engaged in by free people of color. Beyond helping to connect such texts more directly to the communities within which their authors moved, this conceptual shift opens space for a rethinking of the meaning of citizenship in the antebellum period and after, situating the discussion of abolition and emancipation within a broader analysis of African Americans' complex and uneven position in the national polity and their articulations/theorizations of what it means to be part of the nation.

When explored from this perspective, *Incidents* not only can be seen as taking up the concerns and tropes of African American activism in the North but as offering a woman-centered critique and expansion of the notions of citizenship circulating in this black public sphere.[3] Jacobs's explicit politicization of domesticity can be interpreted as marking and rejecting the lurking masculinism of much of the political discourse articulated by free people of color, while simultaneously extending, concretizing, and incorporating women into the vision of substantive freedom being developed within

1. For discussion of *Incidents* in relation to domesticity and sentiment, see Berlant; Burgett; Carby; Foster; Merish; Mills; Peterson; Sánchez-Eppler; Skinfill; Tate; and Yellin. For discussion of *Incidents* in relation to slave law, see Accomando, "The Regulation"; Hartman; and Kawash.
2. For additional discussion of the importance of studying literacy and advocacy among free people of color, see McHenry.
3. On the notion of a black public sphere, see the Black Public Sphere Collective.

African American activist networks in the North. Taking into account *Incidents*'s reconfiguration of discourses of black activism, then, allows us to trace the ways that the text's representation of households and homeownership as material (rather than only allegorical) sites of national belonging complicates contemporaneous African American analysis of the interdependence of public and private spheres.[4]

* * *

Convention[5] discourse's combination of Revolutionary nationalism, caste-critique, and call for contribution to the uplift of the race cast access to political rights and employment irrespective of race as a fundamental American principle. The minutes implicitly argue that once whites get out of the way, African Americans can take up their rightful place as full contributors to the collective betterment of themselves and of the nation. In adapting these rhetorical maneuvers, *Incidents* offers both a more stinging indictment of the role of public policy in shaping the circumstances of ostensibly private life and a more politicized understanding of the household as a site of collective claims for equity. In comparison to the rhetoric of the conventions, and by extension much free black activist discourse, Jacobs's narrative more directly charges (federal) law and legislative (in)action with the responsibility for enabling and maintaining white power/privilege in slavery and in formal freedom, and, reciprocally, the text emphasizes how the material provision and protection of putatively private space functions as a central element of the public rights of citizenship.

Deprivatizing Race, or Incidents *Goes to Washington*

Speaking to the concerns of the convention movement in its mapping of the social topography of white privilege, *Incidents* eschews patriotic paternity in favor of emphasizing the centrality of "home" to understanding the scope and subtlety of state violence and the dimensions of caste, refracting the issues and strategies of the conventions and envisioning substantive social change through a domestic imaginary in which women are central.[6] More specifically, I want to highlight the ways Jacobs's narrative works to present

4. For an extended discussion of such analysis that contextualizes it within antebellum intellectual life and political discourse, see Rael.
5. The National Convention movement (1830–35), a series of meetings among African Americans to develop strategies for claiming full rights as U.S. citizens [editors' note].
6. In *"Doers of the Word,"* Carla Peterson offers an astute reading of Jacobs's effort to develop a vision of "home" and of "local place," but her account does not address the relation between the text's strategies and the specific rhetorical dynamics of Northern black (men's) activism or the specific connection *Incidents* makes between "local" circumstances and national citizenship.

African Americans as national subjects and to foreground the ways law (at the national and state level) takes part in the production of caste. In this vein, the text's depiction of homeownership helps emphasize the extent to which even the most apparently intimate aspects of daily life are impacted by a national investment in whiteness, as well as giving a more material form to the potentially amorphous language of rights.[7]

Jacobs calls on the patriotic affect of her readers rather early in the narrative. Like the conventions' regular returns to the "Fathers of '76," the text also illustrates the intersection of her lineage with that of the nation, but instead of the figure of the soldier-father, the connection is made through the thwarted emancipation of her maternal grandmother.

> She was the daughter of a planter in South Carolina, who, at his death, left her mother and his three children free, with money to go to St. Augustine, where they had relatives. It was during the Revolutionary War; and they were captured on their passage, carried back, and sold to different purchasers. (5) [9]

Rather than offering an interracial patriarchal narrative of national founding, here paternity appears as a means of illustrating the profound gap between dominant narratives and the local experience of American identity. This moment suggests the quotidian racial violence embedded in, yet effaced from, national history, registering the latter's checkered record of (non)commitment to liberty as the denial of home and family to people of color. Simultaneously, the text plays to readers' national sentiment, highlighting the irony of contemporaneous American freedom and African American abjection in an implicit call for the fulfillment of the Revolution's promise of equality for all. This strategy of appealing to the national feeling of readers is suggested further by Jacobs's later citation of Patrick Henry's famous demand, "Give me liberty or give me death," as her "motto" in her escape from her master (99) [88].

This desire for recognition as American, and Jacobs's emphasis on the failure of national policy to express national ideals and to treat African Americans as national subjects, is perhaps most palpable in the chapter "What Slaves Are Taught to Think of the North." In it, she sketches the relation between national policy/identity and the everyday experience of blackness.

7. In this interpretation, I have been influenced by Claudia Tate's interpretation of African American women writers' use of domesticity as an "allegory of political desire," as well as Lori Merish's reading of *Incidents'* "decommodification" of African American women's bodies through the positing of a "homeplace" ("a space where she can *claim possession* of the domestic rather than *be* the domestic"). See 211–16.

> Some [of the slaves] believe that the abolitionists have already made them free, and that it is established by law, but that their masters prevent the law from going into effect [. . .] [One woman] said her husband told her that the black people had sent word to the queen of 'Merica that they were all slaves; that she didn't believe it, and went to Washington city to see the president about it [. . .].
>
> That poor, ignorant woman thought that America was governed by a Queen, to whom the President was subordinate. I wish the President was subordinate to Queen Justice. (45) [42]

Debunking the idea that u.s. "law" and its avatars (figured here as a sword-wielding queen) are necessarily opposed to slavery and working in the interests of African Americans, Jacobs presents as merely "ignorant" the notion that the "masters" are somehow operating in defiance of a federal commitment to black freedom. The passage, though, plays on nationalist feeling, implying its potential to challenge and ameliorate existing structures. Even as Jacobs dismisses the fantasy of the "queen of 'Merica" as nonsense, she offers her own myth of "Queen Justice," who appears as a way of imagining an ideological shift within American governance that would bring its institutional power to bear in support of African Americans. While condemning the foolish misapprehension about the actual workings of politics, the text retains the fantasy of a "Queen" to whom the President is "subordinate," preserving the desire for proximity and intimacy between African Americans and the national government suggested by the slaves' ability to send "word" to the Queen and to have her respond to their concerns—a national figure who acts immediately to redress her subjects' local experience of subjugation. In this way, in Lauren Berlant's terms, the text "dislocates the nation from its intelligible official forms" (226), envisioning the federal government as the horizon of redress while rejecting the idea that existing laws are the only parameters for imagining change. Far from irrelevant, "Washington city" remains central to the text's political vision, appealing to readers' patriotic affect as a means of challenging existing policy while insisting that questions of racial justice demand national answers.

In this vein, Jacobs often inserts reflections on national identity, history, and/or policy at what may appear to be odd moments in the text, drawing on such incongruity to situate apparently local/personal events and dynamics within a national/public frame. These juxtapositions and shifts in scale suggest how racial ideologies operate within a national context that shapes the material possibilities available to African Americans, thereby countering the partitioning of blacks into a non-national zone as in *Dred Scott*. When alluding to national identifications and institutions, which she does consistently throughout her narrative, Jacobs contextualizes them in terms of their effect on members of her family and the community(/ ies) to which she belongs, illustrating reciprocally how nationhood becomes immediate in the lives of those around her and the role that notions of privacy play in shaping the racial politics of federal law and defining whose experience counts as national.

At several points, the narrative abruptly moves to scenes of federal governance—itself traveling to "Washington city." These moments highlight how the distinction made between the personal and the political in government acts and debate naturalizes the effects of institutionalized racism and the production of white privilege. In the chapter "Still in Prison," which refers to Jacobs's confinement for seven years in the attic of her free grandmother's house (a space elsewhere referred to as "the loophole of retreat") located in the same neighborhood as her master, she suspends her discussion of her period in hiding in order to relay the following anecdote about Congressional debate:

> Senator Brown of Mississippi, could not be ignorant of many such facts as these [local tales of a mother of miscegenated children being sold by their father and of the suicide by a female slave to escape the whipping ordered for "some trifling offence"] for they are of frequent occurrence in every Southern state. Yet he stood up in the Congress of the United States, and declared that slavery was "a great moral, social, and political blessing; a blessing to the master, and a blessing to the slave!" (122) [103]

As Jean Fagan Yellin notes, the speech itself was made by Albert Gallatin Brown during debate about the Kansas-Nebraska Bill (299).[8] This somewhat unexpected triangulation between Jacobs's grandmother's house, the nation's capital, and the territories contrasts in its geographic scope rather strikingly with the tightness of the space she inhabits, characterized in the chapter title as a "prison" (a description that itself is resonant with the coercive potential of State authority).[9] Quite complex in its mappings, the passage suggests that debate within Congress is predicated on divorcing decisions in Washington from the violent repudiation of kinship that occurs all the time in slaveholding states, on making the latter irrelevant with respect to what transpires in the former. Not only does this disjunction reinforce the legal fiction of natural racial difference that underpins the defense of slavery by screening from federal discourse evidence to the contrary, it actively secures white

8. On the Kansas-Nebraska Act, see Potter 160–76, 199–224.
9. For alternative readings of the "loophole of retreat" that focus on the nature of the agency it implies, see Burnham; and Kawash 73–83.

supremacy by relegating the concrete effects of racism to the realm of personal life and the discretion of individual masters, thereby effacing the role federal discourse and policy play in maintaining the conditions that make racial subjugation possible.

Later, in "New Destination for the Children," Jacobs again reflects on Congressional (in)action. In the chapter, the father of her children, a white man called Mr. Sands in the text who has bought them from their master, has recently been elected to the House of Representatives, and he has taken their daughter Ellen with him to Washington.[1] His failure to inform Jacobs of Ellen's welfare prompts the following:

> If the secret memoirs of many members of Congress should be published, curious details would be unfolded. I once saw a letter from a member of Congress to a slave, who was the mother of six of his children [. . .]. The existence of the colored children did not trouble this gentleman, it was only the fear that friends might recognize in their features the resemblance to him. (142) [119–20]

In addition to indicating the prevalence of miscegenation as part of plantation life, the above imagines an inversion of privacy in which the sexual exploits of government actors are "unfolded" and themselves become part of the public record. However, more than revealing the truth of slavery, the text suggests how the status of miscegenation as an open secret helps to obscure the primary form of congressional misconduct—the denial of *national* responsibility for racial inequality by writing its effects as the *personal* history of individuals.[2]

This focus on the federal, the text's periodic yet insistent return to scenes of national speech (and silence), offers a dialectical analysis of how ideologies of whiteness regulate the relation between institutions of governance and local experience. In these Congressional scenes, the text simultaneously makes three related moves. First, it asserts Jacobs's ability to comment on national affairs seemingly beyond her personal experience, reciprocally implying that in some sense such affairs are constitutive of the conditions of her and other African Americans' lives. The text also puts the horrendous acts she chronicles, as well as the terror/torture of her own confinement, in relation to acts of governance, most directly by indicating that the men in Congress must be aware of the routine instances of miscegenation, separation, and brutality that occur in their districts. Finally, the narrative implies that the inability or refusal of these men to see such local events as having implications for national debate and law perpetuates a cycle of oppression in which the legal

1. For a discussion of the actual Mr. Sands's record in Congress, see Berlant, *Queen* 234.
2. For an elaboration of the notion of the "open secret" as a discursive structure that exceeds the strict question of disclosure, see Sedgwick 1–22.

(re)production of putatively private institutions, like family, is made invisible. In "Color Blindness, History, and the Law," Kimberlé Crenshaw refers to this perpetuation of racism as "racial marketplace ideology"; "the state cannot interfere to redistribute racial value" due to the government's interested narration/circumscription of its own power to act, declaring certain forms of racist practice as "private" and thus protected in ways that ultimately empty citizenship of its potential content for nonwhites (238). In continually returning the reader to national scenes and symbols and connecting her life and the lives of those around her to federal institutions, Jacobs puts her personal story within a national frame, exposing how ideologies of privacy naturalize white privilege by denying the political character of black subordination and violation in white homes and asserting instead that black experiences of oppression testify to a systemic failure to realize national ideals.

Homemaking as Citizenship

If, as I have been arguing, one of the text's primary projects is to represent African Americans as properly national subjects, its portrayal of (frustrated) black domesticity functions as a way of concretizing what such subjectivity would mean in material, local terms. *Incidents* employs the rhetoric of "home" and representations of the intrusion into and destruction of African American houses as a way of more directly tracking entrenched legal and economic geographies of whiteness and reciprocally offering an expanded notion of citizenship in which the security of black homes speaks to a broader national commitment to individual and collective African American well-being. These scenes of trespass into black domestic spaces vividly demonstrate that the security of putatively private property depends on the possession of a range of civic entitlements; these images of violated domestic space demonstrate the racial allocation of constitutional "privileges and immunities" and thereby extend black activist discourse by politicizing what was often portrayed as women's sphere. Rather than endorsing bourgeois privacy, *Incidents* plays on available forms of sentimental affect, indicating how access to home and family is racially inflected by the law and inverting the supposed interiority of privacy to reveal how it is systemically structured by the public policy of white privilege.

Perhaps the most critical attention has been paid to Jacobs's portrayal of her seduction/attempted rape by her master (Mr. Flint), her consequent liaison with another white man (Mr. Sands), and her hesitation in telling her story for fear of questions about the propriety of her actions. Prior to her escape from Flint, this is the major plotline of the text. In "A Perilous Passage in the Slave Girl's Life," the chapter in which Jacobs's relationship with Sands is revealed, she introduces this part of her story with the following qualification.[3]

> And now, reader, I come to a period in my unhappy life, which I would gladly forget if I could. The remembrance fills me with sorrow and shame. It pains me to tell you of it; but I have promised to tell you the truth, and I will do it honestly, let it cost me what it may. (53) [49]

While the above appears like an apology, it need not be read as a generic deformation of Jacobs's story.[4] Sexual secrets do not signify here as a marker of an individualized privacy. Instead, that supposedly isolated space of personal interiority is turned inside-out, narratively displaying the effects of the political economy of race in the u.s. (or at least in the slaveholding states).[5] She laments,

> But, O, ye happy women, whose purity has been sheltered from childhood, [. . .] whose homes are protected by law, do not judge the poor desolate slave girl too severely! If slavery had been abolished, I, also, could have married the man of my choice; I could have had a home shielded by the law; and I should have been spared the painful task of confessing what I am now about to relate. (54) [49]

Allusions to the relationship between "home" and "law" also appear several other times in the text: once Jacobs has arrived safely in Philadelphia, she notes that Mrs. Durham, the wife of the minister to whom Jacobs reveals her "secret," has "a home made sacred by protecting laws" (160) [135], and in describing her trip to England, Jacobs notes that the homes of even "the poorest poor" "were protected by law" (184) [152]. "Purity" depends upon possession of "homes [. . .] protected by law"; therefore, the "painful task" of revealing this element of her past testifies not to personal failing, but to the need for African Americans to have "home[s] shielded by

3. The term "relationship" is an attempt to describe their connection in a way that neither presents it as a love affair nor as an assault. For opposing readings of this "relationship," and its implications for conceptualizing consent within slavery, see Baker 53–54 and Hartman 106–12. On the gender dynamics of slavery, see Gray White; Spillers; and Wiegman.
4. Several critics, however, do make arguments similar to this one. See Accomando; Cutter; and Skinfill. In *Written by Herself*, Frances Smith Foster notes that for the most part during the antebellum period white women were not reading black women's texts, so that Jacobs's direct address to white women of the North can itself be read less as conforming to available norms than a daring reach across the color line. See 76–116.
5. As both Saidiya Hartman and Karen Sánchez-Eppler have argued, the text's apparent remorse can be read as itself a kind of seduction, an effort to create identification between white Northern women readers and the narrator, as well as to incite their interest and sympathy for the broader program of abolition. See Hartman 105–10 and Sánchez-Eppler 93–104. Hartman brilliantly details the ways in which the law's refusal to recognize the rape of slaves as rape relies upon a parallel narrative of black women as inherent seducers, thereby displacing the blame for sexual violence onto the wiles of its victims (79–105).

the law." Freedom, and by implication citizenship as well, then, appears not as membership in a (white-washed) national "family," but as the government's safeguarding of black people's autonomy in their situated circumstances—black homes whose safety is guaranteed by positive government action.

The chapters "Fear of Insurrection" and "The Fugitive Slave Law" in particular represent the violent dismantling of black homes as a means of confronting readers with the devastating consequences of institutionalized identification with whiteness and its role as a conduit for government control. "Fear of Insurrection" addresses the regime of inspection and accompanying reign of terror that followed Nat Turner's insurrection.[6] Although the stated purpose of the searches conducted was to ferret out evidence of conspiracy and tools of insurgency (firearms, ammunition, etc.), Jacobs explores the twin goals that underlay the immediate rhetoric of public safety: forging interclass white identification and crippling black public participation and expression by claiming authority over black occupied (private) spaces. The whites unassociated with plantations form the majority of the mob of searchers:

> It was a grand opportunity for the low whites, who had no negro of their own to scourge. They exulted in such a chance to exercise a little brief authority and show their subserviency to the slaveholders; not reflecting that the power which trampled on the colored people also kept themselves in poverty, ignorance, and moral degradation. (64) [57]

The unequal distribution of economic resources and its obvious deprivations, then, are displaced by the opportunity to exert power over "the colored people," whose consequent lack of privacy allows the poor whites to prize their own (minimal) property as a privilege of whiteness.[7] The discourse of racial difference authorizes white control of black people, either as masters or as protective agents of a public envisioned as generically white, while simultaneously depoliticizing the very inequalities in wealth that make such a right attractive.[8]

6. Living in Edenton, Jacobs was located in the northeast corner of North Carolina, very near Southampton County, Virginia, in which Turner's revolt took place. See Cecil-Fronsman 83–84 and Parker 41–42. For an assessment of the controls exerted over free people of color in the South, especially in the wake of Nat Turner's revolt, see Berlin 182–216. For a discussion of Turner's rebellion and his "Confessions" that locates them within a larger Afro-American revolutionary ethos, see Sundquist 27–83.
7. For discussion of "common whites" in North Carolina in the antebellum period, see Cecil-Fronsman. Many critics have noted both the imbrication of race and class and the need to read the former as more than merely an aspect of the latter, instead searching for the particular benefits (psychological and otherwise) that attend access to whiteness. See Omi and Winant 24–35 and Roediger 3–17, 65–92.
8. The conflation of legal status in the concept of "colored people" also serves to displace the fact that free people of color could vote in North Carolina during the period this episode represents. The franchise was revoked by the new state constitution in 1835. See Cecil-Fronsman 34.

Thus, whiteness here means the legal power to prevent nonwhites from having authority over certain kinds of space, and as Jacobs indicates, these assaults on households serve political purposes.[9] The supposed threat of an uprising is used to justify an invasion of places occupied by people of color so as to prevent their use for antiracist projects like the forging of community solidarity or the building of interracial alliances. The search of her grandmother's house, for example, involves more than a focused inspection for contraband. As they storm the house, the "soldiers" find a packet of "letters" that sparks their concern. In response to Jacobs's reply that "most of my letters are from white people," the company lets out "an exclamation of surprise" (66) [59], suggesting their horror at finding evidence of the very kinds of crossracial identification that the poor whites' alliance with the slaveholders is meant to prevent. Additionally, the "fear of insurrection" is revealed as a fear of black association, period: "No two people that had the slightest tinge of color in their faces dared to be seen talking together" (64) [58]. Beyond inspecting homes and randomly attacking African Americans, the white mob demolishes the church used by "the colored people." The text does not differentiate here between freepersons and slaves, implying that the church, like the grandmother's house, provides a place in which the boundary between institutionally constructed identities (of race, class, and bondage) becomes permeable.[1] *Incidents*, then, represents the invasion of African American homes as the concrete manifestation of a state-sanctioned regime of whiteness that orders the relationship between persons and place, racially restricting access to various kinds of space as a means of maintaining social control and preventing collective antiracist political mobilization.

Emphasizing the national status of this spatial nexus of white supremacy, the chapter "The Fugitive Slave Law" further puts the local circumstances of black family and community in the context of the federal government's refusal to extend citizenship rights to African Americans.[2] Having escaped from slavery eight years prior to the passage of the law, Jacobs describes its effects in New York, to which she has returned to work for her former employer, Mr. Bruce,

9. The role of the government in this racially differentiated production of the private is foregrounded in the text by the fact that the whites doing the inspecting wear "military uniforms" and function as "soldiers" (63). The Constitution offers support for this use of force in Article I, Section 8: "Congress shall have Power [. . .] To provide for calling forth the Militia to execute the Laws of the Union, suppress Insurrections and repel Invasions."

1. For discussion of interaction between slaves and free people of color in North Carolina, see Parker 29–64, and for the South in general, particularly in the context of church meetings, see Berlin, esp. 284–314.

2. On the Fugitive Slave Law of 1850, see Finkelman; Morris; and Potter. On Jacobs's representation of that law, see Peterson 161.

having earlier fled due to the likelihood of capture. Enforcement of the act initiated "a reign of terror to the colored population," a wave of violence narrated through attention to its wrenching effects on black domesticity and community:

> Many families, who had lived in the city for twenty years, fled from it now. Many a poor washerwoman, who, by hard labor, had made herself a comfortable home, was obliged to [. . .] seek her fortune among strangers in Canada [. . .]. Every where, in those humble homes, there was consternation and anguish. But what cared the legislators of the "dominant race" for the blood they were crushing out of trampled hearts. (191) [157–58]

Registered here as an attack on black households, the law appears not only as a shocking extension of federal power, given the longstanding ("at least twenty years") doctrine of relative state autonomy in matters of recaption, but as an initiative predicated on forms of white supremacist identification that exceed the support of slavery per se. While the act was justified as necessary to the preservation of the Union, Jacobs illustrates how the law consolidates the power of "the dominant race" at the expense of the "blood" of "trampled hearts," defining the nation in ways that imagine African American homes and communities as expendable and thereby casting national interests as de facto white. Jacobs's reference to "those humble homes" foregrounds the failure of the rhetoric of state or local autonomy to protect black people from legally sanctioned violence. *Incidents*, then, alerts the reader to the need for a substantive national commitment to combating the white supremacist understanding of national well-being as consonant with the destruction of black communities. Instead, the text advocates for national promotion of the welfare of African Americans, as represented by their possession of and safety in "homes" of their own. Figures of domesticity in the text, then, can be seen as an effort to reconceptualize national ideals in ways that safeguard black communities rather than disavowing or dismantling them.

Like other activists of color, Jacobs extends this critique of institutionalized racism beyond enslavement per se. *Incidents* offers a vision that exceeds formal abolition in its call for broader antiracist agitation, demanding substantive economic and social equality as inherent parts of the promised freedom of national citizenship—of becoming recognized subjects under the "law." As with the discussion of slavery in its local and federal workings, this aspect of the narrative also relies on the trope of "home" in order to trace (legal) geographies of segregation and racially inflected exploitation, elaborating the workings of what can be thought of, and is described in convention discourse, as "caste."[3] While clearly appreciating the difference between being a slave (albeit a fugitive one) and a freewoman, noting that "I had objected to having my freedom bought, yet I must confess that when it was done I felt as if a heavy load had been lifted from my weary shoulders" and referring to her purchase by her employer Mrs. Bruce as an "inestimable boon" (200–01) [167], Jacobs illustrates the persistence of manifest forms of inequality despite her (practical and then legal) liberation from a master, often doing so by way of subtle yet repeated references to the continued deferral of her access to homeownership.[4]

Household economies play a central role in the text's staging of racial justice. In her "Preface," Jacobs announces her support for abolition, indicating the text's purpose as antislavery propaganda, but she simultaneously indicates that the form of the narrative is marked as much by the racial dynamics of "free" labor as it is by her history in bondage:

> I trust my readers will excuse deficiencies in consideration of circumstances. I was born and reared in Slavery; and I remained in a Slave State twenty-seven years. Since I have been at the North, it has been necessary for me to work diligently for my own support, and the education of my children. This has not left me much leisure to make up for the loss of early opportunities to improve myself; and it has compelled me to write these pages at irregular intervals, whenever I could snatch an hour from household duties. (1) [5]

While her apology for the "deficiencies" in the text is rather conventional, her discussion of the "circumstances" of its production seems quite notable, especially given the fact that she puts more stress on the demands of free labor than the depredations of enslavement. Or to be more specific, she suggests that the lack of education and

3. In his book *Conjugal Union*, a study of representations of the relationship between domesticity and racial identity in antebellum African American narratives, Robert Reid-Pharr contends that "there had to be a clearly definable black body if there was to be a definable black community" (18). While I agree that the black household serves as a site for representational struggle over African American citizenship, access to the public sphere, and the nature of community, antebellum narratives, such as Jacobs's, are also deeply invested in challenging the idea of racial identity, refiguring it as a political rather than merely corporeal issue. The depiction of black houses need not insist, in Reid-Pharr's terms, that "the black body" be "put on [. . .] display," but that ideologies of national belonging be reorganized such that the rights of citizenship, including property holding, cease to be defined by the standardization of whiteness and the abjection of blackness (21). In *Incidents*, then, "the household" does not function "as the primary means of [. . .] producing properly black subjects" (88), but as a narrative vehicle for mapping the spatio-political effects of legalized racial difference and for concretizing the implications of national subjectivity for black people.

4. There are actually two "Mrs. Bruce"s. This reference is to the second one, but elsewhere I do not differentiate since the two characters are not substantially distinguished from each other in the text.

opportunities for self-improvement and self-expression in slavery are not necessarily remedied by freedom per se.[5] Formal freedom reaches its limit in the figure of the "household," which functions for Jacobs as a place of work that barely sustains her attempts to access the privileges of the North.

Later, after bemoaning the fact that she "could not give her [daughter who had been purchased by her father and sent to live with his sister in New York] a home till I went to work and earned the means" (166) [139], Jacobs ironically entitles the next chapter "A Home Found," enticing the reader with the promise of motherly domestic bliss only to disclose the fact that the home in question is not her own but that of Mrs. Bruce and that her place within it is that of a nanny. Since her employer "preferred to have [a nursemaid] who had been a mother" (168) [140], Jacobs arrives eminently qualified, presenting motherhood as itself part of a commercial nexus.[6] Like the discussion of caste within the national conventions, Jacobs's depiction of her domestic work vividly illustrates how African Americans get tracked into certain jobs creating a racialized matrix of dependence that constrains the achievement of individual and collective autonomy. In other words, working in someone else's house prevents you from gaining the economic means to own a home of your own. Thus, "home" registers both the fantasy of freedom as well as the failure of the existing provisions of liberty within the North to secure to African Americans the opportunity to achieve this kind of material security.[7] Domesticity, therefore, opens up in the text into a broader consideration of the concrete meaning of freedom for African Americans and the ways that the formal equality of freedom not only fails to eradicate institutionalized racism but continues to naturalize racial difference/inferiority as a characteristic of individual bodies rather than as an effect of political processes.[8]

5. Hazel Carby offers a similar reading: "She contrasted both her past life as a slave girl and her present condition, in which the selling of her labor was a prime necessity, with the social circumstances of her readership" (48). See also Peterson 149.
6. Many critics have noted the ways in which the text depicts slave motherhood as a form of surplus-value for the master (the most explicitly Marxist of these can be found in Baker 54–56), but I have yet to note any critical commentary on the similarity with which Jacobs depicts her credentials for becoming a nanny.
7. For discussion of property-holding among free people of color, see Berlin; and Rael. In 1860, the percentage of free people of color who were property owners in various regions is approximately as follows: North, 11.7 (vs. 18.1 among whites); Upper South, 9.8 (vs. 19.4); and Lower South 17.9 (vs. 18.8) (Rael 23). For different interpretations of relative class differences among free people of color in the North, see Horton and Horton 77–124; and Rael 12–53.
8. The chapter "Prejudice against Color" provides a brief anatomy of segregationist policies within the North, including seating on boats and trains, service in restaurants, and lodging in hotels. In the nonslaveholding states, in most places, public accommodations, transportation, and education were segregated, where publicly funded education was provided for nonwhites at all, and African Americans were excluded from professions and trades. An example of the latter can be found in the text in its narration of the narrator's son, Benny, being forced out of his apprenticeship due to his race (186). See Horton and Horton; and Litwack.

At the same time that the text renders legible the potential disjunction between legal liberty and material welfare, however, it reinvests in the ameliorative and antiracist potential of the discourse of citizenship. At the end of the above chapter, Jacobs offers an instructive anecdote about her stay in a boarding house in Rockaway, where she encounters both the resentment of white waiters who do not wish to serve her and black servants who resent her demands for better treatment.

> My answer was that the colored servants ought to be dissatisfied with themselves, for not having too much self-respect to submit to such treatment; [. . .] finding that I was resolved to stand up for my rights, they concluded to treat me well. Let every colored man and woman do this, and eventually we shall cease to be trampled under foot by our oppressors. (177) [147]

In this context, the call for "rights" seems to be less a citation of legal precedent than a rhetoric of political and social entitlement based on the demand for substantive equality within the nation. "Rights" appears in the above not as an accomplished political fact, but as a pedagogical and collective process through which both blacks and whites (the ambiguous "they") are educated and mobilized to support the concrete, local manifestation of constitutional promises.[9]

Formal freedom and its failure to deliver full equality are again brought back to the question of "home" in the final chapter. Other critics, though, have interpreted this final chapter as, in the words of Bruce Mills, an "affirm[ation of] the role of domestic values in resolving the national crisis," seeing Jacobs as resuming the idiom of proper (bourgeois) femininity in order to solidify her white female readers' identification with her and her story (256). This reading is supported by the fact that Lydia Maria Child, in her role as editor, advised Jacobs to substitute the ending that we have for a more polemical discussion of John Brown and his raid on Harpers Ferry.[1] In his essay on the change in endings, Mills indicates that despite Child's individual commitment to Brown's cause, her ideas about the

9. For a similar discussion of the broader significance of the language of "rights" as part of African Americans' representation of themselves as national subjects, see Patricia Williams, esp. the chapter "The Pain of Word Bondage."

1. For an extended reading of the significance of this substitution, see Mills. For a discussion of John Brown and the effects of Harpers Ferry on popular sentiment and national policy, see Potter 356–84. Yellin describes the replacement in the following terms: "Child did significantly change the text when she dropped the final chapter and ended the book on a private, personal note with the death of the narrator's grandmother instead of on a public, political note with a discussion of the recent armed attack on slavery" (xxii). As Yellin notes, aside from the ending, Child's editing was somewhat minimal, consisting primarily of a request to elaborate on the violence by whites that followed Nat Turner's rebellion (xxii–xxiii). For a broader discussion of the politics of white editorship in the antebellum period, and its implications for later interpretation, see Andrews 1–31. For a broader discussion of the role of racist affect in the mesh between antebellum abolitionism and feminism, see Sánchez-Eppler 14–49.

difference between an antislavery tract and a novelized narrative led her to push for a less confrontational ending. However, this description of Child's investments need not mean that we must read the text from her perspective. Jacobs's continual reworking of the discursive and institutional relation between the "domestic" space of the household and the "domestic" space of the nation mitigates an interpretation that persists in dichotomizing the public and private. Though ending with Brown would undoubtedly have produced a different effect on the reader than the paean to her grandmother that closes the narrative, the rhetoric of "home" need not be understood as a depoliticizing compromise nor as a deformation of the narrative to suit the tastes of white readers.

Integrating Child's suggestions does not undo the text's employment of key aspects of (white) femininity to propound an antiracist national imaginary in which the black household testifies to the legalization of African American "rights." In a much analyzed passage, Jacobs summarizes her situation with the following statement:

> Reader, my story ends with freedom; not in the usual way, with marriage. I and my children are now free! We are as free from the power of slaveholders as are the white people of the north; and though that, according to my ideas, is not saying a great deal, it is a vast improvement in my condition. The dream of my life is not yet realized. I do not sit with my children in a home of my own. (201) [167]

While celebrating the situated victory of self-ownership, a "vast improvement" over the routine violations of enslavement, she notes the incompleteness of this accomplishment in several ways. Her presentation of "freedom" emphasizes its failure to provide her access to a secure domestic space.[2] Personal freedom does not address the continuing existence of slavery elsewhere, but even more than this, "the power of slaveholders [. . .] [over] the white people of the north," namely, the national matrix of law and policy, must be adjusted before "a great deal" can be done to make freedom into more than a respite from slavery.[3] Moreover, in portraying homeownership rather than marriage as the horizon of her life's dream, Jacobs offers a multivectored political remapping. The text here rejects the way (African American) men's full participation in the public sphere was represented through the image of their control over the private space of the household, in which women were figured as dependents, and it

2. As Christina Accomando notes, "[T]he final image of her life is one of domesticity denied" (170).

3. Frances Smith Foster argues, "It is an ending that directly links her with her readers and it conveys the subtext to Jacobs's entire narrative: that Northern whites are not themselves finally free" (104).

implicitly joins the states' control over slave law and family law as part of an argument for a nationalized commitment to an expanded conception of freedom that cuts across and links these policy domains.[4]

Jacobs's free "condition," then, is not equivalent to possession of a "home of my own," an image, as I have suggested, that connotes an enlarged and concretized definition of the benefits of citizenship as well as a challenge to the institutional connection between whiteness and the legal production/protection of ostensibly private space. This use of "home" as a prism through which to understand the political and legal status of African Americans is made clearer by the preceding paragraph, which records the obituary of Jacobs's Uncle Phillip: "Now that death has laid him low, they call him a good man and a useful citizen"—to which Jacobs adds, "So they called a colored man a *citizen*! Strange words to be uttered in that region!" (201) [166]. The question of black citizenship and its substantive meaning, then, is precisely what frames the discussion of marriage and home. Closing with reference to her grandmother, therefore, does not so much offer a fantasy of domesticity safely sealed away from political conflict as it recalls her familial bonds and her grandmother's house (and its quasi-public functions) in the context of the struggle through abolitionism for a national ideology of citizenship in which African Americans can gain "a home made sacred by protecting laws" (160) [135].[5]

In framing its representation of black families and homemaking in terms of the racialized production of national subjectivity, *Incidents in the Life of a Slave Girl* connects the quotidian circumstances of African Americans' lives to the often abstract principles and seemingly distant practices of national governance. It draws on and extends existing black activist discourse by concretizing the critique of white privilege, inverting privacy into an invigorated call for rights, and politicizing "home" by putting it at the center of its mapping of the political economy of race. Employing a national imaginary in which persons of African descent are included as citizens, then, Jacobs's narrative traces geographies of racial privilege and property rights in order to oppose not only the institution of slavery but the granting of a merely formal freedom. Merging national belonging with the material markers of substantive access to social and economic resources, the text uses the household to register the racist dynamics of government policy as well as to envision the local and material forms that a national commitment to racial justice might

4. On the ideological connection between men's freedom and women's dependence in the antebellum and postbellum periods, as well as the relation between discourses of marriage and states' rights, see Hartman; and Stanley.
5. On the role of Jacobs's grandmother's home as itself a kind of public sphere, see Peterson 158–59.

take. In dialectically conjoining black domesticity and national domestic policy, displacing the image of the nation as a "political family" in order to argue for a political commitment to protecting black families, the text gestures toward the adoption of a positive national agenda in which government institutions at every level work to eradicate the effects of racism in all arenas of American life and to make national ideals and belonging locally meaningful across the color line—a project that to this day remains unfinished.

Works Cited

Accomando, Christina. *"The Regulation of Robbers": Legal Fictions of Slavery and Resistance.* Columbus: Ohio State UP, 2001.

Andrews, William L. *To Tell a Free Story: The First Century of Afro-American Autobiography, 1760–1865.* Urbana: U of Illinois P, 1986.

Baker, Houston A., Jr. *Blues, Ideology, and Afro-American Literature: A Vernacular Theory.* Chicago: U of Chicago P, 1984.

Berlant, Lauren. *The Queen of America Goes to Washington City: Essays on Sex and Citizenship.* Durham, NC: Duke UP, 1997.

Berlin, Ira. *Slaves without Masters: The Free Negro in the Antebellum South.* New York: New Press, 1974.

Burnham, Michelle. "Loopholes of Resistance: Harriet Jacobs' Slave Narrative and the Critique of Agency in Foucault." *Arizona Quarterly* 49.2 (1993): 53–73.

Carby, Hazel. *Reconstructing Womanhood: The Emergence of the Afro-American Woman Novelist.* New York: Oxford UP, 1987.

Cecil-Fronsman, Bill. *Common Whites: Class and Culture in Antebellum North Carolina.* Lexington: U of Kentucky P, 1992.

Crenshaw, Kimberlé. "Color Blindness, History, and the Law." *The House That Race Built.* Ed. Wahneema Lubiano. New York: Vintage, 1998. 280–88.

———. "Race, Reform, and Retrenchment: Transformation and Legitimation in Antidiscrimination Law." *Critical Race Theory: The Key Writings That Formed the Movement.* Ed. Kimberlé Crenshaw, Neil Gotanda, Gary Peller, and Kendall Thomas. New York: New Press, 1995, 103–22.

Finkelman, Paul. *An Imperfect Union: Slavery, Federalism, and Comity.* Chapel Hill: U of North Carolina P, 1981.

Foster, Frances Smith. *Written by Herself: Literary Production by African American Women, 1746–1892.* Bloomington: Indiana UP, 1993.

Gray White, Deborah. *Ar'n't I a Woman?: Female Slaves in the Plantation South.* New York: Norton, 1985.

Hartman, Saidiya. *Scenes of Subjection: Terror, Slavery, and Self-Making in Nineteenth-Century America.* New York: Oxford UP, 1997.

Horton, James Oliver, and Lois E. Horton. *In Hope of Liberty: Culture, Community, and Protest among Northern Free Blacks, 1700–1860.* New York: Oxford UP, 1997.

Kawash, Samira. *Dislocating the Color Line: Identity, Hybridity, and Singularity in African American Narrative.* Stanford, CA: Stanford UP, 1997.

Litwack, Leon F. *North of Slavery: The Negro in the Free States, 1790–1860.* Chicago: U of Chicago P, 1961.

Merish, Lori. *Sentimental Materialism: Gender, Commodity Culture, and Nineteenth-Century American Literature.* Durham, NC: Duke UP, 2000.

Mills, Bruce. "Lydia Maria Child and the Endings to Harriet Jacobs's *Incidents in the Life of a Slave Girl.*" *American Literature* 64.2 (1992): 255–72.

Morris, Thomas D. *Free Men All: The Personal Liberty Laws of the North, 1780–1861.* Baltimore, MD: Johns Hopkins UP, 1974.

Omi, Michael, and Howard Winant. *Racial Formation in the United States, From the 1960s to the 1990s.* New York: Routledge, 1994.

Parker, Freddie L. *Running for Freedom: Slave Runaways in North Carolina, 1775–1840.* New York: Garland, 1993.

Peterson, Carla. *"Doers of the Word": African American Women Speakers and Writers in the North (1830–1880).* New York: Oxford UP, 1995.

Potter, David. M. *The Impending Crisis, 1848–1861.* New York: Harper, 1976.

Rael, Patrick. *Black Identity and Black Protest in the Antebellum North.* Chapel Hill: U of North Carolina P, 2002.

Reid-Pharr, Robert. *Conjugal Union: The Body, The House, and the Black American.* New York: Oxford UP, 1999.

Roediger, David R. *The Wages of Whiteness: Race and the Making of the American Working Class.* New York: Verso, 1991.

Sánchez-Eppler, Karen. *Touching Liberty: Abolition, Feminism, and the Politics of the Body.* Berkeley: U of California P, 1993.

Sedgwick, Eve. *Epistemology of the Closet.* Berkeley: U of California P, 1990.

Spillers, Hortense. "Mama's Baby, Papa's Maybe: An American Grammar Book." *diacritics* 17.2 (1997): 65–81.

Stanley, Amy Dru. *From Bondage to Contract: Wage Labor, Marriage, and the Market in the Age of Slave Emancipation.* New York: Cambridge UP, 1998.

Sundquist, Eric J. *To Wake the Nations: Race in the Making of American Literature.* Cambridge, MA: Harvard UP, 1993.

Tate, Claudia. *Domestic Allegories of Political Desire: The Black Heroine's Text at the Turn of the Century.* New York: Oxford UP, 1992.

Wiegman, Robyn. *American Anatomies: Theorizing Race and Gender.* Durham, NC: Duke UP, 1995.
Williams, Patricia. *The Alchemy of Race and Rights.* Cambridge, MA: Harvard UP, 1991.
Yellin, Jean Fagan. Introduction. *Incidents in the Life of a Slave Girl, Written by Herself.* By Harriet Jacobs. Cambridge, MA: Harvard UP, 1987. xiii–xxxiv.

P. GABRIELLE FOREMAN

From The Politics of Sex and Representation in Harriet Jacobs's *Incidents in the Life of a Slave Girl*†

"Rise up, ye women that are at ease! Hear my voice, ye careless daughters! Give ear unto my speech."—Isaiah xxxii, 9
—Title page, first edition, *Incidents in the Life of a Slave Girl*

Untruth becomes truth through belief, and disbelief untruths the truth. —Patricia Williams

Harriet Jacobs's *Incidents in the Life of a Slave Girl* (1861) was once dismissed and then resuscitated precisely on the basis of its value as "truth" even though it is widely accepted today that "the 'unreliability' of autobiography is an inescapable condition, not a rhetorical option."[1] Although there are explicit markers of distance between "truth" and its representation in the text, contemporary critics tend to accept the transparency between the life of Harriet Jacobs and her narrative self-construct "Linda Brent."[2] For Jean Fagan Yellin, Jacobs's most important critic, treating her book "as if it were gospel truth" has led to one of the most important works of recovery in American literary and historical studies.[3] As Yellin puts it, "you can trust [Jacobs]. She's not

† From *Activist Sentiments: Reading Black Women in the Nineteenth Century* (Urbana, IL: U of Illinois P, 2009), 19–36, 42. Copyright © Cambridge University Press 1996. Reprinted by permission of Cambridge University Press. Page numbers in brackets refer to this Norton Critical Edition.

1. *Incidents in the Life of a Slave Girl* had long been thought to have been composed by Lydia Maria Child, its editor. Until Yellin's 1987 edition, many twentieth-century Black writers, anthologists, and historians denigrated and dismissed the book as well. Among them were Sterling Brown, Arthur Davis, Ulysses Lee, Arna Bontemps, and John Blassingame. See Yellin, "Text and Contexts," 287 n. 2; Yellin, *Harriet Jacobs: A Life*, xvi, xviii, xx; and Blassingame, *Slave Community*, 373. Sidonie Smith affirms the notion of unreliability as she quotes Francis R. Hart in *Poetics of Women's Autobiography*, 46.
2. Jean Fagan Yellin, Mary Helen Washington, Linda Mackethan, and William Andrews, to name a few, all basically accept a one-to-one correlation between Jacobs's life and her representation of it. Yet Andrews argues that slave narrators' "actual life stories frequently dispute, sometimes directly but more often covertly, the positivistic epistemology, dualistic morality, and diachronic framework in which antebellum America liked to evaluate autobiography as either history or falsehood." Andrews, *To Tell A Free Story*, 6.
3. Yellin, *Harriet Jacobs: A Life*, xviii.

ever wrong. She may be wrong on incidentals like the birth order of her mistresses' children—after all she was a woman in her forties trying to remember what happened to her as a teenager—but she's never wrong in substance."[4] Through the lens of the biographer, this approach has brought Jacobs's life into focus. But for the literary critic, choosing this aperture can blur the ways in which *Incidents* foregrounds and obscures the text's multiple messages. The coordinates—right/"wrong," "substance"/incidentals, "trust" [worthy]/liar—are mapped onto *Incidents*, even though modern critics generally accept literary theorist Sidonie Smith's maxim about autobiography's unreliability. Today, truthfulness, as Smith affirms, is viewed as a "complex and problematic phenomenon" that does not emphasize "the truth in its factual or moral dimensions."[5] In this chapter, rather than emphasize the *auto*, the assumed transparent self, or the *bio*, I grapple with interpreting *graphia*, "'the careful teasing out of warring forces of signification within the text itself.'"[6] As its autodiegetic narrator, Jacobs offers her reception communities explicit directions to look for multiple modes of interpretation. These alternatives are not subversively subtextual, I argue, but rather, they are simultextual; that is, they are interpretive paths that offer equally substantive, often competing, simultaneously rendered reading modalities.

When we pay attention to Black simultextuality, we limn the challenges to the truth-telling imperatives associated with slave narratives and with the narrative transparency—the correlation between text and a readily apparent singular meaning—that is considered a keynote of sentimental fiction. Though the challenges Black male narrators launch against such generic expectations are generally celebrated, the figure of the nineteenth-century Black woman is more readily expected to tell just one truth and to embody the truth.

Truth was highly valued in abolitionist rhetoric. Black authors and speakers were valued precisely because their bodies stood in its rhetorical stead and displaced Southern apologist versions of "slavery as it is." Nineteenth-century truth, for the once-enslaved narrator's audiences, was most threatened by exaggeration of the social evils of slavery, in other words, by overindulgence and rhetorical excess.[7]

4. Washington, *Invented Lives*, 9.
5. Sidonie Smith, as quoted in Olney, *Autobiography*, 5.
6. Sidonie Smith, in Olney, *Autobiography*, 20.
7. Lunsford Lane, for example, writes that he chooses "to come short of giving the full picture" rather than to "overstate." See Preface, *Narrative of Lunsford Lane*, available at http://docsouth.unc.edu/neh/lanelunsford/menu.html (accessed November 17, 2008) and Andrews, *To Tell a Free Story*, 115. Solomon Northup also states that the point of his narrative is "to repeat the story of my life, without exaggeration." *Solomon Northup*, 3. William Lloyd Garrison says of Douglass's *Narrative of the Life*, "I am confident that it is essentially true in all of its statements, that nothing has been set down in malice, nothing exaggerated, nothing drawn from the imagination, that it comes short of the reality, rather than overstates a single fact in regard to SLAVERY AS IT IS." Douglass, *Narrative of the Life*, 38.

"Delicacy" and "modesty," virtues extolled in women's and even in African American men's narratives, allowed for and even demanded that narrators systematically come short of the truth.[8] Tracing simultextual signs of "truthfulness" complicates the ways in which *Incidents* is traditionally read and affirms an alternative interpretation: that Dr. Norcom did rape Jacobs, which stands alongside the script that Linda triumphed over Dr. Flint, not only in her fugitive escape, but in her sexual one. The analysis I offer here is not meant to reassert "truth-telling" and "lying" as evaluative axes, or to substitute one reading for another. Rather this commentary calls into question the politics of transparency that often frame both our consideration of *Incidents* and an approach to Black sentimental writing that discourages the recovery of the multivalent nuances that I argue characterize the genre.

This chapter traces the simultaneous modes of address that are manifest in *Incidents in the Life of a Slave Girls*'s loud "silences" and their relation to the truth. Widening traditional categories of exploited and exploiter, I offer an extended reading of homosexual abuse and interrogate how masters link an imperative toward sexualized silence to security from sale. When, for women, bodily expression (that is, pregnancies and pale children) is constructed as punishable speech, the promise of safety that owners offer in exchange for silence is impossible for enslaved women to carry out, much less collect upon. Jacobs turns the politics of ownership, reproductive agency, and naming under slavery on its head as she complicates her children's paternity and so neutralizes her owner's power to sell her by positioning her lover as her probable buyer. * * *

Eenie, Meenie, Minie, Moe, Abuser, Victim, Ally, Foe?

Incidents both advances and simultextually challenges the script that Linda had an affair with the white bachelor Mr. Sands in order to fend off the sexual threat of her owner Dr. Flint. She constantly reiterates that "the degradation, the wrongs, the vices that grow out of slavery are more than I can describe. They are greater than you would willingly believe."[9] This admonition echoes her preface, where she tells her readers that the events related in *Incidents* are "strictly true. I have not exaggerated the wrongs inflicted by Slavery; on the contrary, my descriptions fall far short of the facts" (*InL*, i [5]). How are readers to interpret the narrative tension between a "strict truth" that nonetheless "falls far short of the facts"? The mistrust Jacobs feels for those who will not "willingly believe" the "facts" informs what

8. Edmund Quincy, a white Garrisonian, noted of William Wells Brown's narrative, that it was told with greater "propriety and delicacy" than was Douglass's. See Andrews, *To Tell a Free Story*, 108.
9. Harriet Jacobs, *Incidents in the Life*, 28 [27] (hereinafter cited in the text as *InL*).

Frances Smith Foster discusses as an "implicitly argumentative" mode of address that anticipates such resistance; it is what Robert Stepto might call a culture of distrust.[1] These characterizations point contemporary readers to the politics of nineteenth-century reception and to the ways in which distrust of audiences encouraged authors to gauge the distance between the strict truth that falls short and to undertell their stories to match what we might call delicate expectations, while simultaneously indicating to receptive readers that more is apparent for those who choose to look. Such discursive maneuvering works to "thwart the resisting reader's urge to compete with the author for authority," instead enlisting the reader "as a collaborator," as Foster suggests.[2] These dynamics also spawn rhetorical tactics that respond to multiple expectations, both challenging and simultaneously appealing to readers' racialized assumptions and power.

Incidents seems to both dismiss and genuflect at the feet of authoritative notions of Northern femininity and transparency. Indeed, the text reflects some of the central cultural tensions of the antebellum era. The cult of sincerity that had dominated the previous two decades faded in importance in the fifties. Karen Halttunen argues that the "sentimental typology of conduct," the valorization of transparency of character, was fast being replaced with the laws of polite social performance.[3] She notes that the "most important law of polite social geography was that no one shatter the magic of the genteel performance by acknowledging back regions that alone made the performance possible."[4] *Incidents* reflects that, in an era of shifting truth expectations, the rules of decorum were as compelling as those of disclosure. Understanding an implicit contract with her readership, Jacobs could expect her white bourgeois female audience to play its part—to perceive (but to be "delicate" enough not to admit that they comprehend) the sexually determined Black "back regions" of her textual performance.[5]

1. Frances Smith Foster, "Resisting Incidents," 69 [270]; Stepto, "Distrust of the Reader in Afro-American Narratives," 301–2.
2. Frances Smith Foster, "Resisting Incidents," 70 [271].
3. See Halttunen, *Confidence Men and Painted Women*, 40, 52; and also Smith-Rosenberg, *Disorderly Conduct*, 26.
4. Halttunen, *Confidence Men and Painted Women*, 107.
5. The parlor, Halttunen asserts, mediated between the public and the private. Her "back regions" refer to the indelicate preparation of bourgeois parlor performances—dinners, parties, and the intricate rules of formal visits. Black back regions is a pregnant metaphor that resonates temporally (back when), geographically (back South). One metaphor for white and Black female difference was medically construed as located in the back regions or buttocks (see Gilman, "Black Bodies, White Bodies," 204–42). Jacobs may well assume a bourgeois reception. Such a contract of delicacy is well illustrated in Jacobs's relationship with Mrs. Willis, who never inquires as to the circumstances of Jacobs's children's conception, yet is assumed to know. Jacobs writes of this to Amy Post: "I had never opened my lips to Mrs. Willis concerning my Children—in the Charitableness of her own heart she sympathized with me and never asked their origin—my suffering she knew." *Incidents*, 235.

Jacobs anticipates her audience's interpretative bind, one Lydia Maria Child articulates when she takes pains to explain why she, a prominent white abolitionist, might be associated with so "indelicate" a text. In her introduction Child writes that she presents the "veil withdrawn . . . for the sake of my sisters in bondage, who are suffering wrongs so foul that our ears are too delicate to listen to them" (*InL*, 4 [6]). As Valerie Smith notes, the editor places herself and her imagined readers in the enslaved victim's stead; she substitutes "our" (presumably white) ears in the grammatical place that should call for Black reactions or bodies.[6] Importantly, "ear" as the orifice penetrated by words acts to degender sexual exploitation and to break down oppositions of male/female abuse.[7] By deemphasizing Jacobs's mediation of truth and the politics of sexual revelation and discursive autonomy, Child's introductory claim that as editor she presents the "veil withdrawn," the back regions exposed, stands as *Incidents*' guiding con/text.

In *Incidents*, enslaved men as well as women are sexually terrorized by white people of either sex. In language that characteristically reveals as it also conceals, *Incidents* exposes the homosexual abuse to which male narrators rarely admit.[8] Luke is the slave of a dissipated and sick young owner who has the enslaved man "bare his back and kneel beside the couch, while he whipped him." And, as Jacobs writes in the very next sentence, Luke is forced to serve his owner bare-bottomed, for "somedays he was not allowed to wear any thing *but* his shirt, in order to be flogged" (*InL*, 192 [158], emphasis mine): "As [the young master] lay there on his bed, a mere degraded wreck of manhood, he took into his head the strangest freaks of despotism; and if Luke hesitated to submit to his orders, the constable was immediately sent for. Some of these freaks were of a nature too filthy to be repeated. I left poor Luke still chained to the bedside of this cruel and disgusting wretch" (*InL*, 192 [159]). The language here taps into a familiar anti-slavery critique that explicitly links sexual defilement and the political "despotism" of slavery. It likewise suggests that the North is not safe from the contagion of Southern dissipation, as the young owner had become "prey to the vices

6. Valerie Smith, "'Loopholes of Retreat,'" 222.
7. In nineteenth-century iconographics and physiognomy, ears were construed, as were genitalia, as organs that exposed pathological essence, particularly of prostitutes and sexual women. See Gilman, "Black Bodies, White Bodies," 224. Also see Shawn Michelle Smith, *American Archives*, 68–93, especially 77 and 84.
8. Foster notes parenthetically that "rare indeed is any reference to sexual abuse of slave men by white women, and homosexuality [or homosexual abuse] is never mentioned" in narratives authored by men. "'In Respect to Females . . . ,'" 67. Similarly, Mary Helen Washington maintains that "in the male slave narrative . . . sexuality is nearly always avoided, and when it does surface it is to report the sexual abuse of female slaves. The male slave narrator was under no compulsion to discuss his own sexuality nor that of other men." *Invented Lives*, xxiii.

growing out of the 'patriarchal institution,' and when he went to the north, to complete his education, he carried his vices with him" (*InL*, 192 [158]). Northern pedagogy is ineffective, the text suggests; it cannot purify the patriarchal institution nor fight off the disease of vice and debauchery that Southerners carry with them. Abuse of power, however weakened or weakening, admits no limits in its access to the body politic as represented by the bodies of its enslaved population; each controls by force without consent. By making homosexual exploitation and political abuse analogous, this passage breaks from conventional imagery to assert that the reach of despotic control, of slavery, cannot be contained.

In *Incidents*, white women are also included in a miscegenous sexual politics that so often is characterized by white male desire for ever-available Black female bodies. Indeed, the text "demarcates a sexuality that is neuter-bound, insomuch as it represents an open vulnerability to a gigantic sexualized repertoire that may be alternately expressed as male/female," to borrow from Hortense Spillers.[9] Early on, Jacobs exposes white women with the veil withdrawn by asserting that "from others than the master persecution also comes in such cases" (*InL*, 13 [323]). Critics have pointed out that it is the "whispering" Mrs. Flint who realizes her demand to have Linda sleep in her room, who leans suggestively over her slave's body at night.[1] And young mistresses, too, "hear their parents quarreling about some female slave. Their curiosity is excited . . . and they hear talk as should never meet youthful ears, or any other ears. They know that the women slaves are subject to their father's authority in all things; and in some cases they exercise the same authority over men slaves" (*InL*, 52 [323]). In this passage, sexualized language again attracts varied agents. The "they" in the clause: "in some cases they exercise the same authority over men slaves" can refer to both the young mistress of "they know that the women slaves are subject to their father's authority" and to the Ur-agent-abuser himself, the master/model whose restless nature knows no bounds with enslaved women, and in some cases, "men slaves." Grammatically, Jacobs signals both homosexual violation and also abuse not very complimentary to the reputation of white women. This passage thus transforms some readers, the women of the North she hopes to "arouse" to "realizing a sense of the condition of the two million women at the North, still in bondage" (*InL*, preface [5]) from a state of mirrored identification with the youthful ears of the innocent belle hearing too much to a state of active culpability as "careless daughters" rise up and transmogrify into sexual aggressors.

9. Spillers, "Mama's Baby, Papa's Maybe," 77.
1. Sánchez-Eppler, *Touching Liberty*, 22; Spillers, "Mama's Baby, Papa's Maybe," 77.

Subject to Jacobs's narrative control, both mistress and reader are stripped of their usually protected status and, "curiosity" excited, ears exposed, they are sexualized.[2]

This passage likewise tarnishes planters' reputations through the incestuous inferences it raises. The relation between miscegenous abuse and familial contamination is further confirmed when Dr. Flint insists that his young daughter sleep in his room to justify Linda's presence there. One cannot help but wonder, as critic Sandra Gunning does, "if Flint expects the child to be present while he tries to rape her nurse."[3] These masters contaminate their daughters, introducing young girls to transgressive acts and desires via their fathers' own salacious conduct (*InL*, 52 [47]).

Sexual abuse of enslaved women was neither visible to the law nor did it elicit public stigma for its perpetuators. So it left "other ears" systematically open to the symbolic penetration that "words that sting like fire" represent in *Incidents*. By placing these normalized "relations" center stage alongside recognizable, even actionable, taboos of incestuously tainted and homosexual abuse, these passages both highlight Black women's defilement and raise questions about the role of all of the parties involved. Jacobs stages enslaved women's abuse alongside other sexually oppressive scenarios; she thus highlights illicit behavior sure to get the attention of many readers even if they were deadened to the plight of enslaved women themselves.

Confession and Commodities; Silence and Sale

Jacobs's simultextual descriptions of varied types and agents of sexual abuse evoke sympathy from her audience and also expose their complicity. Indeed, if readers attend to the polyvalent interpretive paradigm the text sets out, the ways through which *Incidents* both embraces and also rejects discursive victimization emerge.[4] The delimited arena of interracial sexual "victimization" is characterized by a lack of explicit expression, at least by the "victims." For centuries, white women only pointed at Black men, and the legal apparatus need not even be brought to bear on them before they were sold, shot, or lynched. Conversely, recognition of the sexual

2. Garfield, "Earwitness," 110, makes a similar argument using a different passage. She writes, "The discerning white reader should find herself in her black sister's place, in the humiliated nakedness of confession; and Jacobs, seizing the agency of discourse in which she is supposedly the logical victim, adroitly unwrites Child's protection of her readership. In the epigraph's mute addendum about bared bodies, the code of black sexuality is subtly revised, the categories of vulnerable black teller and decorous white listener undermined."
3. Gunning, "Reading and Redemption," 143 [289].
4. Carby, Washington, and others argue, I think rightly, that male depictions of Black women as victims deny these women agency in other parts of their lives, and limit women's expressive agency. See Carby, *Reconstructing Womanhood*, 35; Washington, *Invented Lives*, xxii–xxiv.

abuse of enslaved or freed African American women was as alien in concept as it was in fact.[5] What, then, underwrote speech-rights for the enslaved? Literary critic Houston Baker claims that the male slave "*publicly* sells his voice in order to secure *private* ownership of his voice-person,"[6] and so shifts concepts of desire and privatization from a gendered arena (public/private) where the slave is infantilized and feminized to an economically determined sphere where he could own his own person or manhood as agent rather than victim.

When *Incidents* is published, however, the once-fugitive author is already free, so she cannot justify her publishing venture into the masculinized public realm to secure ownership of her person. Nor can she invoke the accepted model of the era in which women writers legitimize their trade by emphasizing explicit ties to an overriding and valorized motherhood. Louisa Picquet (1861) unveils the details of her sexual past only as a last attempt to purchase her enslaved mother; Harriet Wilson (1859) in effect writes in order to "purchase" her son. The Jacobs children, however, were both technically and legally free (despite the fears the narrator expresses), even though illegitimate and Black children were particularly susceptible to involuntary apprenticeship in North Carolina where they were born.[7] Nor does the conventional trope of a mother figure with whom to reunite exist; Jacobs's free grandmother has recently died. Neither does Jacobs make an explicit claim that she is attempting to buy, through this work, a "home of her own" (*InL*, 201 [167]). Nor does she make claim to destitution, another popular justification for women writers' indelicate jaunt into the public sphere. Rather, she asks her abolitionist friend Amy Post to mention that "I lived at service all the while that I was striving to get the Book out. . . . [as] I would [not] like to have people think that I was living an Idle life—and had got this book out merely to make money" (*InL*, 242). If Jacobs refuses to invoke received legitimizing strategies, how does one account for her economy of voice and possession? In some

5. See Angela Davis, "Rape, Racism and the Myth of the Black Rapist," and "Legacy of Slavery." In antebellum Missouri, if a white man forced himself on an enslaved person he did not own, he could be charged with "trespassing." The concept of master/slave rape was inconceivable since someone who owned property could not be a trespasser on it. These relations reveal themselves in recent scholarship as well. In Tushnet's *American Law of Slavery*, for example, when rape is mentioned white men are never the culprit. And though the antebellum social system sometimes recognized that Black-on-Black rape could occur, the legal apparatus of the South refused to give such standards judicial consideration. In other words, legally, Black women could not be raped. See McLaurin, *Celia, A Slave*, 93.

6. Baker, *Blues, Ideology, and Afro-American Literature*, 50.

7. The North Carolina Supreme Court codified earlier state practice in 1855 declaring that the "county courts had power to bind out all free base-born children of color without reference to the occupation or condition of the mother." Bardaglio, *Reconstructing the Household*, 104. However, Sawyer draws up the children's bill of sales in Jacobs's grandmother's name; they are no longer, then, legally under his power.

ways, Jacobs's model is most often predicated upon the politics of representing desire and sexual autonomy. She sells her voice to secure and express private ownership, not only of her body, but of its discursive embodiment—her voice and text themselves.

As Michel Foucault reminds us, "from the Christian penance to the present day sex was a privileged theme of confession," as it was in African American literary history and particularly in the most popular of all early slave narratives, the criminal "confession." Yet the criminal genre's titillation is often resolved in outrage and punishment—the subgenre itself is predicated upon the suppression of the connected realms of Black speech rights and criminal justice.[8] Jacobs's potential confession, we can easily imagine, with cowering victim and salacious owner, could collapse for her readers into the arousal of sadistic pornography. Yet, by strategically undertelling "what the world might believe that a Slave Woman was too willing to pour out—that she might gain their sympathies," *Incidents* makes good use of the implicit expectations of victimization that Jacobs simultaneously shuns (*InL*, 242 [200]). This is particularly true in the scenes of "confession" with Mrs. Flint, Linda's grandmother, and in the extratextual confession described by Amy Post in *Incidents*' appendix.[9] In none of these passages does the text reveal what the once-enslaved girl actually testifies to or confesses. Instead, *Incidents* teases, toying with the acceptable titillation and resolution of confession and absolution without ever really shedding any raiment.

To anti-slavery whites in the North, "blackness and black women in particular signified victimization."[1] While *Incidents* often gives the impression "that the [sentimental] form only allows Jacobs to talk about her sexual experiences when they are the result of victimization,"[2] it is also true that "only when Brent is silenced can she become the object of charity," that she moves, as Gunning asserts, from embodying a delicate tale that situates her as an object of sympathy to telling an indelicate tale that makes her agent and pariah, a potential pollutant to "purer" sensibilities.[3] Marianne Noble maintains that "histrionic victimization is a particularly effective strategy for self-empowerment in a liberal society where most citizens want to be seen as nonviolent and compassionate."[4] Most Garrisonian abolitionists' self-identity hinged on a self-conceptualization that elevated moral

8. See Foucault, *History of Sexuality, Vol. 1*, 61; Sekora, "Black Message", 489.
9. Post's description does not reveal any details when she describes Jacobs's "suffering." She writes, "Even in talking with me, she [Jacobs] wept so much, and seemed to suffer such mental agony, that I felt her story was too sacred to be drawn from her by inquisitive questions." Harriet Jacobs, *Incidents* (Yellin edition), 204 [168].
1. Gunning, "Reading and Redemption," 135 [280].
2. Valerie Smith, *Self-Discovery and Authority*, 222.
3. Gunning, "Reading and Redemption," 136–37 [282].
4. Noble, *Masochistic Pleasure*, 9.

suasion and nonviolence when slavery and its defenders were seen as violent threats to the body politic. But racialized dynamics of speech production preclude "histrionic" positioning for Black victims; again, exaggeration threatens truth-telling. Moreover, the very appellation "sexual victim" exonerates one from guilt, and so from compulsion toward confession, especially when one might offend delicate sensibilities. Thus, perversely, Jacobs must be a sexual *actor* to appropriate speech rights; she does so by expressing agency where male authors most often depict female victimization. This agency exhibits itself in the realm of the illicit: it must produce something to confess.

Confession, then, is the currency with which the text purchases the sanitized (and thus legitimate) attention of its readers. Her much quoted "Pity me and me pardon me, O virtuous reader" (*InL,* 55 [246]) acts to relieve the titillated audience from its excited state; in a sense, by reminding them of their access to and responsibility for virtue, the passage acts to absolve them as much as it seeks to absolve Linda. Through confession, then, *Incidents* converts a religious invocation of pardon into both sexual and political agency.[5] In doing so the narrative "questions the character of a white nation that establishes its moral ideals on a victimizing construction of Blackness" as Brent transforms from "victim to actor on the very terms of the slave woman's oppression," as Gunning points out.[6] Jacobs's victimization then acts with her sexual agency, challenging readers to face their own mirrored complicity as women with sexual power and abusive agency.

Incidents delineates the multivalent relationships between owners, the enslaved, sex, and criminalized speech. Silence, it asserts again and again, ostensibly stands in fungible relation to security from sale. In the first few weeks after Linda has been willed to young Emily Flint and removed from her former mistress's home, Dr. Flint hands a slave mother and her "husband" over to a trader: "you *promised* to treat me well," the mother says. "To which [Flint] replied, 'you have let your tongue run too far; damn you!' She had forgotten that it was a crime for a slave to tell who was the father of her child" (*InL,* 13 [16]). The narrator's use of an indefinite article in the phrase, "a slave," links the mother to a collective of enslaved and abused women. Jacobs similarly switches to the plural when outlining Linda's experience as Flint pursues her. The doctor is uniformly relentless but his approaches and interests are varied: "sometimes he had stormy, terrific ways that made his *victims* tremble" (*InL,* 27 [327], emphasis

5. In *Reconstructing Womanhood,* Carby argues explicitly what Mary Helen Washington maintains, that Jacobs is "informed not by the cult of domesticity or domestic feminism but by political feminism; *Incidents* is an attempt to move women to political action." Mary Helen Washington, *Invented Lives,* xxxii.
6. Gunning, "Reading and Redemption," 144 [291], 146 [203].

mine). This harassment, we can deduce, was physical as well as verbal. As Jacobs writes, "The secrets of slavery are concealed like those of the Inquisition. My master was, to my knowledge, the father of eleven slaves. But did the mothers dare to tell who was the father of their children? Did the other slaves dare to allude to it, except in whispers among themselves? No indeed! They knew too well the terrible consequences" (*InL,* 35 [329]). Did these women form whispering communities of support analogous to those of white bourgeois women who provided each other with advice, solace, and aid?[7] Or did these enslaved women come to understand—as Jacobs suggests—that such sharing constituted punishable speech?

The formula "silence or sale" renders the subject closed to the inquiries of the supportive and/or enraged husband, family, and green-eyed mistress alike. Like Linda's reticence with her grandmother, the sales *Incidents* depicts strongly suggest that at least some enslaved women quickly learn that they can whisper only if they are not the subject; they are required to mute their violation with silence—to reinforce, perversely, their own violation. The shared whisperings "among themselves," then, exclude the assaulted individual whose confirmation of her abuse might actualize the constant threat of sale and endanger others' security as well; her required silence, though it does not ensure her own safety from rape or sale, makes her responsible for maintaining the fragile "security" of her community.

Yet might not the signs of a "favorite" slave's pregnancy, or the child itself, constitute punishable speech? Can her silence perform what is demanded of it? Can it nullify bodily speech? The slave mother who appears early in *Incidents* flings back Flint's commitment—"you *promised* to treat me well"—and he acknowledges their agreement but accuses her of breaching it, replying, "'you have let your tongue run too far; damn you!'" The following comment—"she had forgotten that it was a crime . . . to tell" (*InL,* 13 [16])—concretizes the language of contract represented in the passage. Jacobs transfers the juridical consequences of breaking contracts to a figure of speech, speech that in this nonactionable situation between enslaved and owner nonetheless carries the punitive force of punishment. What is clear, however, is that silence—the enslaved mother's agreed-upon item of exchange—is neither delimited by speech nor defined by its absence. Rather, it is the *issue* who is at issue, for the mother and husband "were both black and the child was very fair" (*InL,* 13 [16]). The evidence is transmitted through her and against her own will, creating a bodily legibility that

7. See Smith-Rosenberg, *Disorderly Conduct,* chaps. 1 and 2, and esp. Auerbach, *Communities of Women,* chap. 1.

is compulsory for it is produced by her owner's seminal inscription upon his own property.[8] Her tongue, in other words, did not have to produce the telling text. No one has to *say* anything; the child's color speaks for itself. The text depicts the slave mother as *coerced* into an "agreement" in which even her agreed-upon part was never tenable. Not only are contracts between slave and master always nonbinding and duplicitous, they will also turn a slave's speech *and* silence against her.

One might argue, then, that because Linda is said to know "too well the terrible consequences" that "as soon as a new fancy took him, his victims were sold far off to get rid of them, especially if they had children"—because she had seen this—she began her affair with Sands (*InL,* 35 [33], 55 [50]). She explains that "of a man who was not my master I could ask to have my children well supported; and in this case, I felt confident I should obtain the boon and that they would be made free." This sentence directly precedes *Incidents*' most oft-quoted "sentimental" lines: "With all these thoughts revolving in my mind, and seeing no other way of escaping the doom I so much dreaded, I made a headlong plunge. Pity me, and pardon me, O virtuous reader!" (*InL,* 55 [50]). What is consistently read as a concession to or internalization of true womanhood also can be read in this context as masked and mocking irony. "Doom's" antecedent is most pointedly not only the threat of sex, the ubiquitous trope of "doom" in a sentimental lexicon, but also the threat of sale.

As a disciplinary device, being sold surpassed almost all punishment, including physical "correction." Owners were advised to get women pregnant and men settled; bonds of affection made unmanageable chattel less likely to run. Following this logic, the pledge not to sell one's slaves was the next best thing to a promise of freedom; in some conservative anti-slavery rhetoric, owners—and the system itself—could be redeemed almost as fully by not selling and separating enslaved families as by freeing them, though abolitionist rhetoricians forcefully displayed how even the best-intentioned owners routinely broke such promises. Jacobs inverts the affective disciplinary dynamics so often manipulated by the planter class to domesticate those they enslaved. "I will never sell you," Flint bellows after Sands offers to buy her (*InL,* 60 [54]). Indeed, Dr. Flint refuses to sell Linda even as punishment: "I have no right to sell her," he avers to a slaveholder he rightly suspects has been commissioned by Linda's "friends." "I mistrust that you come from her paramour. If so, you may tell him that he cannot buy her for any money; neither can

8. See Chinn, "Introduction," in *Technology and the Logic of American Racism,* esp. 7, for a theorization of the politics of bodies used as evidentiary material in systems of subordination.

he buy her children" (*InL*, 80 [70]). By turning words most often figured in narratives as broken promises into an unreserved threat, Jacobs tactically outmaneuvers her own owner and victimizer; she nullifies the loss she most fears and preserves perhaps not her virtue—but her family.

Sexual Truth, Testimony, and Tyranny

Although Jacobs would have at least a segment of her reception community believe that her owner never "succeeded" in his ultimate assault, *Incidents* simultextually suggests that Norcom did rape his much-desired slave girl. Take the entire passage describing Linda's "plunge" as a paradigmatic example. The paragraph that introduces Sands concludes with these words: "A master may treat you as rudely as he pleases, and you *dare not speak;* moreover, the wrong does not seem so great with an unmarried man, as with one who has a wife to be made unhappy. There may be sophistry in all this; but the condition of a slave confuses all principles of morality, and, in fact, renders the practice of them impossible" (*InL*, 55 [50], emphasis mine). The imperative to remain silent surfaces yet again. Though the immediate referent for the narrator's "sophistry" is her justification for Linda's relationship with Sands, there is reason to interpret her words in "all this" rudeness more broadly.

Throughout the text the question of Flint's "restraint" remains unresolved. Some important Jacobs critics suggest that the actual enslaved girl couldn't possibly have eluded her master.[9] One suggests that Jacobs's attempt to "authenticate herself" to an audience that valorizes middle-class mores and values rests on a "great factual lie, for it stretches the limits of all credulity that Linda Brent actually eluded her owner's sexual advances."[1] Why, critics ask, if Dr. Flint could treat Linda "as rudely as he please[d]," did he choose not to? Flint's language ranges from affectionate to authoritative, but his tactics do not explicitly shift from discursively sexual foul play to physically sexual force.[2] He whispers foul words, writes obscene notes, and then becomes a personal threat. Linda reflects: "My master, whose restless, craving, vicious nature roved about day and night, seeking whom to devour, had just left me, with stinging, scorching *words; words* that scathed ear and brain like fire. O, how I despised him! I thought how glad I should be, if some day when he walked the earth, it would open and swallow him up and disencumber the world of a plague" (*InL*, 18 [19], emphasis mine). Despite

9. Frances Smith Foster, "Resisting Incidents," 67 [268].
1. Fox-Genovese, *Within the Plantation Household*, 392.
2. Flint's tactics do include the physical. I thank Richard Yarborough for his suggestion that this physical abuse might be a loophole for a shift to physical sexual abuse as well.

the power of verbalized sexual pollution in the representational economy of both domestic fiction and anti-slavery rhetoric—and even accounting for the damage of such abuse in the life of a teenage girl—this passage displays an imbalance between Flint's actions and Linda's reactions; the passion in her language does not seem to have a direct correlation with what Flint "says." Rather it seems likely that abuse is both mediated through audience expectations and that the text transfers Linda's violated body to the body of the word. By both serving for and providing the trope for physical abuse, words act both to describe her violation and to absorb it.[3]

The narrative supports the supposition that the slave girl could very well have been pregnant with her master's child when she began her relationship with a neighboring bachelor.[4] Jacobs describes what are clearly her own circumstances—a kind mistress, a pious grandmother, a respectable and loving Black suitor—again and again in the third person, insisting that there is no escape from the manifold devices men with power will use to have their way. "The slave girl is reared in an atmosphere of licentiousness and fear," she declares,

> the lash and the foul talk of her master and his sons are her teachers. When she is fourteen or fifteen, her owner, or his sons, or the overseer, or perhaps all of them, begin to bribe her with presents. If these fail to accomplish their purpose she is whipped or starved into submission to their will. She may have had religious principles inculcated by some pious mother or grandmother, or some good mistress; she may have a lover, whose good opinion and peace of mind are dear to her heart; or the profligate men who have power over her may be exceedingly odious to her. But resistance is hopeless. (*InL*, 51 [47])

Incidents exposes the pedagogy of submission that the school of slavery teaches its daughters even in the face of pious mothers and good mistresses, teaching its audience the art of interpretation under these circumstances.

Unable to dodge the explicitly illicit message Jacobs narrates in the third person, her receptive audience is instructed to recognize the complex and conflicting signs of the same story when it is narrated in the first person. Ostensibly referring to the threat of an isolated cottage that Dr. Flint is building for Linda's future concubinage, the narrator notes that

3. Jacobs's transference from the sexual to the rhetorical is developed more fully in Foreman's "The Spoken and the Silenced," 317–18.
4. Timing supports this possibility. She begins her relationship when she is fifteen; born in 1813, Jacobs then dates 1828 or 1829 as the year she begins her affair with Sawyer. Joseph Jacobs is born circa 1829. It is also in 1828 and 1829 that Mrs. Norcom's suspicions get particularly heated. See Harriet Jacobs, *Incidents* (Yellin edition), 54 [49], 35 [32].

> the crisis of my fate now came so near that I was desperate. I shuddered to think of being the mother of children that should be owned by my old tyrant. I knew that as soon as a new fancy took him, his victims were sold far off to get rid of them; especially if they had children. I had seen several women sold with his babies at the breast. He never allowed his offspring by slaves to remain long in sight of himself and his wife. Of a man who was not my master I could ask to have my children well supported; and in this case, I felt confident I should obtain the boon and that they would be made free. (*InL*, 55 [50])

As we have seen, some readers will interpret this to mean that Linda takes "the plunge" with Sands because of Flint's immanent sexual threat. Yet others may recall that Linda has eluded her owner shrewdly on every preceding occasion. The narrative offers several simultextual possibilities at this critical juncture. One is that the analogy of other victims may fully obtain, and that Linda's crisis could well be read as an impending pregnancy. The statement—"I shuddered to think of being the mother of children that should be owned by my old tyrant," a concern she expresses earlier when she wants to be with her free Black suitor—differs importantly from what follows: "I knew that as soon as a new fancy took him his victims were sold" (*InL*, 55 [50]). The first is solely a legal issue that emphasizes Flint's property rights; the second, with its inclusive victimization, implies paternity and sexual possession as well. It is this latter scenario that Jacobs's grandmother and Mrs. Flint are all too ready to believe.

To diffuse "the crisis of [her] fate" as best she can, the narrator complicates paternity and names Sands as her children's father. Hazel Carby suggests that "from [Linda's] experience she knew that Dr. Flint sold his offspring from slave women and hoped that if her children were fathered by Sands he could buy them and secure their future."[5] Carby's language reflects the multiple possibilities embedded in Jacobs's own; if Flint sold "*his* offspring from slave women" and Linda's "children were fathered by Sands," then Jacobs presents no reason for Flint to sell them.[6] Indeed, both the narrator's and her latter-day critic's language imply what neither of them say explicitly: for this mother's strategy to work, Sands's role as father must be contested. Understanding this, Jacobs counters the sexual and familial instability and powerlessness that characterizes paternity (and representations of such issues) under slavery; in *Incidents*, an enslaved

5. Carby, *Reconstructing Womanhood*, 58.
6. Jacobs stresses throughout the narrative that Flint sells the children he fathers. She does not mention his sale of other children, and emphasizes, as Douglass does in both his 1845 and 1855 narratives, that masters often sell children that remind them—and their wives—of their own philandering.

woman names the father of her children and makes that naming important indeed.

Incidents articulates the multiple codes of silence and self-preservation demanded of Black women both North and South. In the first few moments after her arrival, she confides in her first host, a Black minister she "would not deceive" (*InL*, 160 [135]); he responds by warning: "Don't answer everybody so openly. It might give some heartless people a pretext for treating you with contempt" (*InL*, 160 [135]). His words "made an indelible impression upon me" (*InL*, 161 [135]), an impression arguably transferred indelibly onto *Incidents*. Jacobs's own letters to Amy Post express her perception that Southern *de facto* laws of silence rule Northern dictums of disclosure. She writes, "I had determined to let others think as they pleased but my lips should be sealed and no one had a right to question me for this reason when I first came North I avoided the Antislavery people as much as possible because I felt that I could not be honest and tell the whole truth."[7] Those the minister calls "some heartless people," as Jacobs applies his admonition, are an expansive group. As Linda had learned in the South, those who can be trusted aren't easily emotionally and politically classifiable. Linda had been initiated into a slave's understanding of power's relation to trust upon the death of what Lydia Maria Child calls Linda's "kind, considerate friend." This friend, the mistress who teaches her to read and write, then willed Linda to her niece and so, effectively, to Dr. Flint.

Resisting the simple (sentimental) dichotomies of good and bad, Jacobs separates bodily threat, the fear of actual repossession, from the politics of trust and speech. She relocates the relationship of truth to silence to the realm of Northern power relations invoked by the stinging word "contempt." William Andrews's commentary on James Pennington transfers easily: "As a black autobiographer among suspicious whites, [Jacobs] was not morally obliged to deal truthfully with [her] audience if that meant putting [herself] in jeopardy. On such autobiographical occasions self-interest takes priority over truth by claiming it, appropriating it, to its own needs. In an ultimate sense . . . one could lie and still be true—to oneself. Under such conditions willed autobiographical concealments and/or deceptions might be the truest form of self-expression."[8] Jacobs replots received

7. In the same letter Jacobs writes, "I never would consent to give my past life to any one for I would not do it with out giving the whole truth." The tensions between the two statements, between self-protection and possession and layers of consent between an artful narrator and her "trusted" friend Post, and between Jacobs and an untrustworthy public, aptly demonstrate seemingly irreconcilable "warring forces of signification" and truth. Harriet Jacobs, *Incidents* (Yellin edition), 232.

8. In Andrews, *To Tell a Free Story*, 161 (my substitution); Andrews, here, doesn't apply his brilliant analysis of the male trickster narrator to Jacobs. Instead, his reading, too, suggests a transparent relation between Jacobs and her tale.

relations between slave truth and freedom. While in the South an enslaved woman's lips and tongue were muzzled; now North, she seals her lips, the double entendre only too evident, by her own accord.[9] However, this is no imitative adaptation of Northern Victorian mores, discursive or sexual.

By denying others free rein to question her, Jacobs empowers herself on her own terms. She envisions discursive property rights—the license and comfort that make it possible "to be free to *say* so" (*InL*, 174 [145])—as Pennington does, by appropriating them into her own protective economy. Thus she dismisses the legal (and extralegal) economies that bind her and her children to interpretations that grant their bodies to the Master and the master text: "I could not possibly regard myself as a piece of property," she writes. "I knew the law would decide that I was his property, and would probably give his daughter a claim to my children; but I regarded such laws as the regulations of robbers, who had no rights that I was bound to respect" (*InL*, 187 [155]). If, as legal theorist Patricia Williams argues, slavery is a structure that denies Black generative independence, then what Jacobs affirms, in her ironic rhetorical overturning of *Dred Scott* and in her strong claims to nondisclosure, is the generative independence in a discursive realm that is denied her by slavery in a biological one.[1]

Jacobs's symbolic relation to her narrator's trajectory of multivalent address stands in opposition to the seemingly transparent regained candor of most male narrators. As Andrews argues, confessing to morally compromising behavior in slavery "is a traditional rhetorical strategy of antebellum Black autobiography." He suggests that "each [author] takes steps to preserve his bond with the reader by repudiating that behavior and requesting the reader's sympathy for the slave in his tragic moral dilemma. Still, he seems to savor the sufficiency of his invention, performance and manipulation."[2] Although Jacobs disavows the sexual past of slavery, she "clearly delights" in the letter-writing maneuvers enacted from her grandmother's garret, and she does so without ever disowning these activities.[3] Though Andrews's analysis does apply to Jacobs, male authors distance themselves from their trickster past by insisting that it is

9. Jacobs's silence on any personal sexual interest or involvement echoes her construction of her grandmother as a nonsexual being. Though in her twenties when Jacobs escapes to the North, not only does this narrative not end "in the usual way with marriage," never does she even intimate another romantic "lover" after her free suitor moves from Edenton.

1. Patricia Williams, *Alchemy of Race and Rights*, 163. In the infamous 1857 Dred Scott Supreme Court decision, Justice Taney, writing for the majority, declared that African Americans were not sovereign citizens of the United States and had no rights that whites were bound to respect. *Scott v. Sandford*.

2. Andrews, *To Tell a Free Story*, 165–66.

3. Valerie Smith, "'Loopholes of Retreat,'" 215.

the circumstances of slavery that engendered their behavior; their geographical and behavioral change is often symbolized by a change in name itself.[4] That the audience knows their new names—William Wells Brown, Frederick Douglass—signifies that they can gauge Black narrators' "interior subjectivity unmediated by the distance of manipulative representation": "My character, yes, was forced to be duplicitous; but me, your narrator, transformed by freedom, you can trust," they seem to say; "now that I own myself, my name, I share them freely with you."[5] Whereas the men transform from trickster to true-name-trusted author, the narrator of *Incidents* rejects the implied transformation and textual transparency promised in the narrative resolution by the slave narrative paradigm: she becomes the fictive character, Linda Brent.[6]

Flint, Sands, and Willis: South to North, Daddies to Dandies

By collapsing the rhetorical opposition between North and South, Jacobs further complicates her narrator's status as "truthsayer."[7] She envisions her Northern situation as analogous to her life in the South, a geographical coordinate on a racist vector that denies any radical rupture. Indeed, *Incidents* rarely indulges—or lets readers be indulged—in a vision of the North without exposing Northern hypocrisy. Her icy description of her first sunrise "on free soil, for such I *then* believed it to be" (*InL*, 158 [133]), crystallizes her sustained condemnation. Nor is this a critique of the North as a geographical concept, as if it were not peopled with actors who are actively complicit in doing the dirty work of slavery's interests. Yankees, she writes, "consent to do the violent work for [Southern 'gentlemen'] such as ferocious bloodhounds and the despised negro-hunters are employed to do at home" (*InL*, 44 [41]). Comparing Yankees to dogs and poor white trash, her stinging rebukes are hard to ignore.

The Northern space where Jacobs composes the manuscript that will become *Incidents* recalls her Southern confinement in her grandmother's garret. She writes in both places secretly and does not allow her new mistress, Cornelia Willis, the "beloved" second Mrs. Bruce,

4. Andrews develops this fully in *To Tell A Free Story*, 148.
5. For a full discussion, ibid., chap. 4.
6. As Yellin points out in her memoir to Jacobs's publishers and the New England anti-slavery circle active in helping her publish *Incidents*, Jacobs's identity was never in question. By 1862 she had publicly merged her public persona and her private one, publishing an article in *The Liberator* by "Mrs. Jacobs, the author of 'LINDA.'" Yellin, *Harriet Jacobs: A Life*, 161.
7. The Black or Oriental woman as soothsayer has a vivid iconographic history. Examples include Whoopi Goldberg's Oscar-winning portrayal of a medium in *Ghost*. She was only the second Black woman to earn this honor. Black women are featured as oracles, truthsayers, or soothsayers again in *The Matrix*, where Gloria Foster and Mary Alice are all-wise, all-knowing and, in one instance, comfortably ensconced in a humble kitchen making cookies.

entry to her private—soon to be public—world. "Mrs. Willis don't even know from my lips that I am writing a book . . . Let no one see it" (*InL*, 237–38), she comments as she sends a transcript to her friend Amy Post, whose name, in biting contrast to the Willises', appears unchanged in the narrative. Indeed, the description of her physical space at the Willises' echoes her Southern "loophole of retreat": "I must stop for I am in the only spot where I can have a light—and the mosquitoes have taken possession of me" (*InL*, 243), she writes to Post as if she were in Edenton near her gimlet-made garret light "tormented by hundreds of little red insects fine as needle's point that pierced through my skin" (*InL*, 115 [201]).

Jacobs finds herself working in the eighteen-room manor of Nathaniel Parker Willis, a famous newspaper editor less concerned with social welfare than with social status. Willis's biographer describes the manner in which the family lived: "From early spring till after Christmas the family at Idlewild kept open house, almost always having company staying with them. . . . The place had become celebrated through Willis's descriptions of it in 'Home Journal.'" The editor's habit, his biographer notes, was "to breakfast in his own room and write till noon. Sometimes he would take a stroll . . . before dinner. After dinner he would write letters or do scissors work before the afternoon ride. The evening was spent with his guests, or, if the family were alone, he would write again and come down to a nine o'clock dinner."[8] Contrast this with Jacobs's 1854 description of Idlewild. "My friends . . . were here . . . and saw from my daily duties that it was hard for me to find much time to write as yet I have not written a single page by daylight" (*InL*, 237–38 [198]).[9] When Jacobs asks Post to mention in her letter to accompany *Incidents* that "I lived at service all the while that I was striving to get the Book out. . . . [as] I would [not] like to have people think that I was living an *Idle* life—and had got this book out merely to make money" (*InL*, 242 [200], emphasis mine), her characteristic irony communicates her analysis of who, actually, is out to merely make money while laying bare who is most likely to be suspected of trying to profit from their literary production. Capitalizing "Idle" and so linking her life "at service" to Nathaniel Parker Willis's idle and indulgent time at Idlewild, Jacobs underscores the racial, class and gender privileges at work as she labors to write and publish her own book.

8. Henry Beers, *American Men of Letters*, 330.
9. Jacobs writes that she told Mrs. Willis "in the Autumn that I would give her Louisa's services through the winter if she would allow me my winter evenings to myself but with the care of the little baby and the big Babies and at the household calls I have had but a little time to think or write." Harriet Jacobs, *Incidents* (Yellin edition), 237–38. At this point, the Willises had four children (the last child to survive was born in 1857), to whom Jacobs was nurse.

By writing secretly, Jacobs matches her cunning against a new but familiar type: in Willis, the licentious Southern plantation owner is replaced by the Northern confidence man, a "modern industrial version of the trickster."[1] As historian Karen Halttunen explains it, the mid-century confidence man was a person of few values, conscious of his less-than-qualifying social beginnings, who dupes society by his attire, charm, and newly made money to marry into status and leisure. In his day, Willis was often criticized for his dandyism in dress; he attempted to "exemplify himself as the epitome of the fashionable gentleman."[2] While he wrote in the best of style and situations, other authors in his life—his sister Sara Payson Willis Parton (or "Fanny Fern") and nurse Harriet Jacobs—published under pseudonyms and didn't share his fortuitous circumstances. Indeed, in *Ruth Hall* (1854), his sister suggests that he marries Cornelia Grinnell, niece and adopted daughter of the wealthy Honorable Joseph Grinnell, for money. Indeed, it was with her inheritance that they built Idlewild on the Hudson.[3] His first wife, Mary Stace Willis of England, was also well off; her father provided his daughter and son-in-law with £300 per annum—about half of their yearly income.

Willis supported a select group of women journalists, but could not be trusted by those too close to home. Like his sister, Jacobs received no encouragement from Willis. He "is too proslavery," she confides to Amy Post; "he would tell me that it was very wrong [to write a book] and that I was trying to do harm or perhaps he was sorry for me to undertake it while I was in his family" (*InL*, 232). Jacobs keeps her job by playing her own trickster—the faithful servant—and plays her role well enough to convince Willis's most thorough biographer that her "attachment to the interests of the family during the whole period of her service was a beautiful instance of the fidelity and affection which sometimes, but not often, distinguish the relation of master and servant."[4] Jacobs had little confidence in the man; though her "master" and Mrs. Willis, unsolicited, secured her official freedom, she composed her narrative and published articles in numerous journals without their knowledge or help.

Incidents' closing passage disrupts the Northern economy of genteel servitude invoked by both Willis's biographer's and Jacobs's own sentimental language: "I still long for a hearthstone of my own,

1. Haltunnen, *Confidence Men and Painted Women*, 24.
2. Auser, *Nathaniel P. Willis*, 24. His treatment of his destitute sister, who later became known as the writer Fanny Fern, reveals this. She fictionalizes her scathing critique of her brother in the novel *Ruth Hall* (1854). Jacobs's belief that Willis was pro-slavery, or at least in no way anti-slavery, is confirmed by the stated policy of his paper, the *Home Journal*: "It is entirely neutral in politics, free from all sectionalism and sectarianism." Not until after the South seceded did he take a public stance. Ibid., 128.
3. Beers, *American Men of Letters*, 337.
4. Ibid., 285.

however humble. I wish it for my children's sake far more than for my own. But God so orders circumstances as to keep me with my friend Mrs. Bruce. Love, duty, gratitude, also bind me to her side. It is a privilege to serve her who pities my oppressed people, and who has bestowed the inestimable boon of freedom on me and my children" (*InL, 201* [167]). This passage cloaks domestic desire with the justification of motherhood that is then quickly reduced to the "privileges" of service. Yet the language almost seethes, as the careful usage of "bind me to her side" recalls Luke's being "chained to the bedside" of his abusive owner. Linda's barely checked anger at being "*sold* at last" (*InL*, 200 [165]) to the Bruces also serves as a referent that disrupts a closing passage dripping not only with sentimentality but also with an irony that challenges the feminine "fidelity and affection" that characterizes a woman's place within domestic fiction. Jacobs's simultextually appreciative and angry prose both expresses and challenges the costs of a system in which parties suppress the "indelicate" issue, as it were, of division of labor and property exchange.[5]

* * *

What marks this text, I would maintain, is not the central question "Is Linda, or until when is Linda, pure?" Rather, it is how ingeniously *Incidents* challenges the supposed transparency of sentimental fiction and also appeals to and critiques its multiple readerships. Ultimately, this text's overlaid voicings illustrate and complicate Sidonie Smith's contention that a woman narrator "may even create several, sometimes competing stories about versions of herself as her subjectivity is displaced by one or multiple representations."[6] Like the other writings I examine in *Activist Sentiments, Incidents* is characterized by a narrative plentitude that reaches various audiences. Thus, although I contend that reconsidering Jacobs's simultextual representation calls for supplementing the conventional understanding of her plot to add that Norcom might well have "succeeded," in no way do I wish to be understood to ascribe to a binary characterization that she is either telling the truth, the whole truth—or that she is lying; this would beg all the questions I mean to raise here. My work does not attempt to substitute one reading (Linda's escape from Flint's sexual intentions) with another (that Flint really raped her); I resist accepting, or offering, any

5. Linda's "benefactress" says to her when she returns home free: "You wrote to me as if you thought you were going to be transferred from one owner to another. But I did not buy you for your services. I should have done just the same, if you had been going to sail for California tomorrow. I should, at least, have the satisfaction of knowing that you left me a free woman." Harriet Jacobs, *Incidents* (Yellin edition), 200 [166]. Without impugning Cornelia Willis's motives, their exchange can be read to signal that Willis's sincere effusion works to silence Jacobs's feelings of outrage at the broader issues of commodity exchange and power relations.
6. Sidonie Smith, *Poetics of Women's Autobiography*, 46.

critical exegesis as a definitive one. Instead, I mean to call into question the politics of transparency that often have led critics to accept the narrative's principal script—Linda's sexual "triumph"—and that act to smooth away and quiet down the very tumultuous speech to which her contemporary readers might well give ear.

Works Cited

Andrews, William L. *To Tell A Free Story: The First Century of Afro-American Autobiography, 1760–1865*. Urbana: University of Illinois Press, 1986.

Auerbach, Nina. *Communities of Women: An Idea in Fiction*. Cambridge: Harvard University Press, 1978.

Auser, Cortland. *Nathaniel P. Willis*. New York: Twayne, 1969.

Baker, Houston A. Jr. *Blues, Ideology, and Afro-American Literature: A Vernacular Theory*. Chicago: University of Chicago Press, 1984.

Bardaglio, Peter W. *Reconstructing the Household: Families, Sex and the Law in the Nineteenth-Century South*. Chapel Hill: University of North Carolina Press, 1995.

Beers, Henry. *American Men of Letters: N.P. Willis*. New York: Houghton Mifflin, 1885.

Blassingame, John. *The Slave Community: Plantation Life in the Antebellum South*. New York: Oxford University Press, 1979.

Carby, Hazel V. *Reconstructing Womanhood: The Emergence of the Afro-American Woman Novelist*. New York: Oxford University Press, 1987.

Chinn, Sarah E. *Technology and the Logic of American Racism: A Cultural History of the Body as Evidence*. London: Continuum, 2000.

Davis, Angela. "The Legacy of Slavery: Standards for a New Womanhood." In Angela Davis, *Women, Race, and Class*, 3–29.

———. "Rape, Racism and the Myth of the Black Rapist." In Angela Davis, *Women, Race, and Class*, 172–201.

Douglass, Frederick. *Narrative of the Life of Frederick Douglass, An American Slave, Written by Himself*. Edited by Houston A. Baker Jr. New York: Penguin Books, 1982.

Foreman, P. Gabrielle. "The Spoken and the Silenced in *Incidents in the Life of a Slave Girl* and *Our Nig*." *Callaloo* 13, no. 2 (Spring 1990): 313–24.

Foster, Frances Smith. "'In Respect to Females . . .': Differences in the Portrayals of Women by Male and Female Narrators." *Black American Literature Forum* 15 (Summer 1981): 66–70.

———. "Resisting Incidents." In Garfield and Zafar, eds., *Harriet Jacobs and "Incidents in the Life of a Slave Girl,"* 57–75.

Foucault, Michel. *The History of Sexuality, Vol. 1.* New York: Vintage, 1980.

Fox-Genovese, Elizabeth. *Within the Plantation Household: Black and White Women of the Old South.* Chapel Hill: University of North Carolina Press, 1988.

Garfield, Deborah M. "Earwitness: Female Abolitionism, Sexuality, and *Incidents in the Life of a Slave Girl.*" In Garfield and Zafar, eds., *Harriet Jacobs and "Incidents in the Life of a Slave Girl,"* 100–130.

Gilman, Sander L. "Black Bodies, White Bodies: Toward an Iconography of Female Sexuality in Late Nineteenth Century Art, Medicine, and Literature." *Critical Inquiry* 12 (Autumn 1985): 204–42.

Gunning, Sandra. "Reading and Redemption in *Incidents in the Life of a Slave Girl.*" In Garfield and Zafar, eds., *Harriet Jacobs and "Incidents in the Life of a Slave Girl."* 131–55.

Halttunen, Karen. *Confidence Men and Painted Women: A Study of Middle-Class Culture in America, 1830–1870.* New Haven, Conn.: Yale University Press, 1982.

Jacobs, Harriet. *Incidents in the Life of a Slave Girl.* 1861. Reprint, edited by Jean Fagan Yellin. Cambridge: Harvard University Press, 1987, 2000.

Lane, Lunsford. *The Narrative of Lunsford Lane.* Boston: J.G. Torrey, Printer, 1842. Documenting the American South, available at http://docsouth.unc.edu/neh/lanelunsford/menu.html (accessed November 17, 2008).

McLaurin, Melton A. *Celia, A Slave.* Athens: University of Georgia Press, 1991.

Noble, Marianne. *The Masochistic Pleasure of Sentimental Literature New York Age.* Princeton: Princeton University Press, 2000.

Northup, Solomon. *Solomon Northup, Twelve Years a Slave.* Baton Rouge: Louisiana State University Press, 1968.

Olney, James. *Autobiography: Essays Theoretical and Critical.* Princeton: Princeton University Press, 1980.

Sánchez-Eppler, Karen. *Touching Liberty: Abolition, Feminism, and the Politics of the Body.* Berkeley: University of California Press, 1993.

Sekora, John. "Black Message/White Envelope: Genre, Authenticity, and Authority in Antebellum Slave Narrative." *Callaloo* 10 (Summer 1987): 482–515.

Smith, Shawn Michelle. *American Archives: Gender, Race, and Class in Visual Culture.* Princeton: Princeton University Press, 1999.

Smith, Sidonie. *The Poetics of Women's Autobiography: Marginality and the Fiction of Self-Representation.* Bloomington: Indiana University Press, 1987.

Smith, Valerie. "'Loopholes of Retreat': Architecture and Ideology in Harriet Jacobs' *Incidents in the Life of a Slave Girl.*" In Gates, ed., *Reading Black, Reading Feminist*, 212–26.

———. *Self-Discovery and Authority in Afro-American Narrative.* Cambridge: Harvard University Press, 1987.

Smith-Rosenberg, Carroll. *Disorderly Conduct: Visions of Gender in Victorian America.* New York: Oxford University Press, 1985.

Spillers, Hortense. "Mama's Baby, Papa's Maybe: An American Grammar Book." *Diacritics* 17, no. 2 (Summer 1987): 65–81.

Stepto, Robert B. "Distrust of the Reader in Afro-American Narratives." In Sacvan Bercovitch, ed., *Reconstructing American Literary History*, 300–322. Cambridge: Harvard University Press, 1986.

Tushnet, Mark. *The American Law of Slavery, 1810–1860: Considerations of Humanity and Interest.* Princeton: Princeton University Press, 1981.

Washington, Mary Helen, ed. *Invented Lives: Narratives of Black Women.* New York: Doubleday, 1987.

Williams, Patricia. *The Alchemy of Race and Rights.* Cambridge: Harvard University Press, 1991.

Yellin, Jean Fagan. *Harriet Jacobs: A Life.* New York: Civitas Books, 2004.

———. "Introduction." In Harriet Jacobs, *Incidents in the Life of a Slave Girl.* Cambridge: Harvard University Press, 2000.

———. "Text and Contexts of Harriet Jacobs' *Incidents in the Life of a Slave Girl: Written by Herself.*" In Charles T. Davis and Henry Louis Gates Jr., ed., *The Slave's Narrative*, 262–82. New York: Oxford University Press, 1985.

KATJA KANZLER

From "To Tell the Kitchen Version": Architectural Figurations of Race and Gender in Harriet Jacobs's *Incidents in the Life of a Slave Girl*†

The scholarship on 19th-century American women's literature and culture has greatly benefited from understanding domesticity as a discursive operation. From Barbara Welter's seminal work on the 'cult of domesticity' onward, historians and literary critics have described and critiqued what they variously called the ideology,

† From "'To Tell the Kitchen Version': Architectural Figurations of Race and Gender in Harriet Jacobs's *Incidents in the Life of a Slave Girl* and Harriet Wilson's *Our Nig*," *Gender Forum* 15 (2006): 1, 3–5, 8–9. Reprinted by permission of *Gender Forum* and the author. Page numbers in brackets refer to this Norton Critical Edition.

virtues, practice, or cult of domesticity. The discourses these terms reference, however, also have a spatial dimension, which surfaces most insistently in the notion of 'separate spheres' that continues to shape scholarship on antebellum gendered culture(s). For at least two decades, literary and historical scholarship alike has struggled to come to terms with the complex operations of the separate spheres paradigm in antebellum culture, as well as its equally complex reverberations in the scholarship.[1]

In the following, I propose to engage the spatial dimension of antebellum domesticity by exploring architectural figurations * * * to challenge prevailing assumption about the antebellum American home as a culturally coherent and cohesive space that finds its conflicts with the world outside rather than within its own. Quite to the contrary, the structures of domestic architecture allow writers to engage complex systems of social ordering, the spatial signification and enforcement of as well as the resistance against socio-cultural hierarchies. In the context of thus interrogating architecture as a system of cultural signification, I want to focus on the kitchen as the room that most centrally hosts narratives of gender and racial difference. Arguably the epicenter of domestic operations, the kitchen occupies a remarkably marginal space in most narratives of the antebellum home: It commonly figures as the domain of those members of the household who occupied the most inferior positions within the domestic hierarchy—employed, indentured, or enslaved 'servants'—while the 'work' of the mistress of the house unfolded in the parlor. The kitchen thus presents itself as antebellum domesticity's spatial unconscious, the largely concealed flip-side of discourses of bourgeois femininity.

* * *

* * * If we pursue housekeeping as a productive metaphor of selfhood and authorship, there is no way around the kitchen as the gravitational center of domestic work. Extending on Virginia Woolf's famous call for 'a room of one's own,' I will suggest that women have always had a room of their own—the kitchen—and that they did write there. Of course, the conditions for authorship the kitchen offered fall far short of the room Woolf envisioned, but they still circumscribe a valuable feminine literary tradition. In addition, the kitchen presents itself not only as a gendered space—it also bears connotations of class and, certainly in the American South, of race. More than any other room, the kitchen brings the mistress of the house together with (varying numbers of) servants or 'help.' The

1. Cf., for example, the various essays anthologized in Elbert and in Davidson and Hatcher.

work each of them performs in the kitchen as well as the tracks on which each may (or may not) move through the rest of the house are carefully scripted, and these scripts host complex negotiations of gender, class, and race. The kitchen seems to represent a thoroughly paradoxical space as it accommodates both some of the most central domestic operations and the most peripheral members of the household.

Writing the House of Slavery

Turning more specifically to houses built and operated on the basis of slave labor adds another dimension to the web of cultural differences negotiated in writings of the antebellum American home. As scholars working with a wide range of cultural artifacts have emphasized, slavery operates on the basis of a spatial logic. Historian Stephanie Camp notes, "[a]t the heart of the process of enslavement was a geographical impulse to locate bondpeople in plantation space [. . .]. Slaveholders strove to create controlled and controlling landscapes that would determine the uses to which enslaved people put their bodies" (533).[2] This spatial logic of domination provoked equally spatial strategies of accommodation and resistance, which Camp terms "rival geographies" (533). In a similar vein, John Michael Vlach maintains in his study of plantation architecture that "[s]laveowners set up the contexts of servitude, but they did not control those contexts absolutely" (1). Slaves found myriad of ways to appropriate the spaces to which slavery confined them.

Given the material and cultural import of spatial formations for slaveowners as well as for slaves, the architecture[3] of slaveholding properties is charged with particular significance. Their structures and designs organize the complex power relations in the slaveholding household, display the family's social standing, and give material expression to the virtues and values according to which the lady of the house executes her role as mother and wife. In performing such multifaceted cultural work, Southern dwellings participate in proliferating debates about domestic architecture throughout the United States. As Lori Merish elaborates in her study of gender and

2. As Vlach points out, plantations make for only a fraction of slavery's workplaces (7). In the popular imagination, however, especially that vented in an abolitionist context, plantation slavery has become established as the quintessential form of bondage (Sánchez-Eppler 260).
3. Camp and Vlach sometimes use the terms architecture, landscape and geography interchangeably. When I speak of (literary) architecture, I wish to denote (the literary representation of) built structures along with the uses that map them. While my focus rests on homes, sometimes other 'architectured' spaces need to be considered alongside them, such as gardens or outbuildings. Especially Southern plantations, Vlach reminds us, need to be understood as ensembles of 'Big House,' slave quarters, and workspaces (1–3).

material culture, the formation of the discourse of feminine domesticity in the antebellum years entailed a growing concern about the material structures in which this ideal of domesticity was to unfold. Thanks to the value evolving notions of 'true womanhood' placed on the domestic, architectural choices were invested with increasing cultural and 'civilizational' significance.

Accordingly, the structures and uses of domestic architecture appear uniquely qualified for spelling out not only the regional idiosyncrasies of Southern living but also the particularities of slavery. They help define slavery as a 'feminine' concern, a topic that women authors, from their supposedly domestic perspective, would be particularly authorized to address. While most texts spatially conflate the racism represented by the institution of slavery with the South, I wish to include in my discussion * * * part of a broader literary tradition in which authors writing from a variety of perspectives—from abolitionist to pro-slavery—have focused on the architectural formations of the 'house of slavery' to flesh out the 'peculiar institution.'[4] Domestic structures allow writers to stage both the differences and the similarities of slaveholding and non-slaveholding households: They may mark the different—but comparable—organization of workspaces and spaces of residence, stage encounters between slaves and slaveholders, and outline the specific arrangements of domestic labor. If, as many scholars have noted, 'family' figures as the primary touchstone for representations of slavery (again, in texts indebted to a variety of politics), domestic spaces present themselves as the sites where familial relations gain material substance so as to lend themselves to representation. In all constellations, a focus on domestic architecture offers readers outside the South moments of recognition that other aspects of the plantation economy might not. Thus, architecture provides a perceptual angle through which slavery becomes 'readable.'

In exploring domestic architecture as a system of signification, I want to zoom in on the kitchen as the one room where, in text after text, the operations of slavery become most readily intelligible. It is precisely the fact that the kitchen connotes a distinctly feminine labor—and female laborers—that makes it useful for dramatizing the exploitative and abusive nature of slavery. The kitchen unfolds its signifying potential through its strategic use as a setting as well as its architectural contextualization within the house as a whole. From John Michael Vlach's material perspective, the kitchen occupies a curious position on Southern plantations as part, yet not quite part of the 'Big House': Those Southern home owners who

4. Harriet Beecher Stowe's *Uncle Tom's Cabin,* to which I return throughout my argument, may serve as the most widely known representative of this tradition, and so do the many texts written in response to Stowe's novel.

could afford it would relegate the kitchen to a separate building somewhere between the master's house and the plantation's work-spaces and slave-quarters. While pragmatic considerations certainly played a role here, separating the kitchen from the living-space of the slaveowner's family also codified hierarchical relationships "between those who served and those who were served" (Vlach 43). At the same time, cooking of course remained a key domestic operation, resonating with the cultural and affective significance discourses of domestic femininity invest it with. Finally, detaching the kitchen into a separate building diminished the influence of the lady of the house (as well as the rest of her family) over that room, increasingly ceding it to the slaves who work there.

The writings of Andrew Jackson Downing—antebellum America's most influential architect—further help appreciate the cultural significance of the Southern kitchen. As William Gleason notes, architectural guide books of the period, and Downing's among them, remain conspicuously silent about slavery (154). Downing's *The Architecture of Country Houses*, however, offers one telling exception: In elaborating one of his regional designs, "A Small Country-House for the Southern States," Downing identifies two features that distinguish Southern from other modes of architecture—the kitchen and the veranda. In defining their distinctiveness, he needs to make reference to the particular social structures generated by slavery: "A peculiar feature in all Southern country houses is the position of the kitchen—which does not form part of the dwelling, but stands detached at a distance of 20, 30, or more yards. This kitchen contains servants' bed-rooms on its second floor [. . .]" (313). Throughout his discussion of this design, Downing returns to the "detached kitchen" as the one architectural principle that gives spatial expression to the racial segregation underwriting the slaveholding household.[5] Downing thus acknowledges the ways in which domestic architecture reflects the social hierarchies of slavery, and he singles out the Southern kitchen as its most potent signifier.

Antebellum literary conventions offer a rich and varied language to write the houses of slavery. Authors navigate this terrain in often eclectic ways, utilizing and combining conventions of domestic, sentimental, and Gothic fiction along with those of autobiographical and advice writing. In the process, they flesh out an amazing array of literary homes, sometimes taking the reader on grand tours, prying open the last door and directing our attention to the minutest

5. Gleason offers an intriguing reading of the human figures featured in Downing's sketches of the design, which, he argues, pinpoint Downing's ambivalence about representing the "ostensibly unseen labors of the southern slave" (157).

detail, sometimes tightly controlling and delimiting our access to them. Next to the specificities of such spatial formations, the culturalization of domestic architecture the texts work on finds its final context in the act of writing the texts represent—in varying ways, they explore the interplay between writing a house and owning a house, between domestic labor and authorship.

Incidents in the Life of a Slave Girl

The kitchen figures as the central setting in many African American writings of the houses of slavery. Slave narratives, irrespective of whether they detail female or male experiences of slavery, typically set many of their plantation scenes in the kitchen of the 'Big House.' In Frederick Douglass' most canonized narrative, the kitchen accommodates scenes that flesh out the exploitation of slave labor, the violent abuse of slaves, and the dynamics of the slave community that regularly assembles in that room. Harriet Jacobs' *Incidents in the Life of a Slave Girl* certainly participates in this representational practice. At the same time, however, her protagonist's very different—and, as several critics maintain, highly gendered[6]—strategies of escape lend another twist to the architectural figurations in her narrative.

Jacobs' narrative takes its readers through several homes, located in the South as well as in the North, owned by slaveholding as well as non-slaveholding whites, including even one black-owned property. Throughout, the text picks up on the way in which contemporary domestic discourses picture the home as a safe haven, arguing that this promise fails to materialize for African Americans. In a key scene, the house of Linda's black grandmother—a free woman—is easily violated by white raiders as they search for runaway slaves. Even more pronouncedly in the narrative's descriptions of the house of Linda's oppression, the Flints' mansion, the privacy typically associated with 'home' assumes a meaning radically different from that in dominant (white) narratives of the time: The relative publicity of the Flint household, where family and slaves are constantly present, affords Linda some degree of protection. She panics when Dr. Flint announces his plans to build for her a cottage of her own because the privacy of this space would place her entirely at his mercy.

These two episodes involving the Flints' and the grandmother's houses outline a perversion of the public vs. private binarism central

6. Typically, the 'feminine' quality of Jacobs' narrative is located in the strategies of escape it narrates (hiding inside domestic settings rather than fleeing, geared toward liberating her children rather than just herself) and in the generic conventions it employs (sentimental fiction). Cf. Morgan and Gray.

for antebellum culture. For the slave narrator, the connotations of public and private have been reversed: While publicity signifies (albeit limited) protection, privacy signals vulnerability and exposure. Throughout its elaboration of privacy thus perverted, the text aligns the question of African Americans' control over their dwellings with that of control over their bodies—the plot most immediately thrives on Linda's efforts to protect her own sexual integrity. Ownership—expansively defined to encompass economic as well as semiotic control over one's surroundings, possessions, and self—figures as the text's central language for charting the evils of slavery.

Another moment of critique presents itself in the narrative's depiction of the Flint household, where the kitchen plays an important role in fleshing out the insidiousness and perversity of slavery. In thus using the kitchen, the text extends on conventions established in Frederick Douglass' foundational slave narrative which, though narrated from the perspective of a male slave, employs female characters to illustrate the abusive nature of slavery. In a key scene, the young narrator of Douglass' text witnesses the whipping of one of his aunts. He frames this scene—which, symptomatically, takes place in the kitchen—as his first initiation into slavery, "the blood-stained gate, the entrance to the hell of the slavery, through which I was about to pass" (7). Along similar lines, Jacobs' narrator singles out the family's cook as a paradigmatic figure of victimization, subject to constant harassment. Her work in the kitchen regularly exposes her to the whims of her master and mistress. Their preferred mode of disciplining the house-slaves proves particularly vicious:

> If dinner was not served at the exact time on that particular Sunday, [Mrs. Flint] would station herself in the kitchen, and wait till it was dished, and then spit in all the kettles and pans that had been used for cooking. She did this to prevent the cook and her children from eking out their meagre fare with the remains of the gravy and other scrapings [. . .]. The cook never sent a dinner to [Dr. Flint's] table without fear and trembling; for if there happened to be a dish not to his liking, he would either order her to be whipped, or compel her to eat every mouthful of it in his presence. The poor, hungry creature might not have objected to eating it; but she did object to having her master cram it down her throat till she choked. (22) [15]

Alternating between keeping their slaves hungry and force-feeding them, the Flints employ food as an instrument of punishment, a practice whose evilness contemporary discourses would highlight. As virtually the entire South depends on black labor for their sustenance—from mother's milk to gourmet cooking—the Flints' regime of punishment turns a key service the slaves render their masters against them. Where in antebellum writings of the ideal home the preparation of food figures as a labor of love, as material expression of a mother's love of her family, strengthening family ties,[7] it here becomes a service that is forced, occasioning the diners' wrath and abuse rather than their love and gratitude. Food prepared and served, withheld and force-fed this way fails to nourish and sustain; it rather violates and perverts the sacramental potential of food.

Turning our attention to the various homes of *Incidents*, we are presented with almost labyrinthine structures which feature a wealth of secret spaces that help the narrator in her eventual escape. Both the elaborate mansion of some unnamed (slaveholding) benefactress and the humble cottage of Linda's grandmother provide secret rooms that shelter the narrator from her persecutors. Linda finds one of her most stunning hiding-places in the above mentioned mansion: After Dr. Flint pretends to know of Linda's whereabouts, the lady's cook—Betty—removes Linda from the attic, where she had been hiding, to the kitchen, where she conceals her underneath the floor-panels. There, the narrator not only passes one day perfectly protected, she also witnesses several conversations in which Betty involves whoever enters her kitchen, all of which testify that her whereabouts are entirely unknown in the neighborhood.

Betty's kitchen presents itself as a highly polymorphous space: a room many people pass through—servants of this and of other households, merchants, occasionally the master and mistress of the house along with their guests—both a junction within the household and a contact zone to the world outside; yet in midst of this ostensible publicity, the kitchen offers Linda perfect seclusion. The room's secret spaces—its corners, recesses, and the space underneath the floor-paneling—are entirely under the control of the slave-cook. Betty's kitchen both extends on the depiction of kitchens in other antebellum texts—especially their porous boundary to the marketplace—and contrasts with pictures like that of the Flint-kitchen which position this room as the paradigmatic place of slavery's exploitation of (female) slave labor and highlight the vulnerability the slave suffers in the kitchen. Against this background, Betty's kitchen can be read as symbol of resistance, outlining ways in which slaves appropriate the spaces slavery assigns them. There is an unmistakable trickster-quality to Linda's hide-out in Betty's kitchen—it is not only about hiding from but also about eavesdropping on the people who hunt after her, especially the detested Dr. Flint, and hearing about (and rejoicing in) the wrong tracks they are following.

7. Note, for instance, the sacramental mis-en-scène of the meal Rachel Halliday serves in *Uncle Tom's Cabin*.

The episode in Betty's kitchen focalizes the figure of the eavesdropping slave that recurs throughout writings of slavery,[8] which, in turn, draws attention to the pervasive association of liminal domestic spaces with resistance. Precisely because slavery alters the meanings private and public spaces bear for the slave, her resistance needs to unfold in the in-between, in spaces too small or too slippery to control (in material as well as in epistemic terms) for slavery to fully colonize. Jacobs' narrative here invites a postcolonial reading: Homi Bhabha's concept of liminal domestic spaces helps appreciate the architectural dynamics of Jacobs' houses of slavery. The kitchen presents itself there as a place of both oppression and resistance, as representative of the in-between spaces (and of its protagonist, the eavesdropping slave) at once created by and subverting slavery.

Overall, the dwellings in *Incidents in the Life of a Slave Girl* are far from the readily legible structures in that most successful novel about slavery, Stowe's *Uncle Tom's Cabin*. The text shows no ambition to flesh out any of these buildings in detail. Instead, the narrator's attention rests with individual rooms, that are invariably off the tracks the white inhabitants take through their houses. The text's glimpses of kitchens and attics never connect to pictures of entire houses. In contrast to the narrative voice in Stowe's novel, Jacobs' narrator does not seem to feel entitled to owning the houses she chooses as her setting. She rather takes narrative possession of those rooms literary conventions would picture in the Gothic mode—rooms that are neither fully ownable nor knowable. This narrative stance further adds to the narrator/protagonist's framing within a subaltern subjectivity. Next to its appropriation of sentimental conventions, the text uses architectural conventions as a touchstone to both connect with its readers and to flesh out its indictment of slavery.

* * *

To conclude, architectural figurations allow [characterization] and critique [of] the oppressions of slavery. Unfolding slavery in domestic settings not only enables the texts to highlight a specifically feminine experience, it also offers them a cultural register they could expect to resonate with their audience, which chiefly consisted of white middle-class women. The writings of the kitchen on which I specifically focused pinpoint the conflicting negotiation of victimization and resistance the texts engage in, along with the ambivalences of authorial self-fashioning that emerge out of it.

8. Texts as different as Stowe's *Uncle Tom's Cabin* and Hannah Crafts' *The Bondwoman's Narrative* feature eavesdropping scenes at key moments in their plots.

Works Cited

Bhabha, Homi K. "Introduction: Locations of Culture." *The Location of Culture*. London: Routledge, 1994. 1–18.

Camp, Stephanie M.H. "The Pleasures of Resistance: Enslaved Women and Body Politics in the Plantation South, 1830–1861." *Journal of Southern History* 68.3 (2002): 533–72.

Davidson, Cathy N. and Jessamyn Hatcher, eds. *No More Separate Spheres! A Next Wave American Studies Reader*. Durham: Duke UP, 2002.

Douglass, Frederick. *Narrative of the Life of Frederick Douglass, an American Slave; Written by Himself*. Boston: Anti-Slavery Office, 1845. Accessed via *Documenting the American South*. 1999. University of North Carolina Chapel Hill. 1 June 2006. http://docsouth.unc.edu/douglass/menu.html.

Downing, Andrew Jackson. 1850. *The Architecture of Country Houses*. Intro. J. Stewart Johnson. New York: Dover, 1969.

Elbert, Monika M., ed. *Separate Spheres No More: Gender Convergence in American Literature, 1830–1930*. Tuscaloosa: U of Alabama P, 2000.

Frank, Ellen Eve. *Literary Architecture: Essays Toward a Tradition*. Berkeley: U of California P, 1979.

Gleason, William. "'I Dwell Now in a Neat Little Cottage': Architecture, Race, and Desire in *The Bondwoman's Narrative*." *In Search of Hannah Crafts: Critical Essays on* The Bondwoman's Narrative. Ed. Henry Louis Gates, Jr., and Hollis Robbins. Cambridge: Basic Civitas, 2004. 145–74.

Jacobs, Harriet A. *Incidents in the Life of a Slave Girl; Written by Herself*. Ed. Lydia Maria Child. Boston: Published for the Author, 1861. Accessed via *Documenting the American South*. 2003. University of North Carolina Chapel Hill. 1 June 2006. http://docsouth.unc.edu/jacobs/menu.html.

Merish, Lori. *Sentimental Materialism: Gender, Commodity Culture, and Nineteenth-Century American Literature*. Durham: Duke UP, 2000.

Stowe, Harriet Beecher. *Uncle Tom's Cabin*. 1851–52. New York: Bantam, 1981.

Vlach, John Michael. *Back of the Big House: The Architecture of Plantation Slavery*. Chapel Hill: U of North Carolina P, 1993.

Welter, Barbara. "The Cult of True Womanhood: 1820–1860." *American Quarterly* 18.1 (1966): 151–74.

SAMANTHA M. SOMMERS

From Harriet Jacobs and the Recirculation of Print Culture†

* * *

In recent years scholars have energetically responded to calls from Frances Smith Foster and Leon Jackson for greater attention to book history in African American literary studies by demonstrating that we must consider typography (Dinius 55–57), read "histotextually" (Foreman, "*Christian*" 331; Foreman, *Activist* 6–7), remove the geographic limits of our archive (Gardner 11–15), and see the domination and resistance that inheres in the paratext (McCoy 156–57) as we study African American literature. Additionally, in Lara Langer Cohen and Jordan Alexander Stein's edited collection *Early African American Print Culture* (2012), critics reconsider theories of authorship, publicity, circulation, literacy, and reading in light of the racial, social, and economic dynamics at play in the production of early African American texts.

As the proliferation of its usage suggests, *print culture* is an expansive and expanding term that encompasses the technology of print (with all its requisite tools and materials), the literary and nonliterary products produced by this technology (books, newspapers, pamphlets, primers, posters, and broadsides), and the people involved at every stage of these processes (typesetters, editors, printers, writers, booksellers, readers, and newsboys). Yet African American print culture is not something limited to material processes and products—it also exists in the imaginative space of literature. This view of print culture manifests when printed documents are incorporated into the world of a narrative or kept at a distance through ekphrastic description. The decision to reprint or elide a text within a text directly affects a reader's proximity to the imagined world of a narrative, and through the presence or absence of such texts writers produce visual revelations and silences.[1] Acknowledging the presence of print culture within African American literature yields new sites

† From *MELUS: Multi-Ethnic Literature of the United States* 40.3 (Fall 2015): 136–49. Page references in brackets refer to this Norton Critical Edition.

1. My approach to studying the print culture represented in African American literature is indebted to Meredith L. McGill's extended historical study of the practice of reprinting in nineteenth-century America, Leah Price's investigation into the uses of books in Victorian literature, and Cohen's claims about the role of citation in African American textual production (164).

for investigating early African American writers' assertions of authority. Indeed, a broader interpretative field holds great potential for the study of autobiographical texts, where the act of composition continues to dominate our discussions of authorial agency and subject formation.[2] Focusing on the act of recirculation rather than autobiographical composition shifts our emphasis from linguistic declarations to an expanded set of gestures that can demonstrate subjecthood, including the aesthetic act of arranging materials.

Taking [Harriet] Jacobs's *Incidents in the Life of a Slave Girl* [1861] as a case study for this claim, attending to the recirculation and strategic elision of printed documents in the narrative affords us a new lens for registering Jacobs's transition from slavery to freedom—under slavery she is a subject of print; in freedom she becomes an author and arranger working in the medium. While examples of reprinted texts and rich descriptions of print materials proliferate in literature from many periods and specializations, the social and political stakes of this practice are heightened in the case of early African American literature given the dual role of print as a medium that helped to circulate early African American writing as it continued to facilitate the practices of slavery. By practices of slavery, I refer to the everyday transactions and events that helped perpetuate slavery as an institution. Slave auctions, sales, and the posting of runaway slave advertisements are all examples of such practices, and African American writers frequently recirculate documents that helped enable or attest to these practices in their writing.

In his study of eighteenth-century runaway slave advertisements, David Waldstreicher explains that while such texts were "[r]ealistic in intent, they [were] also rhetorical to the core." He further claims that these runaway ads were "in effect, [the] first slave narratives—the first published stories about slaves and their seizure of freedom" (247). This assertion that historical print culture can provide new perspectives on literary genres has been particularly generative for this essay, which pursues something akin to the inverse of this claim. With the recirculation of her own runaway slave advertisement, Jacobs shows us how the same printed text can at once register the terror of slavery and the temporal distance between a text's initial circulation in the world and its recirculation in narrative. *Incidents in the Life of a Slave Girl*, like *Clotel*, reminds us that print lent visual and material form to runaway slave advertisements, publicity for slave auctions, and legislation protecting slaveholders. Yet, for Jacobs and other ex-slave narrators, printed documents that evince their status as slaves signify differently through the act of recirculation

2. Teresa A. Goddu attests to and seeks to modify this critical tendency in "The Slave Narrative as Material Text" from *The Oxford Handbook to the African American Slave Narrative* (2014).

even when the textual medium remains the same.[3] The texts serve a dual function as documentary evidence for the peril and brutality of life under slavery and as an index of the writer's freedom.

While critics such as Valerie Smith, Hazel V. Carby, and William L. Andrews productively detail Jacobs's techniques for reappropriating narrative genres, critiquing "conventional standards of female behavior" (Carby 47) and articulating a black female subjectivity under the institution of slavery,[4] Jacobs additionally demonstrates an awareness of print's potential for strategic reappropriation within her narrative and as part of her escape. When we ground our reading of *Incidents in the Life of a Slave Girl* in Jacobs's recirculation of print, we see her as a critic keenly attuned to her vexing position as subject, author, and arranger of printed matter. This conception of Jacobs as a writer who demonstrates her status as a subject through a changed relationship to print challenges a conventional reading of *Incidents in the Life of a Slave Girl* as one example of the slave narrative genre that "represents the attempts of blacks to *write themselves into being*" (Davis and Gates xxiii). Jacobs's acts of recirculation subtend the claim that the act of autobiographical composition produces the subject. Her critical relationship to print, in slavery and in freedom, demonstrates an awareness that this is not solely a liberatory medium. Jacobs's treatment of print reminds us that media are medial—able to be put to a variety of uses, including liberation, although they are not inherently liberatory.[5] In my reading, Jacobs's acts of recirculation lay bare her efforts to transform printed texts into tools for and evidence of her liberation—this is especially striking when such texts originally justified or ensured her enslavement. By including these printed texts within her narrative, Jacobs asserts her changed relationship to the medium of print through her acts of recirculation as much as her autobiographical composition.

One of the ways Jacobs reveals the power of her transformed relation to print is to draw a distinction between her agency over the medium in comparison to the older generation of slaves and former slaves in her narrative. By the end of *Incidents in the Life of a Slave*

3. This claim follows Joseph Rezek's and Cohen's arguments that formerly enslaved authors exhibit a keen awareness of print as at once a medium for delivering their texts and, for better or worse, distributing their identities. See especially Cohen (162–63).
4. See Valerie Smith, *Self-Discovery and Authority in Afro-American Narrative* (1987), and William L. Andrews, *To Tell a Free Story: The First Century of Afro-American Autobiography, 176–1865* (1986).
5. I am grateful to Jordan Alexander Stein for offering this succinct formulation of a key concept running through the essay. He pursues his own version of this claim in "The Whig Interpretation of Media: *Sheppard Lee* and Jacksonian Paperwork" (2013). I am also indebted to him for helpfully clarifying that this essay seeks to illustrate Jacobs *in the process* of transforming the print materials of her enslavement through her acts of recirculation.

Girl, we do not see Jacobs's grandmother Martha or uncle Phillip progress to a place of asserting control over print or manuscript; instead, Jacobs's grandmother repeatedly exhibits fear and resistance to Jacobs's own manipulation of media. Carla L. Peterson characterizes these moments as evidence of Martha's conservatism and preference to remain within the slave community (158–59). Ultimately, the older generation's uncritical relationship to print and manuscript maps on to Jacobs's portrayal of its inability to exert control over its personal narratives or escape the power dynamics inscribed by slavery. We might read this as Jacobs's own commentary on the prohibitions of literacy under slavery, which prevented Martha and Phillip from gaining full access to the written word. However, by foregrounding their limited engagement with written texts, Jacobs throws her own acts of recirculation into starker relief. She ultimately expresses the difference between herself and the older generation in her treatment of Phillip's obituary, which she frames as his disappearance into text at the end of the narrative.

Another iteration of this conflict between Jacobs and the older generation is her diagnosis of oral tradition as insufficient for her narrative purposes. Paul Gilroy has identified oral culture as an influential antecedent to the written autobiography of black Atlantic cultures, arguing that "Both storytelling and music-making contributed to an alternative public sphere, and this in turn provided the context in which the particular styles of autobiographical self-dramatization and public self-construction have been formed and circulated as an integral component of insubordinate racial countercultures" (200). While we might assume that Jacobs would more aptly oppose writing and print, which she implicates in the practices of slavery, when we examine two examples of oral tradition in *Incidents in the Life of a Slave Girl*, we see that Jacobs does not fit Gilroy's formulation.

Rather than portraying oral tradition with a reverence that would acknowledge this medium as her literary inheritance, Jacobs distances herself from her grandmother's storytelling. After recalling Martha's oral account of the family's re-enslavement during the Revolutionary War, Jacobs concludes, "Such was the story my grandmother used to tell me; but I do not remember all the particulars" (11 [9]). Positioning herself simultaneously as the intended audience for this oral history and a poor receiver of its transmission, Jacobs resists participating in oral tradition. By stating that she does not remember the particulars of the narrative, assigning the story to her grandmother, and locating the scene of the telling in the past, Jacobs absolves herself of any expectation that she should be relied on to retell the story to others in her family. Whether it is the medium's ephemerality, its opposition to the written word, or its perceived centrality to the slave community, this scene does not provide a clear explanation for Jacobs's apathy toward oral tradition. To gain a clearer sense of her objections, we need to turn to a much later scene wherein she cements her dismissal of orality.

Faced with her daughter's imminent departure for boarding school, Jacobs attempts to confess her relationship with Mr. Sands to Ellen. She resolves to speak openly with the girl about her father, but almost as soon as she begins, Ellen interrupts: "O, don't, mother! Please don't tell me any more. . . . I know all about it, mother," she replied; "I am nothing to my father, and he is nothing to me. [I] knew all the time he was my father, for Fanny's nurse told me so; but she said I must never tell any body, and I never did" (283 [156]). This moment of confession—thwarted by her daughter's foreknowledge—represents a second collapse of oral tradition in Jacobs's narrative. In an effort to prevent Ellen from hearing this history from someone who "might not understand the palliating circumstances" (282 [155]), Jacobs musters the courage to deliver her history to the next generation. However, since Ellen has already received the details, Jacobs is denied her moment of confession, and oral tradition is never redeemed in her narrative. Jacobs's loss of authority over the transmission of the events of her life to her daughter discloses the failure of oral tradition to sufficiently organize and deliver her personal history. With this scene, Jacobs portrays oral tradition as a medium that accommodates the disruption of narrative order. As she elaborates her relationship to print, we see she is able to remain in control and utilize the medium's potential to signify in multiple ways.

In the first two examples of recirculated texts in *Incidents in the Life of a Slave Girl*—the law against harboring slaves and Dr. Flint's advertisement for Jacobs—we see the seamless incorporation of print within print that lays bare the duality of a medium that at once circulated the self-authored accounts of free blacks at the same time that it served a disciplinary function in the pursuit of any runaway slave. This pair of texts also attests to the range of techniques used for the recirculation of print since one document is easily recognized by its visual representation on the page while the other is only detectable as part of an imagined scene. Considering the two texts together illuminates the degree of detail attendant in Jacobs's acts of recirculation as the overt presence of the second text reflects back on the subtle recognition of the first. When Jacobs describes Flint's efforts to capture her, we learn that he and his agents intensely search for her at her grandmother's house, and after misreading her empty trunk as evidence that she has departed, Flint moves his search to "every vessel northward bound." Flint's agents physically search the ships, but their efforts are augmented by a peculiar performance of reading. Jacobs explains that "the law against harboring fugitives was read to all on board" (148 [84]). This public scene of reading, described in no further detail than what I have quoted, illustrates Flint's first recourse to print in his pursuit of Jacobs. The implied presence of a physical document from which the agents read from demonstrates Jacobs's careful attention to the role of print in the service of a national discourse of slavery that refuses to acknowledge her as a subject. Additionally, her decision to not reproduce the text of this law within the scene becomes strategic in light of the fact that she includes the full text of her runaway advertisement on the following page.

The textual proximity of the runaway advertisement is underscored by the absence of the law on the previous page. The presence of the advertisement compels the reader into a direct relationship with a printed text that records the ongoing threat of slavery even for those who escaped. This contrast between what the reader is and is not able to read for herself evinces Jacobs's strategy of highlighting the role of print in the construction of African American identity through the terms of slavery. Rather than incorporate the impersonal text of the law into her personal narrative, Jacobs opts to recirculate Flint's representation of her mind, body, and intentions within the pages of a text that seeks to represent the very same things:

> $300 REWARD! Ran away from the subscriber, an intelligent, bright, mulatto girl, named Linda, 21 years of age. Five feet four inches high. Dark eyes, and black hair inclined to curl; but it can be made straight. Has a decayed spot on a front tooth. She can read and write, and in all probability will try to get to the Free States. All persons are forbidden, under penalty of law, to harbor or employ said slave. $150 will be given to whoever takes her in the state, and $300 if taken out of the state and delivered to me, or lodged in jail.
>
> DR. FLINT. (149 [84–85])

This text serves as the conclusion to the chapter titled "The Flight," and as such, it stands alone on the final page of the chapter without narrative commentary. In the preceding prose, Jacobs writes that Flint posted the advertisement "at every corner, and in every public place for miles round" (148 [84]). The fact that this text is reproduced in print means that the advertisement in *Incidents in the Life of a Slave Girl* is and is not the same as the advertisement that was posted "for miles round." This slippage presents the problem that is print's inability to differentiate an original from its copy. Granted, we know that the advertisement located within the book has not been taken down from a lamppost, but the medium is bidirectional. This reprinted advertisement contains the potential to function in precisely the same way as the original once it is torn from the binding of the book and nailed to a separate lamppost. In my view, Jacobs is fully aware of the reprint's insidious potential, particularly since we see her own skillful reuse of print less than fifty pages later. Indeed, this is the very reason Flint's advertisement receives a separate page. Jacobs dares her readers to recognize the competing significations contained within this recirculated text. She confronts the reader with her own terrifying inclusion of a text that sought her capture.

Jacobs's recirculation of this text, which was for years the only record of her physical appearance, places her in a position of authority over the gaze of her former master. The excruciating detail that he provides—that her hair is inclined to curl and there is a decayed spot on her front tooth—records her subjugation while its presence within the narrative affirms Jacobs's transformed relation to the text as she is now the agent of its recirculation. P. Gabrielle Foreman and Sarah Blackwood have noted that there are some important differences between the advertisement that Jacobs includes in *Incidents in the Life of a Slave Girl* and the historical advertisement written by Dr. James Norcom (Blackwood 106–09; Foreman, "Who's" 518–19). As part of her changes, Jacobs raises the reward for her capture from one hundred to three hundred dollars, includes "intelligent" among the descriptors used to identify her, and states that she is able to "read and write" rather than "[speak] easily and fluently" (Jacobs 149 [84–85]; Blackwood 108). This shift from emphasizing speech to reading and writing supports my earlier claim that Jacobs finds oral tradition insufficient for her narrative purposes. With this change, she carefully aligns herself with textual production and consumption rather than the spoken word.[6] Blackwood contends that the differences between the original advertisement and the version in *Incidents in the Life of a Slave Girl* demonstrate that Jacobs composed a fictional advertisement to "[recalibrate] the mimetic capacity of the fugitive slave notice" (96). This claim is part of Blackwood's larger reading of the advertisement as a site for Jacobs to reclaim the power of textual description from Norcom while capitalizing on the conventions of the runaway advertisement to offer proof of slavery's abuses through individualized descriptions of bodies marked by violence and malnourishment.

Jacobs's explanation that the advertisement reproduced on the page was previously posted "for miles round" (148 [84]) is not affected by the historical or fictional status of the advertisement since it purportedly exists within the imaginative space of Jacobs's narrative. What we see on the page was seen by others in the world

6. I thank Howard Rambsy II for bringing this important detail to my attention.

the text describes. Additionally, both the version that is circulated in *Incidents in the Life of a Slave Girl* and the historical advertisement written by Norcom similarly function as records of Jacobs's body and as printed documents that seek to effect her return to slavery. Similar to Blackwood's and Foreman's insightful readings of Jacobs's power and agency in her changes to the advertisement, Martha J. Cutter argues that through her "critical literacy" (209), Jacobs transforms the dominant culture's "language game" (213) to "generate a future where language and abusive power are no longer synonymous" (224). While I share these critics' interest in language as a site for transformation, I would stipulate that Jacobs does not describe her runaway slave advertisement nor does she quote from it within a paragraph. Instead, she reproduces the advertisement with margins and typographic details that render the document's print characteristics legible to her readers—she preserves the medium of print as part of her critical project.[7] For Jacobs, the discourse of slavery and oppression does not exist in the abstract; it is intimately bound to its medium of circulation.

To make one final point before moving on to additional examples, when we read past the portrait of Jacobs and closely examine the final lines of the advertisement, we find a complex entanglement of regional and national discourse within a single locally distributed text. The language of the advertisement reluctantly acknowledges the historical reality of a divided nation. Flint clearly indicates that the Free States are a likely goal for Jacobs's escape, yet his indictment of "all persons" (149 [85]) contrasts with any division the advertisement presupposes with its mention of the Free States in the previous sentence. This brief line reinforces the internal conflict of a nation comprised of regions at odds in ideology yet uniformly governed, at the time, by the 1793 Fugitive Slave Law. The fact that the advertisement in Jacobs's narrative uses the phrase "Free States" instead of "the North" (which is used in the advertisement written by Norcom) suggests a deliberate attempt to underscore the hypocrisy in this name for the region. The concluding lines prove the impossibility for the "Free States," and by extension the nation, to offer any true freedom for an escaped slave with the declaration that a reward will be paid to any person who lodges Jacobs in an out-of-state jail. Through these references, we learn that the advertisement, while physically circulated in a limited geographic radius, positions

7. Depending on the edition of *Incidents in the Life of a Slave Girl*, the typographical details that distinguish Jacobs's prose from her runaway slave advertisement will be preserved to a greater or lesser degree and can, at times, be completely elided. This is particularly true in the case of anthologized versions of the text. Certain threads of my argument depend on the original representation of the recirculated advertisement, and I offer this reading as further evidence for the necessity of preserving typographical distinctions within a text.

itself as part of a national discourse and implies a reader with the potential (realized or readily available) to traverse state boundaries. By recirculating this text, Jacobs reveals the porous boundaries of the local and national print spheres that helped to perpetuate the institution of slavery, but in the next example, we will see how she uses a nationally distributed print publication to affect her private circumstances of concealment.

Once she obtains her hiding place in the garret and the immediate threat of capture subsides, we learn that Jacobs prepares a series of letters that attempt to convince Flint that she has escaped to Boston. The genius of the ruse is that it lays bare the assumptions that epistolary technology carries with it: a letter is produced in a stable location, distributed across a landscape, and received by the appointed audience in a second stable location. As Jacobs plays off these assumptions, she exposes Flint as an undiscerning reader and makes a fool of him when he writes to the mayor of Boston to inquire after her. The letters reveal Jacobs's efforts to assert control over media and deftly reconceive this technology as a means to ensure her safety, illustrate her status as a subject, and secure her eventual freedom. While the letters themselves are part of the manuscript culture of the narrative, Jacobs relies on printed newspapers to guarantee the realism of these fraudulent correspondences and thus demonstrates a critical relationship to print materials even under slavery. Cutter argues that because Flint suppresses Jacobs's letters and reads his own version to her grandmother, Jacobs does not succeed in her "discursive aim." Cutter rightly points out that Flint's intervention means that Jacobs "does not gain control of her voice, or of her representation of herself" (217), but I contend that Jacobs achieves a different kind of control through the composition of these letters—control over information contained in Northern newspapers.

When Jacobs resolves to pursue this letter writing project, she reaches out to her friend Peter to ask for his help mailing the letters from New York and to request copies of New York newspapers so that she can include accurate street names and city locations in her writing. In the scene that follows, Jacobs strategically reappropriates a partial, outdated newspaper to help exploit Flint's assumptions about personal letters. Even the way she procures the newspaper provides an intriguing context for the reuse of print in the world of her narrative. Jacobs writes that Peter "run his hand into his pocket, and said, 'Here is half a one, that was round a cap I bought of [sic] a peddler yesterday'" (193 [108]). The choice to include the detail that Peter's newspaper most recently served a purpose far removed from a scene of reading speaks to the historical reality that print materials quickly transitioned from texts to refuse. In *How to Do Things with Books in Victorian Britain* (2012), Leah Price devotes an entire chapter to the processes of extracting and recycling the raw materials of books (219–58). By acknowledging the newspaper's status as packaging, Jacobs makes it clear that her use of this newspaper is not subject to the ephemerality of its content. Instead, she extracts stable pieces of information from a printed document that assumes its own obsolescence; in effect, she restores this piece of refuse paper to the status of a text. Even the politics of this newspaper are subordinated to her strategic use of the information it contains as she explains that Peter had given her a piece of the *New York Herald* and that, "for once, the paper that systematically abuses the colored people, was made to render them a service" (194 [108]). Jacobs's ability to reuse newspapers—a print form that makes locations and people public—as a tool to protect her concealment represents a subversive use of these textual materials, one that she continues after she escapes to New York by scanning the papers for announcements of Southern slave owners staying in local hotels (295 [158]).

As her narrative draws to a close, Jacobs recounts the events that precipitate her long-awaited freedom by foregrounding the material text that serves as the literal point of convergence between her life as a slave and as a free woman: her bill of sale. In so doing, she reindicts print as a crucial instrument for the practices of slavery by noting the record of slavery that this text preserves:[8]

> So I was *sold* at last! A human being *sold* in the free city of New York! The bill of sale is on record, and future generations will learn from it that women were articles of traffic in New York, late in the nineteenth century of the Christian religion. It may hereafter prove a useful document to antiquaries, who are seeking to measure the progress of civilization in the United States. I well know the value of that bit of paper; but much as I love freedom, I do not like to look upon it. I am deeply grateful to the generous friend who procured it, but I despise the miscreant who demanded payment for what never rightfully belonged to him or his. (300–01 [165–66])

The details regarding the historical legacy contained by the physical document, "the value of that bit of paper" and its usefulness to "antiquaries," reveal Jacobs's sensitivity to the paper trail generated by slavery. When she clarifies her distaste for viewing the bill of sale, she signals a resistance to seeing herself in the record of a transaction predicated on the idea that she was an object. By disavowing

8. Because Jacobs's freedom papers and bill of sale have never been found (Yellin xxxiv), we cannot know whether they were printed or handwritten. There is documentary evidence that some bills of sale from this time were printed blanks on which the parties involved could fill in the details of the transaction. Ultimately, I find that Jacobs's emphasis on the materiality of the document aligns with the narrative's larger critique of print's role in the practices of slavery.

the record of her status as a slave, Jacobs affirms her status as a subject. Her meditation on and resistance to this material text is especially revealing when read against her narration of Martha's and Phillip's deaths on the following page.

Lois Brown asserts that "it is in public writing about dying . . . that one can resurrect some of the most compelling articulations . . . of African American life and agendas" and that early African American obituaries offer their subjects "the prospect of achieving narrative immortality and archival presence because their race and existence are literally imprinted on the public sphere" (136). In *Incidents in the Life of a Slave Girl*, Jacobs's accounts of the deaths of her grandmother and uncle doubly function as her own obituaries for these characters and as a concluding moment of critique. Martha's and Phillip's presence within the space of Jacobs's narrative already ensures them a kind of "narrative immortality," so while Jacobs's treatment of their deaths provides a coda to their stories, this episode is also an opportunity for her to set her transformed relationship to textual media against their unchanged status as subjects, rather than arrangers, of texts. In this way, Jacobs's obituaries become a site for her own "articulation of African American life" under slavery.

After writing of her appreciation for Mrs. Bruce's efforts in securing her freedom, Jacobs transitions to the final moments of her text, in which she reports the deaths of her grandmother and her uncle with overdrawn nostalgia:

> My grandmother lived to rejoice in my freedom; but not long after, a letter came with a black seal. She had gone "where the wicked cease from troubling, and the weary are at rest."
>
> Time passed on, and a paper came to me from the south, containing an obituary notice of my uncle Phillip. It was the only case I ever knew of such an honor conferred upon a colored person. It was written by one of his friends and contained these words: "Now that death has laid him low, they call him a good man and a useful citizen; but what are eulogies to the black man, when the world has faded from his vision? It does not require man's praise to obtain rest in God's kingdom." (302 [166])

In this passage, Martha's and Phillip's deaths are inseparable from the documents that announce them. Phillip's death is completely contained by the printed text Jacobs receives. We never learn who sent the paper that published the obituary nor is it clear where the paper came from beyond "the south." Emerging from such obscurity, Phillip's death mirrors the conventional *ex nihilo* opening of many slave narratives. At the end of his life, the particulars of his death are unknowable in the way that the origins of those born into slavery were so often equally obscured.

By framing Phillip's death as the dissolution of event into material record, Jacobs tempers the honor she recognizes in the gesture of the obituary. In her account, Phillip is denied control of his narrative, and the news of his passing is delivered to Jacobs without ties to community or family. In the lines she records from the obituary, the writer ironizes the posthumous praise Phillip received by explaining its worthlessness once the "world has faded from [the black man's] vision." In this construction, the black man already exists as subject with a gaze fixed on a fading world, yet his recognition by that world as a "citizen" and a "good man" (302 [166]) after his death is insufficient to the task of affirming his status as a subject when his treatment in life proved otherwise.

In the case of her grandmother, Jacobs narrates her passing by remarking only that she received "a letter with a black seal" (302 [166]), reducing the event of Martha's death to a wax marking. As if to clarify the meaning of this seal, Jacobs repeats the quotation her grandmother once offered to her from the book of Job, further denying Martha any original contribution to the record of her death. Martha's personal narrative is subsumed by the medium that records it: the ending of her life is fully expressible through banal materiality and imported text. In the scene on the previous page, Jacobs rejects the vision of herself that is encoded in her bill of sale, yet Martha and Phillip seem trapped by the materials that deliver the events of their deaths. With this conclusion, Jacobs reasserts the narrative and textual control that distinguishes her from the older generation. Whereas she successfully recirculates and repurposes textual materials as part of her narrative, the last time she mentions her uncle and grandmother they are fully contained by texts.

In his influential study *To Tell a Free Story: The First Century of Afro-American Autobiography, 1760–1865* (1986) Andrews elaborates a theory of the African American slave narrative as primarily a project for the formation of the African American subject. He explains that "blacks set about writing life stories that would somehow prove that they qualified as the moral, spiritual, or intellectual peers of whites" (2). While it is clear that a completed autobiography could serve to validate the intellectual, moral, and spiritual aptitude of the writer, in a later statement Andrews argues that it is, in part, the very act of writing the autobiography that accomplishes these goals:

> In a number of important black autobiographies of this era, however, a quest, more psycholiterary than spiritual can be discerned. It is spurred by many motives, perhaps the most important of which is the need of an other to *declare* himself through various linguistic acts, thereby reifying his abstract unreality, his invisibility in the eyes of his readers, so that he can be

> recognized as someone to be reckoned with. Such declarative acts, as we shall see, include the reconstructing of one's past in a meaningful and instructive form, the appropriating of empowering myths and models of the self from any available resource, and the redefining of one's place in the scheme of things by redefining the language used to locate one in that scheme. (7)

The primacy of narrative composition in this account neglects the moments of resistance, subversion, or critique that can also demonstrate a person's status as a subject. For Jacobs, it is not the organization of the events of her life into a coherent narrative but rather her acts of recirculation that position her as a subject. By close reading the print culture contained within *Incidents in the Life of a Slave Girl*, we see Jacobs actively working to transform the materials of her enslavement into evidence of her liberation. She declares herself through the aesthetic act of arranging and recirculating printed texts.

By studying her acts of recirculation, we see Jacobs demonstrate print's potential for radical recontextualization even as she clarifies the medium's role in perpetuating the practices of slavery. Examining the print culture contained within early African American literature can yield new readings of many other texts, including David Walker's *An Appeal to the Coloured Citizens of the World* (1829), Moses Roper's *A Narrative of the Adventures and Escape of Moses Roper from American Slavery* (1838), and Frances E. W. Harper's *Iola Leroy; or, Shadows Uplifted* (1892). By recognizing the agency of early African American authors as arrangers of print, we can not only trace the literary and historical resonances of their works but also recover their position and commentary on the medium that helped their texts to circulate.

Works Cited

Andrews, William L. *To Tell a Free Story: The First Century of Afro-American Autobiography, 1760–1865*. Urbana: U of Illinois P, 1986. Print.

Blackwood, Sarah. "Fugitive Obscura: Runaway Slave Portraiture and Early Photographic Technology." *American Literature* 81.1 (2009): 93–125. Print.

Brown, Lois. "Death-Defying Testimony: Women's Private Lives and the Politics of Public Documents." *Legacy: A Journal of American Women Writers* 27.1 (2010): 130–39. Print.

Carby, Hazel V. *Reconstructing Womanhood: The Emergence of the Afro-American Woman Novelist*. New York: Oxford UP, 1987. Print.

Cohen, Lara Langer. "'Notes from the State of Saint Domingue': The Practice of Citation in *Clotel*." Cohen and Stein 161–77.

Cohen, Lara Langer, and Jordan Alexander Stein, eds. *Early African American Print Culture*. Philadelphia: U of Pennsylvania P, 2012. Print.

Cutter, Martha J. "Dismantling 'The Master's House': Critical Literacy in Harriet Jacobs' *Incidents in the Life of a Slave Girl*." *Callaloo* 19.1 (1996): 209–25. Print.

Davis, Charles T., and Henry Louis Gates, Jr., eds. *The Slave's Narrative*. New York: Oxford UP, 1985. Print.

Dinius, Marcy J. "'Look!! Look!!! at This!!!!'": The Radical Typography of David Walker's *Appeal*." *PMLA* 126.1 (2011): 55–72. Print.

Foreman, P. Gabrielle. *Activist Sentiments: Reading Black Women in the Nineteenth Century*. Urbana: U of Illinois P, 2009. Print.

———."The *Christian Recorder*, Broken Families, and Educated Nations in Julia C. Collins's Civil War Novel *The Curse of the Caste*." *African American Review* 40.4 (2006): 705–16. Print.

———. "Who's Your Mama? 'White' Mulatta Genealogies, Early Photography, and Anti-Passing Narratives of Slavery and Freedom." *American Literary History* 14.3 (2002): 505–39. Print.

Foster, Frances Smith. "A Narrative of the Interesting Origins and (Somewhat) Surprising Developments of African-American Print Culture." *American Literary History* 17.4 (2005): 714–40. Print.

Gardner, Eric. *Unexpected Places: Relocating Nineteenth-Century African American Literature*. Jackson: UP of Mississippi, 2009. Print.

Gilroy, Paul. *The Black Atlantic: Modernity and Double Consciousness*. Cambridge: Harvard UP, 1993. Print.

Goddu, Teresa A. "The Slave Narrative as Material Text." *The Oxford Handbook to the African American Slave Narrative*. Ed. John Ernest. New York: Oxford UP, 2014. 149–64. Print.

Jackson, Leon. "The Talking Book and the Talking Book Historian: African American Cultures of Print—The State of the Discipline." *Book History* 13 (2010): 251–308. Print.

Jacobs, Harriet. *Incidents in the Life of a Slave Girl*. Introd. Valerie Smith. New York: Oxford UP, 1988. Print. The Schomburg Library of Nineteenth-Century Black Women Writers. Henry Louis Gates, Jr., gen. ed.

McCoy, Beth A. "Race and the (Para)Textual Condition." *PMLA* 121.1 (2006): 156–69. Print.

McGill, Meredith L. *American Literature and the Culture of Reprinting 1834–1853*. Philadelphia: U of Pennsylvania P, 2003. Print.

Peterson, Carla L. *"Doers of the Word": African-American Women Speakers and Writers in the North (1830–1880)*. 2nd ed. New Brunswick: Rutgers UP, 1998. Print.

Price, Leah. *How to Do Things with Books in Victorian Britain.* Princeton: Princeton UP, 2012. Print.

Rezek, Joseph. "The Print Atlantic: Phillis Wheatley, Ignatius Sancho, and the Cultural Significance of the Book." Cohen and Stein 19–39.

Smith, Valerie. *Self-Discovery and Authority in Afro-American Narrative.* Cambridge: Harvard UP, 1987. Print.

Stein, Jordan Alexander. "The Whig Interpretation of Media: *Sheppard Lee* and Jacksonian Paperwork." *History of the Present* 3.1 (2013): 29–56. Print.

Waldstreicher, David. "Reading the Runaways: Self-Fashioning, Print Culture, and Confidence in Slavery in the Eighteenth-Century Mid-Atlantic." *The William and Mary Quarterly* 56.2 (1999): 243–72. Print.

Yellin, Jean Fagan, ed. *The Harriet Jacobs Family Papers.* Vol. 1. Chapel Hill: U of North Carolina P, 2008. Print.

WILLIAM L. ANDREWS

From Class and Class Awareness in *Incidents in the Life of a Slave Girl*†

* * *

Over the past thirty years, there has been a substantial outpouring of scholarship devoted to race and gender as depicted and constructed in the pre–Civil War African American slave narrative. But I have found comparatively little study of the representation of class and various degrees of class awareness in these foundational texts of African American literature and culture. Yet the large majority of the sixty texts published during the heyday of the antebellum slave narrative between 1840 and 1865 evince widespread class differences and awareness of class among the enslaved of the American South. The producers of slave narratives often expressed their sensitivity to class distinctions among whites within the slaveocracy. "The slave holders are generally rich, aristocratic, overbearing," wrote Henry Bibb, one of the best-known mid-nineteenth-century fugitive slave narrators.

> They look with utter contempt upon a poor laboring man, who earns his bread by the 'sweat of his brow,' whether he be moral or immoral, honest or dishonest. No matter whether he is white

† From *Auto/Biography across the Americas: Transnational Themes in Life Writing,* ed. Ricia Anne Chansky (New York: Routledge, 2017), 184–97. Reprinted by permission of Taylor and Francis, Ltd. Page numbers in brackets refer to this Norton Critical Edition.

> or black; if he performs manual labor for a livelihood, he is looked upon as being inferior to a slaveholder, and but little better off than the slave, who toils without wages under the lash. It is true, that the slaveholder, and non-slaveholder, are living under the same laws in the same State. But the one is rich, the other is poor; one is educated, the other is uneducated; one has houses, land and influence, the other has none. This being the case, that class of the non-slaveholders would be glad to see slavery abolished, but they dare not speak it aloud. (25)

Andrew Jackson, a fugitive from Kentucky, asked workingmen of the North "whether many of our own northern laborers would deem it a very great crime to eat a pig, or even an ox, that might belong to one who was compelling him to labor year after year without pay" (28). Denunciations of nonslaveholding, as well as slaveholding, whites on the basis of class are not hard to find in slave narratives either. Recalling the violent aftermath of the Nat Turner insurrection in her hometown of Edenton, North Carolina, Harriet Jacobs made no effort to hide her disgust over the "low whites" who, having "no negroes of their own to scourge . . . exulted in such a chance to exercise a little brief authority, and show their subserviency to the slaveholders; not reflecting that the power which trampled on the colored people also kept themselves in poverty, ignorance, and moral degradation" (98) [57]. Jacobs granted that the low whites' "poverty, ignorance, and moral degradation" were less a matter of their own choice than a function of "the power" of the slaveholders to trample the rights of poor whites and enslaved blacks alike. But she still blamed the "low whites" for "their subserviency to the slaveholders."

So did Frederick Douglass when he assessed the motives of white Baltimore dockworkers who assaulted him in 1836 when he worked among them as a slave. In *My Bondage and My Freedom* (1855), Douglass interjected into his account of the assault a two-page comment on, first, the victimization of the white worker "robbed by the slave system, of the just results of his labor" and, second, the strategy by which "the slaveholders" convince "the laboring white man" to regard the slave system as his only protection "from falling to the level of the slave's poverty and degradation" (*Bondage* 310–11). "In cities, such as Baltimore, Richmond, New Orleans, &c.," Douglass continued, "the conflict of slavery with the interests of the white mechanics and laborers of the south . . . is seen pretty clearly" (*Bondage* 309).

But not by the white working men themselves. Still angry over the beating he had absorbed almost twenty years earlier, Douglass in 1855 did not confine his resentment to elite whites who could depend on white workers to blame the enslaved worker, rather than a common master, for their economic fears and anxieties. "In the city of Baltimore," Douglass asserted,

> [T]here are not unfrequent murmurs, that educating the slaves to be mechanics may, in the end, give slave-masters power to dispense with the services of the poor white man altogether. But, with characteristic dread of offending the slaveholders, these poor, white mechanics in Mr. Gardiner's ship-yard [where Douglass was attacked]—instead of applying the natural, honest remedy for the apprehended evil, and objecting at once to work there by the side of slaves—made a cowardly attack upon the free colored mechanics, saying they were eating the bread which should be eaten by American freemen, and swearing that they would not work with them. The feeling was, really, against having their labor brought into competition with that of the colored people at all; but it was too much to strike directly at the interest of the slave-holders; and, therefore—proving their servility and cowardice—they dealt their blows on the poor, colored freeman, and aimed to prevent him from serving himself, in the evening of life, with the trade with which he had served his master, during the more vigorous portion of his days. (*Bondage* 309–11)

Although the slave narrators' views of class differences among southern whites deserve more careful study, I prefer to focus in this chapter on an even more striking, though seldom discussed, aspect of class in the antebellum slave narratives: what narrators wrote about class differences among the enslaved themselves. Bibb was decidedly open and categorical about this social phenomenon. "The distinction among slaves is as marked, as the classes of society are in any aristocratic community," Bibb declared, "some refusing to associate with others whom they deem to be beneath them, in point of character, color, condition, or the superior importance of their respective masters" (33–34). *The Narrative of Lunsford Lane* is notably direct in articulating its author's awareness of the material and social differences that privileged him, as a house slave from his childhood in Raleigh, North Carolina, over his master's plantation workers.

> It is known that there is a wide difference in the situations of what are termed house servants, and plantation hands. I, though sometimes employed upon the plantation, belonged to the former, which is the favored class. My master, too, was esteemed a kind and humane man; and altogether I fared quite differently from many poor fellows whom it makes my blood run chill to think of, confined to the plantation, with not enough of food and that little of the coarsest kind, to satisfy the gnawings of hunger—compelled oftentimes, to hie away in the night-time, when worn down with work, and steal, (if it be stealing,) and privately devour such things as they can lay their hands

> upon—made to feel the rigors of bondage with no cessation—torn away sometimes from the few friends they love, friends doubly dear because they are few, and transported to a climate where in a few hard years they die—or at best conducted heavily and sadly to their resting place under the sod, upon their old master's plantation—sometimes, perhaps, enlivening the air with merriment, but a forced merriment, that comes from a stagnant or a stupified heart. Such as this is the fate of the plantation slaves generally, but such was not my lot. My way was comparatively light, and what is better, it conducted to freedom. (18)

In this evocative passage, Lane details both material and psychological resources that "plantation hands" had but limited access to, such as nourishment, rest, recreation, and friendship, while acknowledging that Lane himself did not suffer from such deprivations. Lane's regard for "the plantation slaves generally" strikes a sympathetic, if slightly sentimental, chord, but the tone is detached and conveyed through a formal diction (e.g., "hie away") that bespeaks the narrator's distance from the field workers. Expressing pity for the "poor fellows" reduced to "devour[ing] such things as they can lay their hands upon," the narrator nevertheless seems to qualify the degree to which, even in death, the plantation hand's "stagnant" or "stupified" heart may fully appreciate the pathos of his condition. The "comparatively light" burden of his own enslavement when contrasted to the miserable fate of the plantation worker seems genuinely to disturb Lane even in the act of recalling his past. Having stated already in his preface "that my condition as a slave was comparatively a happy, indeed a highly favored one" (iii), a status he shared with his wife (11), Lane's repeated emphasis on his "favored" situation in slavery may suggest as much a lingering survivor's guilt as any conscious sense of class superiority. Also worth noting is that Lane credits his favored class status with having "conducted [him] to freedom" (18). While his narrative shows that Lane made concerted and gutsy decisions that led to both his own and his family's liberation, he is one of the few antebellum slave narrators to allude explicitly to a linkage between class in slavery and both the desire for and the opportunity to attain freedom. Nevertheless, a number of slave narrators testify implicitly as well as explicitly to class as a shaping influence on their own lives, on their assessments of many whites and blacks whom they knew in the South, and on their convictions, while they were enslaved, that nothing less than complete freedom was their due.

Incidents in the Life of a Slave Girl is one of the few narratives in which scholars and critics have noted aspects of class as well as caste difference that affect its protagonist's determination to resist sexual exploitation and ultimately attain freedom for herself.[1] But a great deal remains to be explored in *Incidents* with regard to class and its influence on the outlook and values of the various members of what I call the Jacobs-Horniblow clan. In this chapter I will point out just a few features of Jacobs's fascinating autobiography that evoke the class-inflected perspectives and values of the clan's chief representatives in *Incidents*, Jacobs ("Linda Brent") and her grandmother, Molly Horniblow, the "Aunt Martha" of the story.

Strong evidence in *Incidents* indicates that the extended family into which Harriet Jacobs was born constituted a high, if not the highest, class of enslaved and free people of color in Edenton, North Carolina, where Jacobs's story begins. The Jacobs-Horniblow clan, particularly Molly Horniblow, was quite aware of its class position and very strategic in deploying its social assets. Jacobs never says directly that her clan was in one of Edenton's higher classes of people of African descent, but several incidents point directly to the power that the clan wielded and to the importance of Jacobs's class identity to her survival and ultimate escape to freedom.

When I speak of class awareness in these remarks, I'm not talking about what Marxists mean by class consciousness, or what is called "class for itself," defined by a consciousness of one's own class identity based on a recognition of the identity of one's class antagonist. Many slave narrators articulate a highly developed consciousness of their *caste* antagonists among the whites. Narrators like Jacobs, Douglass, William Wells Brown, and Bibb were very sophisticated in their analyses of the bases on which caste consciousness and caste antagonism were enforced and perpetuated by whites, especially slaveholders, in the South. But the antebellum slave narrative takes a more complex and decidedly individual approach to class differentiation, particularly insofar as intraracial class and status differences among the enslaved were concerned. One reason antebellum slave narratives are so interesting from the standpoint of the internal dynamics of class among the enslaved is that the narratives evince such a wide range of opinion about class differences and little unanimity about who is the class antagonist of whom. For this reason I speak of slave narrators as displaying, in many cases, an awareness of class and class differences among the enslaved but not the sort of class consciousness that Marxist analysis attempts to define.

In *Incidents*, the reader discovers in the words and actions of various Jacobs-Horniblow clan members a sense of personal as well as familial identity that is inflected in ways that suggest either a conscious or an unconscious sense of status, just deserts, and merited privilege. The clan's sense of class identity was to a significant degree

1. See Henderson and Kawash. Also relevant is Smith.

a function of the resources and prestige that various senior clan members—Molly Horniblow and Elijah Jacobs (Harriet's father), most importantly—brought to the entire extended family by virtue of their skills—baking and carpentry, in these cases—which allowed Horniblow and Elijah Jacobs to hire themselves out as quasi-wage-earning, but still enslaved, workers. What distinguished the Jacobs-Horniblow clan from the standpoint of class was their access to material resources (such as money and real estate) and social leverage (such as the power to enlist the confidence and aid of class allies, most notably among upper-class whites) that few members of Edenton's enslaved rank and file could have ever wielded. In *Incidents*, the clan's leaders, especially Horniblow, use their class advantages, both material and social, to guard the clan's status and pursue its ends. Because *Incidents* focuses on the life of its author, one should not be surprised that the chief end of the Jacobs-Horniblow clan in *Incidents* was to protect the status and welfare of Molly Horniblow's favorite grandchild, Harriet.

From the opening sentences of *Incidents*, Jacobs provides broad hints as to the class circumstances in which she was born and the advantages those circumstances brought to her. Reading the first paragraph of *Incidents*, one learns that Jacobs was born and raised in an urban area, not on a farm or plantation. Frederick Douglass, who was an urban house slave from the age of eight to fifteen, states in his *Narrative*, "A city slave is almost a freeman, compared with a slave on the plantation. He is much better fed and clothed, and enjoys privileges altogether unknown to the slave on the plantation" (34). A town slave himself, Elijah Jacobs had earned for himself privileges unknown to the large majority of southern slaves, whether urban or rural. His daughter states that her father, a skilled slave (not an agricultural worker), was "considered so intelligent and skillful in his trade" that he was hired out as "head workman" on various projects in and out of his hometown (Jacobs 11) [9]. The privilege of hiring his time to work on his own, for which he was obliged to pay his mistress "two hundred dollars a year," distinguished Elijah Jacobs, from a class standpoint, since only a minority of slaves were allowed to hire their time on an annual basis and otherwise come and go as they pleased.[2]

In an essay on "The Ante-Bellum Negro Artisan," W. E. B. Du Bois characterized the practice of hiring skilled slaves as "naturally

2. By 1860, approximately thirty-one percent of urban slaves, most of them from the upper-echelon skilled ranks, and six percent of rural slaves were working for hire. See Penningroth (53). "Bondsmen and women would gain a measure of independence by being permitted to seek out an employer, negotiate wages and working conditions, and pay the owner an agreed-upon sum. Often they [the hired slaves] were permitted to retain a portion of their wages. Owners on the other hand did not have to bother with negotiating hiring agreements and could expect a good income" (Franklin and Schweninger 134).

resulting in the growth of a privileged class among the slaves. . . . Among this class were many who, free in everything but name, acquired property, reared families and often lived in comfort," despite "the opposition of white mechanics" (31). As long as he paid his mistress her $200 hiring dues, Elijah Jacobs could earn his own wages and "manage his own affairs," unlike the vast majority of slaves subject to daily white surveillance and control. Like a number of self-hired slaves who authored midcentury slave narratives (among them Douglass), Elijah Jacobs lived in his own dwelling with his own nuclear family. His daughter had particularly fond memories of the "comfortable home" she grew up in (11) [9], which was not the home of her mistress but a separate residence presided over by her parents, Elijah and Delilah. In this family dwelling ensconced in Edenton (far from the slave quarters of nearby farms and plantations), Elijah and Delilah Jacobs used their class advantages to raise their children insulated from the worst of slavery's depredations. Hatty Jacobs's class status "fondly shielded" her from the knowledge of her caste status as a slave until she was six years old (11) [9].

Like her fellow North Carolinian and fellow urban slave, Lunsford Lane, who also was ignorant of his own enslavement during his early childhood, Jacobs as a girl belonged to what Lane called "the favored class." As Jean Fagan Yellin says in her magisterial biography of Jacobs, "Molly's cherished granddaughter led a charmed life" even after she was conveyed at the age of six into the home of her mother's mistress, Margaret Horniblow (8). As "grandmother's child," the talented Hatty "enjoyed a privileged place in the black community, where skilled house servants like Molly, who were owned by people of substance, had status" (Yellin 12).

The "status" of Molly Horniblow in Edenton, which placed her and those in the family under her protection in "a privileged place in the black community," established for the Jacobs-Horniblow clan a class identity among the enslaved and free people of Edenton and its environs. Yellin's biography carefully maps the class hierarchies within Edenton's African American population, noting that Molly Horniblow occupied a status close to the top of the ladder, just below that of light-skinned families who could trace their free status back a few generations.[3] At the bottom of Edenton's caste hierarchy were

3. The "highest rank in the black community" of Edenton belonged to free people "who were connected—often by 'blood'—to the white aristocracy." Molly Horniblow "belonged to the next social level, made up of the freed men who had been owned by moderately prosperous white families and the freed women who had been owned by the white aristocracy." Below the Jacobses and the Horniblows were free Negroes descended from "unions between black men and indentured white women" (Yellin 31–32). Below them were the enslaved, who, *Incidents* indicates, were not one undifferentiated mass but were composed of ranks and levels of "status" too, depending on factors such as whether one lived in town or in a rural area, what sort of work one did, and the wealth and social status of one's master or mistress.

rural slaves who did the routinized, unrelenting, punishing agricultural labor that undergirded the economy of the South. Well above the majority of enslaved workers, in terms of class and privilege, were town slaves, particularly skilled slaves like Molly Horniblow and Elijah Jacobs, who could hire themselves out and thereby gain a significant degree of freedom and social leverage despite their enslavement. That Harriet Jacobs was aware of upper and lower classes among even the slaves of Edenton and its environs is evident from this statement she makes in *Incidents* about her hometown's Christmas Day John Cooner festival: "[The Johnkannaus] consists of companies of slaves from the plantations, generally of the lower class" (180) [101]. Jacobs also codes upper- and lower-class slaves in *Incidents* through their dialogue. Everyone in the Jacobs-Horniblow clan, including, of course, Harriet and Molly, speaks in standard English in *Incidents*. The speech of almost all other slaves in the text is recorded in forms of Negro dialect. That dialect serves as a class marker in *Incidents* is further attested by Jacobs's use of dialect to mark the speech of the "low whites" for whom she had such contempt. Jacobs did not treat the dialect speech of other slaves with scorn, but the social respectability of her extended family is evident in the fact that the nondialectal English they speak is no different from the standard English in which the speech of higher-class whites in *Incidents* is also recorded.

Molly Horniblow's status and power in Edenton become clear early in *Incidents* when Jacobs narrates how her grandmother got her freedom in the spring of 1828, when Horniblow was in her late fifties. The redoubtable Horniblow impressed her granddaughter by defying her master's plans to sell her under circumstances that would not place him in bad odor within Edenton's white community. Needing money, Dr. James Norcom informs Horniblow that he intends to sell her, despite "the intention of her mistress to leave her free" and regardless of the fact that "her long and faithful service in the family" had made her a figure of respect and sympathy among established whites in the community (Jacobs 21) [14]. Norcom hopes to mollify Horniblow by assuring her that he will not subject her to the indignity of sale in the standard way, that is, at the town's annual New Year's Day public auction. Norcom plans to manage the sale privately out of specious solicitude for Molly's sensibilities because, he assures her, "he was unwilling to wound her feelings by putting her up at auction" (20) [14].

Why should the ruthless hypocrite whom Jacobs dubs "Dr. Flint" in *Incidents* care about wounding the feelings of a slave woman he contrived to sell? Not to protect his slave, but to avoid jeopardizing his own social reputation by putting a respected, socially well-connected slave on humiliating display on the public auction block.

The private-sale ploy could safeguard Norcom's reputation as a member of Edenton's gentility[4] while making the bitter pill of sale go down a little more easily with Horniblow herself. The enslaver was ostensibly treating his slave with a bit of deference befitting someone of Horniblow's status in Edenton. No doubt Norcom hoped that Horniblow would appreciate his decision not to place her on public display with every other slave, house servant or field hand, who would be subjected to cold stares, physical examination, and noisy purchase on New Year's Day.

Horniblow, however, quickly sizes up Norcom's vulnerability and resolves to exploit it. She "understood very well that he was ashamed of the job," Jacobs notes, adding "she was a very spirited woman, and if he was base enough to sell her, when her mistress intended she should be free, she was determined the public should know it" (20–21) [14]. Ingeniously and very effectively, Horniblow devises her own plan to capitalize socially on her *class* status so as to resist the *caste* status that her master, Dr. Norcom, counted on in deciding when and how he would dispose of Horniblow. While Norcom schemes to escape publicity, Horniblow aims to exploit it. She embraces the public space of the auction block, partly to teach Norcom a lesson that she was not just any slave woman in Edenton to be bought and sold as it suited her master, but more importantly, to engineer her sale in such a way that she could obtain her freedom.

On New Year's Day, 1828, Horniblow appears without her owner's permission at the public auction "among the chattels" ready for auction. Indeed, "at the first call, she sprang upon the auction block" (21) [14], deliberately offering her own body for the opening bid. *Incidents* does not address the obvious questions that readers would have asked as they followed Horniblow to the auction block flanked by "the chattels." How did this enslaved woman get away with openly defying her master's plans for her sale? How could such an apparently disempowered black woman determine where and how she would be sold? Why didn't her master, upon seeing her on the auction block, summarily drag her away from the auction? Why did this white man do nothing to stop this impudent black woman from publicly subjecting *him* to embarrassment?

The answer to all these questions points us back to one source: Horniblow's social status in Edenton. Plenty of "very spirited" enslaved women might have tried to defy their masters on an occasion like this, but only a rare female slave with social clout and prestige amassed over many years would have dared what Horniblow

4. "The doctor was exceptionally sensitive to social position. . . . Because he was a physician, Norcom's [class] rank was high," but he did not occupy the highest echelon of white society in Edenton. The man whom Jacobs chose as her lover, Samuel Tredwell Sawyer, did (Yellin 31).

did that New Year's morning. Nor were defying her master and rendering him powerless to stop her when she stepped on the auction block the most striking indicators of the power of Horniblow's status in Edenton. Her class connections in Edenton gave her an even bigger trump card to play, as the episode makes clear once the auction begins.

After boldly stepping onto the auction block, the old slave, Jacobs recounts, is greeted by a chorus of disapproving white voices. "Many voices called out, 'Shame! Shame! Who is going to sell *you*, aunt Marthy? Don't stand there! That is no place for *you*'"(21) [14]. Jacobs does not identify to whom these "voices" belonged, but it is evident that the people who hissed their disapproval were white Horniblow supporters. Some must have been women, since women were likely the customers for the baked goods and fancy preserves Horniblow made at night to earn her own money while enslaved. The people Horniblow hears once she mounts the auction block are not outraged, of course, by the sight of a human being sold like a horse or a table on New Year's Day. White southerners did not go to slave auctions to protest the proceedings; they went to buy human beings. "On one of these sale days, I saw a mother lead seven children to the auction-block," Jacobs reports. "She knew that *some* of them would be taken from her; but they took *all*" (26–27) [18]. There were no whites at that auction crying "Shame! Shame!" over the sale of this mother or her children.

What upsets the whites at this particular auction on New Year's Day, 1828—and no doubt why they were present at the auction in the first place—is that *Molly Horniblow*, a special and highly regarded slave, was going to be sold at auction. Whites, especially respectable white ladies, would have never set foot in a place as seamy and emotionally distressing as an auction of slaves had they not been forewarned that Horniblow would be there. The protest against Horniblow's sale was not an attack on the southern practice of selling slaves. Those who came to protest were present because they objected to a *particular* slave's being sold. "That is no place for *you*" was the protesters' way of declaring that "Aunt Marthy" did not *deserve* to be classed among the ordinary slaves slated for sale that day. They cried "Shame! Shame!" not because they were ashamed of the selling of human beings on New Year's Day in their town. They simply wanted to shame Horniblow's master publicly for selling such a respectable woman, especially in such a public, undignified way.

As every reader of *Incidents* knows, the auction proceeds despite the vocal protests. But it soon becomes clear that the bidding won't follow protocol. The term *bidding* is actually a misnomer since, Jacobs informs her reader, only one bidder speaks up, offering an absurdly low $50 for perhaps the most valuable, respected, and accomplished female slave in all of Edenton. Yet no one overbids Hannah Pritchard, the 70-year-old sister of recently deceased Elizabeth Horniblow, Molly's former mistress. Doubtless Molly was not surprised in the least by Pritchard's bid or by the absence of any bid in competition. A member of Edenton's white upper-crust, Pritchard would have commanded respect and deference especially in bidding for the Horniblows' Molly. Purchase by a white lady under these highly unusual circumstances confirms Molly Horniblow's status as well as her ability, when necessary, to marshal her long-cultivated alliances with upper-class white women in Edenton to protect her interests. In this case, Horniblow's goal is nothing less than freedom for herself (and for her son Mark Ramsey, whom Norcom also wished to sell, though *Incidents* does not mention this aspect of the case). Pritchard purchased both mother and son, Yellin suggests, with Molly's own money, saved from her earnings and advanced to Pritchard before the auction (Yellin 21). What Norcom learned the hard way in this case was that Molly Horniblow's class and connections among white ladies had trumped his apparent caste and gender prerogatives as a white male slaveholder. A few months later he received even more irritating news that Pritchard had signed manumission papers for Horniblow.[5]

In this episode, the power of class and class solidarity among black and white women in *Incidents* is affirmed in ways that anticipate later interracial class alliances that Horniblow draws on to enable her granddaughter to go into hiding successfully. Class connections and alliances across Edenton's color line factor significantly in Jacobs's successful waging of "the war of [her] life" (Jacobs 31) [20] against Norcom's attempts to control, dominate, and demoralize her.[6] But to reckon fully with the role and effect of class in *Incidents*, we must not ignore another dimension of the class-inflected views and values of the Jacobs-Horniblow clan. If Molly Horniblow's status, connections, and values helped her marshal protective alliances with higher-class whites in Edenton, those same aspects of class distanced the matriarch of the clan from blacks in town whom she felt were beneath her. If Molly evinces strong affinities with what Jacobs calls "the better class" of Edenton whites (103) [60], Molly

5. After gaining her freedom, Molly temporarily became the owner of her son but soon freed him.
6. Jacobs on one occasion during her teens recounts her enlisting a white "lady" in her neighborhood in Edenton to intercede for her with Norcom. Jacobs wanted to marry a free black carpenter and hoped that the good offices of the "friendly" white lady would convince Norcom, who was also a friend of the unnamed lady, to sell Jacobs. "The lady listened, with kindly sympathy, and promised to do her utmost to promote my wishes," but Norcom did not yield (Jacobs 60) [36]. That Jacobs had such connections among white ladies, whom she could depend on "to do her utmost to promote my wishes," is testimony to the class-based leverage that both Jacobs and her grandmother had with important white women in Edenton.

also expresses opinions that betray her sense of moral, not just class, superiority over many enslaved black women of Edenton.

Intentionally or not, Jacobs dramatizes this side of her grandmother when recounting the upshot of Jacobs's revelation of her first pregnancy. Horniblow's initial reaction to the shocking news is to banish fifteen-year-old Harriet for having become "a disgrace to your dead mother" (Jacobs 87) [51], a woman characterized in *Incidents* as "a slave merely in name, but in nature . . . noble and womanly" (14) [11]. Delilah Jacobs, also a comparatively privileged domestic slave, is portrayed by her daughter as a paragon of female virtue, who had been married formally (though not legally, of course) and who had had her children baptized in Edenton's Episcopal church, where the town's highest-class whites and blacks worshipped. Neither Harriet nor her brother John had been born out of wedlock, another factor contributing to the shame Jacobs felt when obliged to confess her sexual transgressions to her grandmother.

It's unlikely that Molly Horniblow's outrage over her granddaughter's "disgrace" stopped at Delilah Jacobs's hallowed grave. Horniblow's extreme reaction to the pregnancy probably stemmed in part from her anxiety over the impact of her granddaughter's behavior on the social reputation of the clan itself. Calling Harriet a disgrace denotes Molly's belief that Harriet could *be* "dis-graced," that is, could lose favor or standing in the eyes of others, socially and morally. By legal definition a slave could not be disgraced, since a slave had no favor or standing to lose, any more than a pig or an ironing board could be disgraced. But as far as the matriarch of the Jacobs-Horniblow clan was concerned, *her* family definitely *did* possess favor and standing, hard-earned and carefully cultivated, which Harriet, the clan's pride and joy, had undermined, if not damaged, by failing to uphold her family's reputation for female sexual virtue. Jacobs was intensely aware of this. Anticipating how her relatives would react to the news of her pregnancy, "I felt wretched. Humble as were their circumstances, they had pride in my good character. Now, how could I look them in the face?" (Jacobs 87) [51].

Horniblow soon put aside her dismay and took her pregnant granddaughter under her protection. For the remainder of Jacobs's pregnancy and for at least five years thereafter, through the birth of Joseph in 1829 and Louisa in 1833, Jacobs continued to reside in her grandmother's home, despite the fact that she remained Dr. Norcom's slave. The doctor's wife had forbidden Jacobs access to the Norcom home, but what is puzzling is Norcom's acquiescence in allowing Jacobs as much as six years of relative protection in the one place in Edenton where Harriet would have most wanted to live and raise her children. The normally vindictive doctor could have sent her anywhere he wanted, except into his own home. He chose—if he felt he had any choice—to permit his fractious and defiant slave and her children to stay in a domicile that he did not control, a space where he sometimes confronted, harangued, threatened, and, on rare occasions, struck Jacobs, but where he knew he could go only so far and only so often. Norcom's permitting Jacobs and her children to live for so many years with her grandmother, along with his grudging acceptance of Molly Horniblow's right to order him out of her house (Jacobs 125–26) [72], cannot be fully explained without reference to the status and class alliances of the Jacobs-Horniblow clan.

In the wake of the revelation of her granddaughter's pregnancy, Horniblow also brought her indignation to bear on the father of Jacobs's unborn child. Seeking a conversation with "Mr. Sands" (Samuel Tredwell Sawyer), aptly named because of his shifty ways throughout *Incidents*, Horniblow goes on the moral offensive with a white man of the highest social standing in Edenton. Here are the opening sentences of chapter 11: "I returned to my good grandmother's house. She had an interview with Mr. Sands. When she asked him why he could not have left her one ewe lamb—whether there were not plenty of slaves who did not care about character—he made no answer; but he spoke kind and encouraging words" (Jacobs 90) [52–53].

Molly's query, as Jacobs phrases it, alludes to a passage in 2 Samuel, chapter 12, in which the prophet Nathan tells King David a story about the betrayal of a poor man by a rich man. The rich man has many flocks and great wealth, whereas the poor man has "nothing, save one little ewe lamb, which he had bought and nourished up: and it grew up together with him . . . and lay in his bosom, and was unto him as a daughter."[7] Yet when the rich man decides to entertain a traveler, he shows no respect for the poor man's beloved "ewe lamb" but instead appropriates it, rather than an animal from his own plentiful flock, to serve to the traveler.

By comparing teenage Jacobs to the "ewe lamb" of the Old Testament account, Horniblow counts on Sawyer's recalling not only Nathan's parable but, more importantly, the pretext of the parable, which was the infamous decision by King David to arrange for the death of Uriah the Hittite so that David could then appropriate Uriah's widow, Bathsheba, to gratify his own desire. Molly's point to Sawyer is clearly judgmental. She aims to shame this member of Edenton's white ruling class by comparing him to King David and herself to the poor man who lost his "ewe lamb." The "ewe lamb," the innocent creature despoiled by the callous rich man, symbolizes Harriet Jacobs. Refusing to blame the enslaved victim of a white man's desire, Horniblow courageously holds Sawyer morally accountable.

7. 2 Samuel 12.3.

The black woman's moral indignation extends through Sawyer to any upper-class white man who could exploit an enslaved woman sexually with no appreciable consequences.

The problem with Horniblow's otherwise admirable upbraiding of Sawyer arises when she poses her rhetorical question: "why he could not have left her one ewe lamb—whether there were not plenty of slaves who did not care about character." Raising such a question subverts Horniblow's moral authority by introducing *class* difference—the difference between the few female slaves who "care about character" and the many who don't—into what starts out as a stark moral contrast based on *caste* distinction, the power of a white man to rob a slave girl of her innocence. After referring in chapter 10 to her clan's "pride in my good character," Jacobs's chapter 11 demonstrates that part of that pride stems from the clan's conviction that they were different from and better than all those "slaves who did not care about character." Jacobs could have portrayed her grandmother referring to "plenty of slaves" whose character had been impugned or assaulted or otherwise outraged by white sexual aggression. Instead, Jacobs states that her grandmother wanted to know why Sawyer didn't help himself to the plentiful female slaves who simply didn't care about character at all.

The language Jacobs assigns to her grandmother shows how Horniblow's class views compromise her attempt to challenge white male caste privilege in Edenton. By dismissing the pretense to "character" of numerous unnamed female slaves in her community, Horniblow places herself in a position not unlike that of the whites who came to protest her sale on the public auction block. In each case, what might have been an opportunity to protest against the *caste* injustices of slavery (whites' selling black slaves at auction, white men sexually exploiting female slaves) ends up being a demand that certain slaves, by virtue of their *class* status, be exempted from inhuman treatment that other slaves must endure without redress. In her interview with Sawyer, Horniblow's entirely righteous indignation is predicated on her conviction that *her* granddaughter did not deserve to be exploited sexually by this white man. The "good character" of fifteen-year-old Harriet—and by extension of the Jacobs-Horniblow clan—should have mattered enough to Sawyer to keep his hands off Harriet. He could have sowed his wild oats with one of those *other* slave women, the ones "who did not care about character." After all, there were "plenty" of them, but only one Harriet.

One of the most complex and intriguing questions that arises when grappling with *Incidents* from the standpoint of class is this: to what extent did Jacobs herself, as either subject or narrator of *Incidents*, internalize the class-based notions of status, rank, and rights that so strongly influenced her grandmother's thought and behavior?

What is a reader to make of Jacobs's statement, "I knew that I was the greatest comfort of her [grandmother's] old age, and that it was a source of pride to her that I had not degraded myself, like most of the slaves" (86) [51]? Does this reference to the morally "degraded" status of "most of the slaves" in and around Edenton indicate that Jacobs shared in her grandmother's class-inflected "pride"? Did Jacobs herself feel that, before her pregnancy, she had been morally superior to "most of the slaves"? Did Jacobs judge "most of the slaves" for having "degraded themselves"? Did she believe that "most of the [female] slaves" had "degraded *themselves*," that is, these slaves bore moral responsibility for their supposedly "degraded" status?

As a former slave who knew all too well about the sexual exploitation of enslaved women, the author of *Incidents* risked exposing herself to moral censure by seeking "to arouse the women of the North to a realizing sense of the condition of two millions of women at the South, still in bondage, suffering what I suffered, and most of them far worse" (6) [5]. In this capacity, Jacobs represented herself as a spokeswoman who sympathized deeply with the mass of southern women "still in bondage." However, Jacobs also was motivated by a strong desire to represent herself as a respectable colored woman of character, who, once self-liberated, affirmed to a black minister in the North, "'God alone knows how I have suffered; and He, I trust, will forgive me'" (244) [135]. Did the contrasts Jacobs introduced into *Incidents* between her own character in slavery and that of "plenty" or "most" of the female slaves of Edenton indicate that their suffering warranted the kind of forgiveness that Jacobs felt her own suffering deserved? If nothing else, *Incidents*'s case for Harriet Jacobs's individual character rests emphatically on the contention that, both before and after her self-liberation, Jacobs had always "cared" deeply about "character." Whether her grandmother or she herself thought that "most of" the "degraded" female slaves cared as much about their character as the Jacobs-Horniblow women cared about theirs leads inevitably to the tangled intersection of morality and class that often complicates the former by revealing the pervasive influence of the latter in the life and life story of Harriet Jacobs.

Works Cited

Bibb, Henry. *Narrative of the Life and Adventures of Henry Bibb, an American Slave, Written by Himself.* New York, 1849. Print.

Douglass, Frederick. *My Bondage and My Freedom.* New York: Miller, Orton & Mulligan, 1855. Print.

———. *Narrative of the Life of Frederick Douglass, an American Slave, Written by Himself.* Boston: American Anti-Slavery Society, 1845. Print.

Du Bois, W. E. B. *The American Negro Artisan.* Atlanta: Atlanta UP, 1912. Print.

Franklin, John Hope, and Loren Schweninger. *Runaway Slaves: Rebels on the Plantation.* New York: Oxford UP, 1999. Print.

Henderson, Carol E. "The Critical Matrix of Caste, Class and Color in *Incidents in the Life of a Slave Girl.*" *Legacy* 16.1 (1999): 49–58. Print.

Jackson, Andrew. *Narrative and Writings of Andrew Jackson, of Kentucky.* Syracuse, 1847. Print.

Jacobs, Harriet. *Incidents in the Life of a Slave Girl.* Boston, 1861. Print.

Kawash, Samira. "Fugitive Properties." *The New Economic Criticism.* Ed. Martha Woodmansee and Mark Osteen. London: Routledge, 1999. 238–49. Print.

Lane, Lunsford. *Narrative of Lunsford Lane Formerly of Raleigh, N.C.* Boston, 1842. Print.

Penningroth, Dylan C. *The Claims of Kinfolk: African American Property and Community in the Nineteenth-Century South.* Chapel Hill: U of North Carolina P, 2003. Print.

Smith, Valerie. "'Loopholes of Retreat': Architecture and Ideology in Harriet Jacobs's *Incidents in the Life of a Slave Girl.*" *Reading Black, Reading Feminist.* Ed. Henry Louis Gates, Jr. New York: Penguin, 1990. 212–26. Print.

Yellin, Jean Fagan. *Harriet Jacobs.* New York: Basic Civitas, 2004. Print.

Harriet Jacobs: A Chronology

1813	Born into slavery in Edenton, North Carolina, daughter of Delilah and Elijah.
c. 1819	Mother dies.
1825	Mistress (Margaret Horniblow) dies. Jacobs becomes property of Mary Matilda Norcom, daughter of Dr. James Norcom.
c. 1826	Father dies.
c. 1829	Begins sexual relationship with Samuel Tredwell Sawyer. Their son, Joseph, born.
1833	Louisa Matilda, daughter of Sawyer and Jacobs, born.
1835	Runs away from plantation.
1842	Escapes to New York City.
1844	Moves to Boston.
1845	Travels to England as nurse for Imogene Willis.
1849	Moves to Rochester, New York, to live with her brother, John S. Jacobs. Her social circle includes several prominent abolitionists, including Frederick Douglass, William C. Nell, and Amy Post.
1850	Returns to New York City and works as domestic servant for Nathaniel Parker and his second wife, Cornelia Grinnell Willis.
1852	Cornelia Grinnell Willis purchases Jacobs and her children.
1853	Publishes "Letter from a Fugitive Slave" and "Cruelty to Slaves" in the *New York Tribune*. Begins writing *Incidents*.
1858	Travels to England in search of a publisher for *Incidents*.
1861	Publishes *Incidents in the Life of a Slave Girl* using the pseudonym Linda Brent.
1862	Publishes "Life among the Contrabands" in the *Liberator*. *Incidents* published in England as *The Deeper Wrong*.
1864	Establishes the Jacobs Free School in Alexandria, Virginia.
1868	Travels to London, England, to raise money for an orphanage.
1870	Moves to Cambridge, Massachusetts, where she runs a boarding house.

1877 Moves to Washington, DC.

1897 March 7, dies in Washington, DC. Buried in Mount Auburn Cemetery, Cambridge, Massachusetts.

Selected Bibliography†

• indicates works included or excerpted in this volume

Accomando, Christina. "'The laws were laid down to me anew': Harriet Jacobs and the Reframing of Legal Fictions." *African American Review* 32.2 (1998): 229–45.

• Andrews, William L. "Class and Class Awareness in *Incidents in the Life of a Slave Girl*." In *Auto/Biography across the Americas: Transnational Themes in Life Writing*. Ed. Ricia Anne Chansky. New York: Routledge, 2017. 183–97.

Berry, Sarah L. "'[No] Doctor but My Master': Health Reform and Antislavery Rhetoric in Harriet Jacobs's *Incidents in the Life of a Slave Girl*." *Journal of Medical Humanities* 35.1 (2014): 1–18.

Burnham, Michelle. "Loopholes of Resistance: Harriet Jacobs' Slave Narrative and the Critique of Agency in Foucault." *Arizona Quarterly* 49.2 (Summer 1993): 53–73.

Carby, Hazel V. "Hear My Voice, Ye Careless Daughters." In *Reconstructing Womanhood: The Emergence of the Afro-American Woman Novelist*. New York: Oxford UP, 1987. 45–61, 183–85.

Cope, Virginia. "'I Verily Believed Myself to Be a Free Woman': Harriet Jacobs's Journey into Capitalism." *African American Review* 38.1 (2004): 5–20.

Crawley, Ashon. "Harriet Jacobs Gets a Hearing." *Current Musicology* 93 (2012): 35–55.

Deng, Chiou-Rung. "Resisting Sympathy, Reclaiming Authority: The Politics of Representation in Harriet Jacobs's *Incidents in the Life of a Slave Girl*." *Tamkang Review: A Quarterly of Literary and Cultural Studies* 41.2 (2011): 115–140.

• Ernest, John. "Reading the Fragments in the Fields of History: Harriet Jacobs's *Incidents in the Life of a Slave Girl*." In *Resistance and Reformation in Nineteenth-Century African-American Literature*. Jackson: UP of Mississippi, 1995. 81–108.

• Foreman, P. Gabrielle. "The Politics of Sex and Representation in Harriet Jacobs's *Incidents in the Life of a Slave Girl*." In *Activist Sentiments: Reading Black Women in the Nineteenth Century*. Urbana: U of Illinois P, 2009. 19–42.

• Foster, Frances Smith. "Resisting Incidents." In *Harriet Jacobs and* Incidents in the Life of a Slave Girl: *New Critical Essays*. Ed. Deborah M. Garfield and Rafia Zafar. New York: Cambridge UP, 1996. 57–75.

Garfield, Deborah M., and Rafia Zafar, eds. *Harriet Jacobs and* Incidents in the Life of a Slave Girl: *New Critical Essays*. New York: Cambridge UP, 1996.

Gates, Henry L. Jr., and K. A. Appiah, eds. *Harriet Jacobs: Critical Perspectives Past and Present*. New York: Amistad, 1997.

Gelder, Ann. "Reforming the Body: 'Experience' and the Architecture of Imagination in Harriet Jacobs's *Incidents in the Life of a Slave Girl*." In *Inventing Maternity: Politics, Science, and Literature, 1650–1865*. Ed. Susan C. Greenfield and Carol Barash. Lexington: UP of Kentucky, 1999. 252–66.

† Compiled by Erica Onugha for this second Norton Critical Edition.

Gomaa, Sally. "Writing to 'Virtuous' and 'Gentle' Readers: The Problem of Pain in Harriet Jacobs's *Incidents* and Harriet Wilson's *Sketches*." *African American Review* 43.2–3 (2009): 371–81.

Green-Barteet, Miranda A. "'The Loophole of Retreat': Interstitial Spaces in Harriet Jacobs's *Incidents in the Life of a Slave Girl*." *South Central Review* 30.2 (2013): 53–72.

Greeson, Jennifer Rae. "The 'Mysteries and Miseries' of North Carolina: New York City, Urban Gothic Fiction, and *Incidents in the Life of a Slave Girl*." *American Literature* 73.2 (2001): 277–309.

• Gunning, Sandra. "Reading and Redemption in *Incidents in the Life of a Slave Girl*." In *Harriet Jacobs and* Incidents in the Life of a Slave Girl: *New Critical Essays*. Ed. Deborah M. Garfield and Rafia Zafar. New York: Cambridge UP, 1996. 131–55.

Henderson, Carol E. "Borderlands: The Critical Matrix of Caste, Class, and Color in *Incidents in the Life of A Slave Girl*." *Legacy: A Journal of American Women Writers* 16.1 (1999): 49–58.

• Kanzler, Katja. "'To Tell the Kitchen Version': Architectural Figurations of Race and Gender in Harriet Jacobs's *Incidents in the Life of a Slave Girl* and Harriet Wilson's *Our Nig*." *Gender Forum* 15 (2006).

King, Lovalerie. "Counter-Discourses on the Racialization of Theft and Ethics in Douglass's 'Narrative' and Jacobs's 'Incidents.'" *MELUS* 28.4 (2003): 55–82.

Kreiger, Georgia. "Playing Dead: Harriet Jacobs's Survival Strategy in *Incidents in the Life of a Slave Girl*." *African American Review* 42.3–4 (2008): 607–21.

Larson, Jennifer. "Converting Passive Womanhood to Active Sisterhood: Agency, Power, and Subversion in Harriet Jacobs's *Incidents in the Life of a Slave Girl*." *Women's Studies* 35.8 (2006): 739–56.

LeRoy-Frazier, Jill. "'Reader, My Story Ends with Freedom': Literacy, Authorship, and Gender in Harriet Jacobs' *Incidents in the Life of a Slave Girl*." *Obsidian III: Literature in the African Diaspora* 5.1 (2004): 152–61.

Li, Stephanie. "Motherhood as Resistance in Harriet Jacobs's *Incidents in the Life of a Slave Girl*." *Legacy: A Journal of American Women Writers* 23.1 (2006): 14–29.

McKay, Nellie Y. "The Girls Who Became the Women: Childhood Memories in the Autobiographies of Harriet Jacobs, Mary Church Terrell, and Anne Moody." In *Tradition and the Talents of Women*. Ed. Florence Howe. Urbana and Chicago: U of Illinois P, 1991. 106–24.

Moore, Geneva Cobb. "A Freudian Reading of Harriet Jacobs' 'Incidents in the Life of a Slave Girl.'" *Southern Literary Journal* 38.1 (2005): 3–20.

Mullen, Harryette. "Runaway Tongue: Resistant Orality in *Uncle Tom's Cabin, Our Nig, Incidents in the Life of a Slave Girl*, and *Beloved*." In *The Culture of Sentiment*. Ed. Shirley Samuels. New York: Oxford UP, 1992. 244–64, 332–35.

Painter, Nell Irvin. "Three Southern Women and Freud: A Non-Exceptionalist Approach to Race, Class, and Gender in the Slave South." In *Feminists Revision History*. Ed. Ann-Louise Shapiro. New Brunswick, NJ: Rutgers UP, 1994. 195–216.

Pratt, Casey. "'These Things Took the Shape of Mystery': *Incidents in the Life of a Slave Girl* as American Romance." *African American Review* 47.1 (2014): 69–81.

• Rifkin, Mark. "'A Home Made Sacred by Protecting Laws': Black Activist Homemaking and Geographies of Citizenship in *Incidents in the Life of a Slave Girl*." *Differences: A Journal of Feminist Cultural Studies* 18.2 (2007): 72–102.

• Smith, Valerie. "Form and Ideology in Three Slave Narratives." In *Self-Discovery and Authority in Afro-American Narrative*. Cambridge: Harvard UP, 1987. 9–43.

• Sommers, Samantha M. "Harriet Jacobs and the Recirculation of Print Culture." *MELUS: Multi-Ethnic Literature of the United States* 40.3 (2015): 134–49.

Spelman, Elizabeth V. "The Heady Political Life of Compassion." In *Fruits of Sorrow: Framing Our Attention to Suffering*. Boston: Beacon Press, 1997. 59–89, 184–89.

Taves, Ann. "Spiritual Purity and Sexual Shame: Religious Themes in the Writings of Harriet Jacobs." *Church History* 56.1 (March 1987): 59–72.

Tricomi, Albert H. "Dialect and Identity in Harriet Jacobs's Autobiography and Other Slave Narratives." *Callaloo* 29.2 (2006): 619–33.

Wardrop, Daneen. "'I Stuck the Gimlet in and Waited for Evening': Writing and *Incidents in the Life of a Slave Girl*." *Texas Studies in Literature and Language* 49.3 (2007): 209–29.

Warner, Anne Bradford. "Harriet Jacobs at Home in *Incidents in the Life of a Slave Girl*." *Southern Quarterly* 45.3 (2008): 30–47.

Wells, Kimberly A. "'The Dream of My Life Is Not Yet Realized': Harriet Jacobs and the Failure of the Ideal." *Griot: Official Journal of the Southern Conference on Afro-American Studies* 26.1 (2007): 65–75.

Wolfe, Andrea Powell. "Double-Voicedness in *Incidents in the Life of a Slave Girl*: 'Loud Talking' to a Northern Black Readership." *American Transcendental Quarterly* 22.3 (2008): 517–25.

Yellin, Jean Fagan. *Harriet Jacobs: A Life*. New York: Basic Civitas, 2004.

———, ed. *The Harriet Jacobs Family Papers*. 2 vols. Chapel Hill: U of North Carolina P. 2008.

• ———."Written By Herself: Harriet Jacobs' Slave Narrative." *American Literature* 53.3 (November 1981): 379–486.